ILL MESSIAH

THE STATION TRILOGY: BOOK THREE

JARRETT BRANDON EARLY

www.jarrettbrandonearly.com

www.illmessiah.com

Maps by Jarrett Brandon Early

Book Cover by BINATANG via 99Designs

Ill Messiah / Jarrett Brandon Early - FIRST EDITION

ISBN: 978-1-7342314-6-5 (Paperback)

ISBN: 978-1-7342314-7-2 (eBook)

❀ Created with Vellum

Dedicated to:

Dad

Thanks for not only allowing, but daring me to dream. And for being my first and, as of right now, only fanboy.

The Isle of God

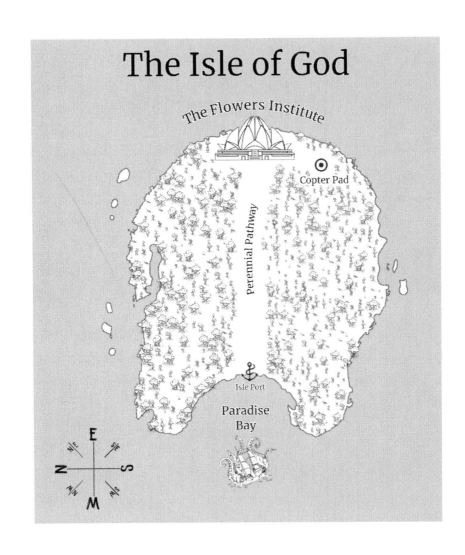

The Flowers Institute

Copter Pad

Perennial Pathway

Isle Port

Paradise
Bay

The Flowers Institute

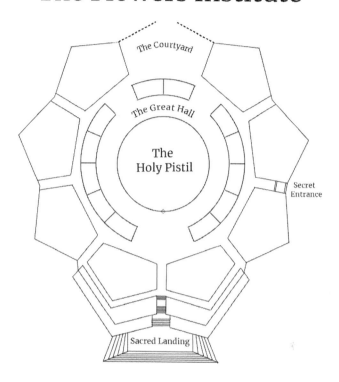

PROLOGUE

Daksha's heels sent echoes down the white marbled corridors of the Flowers Institute, the sounds mirroring the pounding of her heart within her once-frail chest. She inhaled deeply to steady herself. Daksha always felt this rush of excitement and anxiety when walking to update Doctor Flowers on the week's activities. And why would she not? Who wouldn't feel those overwhelmingly sweet, dizzying sensations when meeting God?

If not *the* God, then *a* God.

Her God.

Daksha's footsteps halted abruptly as an ornate, silver mirror that hung along the too-white wall caught her eye. Countless characters and designs adorned the perfectly polished silver, carefully carved into the expensive metal with a master's touch. Just another of the myriad of gifts given to Doctor Flowers by his legion of wealthy followers.

It was not the antique mirror that gave Daksha pause, however. Rather, it was the image that stared back at her, demanding that she take note.

A beautiful, dark-skinned woman looked back, her features in stark contrast to the sickly girl who, little more than a year ago, refused to look upon anything reflective. Thick, wavy hair now covered the bald head that once greeted strangers, its deep surgical scars proving a decorative element that made others look away in either pity or disgust. Or both. A face that was once all angles, with the sunken look of too-thin skin draped over a skull, was now beaming with water and health.

But the most striking difference was the eyes. Eyes that were cold and black, the fire within long dead, had been replaced. In their stead were a pair of golden-brown orbs that always seemed to catch the light just right, sending bright rays back out in a dance of color that screamed *I am here. I am alive. I have value. I will be reckoned with.*

Taking one last moment to admire the person she had become, the person her God had allowed her to be, Daksha smoothed down her white on white pantsuit. She then tightened her grip on her Taragoshi Pastiche custom ream and spun on a heel, continuing her journey to the Holy Pistil, the center of the lotus-shaped Flowers Institute.

Where her God awaited her.

———

THE MASSIVE CENTRAL chamber hummed with power, vibrated with the energy of invisible forces. Daksha found herself looking around as she entered the Holy Pistil. No matter how many times she entered this sacred space, Daksha found herself unable to avoid staring in awe at the achingly beautiful frescoes that surrounded the circular room.

The frescoes were a religious tour through history, depicting modern, recently worshipped deities alongside gods and goddesses of antiquity. As an educated woman, Daksha recognized the vast majority of those who inhabited the colored plaster, but now and then, her brown eyes caught an image that seemed improper, not of this world.

Daksha shrugged these unknown images away rather easily. Her God had selected the figures that would surround the visitors of this most holy of places. Of course He, in his limitless knowledge and wisdom, would know more than a lowly servant, could see beyond the limits of this dark world. Daksha only prayed that He would one day deem her worthy of sharing some of that enlightenment.

Until that day came, Daksha vowed to serve Him in the only way she knew how — by giving her all to Him.

Finally able to tear her gaze from the enchanting artwork that decorated the curving wall, Daksha smoothed down her pantsuit once more and moved forward with all the confidence she could muster.

As Daksha walked, she passed rows upon rows of medical tables that dominated the majority of the Holy Pistil. On the tables, different biological forms in various stages of vivisection lay bare, exposing their secrets to the world. Accompanying each medical table was one or more Taragoshi surgical mechs, their long, multi-jointed, arms carrying out her God's every command, utilizing an endless array of highly specialized instruments and devices. Each mech probably cost several million credits, but what was money to one able to give life?

Daksha took note as she passed the whirring Taragoshi mechs, always curious about her Lord's most recent projects. To her left, it looked like a Spirit Girl was being retrofitted with alternative biological components. To Daksha's right, a large blonde woman covered in painful sores, still awake, stared wide-eyed at the domed ceiling as three mechs worked furiously in perfect unison to rebuild every muscle in her once-weak body. Despite quivering in unimaginable pain, the woman smiled through the agony, understanding that, should she live, she would be reborn as something more than human.

Daksha envied the woman, but was glad that her God might soon have another powerful guardian.

The biological experiments only grew more odd from there. One table held the corpse of a man whose chest had exploded in a large batch of tentacles. Another held a giant slug-like creature that was being dissected, allowing for the careful removal of hundreds of smaller living slugs from the creature's lower cavity.

Daksha shook her head as she progressed, clearing her mind of the often brutal images of her God's important work. It was time for her to focus on her updates.

Daksha began to shake as she closed in on the back wall opposite the Holy Pistil's only entrance. She gripped her ream tighter as she walked, the words she had rehearsed spinning through her mind like a tornado. Her eyes cast down toward the marble floor, Daksha felt when to stop, could feel the power of her Lord's gaze on her feeble frame from above.

Daksha cursed her weakness, cursed her inability to look up and greet Doctor Flowers with a smile. But then her logical side kicked in, as it always did, and corrected her.

It should be difficult, if not impossible, for a mere mortal to match eyes with a God. Especially if that God is your God. And this certainly is your God.

Daksha spoke first, as she always did. "My Lord, I'm here for your weekly updates."

A heavy silence came on the heels of Daksha's words, Doctor Milo Flowers no doubt studying his disciple from on high, easily seeing things that she would never discover.

"Does my form pain you, my child?"

Daksha hesitated before responding. "It does not pain me, Lord. I am just unaccustomed to it."

"But you knew it would come to this, did you not, child?" Doctor Flowers's voice sounded farther away than usual.

"I did, my Lord, but still…"

"Look at me, my child."

Daksha took a deep breath before raising her eyes from the floor, fighting the invisible weights that wanted to pull them back down. Doctor Flowers was positioned similarly to how she found him for the past three weeks, but that didn't make things any easier.

Stuck against the back wall, in the only space void of the magnificent frescoes, was her God. He hung fifteen feet in the air, cocooned in a thick biological resin that hid the entirety of his body save his beautiful face. The cocoon had grown much thicker since Daksha's last visit, and she could see hard plates forming just beneath the cloudy mucus.

Two extra-tall Taragoshi surgical mechs attended to Doctor Flowers, one injecting the cocoon with a variety of colored liquids while the other ran constant diagnostics for later analysis.

While her Lord could, and often did, disappear completely into the cocoon, a small crevice near the top allowed him to press his face out to meet with his followers and conduct his necessary work with the mechs. Doctor Flowers did that now, the jellied slime that covered His face doing nothing to conceal the power in his bright blue eyes.

Daksha's golden eyes met her Lord's blue orbs, and for a second she feared that lightening would strike, linking the two for a too-brief moment before her brain liquified from the power of the connection.

Flowers smiled beneath the ooze. "There now, that's better. What of the world outside these walls? How are my plans proceeding?"

Daksha gripped her Pastiche ream. She hated delivering bad news to her God. "Most are going accordion to plan, my Lord. But in some areas, there are…setbacks."

Flowers's too-blue eyes went wide under the gunk. "Go on."

Daksha collected herself, steeled her resolve. "The proposed Bhellum Petal has hit a snag. Actually, more than a snag, my Lord. It appears that it will take much more to pry the land from its current owners, who seem unmoved by offers of monetary gain."

Flowers's eyes looked into the distance as he thought over this new development. "So Viktor Krill is not the ally that I hoped he would be. And after all I had given him. What a pity."

"Do you want this man destroyed, my Lord? This… Viktor Krill?"

Flowers reflected on his former partner-in-crime from another world. "Not yet, my child. Viktor Krill is a notorious loner. His reluctance to join me, while admittedly disappointing, does not necessarily reflect an active opposition to my plans. Do nothing. But keep an eye on him."

"As you command, my Lord. And the proposed Bhellum Petal?"

"Leave it be. We don't need it. I had more than two dozen locations selected, most of which panned out. Construction on an additional ten Petals have already begun with extreme haste. We will soon have twenty-five Petals with fully functioning Divine Anther systems. That will be more than sufficient for the Great Conversion."

Daksha was taken aback by this news. "My Lord, I knew you were looking at other locations, but I had no idea that ten had already been selected. And ground has already been broken?"

"You think you are my only Disciple, Daksha? You think I would divulge all my plans to any one human?"

Daksha's eyes fell back to the floor as she was dizzied by the news that there were other disciples more trusted by her Lord. Her mind spun with possible challengers for her God's attention. She landed on one name. *Nieve.* Anger filled the usually even-tempered woman. *That fucking bitch, how dare she conspire to keep me out of the loop. I'll kill that..."*

"Any good news, my child?"

Daksha was immediately brought back to reality and found herself staring at her God's cocoon, shaking uncontrollably in hatred. She pulled herself together.

"Of course, my Lord. The remainder is good news."

"Please, do tell. I would hate to think that my Daksha has only brought me disappointment."

Daksha winced at her God's barb. "Everything else has gone according to plan, my Lord."

"Go on."

"Anton Carlyle has done as you commanded, purchasing every available news and media outlet. I think the bastards caught wind that this directive came from on high because even the lowliest trash station and paper were asking ten times their worth. Maxim Global took quite a hit due to the mass buys, but you now control the vast majority of the world's media coverage. We now should be able to avoid any significant PR blowback. The public has only us to tell them what is going on. Our story is the only story, the only truth."

"And Anton?"

"He was certainly distraught to have to take it on the chin by so many businesses deemed unworthy of his attention, but he serves you faithfully."

Flowers's too-blue eyes began to cloud over, as if other, more godly issues were beginning to impede on their mortal discussion.

After a beat, however, they cleared and Daksha's God was back with her.

"Money means nothing now. Anton sees this. It is his human pride that stings him. But that will soon be eradicated. For everyone. Now, tell me about our political affairs."

"Obviously, the Centrus Affiliation is under your thumb." Daksha paused for a second, uncomfortable with her choice of words. At this time, her Lord was entirely encased in his cocoon, with no hands to be seen. Luckily, Flowers seemed unfazed, so she continued. "Brayden Yorsaf has not only made sure that all the member countries are in loyal alignment, but he has begun to manipulate those outside of the Affiliation. Several successful campaigns have already been executed to replace your critics with those loyal to our holy cause. Numerous Presidents, Prime Ministers, Chancellors, Premiers, and Chiefs outside the Affiliation are now Blossoms of the New God. They have to hide this from the public, obviously, but their loyalties are certain."

"And my religious… competition?"

Daksha smoothed down her pantsuit once more. "That has proven a bit more… challenging, my Lord."

"Has it, now?"

"Willard Hillmore is doing his best, converting thousands by the day, but the usual infidels remain a problem, even as their numbers dwindle. Some of them are even banding together, combining their heathen efforts under a new banner — the Protectors of Man."

Doctor Milo Flowers chuckled within his cocoon. "I have to give them credit, it *is* an apt name. But they miss an obvious fact."

"Enlighten me, Lord."

"The Age of Man has already ended, but no one has taken notice. They are protecting the ghost of a memory, which is an impossible task."

"They are worms beneath your greatness, Lord."

Flowers's blue eyes grew serious. "Careful how you speak of worms, my child. Worms embody the true chaotic nature of biological existence. Cut them in half and watch one become two. They eat death and excrete life. You should wish you were more like a worm, Daksha. You all should."

Daksha's golden eyes filled with tears, her Lord's admonishment burning her skin like an army of fire ants. "Of course, my Lord. Thank you for correcting my thinking."

"And what is Devout Willard going to do about these… Protectors of Man?"

Daksha cleared the wetness from her eyes and collected herself. "Devout Willard has named himself the Grand Commander of a new arm of the Blossoms aimed at seeking and destroying those who refuse to recognize the one true God."

Flowers seemed amused beneath the layers of ooze. "And does this army have a name?"

"Yes, my Lord. Willard calls them the Thorns of Reckoning."

Flowers laughed again, his eyes flashing as he did. "Yes. Yes. Every Blossom needs protection from those who would attempt to pick it, jealous of the beauty of its existence. What could be better and more natural than a thorn? Tell Willard that I approve. Tell him to show no mercy. Tell him that the death he must cause is not an end, but a painfully gorgeous beginning. Tell him to remind his soldiers of this as they carve up our enemies."

"I will, my Lord. But it will have to be via letter. Devout Willard has shunned all technology, stating that it is an affront to your natural godliness."

"That will surely slow his investigations, will it not?"

"I have a team using the most advanced surveillance and investigative innovations, feeding him constant intel through non-digital channels. Information is a bit delayed because of this, but it is the best we can do. This is *Devout* Willard, after all. My team and I will be his eyes and ears, and Willard the blade. Together, we will carve out the plague that is the Protectors of Man."

"Anything further, my child? I have much… work… to do within these biological walls."

Daksha's pulse began to race for this delicate part of the conversation. "One more thing, Lord. There have been more unplanned

Blooms. Not a huge amount, but enough to draw eyes. Some are growing concerned that this could impact plans for the Great Conversion."

Flowers did not speak as he mulled over this news. His moment of pause felt like an eternity to Daksha. "Although I was hoping this would be avoided, I am not surprised by it. When you set a billion traps, a few are bound to go off prematurely. I have found shocking variance in what I once thought was the offensively simplistic human form. I accounted for as many variables as possible, but there will always be outliers, rare Blessed Carriers that do not need the Divine Anthers' Spores to trigger the Charismata."

"What would you have me do, Lord? Have them destroyed?"

Flowers's painfully blue eyes went wide with anger, and the cocoon started to shake. "How dare you?! Foolish girl, do you not see?! The Bloomed are holy! They are what you all should strive to be! They have ascended to a level of existence that all of you will have to work to reach! And you would abort my favored children?!"

Tears once again enveloped Daksha's eyes and rolled down her dark cheeks. She collapsed to her knees as her chin hit her chest, daring not to look at her furious God. "Forgive me, my Lord. I *am* a foolish girl. Please teach me."

After a terrifying moment, the cocoon's agitation subsided. "Stand, my child." Daksha did as she was told, but still did not look at Milo Flowers. "It is not your fault. I often forget that you, even the best of you, are still primates under all that hairless skin. But we will soon change that, will we not?"

"Yes, your Holiness. Thank you for your infinite understanding, my Lord. What would you have me do?"

"The Bloomed, beyond being holy entities, could prove extremely useful. I may be able to create a direct connection to them, giving me eyes around the globe."

"I thought *we* were your eyes, my Lord."

"You are my indirect eyes, my child. This would give me direct vision to the world at large. I must pray on this in my Chrysalis. There are things I will need to... change to accomplish this divine task. In the interim, tell my Blossoms that they are to seize and protect any of the Bloomed that they find. Tell them that the Bloomed are holy, despite their shocking appearances, and are not to be harmed. Until I can establish a direct divine connection, it will not be easy to capture them. Many of our Blossoms might fall in the act. Tell them this sacrifice will be noted and appreciated. Tell them that doing God's work is never easy."

"It will be done, my Lord."

"Good, now leave me. You have burdened me with more tasks, and relieved me of very little."

"I am sorry, my Lord."

"Do not be sorry. Be better. We must all be better."

"Yes, my Lord."

"Now go."

With that, Doctor Milo Flowers's face vanished as he disappeared deeper into his Chrysalis. Daksha turned and began her long, unsettling walk out of the Holy Pistil. As she passed the various Taragoshi surgical mechs conducting their gruesome work on the multitude of forms strapped to metal tables, Daksha reflected on the meeting with her God.

It did not go as well as she had hoped, and she was properly reprimanded by the Lord, but things had gone much worse for many others. And it could have easily gone terrible for Daksha.

Instead of exiting the Holy Pistil on two legs, she could have ended up strapped to one of the many surgical tables, only to eventually exit her Lord's chambers on many more appendages, her humanity prematurely stripped away.

PART I

TWISTED ODYSSEY

1

"Can you smell it?"

Marlin Hadder tilted his nose into the air, tying to catch something, anything, on the shifting breeze. "I got nothing."

"Try harder," said Viktor Krill angrily. Krill's usually stoic demeanor had vanished over the last several minutes, putting Hadder on edge. If something was enough to concern the world's greatest killer, then it sure as hell needed to worry Hadder as well. "Close your damn eyes and try again." Hadder did as he was told. Krill's voice calmed. "Use your abilities. Cut off your other senses. Redirect their energies into your Wakened olfactory nerves. Run the analysis. What do you sense?"

Hadder froze in place as his other senses dimmed, leaving him in a world of numbed darkness, where there was nothing to surround him but a medley of odors. From this bouquet, Hadder began to pick out distinct smells. The last of the morning dew was slightly sweet against the sharpness of pine. The gamey pelt of a squirrel was detected as it brushed against a fruity flower, knocking loose bitter spores. Deeper into the wooded area, the freshness of a stream served as the backdrop for something… unnatural. Hadder used his Wakened abilities to push away all other smells, focusing on that singular scent that did not belong, that appeared as offensive as a black stain on a white wedding dress.

"What *is* that," asked Hadder.

"Tell me what you detect. Describe it."

Hadder focused once more. "It is something rotten, but not in the natural sense. It is not a carcass, but the odor of death envelops it. It is striking out against me, and only my Wakened control is keeping my breakfast in my belly." Hadder opened his eyes, hazel orbs drifting toward Krills's black counterparts. "What *is* that, Viktor?"

Krill looked around the small forest that he had entered on an uncomfortable hunch. A strange tingling on the back of his neck had forced him to stop their Taragoshi Monocycles just as they had exited the minor city of Durnish. Krill had followed that worrisome intuition, having learned to trust all his gut feelings in all things, as it took the unlikely companions off the main road and into a rural landscape dotted with backwoods.

"Remember those rumors we heard back in Renneleer?"

"About the freak that was tearing loners apart?"

"That's the one. You discarded them as embellishments, as potential effects of remaining Slink abuse. But I detected real fear and honesty in the stories, even if I, too, found them hard to believe. But there was something else."

"What?"

"A particular smell. There was a distinct odor that blanketed the city of Renneleer, one that I had never experienced before. Until now."

"And you thought that this… smell… was enough to drag us out here? In the middle of nowhere?"

"I did. And if you were half the student you should be concerning your Wakened abilities, you would, too."

Hadder sighed but kept several potential quips to himself. After all, he had to admit that Viktor Krill was the expert here, a master of things that Hadder was just beginning to understand. "Very well. What do we do?"

"We hunt, of course. Follow me. And try to keep up this time."

A comeback began to form on Hadder's lips, but Krill had disappeared into the woods before it could be given voice. Hadder settled for a deep sigh before taking off after Krill, moving faster than any human in history. Save one.

———

Traveling at such speeds, Hadder had no idea how far the pair had traveled, but in less than ten minutes, he found that Krill had stopped with his fist held aloft, commanding Hadder to follow suit. Hadder skidded to a stop, cutting a deep swath in the soft forest floor.

"What," mouthed Hadder to Krill, unwilling to betray their position any more than he already had.

In response, Krill merely pointing ahead before putting his fingers to his lips and motioning Hadder forward. Together, the companions snuck ahead.

As they carefully progressed, Krill tapped his finger to his nose and looked questioningly at Hadder. Hadder inhaled deeply and could not deny that the putrid odor had grown significantly stronger, threatening to bring water to his eyes. Hadder nodded in agreement.

After a few tense minutes, the pair came upon a thicket that blocked any view beyond. They approached the dense brush simultaneously and slowly peeled away limbs and leaves to glimpse what lay ahead.

On the other side of the thicket sat a large clearing, in the middle of which a singular man knelt in prayer, his body quivering uncontrollably. The man, as white and average as anyone Hadder had ever seen, foamed at the mouth, his words coming out in a fit of guttural coughs. The stranger took breaks from praying to scratch at his skin, tearing deep fissures into his flesh, as if it had somehow offended him. As if it was an alien that did not belong.

While disturbed by the scene, Hadder found himself pitying the distressed man, wanting to offer whatever solace he could to alleviate the suffering.

Without thinking, Hadder tore through the thicket, barely dodging Krill's hand that shot forward to stop him, and found himself thrust into the clearing.

The praying man spun on his knees to face Hadder, his shaking becoming full-on convulsions. The man's bloodshot eyes went wide when he saw Hadder, and his hands, formerly clasped together in prayer, went out wide toward the visitor, as if begging for assistance. He spoke through foamy discharge, his words only audible due to Hadder's unnatural hearing.

"Please. Help. Me. Please. Help."

As Hadder moved cautiously toward the desperate man, he tried to converse with the pitiful creature. "What is your name, friend?" The man's red-tinted eyes vibrated back and forth in thought, as if he was having to retrieve the information from the deepest recesses of his mind. "Do you have a name?"

After several seconds of coughing, punctuated by the excretion of a vile green substance, the man responded. "Benn. Benn."

"It's good to meet you, Benn. Now, can you tell me what's ailing you? Why are you suffering in such a way?"

Benn fought through the convulsions, rose to his feet, and began to walk to Hadder on unsteady legs. Hadder, unsure if the man could make it that far, also moved forward, willing to meet Benn in the middle. As the distance began to close, a voice could be heard from behind.

"Marlin Hadder! Get away from that creature at once!"

"His name is Benn, Viktor," Hadder called over his shoulder. "And if you can't tell, he needs our assistance!"

"Marlin! You are in danger!"

Hadder laughed off the warning, but halted his advance. Benn did not, and continued to advance in shuffling steps. Hadder turned to face Krill, who now also stood in the clearing, his tan face one of legitimate concern, which once again disconcerted Hadder.

"Danger how? Aren't we the two most dangerous humans in the world? What have we to fear from a sick man?"

Krill, instead of heading toward Hadder, moved off to his right, as if to flank Benn. Krill spoke as he moved. "That is more than a sick man, Marlin."

Hadder's face twisted in confusion. "What else could it be?" Benn drew closer.

"An abomination."

Hadder looked to Benn, who was now only ten yards away, before returning to Krill. "What are you seeing that I am not, Viktor?"

"Everything. Get away from him. Now!"

Hadder's gaze swept back to Benn, whose pained gait was starting to quicken as he drew closer. Although Benn was certainly going through something strange, Hadder detected nothing dangerous, especially for two Wakened humans. "I see nothing that can harm us, Viktor. Benn needs our…"

Before Hadder could finish his sentence, something burst from Benn's chest, tearing a hole in the man's white t-shirt. A brownish-grey tentacle raced at Hadder, striking him in the shoulder before he could react, so stunned was he by the unimaginable occurrence. The hit sent Hadder spinning away to land awkwardly a dozen feet away, leaving his mind as off-balance as his Wakened body.

When he settled, Hadder immediately withdrew his crystal hand-guns from their shoulder holsters and aimed them at Benn, although he did not fire. It wasn't that he did not *want* to fire, but, rather, Marlin Hadder found that he *could not* fire. The scene unfolding before him was simply too appalling.

The tentacle that had struck Hadder was soon joined by a dozen others, tearing their way free from the front, back, and sides of Benn's t-shirt. The tentacles writhed in the air threateningly as Benn's face contorted in a mask of pain. The guns in Hadder's hands grew heavy as the reality of what he was witnessing began to weigh on him.

A voice from behind the transforming Benn ripped Hadder from his frozen state. "What are you waiting for, Marlin?! Shoot the goddamn thing!"

Hadder shook his head, as if the horror before him was a hood that could be cast away, and aimed his handguns. Just as he was about to pull the trigger, Hadder's eyes met Benn's, and the deep sadness that the Wakened human found there held his finger.

And then Benn was no more.

Benn's face, formerly a mask of suffering, shifted before Hadder. Eyes previously filled with sadness and fear glazed over. When the orbital cloudiness eventually vanished, a wild expression of ecstasy had replaced the previous one of horror. Benn, once looking as if he was enduring more pain than Hadder had ever known, now appeared in the grips of a religious experience, his mouth agape, as if he was trying to ingest the beautiful world surrounding him.

Hadder tried to reason with this new face, doing his best to ignore the tentacles that still soared through the air before him. "Benn! Are you still there? Benn?"

Benn's wild eyes once again met Hadder's, and a great grin broke out on the transforming man. Just as Hadder again attempted to speak with Benn, deep fissures appeared on the man's face, splitting his head down the middle and again just under his eyes. With one last frenzied laugh, Benn's face opened up along the fissures, reminding Hadder of a vampire squid, and turned itself inside out, revealing a singular round eye above an enormous, tooth-filled maw beneath.

"Fuck me," cried Hadder as Benn took off towards him, the man's legs no longer unsteady or weak. Hadder steadied his arms and fired round after round into the charging Benn. The bullets sank deeply into the changeling's chest and plunged into the frenzied tentacles with no effect. Benn closed the distance with uncanny speed.

Two tentacles shot out towards Hadder, who had no time to think, only react. He shot up straight into the air, higher than anyone in history had ever jumped, allowing the tentacles to pass far beneath him. As he rose, Hadder fired both guns downward, this time aiming for Benn's newly revealed "face." Although he missed the lone eye, holes appeared surrounding the rage-filled orb as bits of flesh and bone flew away.

As Hadder shot down from above, Viktor Krill launched his attack from behind. Knife after knife plunged into Benn's exposed back, sending the creature into an increasing craze. Benn spun to face Krill, ignoring the bullets raining down on him. As he did, long talons slid out from the ends of their tentacle sheaths, promising to slice into soft skin and puncture vital organs.

Krill, never one to shy away from horror, waded into battle, tired of fighting from afar. He ducked and dodged as the hooked biological weapons swung for his face and chest, swinging his knives with matching fury and severing several tentacles, sending them to the forest floor to writhe around like earthworms on hot cement.

As the battle between Krill and Benn played out, Hadder began his descent. Seeing his handguns having little effect, Hadder neatly slid them back into their holsters as he fell and cocked up his right knee. Preoccupied with Krill as he was, Benn didn't even react as Hadder ambushed him from on high, landing atop the beast and driving his knee with impossible force into its shoulders, driving it to the ground.

Hadder sprung away before any of the barbed tentacles could strike, joining Krill. Both humans looked upon Benn with renewed shock, wonder, and respect.

"Shit, Benn, you're a hard man to like," said Hadder, speaking behind wide eyes. Benn rose once more, his single orb wide with anger, his mouth releasing a guttural cry not of this or any other world.

"That's because he is *not* a man, Marlin. He is something else. Something unnatural."

As Krill spoke, Benn began to convulse once more, tentacles flying in the air. Those that were cut by Krill sent a brownish goo cascading into the air to fall like an apocalyptic rain shower. Hadder took an impulsive step back to avoid the terrible substance.

"You're a Wakened human, Marlin. It can't do anything to you."

Hadder looked to Krill. "And others?"

Krill shrugged, his black eyes filled with limited concern, as if to say, *who knows what affect the unnatural can have on the weak.*

"Unnatural, you say?"

The strange but familiar voice demanded Hadder and Krill's attentions, forcing them to once more look upon Benn, who had issued the question. Hazel and black eyes fell upon Benn, who had ceased his shaking and was now sporting a single eye of the lightest blue. Benn's tentacles no longer swung chaotically in the air before him, instead appearing statuesque, cocked back like loaded crossbows, daring anyone to come near.

Hadder scoured his memories for the source of that ghostly voice that was now emanating from the sad creature known as Benn, trying desperately to scratch the itch that had appeared in the recesses of his brain. Luckily, Krill answered the query before Hadder could go mad trying to solve the puzzle.

"I would say that it's good to see you again, Milo, but we both know that is not true. Especially given the vessel that you have chosen. You couldn't have picked a more offensive messenger?"

Fucking Milo Flowers, thought Hadder, the voice immediately becoming painfully recognizable. That rage-filled little twist of a man who served at the feet of Albany Rott had always set off warning signals in Hadder's mind, but speaking through the fanged maw of a monster? This went far past Hadder's concerns.

Benn, now Flowers, shifted his giant blue eye from Krill to Hadder before returning to Krill. "I asked you a simple question, Viktor? What makes the form you see before you *unnatural*?"

Hadder stood in shock as Krill responded. "You know goddamn well what makes it unnatural, Milo."

"Do I now? I see before me two biological organisms that have never existed in this world's history. Are you two, therefore, also *unnatural?*"

"You know what we are, Milo. We are the full potential of Albany Rott's creation, by definition the most natural form of humanity. You, in this form, however…"

"Ahh, but that is where our thinking differs, does it not, Viktor? You always thought Rott's biggest crime was limiting our abilities as humans, while I believe that his most egregious insult was limiting life at all. Life needs no bounds, it should spring at will from every pore, every cell, every warm crevice."

"What you are describing is cancer, Milo. *You* are a cancer."

Flowers chuckled from within his hideous flesh puppet. "And what makes cancer so bad? It is life raging for growth, demanding to be noticed, refusing to be locked in to normal standards. Where you see cancer, I see life challenging the status quo. I respect that. I aim to give the ultimate power back to life, to flourish without borders."

Now it was Viktor Krill's turn to chuckle dryly. "Who are you kidding, Milo? You are a rage-filled little rat. I don't know what happened in your first life, or if you were simply born a nasty little weasel, but you've always hated humanity, always angled for its demise."

"And what about you, Viktor?! Who worked with me to decipher the Great Code, to unlock biology's potential? It was you! You were my greatest success. And now you are my greatest disappointment."

"It seems we never truly understood each other, Milo. I had two intentions. The first was to escape Rott's prison, which I stand by. The second intention was admittedly dark. But it was to dominate, to control; not to destroy. Not to watch the world burn."

Benn smiled, showcasing rows of sharp teeth within his oversized maw. "When you want future crops to come in faster, thicker, and with more yield, do you not set ablaze the former? From the ashes of man, a new world will flourish in perfect balance."

"With you as the messiah?"

"Why not?!" Flowers's rage had returned under Krill's questioning. "I don't take life! I redirect it! I translate it!" The too-blue eye moved to Hadder. "I *give* it." A smile returned to Benn's mouth. "You never thanked me for saving your life, Marlin."

Hadder finally found his voice. "That was Rott's doing, not yours."

"Nevertheless, they were my hands that pumped life back into your dead heart, that closed the holes made by your angry girlfriend." Hadder's Rage surged to the surface, and he moved forward, only to be stopped by Krill's outstretched arm. Flowers laughed once more. "Ahh, yes, there's that Rage; I know it too well, Marlin. I must say, I was surprised and even a little perturbed by Rott's interest in you, but I know now what he saw that I did not. I thought you would surely die during the Great Battle for Station. Then, I thought Rott would certainly cast you aside once he was able to return home. It looks like I was wrong on both accounts. I will not underestimate you again."

"Enough," cut in Krill. "You have gone completely mad, Milo. I know your end game."

Flowers shot an angry glare at Krill. "I don't doubt you do, Viktor. But that doesn't mean you know how I will get there. Or how to stop me. And do you know why, Viktor? Because you cannot stop me. You are Wakened, the first of your kind, the greatest that any human can ever hope to be. But I am no longer human, Viktor. I am so, so, so much more…" Flowers's voice grew farther away as he spoke, as if he was slowly exiting their bizarre conversation.

"You are a rat, Milo. You will always be a rat."

Flowers laughed softly at the jab. "You know, I haven't been called that in a long time, Viktor."

"Rat?"

"Milo. I have transcended that name. I go by many other titles now."

"And what are those?"

The voice became increasingly distant, as if Flowers was growing bored by speaking with mere mortals. "The usual. His Holiness. My Lord. God. Messiah. The same things that you both will soon call me."

"That will never happen," said Hadder.

"You may be right, Marlin. You both will probably die long before you have the chance to kneel before me. What a pity."

Krill spoke again, a thin layer of fear coating the killer's words. "Don't do this, Milo. It's not too late to stop."

"Life cannot stop, Viktor. It should not stop. It should be without bounds." A heavy silence fell over the tense trio. "You know, none of this could have come to be without you, Viktor." Hadder looked over to see Krill wince at Flowers's words. "We worked secretly arm-in-arm for countless Haelas, Viktor, discovering Rott's restrictors and removing them, allowing life to flourish, uncovering dark gifts and creating new organisms. Together, we have toppled our Creator, and you want to dash off before He smashes to the ground, denying yourself the greatest of accomplishments in the cosmos. Well, I will be there to take His place. I would like you to be there with me."

"I will not."

"Very well, Viktor, then do me this one favor. Allow me to officially pay back your contributions to this world's metamorphosis. Do not actively oppose me. Find a little corner of the world and claim it as your own. I will leave you be. This will be my gift to you."

Krill's mind spun with thoughts and dark memories. It was not Milo Flowers that stole his adopted daughter from him. It was not Milo Flowers that locked him away in a sunless city for eternity. It was not Milo Flowers that forced him to send away his son for protection.

Doctor Milo Flowers did none of these things directly, but his pale little hand had been moving pieces in the background for some time now. The ripples of his dark covert actions had already struck tens of thousands, causing irrevocable harm. And the collective pain of billions would follow.

"I do not deny my responsibility in your wicked rise, Milo. I do not deny that I once hated the world as you do now. I do not deny that I wanted to run a knife across the throat of humanity. But that horrible man is dead, and this Wakened human is all that remains. A Wakened human who cannot allow you to do this."

Benn's twisted form remained unmoving. "That's a shame, Viktor. But my conscience is now clear. I will feel nothing when my Blossoms skin you both alive."

"You have never felt anything but rage and hate, you ridiculous little man."

Benn's too-blue eye darkened. "The same was said about you, Viktor Krill. But did you feel something when that whore daughter of yours was eaten alive by a Slink of your own construction?"

Flowers had barely completed his sentence when Krill shot

forward, moving faster than the bullets from Hadder's guns. Within the blink of an eye, Krill was upon Benn, diving forward with twin blades held out before him. The tentacles sprung to life and swung inward like a bear trap, but they reacted too slowly as Krill was already inside their reach.

Krill entered Benn's chest like a missile, his blades cutting open an entry that was widened by Krill's torpedoing body. Hadder came in directly behind his companion, moving blindingly quick, collecting as many tentacles in his two hands as possible, holding them at bay and preventing further attacks. Two tentacles remained free and slammed against Hadder's dark suit, but they were luckily disarmed by Krill's earlier attack.

With Hadder holding several tentacles out wide with each arm, Benn released a raspy scream that echoed across the chilly forest, sending birds scrambling from treetops and small critters retreating into the safety of burrows. Hadder stared deeply into Benn's lone eye, now brown and bloodshot again, and watched as it went wide in pain, Krill's unforgiving knives doing horrible work to the changeling's back. With one last terrifying cry, Benn split in half down the middle, an enraged Viktor Krill coming into focus as he took hold of each side of the vampire squid's head and pulled the pitiful man apart. It was a clean tear, following where Krill's knives had already carved a deep crevice.

Hadder released the tentacles, allowing them to follow both halves of Benn's body to the forest floor, and stepped back.

"Marlin, move back," called Krill, and Hadder did as he was told, backpedaling away from the twin mounds of flesh. As he did, a thick vapor began to surround the carcass before it exploded into a cloud of spores, sending Hadder retreating even faster. His speed caused him to trip over a random stick and fall to his backside, his hazel eyes never leaving the spore cloud that was rising into the air. Eventually, a draft of air caught the cloud and sent it soaring above the tree line and away from the clearing, until it was finally no longer visible.

Krill collected his knives and joined Hadder, sitting next to his companion on the forest floor. The two Wakened humans stared in silence at where the man once known as Benn had fallen. Their calm scene was broken, however, when a bright-green stalk suddenly burst forth from the dark stain that once held Benn's remains. It thickened as it rose towards the blue sky, becoming twice as tall as a man and ultimately ending in a bud the size of a card table. After a brief pause, the bud exploded into an enormous tubular blossom that shifted in color from green to blue to red as it swayed slowly in the shifting winds.

Hadder looked from the wondrous blossom to the dark stain that surrounded the stalk's base. "Humicast."

"What's that," asked Krill from beside Hadder.

"I saw blossoms like that in Lester Midnight's Biomass display. He said that only the excretion of humans could provide the fuel, or *humicast*, needed to grow them." Hadder met Krill's questioning black gaze. "Is that all we're destined to be, Viktor? Humicast for Milo Flowers's new blossoms?"

Krill looked to the giant flower before returning to Hadder. "I think we need to have a serious talk, Marlin. Things are much worse than I anticipated. And, moreover, we are no longer flying under Milo Flowers's radar. From here on out, it's going to get pretty nasty."

"You know the horrors that I've seen, right?"

"Yes. And I know what I've seen. And still, I fear we have both simply witnessed the tip of the nightmarish iceberg that stands before us."

"Fuck."

"Exactly, Marlin. Fuck, indeed."

———

MARLIN HADDER and Viktor Krill sat silently in the clearing for a long time, staring coldly at the alien blossom that had sprouted where the pitiable man named Benn had fallen. The weight of a hundred questions pressed heavily upon Hadder's shoulders, but he kept these to himself for now. He simply waited, knowing that Krill's mind was whirling like a computer, testing variables and factoring them in with constants. As this world's sun finally began to creep behind the forest's tree line, Krill finally spoke.

"I never cared much for Doctor Milo Flowers. To be honest, I always found him to be a loathsome little vermin. But in Station, we shared interests. We shared curiosities. We shared goals. And most importantly, we shared a hatred for our fellow man."

"Milo Flowers also has the Rage. I saw it in him the first time we met at Rott Manor. It is a different kind of Rage from the one that inflicts me. I felt it then, and know that he did as well. We were like two travelers from the same small town who ran into each other in a foreign country. We should have felt a kinship. Instead, we hated each other all the more for it."

Krill nodded absently. "Flowers and I wanted to unlock the human body's potential, infuriated that Albany Rott would place restrictors on his creations. Then I wanted to escape Station, enraged that I was being kept as a lab rat for celestial enjoyment. Finally, I wanted to prove my strength, more to myself than to others."

"And that is where you and Flowers differed."

Krill picked up a small stick from the forest floor and broke it as he spoke. "Yes. To be truthful, I didn't give much thought to what that little twist really wanted. To me, he was simply a tool to be used, no different from the many I wielded both before and after him. I wanted to make the world pay for the pain I endured in my younger days. I needed everyone, especially myself, to know my strength, to respect it, to fear it. But my endgame was about control, about power."

"And Flowers?"

"He always alluded to it, but I refused to listen. I never thought he could escape Station. I never thought Albany Rott would let him get this far. I was so myopic at the time, so singularly focused, I missed all the clues."

"What does he want, Viktor?"

"Milo Flowers knows that Rott cares nothing for this world. He spent more time with Rott than anyone in history, save yourself, Marlin. He would have figured out by now that Rott was simply looking to punch his ticket home, which he has successfully done."

"Which means?"

"Which means, Marlin, that this world is without a god. Doctor Milo Flowers aims to fill that role."

Hadder's gaze returned to the Benn stain. "And how does what we just saw fit in with this desire?"

Krill's black eyes flashed dangerously. "I said he wanted to be a god. I didn't say he wanted to be a god of man."

Krill's words snapped Hadder's attention back to the killer. "What the hell does that mean?"

"I wanted to control mankind. Flowers wants to remove mankind. Your Rage is something you have struggled with your entire life. Flowers's Rage is a loving partner, something he has nurtured and fed over time."

"Can't you give me a fucking straight answer, Viktor!" Panic was beginning to settle over Hadder like a shroud.

Krill ignored the outburst. "Flowers believes in life unencumbered. And there is nothin more encumbered and rules-based than the human form. Flowers hates humanity, he hates the body that he has felt trapped inside." Krill paused for effect. "Doctor Milo Flowers aims to be a god, but not the god of this world as we know it. He wants to be the god of a new world, where humanity's existence has been erased, replaced by lifeforms that constantly change and shift, that consume and kill and birth without rhyme or reason."

"It sounds like Hell."

"It will be."

An uncomfortable silence settled over the clearing before it was broken by Hadder. "You helped create this monster."

"I did."

"You have known of Flowers's existence in this world for some time now."

"Not that long, I assure you. Literally, a few days longer than you."

"Still, I have felt no desperation on this journey of ours. Despite knowing what Milo Flowers can be and what he wants, I have seen no determination in your actions or attitude. Why is that, Viktor? Where is that Wakened villain who toppled the Muck and united its warring gangs? Do you *really* care?"

Krill's dark eyes flashed once more, and Hadder's body tensed for a possible attack. "If I am guilty of anything over these past weeks, *Marlin*, it is that I have significantly underestimated Flowers's ambitions and abilities. I knew what he wanted, but I never gave much thought to what he could truly achieve. I thought he would seize control of some far-off province, where he could resume his experiments and surround himself with his creations. He would play Messiah in a contained world of madness, and the rest of the world could simply look the other way."

"And now?"

"And now it seems as if there will be no other way to look."

"Tell me what's happening."

Krill sighed deeply before continuing. "It appears that the good Doctor is aiming to transform humans on a massive scale."

"How massive?"

"Is everyone massive enough for you?"

"Impossible."

"Is it?" Krill nodded towards the large blossom. "Benn is not the first that this has happened to. There will be more."

"What is changing them?"

Krill sighed again. "I don't know, Marlin. But if I had to venture a guess, it's something in the food supply. Or the water." He looked up. "Or in the air."

"Fuck me, Viktor!" Hadder placed a suit sleeve to his nose and mouth and spoke into the cloth. "Are we safe being out here!?"

Krill reached over and angrily ripped Hadder's arm down. "Don't be a fool. We are Wakened humans, the only pair in history. Never forget what you are! We have masterful control over our bodies and chemical makeup. We cannot be changed unless we allow ourselves to be."

"And others?"

"They will not be so lucky."

"If it is as you say it is…"

"As I am guessing," Krill corrected.

"If it is as you are guessing, then why aren't we seeing these changes everywhere? Why aren't there millions of others like Benn?"

"I don't know, Marlin."

"What? How do you not know!?"

Krill lost his patience with Hadder's questioning. "I'm a Wakened human, not a goddamn omniscient being! I don't fucking know!"

Hadder held up his hands in mock surrender, not wanting to push his dangerous friend any further. "Fine. What now?"

Krill had drawn one of his knives and now spun it masterfully in his hand as he thought out loud. "Flowers is putting something out into the world on a mass scale, whether in the food, water, or air. But it is seemingly affecting very few, thus far. Why is that? Does it need to build up in the body? Does it have a delayed reaction? Does it need a trigger? Too many questions need answers, Marlin."

"So where do we look for these answers?"

"No one knows where Doctor Flowers is now. He hasn't been seen in public in months, and the location of the Flowers Institute is carefully hidden."

"So where does that leave us?"

"If we cannot reach the source, then we will continue with our original plan. We will travel to satellite campuses of the Flowers Institute and learn what we can from these Petals. We know that they are scattered across the globe and are easily found."

"What do we hope to find at these Petals?"

Krill rose to his feet, his knife still spinning in his tan hand. "I thought that they would be nothing more than the public faces of Doctor Milo Flowers, institutes that did good while the real horrors took place far in the background."

"And now?"

"And now I think that they all must be lending efforts towards the creation of horror, and not in the background. Rather, right before everyone's open eyes." Krill looked down at Hadder. "Get up. You wanted to see my desperation. Well, here it is."

Hadder did as he was told, brushing dry pine needles from the seat of his suit pants. "Good to see." Hadder looked down and frowned at a brown stain on his white dress shirt. He then looked at Krill's white suit, which was spotless despite traveling through the chest of poor Benn, except for some fire damage on one sleeve. "Do you ever miss it?"

Krill's face twisted in confusion. "Miss what?"

"Station."

"What makes you ask that?"

Hadder nodded to Krill's outfit, the white suit being the only remaining tangible evidence of the sunless city's existence. "Your clothes. You just crawled through the body of another and came out clean on the other side."

Krill thought for a moment. "I miss some benefits of the place, not the place itself. Do not kid yourself, Marlin. It was a prison. It was an experiment station where the subjects were scheduled to be exterminated after the test. Do I miss it? No, I do not."

"I do."

"That's because you think so little of yourself, and what you can become."

"How's that?"

Krill shook his head and slipped his knife back into one of many hidden sheaths. "No. No. Nope. Enough goddamn questions. You also have a Wakened mind, Marlin. It is time you started using it alongside your physical abilities. Let us get back to our monocycles. This battle and these dark thoughts have left me ravished." Krill inhaled deeply. "You asked if I missed Station. I do not, and never will. But already I miss the smell of the Muck's chowsets and the endless options that they offer. Already I miss the cool breeze that would cut between the Towers as the sun began to set behind Cyrix Headquarters."

"And your friends?"

Krill stared off into the woods. "Yes, I suppose I miss some of them, too."

"And Mayfly Lemaire?"

Instead of answering, Krill took off into the forest in a blur, back the way they had entered the clearing. While he could easily address questions about false gods, gruesome transformations, and Hell made real, it seemed that some topics were too painful even for the world's greatest killer.

Marlin Hadder understood how Viktor felt as he sped after his companion, the world becoming a stain of color around him.

2

As Nieve passed Daksha in the quiet hallways of the Flowers Institute, both women nodded out of formality, the ghosts of smiles on their lips reflecting a wide spectrum of emotions, none of them civil.

She really wants me dead, thought Nieve as the impossibly thin woman made her way to the Holy Pistil, responding to a summons issued by her God. A cruel grin took over Nieve's mouth. *I can't wait for her to try.*

The two women, Doctor Milo Flowers's closest confidantes, couldn't have been more different. Daksha, dark and athletic, brilliant and calculating, hated Nieve for what she was — a rich girl with an eating disorder who used their Lord's gift to support her body dysmorphia. Nieve laughed at the thought. Yes, her God had made it so that her extreme thinness was not only maintainable, but empowering. She could now eat what she wanted and not gain a pound. She could break the bones of women who thought her weak because of her skeletal build. She had the perfect body, now without all the guilt, shame, and health concerns.

This is why Daksha hated her, for wasting God's talents. But that is not why Daksha *should* hate her. Daksha should have despised her for a multitude of other, more weighty reasons. As a rich girl with blond hair and blue-green eyes, Nieve's family name rang out among the upper classes who ran the world, making her an invaluable commodity to her Lord. She was not looked down upon in discussions with other strong women like Xioxian Chan, CEO of Taragoshi Robotics, who looked upon Daksha as one would a mail courier.

While Daksha was undoubtedly smarter, she should have abhorred Nieve for her superior degree from a school that would have never accepted a lowly dark-skinned girl from nowhere. Nieve's grades weren't great, but they were adequate, and her years at the Killmore Academy saw her rubbing elbows with the sons and daughters of the rulers of the planet. Nieve sharpened her talons as President of the Academy's largest sorority, learning about and noting the dark, embarrassing stories of the world's elite. Nieve now wielded her knowledge of these secrets like a katana, making the necessary cuts to bend powerful men and women to her Lord's will.

Daksha should have been disgusted by how easily Nieve navigated the social waters of world politics, carefully manipulating her accent, tone, pace, and language to steer conversations in directions that benefited the New God.

These are the reasons that Daksha *should* have hated her, not because of her tiny fucking frame.

Enough thinking of that vile woman, Nieve screamed internally, focusing her attentions on the matter at hand. Her Lord had summoned her, and she needed to be mentally prepared, lest she exit the Holy Pistil wearing a much different form from the one she had entered with.

Nieve cleared her head as she walked, her white pencil skirt and matching white blouse feeling ten sizes too large as she moved, which Nieve loved. She ran updates and figures through her mind, never knowing what information her Lord would want from her.

As Nieve approached the lone entrance to the Holy Pistil, she nearly dropped her Pastiche ream.

Standing next to the massive golden sliding doors of the Holy Pistil was a mammoth man who gave chills to all forced to look upon him. Cement Felix casually leaned his seven-foot frame against the wall, and Nieve feared that his weighty girth would crack the beautiful marble. Felix's inhuman muscles bulged under a custom blood-red suit. Apparently, her Lord's all-white dress code did not pertain to his beloved Anointed Champions.

Cement Felix failed to hear Nieve's approach, so engrossed was he in watching as he ran his oversized machete across the top of his left hand. He smiled in glee as its sharp edge refused to make even the slightest cut on his impenetrable grey skin. Nieve decided to speak first, not wanting to be considered "uppity" by her Lord's premier killer, a word the grey behemoth enjoyed throwing around, especially at the women of the Flowers Institute.

"Felix, good to see you. Do you also have a meeting with His Holiness?"

Cement Felix's large blade froze as the Champion swung his terrifying face toward Nieve, almost causing the woman to trip as she approached. Felix's face matched the rest of him, a bulbous grey nose sitting above grey lips. The giant man grinned wickedly as Nieve stopped, showcasing teeth that looked more home in a shark's mouth than a human's. But was Cement Felix really still human, after all?

"Nieve. You still live? I would have thought the weight of your responsibilities would have folded that sticklike frame of yours. Tell me. How long do you think you could last with a man like me? How long would it take before those bones turned to dust under my thrusts?"

Felix's voice sounded like a boulder come to life, while his disconcerting light pink eyes flashed threateningly. Nieve took a deep breath, at home dealing with dangerous men, and reminded herself that Felix had nothing specifically against her. Cement Felix hated everyone save their Lord.

"That's enough, Felix," said Nieve, putting her best mothering tone into the statement. Felix just stared for a moment before bursting into harsh laughter, its deepness threatening to chip bits off the many ornate statues that decorated the hall.

Felix's enormous head moved back and forth as he roared in amusement, causing the singular braid that hung over his left shoulder to dance before Nieve. With the right side of Felix's head heavily scarred, as if someone had taken a blowtorch to it, hair only grew on the monster's left side, which he took great pride in. The hair that sprouted on that lone side was thick and luxurious, carefully maintained and worked into ever-changing, mesmerizing braid designs. These braids always ended in a collection of finger bones that swung noisily from the end, a grim reminder of those who opposed the New God.

"My deepest apologies, Nieve." There was no hint of remorse in Felix's gravelly voice. "I forget that you Faithful are without senses of humor."

Anger welled up in Nieve, overwhelming her fear of the dangerous Felix. "Are you not faithful, Felix? Do you not believe that our God is the true God? Do you doubt Him? I think our Lord would be disappointed by these words. Perhaps I should share them with Him."

Another deep laugh assaulted Nieve. "Stupid woman. I am more loyal to Doctor Flowers than any on this miserable world, including yourself and that burnt-skinned whore Daksha. But I do not follow him because he is God, which I do not doubt. I follow him because he shares my views of this planet. Namely, that it must be purged and reconstituted without rules, without limits, without false morals. Doctor Flowers is making this happens, and I am one of the few among the humans who can protect Him as He does."

"You are not a human. You are an ogre in a suit."

Felix's pink eyes went wide. "Ah, so that is why you detest me so. The idea that our God may favor an ogre like me over a human like you must eat at you. It must threaten to consume the little meat you have on that repugnant body of yours."

Nieve internally winced at Felix's words, but she showed nothing. Felix may have been cement, but Nieve was steel. "You think him not a god?"

Felix thought for a moment. "He is *a* god. He is *my* god. But that is not why I follow him. And *that* is why I will always be more loyal than you. *That* is why I will always be his favorite."

Felix's words hit Nieve like an ice bath. "I don't have time for this. Is our Lord prepared to see me?"

Cement Felix waved his machete toward the large golden doors. "Doctor Flowers is waiting. I can speak to him later, clean up any messes you may have left behind."

Nieve almost launched a verbal attack on the grey thug, but stopped herself. Felix had already mentally dismissed her and was picking at his thick, red-painted fingernails with the point of his machete.

Nieve exhaled deeply, ridding herself of any anger, fear, and resentment aimed at the Anointed Champion, and turned toward the large golden doors, which silently slid open when her palm touched the metal.

Nieve flung aside all residual negative feelings before stepping into the Holy Pistil, wanting her Lord to feel only love and dedication from his loyal servant.

———

"You seem unwell, my child. What distresses you?"

Nieve stared into her Lord's too-blue eyes as he spoke, his face jutting out from his Chrysalis. Unlike that idiot Daksha, Nieve had no issues looking upon her God's changing form. In fact, she found it hard to look away. That was how beautiful she found the New God, and how deep her love for him ran.

"I'm sorry, my Lord, it's just that Cement Felix waits outside the Holy Pistil. I always find his presence... off-putting." Nieve left it at that, understanding that she was speaking ill of one of his Anointed Champions.

"And he said some uncouth things to you?"

"He did, my Lord."

"I'm sorry, my child, but we must forgive Felix of these minor transgressions. The reaction that he elicits from you and the others is the very reason he is so valuable to me. Every god needs his protectors, and they are almost always demons in the flesh. But Felix is as loyal as he is vicious, and that is all you need to know."

"Of course, my Lord. I was not complaining, simply responding to your query."

"And I appreciate your honesty, Nieve. I would now request more of the same for this conversation."

"Always, my Lord."

"Do you know of Viktor Krill, Nieve?"

"Only tangentially, my Lord. Daksha was much more involved in that failure." Flowers smiled at Nieve's obvious jab at her perceived competition. "I know that he was instrumental in Cyrus Bhellum's death and our inability to purchase the land necessary for the proposed Bhellum Petal. Other than that, I do not know much."

"Viktor Krill was one of my early projects. He played a key role in escaping my former prison and is partially responsible for much of my divine knowledge."

"Then he is holy, my Lord?"

Flowers thought for a moment within his cocoon. "He is not. Oh, how I hoped he would be, but he is not. I thought he would lead my Anointed Champions, be First among them, but, alas, he has chosen another path. I gave him godly powers, and, in return, he has turned his back on his creator. He is not holy, Nieve. He is wicked, the most wicked human on this planet, and soon he will try to impede our divine work. In short, he must be stopped."

"He sounds terrible, my Lord. What would you have me do?"

"The vile Viktor Krill must be captured. Alive, if possible. But dead is acceptable."

"Shouldn't be too hard to catch one man."

"Viktor Krill is not alone. He travels with a man named Marlin Hadder, another human who owes his life to me. They have banded together, two hurricanes of fate, joined as one to destroy your Lord."

"But still, they are just two men. We will have them in our capture by the week's end."

"Do not underestimate them, Nieve. All that have are now mere energies flowing aimlessly through the cosmos. I made Viktor Krill into the most powerful human in history, and I am confident that he has done the same to Marlin Hadder, who has his own hidden... talents."

"But surely, they can be stopped, my Lord."

"Of course they can. They are still men, not gods. But we must do everything to slow their progress. We will water the ground and watch them come to the surface like the worms that they are."

"I thought you loved worms, my Lord."

"I do, Nieve. And I love my creation that is Viktor Krill. But he is beneath me. Worse, he is actively working against me. Thus, he must be destroyed."

"Understood. How should I water the ground, my Lord?"

"Use your connections at the banks. Track their current location before freezing their accounts. They are both resourceful men, but this should impede them a bit."

"Consider it done. Would you also like me to contact Anton Carlyle? Their faces can be plastered on every news outlet owned by Maxim Global Media."

"Yes, that will be done, my child, but let us leave that to Daksha. She seems to have a real rapport with the curmudgeonly Carlyle."

Nieve took an involuntary step back, as if one of the tall surgical mechs working on her Lord's Chrysalis had stopped to run a scalpel across her too-tight belly. Flowers noted her discomfort and smiled.

Nieve struggled to recover. "Of course, my Lord. Is there anything else that I can do to help apprehend these heathens?"

"Yes, Nieve, there is something that you can do. Something that only you can provide."

Nieve perked up at this. "Just speak it, my Lord. It will be done."

"Do you still regularly speak with Xioxian Chan?"

Nieve smiled brightly, recognizing that her close relationship with the Taragoshi CEO would assist her Lord and his divine work. "We remain close friends, my Lord."

"Good. Very good."

As Flowers spoke, a scream echoed across the Holy Pistil before fading away, leaving only the general hum of the surgical mechs behind Nieve as a hundred experiments were conducted on a hundred specimens, all moving closer toward divinity.

————

DESPITE THE HORROR that they had just witnessed, Viktor Krill had no problem finishing off three meat pies from a chowset in the small town of Yeffik. Following the first bite of each pie was commentary on how it couldn't hold a candle to the Muck's food vendors. Although Krill would never admit it, Marlin Hadder could tell that the killer missed his adopted home. Perhaps the only home the enigmatic Krill ever knew.

Hadder and Krill spoke little during their pitstop, neither needing to tell the other the stakes of this latest adventure. Their conversation with Milo Flowers, via the unfortunate Benn proxy, cemented what needed to be done. At all costs.

They needed to destroy Doctor Milo Flowers. To accomplish that, they needed to find him. The location of the Flowers Institute was a heavily guarded secret, unknown to all but those closest to the false god. Among those trusted by Flowers were world leaders, corporate heads, and the directors of the Petals, known pretentiously as Arch-Soothers. While the first two groups would be hard to infiltrate, the Petals were notoriously open, welcoming the sick from around the globe to receive "holy restoration" or the "healing touch."

While the Flowers Institute itself was cloaked in secrecy and shadow, the Petals were the targets of a marketing blitz, their locations endlessly shared via commercial and their success stories repeated ad nauseam on almost all media channels. Millions flocked to the Petals to cure an array of maladies, both significant and trivial, and none were ever turned away or charged for services.

They were the perfect places for Hadder and Krill to sneak into and find answers.

The closest Petal was almost four hundred miles away, in the burgeoning city of Crimmwall. If one were to look at it quickly, Crimmwall would have appeared the same as Bhellum thirty years prior, a port town that served as the central hub of the region. Whether by boat, plane, or automobile, thousands flocked to the Crimmwall Petal on a weekly basis, most to receive holy treatment, but many to simply bask in the holiness of the New God.

Hadder's stomach groaned at the thought.

Thus, it was decided that Hadder and Krill would travel to Crimmwall, infiltrate the Petal, locate the Arch-Soother, and force them to give up the whereabouts of the Flowers Institute. Hadder had voiced concerns that one so devout may not be willing to divulge such secrets. Krill had no such worries that they would spill their guts, both literally and figuratively.

And so, Hadder and Krill found themselves on the Abstract Highway that ran across the continent, their Taragoshi Monocycles weaving in and out of traffic, gobbling up the kilometers that sat heavy between themselves and the Crimmwall Petal. The tiny earbuds that Hadder wore pumped this world's version of synthwave into his head as he pushed forward, tearing past auto-taxis and rail trailers, alike.

Viktor Krill matched Hadder's speed, even moving far ahead of his companion occasionally, with no music to backlight his journey. Instead, a different kind of soundtrack played in Krill's mind. The laughter of a young girl and her adopted brother melded with the faux anger of a black-skinned queen, forcing Krill's hand down on the throttle, as if speed could help him escape painful memories.

Unfortunately, they always managed to keep pace.

On they traveled for over an hour, the two most dangerous men in history making good time towards their goal, as if they were destined to quickly accomplish their urgent task.

And then fate stepped in to show them otherwise.

With Krill neck-deep in dark thoughts, Hadder was the first to notice the change. Vehicles on the highway that recently soared past were now mere smears of color. Hadder looked down to see the monocycle's speed increase to suicidal levels as the motor's RPMs rose dangerously high.

Hadder focused his Wakened reflexes on keeping the cycle upright and away from others on the road. He looked to his left to see that Krill was in a similar predicament, offering Hadder a weak shrug as his monocycle, too, accelerated beyond safe parameters.

On the companions flew, the scent of burning rubber tickling their noses as both monocycles pushed past intended limits, only their Wakened abilities keeping the vehicles upright. And then those, too, were rendered meaningless.

This time, it was Krill who noticed the change, first. He motioned desperately to Hadder, who saw him as another auto-taxi passed between in the blink of an eye. Krill's fears were quickly proven correct as Hadder confirmed that his steering, too, was no longer under his control. He signaled back to Krill, echoing the warning.

Both monocycles were now controlled by another.

While panic enveloped Marlin Hadder, Viktor Krill, no stranger to deadly situations, reacted. The notorious killer carefully stood on the seat of the monocycle and directed Hadder to do the same. Despite the dire situation, Hadder shook his head in the negative, terrified of attempting such a risky maneuver. Krill screamed into the tornado-like wind, and although Hadder could not hear him, he could make out the words.

"You must! Now!"

Swallowing down his fear, Hadder raised his feet and placed them onto the monocycle's seat before carefully standing, leveraging all of his Wakened abilities to keep his balance and prevent flying off into traffic. When Hadder had finally attained some sense of equilibrium, he looked once more at Krill.

"Now what?!"

Instead of responding verbally, Krill held up a finger, as if to say, *now we wait.*

Several uncomfortable moments passed before the endgame reared its ugly head. Both Taragoshi Monocycles, now traveling in tandem, started to veer to the left, crossing numerous lanes of traffic, narrowly missing devastating collisions before entering the medium that separated directions of the Abstract Highway.

Hadder's hazel eyes went wide and met Krill's equally large black orbs as both came to a singular realization. *We will be smashed against oncoming traffic.*

Hadder and Krill, using their uncanny talents, sustained perfect balance as the monocycles bounced over small obstacles within the medium before entering the opposite side of the Abstract Highway, where enormous vehicles bore down on them at blinding speeds.

Hadder looked to Krill for guidance, but the Wakened killer merely pointed up at his questioning glance. He shrugged desperately, and Krill pointed up more emphatically, his accompanying words lost in the raging winds.

Seconds later, the time for planning had come to a quick end as both monocycles cut a line across the highway to intercept a large rail truck coming from the opposite direction. Due in equal parts to Krill's direction and an odd innate reaction, Hadder jumped straight up milliseconds before his cycle was obliterated by the oncoming rail truck, celebrating silently when he saw that Krill that done the same.

Time slowed to a jog, and then a crawl, as both Wakened humans soared high into the air, scores of vehicles passing beneath them, any of which would prove deadly should his soft body meet their speeding steel.

As the companions reached the zenith of their jump, Krill pointed towards an impressive auto-van in the distance, trailing the rail truck that had stuck their monocycles by several hundred meters.

Hadder nodded and angled his body as the pair began to descend, diving like an arrow toward the road to intercept the approaching auto-van. Krill followed suit, and the companions soared through the air like synchronized swimmers, perfectly mirroring each other's every move and reaction. The air resistance pushed the skin of their faces back into grim smiles, and Hadder thought, *at least I will leave behind a merry corpse.*

Speeding bodies and racing auto-van closed the distance that separated them. Just as Hadder and Krill's heads were about to smash against the van's curving windshield, both men executed perfect somersaults, spinning in midair as knees tucked into chests.

As heads spun away from the auto-van, legs were thrown back down with impossible power, caving in the plexiglass barrier as both mean tore into the vehicle like human torpedoes. Luckily, the auto-van was empty of passengers, for the plastic windshield failed to halt Hadder and Krill's momentum. Instead, the Wakened humans careened through the entirety of the speeding metal carrier, taking out all four rows of seats with their twisting, out-of-control bodies. Only the back of the auto-van, which luckily had no rear door or hatch, brought the companions to a full stop. Hadder groaned loudly upon realizing that he had lived through the ordeal.

"Marlin, are you ok," asked Krill from the opposite side of the auto-van as he tried to extricate himself from the wreckage.

"Fuck! That hurt."

"I didn't ask you if it hurt. I asked if you're ok."

Hadder attempted to move, and found that he could. Although he ached everywhere, nothing seemed too out of sort. "I think so. I don't think anything is broken."

"Of course it isn't. You're a Wakened human. It will take more than that to break us." Krill threw the last of the ruined seats off himself and stood. He offered Hadder his hand and pulled him free from his prison of debris.

The companions stood uneasily in the still-speeding auto-van. After brushing bits of plastic and cushion from their suits, Hadder spoke first. "Well, that was close. What the fuck was that?"

"Taragoshi."

"What?"

"Remember that commercial I showed in Bhellum's office? The one for the Flowers Institute?" Silence from Hadder followed. "Come on, Marlin! Use your damned Wakened mind!"

Hadder jumped from Krill's admonishment. "Ok, ok, just give me a moment! Fuck, man, we just nearly died!"

"Not so nearly. Now, do you remember?"

Hadder's Wakened mind spun back in time, to when he first met the notorious Viktor Krill. The Flowers Institute commercial played on the back wall. An older asian woman spoke into the camera. Her title appeared below her...

"Xioxian Chan was there. She is the President of Taragoshi Robotics."

"That's right. That wasn't so hard, now, was it?" Hadder frowned at Krill. "I fear that our little discussion with Flowers back in the forest has moved me and, by proxy, you, from the potential ally column and into the active opponent category."

"Meaning Flowers's followers, including Taragoshi, have started to take notice of us. And they've decided that our little trip needs to be stopped."

Krill's black eyes went wide with false surprise. "There's the Wakened human that I spent so much effort in creating! Thanks for joining the party."

The auto-van continued down the highway. Hadder looked around his destroyed surroundings. "Well, what now?"

Krill also looked around. "First, we need to get control of this..." Krill's voice faded off.

"Yes? Get control of this..."

"Goddammit."

Hadder grew concerned once more. "What is it, Viktor?"

Krill nodded to the front of the auto-van, just below the ruined windshield. There, in bright chrome along the dashboard, it read *Taragoshi Motors*. "Godammit," echoed Hadder, and just as he did, the loud *click* of doors locking filled the auto-van's cabin followed by the lurch of the vehicle's acceleration.

Both Hadder and Krill looked out of the gaping hole in the front of the auto-van to see that traffic had slowed to a crawl down the highway. They tore their eyes from the scene and stared at each other knowingly. They were locked in a metal box that would soon ram into a near stationary object at a ridiculous speed. Even their Wakened bodies would be mangled in the violent collision.

As always, Krill reacted first. "Marlin, on three, kick the holy hell out of this sliding door."

"But, it's…"

"Just do it, man! One, two, THREE!" On Krill's call, the pair front kicked the right door panel of the auto-van, their uncanny strength significantly bowing the thick metal. "Again!" The metal sliding door cried out as Wakened legs assaulted it. "Once more!"

With a great *snap*, the auto-van's large side door flew off into the distance, cascading with a red roadster to cause a multiple-vehicle pileup. And still the auto-van raced on toward the upcoming stopped traffic.

"This is where we get off," stated Krill matter-of-factly.

Hadder watched as the road sped by beneath him. He looked back through the now-open side to see all manner of vehicles surrounding the van. "We're gonna be smashed to pieces."

"Trust your Wakened instincts. Trust your Wakened reactions. And roll. Now go!"

Hadder did as he was commanded, understanding that additional thinking would only lessen his resolve. He leapt from the speeding auto-van, clearing his mind as he did, allowing the rare gift he was given to take over, allowing it to drive his actions. Hadder hit the pavement at a ridiculous speed and was shocked to find that his legs kept pace for several strides before succumbing to imbalance.

As he fell, Hadder's Wakened abilities kicked in, slowing time and tucking him into a neat ball that somehow protected his head and other vulnerable areas. He rolled countless times, his body bending here, twisting there, always moving in a way that would minimize irrevocable damage.

After a dizzying journey, Hadder's momentum finally slowed enough to spring back to his feet. Time still slowed, he looked around frantically to find that he was now on the far side of the highway, almost out of harms way. Unfortunately, he also noticed that an auto-taxi was upon him, meters away from his fragile body, leaving no time for either the vehicle to stop or Hadder to move.

Hadder was a dead man. Again. With only time to close his eyes against the coming onslaught.

The collision came in a rush, but not from the front as he had expected, but from the side. It drove the wind from Hadder's lungs as he was sent airborne once more, soaring away from the highway, over the railing, and down the embankment that bordered the busy road.

Hadder tumbled down the steep hill and, despite flipping head over heals, was thankful to feel soft grass under him rather than unforgiving asphalt. Moments after Hadder had finally stopped rolling, his mouth filled with dirt and grit, Krill joined him, gracefully skidding to stop next to his Wakened partner.

Above and behind the pair, the sounds of metal smashing into metal filled the air, and was soon joined by rising pillars of smoke and the acrid smells of exhaust, burning rubber, and leaking batteries.

Once more, and this was getting embarrassing, Krill reached down to help Hadder to his feet. Despite his feeling of inadequacy, Hadder detected no judgment in Krill's dark eyes.

"Would you call *that* nearly dying," asked Hadder, trying to inject some levity into the situation.

"For you? Yes. I remained in full control the entire time."

"Good for you." Hadder looked down to see that his suit was completely shredded from their narrow escape. "Shit!" He looked over to Krill and noticed that the killer's white outfit still looked pristine, with only the burns on its sleeve to detract from its brilliance. Hadder shook his head and sighed. "I guess that eliminates Taragoshi vehicles from our options."

"I fear it is much worse than that," responded Krill, taking Hadder by the crook of the arm and pulling him along, moving farther from the destructive sounds of the highway above.

Hadder almost asked why, but thought better of it, instead using his own Wakened mind to ponder the possibilities. After several seconds, he had reached a hypothesis.

"You think Taragoshi has shared our info with the other transportation companies?"

Krill kept the companions moving. "I do."

"Under what pretense?"

Krill shrugged. "Taragoshi is by far the leading technology

company in this world. They can make up any story they want. There are plenty of fears for them to take advantage of."

"For example?"

Krill shrugged again. "They can claim that we are anti-robotics, anti-AI zealots, working to steal secrets and undermine technological prosperity. It's not like those groups don't exist in spades in this world."

"So, we'll need to be careful with the transportation we use. Shouldn't be that big an issue."

"It's worse than you think, I fear."

"How so?"

Krill continued to lead Hadder away from the highway, away from modern society. "Milo Flowers's reach extends exponentially by the week. I don't think his powerful followers are limited to Taragoshi. My guess is that, very soon, we will discover that our credit accounts have been locked and that we are wanted by every municipality and police force in the country, if not the world."

"Shit! How will we get to the Crimmwall Petal now?"

Krill maintained his pace, always moving away from the congestion of the exploding highway, as Hadder limped along beside him. "We have notes. They still spend everywhere. Especially in the shadowy realms we will now need to traverse to accomplish our goal." Krill stopped suddenly and looked at Hadder. "You know how to move like a phantom, don't you?"

Hadder thought back on his most recent exploits, to the times since his first death. In none of those stories did Marlin Hadder manage to fly under the radar. "I might need a refresher."

Krill shook his head and began walking once more. "Well, you had better learn quickly. From this point on, you and I are atop this world's most wanted list. There are spotlights everywhere, and we will be surrounded by betrayers, by exploiters. Learn to love the shadows, for the light is now our enemy. Now, let us be away from this place. They will begin looking here."

Hadder stopped for a moment and stole a peek behind him. In the distance, the air was thick with black smoke and the skies began to fill with uni-copters investigating the sudden pileup.

Hadder looked up and watched as this world's sun began its daily trip below the horizon. He sighed heavily and moved painfully to follow Viktor Krill once more, deeply bothered by the fact that he would once again have to shun the day's light, fearful that this would once more become a permanent thing.

3

Daksha slowed her walk as she made her way along the cobbled path through the Flowers Institute's beautiful courtyard. She always did. No matter how many times she crossed through its lush gardens and walked along its crystalline bridge over the artificial pond, her breath never failed to catch in her chest.

Along the edges of the courtyard, a variety of flowers never seen on this planet threatened to burn out eyes with their beauty. The strange fertilizer that sat at the base of the large plants gave off a sickly sweet scent, filling the enclosed space and bringing water to visitors' eyes.

When Daksha looked down through the clear bridge, bizarre creatures could be seen frolicking in the pond below, curious things with human faces that could best be described as oversized sea monkeys from the backs of comic books. Some periodically leapt from the water to snatch a large chunk of pollen from the air that was gently released by one of the many umbrella-shaped blossoms. Others would patrol up and down the multiple streams that originated from under the walls of the Institute to feed into the magical pond.

Throughout the water, colors of the spectrum swirled along

hidden currents, mixing with fantastic starlight that permeated the liquid, creating a wholly enchanting scene.

One that only Daksha's god could conjure.

The dark-skinned woman swallowed back a sudden urge to cry and quickly regained her composure. Unfortunately, that composure was soon lost again as Daksha stepped from the crystal bridge, rounded a corner, and almost stumbled headlong into the gangly Seth Whispers, one of her Lord's four Anointed Champions.

The bizarre man, standing at over eight feet in height, was one of the few on the island who could look directly into the flowering blossoms of her Lord's creation. Seth did that now, inhaling deeply of the sour pollen that decorated each bloom. It was said that her Lord's pollen had both psychedelic and aphrodisiacal effects on those who ingest it, so Daksha was unsurprised when Seth's face was flush when he finally removed his head from the flower.

Seth Whispers seemed nonplussed by Daksha's appearance, which made sense given that he was the most stealthy of the Anointed Champions. He probably knew Daksha was going to cross through the courtyard before she did, which made their meeting all the more worrisome.

Seth took a step back on unsteady feet, probably an act. Despite his face being ruddy from the inhalants, the rest of the whiplike man's skin was bone white, a sickly color that mirrored the creature's grotesque behavior. Seth's too-wide grey eyes went even wider as he feigned surprise at seeing Daksha. His giant pale hand rose and tipped the black fedora that he wore on his comparably peanut-sized head.

"Ah, my lady, I failed to notice your arrival. As always, you are the definition of beauty and grace. My day is so much brighter for being able to take you in."

As always, despite being repulsed by the stick man, Daksha was forced to lean in to hear Seth's words, which always came under his foul breath. Her lips reactively twisted into a scowl at Seth's sweet statements, which were always thinly applied over an obvious foundation of hatred and rage. His "gentlemanly" demeanor fooled no one, especially the women who were forced to endure his sloppy, disingenuous advances.

Seth Whispers was a tumor in human form. Still, Daksha was thankful that it was *this* Anointed Champion that she ran into, and not Batti Bat or Yuki Donna. Seth Whispers she could handle, but those two demons…

"What sweet words. It's good to see you, Seth. I see that you are enjoying our Lord's gifts on this beautiful day."

Seth laughed awkwardly and wiped the purplish pollen from his face without taking his large eyes off Daksha. They danced along her frame, forcing her to unconsciously run her hands along her pantsuit, as if to prove to herself that clothing still covered her body. Seth licked his white lips as his grey eyes ran up and down, and Daksha grew horrified to think that another of this fiend's gifts could be to see through clothing. The idea that Seth Whispers was currently memorizing the view of her naked dark skin was enough to almost make Daksha vomit onto the cobbled pathway. But she did not.

Seth's eyes finally met Daksha's. "In more ways than one, my lady." It took every ounce of Daksha's control not to roll her golden eyes at the ridiculous Champion. "And where might you be going? Perhaps we can share a meal if the mood is striking you and your belly has found itself needing nourishment?"

Daksha wanted to say that her belly was currently filling with bile, but resisted the urge. This was, after all, one of the Anointed Champions she was speaking with, and that was no small title. "A most generous offer, Seth, but I have pressing business for our Lord. And as you know, he is great in all things, but patience is not one of them."

Seth's pixie nose flared in the air far above Daksha, as if he could smell the lie in her words. Maybe he could. Seth's disconcerting eyes went briefly wide once more before returning to their regular saucer shape. "Just as well, my lady. I just remembered that I also have a pressing engagement. I have been tasked with making the rounds this afternoon, a noble job if there ever was one. Our Lord's faith in my abilities is a boon to my confidence. And my libido. Another time, on another day, I will prove my worth to you. Until then."

And with that, thinking he had just hit a walk off home run, Seth Whispers turned on the heel of a black and white dress shoe, and tore down a side path that would lead to an alternative courtyard exit. His impossibly long strides carried him away faster than Daksha could ever hope to run, something she always needed to keep in mind.

As he loped down the pathway, Seth's twin odachi swords, each too long for any normal human to ever wield, bounced gently on his bony back where they were strapped. Daksha wanted to laugh at the foolish Champion. But then she remembered how Seth had split a young resident cleanly in half with one of his long blades after she had innocently giggled at one of his clumsy attempts at courtship. When Seth had noticed the look of horror on Daksha's face, he simply shrugged and said in a low voice, "The young lady besmirched my honor. I had but a single choice."

Daksha shook away the grim memory as Seth passed out of sight. Her once pleasant jaunt through the courtyard ruined, Daksha quickly passed through the remainder of the courtyard and reentered the Institute's outer hallway. In only a few minutes, she had reached her destination – Nieve's office.

Daksha stood in the open doorway for a moment, waiting for the bony woman to notice her. Nieve was absorbed in her Pastiche ream, pounding away at the holographic keyboard that was transposed on her white office table. Beside the ream was a small pile of sunflower seeds, probably the woman's lunch and dinner.

Daksha loudly cleared her throat, the anticipation of this conversation becoming too much to handle.

Nieve looked up from her work and frowned before regaining control of her friendly facade. "Daksha. To what do I owe the pleasure?"

Daksha did her best to hide her glee, although a thin smirk managed to sneak through onto her lips. "Oh, nothing much, Nieve. I just heard about the fiasco out on the Abstract Highway and wanted to see if there is anything I can do to help."

Nieve's false smile finally faded. "It's under control, Daksha. Everything is under control."

"Is it? Because I heard that you had Viktor Krill in your grasp, and you lost him. He *and* that impotent partner of his. Both escaped and are now..." Daksha put her dark fingers to her mouth and blew. "Gone. Lost to the world."

"And how is that *my* fault? These are not normal men; they will not be captured so easily. Maybe where you come from, everything is expected to come easy, but from where I sit..."

"How dare you?! From where I come from? You forget yourself, Nieve, and who you are, and who you are speaking with! You are the girl born with the silver spoon. It matters not that you refuse to eat from it."

Both women stared daggers at each other from across the office. Even for Daksha, referring to Nieve's food issues was a low blow. Daksha and Nieve may have been competitors for their Lord's love and trust, but they both still served the one true God.

"What is it that you want, Daksha? Or do your juvenile insults comprise the entirety of your purpose for today's visit?"

Daksha bristled at the response to her attack. "Your failure has not gone unnoticed. The capture or elimination of Viktor Krill and his associate Marlin Hadder is no longer your directive. It is now *our* directive."

Nieve stood up in a huff. "Says who?!"

Daksha smirked at her adversary. "Says the New God. I just came from the Holy Pistil. It appears that Viktor Krill is beyond your lone scope of abilities. He is now *our* quarry."

"And what do you plan to do?"

"I don't *plan* to do anything. I have already done it."

"Care to share it with me?"

"I will. Because I must."

"Get on with it, Daksha."

Daksha idly smoothed down her pantsuit as she spoke. "Well, leveraging my close relationship with Anton Carlyle at Maxim Global Media, Viktor Krill and Marlin Hadder are now the world's two most wanted men. As we speak, their faces are displaying across every channel and broadcast in the known world."

"And what charges did you trump up?"

"The usual. Enemies of the state. Terrorists. Threats to the public. I threw in sex trafficking of minors and animal abuse to make sure that the entirety of the world despises them."

"How clever," said Nieve through gritted teeth. It obviously pained the woman to have to offer her rival a compliment.

Daksha shrugged, barely containing her joy. "I thought so. I also have a call in to Roanda Marks at Universal Bank to freeze any of their accounts, limiting their options."

When Nieve's face twisted in confusion, Daksha knew that she had made an error in her desperate attempts to jab her colleague. "What do you mean, you have a *call in*? You weren't put through immediately?"

Daksha straightened. "Well, no, but I'm sure she'll return my call shortly."

Nieve angrily shook her skull-like head. "It is no wonder why our Lord sent you here. I'll contact Roanda as soon as I've finished here. Her son Fillip and I had a *thing* one summer, and she's always like me."

"But I already…"

Nieve smiled wickedly. "Oh, come on now. Did you really think the head of the world's largest bank is going to speak to some dark-skinned nobody from nowhere?"

"But, I…"

Nieve's smile grew vicious. "You still haven't learned how this works, have you, poor Daksha. It doesn't matter to most of these people, to this old money, that our Lord favors you. Our Lord's favored trash is still trash. And unworthy of their time or attention. But I thank you for the update. I'll take care of this before the end of the day. It has been too long since I have caught up with Ro."

The use of the familiar "Ro" stung Daksha deeper than it should have. It was a pointed reminder that no matter how high Daksha climbed, there would be glass ceilings that she could not penetrate.

Daksha laughed bitterly, tossing aside the injury like an itchy blanket. She reminded herself that this was a fleeting power dynamic; that soon, after the Great Conversion, money would no longer have value, and only her Lord's Faithful would wield true power.

Daksha painted a smile onto her dark face. "Then I will leave you to it. I will talk to Xioxian Chan once more, and ask that she speak with the Collective. Soon, every vehicle with AI or recognition software will be off limits to these heathens."

Daksha's smile widened when Nieve had no slick retort to this comment. Everyone knew that Xioxian Chan was a self-made woman, had risen from the dirt to sit alone in the world's robotics pantheon. Nieve's pedigree would hold no sway over the robotics magnate, Daksha's legitimate friend.

Nieve laughed in a huff and popped a sunflower seed into her mouth. It was as close to a called truce as the frail woman would ever come. "Then I suppose we both have our tasks…"

Daksha waited for Nieve to finish, but soon realized that the uppity woman would not even dignify her with a proper dismissal. Anger swelled up in the dark-skinned woman, faster than she could reign it in, and culminated in her spitting a brown loogie onto the marbled floor, just within Nieve's spotless office.

Nieve's face scrunched up in disgust, and Daksha beamed with pride. If this skeleton thought her trash, then best to leave her with something to clean up.

With that, Daksha began to storm away, but something held her back. There was something more that needed to be said. "Oh, I almost forgot."

"What else could you possibly want, Daksha? Or would you like to take a hot shit on my desk? That's probably par for the course where you're from."

Daksha wanted to leave in a rage, but found that she could not. This had to be voiced. "Seth Whispers. He's been prowling around the Institute today. He's high on pollen. You should be careful as you move about. Take some residents with you."

Nieve's angry face fell, as if someone had thrown ice water onto their campfire. She stumbled over her words. "Yes. Well. Thank you for that. It is noted."

Daksha nodded briefly and then sped down the white hallway, a strange mix of emotions swirling within. Nieve was her adversary, to be sure, but she was also a woman and a servant of their Lord. And Daksha would be goddamned if she let a sexually charged, blade-wielding toothpick harm an invaluable asset.

The Anointed Champions might be her Lord's protectors, but even Daksha had her limits to what would be tolerated. They may be necessary evils now, but once the Great Conversion was eminent, Daksha swore that the Champions would be the first to burn under the fires of the New God's reign.

———

HADDER AND KRILL walked all night through small, dense forests and sped across vast empty plains, two shadowy blurs against the midnight backdrop. Four ears kept to the sky to detect the dim hum of spy drones or louder flutter of manned police copters.

Every time the cold night air threatened to cut too deep, Hadder used his newly acquired Wakened abilities to push the pain away, redirecting it to further fuel his muscles, which now never seemed to tire.

On the reluctant companions traveled in silence, the weight of their current predicament slowly beginning to hang heavy as a once-difficult task quickly grew more impossible by the moment.

Hadder false-started a hundred conversations with Viktor Krill, always stopping himself just as breath was about to form words. Instead, he pushed on in silence, the voices of dozens of lost friends and family creating an uncomfortable symphony in his mind. As Hadder tried to shake these memories to no avail, he looked over to see Krill's black eyes directed at the ground and knew that he, too, was struggling with sounds from the past. Hadder sighed deeply and waded back into the discomfort of personal history.

Luckily, a short time later, both men, or humans as Krill would call them, found their disturbing playlists paused. The bright lights of a distant city came into view several hours before the first rays of morning would begin to rain down like spotlights.

Hadder squinted at the collection of light, as if his Wakened eyes would allow him to read the welcome sign from twenty miles away. They did not.

"What city is that, Viktor?" Krill remained silent, and Hadder could almost hear the complicated network of gears turning over in his too-sharp brain.

"That should be Kharras. If we had stayed on the Abstract Highway, we could have bypassed it completely. And we would have. It is a shit hole. Bhellum without the charm."

Hadder kept his thoughts about the city of Bhellum to himself, not wanting to upset his dangerous running mate. "And how do you know of this Kharras?"

Krill's dark eyes shot over to Hadder, almost tearing up with annoyance. "Marlin, I ruled over a drug empire that was spreading across the continent like wildfire. It was my job to know these things. And Kharras was to be one of our next strategic hubs. It is not heavily policed in the same way Crimmwall is, and would have proven the perfect staging ground for our southern expansion efforts."

Hadder couldn't resist. "Sorry for shitting on your plans."

Krill's black orbs flashed with danger, causing Hadder to involuntarily tense. "Don't ever think that you and that pompous fallen angel had anything to do with my downfall. It was corrupted from within long before you two found your way to Bhellum. And be glad for it. Because if I was at full strength when you arrived, Marlin Hadder, you would be in the cosmic reaches now, and not traipsing through dirt to confront a powerful false god."

Hadder had recovered from Krill's anger, his own Rage now bubbling to the surface. "So, I should be glad for not being reunited with my family in the energy of the universe? I should be glad for being dragged along across deaths, only to find myself coupled with a villain to face a demon messiah who seems to have the support of the world? Is that what you're saying?"

Hadder's speech picked up as he continued, and the coating of threat in his voice thickened with every syllable. The Rage began to take over.

Krill saw this clearly and, although he feared nothing, his black eyes softened. The two Wakened humans may have been destined to battle each other at some point, but this was certainly not the time or place. Krill held up his hands in surrender.

"All I am saying, Marlin, is that, yes, I know this city. Its seedier edge may be able to benefit our cause. Money talks in places such as Kharras, and questions are rarely asked when ample notes are produced."

The Rage melted away like wax before a flame, leaving Hadder with only residual embarrassment. Krill nodded, understanding only too well the constant battle against anger that left one invariably hollowed out, with only negative emotions to fill the space.

With the tension finally released, Hadder found his voice once again. "On to Kharras?"

Krill shook his head, sending his ponytail swaying behind him. "It will be light soon. Better to camp out in those trees over there." Krill pointed to a small grove ahead and to the left. "Like I said, the darkness is our friend, especially given our current situation. Perhaps that will change soon, but for now…"

Hadder simply nodded and followed the notorious killer, the Rage's quick appearance and exit leaving him exhausted for the first time since his Wakening.

It seemed that even Wakened humans were not immune to the effects of the Rage, this intangible enemy that had accompanied Marlin Hadder throughout his many lives, the only shadow that required no source of light.

———

MARLIN HADDER and Viktor Krill laid on their backs on opposite sides of a small fire, the copse surrounding them offering protection against prying eyes. Two sets of eyes, hazel and black, stared up at the night sky through a break in the foliage above. Wakened minds raced, neither truly understanding what the other was thinking.

As usual, it was Hadder who finally broke the relative quiet. "I'm not tired." He thought better of his words. "I mean, I *am* tired, but I'm not sleepy. How long do you expect us to stay here?"

"Until dusk."

"Dusk? That's fucking…" Hadder did the math in his head, something even his Wakened abilities had struggled to improve. "…fourteen hours from now. What do you expect me to do in that time?"

"Rest. Recharge."

"But I'm not tired."

Krill rolled over onto his side to face his endlessly annoying companion. "Marlin. You are a Wakened human now. Your body does not tell *you* things. *You* tell your body things. Like when to rest and for how long."

Hadder continued staring at the stars, refusing to meet Krill's glare. "I guess you failed to mention that during our fifteen-minute Wakened human orientation."

Krill fought back the urge to dive across the small flames and throttle the only other person in history to share his unique moniker. With those feelings sufficiently suppressed, Krill then had to push down chuckles that were rising from his chest, understanding only too well the confusion that accompanied a Wakened body.

"Marlin, you have to remember that you are no longer riding shotgun in an old jalopy; you are driving a muscle car, and it will do as you command."

"Meaning?"

Krill let out an exasperated sigh and flipped onto his back. His dark eyes squinted at something in the heavens before he continued. "Meaning, if you tell your body to rest, it will. That could be for one hour, or twelve. Our Wakened vessels can store energy in ways that these false humans could never hope to replicate. A twelve-hour revelry could mean that we can go a week without sleep again. Which could very well be in the cards for us. Do you understand?" Krill waited for a pause.

Hadder's silence told him everything he needed to know. "Clear your mind. I understand how difficult that is, but you can do it. Once all else is gone, the only things that will remain are commands. Commands that your Wakened self *will* obey. Shut everything off. Only then will you…"

"What the fuck is that?"

Krill cursed under this breath, hoping that Hadder would not have noticed the abnormality in the night sky. He should have known better. Even an infantile Wakened human would not miss such a thing.

"What?"

"*That!* That pink dot in the sky."

"It's nothing."

"I don't think so. No, scratch that. I *know* it's not nothing. I'm a depressive person, Viktor, which means I've spent more time than most staring at the stars. I know this may be a different plane of existence, but I'm pretty sure the contents of the universe haven't changed that dramatically. And I don't ever remember seeing a pink dot up there. A fucking *bright* pink dot." Krill's silence, drenched in obvious hesitance, told Hadder all he needed to know. "What is that, Viktor?"

Krill gave himself a moment to collect his thoughts before responding. "I don't know, Marlin. That is my honest answer."

"But you have an idea?"

"Yes."

"And that is?"

"God's judgment."

Now it was Hadder's turn to flip onto his side to stare at Krill across the flames. "What was that?"

Krill refused to face his companion. "I believe that is God's judgment."

"What the fuck do you mean by that?"

Krill's mouth twisted in uncertainty before he, too, rolled onto his side. This was something that needed to be said face to face. "I think that…" Krill pointed to the pink spot. "…is God's judgment. It is coming for this world. And we will all burn when it arrives."

Hadder twisted in discomfort. "What the hell are you talking about? Why would that prick give a shit about what's going on here?"

Once again, black eyes met hazel, firelight dancing in both sets of orbs. "He. Or she. Or it. Or whatever it is, dislikes the fact that there is a new messiah in town. I think He is taking it as a personal slight."

"So?"

"So, when you throw rocks at God, expect to get asteroids in return."

"But He must have known this would happen."

Krill smiled knowingly. "Remember, He bet against it. With Albany Rott coming out the victor in their wager. I don't know any gods, but my guess is that they are not partial to losing."

"So, you're trying to say…"

"I am not saying anything, Marlin!" Krill rolled once more onto his back. "Apart from this — get some rest. Command your body. Store your energy. I fear that this may be the last good repose we get for a long time. Now leave me alone!"

And with that, Krill closed his eyes and was gently snoring seconds later. Hadder gave it several minutes before following suit, finally putting his back against the cold ground. The last thing Hadder saw before forcing his body to shut down was the pink dot against a black backdrop, as if the narrow tip of God's accusatory finger aimed directly at him, blaming him for the faults of humanity.

Hadder wanted to argue against the accusation, but found that he could not.

4

Marlin Hadder and Viktor Krill strode casually into the city of Kharras shortly after nightfall. Although not comparable to the Neon City, Kharras came alive with light of its own, a muted Bhellum covered in a blanket of its own neon luminescence. Hadder looked over as they entered the dome of brightness and watched as the corners of Krill's lips twisted in a slight smile.

Perhaps Viktor Krill missed his home even more than he was letting on.

Hadder breathed in deeply and could smell much with his Wakened olfactory nerves. In addition to the usual scents of street food, garbage, and exhaust, Hadder detected much more under the surface. He decided to share his findings with Krill, who undoubtedly had already made similar discoveries.

"I smell desperation, a loss of hope. There is blood in the air here, not unlike Bhellum. This city is rotting from within, but is without a fresh coat of paint like the Neon City. They feel like sister cities in many ways."

"More like father and son," corrected Krill. "But you are right. This city festers. The open sores are obvious to any who would dare to take an honest look." Krill inhaled. "There is Slink here. Not a ton, but enough to make someone very wealthy, especially given that the supply has now ended."

"Are all the cities of this world like this, Viktor? All the ones I have visited seem to share similar qualities, none of them positive."

"This world appears sick, Marlin. There is a malady that I cannot put my finger on, but this world is feeling it increasingly every day." Krill spun his dark eyes toward Hadder. "It is the perfect environment for the rise of a new messiah, for the deification of a false god." Hadder nodded solemnly as an auto-taxi sped past, temporarily blocking out the sounds of a screaming woman from a nearby alley. "Come. Enough dwelling on the issue. Let us find a solution to our current situation. And quickly. The longer we linger, the more eyes will fall upon us."

———

HADDER ACTED as lookout as Krill worked at the MBU, or mobile banking unit. He leaned backed into the shadows as an eight-wheeled law enforcement tank roared past, filled with Loaded police and topped with riot control auto-turrets. Hadder exhaled as they passed, never thinking that he would actually miss Bhellum's inept Bobby Bots.

Viktor Krill let out a short curse from behind before joining Hadder. "Accounts frozen, as I imagined. I was hoping that we would have time for one last withdrawal."

"Don't you have any other accounts? Secret accounts? I thought you were supposed to be some great villain."

"Of course I do, you fool," snapped Krill. "But those cannot be accessed with a simple MBU. No matter. I didn't need the money; I needed the information. The reach of the Blossoms is as far and deep as I feared."

"Won't they be able to pinpoint where you tried to access your account from?"

Krill shrugged. "Probably. Which is why we need to be moving. If all the autonomous vehicles weren't already dead to us because of our handprints, they certainly are now that our credit accounts are locked." Hadder looked confused. "They don't take notes, Marlin."

"Which means?"

"Which means that we need to secure more traditional means of transportation, old school automobiles or motorcycles like those from our world that are not connected to the Globe-net, and start with a key."

"They still have those here? I certainly haven't seen any."

"I admit, they are few and far between, but they exist. They mainly exist in collections of the very wealthy. You know, what was once old and outdated is now popular and desired due to rarity."

Another police tank came into view, forcing Hadder and Krill deeper into the darkness. "Certainly not lacking for police presence in Kharras, are they?"

Krill stepped back into the neon light as the tank passed. "The city still thinks it has a chance to recover. It has yet to resign itself to its dark fate. But it needs to. They are only making things worse. Villains running a city might not sound ideal, but it often ushers in a stability that law enforcement could never provide. Plus, I remember hearing that the Kharras Police Force is unloved by criminal and citizen, alike. In their efforts to save their jobs, to prevent them from being turned over to superior Taragoshi Auto-Enforcement Squads, the KPF is especially brutal, going out of their way to prove how hard they are on crime. From what I've heard, all they've accomplished is pissing everyone off, from villain to resident to business owner."

Hadder's head swiveled up and down the busy boulevard that sat only a few yards from the companions. He began to feel very naked under the glow of the neon light. "Viktor, I think we should be moving."

"Right you are. Come, let us do some investigating. I have the notes that pry lips loose. We should be able to locate some classic vehicles in short order."

"Do you have enough notes to purchase one of those, as well."

Viktor Krill smiled darkly, and an evil twinkle appeared in his black eyes. "I do. But we're not going to need them."

———

THE WAKENED PAIR's exploration of Kharras and subsequent inquiries uncovered much. Marlin Hadder and Viktor Krill were wanted on a global scale, their names and "faces" plastered on every news outlet encountered across the city. Luckily, this world had no actual photo of Marlin Hadder, forcing them to use a poorly rendered drawing of the man who retained similarities to several million other adult males. Viktor Krill was even luckier, as the photo used on each telecast was borrowed from the Cyrix Industries executive archives. The photo displayed an affable blue-eyed man with short blond hair and an impish smile, the opposite of the swarthy Krill.

Despite this good fortune, Hadder and Krill remained careful, walking in the darkness of the city, when possible, and interacting only with those who maintained an obvious distaste for the law. While Hadder was no novice to the seedier side of life, Krill was an obvious master. He could immediately sense whether a person would prove useful to their search, or a waste of time. Answers to Krill's questions came fast and true because of either intimidation, broken bones, or an exchange of notes, each one bringing the companions closer to their prize.

During their investigation, it became clear that the city of Kharras was on edge. Police tanks continued to pass, each stuffed with Loaded bodies. Everywhere that Hadder and Krill visited, there was evidence of Milo Flowers. It was as if thin cables were rushing up from the city to meet a great control bar in the sky, an invisible hand manipulating all beneath it.

Alongside the weathered neon, Kharras was decorated with another kind of wrapping. Signs, posters, and graffiti covered the city, lovingly applied by the Blossoms of the New God. Each notice bore the lotus symbol that Doctor Flowers had adopted, and called for complete devotion to this world's most recent messiah. Interspersed among these fairly innocuous messages, however, there were other, more deliberate directives.

Marked with a horizontal line with three small triangles attached, one centered on top and two others to either side beneath, points facing out, these posters were of the darker variety.

Those who do not acknowledge His Holiness are devils disguised.

Walk in His light, or burn in OUR fires.

The New God is the only God. Either surrender to His love or OUR wrath.

Report anything against the New God to the Thorns and be handsomely rewarded.

After seeing several such messages, Hadder's curiosity could take no more, and he asked a particularly grizzled street bar vendor with missing teeth about them. Hadder choked down the unpleasant home brew as the woman answered.

"You must be new here, honey. Them's the goddamn Thorns." Hadder's face remained blank. "Fuckin' hell, you are green to Kharras, ain't cha. The Thorns? You know, the Thorns o' Reckoning?"

"I am unfamiliar." Hadder put an extra note on the filthy bar top that separated himself from the equally dirt-covered woman. She took an anxious look around before sliding the note into her stained apron pocket.

"The Thorns o' Reckoning. They's the Blossoms new muscle, as if those fuckers ain't nasty enough."

"What are they doing here?"

Another nervous look around. "They's a bunch of fuckin' killers. Scoopin' up anyone who might be against they almighty New God. Group o' goddamn witch hunters if you ask me. They don't need any evidence to pick you up, no they don't. Even got the police scared of them." One last swivel of her pruned head. "Gonna be a showdown soon, I'm tellin' ya. Best stay clear of those white-on-white bastards." The woman spat a brown loogie onto the street to accentuate her point.

Hadder threw another note onto the table as thanks and chugged the remainder of his offensive beverage. The pieces began to fall into place. While in Kharras, he and Krill had seen numerous men and women in white trench coats overtop white skinsuits, always in hushed conversations with the city's more deplorable element. Their eyes shifted quickly as they listened to the most recent gossip, fanatical faces crying out that everyone is guilty until proven innocent. And no one was innocent.

"I have what we need." Krill's voice angrily cut into Hadder's inner monologue, causing him to jump. Krill immediately assumed the worst and tensed, his tan hands reaching for his hidden knives. "What is it? Threat?"

Hadder waved him away. "No. It's nothing. But we need to talk."

"Fine, just let me get a drink."

Hadder put a hand on Krill's suited shoulder and leaned in, not wanting to upset the street bar's proprietor. "Not here."

A few minutes later, Marlin Hadder and Viktor Krill found themselves in an alley bar barely bright enough to see the liquid contents of the glass in one's hand. Across the small bar, most could not distinguish the faces of the patrons that occupied the space, except when a lit cigarette was brought up to dry lips. It was the perfect location for clandestine conversations.

Krill downed most of his drink in a single gulp. "What is it, Marlin?"

Hadder took a long drag from a joint he had bought while Krill was making inquiries. As the smoke rolled into his lungs, he wondered whether that particular Leaf had come from Old Tens. He found himself hoping so, for he had grown to like the veteran gangster. Hadder responded to Krill as he exhaled.

"Those strangers in white we have seen across the city..."

"The ones I told you were outsiders?"

Hadder nodded. "The same. You were right. Turns out they are part of some fringe group of the Blossom that call themselves the Thorns of Reckoning. They..."

Krill cut in. "I can already guess what they do, Marlin. The same as any extremist religious group has done over the millennia. They accuse, they imprison, and then they murder. They use their fanaticism as an excuse to live out their dark fantasies. Fantasies that were there long before they found their *new* god. But now they can justify the blood that they so desperately want on their hands."

Hadder took another pull from his joint before handing it to Krill. "Well, they're here, and they're searching for someone."

Krill sent a plume of smoke into the dark distance of the bar. "They are looking for anyone they can string up, bloodied and mangled, and point at to say, *this is what happens when you fail to do as we command.*"

Hadder tried to keep Krill on track. "In any case, they are here and looking for trouble. I think that's why we're seeing such a police presence." Hadder thought for a moment. "Fuck, you don't think they're looking for us, do you?"

Krill handed back the joint and finished his drink. He then ordered two shots before turning back to Hadder. "Yes, Marlin, I think they are looking for us, and anyone else that may not be as insanely loyal to the New God as they are. But remember, they have only our names, not our faces. And, anyway, do you think I fear these Thorns, or anyone else this world has to offer?"

Hadder had a retort loaded, but did not fire it. If it was considered too personal, too painful, a fight would have resulted that could end them both. Hadder shifted gears. "I do not. But it is something we need to be aware of."

A pair of shots appeared on the bar in front of the companions. Krill took one and shoved the other at Hadder. The only two Wakened humans in history threw back the shots in silence.

Krill continued. "You are right, and we are aware. Now, on to the important stuff. I have found us a ride."

"That's great. What are we waiting for? My skin is crawling under the neon gaze of this border town. It's Bhellum without the charm, or the Spirit Girls."

Krill chuckled at the mention of his beloved Spirit Girls. "I understand the feeling, Marlin, and couldn't be more sympathetic. But it won't be so easy."

"Elaborate, please."

"Taragoshi and the other corporations have put forth a ton of effort in removing these vehicles from the world. They really don't like not being able to track everything and everyone. Their lobbyists have gone to great lengths to pass extremely limiting vehicular exhaust regulations that older models simply cannot adhere to. Unless they are customized."

Hadder's face twisted confusedly. "I don't understand."

Krill ordered two more shots, which concerned Hadder. *Was there to be bloodshed this evening?* Krill continued. "Well, we can't simply go to a junkyard because we don't have the time necessary to rebuild a vehicle. But we also cannot simply buy a shitty used car, especially since we are going to take it on the interstate. The Interstate Control Bots scan vehicles to determine exhaust levels and test a myriad of other regulatory variables. We would be forcefully stopped within fifty miles outside the city."

"Sounds like we're running out of options here."

"We are down to one. But one is decidedly better than zero."

"And that is?"

"Patton Yellich."

Hadder sensed danger in the air and silently ordered two more shots. "And who might he be?"

"The former big dick of Kharras."

"Former? He no longer holds that title?"

Krill shrugged. "He is still a key figure in the city, but he shares that power now with the Blossoms."

"Are they aligned?"

Krill scoffed at the question. "Anything but, Marlin. Patton Yellich might be the typical corporate shark, but he is also quite a pious man. He is a diehard Israalii, very much akin to the Hebrews of our world. Needless to say, his beliefs have heavily bumped heads with those of the Blossoms."

"And Patton Yellich matters to us, why?"

Krill threw back another shot of liquor, and Hadder followed suit. "Because, dear Marlin, Yellich is also quite the fanatic. But his obsession is for classic automobiles. Not only does he buy and restore them, but he puts millions of credits into making them street legal, meeting all the demands of the Global Environmental Order. These rebuilt rides address all of our needs. They adhere to the modern codes without tracking the drivers or passengers."

"And where are these metal saviors of ours?"

Krill offered a *tsk-tsk*. "Careful with your choice of words, Marlin. You never know when a Thorn is lurking in the shadows."

It may have been the liquor starting to kick in, but Hadder quickly grew impatient. "Where?"

Krill shrugged once more. "In his personal museum, of course. A glassed-in garage that is connected to his mansion. At the top of the hill. I believe the locals call it Kharras Knoll."

Hadder took one last drag before putting out the joint's cherry on the damp bar top. He moved to get up. "Then what are we waiting for?"

Krill put a hand to Hadder's chest, stopping him mid-rise. "It is a little more complicated than that."

Any goodwill that came from the liquor exited in a huff. "How so?"

"As I said, it appears that Yellich's dedication to his religion has run him afoul of the Blossoms. Yellich has supported the Kharras Police Force for decades, buying him some much-needed loyalty during this time."

"What are you trying to say, Viktor?"

"I'm saying that Yellich's mansion is heavily guarded, by both a personal security force and Loaded police units."

"So it won't be a simple smash and grab job?"

Krill's black eyes flashed, even in the dimness of the smoky bar. "Oh, there will be smashing and grabbing. But it will also require some sneaking. And killing. We have a few hours until sunrise. Do you think you're up to it?"

Hadder rose from his stool once more, and Krill made no move to stop him. He loudly cracked his neck. "Of course, I'm up to it." Instead of moving toward the exit, however, Hadder turned to face the shadowy bartender. He held up four fingers. "But let's finish our drinks first."

Krill nodded knowingly. Murder was never a pleasant experience for most, especially when there was nothing personal at stake. Few things could dull the twang of guilt that accompanied the taking of lives.

Copious amounts of liquor, however, could do the trick.

————

Viktor Krill moved like a phantom, and Marlin Hadder followed. Despite his Station-sourced white suit, Krill disappeared into even the smallest shadow, as if the darkness expanded at his whim to consume him and the tailing Hadder.

Krill's intel had proven correct. In addition to a large security detail dressed in expensive suits and armed with small machine guns known in the Muck as Stutters, Loaded police also patrolled the grounds of Kharras Knoll. Fortunately, there were not as many police present as the companions feared, with most still making rounds across the city searching for vigilante groups of Thorns.

Guards and police on the outer edge of the Knoll were easy to slip past, with large gaps appearing between their security routes. As Hadder and Krill drew closer to Yellich's mansion, however, the number of bodies became greater, more compact. Soon, their strategy of stealth would no longer be enough.

And then the killing would have to start.

Patton Yellich's residence was a sight to behold, a residence that screamed wealth and power. For such a man to be on high alert was a testament to the power and perceived threat of the Thorns of Reckoning.

Yellich's mansion was a four-story monstrosity that encompassed most of Kharras Knoll. The structure was curved, appearing as a quarter-circle from above, as if its arms were open to embrace the city below as a child. And from what little Krill was able to learn about Patton Yellich, that was how the man felt. Kharras was his child, duty bound to obey his commands, and he, in turn, was responsible for its protection, especially against outsiders like the Thorns.

To the left of the main domicile, sitting against the building like a tumor, was the glass-encased garage-slash-museum, home to dozens of classic automobiles. Using their Wakened eyes, Hadder and Krill discovered much about the transparent enclosure without having to draw too close.

For starters, it couldn't be opened from the outside; there was no keypad or keyed entrance door. This meant that the only access to the garage would be from the main building, something the companions would have liked to avoid entirely.

Next, the only way to remove cars from the museum was through a wall panel in the rear that swung up like the garage doors of Hadder's old world. With military-grade laminated security glass comprising the structure, simply ramming an automobile through the wall was out of the question. This rear exit led to a secret service road that wove its way down the Knoll through a thick forest, against which the entire city was built. Krill recently extracted this information when the pair ran into a former Kharras Knoll gardener in the city's red-light district, along with a couple of the man's teeth.

It seemed that Yellich had earned the loyalty of even his departed employees. But no one remained silent for long when questioned by Viktor Krill.

The Wakened pair spent several minutes taking inventory of the situation from deep within the shadow of a small copse of trees that sat in the "front yard" of the mansion. With variables finally calculated and weighed, Krill leaned in to whisper.

He nodded to the left and right of their hiding place. "We have to dispose of those two." Krill looked seriously at Hadder. "And I mean *dispose*. We can't have them waking up and shooting us in the back." He nodded to other places. "And them. And them. And he might have to go for good measure."

Hadder's stomach tied itself into a knot, but he reminded himself that everyone was dead anyway if they failed in their mission. Or at least everyone would wish that they were dead. "And then what?"

Krill looked up. "And then onto the roof. From there, we'll elimi-nate the rooftop guards and gain access to the house. No idea what we'll find in there, but it shouldn't be anything we can't handle. Once in the museum, we open the rear door, even if I have to hack it, and then we are off into the night. With any luck, we will be in Crimmwall by lunchtime."

"Sounds so simple."

"It rarely is. Clear your mind. Ready yourself."

Hadder did as Krill showed him, stripping all unnecessary thoughts and worries from his brain while carefully manipulating his internal chemistry, loosing an adrenaline drip that would feed his Wakened abilities and transform him into a superman. The world around him grew clear, and the near future turned from gas to solid as he saw how every movement, every action would feed into the next. His pupils the size of quarters, Hadder nodded to Krill.

Krill began to move, but stopped. He faced Hadder one last time, his black eyes flashing as they always did before blood began to fly. "These are not men, Marlin. They are obstacles. They are nothing. We succeed, or all is lost. Understand?"

Hadder simply nodded once more. Words were no longer necessary.

Krill waited half a beat before taking off like a bullet, a streak against a dark night. Hadder followed.

Krill cut to the left and Hadder went to the right. Despite moving at blinding speed, the world slowed before Hadder. The guard that he raced at was in the middle of lighting a cigarette. He looked up as Hadder reached him, but his eyes didn't even have the chance to go wide. Hadder's fist shot out like a piston, crushing the man's throat and leaving him a wheezing mess on the cold, dewy grass.

Hadder refused to slow, silencing the voice in his head before it could even speak. He sped on, targeting his next *obstacle* and moving in. This guard managed to see Hadder a moment before his arrival, and had even begun to raise his Stutter at the blur approaching him.

Hadder moved like a Russian ballerina, stepping neatly into a front kick that shattered the Stutter in the guard's hand before twirling into a spinning elbow that connected squarely with the side of the man's neck. An audible *pop* emanated from the strike before the guard's limp body fell into one of the ground's many gardens.

Hadder moved on, sparing only a single glance to his left to ensure that Krill was also on schedule. Unsurprisingly, he was.

As Hadder closed the distance to the house, the two final lower ground security guards on his side noticed his presence and began to swing their Stutters up from their shoulder harnesses. Making a hundred calculations in a millisecond, Hadder realized that he could not reach them before Stutter rounds began to ring out into the night, drawing unwanted attention.

In a flash, Hadder withdrew the twin crystalline handguns taken from the dead pimp Higgins. With a single smooth movement, still running at a full sprint, Hadder fired two muffled shots, each striking a guard between the eyes before an index finger could pull the Stutter's trigger.

Hadder reached the two guards before their minds even fully registered that they were dead. He caught both men by their ties and gently lowered them to the ground to minimize noise. He then kissed his twin guns, quietly thanking Krill for finding him silencers that fit the unique barrels of the custom weapons, before sliding them back into their holsters beneath his suit jacket.

And just like that, Hadder found himself with his back against Patton Yellich's mansion. He looked over once more and found that Krill was in a similar position. The Wakened humans nodded their congratulations to each other.

Viktor Krill smiled, a white slash against his tan face, and pointed up. And then he was gone.

Krill flew up the mansion's stonework as easily as he would a runged ladder, his hands and feet finding purchase where a normal person never could. Hadder marveled at his companion for a moment before reminding himself that he, too, had such abilities.

Hadder spun and began to climb. Small protuberances in the stonework felt like enormous handholds. Shallow seams between the stones might as well have been deep shelves, allowing Hadder's feet to easily balance on them.

In no time, Hadder had reached the top of the mansion's imposing face. He easily hung from the lip of the roof and carefully peeked over the edge to glimpse the building's flat top. Half a dozen armed security patrolled the rooftop, looking out into the darkness for any signs of danger. Unfortunately for them, all of their eyes aimed into the distance, trusting those who guarded the ground level to identify immediate threats.

Hadder looked to his left a final time and found that Krill, too, hung from the roof's edge, his head just above the top of the building. Hadder watched as Krill studied the guards' patterns, calculating the perfect opportunity to strike. Seconds later, Krill swung his leg over the edge and rolled silently onto the roof. Hadder followed.

Now the companions were in perfect sync. Their rolls neatly transformed into low runs, with Krill cutting to the left while Hadder went right. Hadder imagined knives appearing in Krill's hands as if by magic, spinning out into the dark night to find homes in soft necks.

Hadder's own weapons materialized almost as magically, their crystal barrels aiming at skulls as if drawn to them by an unseen force. Muffled shots rang out, blanketed by the heaviness of the night, and shadowed bodies fell hard to the cold rooftop.

The final guard on Hadder's side of the roof, sensing that something was wrong, swung his stutter at the streak of darkness that was racing his way. Just as his finger began to press against the trigger, the guard's shoulder exploded in pain as a bullet ripped through the muscle. The man's pain was fleeting, as a second bullet tore through the center of his head. Before the world went black for the guard, he found himself in the arms of his killer. Although shrouded in darkness, there was a light bleeding through the shadowy figure, who gently lowered the dying man. The strange figure whispered into the guard's ear. "I'm sorry. Go back to the universe, my friend." A small smile crept onto the man's lips. And then he died.

Hadder stood up in a crouch and looked across the rooftop. Unsurprisingly, only one other silhouette could be seen standing against the starry backdrop. Hadder and Krill met at the roof's center.

"Nice work," simply stated Krill. "We need to move quickly. In short order, someone's either going to find one of the bodies below or notice that the patrols up here are missing."

Hadder looked around and made an observation. "No one was watching the rear of the building. Does Yellich have that much faith in his secret forest path?"

Krill shrugged. "Probably has some cops stationed around the path's hidden entrance on the other side of the Knoll. Anyway, that's not our concern. Come, let us get in and be out like an executive's lunchtime quickie. If we leave this place in rubble, it will only complicate our escape from this miserable city."

"Agreed. Let's go."

Hadder and Krill easily located the rooftop's small set of stairs and followed them down into the mansion. As guards would frequently have to enter the mansion for breaks and to relieve themselves, there was no alarm triggered when the Wakened duo entered the living space. They moved like spirits through the impressive home.

Patton Yellich's home was beautifully crafted and tastefully decorated, all warm hardwood peppered with art and artifacts from decades prior. For most people, this would have been a time to gawk at the collection and expression of wealth. To take in that which was usually reserved for the elite.

But Marlin Hadder and Viktor Krill had seen so much more than the average person. They had both walked the mystical grounds of Rott Manor. They had both traipsed through Cyrix Industries Headquarters. They had both lived in a city of night, where everything glowed and sparkled and pulsed with magic.

Kharras Knoll simply could not compete.

While numerous domestic helpers surely serviced the mansion, they were all undoubtedly still comfortably asleep in their beds given the early hour, unaware of the phantoms moving silently just outside their bedroom doors. Despite the silence, Hadder and Krill took no chances. They moved quickly but carefully, slinking from shadow to shadow, always cognizant of areas that were particularly vulnerable to being viewed. Instead of using the ornate staircases, Krill simply leapt over the railings, landing softly like a cat some twenty feet below.

Hadder did the same, and gave a quiet thanks to the heavens when his ankles didn't disintegrate under the impact.

No additional security was found in the home, nor were any recording devices spotted as the companions made their way down. This was in line with the information that Viktor Krill had obtained during his interrogations. Patton Yellich, despite being a public figure, was very protective of his personal life. With no wife or children, rumors ran rampant that Yellich was a sex maniac, or a collector of illegal animals, or ran a secret cabal. Looking around, Hadder could only glean that Yellich was an older gentleman with impeccable taste who wanted nothing more than to be left alone in his off hours. Hadder could relate.

Only one thing was apparent as the pair continued their trek to the bottom floor – Patton's Yellich's religion was central in his life.

Evidence of his Israalii devotion could be found throughout the mansion, from tapestries with six-pointed stars, to marble statues of hands with eyes on the palms, to paintings with scripts that looked to be a variation of the Hebrew alphabet. If Patton Yellich was guilty of anything, it was not kissing the ass of the New God.

Hadder's hazel eyes passed easily over Yellich's collection of religious artifacts as he stalked from one hallway to another. He remained careful not to knock anything over, more fearful of breaking something of sentimental value to the homeowner than of making noise.

Hadder had almost slipped out of a large room dedicated to ancient weaponry when a dark corner of the room gripped his attention. There, on a triangular pedestal tucked neatly into the corner, rested a small dagger. It looked older than time itself, with a simple bone handle from which sprung a gleaming, curved blade. Just beneath the weapon, a quote was crudely carved into the pedestal's soft wood, a feature quite improper in Yellich's neatly manicured abode.

The False must be opened to expose the Great Lie.

Hadder stared at the words for several seconds, tilted his head in curiosity as something stirred deep within him. His eyes locked onto the bone handle, where someone had burned *YHWH* into the hilt. Hadder began to trace the gentle curve of the metal when an urgent whisper tore him back to reality.

Krill had returned to the weapon room's doorway, and was now demanding that they move on. Hadder held both hands up and nodded in acquiescence. He moved to join Krill, but not before deftly pocketing the mysterious dagger. Krill began to shoot Hadder a curious look, but thought better of it and simply turned to leave.

Minutes later, Hadder and Krill had not only successfully reached the first floor, but had also traversed the mansion and were now approaching the far end of the building that kissed the automotive museum. It was all so easy. Too easy.

"I guess this is it," whispered Hadder as they came upon the large double doors that would swing into the glass enclosure. Krill didn't respond, his black eyes shooting back and forth as if searching for something. "What is it, Viktor?"

"Something feels off. It is as if a great evil is sweeping in."

Hadder shook his head. "Whether that's true, we need to move. Get this fucking door open."

Krill shook his head, as if tearing away invisible cobwebs that had encased him, and moved toward the keypad lock that protected the museum. He removed a small electronic device from this suit pocket and attached it to the keypad via three thin wires. Krill then went to work.

Hadder looked around anxiously, his senses beginning to tingle with worry. His Wakened mind raced. How could things feel so wrong when everything looked so in place, so right?

His worries came to fruition a moment later when alarms rang out across Kharras Knoll. Lights across the grounds, including those in the mansion, sprung to life, temporarily blinding the two Wakened humans. Hadder spun to Krill.

"What did you do?!"

Krill simply shrugged as he continued his work. "Nothing to set any of this off. I think Kharras Knoll has other visitors."

"Well, hurry, then!"

"Do you see me slowing, even with your stupid words doing everything to impede my progress?"

Hadder found it hard to argue as Krill's fingers persisted at a blinding pace, slamming code after code into his thieving device. Gunshots exploded just outside the mansion, followed by the screams of dying men.

"What is going on out there," asked Hadder.

"Shut up!"

Several more tense minutes passed, the sounds of gunfire and death screams melding with calls of bloodlust to create a cacophony. Hadder took out his twin handguns once more, his fingers twitching on the sensitive triggers. After what felt like an eternity, the great double doors silently slid open on hidden motors.

Krill took no time to celebrate. "Let's move."

Just as the pair moved to enter the now-bright museum, a soft voice cut between the men.

"You shouldn't be here. I have to ask you to leave."

Hazel and black eyes spun to face the stranger. Standing before them, her hands stuffed defiantly in the front pockets of a thick robe, was an older woman with a raisin face, her mouth twisted in a disapproving frown. Shockingly, she seemed immune to the gunshots and screams that pounded the mansion walls from just outside.

When Hadder and Krill remained unmoved, the aged maid spoke again, more angry this time. "Well, I gave you boys the chance. You leave me no choice but to call…"

Krill's right arm swung up, knife in hand, ready to deliver a killing blow. Hadder caught his wrist neatly at the top of the attempted throw. The Wakened humans matched glares.

"She doesn't need to die," insisted Hadder through gritted teeth, using all his strength to keep Krill's arm at bay.

"Who said anything about killing her, you fool," retorted Krill, his free left arm shooting out, sending a second knife speeding toward the old woman.

"No," cried Hadder, but he clipped his defiant outburst short as the butt of the weapon grazed the elder's temple, cleanly knocking her unconscious.

Krill shook his right arm free of Hadder's grasp. "You ever stop me from completing a necessary task again, and I'll introduce you to that permanent death you've been chasing. Let's go." Hadder bit back an angry response and followed Krill into the museum.

Inside the glass garage, automobiles of numerous makes and models, foreign but similar to those of decades prior in the companions' former world, sat around polished and desperate to be driven. Outside the museum, chaos reigned as gunshots and screams continued to desecrate the once quiet grounds.

While the brightness of the museum made it almost impossible to see out into the darkness of the night, bullets slamming against the laminated security glass told Hadder and Krill that they could easily be seen within.

The alarm clock in Hadder's mind began to ring. "Pick one and let's go." He looked down into the nearest car, a pale blue winged vehicle that looked similar to a 1960s-era Chevy Impala. "Looks like the keys are in all the ignitions. You work on getting that fucking rear door open, I'll get the car in position. Which one do you want to take?"

"Yes, I'm curious about that myself," said a soft voice ahead and between two large classic trucks.

Twin handguns and knives appeared in hands as the two Wakened humans crept forward, ready to eliminate anything encountered. Their weapons remained frozen, however, when they came upon an old man in silk pajamas and a matching sleep cap who still seemed to be recovering from a deep slumber.

As he calmly cleaned round glasses on his shirt, Hadder and Krill saw that a small cot, covered in thick blankets, sat behind the man, wedged between the pair of pickups.

"Who are you," asked Krill as the elder placed the small frames onto the bridge of his delicate nose.

"I should be asking you that, young sir. After all, this is *my* home, not yours."

"So you are Patton Yellich," concluded Hadder. "Why do you sleep out here?"

The old man shrugged lightly, as if he didn't have a care in the world, as if two armed intruders were not staring him down while a war raged on mere meters away. "I feel most at home here, among relics of the past. I consider myself quite the relic these days. Only between these quiet beasts can I sleep. Only here do I feel safe."

"And yet, you are anything but safe," said Krill.

"Yes, I can see that, young man. But you didn't answer *my* question. Or maybe I need to express it more directly. Who are *you*?"

Krill looked to Hadder. "We don't have time for this." Back to Yellich. "Which is your fastest vehicle, old man? We are going to need to… borrow it."

Yellich pointed his chin to the right, sending his night cap swinging behind him. "The Comet. Black two-door. Three cars down on the right." Krill nodded and went to find it. Yellich faced Hadder. "Before you go, tell me who you are."

Hadder thought for a moment, labels with no adhesion flying in and out of frame. It was a loaded question, full of fear and mystery and anger and power. It was a question that Marlin Hadder was unable to answer. So Yellich answered for him.

"Are you the Yaasha?"

"The what?"

"The Yaasha. The Savior of Man."

Hadder shook his head in the negative. "Mister Yellich, I'm just someone trying to steal your car. Nothing more."

Yellich stared at Hadder through his round glasses with slitted blue-grey eyes. "I think not. Listen to me, we haven't much time. They are coming. They are here. You must not fail in your mission. Whatever happens, do not lose the faith. You are the Yaasha. You are our only hope."

The words hit Hadder like an accusation. They were the words of Acid Boy Gash, a rough translation sent through a different medium. "I'm just a sad guy who doesn't know who he is or why he is here."

"And yet, you keep on."

"I do."

"That is all I ask. And now, you'll excuse me as I drift back into my old thespian days." Hadder's face twisted confusedly, and his lips began to form the words of a question before Yellich beat him to the punch. "I will *NOT* renounce my Israalii heritage, you heathen! The New God is a false god!"

Hadder was at a loss, unaware of the game that Yellich was playing, until he felt the hairs on the back of his neck stand up, could almost see the shadow of evil that swept into the bright museum. He turned back toward the main residence.

There, just inside the large double doors, stood a dozen heavily Loaded men and women clad in white skinsuits, many of which were splattered with crimson from dead police and deceased Kharras Knoll security. At the head of the small battalion stood a lone man, tall and imposing. His long white hair was pulled into a neat bun that sat above his tan, middle-aged face. A neatly trimmed white goatee matched the hairstyle, as did the man's own white skin suit, over which he wore a long white trench coat. Atop one fanatical green eye, so light that it appeared almost yellow, three rows of thorns were tattooed across the man's forehead. A white eyepatch completed the look, rough scars peeking out from where the soft material ended.

It only took a moment for Hadder to size up this new character. He was a fanatic. He was an asshole. Furthermore, he was dangerous.

The dangerous asshole spoke. "Please, do not let me stop your seemingly godly work, my son. I, too, would like to see this heathen come around to the New God. The *only* true god."

Hadder's mind spun with this new plot twist. He stumbled to find the words. He struggled to quickly craft a strategy. Luckily, Yellich was far ahead of him.

"Are these your dogs, Willard? Did you not already tell them that I will not be swayed? My god gives me strength. The *one, true* god!"

The man called Willard held out his hands in faux surrender. "They are not mine, Patton. I'm just a fan." He faced Hadder. "You are doing the New God's work here, son. And I commend you for that. What is your name, if you would be so kind? In fact, I would like nothing more than *both* of your names. After all, proper credit requires proper titles."

Hadder turned to see that Krill had returned from the back of the museum. He smartly kept his knives tucked away as he approached, his black eyes taking everything in, his Wakened mind calculating a thousand variables. "I am Mikk. And my colleague here is Keeth." Hadder's brow wrinkled, and he mouthed the question – *the Stones?* To his credit, Krill was able to ignore him. "We have work to do on this heathen. If you intend to get in our way, we are going to have a serious problem." Hadder marveled at his companion's ability to pivot on a dime.

The eye-patched man laughed, creating a dry, cold sound. "You have me all wrong, Mikk. We are brothers-in-arms, running toward the same glorious goal. I am Willard Hillmore, some call me Devout Willard. I am the Grand Commander of the Thorns of Reckoning. Perhaps you have heard of us?"

Hadder finally understood the role he was to play. He cut in. "Heard of you? We've been trying to get your attention for weeks. Your representatives are less than inviting, even when being gifted the services of two believers."

"Believers with extraordinary abilities," corrected Krill.

Devout Willard shook his head in apology while showing his too-white teeth. "You have my sincerest apologies, my sons. Our group is a tight-knit one, suspicious of outsiders. Many try to curry favor with us. Most are full of malarkey." Willard's lone eye flashed. "You two, however... We have been watching Kharras Knoll for some time and observed your entire invasion. To call it impressive would be an understatement. You both move as if touched by the New God himself, may he guide us forever."

Krill jumped at the opening. "We feel the same. Keeth and I were mercenaries, completing missions for governments around the globe. But since we accepted the New God into our hearts, our skills have increased tenfold. We have become empowered through our faith in Him."

"I can see that," responded Willard. "And your clothing mirrors your devotion." The companions both shot a glance at Krill's white Station suit. Hadder cursed under his breath when looking down at his cheap black suit that he bought secondhand earlier that evening. "But your friend Keeth's…"

"Soiled in a battle with some non-believers," Hadder cut in, thinking on his feet. "I did not want my faith to appear similarly stained, so I discarded it. This…" He pulled at his suit jacket. "Is a temporary replacement."

Willard waved away the excuse. "I was only kidding, my son." He obviously was not. "Tell me, what were your plans for our mutual friend here. Patton Yellich."

Krill once again took the lead. "After persuading him to renounce his dead religion and follow the New God, we were going to turn him over to the Thorns. To you, Devout Willard. We thought that might finally earn your attention."

"Not only my attention," said Willard, "But my appreciation. And I am rarely appreciative beyond my undying gratitude towards our Lord. It is a good feeling to have." He directed his next words at Yellich. "But there was no way that these two honorable men, no matter how skilled they are in violence, were going to sway you against the old ways. Isn't that right, Patton."

Yellich bowed slightly, a hint of disgust apparent under his serene facade. "You know me only too well, Willard."

"You see, my sons? The truth, straight from the heathen's mouth. Let us not waste time on futile efforts. We will take the infidel, and through suffering may his soul be cleansed. Perhaps the New God will still accept him in the end."

Hadder's stomach churned at the thought of what awaited the sweet old man who stood before him. Krill, as always, was the faster to react.

"As we always intended, Devout Willard."

A dark smile crept onto the thin lips of the Thorns' leader. "It is settled then. Thorns, take Patton Yellich. His crime is blasphemy. The penalty is death." The white-clad Thorns, with military-grade shoulder turrets, moved forward in careful precision. Two angrily wrenched the elder's arms behind his back, while another kept a large hand cannon locked onto the bespectacled man's face.

Patton Yellich refused to cry out or even frown. Instead, he shot a serene, knowing look at Hadder before he was dragged back through the museum and toward the main house.

Shortly, only Hadder, Krill, Devout Willard, and a few Thorns remained in the well-lit glass garage. Hadder considered murdering the lot of them there and then. But Viktor Krill had other plans.

"We now have your attention, Devout Willard. And, apparently, your appreciation. May we also find a place among your Thorns?"

A female Thorn with a shaved head stepped forward to whisper something into Willard's ear. He brushed her away angrily. "You two not only have a place, but a place of honor. To call you both Thorns seems inadequate. While we all pierce and injure those who stand against the New God, you two will cut straight to their hearts. The New God has meant for us to cross paths. He has made it so. Mikk and Keeth, you will be our daggers. You will carve out the cancer that is the non-believers, ushering us closer and closer to the Great Conversion. Welcome. Welcome to the Thorns of Reckoning."

Hadder and Krill, unaware of how to react, both bowed deeply in unison, hoping that this would be an acceptable reaction. As they all made their way out of Patton Yellich's beloved museum, the Wakened pair met eyes and shared volumes of unspoken words.

They were now the Daggers of Reckoning, and the irony was not lost on Marlin Hadder. In fact, it screamed into his ears as a tortured man might shout his final words.

As Patton Yellich would cry out soon enough.

5

Daksha sat cross-legged on the hard marble floor, knee-to-knee with the other Chosen who had gathered in the Holy Pistil. The dark-skinned woman looked around and found that more than those who called the Isle of God home were in attendance. In addition to the Isle residents, several prominent disciples from around the globe had joined the weekly sermon. Daksha was unsure what made this week's address so special, but she couldn't blame anyone for not wanting to miss the chance to hear the words of God.

To Daksha's right, Anton Carlyle, the mogul and majority owner of Maxim Global Media, sat quietly on the floor like a schoolchild. His five hundred-credit haircut looked improper sitting above a smiling, stupid face that expressed wonder and total obedience.

Carlyle had traded his tailored suit for loose-fitting white sweats, as they all had. Perhaps comfort would make them more receptive to the Lord's words. Perhaps it was a way of visually expressing their shared devotion. Or perhaps it was simply a way to control. In any case, they were all happy to abide.

Daksha's lips turned down as she looked to her left. There, sitting next to Nieve, chatting away as if they were old family friends, which they were, was Roanda Marks, Head of Universal Bank. While Daksha knew that Anton Carlyle would be joining them, the appearance of Marks was quite the surprise. Very little escaped Daksha's notice on the Isle, so the fact that Marks was able to land her executive copter and enter the Holy Pistil right under her nose gave the devotee pause. Was she losing her place in her Lord's heart? Had another already usurped her?

As if reading her mind, Nieve looked up from her quiet conversation with Marks. She smirked at Daksha, obviously sensing her unease, before reengaging with the powerful businesswoman.

Daksha threw a silent curse her way before moving on.

While the hundred top disciples sat humbly on the floor, awaiting the New God, four others slowly paced behind them, the unspoken rules not applicable to them. Daksha's stomach churned as she accidentally made eye contact with Seth Whispers, who sickeningly tipped his fedora toward her with one hand as he blew a kiss with the other. Daksha could almost see the foul kiss soaring across the Holy Pistil from the wicked man and felt like dodging out of the way, just to be sure. Seth's grey eyes went wide and wild as he saw the discomfort he had caused, yellowed teeth appearing from behind white lips.

The uneasy moment was finally broken by another of the Anointed Champions. Yuki Dona elbowed Seth Whispers as she passed. "Pay attention, you toad. Many outsiders here today."

Seth laughed. "Look who's calling who a *toad*."

Yuki Dona paused for a moment, her small black eyes considering the gangly man. Standing at more than two and a half feet below Seth Whispers, Yuki seemed no match for the giant at first glance. But like anything in life, first impressions were often incorrect. And dangerous.

Yuki Dona was poison, figuratively and literally. Her long black nails, if they drew blood, would usher in death, as would the twin sai that sat on either side of her hips. With tight cornrows, dark make-up, and sleeveless black unitard, Yuki Dona was a beautiful nightmare, as several men on the island had discovered too late. Even her skin was toxic, sending multiple amorous partners into a psychotic tailspin, giving Yuki no option but to slit their throats after she had reached her climax, which is what she wanted all along.

Yuki's sexual appetite was so strong that Daksha, with support from the New God, forbid her from taking high-ranking disciples as partners. Instead, they began to ship lovers in on a monthly basis, mostly against their wills. Yuki Dona didn't seem to mind.

Yuki Dona was lightning quick, deadly accurate, and disinterested in mercy, a true Anointed Champion through and through. And that was without making mention of her true Anointed ability, which almost none lived to recount.

In the end, Yuki Dona decided to ignore Seth Whispers's words and walked on, knowing that disrupting one of the New God's sermons would end badly for her. Yuki was a nightmare, but she was a nightmare of her Lord's imagining. She stalked the world by His grace.

Deep, booming laughter from the far right stole Daksha's attention. There, balancing lightly on tree trunk legs, stood the fourth and final Anointed Champion, Batti Bat.

Batti Bat was the largest creature outside the ocean that Daksha had ever seen. While not as tall as Set Whispers by over a foot, Batti Bat was five times as wide. Every time Daksha looked upon the Champion, she was shocked that such weight and girth could be supported by only two legs, regardless of their own impressive size. Batti Bat looked swollen, as if she was ready to pop from whatever substance had been forcefully injected into her being. The woman looked like if she laid down, she would remain there forever, unable to rise again.

This, of course, was another trick of the eyes. Batti Bat could move like a dancer when she desired, could be upon you in the blink of an eye. And when she was upon you, there was no escape. Although they utilized varying strategies, Batti Bat was every bit as indestructible as Cement Felix. But where Felix used a rocklike exterior to protect his vitals, Batti Bat relied on layer upon layer of blubber over thick muscle to guard her organs. While a blade would flash off Felix's rough exterior, it would neatly slice into Batti's meaty flesh, failing to draw blood or affect the giantess in any meaningful way. By the time an attacker realized his or her mistake, it would be too late.

Like Yuki Dona, Batti Bat had an insatiable appetite, but hers was not of the sexual variety. Batti Bat demanded meat, and she would take whatever was before her, whether that be beef, or chicken, or pork.

Or human.

Daksha once stumbled upon Batti as she was interrogating a known dissenter in one of the smaller gardens surrounding the Institute. Her fat face reddened as she screamed accusations at the man, who quivered in fear before her. Batti's unattractive bob haircut bounced as she yelled, her red-stained white moo moo dress swaying back and forth violently as the Anointed Champion grew increasingly agitated.

The interrogation built to a crescendo. Then, inexplicably, a giant, shark-toothed maw opened up on the Anointed Champion, who dove at the frightened man. Batti was able to fit half the traitor's head into her impossibly enormous mouth before biting down, cleanly cleaving the man's head in half. A geyser of blood shot forth from the opening, showering the Champion in crimson rain as she loudly chewed on brain and bone.

Daksha shook her head as if to physically toss the dark memory away. She spun back to face forward, leaving the Anointed Champions to their patrols as the Taragoshi surgical mechs whirred in the background, continuing their endless work on countless specimens, conducting unknown experiments.

The Chosen in attendance went on with their chatter until a voice silenced them all.

"Shut up, you fools! He comes! The New God is coming!"

Anton Carlyle's words were thick with zeal as he leaned forward, hands on knees, his eyes even wider with wonder. The Holy Pistil fell deathly silent, and even the Taragoshi mechs somehow quieted their work.

Through the slit near the top of the Chrysalis, the face of Doctor Milo Flowers slowly appeared, the New God's too-blue eyes taking in all beneath him. It took the Lord a while to speak, as if he had to rediscover words after traveling the cosmos within his blessed cocoon. When he did finally speak, his voice was calm but powerful, soothing yet demanding.

"It is wonderful to see so many of my favored children gathered here today." Flowers's eyes swept left and right, and a small smile formed on his lips when they ran across one of his Anointed Champions standing in the rear. "We have accomplished so much in such a short period of time. We have cast aside the false prophets. We have turned many non-believers into loyal supporters. And we have fed heretics their just deserts." At this, a small celebration rippled through the collected Chosen. Flowers gave them a moment before continuing. "But now, as we sit on the precipice of ultimate success, I need you now more than ever, my loyal disciples. The Great Conversion is upon us, and we must ensure that humanity is ready to take the next step."

"What would you have us do, my Lord?" The man who spoke was sitting directly to the left of Daksha. She searched her memory for his name and shortly found it. He was Bartholomew Flemming, a forty-something prince from a small but influential country within the Centrus Affiliation. As a close friend of Brayden Yorsaf, it was no surprise that Flemming quickly turned his back on his prior religious upbringing to follow the New God. The middle-aged prince smelled of cinnamon and money. Daksha did her best not to roll her brown eyes at the spoiled royal.

Doctor Flowers vanished back into his Chrysalis for a moment before reappearing to address Flemming's question. "In addition to your usual duties that entail the spreading of my word, I require you all to work more closely with the Petals. The Arch-Soothers are doing a commendable job, but many of them are little more than spiritual leaders. Their words move hearts closer to my own, but now, I need bodies to be moved, as well."

"How can we do so, my Lord? How can we best serve you?" The voice was heavy with an accent. Daksha peeked over and saw that Omye Leenawa, the head of the southern continent's largest mining corporation, had spoken. Leenawa's light green eyes stood in stark contrast to his dark, almost black, skin.

Doctor Flowers's eyelids began to fall over his too-blue eyes, as if speaking with mere mortals was a significant drain on his holiness. He snapped them back open with effort. "All of you gathered here... my followers... my Chosen... you are titans of industry, leaders of men, masters of operational efficiency. I ask that you tap into those valuable skills, that you swing them like a scythe for your Lord." A smattering of cries and declarations of faith emanated from the white-clad group. "When you leave here today, many of you will be assigned to a Petal. I expect you to take an active approach to their management. Consider this a holy task. Nieve will distribute the assignments as you leave the Isle."

Daksha's pulse began to race and a cold sweat appeared on her brow as she realized that she had been overlooked for an especially vital responsibility.

Curse that bitch Nieve!

Anton Carlyle spoke up once more. "We thank you for your trust in us, my Lord. But what is your goal for these appointments? What are the KPIs on which we will be judged?"

Spoken like a true corporate douche, thought Daksha, although she kept this to herself.

Flowers lazily swung his eyes to Carlyle. "A fair question, my child." Back to the crowd. "The Divine Anthers are now fully operational. They fill the skies with life, they charge the air with my glory. The world is primed for the Great Conversion. But we need more Blessed Carriers to ensure a swift victory. They are critical to our ultimate success, acting as both proselytizer and crusader. Therefore, we need to increase the throughput of our Petals. Get people in, implant the Charismata, and release them into the world. Do not ask me how to do this, for that is why I have brought you all here."

A brief silence fell over the Holy Pistil as the Chosen considered their new orders. "It shall be done, my Lord," cried out Xioxian Chan, who was also among those in attendance, and her exuberance proved intoxicating as all the others quickly announced their fealty and excitement for the Great Conversion.

As the brief celebration died down, a small woman that Daksha recognized as Beatrice Sturns, Managing Director of the Planetary Economic Alliance, stood up sheepishly. "My Lord, I know you have much to do, and much that weighs heavy on your godly mind, but could you tell us about the Great Conversion again? Hearing of it again would truly buoy my faith for the coming efforts."

"Is your faith so weak that you need reassurance?!"

Daksha wasn't surprised to see that it was Nieve who cut down the powerful woman. She always felt the need to prove her dedication by questioning that of others. Luckily, Daksha's Lord was too divine for such cheap tricks.

"Now, now, Nieve," said Flowers, his blue eyes looking up, as if he was already traveling far away in his mind. "What child doesn't like to hear sweet reassurances from their parent? If hearing of it again will embolden you, so be it."

Heads bobbed eagerly atop the seated Chosen. "My heart would love to hear it from your lips once more," said Omye Leenawa, giving voice to the hopes of the others.

Doctor Milo Flowers's too-blue eyes rolled around in his head far above the Chosen, as if he was receiving information directly from the Heavens. After a moment, he spoke.

"For ages, we traveled the cosmos, free energy that existed without limits or controls. To call it orgasmic would be to vastly underrepresent the unimaginable pleasure that was experienced in formless existence." The followers rocked gently back and forth, entranced by their Lord's words. "But the Old God eventually grew bored, and cared nothing of our unending rapture. He decided to combat this ennui the only way he knew how. He created.

"Unfortunately, he needed raw materials to complete these projects." Flowers's blue eyes lowered, taking in each one of the Chosen in turn. "We... our energies... were those materials.

"Ripped from a limitless state of being, we were thrust into a world with nothing but restrictions and borders. We were promised life, but that was proven to be the Great Lie. And the Old God was proven to be the Great Betrayer. For it was not life that we were given, but a prison!" The Chosen muttered loudly, curses bubbling to the surface like poisonous gas released under a lake. "We were given these *shells* that are so much less than our true spirits. We were given frailty and needs and broken minds. This is *NOT* life!"

More furious agreement exploded from the followers. Doctor Flowers allowed them a moment to express their outrage before continuing.

"The definition of life is *the capacity for growth through metabolism, reproduction, and the power of adaptation to environment through changes originating internally.* Tell me, do you feel free to change? Do you feel free to adapt? Daksha, did you feel empowered to change when sickness took over your body?"

"I did not, my Lord."

Flowers moved on. "Xioxian, could your son adapt and heal his broken spinal cord?"

"He could not, your Holiness."

"Omye, was your infant able to control her hydrocephalus? Could she stop that demon fluid from building up in her soft brain?"

"She could not, my Lord."

"We were given a raw deal, my children. We traded total universal freedom for life, but found ourselves in a fleshy prison that we could not renovate. This is *not* the life that we were promised. The Old God reneged on his promise, and has abandoned us. That is why I must take up the mantle and lead you as the New God." Cheers floated up to Flowers from below. "I will give the world the life that we were promised, void of limits, void of boundaries, void of impossibility."

"What exactly is the Great Conversion, Lord?" Daksha couldn't tell who posed the question, but it was dangerously close to heresy. Luckily, her Lord didn't seem to take offense.

"The Great Conversion is where we will cast aside these human confinements. The Great Conversion is when life will finally be allowed to flourish the way we were promised — unencumbered, as when we all soared free as nebulous energy. Only then will you experience Rapture once more."

"When will the Great Conversion happen, Lord?" Another voice that Daksha couldn't place. Was she falling so out of favor?

Her Lord's eyes grew heavy again. "I will initiate the Great Conversion soon, when my own transformation has nearly concluded. When Theosis is complete, I will exit this Chrysalis as the New God and will reshape the world, using amorphous life to finally deliver on the promise that we were originally given."

"Will it hurt, my Lord? The Conversion?" This time, the words came from a man Daksha knew well.

"What that is worthwhile is not painful? Mothers, was the indescribable joy of motherhood not prefaced by the pain of childbirth? Athletes, was the thrill of victory not made sweeter by the pain of competition? Daksha, how did it feel when I healed your illness?"

"It was excruciating, my Lord."

"And after?"

"I could have floated home, my Lord."

"Felix, my Anointed Champion, how did it feel to receive my holy gifts?"

"I felt as if my soul had been ripped in half, my Lord."

"And after?"

"I stood only below my Lord in greatness."

"Felix, would you do it again?"

"A thousand times, yes."

"Daksha, would you do it again?"

"A million times, yes."

Flowers looked back out into the Holy Pistil with his icy blue eyes. His voice began to fade away, and his face slowly pulled back, as if the Chrysalis was dragging him back in, demanding a return to Theosis. "My children. Fill the Petals with believers. Churn out more Blessed Carriers. The Great Conversion is upon us. We will rip off the shackles of false life. The next time you see me, you will look upon the New God. I will reward those who have served me well with Rapture. I will celebrate with my Chosen as we reconstitute the world.

"And I will burn the rest."

———

MARLIN HADDER AND VIKTOR KRILL, now known as Keeth and Mikk, exited the front of the mansion along with the Thorns of Reckoning, including Devout Willard and a bound Patton Yellich. The grounds, once beautifully manicured, were now nothing more than the ravaged remnants of a war zone, complete with bullet-ridden trees, trampled flower beds, and corpses laying haphazardly in a multitude of positions. The dead were mostly police and security forces, a testament to the fighting abilities of the ridiculous-looking Thorns.

"Looks like they didn't stand a chance," commented Hadder to Willard, nausea building as he worked to build a relationship with the despicable man.

Devout Willard's green eye flashed. "Thanks to you and Mikk. We were in a good position, hiding as we were in the rear woods, but once you two eliminated the rooftop soldiers, it became a simple shootout, a numbers game. We had the numbers, and the New God, on our side."

A chorus of *Amen* broke out among the Thorns.

Krill's black eyes looked down Kharras Knoll. "I'm surprised the fighting has not brought the attention of the local police. I am sure the battle was heard below."

A smug smile appeared within Willard's white goatee. "Yes, well, old Patton thought that a lifetime of support and service would buy him loyalty. And it did, for a while. But what are credits and warm fuzzy feelings compared to a knife held at one's throat? He thought his little hidden trail through the backside of Kharras Knoll would remain a secret, protected by the officers he has fed and clothed for generations. But they gave it up quite easily, some for trinkets, others for their lives. Similarly, I made sure that no reports would be filed or investigated regarding tonight's skirmish atop Kharras Knoll." Willard chuckled dryly. "They didn't even bother to tell their own on Patton's payroll, the dead officers you see surrounding us. The Kharras P.D.

couldn't have been less impressive. In the end, they all proved corrupt. But then, they are not Thorns, so I expected nothing more from such a low moral group."

Willard then began to shout orders to the other Thorns, directing them to drag all the corpses back into Yellich's mansion. Random gunshots rang out within the building, and Hadder watched Yellich flinch with each *bang*. Tears began running down the old man's cheeks to swan dive to the ground, as if he was pouring out a tribute to each of his fallen house servants.

Devout Willard saw Yellich's reactions and began to address his nemesis. "Come now, Patton, you knew it was going to end this way. You tried to stand in the way of *God*. You had to know that it wouldn't end well for you."

Yellich raised his wet face to meet Willard. Beneath the obvious sadness, Hadder sensed real determination, an iron hand within a silk glove, and admired the man for it. "There are times in life when we understand the sacrifices that we must make. Just because we anticipate them, just because we understand their necessity, this does not make them any easier, or less sorrowful."

"Are you sure it is not fear that you feel, Patton. Fear of the New God's retribution?"

Yellich's face turned to stone, and Hadder almost smiled when he saw that Willard took a small step back from that glare. "It is not. I fear nothing, for I know that my God, the *true* God, will welcome me into His warm embrace when I pass from this world."

"Then why the long face, my old friend?"

"Because I am going to miss my home. Now don't speak to me again, you vile parasite of a putrid idol."

Devout Willard laughed loudly, an obvious attempt to cover the pain of Yellich's barb. "That's what I like about you, Patton. You are a true believer. A *loyal* true believer. You believe in the wrong thing, but still… It's too bad your police friends did not repay your fealty in kind." Willard turned to the female Thorn with the shaved head. "Once all the bodies are in the house, burn it to the ground. Patton maintains one of the greatest collections of artifacts from the old, dead gods. These fragments of the past are simultaneously irrelevant and dangerous. Best to wipe the slate clean, start a new page for the New God."

The bald woman nodded once. "Anything else, Grand Commander?"

Willard thought for a moment. "Yes. Have three of the vehicles removed from the museum before the fire. We'll take them with us."

"Which ones, Commander?"

"Surprise me."

The female Thorn went off to execute her assignments as Willard turned back to face Hadder and Krill. "I must admit, old Patton and I have much in common. I, too, have a soft spot for the old ways, the simpler times." He grew serious. "As long as those things don't interfere with the New God." His face relaxed once more. "All of this… technology… it's just not for me. I prefer not to be tracked everywhere I go. Where's the surprise in that! I don't need to be looped in to every development, much to the chagrin of my righteous colleagues. I need but a cause, and a target, and God's will."

Krill decided it was time to cut in. "We, too, only need a target. Give us one, Grand Commander, and we will lay the quarry at your feet in short order."

Willard slapped his hands together excitedly. "Oh, but I do love new, shiny toys. And you two might just be the shiniest toys in my collection. Do not worry, Mikk and Keeth, I will soon have a plethora of holy assignments to bestow upon you. But now, we have the greatest quarry of them all, isn't that correct, Patton!"

As Hadder's concern grew for the elderly man, he was unable to keep his curiosity in check. "What will be done with the heathen? He obviously will not come over to the light of the New God. Nor does it seem like he will repent."

Willard grew serious again. "Oh, he *will* repent. Patton is a tough nut to crack, I'll give him that, maybe the toughest. But crack he will. And repent he will. My Thorns of Reckoning have an encampment just down the backside of Kharras Knoll, deep within the woods outside the city. We've been here for several weeks, gathering intel, growing our influence in the city, converting heathens into believers. We've been ready to strike for several days, but needed a sign from God." Willard's yellow-green eye took the companions in. "When you two swept in, with abilities only attributable to the New God, I knew the time was upon us."

Hadder couldn't help himself. "We should kill him now. He does not deserve to breathe the same air as the New God."

Willard chuckled lightly. "I love the passion, Keeth, I really do. But this is Patton Yellich, one of the leading figures in the movement against the New God. Some say he has close ties to that awful group who ironically call themselves the Protectors of Man. I'm afraid a simple death is not in the cards for dear Patton, nor do I think he wants it. Old Patton loves the attention, he craves it. We will simply give him and the Thorns the show that we all so desperately want and deserve. And when Patton finally states that the New God is the only god, when he repents and begs for forgiveness, my Thorns will be there to record the divine declaration. This pronouncement will be circulated around the globe, using technologies that I care not about, and those that once stood against the holy tide will crumble at last."

Krill's black eyes met Willard's lone green orb. "And if the Protectors of Man still refuse to bend the knee?"

Willard took Krill by one arm, and Hadder by the other as he walked between the two Wakened humans, leading them toward the back of Yellich's mansion. "If the Protectors of Man do not disintegrate at the sight of Patton Yellich's Holy Confession, then I will be forced to release my dogs of war, my Daggers of Reckoning, upon them."

Krill, always one to play a role, smiled darkly. "Then I hope, selfishly, that the Protectors of Man are made of tougher stuff than the others Keeth and I have come up against."

Willard couldn't hide his excitement. "Are you both so thirsty for the blood of the heathens?"

Hadder jumped in. "Nothing else satiates us."

Willard, flanked by white-clad Thorns, pulled Hadder and Krill around the side of the house and in the direction of a small, almost invisible slit in the thick forest that butted up to the mansion's rear. "Do not fret, my new friends, there are always enemies of the New God that need disposal. And if we cannot find any, we will conjure them, for the horror of the message is so much more vital than the accuracy of the act."

6

The Thorns of Reckoning's encampment was massive, holding almost two hundred members of the elite fanatical fighting force. Sitting less than a kilometer inside the thick forest that cupped the northern edge of Kharras, the Thorns' sprawling camp was hiding in plain sight, Devout Willard's silent challenge to those who would dare voice opposition to his divine cause.

White military grade dome-pods peppered the forest installation, each housing two Thorns within its plastic walls. The dome-pods were organized in some manner that Hadder was unable to identify, perhaps by rank, specialty, or devotion. Between sets of dome-pods, large caches of military weaponry floated silently on hover pallets, making them easy to transport despite their significant weight.

Devout Willard may not have liked technology, but he sure as shit was supported by a lot of it. Hadder snickered as he moved deeper into the encampment, thinking that this was probably the least of the Grand Commander's hypocrisy. The Thorns who had remained behind as their brethren attacked Kharras Knoll tossed suspicious looks at Hadder and Krill before erupting into applause at seeing Patton Yellich trailing them in plastic ties.

The first rays of morning cut through the canopy of evergreens to light the victorious return. Shouts of, "The heathen must repent," and "The New God's judgment is upon you," rained down on poor Yellich as he stumbled every few steps, the old man unused to such physical exertion.

Viktor Krill walked in silence, his black eyes studying his surroundings, his Wakened mind taking note of everything, mental projections accounting for a thousand variables. Hadder tried to do the same, but found that his growing hatred for the Thorns was impeding his ability.

"Well, what do my Daggers think of the mobile base? Quite impressive, don't you think?"

Willard's voice ripped Hadder from his dark thoughts. He struggled to locate a response. "You've done great work here, Grand Commander. Able soldiers Loaded with the best Military Combat Enhancements. Organization seems top-notch. The Thorns are everything I hoped they would be."

"I'm glad I have your approval." Willard's words were thick with sarcasm, reminding Hadder to tread lightly with this fanatic. "We can be packed up and on the move in less than thirty minutes. And the way we travel, the targets never see us coming until it is too late. Of course, it is already too late for all the non-believers, but you catch my drift."

Krill, having completed his analysis, joined the conversation. "And where are these next targets, Commander? The need to spill the blood of heretics is a constant itch we must scratch. Inertness does not sit well with us."

Willard chuckled. "If I had been gifted with the holy abilities that you two possess, I, too, would want to be constantly on the hunt. Alas, I am just a feeble old servant of the New God, and must plan accordingly. But do not worry, my Daggers, the next targets are already selected and filed away." Willard tapped his head with his finger. "One of them, a particularly offensive young woman, is said to be not far from here."

Hadder couldn't resist. "What is her crime?"

Willard threw a green eye Hadder's way. "The same as all the others – opposing the New God. Apparently, she has quite the following in the cyber world, not that I follow that cursed medium. But our youthful Thorns monitor it closely, and report back the terrible things that she has been saying about the New God. She must not be allowed to spew her poison into the eyes and ears of the unconverted."

Krill jumped in. "I'm convinced of her guilt. Do we head out today?"

Hadder felt a jump in anxiety as a realization hit home. Krill must have taken stock of their current situation and deemed it dangerous. On the road, the companions' options opened up, leaving them a variety of strategies to employ and tactics to unleash. But locked into this encampment, surrounded by Loaded Thorns, the threat of their unmasking always lurking...

"Not today, but soon, my son," responded Willard. "We have captured the greatest antagonist yet in the story of the New God. Patton Yellich has been secretly funding organizations around the globe to obstruct the inevitable progress of the New God. Isn't that right, Patton! Tonight, we will celebrate the heretic's capture, hear his repentance, and bask in the light of the New God. Tomorrow, we will continue our divine efforts to purge this world of the non-believers before the Great Conversion is upon us."

Krill frowned almost imperceptibly. "We look forward to watching this infidel burn in the fires of the New God's judgment. Now, if you would be so kind, Keeth and I must replenish our energies. It was a long night of battle."

"Of course, of course," replied Willard. "Ebben," he shouted to a reedlike Thorn who walked ahead of them. "Ebben, who was it that passed into the Lord's warm embrace last night?"

"Mason, Grand Commander," responded Ebben, who didn't look up from the ream on which he was working.

"What dome-pod was he in?"

"He had 29 all to himself, Grand Commander."

Willard nodded, quite pleased with the news. "Mikk and Keeth, you have dome-pod 29 all to yourselves, compliments of your new brothers-in-arms, the Thorns of Reckoning. Ask around, and you'll find food and whatever necessities you need as well. We are…"

"Grand Commander," shouted a short, unimpressive-looking man who suddenly ran at Devout Willard. Popping out from behind a dense thicket of shrubbery as he did, the little man was upon Willard before any of the Thorns could react. Willard's face transformed into a mask of terror. A brave man he was not.

Hadder reacted on pure instinct, his Wakened body moving before his brain could deliver instructions. Quickly, faster than human eyes could follow, Hadder cut in front of Devout Willard and punched out, his left fist moving forward like a piston. Knuckles met the soft tissue of the stranger's throat, and only with great effort was Hadder able to pull back to keep his hand from exiting out the back of the man's thin neck.

The little man fell to the ground and began wheezing, trying to collect oxygen through a crushed windpipe. As he did, the surrounding Thorns finally started to react, bringing weapons to bear and aiming them at the would-be assailant.

Willard, shock wearing off, looked down at the man and spoke though his frightened anger. "Who are you?! Another accursed member of the Protectors of Man?! You cannot kill he who walks in the Lord's light, you foolish worm! Answer me!"

As Willard screamed, he began to kick the little man, who didn't seem to notice the strikes, which were comparatively inconsequential next to his broken trachea. Willard continued his battering until a middle-aged Thorn with a military crew cut and special patch on his white skin suit ran toward the fracas. Willard halted his assault to address the newcomer.

"Gillis! Is this the kind of operation you are running in my absence?! You not only allow a stranger into the encampment, but turn a blind eye as he hides, waiting to assassinate your Grand Commander!?"

Gillis slid to a halt, and his tan face went white under the admonishment of his terrifying leader. "My sincerest apologies, Grand

Commander. But he is no stranger. He is a Blossom Runner who found the base last night. Said he has a message directly from the Flowers Institute."

"And that gives him the right to run up on me like a common cutthroat?"

Gillis looked like he wanted to be anywhere else. "He was... very eager to speak with you."

The exasperation was clear on Willard's face. "Well, what was the message?"

Gillis shrugged helplessly. "He wouldn't tell us, sir. Said it was for your ears only. Something about a new threat. That's all I was able to gather."

Willard frowned and kneeled over the Blossom Runner. "Tell me your message, young man. Tell me before you walk into the New God's light."

The small man attempted to speak around his mangled throat, but only a few words, bookended by sickening gasps, managed to escape. "Krill... Hadd... Pow..."

Hadder and Krill exchanged worried looks as Willard stood up angrily. "What is he saying? Kill-had? Pow? Oh, this is beyond pointless!"

Gillis shrugged once more. "I'm truly sorry, sir. As a Blossom Runner, he was allotted more freedom than we would usually allow."

"Well, can he be saved?"

A female Thorn was already next to the fallen Runner, examining his wound. She looked up and shook her head. "He doesn't have long. There's not much I can do. Everything is too crushed to even make an adequate breathing hole."

Willard sighed heavily and waved the situation away. "Let it be. My love of the New God knows no bounds, but let the light strike me dead if the Flowers Institute doesn't unnecessarily feel that every little advancement requires an emphatic proclamation. I'm confident that we have already known for some time whatever it is that this man was trying to say. Isn't that right, Blossom Runner?" The Runner's eyes went wide as the Blossom redoubled his efforts to speak, increasing the volume and desperation of his wheezing. Willard's pale hands went to his ears. "Oh, that noise! Like nails on a chalkboard to me. Will someone please put this Blossom out of his misery? Let him walk into the light of the New God."

The surrounding Thorns looked at each other questioningly, none of them wanting to complete the grim task. An uncomfortable silence, save the Runner's dying breaths, fell over the group. Through that heavy quietness flew a sharp blade which buried itself deeply in the downed Blossom's chest, cleanly stopping the small man's heart. Everyone looked over in shock to find Mikk, the newest Thorn, standing easily, a second knife spinning deftly in his hand.

Willard, after the immediate shock wore off, cackled in delight. "Oh, but look at how my Daggers are already pulling their weight. Thank you, Mikk, for taking care of that unpleasantness. My Thorns should take note. Dirty deeds are best done quickly. The longer you wait, the more filth gets under your nails." The other Thorns shot Hadder and Krill more unpleasant looks. "And you, Keeth, you have my sincerest gratitude. Although it turns out I wasn't in danger, your swift actions have proven that there is no one better to guard my holy flanks. Thank you."

Hadder bowed dramatically. "You are a beacon of the New God's light. Without our beacon, we would be lost in an ocean of non-believers."

If Devout Willard smiled any wider, his face would have cracked in half. "What a prosperous evening we have just enjoyed, proof of the justness of our cause. Now, if you will excuse me, I must discuss tonight's ceremony with the team. Remember, dome-pod 29 is all yours. Thorns, make sure my Daggers have everything they desire."

And with that, Willard walked off with Gillis and a contingent of Thorns. None stuck around to show Hadder and Krill to their tempo-rary quarters. The companions began to walk together, free from potential eavesdroppers.

"Laying it on a bit thick there, aren't you, Marlin?"

Hadder shrugged. "He's a dog who likes to be petted."

"So, you save him from a potential assassin?"

"But it wasn't an assassin. It was someone with a message about us."

"But you didn't know that."

"What are you getting at, *Mikk?*"

Krill smirked to himself. "Just making sure that you are not starting to buy into this New God bullshit. I need to make sure you are not going to crush my trachea when I turn away, looking to score points with Devout Willard."

If Krill was trying to upset Hadder, he was doing a good job. The embers of the Rage began to flare up deep within the newest Wakened human. "Ask me again how much I care about Devout Willard. After I stick his fucking head on a pike." Images of the fiend Skeelis assaulted Hadder.

Krill's smirk did not change. "Oh, I will."

———

AFTER A QUICK MEAL of rehydrated rations, Hadder and Krill retired to dome-pod 29, dodging the cutting, suspicious looks of Thorns on their way across the encampment. Upon arriving at the dome-pod, Krill unceremoniously spilled the previous occupant's personal belongings onto the forest floor before allowing the small plastic door to close behind him.

The companions spoke little, understanding that each dome-pod could be outfitted with listening devices. Instead, they quickly agreed that one would rest while the other stood guard, neither Wakened human particularly comfortable in the lion's den.

Krill rested first, and Hadder used the hours of conscious silence to reminisce about Emily and Mia, his wife and daughter from several lifetimes ago. His Wakened mind allowed him to better control his memories, permitting only those that brought a smile to his face, leaving the images of twisted metal and tiny blood-covered hands in the dark recesses where they belonged.

When Krill finally rose, Hadder laid down atop his military cot and passed almost immediately into a deep slumber, rocked to sleep by sweet recollections. Unfortunately, even a Wakened mind could not control the subconscious.

Marlin Hadder twisted and turned as he slept, tormented by ghastly images that seemed all too real.

An enormous worm splits in half, light that is truly darkness pouring forth from the wound, blinding all who had gathered to marvel at its glory. A plague sweeps across a sea of humanity, twisting flesh and bending bone as screams of terror roll across the landscape. Those who remain unchanged are doomed to an even more horrid existence, surviving among nightmares that all served a demon god. All the while, a pink judgment rushes toward the planet, an indictment of heavenly proportions. There is no hope.

Hadder sat up straight, covered in a cold sweat, torn from rest by both his terrifying dream and the sounds of battle just outside his dome-pod. Hadder took a brief look around and, seeing no sign of Viktor Krill, plowed through the dome-pod's sliding plastic door, taking no time to properly open it.

Hand already on one of his crystalline handguns, Hadder slid to a stop, feeling foolish as he was confronted with the truth of the noise.

In a large space between groupings of dome-pods, lit by the day's dying light, Viktor Krill playfully sparred with six white-clad Thorns. Or, to be more accurate, Krill playfully sparred while the half-dozen Thorns did their best to the harm the newest recruit. Hadder removed his hand from under his coat jacket and quietly joined the other spectators to watch the show.

The Thorns showcased deft footwork, skilled strikes, and considerable tactical abilities. But these were of no use. Viktor Krill, his hands absent his usual blades, easily ducked kicks, blocked punches, and avoided traps as he circled in and out of engagements, breathing easily as his opponents began to pant heavily. After some time, Hadder could tell that his Wakened colleague was growing tired of holding back. When he finally spotted Hadder among the crowd, Krill decided that he had learned enough in this little exercise.

Krill's surreal defensive maneuvers instantly transformed into blinding offensive strikes. Where he once ducked a head kick, he now punched out, shattering a female Thorn's tibia. He followed this with a spinning back fist that somehow connected perfectly with the jaw of a large Thorn who was rushing at his exposed backside. The sickening, audible cracking of bones echoed across the encampment, slowing the remaining Thorns.

Making Viktor Krill's job even easier.

In short order, all six of the Thorns were left writhing on the ground, some injured, others merely hurt. Although they looked upset, Hadder almost laughed aloud, thinking how lucky they truly were. Had Viktor Krill wished it, six corpses would have littered the sparring ground in place of bruised egos.

The Thorns in attendance whispered among themselves, some grateful for the powerful new allies, while others voiced concern over *unnatural* abilities. Krill joined Hadder, a smug smile pasted onto his tan face.

"You are finally awake. Sorry for not waiting. You were moaning and whining in your sleep, and I couldn't take it any longer."

"So, you came outside and couldn't help yourself?"

Krill shrugged as the pair began to walk away from the crowd of Thorns. "They were training and wanted to know what made us so special. I decided to show them."

"And show our hand."

Krill snickered. "Many of them saw us in action already back at Kharras Knoll. And the others needed... proof. Plus, it gave me an opportunity to test their abilities, for when the time comes."

"And what did you learn?"

Another shrug. "They are all above-average fighters. Some of them are even good. But they should prove no difficulty for us. There is not a Liquid Tye among them."

"Who?"

Krill waved Hadder's question away. "Never mind."

Hadder thought for a moment. "Well, six unarmed Thorns may not be a challenge, but what about a hundred and fifty of the bastards, all Loaded to the teeth? Because that's what we're going to face if our cover is blown."

Krill stopped walking and turned to face Hadder. "If our cover is blown, then we're going to find ourselves in a mountain of shit we may not be able to climb out of. So, I suggest that regardless of what happens tonight, you keep your shit together and that Rage of yours in check. Until…"

"Until what?"

"Until I give you the signal to unleash it." Krill looked around, making sure no Thorns were in earshot. "And then you had better let it feed like it has never fed before."

"And how will I know to unleash it?"

Krill spun Hadder by the shoulder as the pair began to walk once more. "Easy. You will see me start killing people."

———

"THAT AREA IS off-limits to all but the Grand Commander!"

Hadder paused fifty feet from the strange construction, the demands of his curiosity almost audible. Ahead of him, guarded by five Loaded Thorns and positioned well away from the rest of the encampment, sat a rather strange structure. A cube of ten feet on each side, it was made of thick glass that reflected the surrounding forest, causing it to almost disappear amidst the spread of green and brown, especially as dusk was drawing to a close.

Hadder looked to his right and found the source of the proclamation. Standing there, shoulder auto-turret aimed at Hadder's chest, was the reedlike Thorn known as Ebben. Hadder started to run Krill-like calculations in his Wakened mind. He considered the speed with which he could close the distance before the auto-turret could fire. He thought about the five bullets he could put in the five guards' heads before they would be able to signal an alarm. He ran through the percentages, deciphered the odds.

And found that the reward was not worth the risk.

"Sorry… Ebben, was it? I must have gotten a bit turned around. I'm simply looking for this evening's bonfire."

Ebben's eyes went narrow above his narrow body. "The Holy

Beacon is on the other side of the encampment this evening. It is not full dark yet, so you still have time before you are expected."

"Ah, thank you." Hadder was unable to hold back the words. "And what, may I ask, is that unusual erection? It seems so out of place."

"That does not concern you?"

"Even as a Dagger of Reckoning?"

A smirk crept onto Ebben's thin lips. "Yes, even as that. So, unless you are the Grand Commander, which you are not, or the New God himself… Wait. Are you claiming to be the New God?"

The Rage began to tickle Hadder's insides. He forced a smile. "No, of course not. I would never claim such a thing."

Ebben's smirk mutated into a full-on sneer. "Then I guess it is none of your concern."

Hadder pushed down the urge to shatter the skinny man's knee. He offered a slight bow instead. "No, I guess not. In that case, I am off to the Holy Beacon." Hadder threw one last look at the mirrored cube, and, as he did, swore he heard a great bellow emanate from within, muffled by the thick, perhaps two-way, glass. The five Thorns, to their credit, did not react.

Hadder disguised his surprise and turned to leave the secretive area, passing Ebben on his way back towards the encampment. Ebben's soft voice brought Hadder to a momentary stop.

"Do you know what I like best about the Holy Beacon, *Dagger* Keeth?"

Hadder refused to turn back to face the suspicious Thorn. "No. Tell me."

Ebben spoke to Hadder's back. "The Holy Beacon always seems to shine a light on the truth of a situation, the truth of a man. Or a couple of men. It is why Patton Yellich will be the guest of honor this evening."

Hadder responded over his shoulder. "And I trust you will be in attendance?"

A soft laugh trickled out from the lanky man. "Oh, I wouldn't miss this Holy Beacon for the world."

"Good, I'm delighted to hear it," said Hadder as he walked back to the encampment. *I'll be sure to kill you first if things turn sour.*

———

THE STARS COULD BARELY BE SEEN through the thick, piney foliage that sat heavy above the night's show. Below, the Thorns had erected a massive bonfire using dry timber to minimize smoke, ensuring that all around had a clear view of the giant wooden spike driven into the ground just beside the Holy Beacon.

Dangling just above the sharpened end of the wooden spike, held firmly in place by a rudimentary pulley system attached to the thick branch of an overhanging tree, sat a frightened Patton Yellich. Stripped of his clothing, with his arms bound in the back, the old man looked like a pig prepared for the slaughter.

Which is precisely what he was.

Despite his terror, Yellich's cheeks remained dry, and he did not cry out. He simply hung there. A man at ease with the shitty hand he was dealt. A man who had accepted his fate, regardless of how terrible it was certain to be.

Marlin Hadder's respect continued to grow for the man who refused to bow before a false messiah.

The Thorns of Reckoning silently surrounded the bonfire in their white skinsuits, their eyes wide as they stared deeply into the Holy Beacon, expecting the New God to step through the flames at any moment. Between the large circle of Thorns and the Beacon, there was only Devout Willard Hillmore, his white cape swirling dramatically behind him on drafts of hot air. Willard held up his right hand, showing long, sharped nails coated in white lacquer, and Hadder could almost feel the Thorns' eyes shift from the bright fire to their backlit leader.

Marlin Hadder and Viktor Krill, known as Keeth and Mikk, had been given a spot of honor among the Thorns and stood on the inside of the donut-shaped audience, positioned closest to Devout Willard. Krill shot a black-eyed look Hadder's way, a reminder of their earlier conversation. Hadder recalled every word from his Wakened companion.

"This Holy Beacon will be a test, Marlin. While everyone else is watching Yellich's painful demise, Devout Willard will no doubt be watching us. If we are true believers, then the death of a heretic, no matter how gruesome, will be completely justified. You must control your reactions to what is put before you. And you must control that famous Rage of yours. Failure to do so will result in a fight I'm not sure we both come out of..."

Hadder simply nodded at Krill, a muted response of understanding. Just as he did, Devout Willard began to speak to the gathered Thorns.

"It was with this appendage," said Willard, shining his lone green-yellow orb onto his uplifted right hand, "that I proved my loyalty to Doctor Milo Flowers, the New God." Willard turned his gaze back onto the audience. "He told me that it was in Man's nature to betray, that it was a core attribute of our vile Creator. He wanted to know how I could possibly demonstrate that this was not in *my* nature, that He could trust me implicitly with His grand plans and darkest orders." Willard paused a moment for effect, letting only the crackling of the Holy Beacon fill the dead air, his right hand still held aloft. "Of course, there were no words that could properly express the love I had for the New God, nor the lengths to which I would go to execute his divine orders. So, I did the only thing that came to mind.

"I clawed my eye out with this very hand. After ripping it from my head, I held it out to the New God as proof of my fealty. Proof of my loyalty. Proof of my love. The New God has never doubted me since. And when He offered to replace my missing eye with one that could see further than any other, across continents and into cyberspace, I refused. Let my self-inflicted wound remain as a testament to my faith, as a badge of honor, as proof of my God's trust in *me*. Do you all trust me?!"

The Thorns exploded simultaneously in response. "WE TRUST YOU, GRAND COMMANDER!"

Devout Willard finally lowered his arm and began pacing before the bonfire. "Good! Then you trust that the man who hangs above us like curing meat is not simply a man, but a devious heathen! Not only does he not accept the New God, but he actively works against Him. For too long now, Patton Yellich has pulled strings behind the scenes, funding entities like the devilish Protectors of Man, doing everything possible to slow the progress of the New God.

"But you cannot slow an avalanche! Can you, my Thorns!?"

Another coordinated response followed. "NO, GRAND COMMANDER!"

"And, so, given his countless crimes against God, Patton Yellich has been brought here before us to answer for his sins. But our God is a forgiving God, is He not, my Thorns?"

"HE IS, GRAND COMMANDER!"

A wide smile broke out on Devout Willard's face as he took in the moment. "And that is why, despite his transgressions, we will offer this infidel one last chance to accept the New God. His life is already forfeit, that cannot be undone, but the manner in which he meets the New God can now be adjusted." Willard looked up to the naked Yellich, who swayed slightly over the wooden spike, sparks from the bonfire racing up to singe the old man's pink skin. "Patton Yellich, the New God loves you! Return his love and enjoy a painless death that will quickly usher you into His warm, waiting arms. What do you say?"

Yellich looked briefly at Hadder before turning his blue-grey eyes toward Willard. "Willard Hillmore! Your collection of blind idiots do not know who you are really are, but I do! I recall reading about a young man who was chased out of numerous religious sects for misbehavior and conduct unbecoming the clergy. Do you remember that man?"

Although Willard laughed aloud, Hadder could see that the white-clad man seethed beneath the surface. "I remember him, Patton! Do you know why he never fit in? It was not because he was false, but because those religions were false! Does it not make sense that a true believer would flunk out of a false religion?"

Now it was Yellich's turn to laugh. "It would make sense. But it was not a difference of theological opinion that found you on the outs, was it Willard? I believe it was the murder of a pregnant teenager in one case, and the disappearance of a religious rival in another. Does that sound right?"

Devout Willard looked ready to explode, his pale face red with anger. "History will speak of only two times, Patton! That before the New God, which matters not, and that of the New God, in which we now find ourselves. We have all made mistakes. We have all sinned. But those who have given themselves over to the New God have been absolved. And those who have not now find themselves hovering over a knife's edge."

"What do you want from me, Willard? I find interacting with you to be even more loathsome than watching one of your New God's transparent infomercials!"

"Admit your folly!" Devout Willard was beginning to lose control. "Admit that the New God is the only God! Accept Him and accept your much gentler fate!"

Yellich launched a thick loogie from his thin lips. It flashed like a comet as it soared over and past the Holy Beacon to land with an audible *splat* against Devout Willard's forehead before running down to soak the Grand Commander's white eye-patch.

As Willard angrily wiped away the saliva with the sleeve of his trench coat, it took all of Hadder's willpower not to cackle aloud. To the Thorns' credit, no laughter could be heard from the hundred plus gathered around the Holy Beacon.

As Willard cleaned himself, Yellich followed up on his spewed response. "I admit only one thing, and I consider myself particularly blessed to be able to shout this from such a prominent position, where all of you small-minded beings are forced to hear me! Doctor Milo Flowers, whom you call the New God, is a worm! He will eat the world, including all of you within it, and will force life to exist within only his vermicast. His shit!" Yellich began to laugh maniacally. "You fools are not the chosen ones! You are simply too stupid to realize that you are volunteering to be turned into shit!"

"Enough," roared Devout Willard from below, enraged that his grand show was not going according to plan. "Patton Yellich! Do you accept the New God as the only God?"

"I do not!"

"Lower him!"

The pulley above Yellich began to creak as the naked man slowly fell, moving inexorably toward the sharped point of the massive wooden stake beneath. Three Thorns stood at the base of the stake, preventing it from being kicked aside by Yellich, while also aiming it towards Willard's selected target.

As the inevitability of what was to come became clear to Hadder, his stomach began to churn, threatening to displace the military rations he had consumed hours earlier. It was then that Krill's words repeated in his mind once more, forcing Hadder to tap into his Wakened abilities to control his body as no other could.

Yellich's feet passed the wooden point, and then his knees, before the man finally came to rest, his backside hovering just above the three-inch thick instrument of impalement. Sweat poured from Yellich's naked body as he drew dangerously close to the Holy Beacon. Death, it seemed, awaited poor Patton Yellich on multiple fronts.

Firelight danced in Devout Willard's yellow-green eye, and a smug smile remained perched on his thin lips. When Yellich's decline ceased, he spoke once more to the condemned man. "Enough of this, Patton! You have proven your toughness. Now show your compliance. Declare the New God, the only true God! Tell the world that you have seen the error of your ways! Ask for the New God's forgiveness! I swear to you that it will be granted!"

As Willard spoke, Hadder felt Krill's elbow jab his side. When Hadder turned his head, Krill nodded to a female Thorn across the Holy Beacon. Hadder followed Krill's gaze and found the woman, a small recording device in her pale hands, lens fixed on the helpless Patton Yellich. Hadder nodded, his assessment matching that of his companion's.

The Thorns of Reckoning would record Patton Yellich's confession-slash-epiphany alongside his ultimate demise. Then, they would undoubtedly edit the hell out of the footage and use it to demoralize the few groups who still dared to stand against the Blossoms of the New God. It was almost beautiful in its simplicity and brutality.

Hadder looked back up to Patton Yellich, who seemed to be praying quietly to himself, his skin beginning to grow red and bubbly as the Holy Beacon continued to be fed by Thorns from below.

"Patton! Can you still hear me? Confess! State that you were wrong! State that you now see the light of the New God! State that only through His grace and love can the world finally be healed! State…"

"Will you shut the hell up, Willard," screamed Yellich from above. "I'm trying to make peace with *my* God. The only *true* God! The last words I want to hear are His, not yours!"

A dark smile replaced Devout Willard's smug one. This is what he wanted all along. "Very well, Patton. Just remember, you had a choice, which is more than most are given." To the Thorn manning the pulley system, "Lower him once more! Slowly."

As poor Patton Yellich descended again, he closed his eyes tightly, as if shutting them would also help to shut out the pain that was to come.

It did not.

The sharpened stake, guided by the Thorns of Reckoning, slipped between pink thighs and thick buttocks before entering Patton Yellich through the most sensitive of cavities. As Yellich fell, inch by inch, impaling himself further on the demon pole, a small cry began to escape the brave man's lips. That small cry grew into a wail, which morphed into a scream of misery. In short order, the man's cries of agony spread across the encampment like a ghost army.

While most eyes remained locked on the impalement taking place over their heads, Hadder and Krill could feel Willard Hillmore's singular orb on them, searching for any sign of compassion, unease, revulsion, or anger. While Viktor Krill was sure to give the man nothing, having executed gruesome impalements himself, Marlin Hadder worked hard to keep his emotions at bay. Although his hazel eyes stared at poor Patton Yellich, Hadder turned inward, stopping the signals that produce bile, pausing his stomach in its attempt to empty itself, and slowing his breathing to pre-Holy Beacon levels.

But the Rage was one thing that even Hadder's Wakened abilities could not control. It flared to life, its flames fanned by Yellich's audible suffering, leaving Hadder's body humming with an overwhelming desire to destroy. The Rage flashed across Hadder's eyes and swam under the calm surface of his skin. Hadder's Wakened abilities fought a silent war agains the Rage, a dark serpent hidden under black silk.

Viktor Krill looked over and noticed that the Rage was present in his partner, but also saw that he was cloaking it well. To the untrained eye, to Devout Willard's eye, Marlin Hadder looked to be in the throes of fanatical ecstasy.

Devout Willard smiled at the response of his newest weapons, the Daggers of Reckoning, and turned his attention back to Patton Yellich.

The wooden pole was now a foot inside the non-believer, his blue-grey eyes wide with the horrific truth of the pain. Willard rose his clawed hand once more, and Yellich's downward movement ceased.

"Hurts, doesn't it, Patton! Trust me, this is nothing compared to an eternity of damnation! Let's end this charade. Confess! Declare the New God as the true God! Tell the world how you finally see His light! Then this can be over. What do you say?"

Patton Yellich, with a foot of wood burrowing through his intestines, spoke through quivering lips. He struggled to form proper words. "F-f-fools! You all w-w-worship a w-worm! A f-false M-m-messiah! Y-you... w-we... deserve all that c-comes to us. L-look around! Y-you are the f-f-fall of m-man!" Yellich looked down as he talked, his glazed-over eyes meeting as many Thorns as he could. A bloody bubble escaped his mouth as he began to laugh crazily. When Yellich finally stopped howling in humor, he spoke again, his words now clear and crisp. "You all worship a worm! The true God sees and has already passed judgment. You will all be drowned in a pink light. Only the Yaasha can save you."

Many of the Thorns began to shift uncomfortably under Patton

Yellich's small speech. While his monologue meant little to the audience, the clarity and conviction with which the dying man spoke lent real weight to the words, crushing many who fell under them. Devout Willard saw this and decided that enough was enough.

"Let it be never said that the New God does not give chances! I always pegged you as a hopeless heretic, Patton, but never as an irrational idiot. It appears that I, too, can be wrong. Complete the impalement!"

And with that, Patton Yellich was lowered once more, his blue-grey eyes becoming even wider, as if he was taking in the entirety of the world for the first time. Yellich shook violently as his body fell, scorch marks appearing where the Holy Beacon's flames had reached up to scratch at the soft flesh of the man who spit at God. Yellich began to pray softly once more, his lips racing to spit out silent words that only his God would ever hear.

After several excruciating moments that felt like an eternity, Yellich let out a loud gasp as the point of the pole finally reappeared, exiting the top of the elderly man's chest. Tears poured forth from Yellich's eyes as his skin began to bubble and blacken from the increasingly violent Holy Beacon.

"Last chance, Patton," screamed Devout Willard from beneath. "We can end this now! Call out for the New God's forgiveness! He will grant it!"

Just then, a wave of serenity fell over the face of Patton Yellich, and a small smile crept onto his blood-stained lips. He looked down across the sea of Thorns, his blue-grey eyes searching until they stopped at Marlin Hadder. Yellich smiled, the skin of his forehead beginning to fall away from his skull. "Yaasha! Tell God that they know not what they do! They are foolish children, playing at games that they do not understand! They…"

Yellich could not finish his sentence as his lips burst into flame and peeled away from his teeth, leaving the man with a grim smile that passed judgment over all those who looked upon it. The Thorns began to whisper uncomfortably among themselves.

Devout Willard, sensing that he was losing control of the scene, took charge. "And so ends the sad life of the man who thought he could stand against God. Patton Yellich, you deserve no more of our attention! Goodbye! You will not be remembered!" Willard nodded to the men who had been manning the impalement pole but were now standing with the rest of the Thorns to escape the heat of the Holy Beacon. They moved in quickly, the fire already moving in to singe their holy white skinsuits, and kicked at the pole which held poor Patton Yellich aloft.

After several swift kicks, the pole, and Yellich with it, fell across the Holy Beacon, the naked man landing neatly atop the pyre as if he were the recipient of a religious funeral. As Yellich came to rest neatly on his side, his eyes stared out through the flames, reaching out to Marlin Hadder, who could almost feel the connection between hazel and blue-grey orbs.

Kill them. Kill them all.

Just as Hadder began to send a message back, Yellich's eyes exploded in their sockets, the flames of the Holy Beacon melting away all remaining skin and soft tissue.

And Patton Yellich, a man Marlin Hadder did not know, but respected as much as any other, died.

"Did you get it?!" Devout Willard's desperate words pulled Hadder back to reality. The female Thorn with the recording device ran over to Willard and began showing him the footage.

Willard nodded as he watched the small screen. "Good. Good." The woman said something that Hadder could not hear. "No, just dub over it. Very few outside Kharras know Yellich's voice. Use a stock confession or get a new one. But whatever you do, get it done quickly. I want this up by the start of the workday."

The female Thorn saluted before running off toward the encampment. As she left, Ebben approached Devout Willard, a strange look twisting his hawk-like features.

Willard's lone eye went wide, and his jaw fell at the news that was being delivered. He nodded absently at the lanky Thorn, who also took off back toward camp, but not before throwing Hadder and Krill a look of dark amusement.

Devout Willard paced for several moments in front of the Holy Beacon before a wide smile broke out on his goateed face. He addressed the audience, which was beginning to turn back to their dome-pods for the remainder of the evening.

"My Thorns, do not leave! We have a most unexpected, most divine treat at this late hour. Please! Stay where you are, warm yourselves by the Holy Beacon!" Willard's yellow-green eye fell on Hadder and Krill, known as Keeth and Mikk. "You'll kick yourself forever if you miss your chance to converse with God."

7

M arlin Hadder and Viktor Krill shared a concerned look before inconspicuously taking a few small steps back, attempting to blend in among the collection of Thorns. An unseen force tugged at Hadder, warning him that danger was in the air, another dark benefit of his Wakened state. He didn't have to look over to know that Krill was battling similar feelings. Both companions remained on edge.

Minutes dragged on in the chilly night. Willard Hillmore stood alone in the center of the gathered white-clad hunters, his eye staring into the Holy Beacon as his lips moved silently in prayer. As the wait continued, a thin mist descended upon the forest, as if the dead had come to see the show for themselves.

The murmuring of Thorns from across the Holy Beacon foretold the return of Ebben and his entourage. Moments later, a gap appeared in the disc of Thorns, allowing the passage of Ebben, his men, and a large container that trailed them on hover-pallets.

Hadder's breath caught as he recognized the glass cube from earlier in the evening. He recalled his Wakened ears catching sickening inhuman cries from within the evil-looking box. Krill's black eyes shot over and Hadder could feel his partner's questions, but he didn't return the look, for he had no answers, only worries.

Krill, receiving no response from Hadder, returned his dark gaze to the glass cube and turned inward, readying himself for a potential battle. Hadder did the same, now and then fanning the Rage that remained from Patton Yellich's horrible death.

Ebben and his men brought the hovering cube around to the front of the Holy Beacon, where Devout Willard welcomed it warmly with open arms and sweet words. Once positioned before the giant bonfire, the hover-pallets came to a silent halt as Ebben's men took position to either side of the cube, their weapons at the ready. Ebben marched over to Willard and whispered something in the one-eyed man's ear before joining the other guards in armed readiness.

Devout Willard, looking anxious for the first time, took a moment to collect his thoughts before he addressed the Thorns of Reckoning. When he finally spoke, his words carried easily across the misty evening air, as if propelled by an unseen force.

"My Thorns! As you know, our holy mission has been a two-fold one. Primarily, our goal is to hunt down those who oppose the New God and his divine plans. But recently, we were given a secondary goal, one presented to us straight from His Holiness. This directive was to remand, unharmed, any Bloomed Men that we find.

"We do not question the New God, who is all knowing and wise, so we did what was asked of us, losing several loyal Thorns in the capture of a Bloomed Man outside the small city of Ninnicla. That Bloomed Man has been with us, offering very little in the way of spiritual guidance or a raison d'être." Devout Willard paused for effect. "That is, until tonight!" Low conversation erupted among the gathered Thorns. Willard silenced them with an upheld claw. "Tonight, the Bloomed Man will enlighten us, for he is the conduit and the voice of the New God!" To Ebben, "Release him!"

Ebben leaned toward the glass cube, which reflected the surrounding Thorns, and fingered a code into a small, almost invisible keypad. A high-pitched *hiss* escaped the top of the cube as the glass side facing Hadder and Krill fell forward on bottom hinges. The top of the two-way glass panel hit the forest floor loudly, creating a ramp down from the hovering reflective container. From within the gloom of the cube, something began to push toward the light of the Holy Beacon.

Something quite *unholy*.

The Bloomed Man slithered ahead, looking nothing like the man from which it was created. The body was like that of a centipede, with dozens of small "legs" pushing it along down the glass ramp. While half of the 12-foot-long creature remained on the ground, launching it forward on its cilia-like rowers, the upper trunk soared into the air, showcasing its flattened, segmented body. In addition to the small legs that swam in the air uselessly, the Bloomed Man had four giant appendages near its head, each ending in a scythe-like claw. The Bloomed Man's head was similar to that of Benn's, with thick layers of face peeled down to reveal a grisly blob of flesh underneath that contained nothing more than two round eyes above a shark-toothed maw. Unlike Benn, two giant antennae rose from the Bloomed Man's head, completing the centipede-like appearance.

The Bloomed Man completed the journey down the makeshift ramp and paused before Devout Willard and the Thorns of Reckoning, as if it were a celebrity posing for adoring fans. After a moment of stunned silence, Devout Willard found his voice.

"My Lord, is that really you? If so, please address us, your most loyal servants."

The Bloomed Man turned its grotesque head left and right, its antennae twitching in the misty air. "It is I, Willard, the Absolute Being. I have traveled across the world to speak with you and my Thorns."

Viktor Krill nudged Marlin Hadder, who was just about to do the same, as the voice that escaped the twisted creature before them was unmistakable, as were the pair of painfully light blue eyes that dotted the abomination's head.

Doctor Milo Flowers had come again. There would be bloodshed.

Devout Willard looked to be near hysteria as he spoke again.

"What a divine honor, my Lord! We are but slugs before your greatness. Command us!"

The Bloomed Man spun to face Willard. "I have *tried* to command you, Willard, but you have proven a hard man to connect with."

Devout Willard's face slackened as if he had just witnessed his own death. He stuttered a response. "M-my apologies, my Lord, but I trust only your word, not messengers whose loyalties are never truly known, or directives over the vile digital world that is an affront to your physical godliness."

The Bloomed Man chuckled within his centipede frame. He turned to face the Thorns. Hadder and Krill dropped their heads reflexively. "The devout are rarely flexible, are they, my Blossoms?" The crowd laughed maniacally at the non-joke. "That brings me to why I have come to you today, Willard. As you can see, I have found a way to create a direct connection to any Bloomed Man. They are holy creatures, shining examples of life without barriers. With one in every Petal or Blossom company or Thorn detachment, I can deliver my divine word to my loyal followers. The Bloomed Men are my conduit to the world as I complete Theosis. Now do you understand their importance?"

If Willard Hillmore bowed any lower, his head would have touched the dewy ground. He spoke as he rose back up. "Of course, my Lord. They are sublime, your divine proxy, and will be treated as such."

"Good. Then what updates have you for your Lord?"

Willard almost tripped over his words in his excitement to deliver the recent news. "You just missed quite a show, my Lord. We captured Patton Yellich last night, one of the key conspirators for the so-called Protectors of Man. He was brought before the Holy Beacon and given the opportunity to repent."

"Did he?"

"He did not, my Lord. Therefore, he was appropriately punished before his sins were burned away atop the Holy Beacon."

"And the Protectors of Man?"

"With Yellich's substantial support gone, they will wither away, as do all heretics. We already have their other leaders in our sights. My Thorns will draw their blood in short order."

"A job well done, Willard." Devout Willard's face almost split from the smile that engulfed it. "Now, any word on the two wicked men that I warned you about?"

Confusion twisted Willard's singular eye. "What wicked men, my Lord?"

The Bloomed Man sprung right as if launched by a cannon, propelled by hundreds of tiny legs. He loomed large over Willard, who trembled under the light blue gaze. "Nieve had a messenger sent to your encampment, warning you of Viktor Krill and Marlin Hadder. Did you not receive such a message?"

Willard shuddered under the examination. If not for the Rage and tension, Hadder would have laughed out loud.

"I did not, I swear it, my Lord!" Devout Willard's mind raced under the blue stare of the New God. "Wait! Wait! A messenger was here this morning. He came at me in a rush, like an attacker. My loyal Dagger Keeth saved me at the last moment. We had no idea he was an emissary from God. We swear it!"

As Willard spouted excuses, Hadder and Krill tried to disappear back into the Thorns, but found that they could not without drawing attention. The Thorns, enraptured by the appearance of the New God, had pulled in tight, leaving no room for escape.

The Bloomed Man continued. "Then you know not of the twin demons that haunt our land, wanting nothing more than to put an end to my holy work?"

"Just give me a name, my Lord! Your enemy is my enemy!"

"I already gave you two names, you sniveling fool!" With that, the Bloomed Man slid away from Devout Willard, who looked ready to melt into the ground, and approached the circle of Thorns, far to the left of Hadder and Krill. "You are the Thorns of Reckoning, are you not?"

A chorus of voices followed in the affirmative.

"You are the New God's greatest hunters, are you not?"

"We are, my Lord!"

"Then you should have no problem in bringing me two lowly humans – Viktor Krill and Marlin Hadder."

Devout Willard cut in. "We know not those names, my Lord! Who are these heathens?"

The Bloomed Man slid loudly along the forest floor, following the circle of Thorns, coming back toward the companions, who both kept their heads down in apparent penitence.

"They are our greatest enemy, Willard, perhaps even more loathsome than the Protectors of Man. They must be stopped at all costs. If left to roam, they could… Well, hello there."

Hadder's heart skipped in his chest as he felt the weight of light blue eyes atop his bowed head. Krill similarly kept his eyes on the ground, his body coiling for a fight.

The Bloomed Man stopped his circular journey and spoke to Willard again without looking at the Thorn leader. "Willard, who are these two gentleman before me?"

Devout Willard cocked his head to see whom the Bloomed Man was referring to. "Those are my Daggers, my Lord. Keeth and Mikk. They were instrumental in the capture of Patton Yellich. Their skills in violence far surpass any I have ever witnessed. They are an invaluable addition to your holy cause."

"Are they now?"

Devout Willard looked confused once more. "Is there a problem, my Lord?"

The Bloomed Man stood fifteen feet in front of the companions, his antennae swinging to and fro as his small upper legs waved frantically in the air. "No problem, Willard, but let me finally deliver the message that you refused to accept. Are you ready?"

"I am always ready to receive the word of God, my Lord."

"Here is the message: *Devout Willard, you and the Thorns of Reckoning are to capture or eliminate a priority threat in the form of two men – Viktor Krill and Marlin Hadder. Although their names are painted across digital media, the likenesses expressed there are either incorrect or unhelpful. While Marlin Hadder is unremarkable, Viktor Krill can be recognized by his black on black eyes, white suit, and long black hair. They are to be approached as a Class One foe, and all resources should be deployed to ensure their capture or elimination."*

As the Bloomed Man recited the undelivered message, the Thorns surrounding Hadder Krill slowly began to draw back, forming a small circle around the pair while opening up a direct visual line to Devout Willard and the New God. Fingers went to triggers and shouldered auto-turrets swung in their direction as blades discreetly appeared in Krill's palms.

Devout Willard's lone eye went wide with understanding, looking as if it might pop out and join its missing counterpart. "But, but, my Lord, I saw these men battle their way into Patton Yellich's mansion. With my own eye, I watched as they murdered their way to the wanted heretic. I caught up to them just as they were questioning the bastard Yellich, demanding his conversion to the cause of the New God!"

The centipede creature looked unimpressed. "Is that what they were doing, Willard?"

"I, I, I… was so sure of it, Lord."

"Or perhaps, you were so transfixed by their violent abilities that you filled in the gaps with your own wishes, your own dark desires? More tools of death for you to wield? More power for Willard Hillmore?"

Devout Willard fell to his knees before the Bloomed Man, his hands held out in prayer. "Please, my Lord! I am but a foolish, humble servant! Forgive my transgressions! They all stem from my deep love of the New God! I will make sure to read all…"

The Thorn leader's words were clipped off as a scythe-like claw tore through the top of his head, exiting in a spray of blood and gore beneath his chin. After a brief pause, the Bloomed Man pulled his long arm forward, ripping Willard's face off and sending a loose collection of flesh and bone to hit the forest floor with a loud *splat*.

As the Thorns of Reckoning looked on in horror at their fallen leader, the Bloomed Man scurried back up the glass ramp on tiny legs. He paused just inside the cube and turned around, facing Hadder, Krill, and the stunned audience. The light blue eyes cut a path across all in attendance, bringing some to their knees.

"Thorns of Reckoning. No one is bigger than the holy cause. Nothing begins or ends with the death of one man. Continue your work. Search out the non-believers, bring them down. Protect the Bloomed Men, including this one. Burn all who stand in your way. The New God demands this. The Great Conversion is upon us. All who stand with me will be rewarded with Rapture. Now, lock me away; I will come to you again soon. And finally..." A long arm came up, the singular claw at the end dripping with gore and pointing directly at the Wakened humans. "Exterminate Viktor Krill and Marlin Hadder!"

Black eyes met hazel, and one word could be read on the lips of the notorious killer.

"*Up!*"

Just as barrels swung around and auto-turrets surged to life, Marlin Hadder and Viktor Krill leapt straight into the air as if accelerated by dynamite. Ten feet passed, then fifteen, then twenty, then thirty. In the blink of an eye, Hadder and Krill found themselves slamming against the piney canopy that hung heavy over the forest.

The Wakened pair balanced themselves easily on the lower branches of the thick, healthy trees and made their way toward opposite trunks, chased by a barrage of bullets from below. Hadder looked down to see Ebben close the cube that contained the Bloomed Man, while the other Thorns attempted to make out their foes through the mist and flickering shadows.

As Hadder took stock of the desperate situation, Krill acted, using his knives, hands, and feet to rip away large, leaf-filled branches, sending them down onto the Holy Beacon. The waterlogged boughs hit the raging fire with a hissing moan before releasing a more visual complaint. Smoke began to billow from the fresh kindling, rolling off the Holy Beacon like a swarm of angry Manikins to engulf the chaotic Thorns, who were still firing randomly into the trees above.

One task complete, Krill took to the air again, soaring some twenty feet to land heavily against the trunk of the tree that Hadder currently inhabited. "That should level the playing field a bit, Marlin. Are you ready?"

Hadder did not answer, his eyes caught by something below. The remains of Patton Yellich had been knocked from the top of the Holy Beacon and now laid near the base of the pyre, barely visible through the cascading smoke. The man's empty sockets reached out to Hadder, the word *Yaasha* echoing louder than any gunfire. Yellich's skull looked frozen in a silent scream, one that demanded retribution.

The Rage swallowed Marlin Hadder, encircling his Wakened abilities like a lover's legs.

"Marlin! Marlin! Are you ready?! I need to know that…"

Marlin Hadder finally looked up from the Holy Beacon to face Viktor Krill. When Krill saw what danced behind those hazel orbs, he nearly fell from his perch. Krill simply nodded, comforted by the fact that his partner was indeed ready, for the Rage was there with him.

"Kill them, Marlin! Kill them all!"

With that, Krill sprung away once more, disappearing into the shadowed canopy of trees. Hadder looked down again, bullets whizzing past, and searched until he found what he was looking for. Upon locating his quarry, a grim smile appeared on Hadder's lips. He removed the crystalline handguns from his jacket and jumped.

And descended into chaos.

———

JUST BEFORE HADDER hit the ground, he sent a bullet flying that tore through the forehead of Ebben, making good on a silent promise.

He rolled as his feet touched the forest floor, staying hidden within the thick smoke and mist. Screams from across the Holy Beacon told him that Krill had similarly entered the fray, his knives cutting through Thorn flesh while knees and feet crushed bone.

Hadder moved like a wraith, each bullet finding purchase in the skull of a white-clad man or woman. Now and then, something bit him in the shoulder, or hip, or thigh, and Hadder had to turn inward, using his Wakened abilities to turn aside the pain, redirecting it to feed the Rage.

In time, he left the Holy Beacon behind, choosing instead to take the fight to wider grounds, where the Thorns' numbers meant less. Hadder slipped from the shadow of a tree to crush a skull with the remnants of an auto-turret. He leapt from behind a dome-pod to silently choke out the female Thorn whom he had encountered in Yellich's garage. When the crystalline handguns ran out of ammo, he collected the weapons of fallen Thorns, using scatter rifles, Stutters, and las-cutters to sweep death across the encampment.

And still the Thorns came.

Despite their superior abilities, the sheer number of enemies eventually began to catch up with Hadder and Krill. Every so often, a bullet would find its home, sinking deeply into Wakened flesh. From time to time, a punch, or kick would slip past defenses, bruising muscle or damaging bone. Occasionally, the tip of a desperate finger would shoot up to scratch at a vulnerable black or hazel eye.

The Wakened humans were winning. But they were taking real damage. They were getting fucked up.

The fighting stretched into the wee hours of the morning, when the smells of the forest began to shift, preparing for the rising sun. Wherever Hadder moved, he left a trail of blood that was leaking out from countless wounds. When his muscles began to falter, the Rage took over, using up its own limited resources.

Hadder trudged through the encampment, more hunter than hunted now, looking for the few remaining Thorns, so he could finally rest, or die. As he stepped into a small clearing, his Wakened senses came to life, warning him just as shots rang out from a thicket to this right. Hadder, moving with blinding speed, brought up the Stutter that he had borrowed from a dead woman and sent a dozen rounds into the dense bushes just as several bullets tore through his chest.

A thick silence followed the explosion of violence before two bodies in white skinsuits fell forward from the overgrowth, hitting the ground with loud thuds. Hadder also fell, to his knees, thankful that he took two more before his body gave out.

This gratitude was short-lived, however, when one last Thorn, the tanned man named Gillis, escaped unscathed from the thicket, a handgun hanging low in his right hand. Hadder tried to raise his Stutter in defense, but found that his arms would not answer his call, no matter how loudly the Rage screamed at them.

The Thorn limped over to Hadder, his left leg stained red from a deep knife wound. A bloody smile appeared on the Thorn's lips as he brought the handgun up slowly, aiming it at the defenseless Hadder.

"I will be rewarded handsomely by the New God for this. The Rapture is all but mine!"

Hadder laughed aloud and spit a wad of blood at the approaching assassin. "Rapture? Do the Bloomed Men look happy to you, moron? Does it look fun to be a twisted freak?"

The Thorn smiled sweetly, as if dealing with a child who did not know better. "The Bloomed are but carriers to stock the Flowering Horde. The true believers, like the Thorns of Reckoning, need not fear that ending. We will only experience the Rapture. Something a heretic like you will never know."

Hadder spat again. "We'll see about that. Now, make sure you don't miss, you fucking future slug! Come on, right between the fucking eyes!"

"As you wish, Marlin Hadder," said Gillis as he pulled the trigger, sending a bullet spiraling at Hadder's forehead. Hadder tilted his head down a few centimeters as the projectile closed in.

The bullet exploded against Hadder's skull, sending the man flying backwards to fall into a black pit of unconsciousness.

But not before he saw a blur of white fly from the trees to swallow Gillis in a flurry of blades.

———

MARLIN HADDER WOKE WITH A START, fearful that he would find himself hovering naked over of the point of a wooden stake. Instead, he found himself shirtless inside one of the Thorn's dome-pods, Viktor Krill laying next to him, fast asleep.

Hadder looked down to find his wounds tended, covered in bloody bandages and gauze. He reached across and carefully removed the dressings that ran across his chest. Gently tearing away the last of the wrappings, Hadder was shocked to find that the holes had nearly healed, showing nothing more than the tender flesh of a new scar.

He kicked the sleeping form next to him and was met by curses as Viktor Krill rolled onto his back, showing a collection of his own injuries, from slices and holes to bruises and contusions.

"What do you want, you bastard," yelled Krill, responding to being unceremoniously stirred.

"How long?!"

"How long what?"

"How long have I been out?"

Krill sat up, angrily wiping the sleep from his dark eyes. "You mean, how long have you been out since I saved your ass?"

Krill's words hit Hadder like another round of bullets. He immediately softened. "Yeah, since you saved my ass, I guess. Thanks for that."

Krill stretched out uncomfortably, looking like he was testing joints that would never again work as they once did. "Don't mention it. Especially since it was more due to that goddamn Elevation than me. How many times is that now? You really ought to thank the manikin that…"

"Viktor!"

Krill stopped in his tracks, noticing the hints of Rage in his companion's voice. "A week. Maybe less. I've been in and out of consciousness."

"Did we kill them all?"

Krill grimaced, as if it hurt to think. "We must have. Had any Thorns escaped, I'm sure an army of Blossoms would have descended upon these woods as we recovered. And we wouldn't be having this discussion."

"What about the Bloomed Man?"

Krill smiled grimly. "Still in its box, as far as I know."

"We should give it a grand sendoff before we leave."

"You read my mind."

"And when should be we going?"

Krill considered the question for a moment. "The longer we remain, the greater the chance that some clueless hiker will stumble upon this massacre. And the smell is growing by the day. It will attract attention in short order."

"You didn't bury them?"

Krill shot Hadder an angry look. "I barely had the strength to wrap your wounds, much less bury a battalion of swine."

"They were just men. Confused men."

"Fuck them."

Hadder sighed, but decided against pushing the issue with his volatile partner. "Fine. I ask you again. When are we going?"

"Tonight, as soon as the sun retires. I want to put some distance between us and this cursed woods. Already its memories haunt me."

"Very well. But until then?" Hadder peaked out of the dome-pod's sliding plastic door. "Looks like we still have several hours until sunset, and I'm all slept out."

Krill rose uneasily to his feet. "Good. That gives us time to shop."

"Shop? Shop for what?"

Krill laughed dryly. "Did you forget where we are, Marlin? There is a vast collection of military-grade weapons just outside this pod. And I, for one, don't intend to leave here until I am sufficiently Loaded."

Hadder joined Krill in getting to his feet, groaning the entirety of the trip. "Sounds good to me. If we're going to keep fighting against such desperate odds, I could use a few weapons to back up my pistols."

Krill smiled once more. "Then let me lead the way. Consider me the salesman of the year. My prices can't be beat. My wares are almost without cost."

Hadder caught Krill's shoulder as he began to exit the dome-pod. "Those wares cost the lives of two hundred men and women, Viktor."

Krill violently shook loose of Hadder's grip. "Like I said, these weapons are practically free. And those men and women, like everyone in this world, were already dead long before we arrived;

they were just too stupid to realize it." Krill slipped through the dome-pod's entrance, but kept talking, more to himself than to Hadder. "Just like we've already lost, but we're too stupid to accept it."

———

"YOU THINK THAT'S ENOUGH," Hadder asked as Krill stuffed another wad of plastic explosive under the reflective cube, both men ignoring the inhuman moans emanating from within the glass prison.

Krill stepped back to admire his handiwork. "This should be enough to vaporize the cube and the freak within." Hadder's doubtful look forced Krill to continue. "I have some experience with plastic explosives. Do you?" Hadder shook his head in the negative. "This will all be gone in a flash. It won't feel a thing, which is a pity."

Hadder wanted to feel some kind of satisfaction, but found that he could not. "He was just a man, Viktor. He didn't ask for this. Just like Benn, before him. The Bloomed Men are victims, too."

Krill turned back toward the small fire they had built a small distance away from the site of the Holy Beacon. Krill spoke as he pushed past his companion. "Careful, Marlin. Sympathy is a shortcut to a knife in the back. You, of all people, should know that."

After some time alone, staring at his reflection in the Bloomed Man's cube, Hadder made his way to the fire to join his Wakened counterpart. A pair of large burlap sacks sat near the fire, full of weapons taken as trophies of a won battle. The two men sat alone in silence, only the crackling of burning wood filling the heavy air, as night came on in a rush, revealing a starry kaleidoscope through the dense canopy of trees.

"Has it gotten bigger," asked Hadder into the tense quiet, not having to expound any further.

Krill stared up with black eyes, spotting the pink spot through the piney branches above. "Maybe. A bit."

"What does it mean?"

Krill considered several explanations before selecting the one that would least distress his sensitive colleague. "Just means we are closer."

"Closer to what?"

"I told you before. Judgment. God's judgment."

Hadder looked over to Krill, who kept his dark eyes pointed up. "I heard what you said earlier today, about us already having lost, but refusing to accept it. What did you mean by that?"

"Dammit, Marlin, I do not talk in riddles. I meant what I said. Nothing more and nothing less."

"Then you really think that all is lost?"

"I do."

"Then why?"

"Why what?" The irritation was clear in Krill's voice.

"Why take this journey with me? Why not live out your remaining days on some beach with a harem of Spirit Girls, laughing at the *non-humans* that you so obviously despise."

Krill spun off his back and onto his side, his black eyes locking onto Hadder. There was danger there, but Hadder was beyond caring. "I no longer despise those unwilling to push their bodies to meet their full potentials."

"You mean normal people."

"Yes, I no longer despise them. I have already proven that they are beneath me in every way possible."

Hadder sighed loudly. "That doesn't answer my question, Viktor. In fact, it only causes me to ask it again, this time louder. Why take this journey with me? If you have no respect for these *non-humans*, and think that this war is already lost, why are you here?"

Krill rolled onto his back. "I don't have to answer your questions."

The Rage appeared then, unexpected, flaring to life and threatening to overtake Hadder. He spoke through it, his words becoming coated in its perfume. "Yes, you do!"

Quickly, Viktor Krill was on his feet, facing Marlin Hadder, a knife already in his right hand. Hadder stood in the blink of an eye, his fists balled into miniature wrecking balls. "I take commands from no man, least of all a sniveling weakling like you! Your muscles and mind may have been Wakened, but your soft, gooey center remains, Marlin. I can see it, even if no else can. Don't make me open you up to prove it!"

"Tell me why!"

"Fuck you!"

With that, Hadder lost control of the Rage and, before he knew it, found himself charging at famed killer Viktor Krill, who awaited him with both blades drawn and ready. Time slowed as the Wakened humans approached each other, fists playing a dangerous game with knives.

Hadder spun away from one deadly edge, only to encounter the second just behind it. Hadder ducked just beneath that one, feeling a trickle of blood appear atop his head, before punching out with all his might, catching Krill in the sternum with a piston-like straight punch.

As Hadder connected with his blow, a blinding pain exploded within him, a reminder of the dozen nearly fatal wounds he had recently suffered. He doubled over on the ground in excruciating agony as tendered skin was pulled open by inconsiderate actions. Hadder desperately sucked in air as warm blood began to flow from various areas of his body.

Hadder looked over to find Krill in similar straits, his companion on all fours coughing up thick ropes of ruddy mucus. Krill managed to speak through the upheaval. "That was... a bad... idea."

"Tell me about it," echoed Hadder, trying to catch his own breath. After several moments, both Wakened humans fell back onto their respective backsides, staring at each other across the weakening fire. "I still need to know, Viktor."

"Why do you *need* to know, Marlin?"

"I need to know that I'm not in this alone. I need to know that you aren't going to bail when things get too dark."

"And what if you are in this alone, Marlin? Will you, too, simply pack it up and retire to your Spirit Girls?"

Hadder considered the question. "No. But at least I can plan for that."

"Fine. Ask your question once more."

"Why are you on this journey, Viktor, when you think it is a lost cause? Have you uncovered such love in your heart for the people of this world?"

Firelight danced in Krill's black eyes as he responded. "I think you know that is not the case, Marlin. I hate most and feel nothing for even more. But there is good to be found, not only in this world, but in all the realities of man. Friends taught me that. Family... taught me that."

"So, it is regret that drives you?"

Krill laughed bitterly. "No, Marlin. I know I have done wrong. I know that I have killed many that did not deserve that fate. But, although I know that I have committed the greatest of sins, I feel nothing. And *that* is why I am on this journey. If I cannot be subjected to the internal suffering that most endure after wrongdoing, then I need to make amends in other ways. This is my other way."

Hadder's look softened as he considered his companion's plight. "You don't have to do this, Viktor. No one would know any better if you fled to the farthest corner of the world, watched the planet burn from afar."

"You would know."

"Yes, but who am I? I am no one."

Krill snickered. "Yes, keep believing that."

"Come again?"

"Nothing. Listen, Marlin, we have both suffered greatly, before and after our rebirths. You have never inquired as to the source of my pain, and I respect you all the more for that. My life before Station was not a happy one. I was robbed of the ability to feel for others. Or so I thought. This left me cold to the world. I sought power to fill this void, but it did not. Only proof of the love of others, of the general goodness of some, even in the capital of evil, led me to believe that there are things worth saving from the fire. That I could be more than a killer. I saved some. But I failed at saving who mattered most. I need to pay for this. And if my broken spirit will not allow me to suffer for all those I have wronged, then I need to pay in another way."

Hadder cut in. "In waging a war that you cannot win."

"That is correct."

"That's a fucked up way of thinking, Viktor."

"Says the man who marched into the Muck with a billion credits at his disposal."

"You also have a billion credits, Viktor."

"I *had* a billion credits, Marlin. Not anymore."

"So, we're off to die in a war that cannot be won? To watch helplessly as the world twists into horror, just before God burns us all with his pink asteroid of judgment?"

Before he could answer, an alarm went off on a ream that Krill now kept at his waist. "It is time, Marlin. Let's go." Krill rose and crossed the firelight that spread across the vast clearing. He collected the burlap bags before grabbing Hadder's arm as he passed, dragging his partner along with him.

"Are you going to answer my question," asked Hadder as he was being pulling along.

"We are off, Marlin, that is to be certain. To die in a war that *cannot* be won? Well, that is hard to tell. I spoke out of pain and frustration earlier. With my Wakened mind, I am forced to look far ahead, to see all the various possibilities. When you do that, one thing becomes painfully clear. Given a long enough tail, full of enough iterations, anything is possible."

"Including saving the world from a false god while convincing the real God that we are worth not obliterating?"

Krill laughed. "Including that." He turned Marlin to the right. "I am fairly confident that the main road is this way."

Just as the Wakened humans began to cut toward civilization, the glass prison behind them detonated, sending a pillar of fire and smoke up through the forest canopy. All within twenty miles would soon know that something monumental had occurred in the woods near Kharras, which the Anton Carlyle-controlled media would soon dub "Heretic Grove."

Marlin Hadder and Viktor Krill never turned around as the world exploded at their backs.

———

HADDER SQUINTED HIS EYES. Despite the forest being cloaked in deep night, his Wakened vision took in more than most saw in daylight. "Is that what I think it is? Please tell me that I'm not dreaming. I can't fathom walking much farther in this condition, carrying this goddamn bag."

Krill smiled as he walked, grimacing sporadically from deep wounds not yet healed. "That, my fellow human, is indeed what you think it is. It looks like luck is on our side for once. Let us hope not for the last."

Ahead of the two injured companions, barely visible through the trees and hidden under a thick layer of pine-covered branches, sat three vehicles. As Hadder and Krill drew closer, midnight black paint could be seen peaking out from beneath one of the piles of natural camouflage.

After entering the small clearing that was home to the hidden treasures, Hadder dropped his burlap burden, quickly limped over to the far left, and ripped away some foliage, unveiling the black two-door muscle car underneath.

Krill caught up a short time later after setting down his own sack. "Well, if it isn't our old friend the Comet. One last gift from Patton Yellich, I suppose."

Hadder's stomach churned at the thought of the deceased *non-believer*. "There are two other ones here. Which one do you want to take?"

Krill chuckled. "Stop, Marlin. We both know you are already in love with the Comet, as am I. Be a lad and uncover it for me. I'm sore where some asshole fucking punched me."

Hadder joined in the laughter as he removed the remaining branches from Patton Yellich's antique automobile. As he did, Krill looked around the darkened clearing, staring deeply into moonlit shadows.

"There, Marlin! Between those trees. It looks like a small path, just large enough for a car. Any bets that it leads out to the main road?"

Hadder wiped the residual pine needles from the beautiful muscle car, deaf to Krill's words. "What do you think the odds are that it's unlocked, and the keys are in there?"

"If they are not, I can get in and hot wire the damned thing."

Hadder looked over at Krill, his hazel eyes narrowing. "Another thing I can't ask you about, I assume?"

"Correct."

Hadder tried the door handle of the Comet. It opened smoothly, showing the care with which Yellich treated his prized collection. He then slid smoothly into the car's black leather seat, inhaling deeply as he did, bringing back memories from another life in another world.

"Any keys?"

Hadder looked at the ignition and then at the old school ashtray before shaking his head in the negative. Just as he was about to exit, however, a hundred scenes from movies of his youth bubbled to the surface, forcing him to check one last place. Hadder pulled down on the antiquated sun visor and almost called out in glee as the keys fell with a *clink* onto the lap of his matching black suit pants.

He held them up for Krill to see. "Looks like you won't get the chance to destroy this dashboard, Viktor. Going to remain cherry for a while."

Krill shook his head in disappointment. "A pity. I was excited to try out my old skills. Now hop on out."

"Hop out, why?"

"So I can drive."

Hadder did jump out, but not in acquiescence. "What makes you think you're going to drive?"

Krill's black eyes flashed. "Let me think... I just saved *your* life back in the woods. I could have ended *you* in the Cyrix Office Suite, but aimed for that obvious Elevation instead. And, let me see, what else? Oh, that's right! I fucking Wakened *you*!"

Now it was Hadder's eyes that flashed dangerously. "I seem to recall preventing Albany Rott from erasing you."

Krill's jaw fell open. "What?! You know I had that devil dead to rights!"

Hadder shrugged. "Did you? Maybe. Maybe not."

"You have got to be kidding me! I would have ended his reign of tyranny once and for all if not for you, *Marlin*!"

"Maybe."

"I created you!"

Hadder's face grew deathly serious. "Like you helped to create Milo Flowers."

Krill stepped back as if he had been struck with a pipe. "I did no such thing."

"Where do you think he learned about the secret of the human form? The ability to treat flesh and bone like soft clay?"

"He would have learned that without me."

"Perhaps. Maybe not."

An evil grin crept onto the tan face of Viktor Krill. "And what about your role in the deification of Doctor Milo Flowers?"

Hadder let out an exasperated laugh. "I had nothing to do with Milo Flowers. I met the man once." He paused. "Well, twice if you count when he brought me back from the dead."

"I count that. I'm sure he learned a lot from that experience."

"But that's it! I didn't collaborate with him as you did, Viktor."

"No. You did not. But do you think Milo Flowers could have escaped from Station without you turning the city on its head? All eyes, including those of the red variety, fell onto you, Marlin, allowing Milo Flowers to slip unnoticed through the back door."

"Albany Rott let him leave! We know that!"

Krill shrugged. "Perhaps. Maybe not."

"You're not driving!"

"The hell I'm not!"

Both Hadder and Krill reached into their jackets to retrieve the weapons they kept there, determined to let the other know that death was always just around the corner. Both men cried out in pain as the wounds in their shoulders, chests, and abdomens tore open anew, sending both Wakened humans to their knees.

Krill spoke first after catching his breath. "It seems like our Wakened brains do not learn very fast."

"I concur." Hadder used the Comet to get back to his feet before tossing the keys to Krill, who plucked them out of the air. "Fuck it. You drive. Age before beauty and all that. I'll put the weapons in the back seat."

Krill nodded as he, too, rose to his feet, holding his side as he did. "I knew we could peacefully reach an accord. All it took was a little communication."

"And some critical injuries."

"Yes. Those, too."

Hadder moved past Krill and collected both burlap bags of military-grade weapons as Krill settled into the Comet's seat and dropped the passenger's seat forward. Hadder grunted loudly as he hefted both sacks into the automobile's back seat before joining Krill in the front.

"You remember how to drive one of these, Viktor?"

In response, Krill turned the key in the ignition and was greeted by a roar that shook the Comet on its frame. Both Wakened humans grinned like schoolboys. "I think it will come back to me."

As soon as the words came out of Krill's mouth, he shifted directly into second and floored the accelerator, cutting the steering wheel hard as he did. The Comet spun in a circle on the forest floor before Krill straightened the wheel, sending the car streaking to a small gap between two healthy pine trees.

Hadder closed his eyes as they sped toward the barriers, and yelped in delight as the Comet passed neatly between the twin trunks, no more than a few inches of clearance on either side.

Krill cackled in laughter as the Comet tore through the small forest path, eventually leaping over a pile of brush meant to conceal the secret passage.

The Comet fell loudly onto the main road, its shocks groaning under the strain, and fishtailed across several lanes before Krill got the beast under control and floored it.

True to its name, the Comet took off like a celestial body, streaking across a galaxy of pavement. As Krill drove, Hadder reached into his jacket and was delighted by what he found there. He retrieved two joints, both in rough shape from multiple battles but salvageable.

Hadder straightened them out, lit both, and gave one to his companion, who accepted it without word.

Together, the only two Wakened humans in the world sped off into the night, away from Kharras and toward the next vile step in their hideous adventure. As the Leaf smoke filled their lungs and eased their pain, both companions took solace in the fact that, at least for now, they were invisible. They were once more the hunters, determining the time and place of attack. They would find Doctor Milo Flowers and make him pay the ultimate price for his crimes against humanity.

But, meanwhile, Marlin Hadder was going to enjoy this drive, enjoy this smoke, enjoy these stars, and enjoy riding in one of the greatest creations that this world had to offer.

The Comet tore down the highway, a black smear on a neon world, under the cold inevitability of pink judgment.

––––––––––

"What in the world did *he* want?"

The boy shrugged, trying to act nonchalant, but the act didn't fool his caretaker.

The woman's visor issued loud *clicks* as it adjusted to focus on the boy's dark face. "Well, you met for a long time for nothing."

The boy shrugged again. "He gave me something that we may need."

"Need for what?" The visor fell to the small disk in the boy's hand. "Is that it?"

"Yes, ma'am."

"And what is on that disk, pray tell?"

The boy shrugged a final time. "Maybe nothing. I'll have to run some tests."

"And if these tests prove successful?"

The boy took a deep breath and exhaled loudly, unable to bring himself to lie to the woman who had become his second adoptive mother. "It could allow me to hack into any synthetic operating system. Even Taragoshi's."

The woman's knees almost gave out as the boy's words struck her. "To what end?"

The boy looked up with soft brown eyes. "To override their core protection protocols. To make them do whatever we want. Whatever we need."

Now the woman *did* have to sit down as her legs became jelly. "And why would that be necessary?" Silence. "Darrin? Why would that be necessary?"

Darrin Krill shuffled uneasily from one foot to the other. "He's not just any man, Miss Sammi. I think he's more than that."

Sammi Tott collected herself and stood once more on unsteady legs. "What makes you say that, sweetheart?"

"He knew about Father."

Sammi's visor refocused uncontrollably due to a sudden bout of anxiety. "And what did that red-eyed man say about your father?"

Darrin held the disk against his chest as if it was the most valuable item in the world. "He said that Father is fighting a god. And that *this* could prove to be the difference in the fight."

Sammi swallowed hard. "And if this god wins?"

Darrin Krill stared at Sammi Tott, brown eyes and empty sockets both having witnessed too much of the world's cruelty. "If this god wins, the world will collapse into…"

"Into hell," Sammi guessed for the boy.

Darrin shook his head. "No, ma'am. Hell sounds much better than this would be."

PART II

VILE SATELLITE

8

"They have… disappeared, my Lord."

Nieve's empty stomach issued loud protests as the words escaped her mouth, so nervous was she at breaking the unfortunate news to her god.

Doctor Milo Flowers's too-blue eyes rolled back into what was left of his head before returning to focus again on Nieve. As of late, the New God was having a hard time focusing on trivial matters, his theosis required increasing amounts of his attention and energy.

"How is this so?"

Nieve anxiously cleared her throat. "I don't really know, my Lord. They vanished for a bit after the failed highway attempt, but word of a black-eyed man making indelicate inquiries trickled out of the city of Kharras. Around that same time, there was a… disturbance at the mansion of one Patton Yellich. Patton Yellich was one of your key detractors, my Lord. He was a heretic and…"

"I know who Patton Yellich is, Nieve."

"Of course. My apologies, Lord. Patton Yellich went missing amidst the… disturbance. We think Viktor Krill and this Marlin Hadder may have been present."

"Go on."

Nieve shuffled uncomfortably, giving silent thanks to the New God that Daksha was not there to witness this scene. "Well, that's all, my Lord. They haven't been seen or heard of since." Nieve needed to deflect a little blame. "It would have been nice if Daksha had gotten us some photos of the men which were actually accurate. Viktor Krill's, in particular, was especially erroneous." Doctor Flowers's godly eyes pressed down hard on Nieve's small chest. "They can't have gotten far, as we have trackers on every vehicle in the known world. They must be on foot, which would greatly slow their progress." The empty words flowed out like a waterfall. "Also, Devout Willard and the Thorns of Reckoning were last known to be stationed around Kharras. Perhaps they have already been captured; perhaps they are already dead!"

"Viktor Krill and Marlin Hadder were brought into the Thorns' encampment, Nieve, along with Patton Yellich. In a forest just outside Kharras, as you theorized."

Nieve almost fell to the floor in relief. "Oh, what wonderful news, my Lord. I assume all the heathens have been dealt with in appropriate fashion. Where would you like Devout Willard to point his sword next? If I may be so bold, Clinton Voss continues to be a problem. I think we should..."

"Devout Willard is no more, Nieve," Flowers cut in.

What little blood was present drained from Nieve's skull-like face. The words barely slipped past her suddenly dry mouth. "Beg your pardon, my Lord?"

Doctor Flowers's eyes rolled once more back, then returned. "I was there, Nieve, via my Bloomed proxy. I was there. I saw the charred corpse of Patton Yellich."

Nieve spoke desperately. "Well, that's great, my Lord. Yellich was one of your most staunch and influential enemies. His death is a great victory."

Flowers went on, as if Nieve had never spoken. "I also saw the faces of Viktor Krill and Marlin Hadder, among my most trusted Thorns. They had been granted positions of authority within the Thorns of Reckoning."

Nieve's twig-like legs began to give out. "This cannot be, my Lord. I sent a messenger to the Thorns, warning them of Krill and Hadder, even describing the former's black eyes. Perhaps it was a trap set by Devout Willard. He was always crafty. Perhaps it was all a ruse to lull the dangerous non-believers into a state of comfort before ensnaring them and erasing them from this world."

Flowers let out a great sigh, which caused a ripple to run down the entire Chrysalis. "How is it that I, trapped in this prison of Holiness, know so much more than you, Nieve?"

Nieve's jaw fell open, but she managed to form a retort. "You are a god, my Lord."

A joyless laugh emanated from the Chrysalis. "That may be, but my energies are better spent elsewhere now. Wouldn't you agree?"

"I always agree with His Holiness."

Another sigh. "Speaking with you has tired me in a way that even Theosis does not. Let us bring your better informed colleague into the mix, shall we?" Nieve's heart sank even before her god released his next sentence. "Daksha, are you there?"

Nieve didn't bother to turn around; her accursed colleague's heels marked her approach loudly against the hard marble floor of the Holy Pistil.

Had the bitch been standing outside the entire time? Oh, how the bitch must have loved watching Nieve squirm. Damn her! If only it was Daksha who was strapped to one of the many surgical tables strewn across the Holy Pistil. Oh, what price Nieve would pay to see that. She would gladly...

"I am here, my Lord." Daksha's irritatingly sweet voice ripped Nieve from her revenge fantasy.

"Finally, someone competent."

Her Lord's words were enough for Nieve to want to end her life then and there. Had she a blade on her, Nieve would have spilled her bowels onto the white floor in a show of faith and atonement. Alas, she had no physical blade, so Nieve was forced to accept the verbal dissection.

Flowers continued. "Daksha, Nieve here seems to think that Devout Willard and the Thorns may have laid a trap for Viktor Krill and Marlin Hadder. Nieve here seems to believe that both men have been dispatched, and we should move on to the next problematic heretic. Would you concur with her assessment?"

Daksha's chin rose as she prepared to answer. Nieve knew she was fucked.

"I would not, my Lord."

"And why is that?"

"First, it is not an assessment, my Lord. Assessments are based on an analysis of data. It appears that our Nieve has no tangible data to speak of, only hopes and dreams, much like a young girl."

Nieve was unable to hold her tongue. "Just tell me what you know, *Daksha.*"

A feint smile painted the corners of Daksha's mouth as she raised her Taragoshi Pastiche ream and spun it to show Nieve. The thin woman's eyes went wide at the images of a forest littered with the dead, rotting bodies of men and women in white skinsuits.

"This is what remains of the Thorns of Reckoning. What was found — almost two hundred deceased wearing the garb of our Lord's elite fighting force. What was found — one Devout Willard Hillmore, his head torn apart almost beyond recognition. What was found – the burned remains of one Patton Yellich, may his soul burn forever in whatever hell awaits him." Daksha paused for effect. "What was not found – the body, living or dead, of one Viktor Krill and the body of one, living or dead, Marlin Hadder. What was not found – a cornucopia of military-grade weapons once belonging to the Thorns of Reckoning. What was not found – one antique automobile once belonging to Patton Yellich, void of recognition technology or tracking software."

Nieve stumbled to find the words under the weight of her Lord's blue eyes. "I had no way to know, my Lord. You remember Devout Willard! He was terrible at communication! He had us all in the dark regarding his plans and whereabouts! Even my messengers had a hard time reaching him! I…"

"Enough," roared Flowers, silencing the blathering woman beneath him. "The Thorns of Reckoning are no more. Devout Willard is no more. And I have lost a divine Bloomed Man. Daksha, what are we doing about this disaster?"

Daksha took a confident step forward. Nieve almost wretched. "The news crews that were first on the scene are obviously under strict instruction from Anton Carlyle to contact me before releasing any stories that are even remotely close to touching on the subject of the New God." Daksha cut a quick glance at Nieve. "It seems my relationship with the man has worked in our favor once more."

"Go on, my child."

"We have been able to spin the story. We have reported that a peaceful, religious gathering for the New God was descended upon by vicious, heavily armed heretics who killed all in agnostic bloodlust. We showed Devout Willard as a holy man who had healed thousands. Furthermore, we tied more than a few missing children reports to the act, stating that they were lovingly adopted by the New God's followers before being cut down by the non-believers." Daksha's sly grin broke into a smile. "My Lord, I am fully confident that I will spin Nieve's horrible failure into a great victory of faith, one that will garner you hundreds of thousands of new converts."

"How the hell is this *my* failure?!"

"Silence, foolish child!" Flowers's outburst almost put Nieve onto her backside. He continued, "What now, Daksha?"

Daksha cut one more glance at the admonished Nieve. "Patton Yellich is dead, my Lord. That is no small victory. He was not only the spiritual leader, but the financial head of the Protectors of Man. With him gone, I am confident that they will splinter, fragment, and, ultimately, disappear. That leaves only Viktor Krill and Marlin Hadder. Just tell me how many resources you would like dedicated to their eradication. I will succeed where others have failed."

Nieve had to restrain herself from digging her long nails into Daksha's golden eyes.

Doctor Milo Flowers retracted into his Chrysalis momentarily before peering out once more, his face covered in a thick goo. "Leave them."

Now it was Daksha's turn to appear shocked. Nieve drank it in. "Come again, Lord?"

"Leave them. My Theosis is proceeding much faster than expected. The Divine Antlers are priming the world for the Great Conversion. Since my last Holy Delegation, the Petals are churning out more and more Blessed Carriers by the day. Our location is an immaculate secret. My ascension is now inevitable. I do not want us to lose sight of what is truly important." Another blue eye roll. "Let Viktor Krill and Marlin Hadder have their adventure. If they ever manage to reach me, it will be far too late. I almost welcome their appearance. There will be no greater revenge than having them bow before me, helpless, as the world twists around them. Then, they will see the true difference between godly powers and the one, true God."

Both Daksha and Nieve exchanged concerned looks before Daksha spoke. "Are you certain, my Lord, I could easily..."

"Enough! Enough distractions. When the Great Conversion occurs, when my Theosis is complete, a million Wakened humans will not be enough to stop me!"

Daksha and Nieve's faces both twisted at the strange term – Wakened humans.

Flowers went on. "Continue pushing the Petals. Continue creating Blessed Carriers. And most of all, do not bring inconsequential issues to me! Have you no idea what I am doing within this Chrysalis?! Have you no idea the toll that it takes on me?!"

Both Daksha and Nieve fell to their knees under their Lord's anger and disappointment. They said in unison, "We are sorry, Lord!"

"Indeed, you are. Now, leave me. Focus your efforts where they will matter."

Again in unison, "Yes, Lord!"

The women rose and began to exit the Holy Pistil. Their lord's voice from behind gave them both pause.

"Daksha! Something escaped me. Remain for a moment."

The two women shared another look, but not one of smugness or jealousy or accomplishment. For neither knew whether staying behind was to be a mark of praise or reprimand. And if it was a reprimand, what the punishment would be.

"Of course, my Lord. Nothing would please me more."

The mechanical surgeons whirred in the background, always working away at slicing flesh, breaking bone, and bending the definitions of life.

———

"YOU ARE DOING WELL, Daksha. I especially like the work you are doing with Anton Carlyle. In these times, reality is that which is told through the media. I will change all this, of course, but am happy to take advantage where opportunities currently present themselves."

Daksha beamed at the compliment. "Your kind words warm my undeserving heart, my Lord. Even as we speak, the Tragedy at Heretic Grove – that is what we are calling it – is a story that is quickly spreading across the globe. It is a story illustrating the evil lengths that those who oppose the New God are willing to go."

Milo Flowers nodded lightly. "It is a name worthy of the travesty. The loss of Devout Willard and his loyal Thorns of Reckoning is significant."

"But one I hope to transform into a great victory, my Lord. A victory of conversion and faith."

A small smile touched Flowers's gooey lips. "Yes, I see that, my child. Tell me, Daksha, as you turn lemons into lemonade, it seems like your colleague is having a hard time utilizing the wondrous ingredients I have given her."

A trickle of worry ran down the dark-skinned woman's spine. "Are you referring to Nieve, my Lord?"

"I am. Tell me your opinion of her. And, please, do not be shy."

Daksha's hands formed knots as her eyes dropped to the marble floor just beneath the massive Chrysalis. This was her chance to be rid of her rival, to make the sticklike rich girl pay for all her attempts to steal away the attention and love of the New God.

Attention and love that should be reserved for Daksha alone.

Her mind spun with Nieve's many missteps, miscalculations, errors, and misconceptions, all carefully catalogued in Daksha's computer-like brain, ready to be retrieved for this exact moment.

"Few get away with making God wait, Daksha."

Daksha almost collapsed as her Lord's words tore her from her whirlwind of memories. "No, of course, my Lord. My sincerest apologies, my Lord. I just want to make sure I give you my most accurate assessment of the woman."

"And that is?"

Daksha steeled herself. "Nieve is a product of her upbringing. Her entitlement causes her to look at the world in a way that is not reflective of reality."

"Meaning?"

"Meaning, Lord, that she is a rich girl. She always expects things to go according to plan. She thinks things will go right the first time around and does not plan for when they do not." Daksha hesitated, but needed to get this off her chest. "The wealthy are like that. They often do not see the struggle it took to accomplish a thing, the many iterations, failures, and adjustments that were necessary to successfully complete a task. They put orders in and are only notified when achievements are realized. Thus, Nieve's strategy is lacking, as is her ability to pivot, to turn lemons into lemonade."

Milo Flowers's eyelids were beginning to fall again, as if listening was draining his limited strength. "I see. Is that all?"

Daksha wanted to leave it there. She wanted to watch as Nieve was torn from her sleeping quarters and dragged, kicking and screaming, through the Flowers Institute by one of the Anointed Champions, who would take her somewhere deep and dark to inflict awful punishment. This is what Daksha wanted to do. Unfortunately, Daksha found that she could not.

A disappointed sigh fell out of the woman. "No, that is not all, my Lord. My love for you will not permit me to be less than fully honest. I detest Nieve, my Lord. I have always hated her ilk. I hate them for the loathing they have always kept in their cold hearts for me and my kind, for all others beneath their societal station." A pause. "But Nieve is a true believer, my Lord. She loves you with all her heart and would die for you, as we all would. And while her mind is limited and her perspective is cloudy, she has contacts that I could never hope to develop, contacts that only respond to select last names. She navigates the waters of the old regime better than I ever could ever hope to, slowly tilting more and more in your favor."

A silent moment passed between god and disciple. "That hurt you to say, did it not, my child?"

"It did, my Lord."

"Good. Anything worth doing rarely comes without pain of some sort. Do not fret. Nieve's stay of judgment is extended. But her disappointments are becoming borderline habitual, and we cannot have that at this critical juncture. The Great Conversion is upon us. My Theosis is almost complete. We all must successfully play our parts. Nieve is no different."

"Then she is safe, my Lord?"

"For now. But I will not be able to tolerate another failure."

"And if she fails, my Lord? What awaits her?"

"What do you think, my child?"

Daksha did not want to answer, but her Lord had asked a question. "Excommunication, my Lord? Death, my Lord?"

Flowers's too-blue eyes went wide, almost crushing the small woman under their gaze. "Do you think so little of me, my child?"

Daksha fell to her knees as tears immediately began to stream down her dark face. "Of course not, my Lord! But our work for you is holy! We have sworn our lives to you! We would all gladly die should you but command it!"

"Rise, my child." Daksha did as she was directed. "You said it yourself, Nieve is a true believer. What kind of god would I be if I tossed aside such a loyal servant? No, Nieve would remain in my godly care, but in a role that would require much less of her."

Daksha nodded rapidly, delighted to hear that the New God would not simply exterminate one of his own. Her heart swole as another piece fell into place, the larger picture reminding her that she made the right decision in throwing her life behind Doctor Milo Flowers.

"That is wonderful to hear, my Lord. I will redouble my efforts to ensure that the Great Conversion goes according to plan. And I will work more closely with Nieve. Her faith in the New God sometimes blinds her to the world's realities, but there is value there, nonetheless."

Milo Flowers's eyes once more began to roll back as his head slipped slowly into the Chrysalis. He spoke as he retracted, his voice sounding far off, as if he was already sitting shoulder to shoulder with his equals in the cosmos. "Yes, there is value there, Daksha. There is value in all of you. As disciples. Or Blessed Carriers. There is always value. You may go…"

As Flowers's face slid back into the massive cocoon, Daksha turned on a heel and began the long walk out of the Holy Pistil. She did her best to keep her eyes straight ahead, lest they fall on one of a hundred of horrific experiments being conducted by the surgical mechs.

While Daksha kept her eyes locked forward, she also tried to ignore the final words of the New God, those that reminded her of the fate that awaited them all upon failure, the promise of becoming Blessed Carriers.

Daksha marched on, ignoring the screams of those strapped to cold metal tables. Ignoring the incessant whirrs of the surgical mechs, who cared nothing for this world or the one that was to come. Ignoring the laughing faces of the angels that populated the frescoes surrounding the Holy Pistil, those that found hilarity in the troubles of humanity.

But Daksha found that she could not ignore her Lord's final words. And the inherent threat that they contained.

9

Within a half-hour of the Comet flying down the dark highway, Marlin Hadder had passed out in the passenger's seat, the Leaf having massaged his brain with its smoky tendrils.

More nightmares invaded Hadder's sleep. A wave of Bloomed Men tore across the world, consuming and changing all in its path, horrific locusts altering the very essence of the globe. As they ate and mutated, killed and created, a blinding beacon in the rear urging them on — an entity draped in light, a New God. He met eyes with Hadder and smiled as if to say, *I won,* or *You lost,* or both. The New God raised his glowing hand in the air, and Hadder felt his resolve vanish under that unsaid command. Hadder's legs gave out, his knees began to bend...

"What do we have here? Marlin!"

The voice of Viktor Krill stole Hadder from the nightmarish landscape, leaving him panting heavily, covered in cold sweat in the arms of the Comet's black leather.

Hadder shook loose of the dark images, used his Wakened abilities to slow his heart rate, and looked around. Just as when he fell asleep, this portion of the highway was dark, with only small hover globes lighting the path from above and neon color-markings outlining the road's edges and lanes.

Up ahead, however, the Comet was closing in on a rather unusual vehicle, one of the few others on the road at this time. It was no doubt some kind of military or police prisoner transport, with thickly armored sides protecting its driver and escort. Prisoners were piled into the vehicle's rear flatbed, around which a thick cage coursed with deadly electricity to prevent any escape attempts.

Krill accelerated, and the Comet smoothly moved into position just behind the transport.

"What makes *her* so special," asked Krill as their Wakened eyes moved through the darkness, past the glowing outside cage, and into the hold. In the center of the electrified cage, surrounded by regular prisoners, stood one apparently exceptional detainee.

Even with their superior visions, it was hard to tell from this distance, but to Hadder and Krill it looked as if a woman was standing in the center of the flatbed, cocooned in a single-person standing restraint. Thick cables of carbon fiber ran across the woman's sleight frame from neck to shins, attached to a flat metal board that ran behind her and was welded directly into the vehicle's bed. To complete the suffocating look, a muzzle had been placed over the woman's head, preventing her from biting, or spitting, or maybe simply saying unkind things.

"What the fuck could she have done to deserve that," asked Hadder.

"I don't know, Marlin, but I think we should investigate."

With that, Krill shifted into the left lane and accelerated, pulling the Comet even with the transport.

Hadder studied the vehicle. "Definitely was police-owned, but not anymore. Check it out."

Krill looked to where Hadder directed and found that the mono-grammed KPF, meaning Kharras Police Force, that sat heavy on the side of the transport was stenciled over with the white five-petaled lotus of the Blossoms of the New God. The Blossoms controlling the vehicle began to look over at the Comet, but Krill drifted back into the darkness before they could gain any useable intel. The Comet fell back into the darkness of the highway.

"What do you think, Marlin?"

"I think the enemy of our enemy is our friend."

"I agree."

"And I think any friend who needs all that to be restrained could be an especially valuable friend."

"I couldn't have said it better myself."

"Do you have a plan?"

Viktor Krill smirked as he floored the gas petal and sped off ahead of the transport. "I always have a plan, Marlin. But we'll need to get some things out of the back seat. How are your wounds?"

"They hurt like hell. But I'll survive."

"You'll survive. But can you kill?"

"Always."

"Good man."

———

EAMON FLICKED his ash out of the open window with one hand while steering the transport with the other. His comrades, as usual, complained next to him.

"Hurry it up, will you? It's fucking cold outside," said Cris from beside him.

Jarvis chimed in right after. "Yeah, and I don't like that fucking window open. This thing is bulletproof for a reason. And the glass ain't truly bulletproof if it ain't up." He concluded by looking around nervously.

Eamon laughed at the fear that surrounded his five fellow Blossoms, leftover trauma from what had happened back in Ranierra, a small town just outside Kharras. "What's the matter, boys? Scared that the Twat's friends will come to rescue her? Ha! They don't even know where she was. The Budd told us that much." A silence fell over the transport cab. "Oh, don't tell me," cried Eamon in a voice that he hoped carried his disappointment. "Don't tell me that you alls are afraid of the Twat escaping the stand-trap and scaling the electric fence, only to come ripping through this tiny window to make you alls shit your pants again. Tell me that's not what you alls are afraid of! Tell me!"

The five other Blossoms simply looked to each other, each silently agreeing that, *Yes, we are afraid of that very thing.*

Eamon scoffed before tossing his cigarette into the dark night and pressing the control to raise the window once more. "There! Are you pussies happy now?!"

"We are, boss. Thanks," responded Jarvis. It took all of Eamon's willpower not to lunge over and shatter the thin man's long nose.

Eamon placed both hands on the steering wheel, unnecessary given the vehicle's automatic controls. But with the Twat in the back, Eamon wanted to stay sharp. And overriding the auto drive for manual control kept him awake and sharp.

For his men, Eamon wanted them sharp, but not tense. He decided to fill the quiet with supportive words. "Listen, boys, I know the Twat took a real bite out of us back there, but she's in the back, and we're up her, ya dig. She lost and we won. She's gonna be spilling her guts, both literally and figuratively, in a bit, and we're all gonna get handsomely rewarded. So, relax. Bask in a job well done and... what the fuck is that?"

Five pairs of eyes joined the sixth in looking down the dark highway as a strange vehicle quickly came into focus. The antique-looking car was as black as the surrounding night and was slowly riding along in the transport's lane.

This, however, is not what was disconcerting to the six Blossoms. What *was* disconcerting were the two automatic gun turrets that had been placed atop the vehicle, alongside a dark-suited man who was sitting on the edge of the open passenger-side window. The stranger's elbows were resting easily atop the black car's roof, pointing the barrel of an obnoxiously large gun at the transport.

"Go around them, man," cried Noles, the fear in his voice irritating Eamon.

"We're in a fucking transport tank, you cowards! We are impenetrable! I will simply run them off the road." With that, Eamon slammed his foot against the accelerator and smiled as the behemoth responded, surging ahead on modern innovation.

The black car reacted and easily maintained the distance between the two vehicles. As it did, the man in the black suit fired his first shot, sending a large projectile to smash into the transport's bulletproof windshield. Despite the loud noise that threatened to burst eardrums, the glass held.

Eamon laughed as he drove. "See! The fools have nothing for us."

Another projectile slammed into the windshield, and although no cracks could be seen, a loud groan could be heard just after impact.

Eamon sneered. "That's it! I'm launching the forks, boys!"

Before he could, a third oversized missile struck the windshield, immediately followed by loud popping sounds from the window's edges. Eamon's right hand shook as he moved it to the central control panel and keyed in the code for the transport's defenses. A few selections later, and Eamon had brought up the option for the electro-forks.

Another rocket plowed into the windshield, which let out an audible moan along the length of its top.

As the Blossoms all reached for their Stutters, two giant forks extended from the front of the transport, blue electrical flames jumping across the prongs of each. The electro-forks reached for the too-black intruder, but it roared in protest, accelerating far ahead to disappear into the distance of the poorly lit highway.

Eamon let out a great sigh of relief as Jarvis and Cris cried out in victory. A smile returned to his chapped lips. "What did I tell you boys?! No one can harm us! We have the New God on our side! Everything else pales before his... fuck me!"

The black vehicle flew back into frame before Eamon could complete his devotion, the man in the dark suit now perched lightly upon its trunk. Given that the car was now moving considerably slower than the transport, the armored vehicle and its electro-forks closed the distance quickly.

Just as the blue-tinged prongs were to touch black metal, the dark-suited man launched himself at the transport, soaring through the air like a dart. His legs unfolded into a double kick just as he was about to connect with the windshield.

The last thing that Eamon saw before the *indestructible* windshield gave way and assaulted the six Blossoms was the black car ahead accelerating out of reach of the electro-forks.

And the roof-mounted auto-turrets spinning to life.

———

MARLIN HADDER KICKED out with all of this Wakened strength, which ripped at his numerous half-healed wounds. Fortunately, he was rewarded with an explosive cracking sound as the unbreakable windshield ripped away angrily from the rivets that connected it to the transport frame.

Hadder had but a moment to enjoy the fact that his earlier distance attacks had sufficiently weakened the windshield's structural integrity before he was thrown into a shit storm of violence.

Hadder fell hard against the loose windshield, which cracked neatly into three pieces, cutting and crushing those under its clear mass, before rolling gently to the floorboard. He let out a pained groan just as turret shots rang out from the outside.

The Blossoms above Hadder screamed as they attempted in vain to duck and dodge in the incoming onslaught. As they thrashed, several were sliced along their hands and arms by the broken windshield's sharp edges.

Two Blossoms almost immediately took bullets to the head. Two others held up pieces of the windshield as makeshift shields, blood running down their arms from where the glass cut into their soft palms. A third dropped to the floorboard to join Hadder, who shot the man through the heart with one of his crystalline handguns.

As the other two Blossoms trembled beneath the auto-turret attack, Eamon did his best to keep the transport on the road, under no illusions that he would survive in a square fight with the two assassins. Eamon pushed a large windshield piece away and leaned his head to the left, allowing the transport frame to offer some protection from turret fire, and accelerated, hoping that his electro-forks could end this battle once and for all.

Every time Eamon lunged forward; however, the black antique followed suit, easily maintaining the distance between them. Until it didn't.

Eamon, still hiding behind the transport frame, grew concerned as the sounds of gunfire stopped, replaced by the tornado-like winds that sped past his ears. He ignored the whimpering of the surviving men next to him and gambled a peek around the transport frame.

Eamon let out a surprised exhalation of relief as the black automobile was no longer in front of the transport. Determined to take advantage of this break in the attack, Eamon quickly put the transport into auto-drive and reached into his side holster to retrieve his pistol.

A dark smile appeared on Eamon's lips as he considered shooting the two remaining Blossoms along with the dark-suited assassin, earning himself all the acclaim of the Twat's capture.

Just as Eamon began to point his pistol in the direction of the floorboard, a loud whistle to his left stole his attention. Eamon's eyes went wide as the black antique appeared next to him, just meters from the transport. From within the car, a figure cloaked in shadow moved in the driver's seat. As the vehicles passed under one of the highway's hover-globes, Eamon's fear morphed into terror as the man in the car was illuminated. He was wearing the smile of a wolf who had cornered its prey.

Eamon smiled back before swinging his gun back around at the black sportster. Just as the pistol's barrel was in line with the grinning man, a knife crossed the distance with blinding speed, burying itself to the hilt in Eamon's throat. Eamon reached up and removed the blade, immediately regretting the move when a river of blood began to run down the front of his white shirt.

What the fuck just happened, Blossom Eamon's last thought as he slumped over the transport steering wheel, which was now under auto-drive control.

Hadder, also detecting the break in auto-turret fire, looked up to find the driver quite dead, and turned his attention to the two remaining Blossoms. The men remained huddled under their windshield shards, too terrified to move or consider a return attack. Hadder began to rise with his handguns, but thought better of it and returned them to their shoulder holsters. Instead, he removed the blade that he stole from Patton Yellich's mansion and leapt up, using his Wakened abilities to block out the burning pain that ran across his body.

Hadder's first strike flashed out like lightning, curling around the Blossom's shard-shield to drive the strange blade deep into the side of the man's neck. The Blossom brought his piece of the windshield around much too late, but still managed to carve a deep wound along Hadder's forearm.

Hadder cursed under his breath, withdrawing his blade from the mortally wounded Blossom and spinning away from the sharp glass. As Hadder spun, he shifted his grip on his dagger, holding it blade down, and drove it backhand toward the lone remaining Blossom.

Despite the Blossom having his windshield piece in position for the block, Hadder's Wakened strength proved too much. Hadder knocked the glass from the defender's hands, allowing the blade to find purchase in the man's chest, inches above the heart, precisely where Hadder had intended.

Leaving his hand on the blade buried in the screeching Blossom's chest, Hadder reached over and pressed the *Controlled Stop* button on the auto-drive menu. After several seconds, which probably felt like an eternity to the injured Blossom, the transport slowed, moved carefully to the right, and came to a cautious stop along the highway's shoulder.

A few moments later, the Comet came to rest just ahead of the parked transport. Viktor Krill exited the Comet, looking as delighted as Hadder had ever seen him.

Soft whimpering to his right reminded Hadder of the Blossom that he purposely left alive. Hadder removed his dagger from the man's chest, grabbed him by the white shirt, and tossed him easily through the front of the transport.

The Blossom soared over the front of the transport and landed heavily on the pavement, letting out a cry of pain as he did. Viktor Krill placed a Verrato high-top on the Blossom's head, pinning him to the ground. He lit a cigarette before looking up at Hadder with black eyes.

"I think that went quite well."

Hadder began to climb gingerly down from the transport, blood leaking out from his suit jacket's right arm. "Easy for you to say. You weren't a human bowling ball."

Krill shrugged, exhaling a plume of smoke as he did. "You're alive. I'm alive. They're all dead." He looked down. "Well, except for this poor bastard, but that will be rectified in short order." The Blossom let out a loud groan. "I don't know about you, but where I'm from, we call that a successful venture."

Hadder reached the ground, attempting to shake away the pain in his arm. "We're from the place, Viktor. Remember?"

"Unfortunately, I do."

"What now?"

Krill took one last drag before flicking the cigarette into the dark of night. He shifted his black eyes to the young Blossom beneath his shoe. "Now we find out what makes that young woman in the back worth all this effort. Now we find out who she is to the Blossoms of the New God."

———

"YOU SEE anything in the central console options," shouted Hadder to Krill, who was in the cabin of the transport.

"Nothing," came the response from up front. "The release panel must be back there. Can you see it?"

Hadder limped around the transport's electrified flatbed, surprised by the continued silence of the captives within. After some searching, he found what he was looking for along the passenger's side of the cage.

Hadder reached over and carefully slid the panel cover up, revealing the mechanism for releasing the prisoners. "I found it!"

"What does it look like?"

Hadder studied the panel for a moment. "Looks like we got a dual release system. There's a key pad for a code *and* a palm reader."

Krill jumped down from the transport. "Got it. Join me up front."

Hadder returned to the front of the transport, where Krill had handcuffed the remaining Blossom to the vehicle's grill using restraints they found in the armored unit's glove compartment. The Blossom sat sadly on the ground in a daze, the wound in his chest making his breaths come out in ragged wheezes.

Krill kicked the man's white pants to get his attention. "All right, your turn, sweetheart. We've got some questions for you. Answer them to my satisfaction, and I might let you live. Play games, and I'll show you a game of my own creation. It's called *roll your head down the highway.* Are we clear?" The Blossom nodded dumbly. "Good. Now, what's your name?"

"Noles," said the Blossom, sounding unsure of himself. He then repeated it with more conviction. "My name is Noles."

Krill continued the interrogation. "See how well this is going? Keep it up, Noles. Tell me, Noles, what is so special about that young lady in the back? Who is she to the Blossoms, and why is she restrained so aggressively?" A silence followed. "I asked you a question, boy!"

Noles flinched as if he was about to be struck. "I'm sorry! I'm trying to think of how to best answer, ok, man?"

Krill rolled his black eyes. "Let's start slower. Perhaps I overwhelmed you. Who is the woman in the back?"

"That's the Twat, man."

Both Hadder and Krill's faces showed confusion. "Is that her legal name," asked Krill.

"Of course not. That's just what me and the boys call her. Nobody knows her real name, man."

Hadder cut in. "And what makes her so special? Why does she get a nickname and VIP accommodations?"

Noles didn't answer right away as his attention drifted once more to his leaking chest wound. A swift kick by Krill brought him back.

"Ahh, shit, man. Ok. Ok. She's a butcher, man. A goddamn butcher."

"Go on," prodded Krill.

"She's been hunting Blossoms around this region for several weeks now. Groups of us have been found cut all to hell. She don't look like much, which is why she can get in and out before anyone knows what kind of twat she really is."

"And what kind of twat is she," demanded Krill.

Noles met Krill's dark eyes. "The killing kind, man."

Hadder jumped in again. "So, you finally caught her. Why capture her at all if she's such a threat? Why not just eliminate the threat and claim your prize via her corpse?"

"She's more than that."

"How so?"

This question was met with more silence. Krill, already tired of the little Blossom, jammed his thumb into the man's open wound. The Blossom screamed out in pain.

"Protectors! Protectors, man! The Twat is one of the Protectors of Man, man! Probably one of the highest-ranking Protectors!"

"That doesn't answer my question," Hadder continued. "Why not kill her?"

Krill dug his thumb deeper into Noles, who cried out again.

"Fuck, man! Stop! Just stop! I'll tell you, man!" Krill removed his thumb and wiped the blood on Noles's white shirt. "We think the Protectors of Man have their base somewhere around Crimmwall, but no one can find it. We were taking the Twat to the city…"

"What city?"

"Fuck, man, ain't you listening? To Crimmwall, man. There's a major Petal there and some really high-up Blossoms. We take the Twat there, get the credit we deserve, and they're the ones that have to carve the hidden Protector location out of her. Win, win, man!"

Hadder was growing more interested in the female captive by the moment. "You boys don't have a lot of faith in yourselves, do you? You didn't even consider getting the location out of her yourselves?" Noles let out a wheezing laugh. "What's so funny?"

"You've obviously never seen the Twat in action, man."

"Fair enough. But if your group couldn't get it out of her, what makes you think the Blossoms in Crimmwall will be able?"

Noles's eyes were beginning to roll back into his head. Still, he responded. "They have... special skills, man. They can... create monsters, man. No one wants to become a monster, man. Not even the Twat..."

Krill looked down at Noles with distain. "I think that's all we are going to get out of this pissant." Back to Hadder. "Looks like we stumbled upon something valuable here, Marlin."

"If we can get it unlocked."

"Good point." A final kick brought Noles's eyes back into focus. "Noles! We need the code to unlock the back cage."

Noles's head began to loll from one side to the other. "Sure, man. Whatever you need, man. It's..."

"Noles!"

"Fuck, sorry, man. I slipped away for a bit. The code is... 57... 3... 9... 1."

"Are you certain?"

"Pretty sure, man."

"And the palm print? Whose palm print is needed?"

Noles chuckled lightly under his breath, like a drunk man laughing at his own internal joke. "Not me."

"Noles!"

"Fuck, man, I don't know! Not! Me! I don't remember whose print was used. Could have been any of the boys."

Krill swung his dark gaze to Hadder. "Marlin, go punch in the code and see if this little runt was telling the truth. I'll figure out the palm issue."

Hadder did as instructed, returning to the security panel beneath the hissing cage. He keyed in the five digits that Noles provided. The pad chimed and lit up in green.

"Accepted, Viktor," Hadder called back to the front of the

transport.

"Good," Krill answered back. "Give me moment."

As he waited, Hadder stared up through the electrified bars. His eyes naturally fell upon the young woman who was strapped to the standing restraint. Hazel eyes rose until they finally found the muzzle that wrapped around her head. Dark eyes stared out from beneath the mask, and Hadder could tell that she was studying him, analyzing potential paths of attack.

If he were not a Wakened human, Hadder would be terrified.

Viktor Krill appeared from the front of the transport, a small bundle in his arms. "Here, try this one," he said as he tossed something at his companion.

Hadder plucked the object out of the air, but almost dropped it after recognizing it for what it was — a freshly cut hand. "Fuck me, Viktor! You could have at least warned me!"

Krill shrugged lightly, poorly attempting to keep a grin from his lips. "I didn't know you were so squeamish."

"I'm not," Hadder snapped back. "But a little heads up, huh?" Hadder looked at the pale hand. "This isn't even the correct hand, Viktor. It's a right-hand palm reader."

Krill looked down and dropped half of his load onto the pavement. "No worries. I got them all."

A light laugh with a distinguishable lilt escaped the woman in the standing restraint.

Hadder and Krill shared a look. "Well, at least someone enjoys your antics, Viktor. Toss me a righty."

It took several tries, but the fourth hand that Hadder held up to the palm reader was accepted. He then had to re-key in the numerical code, which reset after the first incorrect palm attempt.

The entire security panel lit up green, followed by the audible click of a released lock and the muting of electrical hissing.

Krill yelled back to the front of the transport. "It worked, Noles! You're lucky! Your hand was next!"

"You just can't help yourself, can you?"

Krill slapped Hadder on the back as he moved into position behind the transport. "Open her up, Marlin. Let's see what we've won."

Hadder reached up and pulled on the large lever. It moved smoothly, freed up via the correct code-palm combination. The transport's giant gate swung out, forcing Hadder and Krill to step back out of its path. The companions then stepped up into the transport's flatbed.

"Look at this sad collection of shit," remarked Krill as they took inventory.

Hadder found it hard to disagree with Krill's assessment. Looking around, he found the grimiest collection of men and women he had seen outside the Muck's Jungle. Sitting in neat rows along each side of the flatbed, they were all pinned to their seats by thick bars that ran across their laps like rollercoaster restraints. Each detainee cast their eyes to the floor of the transport, as scared of their rescuers as they were their captors.

Krill finally addressed the unimpressive group. "Who are you all? Why did the Blossoms imprison you?" Silence followed. "I asked you a question!"

If the dirty collective could have jumped out of their seats, they would have. Finally, a woman with long, unkempt hair spoke. She looked to be in her sixties, but was probably in her late thirties. "We done nothing wrong! Did we, y'all? They just took us, saying we were some kinda protectors of man, or some nonsense. Do we look like protectors to you?"

"Indeed, you do not," responded Hadder, noting the trail marks along the woman's too-thin arm.

"Then why go through the trouble of rounding you all up," asked Krill.

A soft voice filtered out from behind the muzzle of the girl known as the Twat. "They honestly don't know anything. I can probably be of more help with your inquiries."

Hadder and Krill met eyes. "What do you think, Viktor?"

"I think we need to be moving faster, regardless of what we do. This highway won't stay empty forever."

"Good point." With that, Hadder found the release button along the back wall of the flatbed, out of reach of the prisoners, and pressed it. The large bars fell forward loudly, freeing the captives to either side of the transport. With nothing holding them to their seats, man and woman alike poured out of the transport, half of them falling out of the back of the flatbed to painfully hit the pavement below.

The junkies said nothing to the two men who freed them. Instead, they simply ambled off into the fields and forest that ran alongside the highway. Hadder laughed to himself. To a junkie, this may have been just another day on the stroll.

"Don't let her go, man," came a delirious cry from the front of the transport. "She'll kill us all, man! You, too, man! Even you!"

Krill and Hadder both turned their full attentions to the woman in the restraint. Krill, standing before the woman, spoke first.

"I think young Noles is talking about you, miss. Is what he is saying true? Are you going to kill us if we free you?"

The woman's eyes and head fell in subservience. "Of course not, good sirs," she replied in soft, birdlike tones. "That would be an awful way to show my gratitude, wouldn't it, now?"

"Very well. Marlin, do you see the releases back there?"

Hadder, still in the rear of the flatbed, took a brief look around and found several mechanisms along the back of the standing restraint. "Yeah, they're right here, Viktor."

"Then, by all means, set our girl free."

Hadder slid three buttons from left to right, from red to green, and stepped back as groups of carbon fiber cables retracted back into the rectangular base unit, unbinding the woman's shoulders, arms, hips, and legs.

As soon as she was released, the woman's muzzled head snapped back up, and, along with it, her right fist. She punched out with blinding speed, with force that would have brought a horse to the ground. The skillful maneuver would have been enough to defeat any man or woman in the world, regardless of size.

Unfortunately for the woman, it was not a man or woman who was the target of her attack, but a Wakened human.

Viktor Krill neatly sidestepped the surprise blow, and was able to deftly turn aside the front kick that was heading toward his testicles. He then blocked three more lightning-fast strikes, marveling at the speed of the masked woman.

If the woman was shocked by Krill's own extraordinary abilities, she did not show it. She kicked off the standing restraint, sending herself flying at Krill, her thin arms searching for space under his chin and around his neck. Krill rolled with her, however, tossing the woman off the back of the flatbed, where she landed cleanly on all fours before springing to her feet.

The woman attempted to slam the back gate shut, but Krill was able to kick it open before the lock caught. He then flipped off the transport, landing opposite the woman, cutting off her retreat into the fields.

Dark eyes went wide under the muzzle. "One of those strikes should have landed. Who *are* you?"

Krill smiled and held his tan hands out wide. "That was my question. But you need to know, you are not the only killer in this world, my dear. And although you are good, excellent, in fact, you are far from the best. You are looking at the best."

"I see," came the soft voice, "then I have no choice but to surrender. Will you accept my…" While the woman never finished her question, it was punctuated by an attack. A knife taken from Krill's coat pocket during their brief tangle flew from her right hand, heading for the face of the notorious killer.

The woman smiled briefly under her mask before it transformed into a frown as Krill's hands moved quicker than her eyes could follow, snatching the knife out of the air as it was mere inches from connecting. At the same time, a second blade came from behind to rest neatly against the woman's soft throat, forcing her chin up in surrender.

Krill laughed aloud as he redeposited the knife into his jacket pocket. "Impressive. Very impressive. But what, exactly, were you hoping to accomplish with that show, miss?"

The woman spoke around the knife at her throat. "I don't just go along with anyone. I needed to test your skills to see if you were worthy of my company."

"And how did you find our… skills?"

"You should be dead." Hadder's knife started to bite into her skin. "What I mean is that any other person would have been defeated by those combinations I threw at you."

"So, you find us… acceptable companions?" The woman nodded as well as possible with the blade cutting into her neck. "You do realize that we are the ones that rescued you, right?"

The woman continued to speak from beneath the muzzle. "I don't know who you are. Perhaps you're just another group of Blossoms, trying to steal the glory of my capture for yourselves. Your outfit certainly had me drawing those conclusions."

Krill looked down at his beloved white suit. "You know, I rocked this look long before the goddamn Blossoms did." The woman simply shrugged. "And now you are sure we are not Blossoms, are you?"

"You don't fight like Blossoms."

"And how do they fight?"

"Like cowards."

"Fair enough. Marlin, I think we can dispense with the show of force." Hadder slowly removed the knife from the woman's throat, keeping himself primed should another attack come. "My name is Viktor Krill. And the gentleman behind you is Marlin Hadder. We were passing this Blossom transport when we noticed you in the back of it. You appeared to be valuable cargo. Valuable cargo to the Blossoms is valuable cargo to us, as well."

"If you're thinking of selling me, I promise that the sale will not go well."

Krill laughed again. Hadder could tell that his companion fancied this woman's attitude. "I would not think of it, dear woman. What I mean is that my partner and I are not fans of the Blossoms of the New God."

"That's putting it lightly," Hadder added.

"We were interested in you because, if you're considered this much of a danger to them, then perhaps you could be of value to our efforts. Enemy of my enemy, and all that."

"Can I take this muzzle off, please. It's really hot in here."

"Oh, where are my manners. You are welcome to remove it."

The woman reached up and undid the leather buckles in the back of her muzzle. When she removed the mask, Hadder's heart jumped in his chest.

"There. Much better."

The woman was a light-skinned asian with slim, delicate features. Dried blood surrounded plump lips, as if she had stepped from the pages of a vampire novel. Her hair was short, barely touching her shoulders, and slicked back, as if it were always wet, even when it wasn't. She wore tight khaki cargo pants with a slim-fitting white t-shirt. Nothing about the woman screamed "danger" or "killer," which made her the perfect assassin.

The woman wiped her face, as if she could still feel the restrictive leather there, before meeting Krill's black eyes with her own dark brown. "Nice to meet you, Viktor Krill." She turned to find Hadder. "And you, Marlin Hadder." Her eyes fell to the knife in Hadder's hand and rested there for a moment. "Where did you get such a unique knife?"

"From a friend," was all that Hadder said in response.

Krill broke the strange pause in conversation. "As I said before, we *really* do need to be going."

The woman shook her head, as if to clear away the image of the knife in Hadder's hand. "Yes, of course. Listen, they took some things from me that are very dear. Could I please retrieve them?"

Krill answered. "If you get them in less than a minute, then go ahead."

The woman nodded. "I watched where they stashed them." With that, she made her way into the shattered remnants of the transport cabin, emotionlessly pushing aside corpses as easily as she did slabs of broken windshield. She reached behind the seats and, after rummaging around for several seconds, came back with a neatly folded brown trench coat. She dropped back down to the pavement.

"That coat must mean a lot to you," remarked Hadder.

The woman seemed surprised by his words, so relieved was she to have found her belongings. "Oh, yes, I do appreciate a good coat. But that's not really what I needed to find." With that, the woman unfolded the trench coat to reveal a katana sword within, encased in a beautiful redwood scabbard. Her eyes danced along its length. "This. This is what I was looking for."

Krill came around the transport. "Ah, a blade. A woman after my own heart. Marlin, take note." To the woman, "My colleague here favors guns, much to my chagrin."

The woman spoke as she donned the trench coat. "Well, whatever gets the job done, right?"

"That is right," agreed Hadder, tired of Krill's jabs about his choice of weapons.

A voice cut in. "I'm telling you, man! She's gonna kill us all, man! You better do her now, man!"

The woman nodded toward the front of the transport. "Friend of yours?"

"More like a friend of yours," said Krill. "One of your captors."

"Do you need him?"

Krill read the woman's blank, beautiful face. "We do not."

"Do you mind if I…"

"Be my guest."

The woman moved around to the front of the vehicle, Hadder and Krill on her heels. Noles immediately began to blather as she came into view. Everyone ignored him.

"We never got your name, miss," ventured Hadder.

The woman spun back to Hadder and Krill. As she did, she pulled the katana free from its sheath and drew a neat line in the air before her. As she completed her spin, she flicked out with her right hand, tossing a rope of blood from her blade to land audibly onto the black pavement.

"I'm so sorry. Where are my manners?" As the woman spoke, the top of Noles's head slid off and fell to the ground, sounding like an empty coconut. She returned the sword to its scabbard. "My name is

Su. Su Anorrak. I have much to thank you both for, but this is not the time nor the place. Shall we?"

Unsurprisingly, Krill was able to recover more quickly than Hadder. "We shall. This way, Su."

The trio made their way to the Comet, which brought a massive smile to Su's lips. "Now, *this* is a car." She took a longer look. "It looks familiar. From where did you get it, may I ask?"

Krill spoke as he removed the auto-turrets from the roof and placed them in the trunk. "You can ask whatever you like, Su. But not here, and not now. Let's all get a few miles down the road. Then, I'll feel more like a chat. Agreed?"

Su nodded in agreement. "Just one more thing."

Krill sighed. "What's that?"

"Shotgun!"

Hadder's head snapped back. "What? *We* rescued *you*."

"What does that have to do with shotgun?"

Krill grinned wickedly. "She's got you there, Marlin. In the back."

Hadder cursed under his breath as he climbed into the back of the Comet, his testicles painfully hitting the front passenger's inclined seat as he did.

Hadder settled into the back seat, exhaustion finally taking hold as adrenaline began to fade. Krill and Su did the same up front.

Krill turned the key in the ignition and the Comet roared to life. "Well, Su, now it's time to find out if you were worth all of this trouble. Where to?"

Su stared ahead, the trauma of her imprisonment already long gone. "It seems that you boys aren't exactly fans of the New God. Therefore, I assume you're going to want to meet some other fellow heretics, as they call us."

Hadder spoke up from the back. "Are you talking about the Protectors of Man? Can you take us to them?"

Su laughed lightly once more, a sharp knife carving easily through Hadder's thin will. "I would hope so."

"What do you mean?"

"Well, I *am* one of the founding members."

"Looks like our man Noles was telling the truth. Prized cargo, indeed," said Krill. "I ask again. Where to, Miss Su?"

"Crimmwall. And step on it. The earlier we get into that horrid city, the better. Even Blossoms aren't fans of the early morning."

With that, Krill sent the Comet soaring down the dark highway toward Crimmwall, putting them back on track after a valuable detour.

Hadder leaned forward between Krill and Su. "Tell me, Su, are all the Protectors of Man like you?"

Su giggled, as if she were a schoolgirl between classes. "Not at all, Marlin." Hadder nodded and fell back into his seat. "No, we have some legitimate characters in-house. Take my sister, for example. She's a really dangerous bitch, pardon my language."

Hadder looked up and found Krill's eyes in the rearview mirror. Both cracked uneasy smiles as they tore down the neon-marked highway, the Comet moving inexorably closer to the New God and the end of their journey.

10

After several miles of silence, curiosity got the better of Marlin Hadder.

"How did a woman of your talents get herself caught by a bunch of no-talent Blossoms," he asked from the back seat.

"Budds."

Hadder's face scrunched up. "Come again?"

"Budds."

"I'm not familiar."

Su Anorrak let out a sigh. "Budds. Child Blossoms. Over the past few weeks, the Blossoms have been incorporating children a lot more into their plans, especially street kids." Viktor Krill fidgeted uncomfortably in the driver's seat. "They use them as spies, as bait, as traps."

"And which of those caught you."

"All three, I suppose. I was deep undercover, my mission well underway. I thought I was being careful, reading all the signals correctly. But kids can be tough to read. Half the time, they don't even know what they're doing or what they believe. One street kid made it known that another child was in trouble with some local toughs. I went in to save the day. Turned out that I walked into a trap." Su cursed under her breath, which came out as if a songbird had sweared. "I've always had a soft spot for kids. My sister said it would be the death of me. She was nearly right."

"Trap or not, I'm still surprised that those bums were able to take you."

Su shrugged. "Well, it wasn't exactly a square fight. I think I did pretty good considering there were twenty of them."

Hadder leaned forward. "You mean to tell me that you walked into a trap and still managed to kill fourteen Blossoms?"

Su shrugged again, seemingly unimpressed with herself. "In their defense, I think they were under strict orders to capture me alive. Otherwise, it might have been a different story."

"Still, a commendable kill count," remarked Krill. "What were you doing out there alone? Where was your backup?"

"I work alone. My missions tend to go best when I go out solo."

Krill pressed on. "And what was your mission?"

"At first, it was simple. Hunt Blossoms. Kill Blossoms. My kind of mission." Su looked over to Krill. "Have you ever been on a hunt, Viktor? With no ulterior motive but to eliminate?"

Krill smiled darkly, his black eyes never leaving the road ahead. "Once or twice."

"Then you know the joy that comes with it."

"Intimately."

"I was doing well, even earned that stupid nickname. But then I got word that the Thorns of Reckoning may have entered the area. My mission changed. I went from being able to simply kill to having to investigate. I guess that I'm better at one of those things than the other…" Su trailed off, and Hadder and Krill, understanding the need for post-failure reflection, allowed her a reprieve.

For a while, only the loud purr of the Comet filled the air with noise. After sufficient time had passed, Hadder continued the questioning.

"What were you investigating regarding the Thorns of Reckoning? They couldn't have been hard to find. They don't strike me as the type to move quietly."

Su shook herself free from self-criticism. "You're correct, Marlin.

Many of them move out in the open, heads held high like their shit don't stink, excuse my language. But I wasn't looking for just Thorns. I was looking for the head Thorn, a man who goes by the name of Willard Hillmore. Thorns are far more talented than their Blossom cousins, so I wasn't under any illusions that I could take them all out once I discovered their encampment."

"So, what was the plan?"

"Simple, really. Find the Thorns of Reckoning's camp. Get word back to the Protectors of Man. Track the Thorns until the Protectors arrive."

"And then what?"

Su spun to face Hadder, and he almost fell back into his seat from her distinct mix of beauty, determination, and anger. "War, of course." She returned her perfect face forward. "But, alas, I failed and the Thorns of Reckoning will continue to torment innocents across the region. My superior *will not* be happy with my report."

"What will you do now," asked Krill, a whisper of self-satisfaction in his voice.

Su rubbed the hilt of her katana absently. "Go back, get reprimanded, regroup, and go back out there. The Thorns are out there, and I *will* find them."

Krill, unable to contain it any longer, began to chuckle under his breath. Su noticed it immediately.

"What's so funny? Many lives will be lost because of my failure."

"Oh, I wouldn't worry about that."

"Elaborate. Please."

"You want to tell her, Marlin?"

Su spun in her seat once more. "Tell me what?" Her dark eyes, dancing with intensity, froze Hadder in place. "Marlin!"

Hadder snapped out of it. "You don't have to worry about locating the Thorns of Reckoning, Su. Viktor and I already found them."

Su's face twisted. "What do you mean, you found them? You saw a few Thorns, or you discovered their encampment?"

"We discovered their encampment."

"Where?"

"In a forest just outside Kharras."

"And you could locate it again?"

"We could."

Su's soft face broke into a wide smile that showcased too-perfect teeth. "Oh, that's wonderful news!" Her eyes swung wildly back and forth as she began to talk to herself aloud. "I'll brief Clinton as soon as we return. We can be back on the road in a few hours. With any luck, we'll be able to return with our army in tow before they depart. I think I can..."

"Su." The woman continued. "Su." She kept thinking aloud. "Su!"

Su finally pulled out of her maniacal plotting. "What?"

"You don't need to go back. None of you need to go to the encampment."

"Of course, we do."

"No, you don't."

Su's pale hand crept up to the hilt of her blade. "And why is that?" There was danger in her soft voice.

"Because they're gone. They're all gone."

Su's mouth fell open in disbelief. "Gone where?"

"Gone. Gone, as in dead. Gone."

"You lie."

"I swear to you."

"And Willard Hillmore?"

"You mean *Devout* Willard?" The name made Su's eyes go even larger. "Yeah, he's gone, too."

"Impossible." Su swung to Krill. "Viktor? Is this true?"

Krill's face remained impenetrable. "I'm afraid so, miss. Marlin and I, through no fault of our own, found ourselves dragged into the Thorn encampment under false pretenses. Some things transpired, and our cover was blown. We had no choice but eliminate them all." His black eyes shot over to Su. "Had we known that an authentic killer such as yourself had called dibs, perhaps we would have saved the best bits for you. But we did not. Apologies, miss. I know all too well the pangs of losing a quarry to another hunter. But there will be others. There are always others..."

"Impossible," Su repeated. "There must have been hundreds of them."

"Nearly two hundred. Wouldn't you say, Marlin?"

"About that," Hadder agreed.

"Impossible." Su looked at Hadder and Krill with renewed respect. "Who *are* you two?"

Hadder had no clue where to start, so Krill responded for him. "Just a couple of humans who were looking for an untraceable car."

"Nothing more, I suppose," replied Su doubtfully.

"Nothing of note, for now."

Su shifted her attention back to the dark road ahead. "Very well. I suppose there will be time for more context later." She thought for a moment. "Forget my selfish feelings. This is great news. With the Thorns of Reckoning gone, we can really start to gain momentum for those who oppose the New God." Su began to think aloud again. "I'll have Clinton contact Yellich as soon as we arrive. We need his counsel now more than ever. If we can…"

A wave of nausea struck Hadder, but he knew that he had to cut in. "Do you mean Patton Yellich, Su?"

The beautiful butcher immediately paused. "I do." She flashed her almond eyes toward the back seat. "How do you know Patton?"

"I told you we required an untraceable ride," said Krill.

Realization dawned on Su. "I thought this car looked familiar. From Patton's private collection, I take it."

"You take it correctly."

"Well, you better keep it in good shape. If there is anything that Patton loves more than humanity, it is his antique cars."

"He won't be needing it back," stated Krill flatly.

Panic started to show on Su's face. "And why is that?" Her question met with silence. "Marlin?!"

"I'm sorry, Su. Yellich was taken by the Thorns. He didn't make it." As the news hit home, Su sank lower into the Comet's black leather, twin rivers running down her face. At that moment, the assassin looked like anything but the killer she was. "Was he important to the cause?"

Su stared ahead. "Patton Yellich *was* the cause. He was *the* Protector of Man. The rest of us just followed in his footsteps. Poorly."

Hadder had no words for the woman. Fortunately, Viktor Krill did.

"Patton Yellich died bravely. He died like a warrior. We should all be so lucky. The universe will readily accept his energy."

That seemed to console Su, who simply nodded as she stared out into the night. Miles more flew under the Comet's wheels before the woman spoke again.

"Tell me. How did Willard Hillmore die?"

This time, Krill did crack a smile before answering. "Devout Willard screamed like a bitch, just before his face was ripped in half by a weapon of the New God's creation. Forest scavengers are eating his corpse as we speak."

Another heavy silence passed. Su Anorrak wiped the last remaining wetness from her cheeks. "Good. Fuck that piece of shit." A look of embarrassment crossed her soft face. "Apologies for the language."

———

THE SUN WAS JUST STARTING to appear over the horizon as the Comet covered the last remaining distance to Crimmwall. The city was massive, larger than Bhellum even, and kissed the eastern coast. Similar to the other cities Hadder and Krill had seen, Crimmwall was outlined in this world's ubiquitous neon, although not nearly as blinding or gaudy as the Neon City or even its copycat metropolis of Kharras.

The companions remained quite as they neared the city, both to study their newest location and to give Su Anorrak, whose head bounced gently off the Comet's side window, a few more minutes of much-needed rest.

Drawing closer, both companions sensed danger and violence in the air, but not the same decay that sat heavy under Bhellum's false veneer.

"Looks like Crimmwall hasn't started to die in the same way Bhellum has," venture Hadder as buildings and skyscrapers came into focus.

"It also hasn't developed any personality," snapped Krill, always surprisingly sensitive about his adopted home.

Su shifted in the passenger's seat before stirring herself awake.

"I'm glad you're up," said Krill. "I need to know where we are going."

"I'm sorry. I didn't even know I fell asleep." A good morning kiss crossed Hadder's mind before he was able to toss the image aside.

Krill waved away Su's apology. "Even killers need rest. Better now than when we are surrounded by Blossoms. How far in are your people?"

Su leaned forward as she thought. "Pretty deep into the city. But I think we should get out just inside the city's borders."

Krill's eyes narrowed, and Hadder could tell that his companion disliked the idea of abandoning the beloved Comet. "I don't understand. This ride is completely untraceable. Let's take her as far as we can."

Su shook her head. "Which will be just inside the city. Don't let your love for this beautiful automobile cloud your judgment, Viktor. It *is* untraceable. And it *isn't*. You think an antique like this won't be noticed?"

"Noticed perhaps. Nothing more."

Su went on. "Look, I don't know where you guys have been, but Crimmwall is a different monster. The CPD answers directly to the Blossoms of the New God; they have for some time now. And the Blossoms have directed the police department to identify, capture, and bring forth for questioning anything out of the ordinary. *Anything.*"

"Sounds like a goddamned witch hunt," remarked Hadder from the back.

Su turned to address Hadder. "And are we not three *witches* working against God?"

"The *New* God," Hadder corrected.

"Same difference to these idiots." Su turned back toward the city rising to meet them. "Look, this isn't Kharras or one of those smaller municipalities that you may have passed. Those cities and towns still maintain a bit of sovereignty, regardless of how tenuous it is. Crimmwall, however, is under the firm grip of the Blossoms, who squeeze every chance they get."

Krill couldn't help himself. "What about Bhellum?"

Su snickered. "Bhellum? Even the Blossoms aren't able to wrangle that war zone. Horrible rumors out of that place." Hadder stole a glance into the rearview mirror to find Krill grinning ear to ear. "Anyway, you need to believe me. You take this car into Crimmwall, and we will have the CPD and its army of support drones on our butts before we reach the city center."

Viktor Krill mulled over Su's words. Finally, he reached a decision. "Fine. I defer to your knowledge of your city. But at least take me somewhere where I can stash the Comet. If I make it out of the Crimmwall alive, which I plan to do, this girl is coming with me."

Su giggled. "Not a problem, Viktor. Take the South 5 Exit when you see it and keep right at the split."

"Understood... What the hell is that?"

Su leaned across Krill to look. "What?"

"That!"

Hadder scooted to the left to see what Krill and Su were gawking at. As the highway sloped down to Crimmwall and the coast, a giant building rose just to the north of the neon-coated city.

Hadder's jaw fell open as the sheer mass of the building became increasingly clear. "Is that what I think it is?"

"What else would it be," replied Su. "That's the Crimmwall Petal, founded on the bones of the old sports coliseum. That's where the monsters are made." She paused for a moment to let it sink in. "Is it all that you imagined?"

Hadder had to force himself to breathe again. The Crimmwall

Petal appeared as a too-white teardrop on the horizon, its point reaching up to heaven, so close to the water's edge that it almost looked to be partially submerged in the ocean. And perhaps it was. The Petal was to the far north of the city, which meant that the building must be colossal to be obvious from such a distance.

The Crimmwall Petal pulsed gently in the retreating night, as if the New God's blood pumped through the white stonework. And perhaps it did.

Krill recovered from the image of the vile satellite. "If any of Milo Flowers's minions had yet to fully buy in, approaching that building would be enough to drive them into fanaticism."

Su leaned back in her seat. Her voice came out in little more than a whisper. "People pour into the Crimmwall Petal day and night. And many, many more, as of late. They arrive in cars, buses, and even private passenger drones. Ships dock and release thousands of converts daily. The Petal has its own port, you know. It has become hard to calculate how many millions have already crossed over into the Crimmwall Petal. And it is but one of a dozen Petals around the globe."

"Millions entered the Petal," said Krill, "but how many have exited?"

Su thought it over. "Almost all who enter seem to be allowed to leave."

"Well, that's good."

Su's voice could barely be heard. "Depends on what they were forced to take with them."

"What's that," asked Krill, although Hadder knew that his Wakened partner heard perfectly well what the female assassin had said.

Su sat up straight, a seeming return to her more normal self. "We're coming up on the South 5 Exit. It'll be on your right. It's easy to miss."

Krill's tan knuckles whitened as he gripped the steering wheel. "I hope you know what you're doing, Su."

Su stared absently out the window at the city she once knew.

"Nobody knows anything anymore, Viktor. But we're doing the best we can. There's no blueprint for fist-fighting pure evil."

"Of course there is," responded Krill as he crossed over to the far right of the highway. "You keep punching until one of you is dead. And pray that the corpse disposed of at the end isn't your own."

———

VIKTOR KRILL LOOKED AROUND DOUBTFULLY. The service station on the outskirts of Crimmwall looked anything but safe. A graveyard of older model Taragoshi, Teeler, and even Cyrix vehicles surrounded the trio. Random sea urchins and undesirables popped in and out of Krill's periphery. As Su Anorrak spoke to a dirty giant of a man in filthy, oil-stained overalls, Krill cut in.

"You sure she's going to be safe here?"

The man ran greasy fingers over his thinning hair, pasting it to his scalp. "You mean your car?"

Krill took a threatening step forward. "Of course, I'm referring to my car. The one you are being given for safekeeping."

The chubby man's face scrunched up. "Well, sure, she'll be safe. Why do you ask?"

Krill took another step toward the man. "Because I look around, and I see a hundred threats a stone's throw away, and very little between them and my girl here."

"You mean your Comet?"

Another step forward. "Are you trying to wind me up, fat man?"

Hadder put a hand on Krill's chest. "You'll have to forgive my friend here, Mister…"

The mechanic touched the name-patch on the breast of his overalls. "Terry. Just Terry. Ain't no misters here."

"Terry," Hadder conceded. "It's just that my friend here has developed quite an attachment to this fine automobile. He wants to make sure that it will be kept safe."

Terry shifted his attention to Krill. "You ain't got to worry about your ride, mister. Everyone this side of Crimmwall knows what happens if you get caught stealing from old Terry."

"Terry is a good friend of the Protectors," added Su. "A *known* friend. To mess with him is to mess with us. And despite what the Blossoms think, *we* control Crimmwall's underworld."

"Plus, we got Lil Terry over there watching the compound. Ain't nothing getting past Lil Terry."

Hadder and Krill looked over in unison to the small dog Terry was pointing at, sitting obediently to the side. With long white hair that nearly covered his eyes, Lil Terry looked to be as dirty as his master, and twice as stupid. Krill nodded toward the dog.

"*This* mongrel is what is supposed to make me feel better?"

Terry's face grew serious, as if he would put up with any personal affront, but not one directed at his canine companion. "I know he don't look like much, but Lil Terry has more trophies to his name than any of you, I'll wager. Got a collection of finger bones in the back from men and women who tried their luck with Lil Terry and came up with the short end of the stick, if you catch my drift."

Su patted her large friend on his bare shoulder. "We do, Terry. I'm certain that Viktor meant no harm."

Terry turned his eyes downward to look at Su. His features immediately softened. "Some friends you got here, Miss Su. Talking down on Lil Terry like that."

"They're new friends, Terry. And I'm just learning the nuances of their personalities." Su tossed a dangerous look Krill's way. "One of which is Viktor's indelicate manner when speaking with others." She leaned in conspiratorially. "Plus, we *need* them. We *really* need them."

Terry nodded, understanding the gravity of what Su was trying to convey. He turned to Krill. "Tell you what, Mister Viktor, I'll keep her in Bay 3. Now, that's my own personal bay where I house all my interesting projects. I'll clear out some things to make room for your girl there. Bay 3 is right next to my and Lil Terry's sleeping quarters, so ain't no one gonna get near her without us hearing them. Ain't that right, Lil Terry." The dog barked in agreement. "Plus, I tell you what. I'll even put wheel locks on her to put your mind at ease. How's that?"

Krill's black eyes ran back and forth across the service station, his Wakened mind tallying a hundred threats to his Comet.

Su's voice pulled him from his analysis. "Viktor! I said, I assume that is sufficient?"

Krill finally threw his hands up in surrender. "Fine. Fine." He rose a single finger up, pointed it at Terry. "But if my girl gets stolen or hurt, I'm coming after you." He swung his finger to Lil Terry. "And you." Lil Terry growled under Krill's black gaze.

Having said his piece, Krill took one last look at the Comet before picking up the two burlap sacks at his feet and walking out of the service station. He looked up as he did, and found a bright neon sign that read *Terry's Tow and Repair.* Under the large sign, a smaller one below it glowed in similar neon and blinked *the Home of Lil Terry.*

Krill shook his head as he passed under the twin advertisements, promising himself that *both* Terry and Lil Terry would be launched into their respective signs should anything foul befall his Comet.

Hadder, Su, Terry, and Lil Terry watched as Krill marched off. Hadder loudly cleared his throat.

"You'll have to pardon my companion. What he lacks in decorum, he more than makes up for in a hatred of almost everyone. But he's good with his hands. And knives. And guns. And anything else you can kill with."

Terry swung a meaty hand in the air, waving away any residual hard feelings. "From the way he carries himself, I'm just happy he's on our side."

Hadder simply nodded. "You have no idea."

Lil Terry barked in agreement.

Su watched as Hadder and Krill shifted their burlap sacks from one shoulder to the other.

"You could have left those with Terry, you know."

Hadder spoke for both of the Wakened humans. "No offense, Su, but these are military-grade weapons and combat enhancements."

"You don't think the Protectors have similar weapons?"

"Honestly, I don't know. But I know what these cost."

"Which was?"

"About two hundred lives."

Su almost said something, but swallowed back her retort. She, as well as anyone, understood the strange connection that accompanied the spoils of war. "Very well. It's not much further anyway."

As the trio walked the backstreets of Crimmwall, Hadder stared up at the blue morning sky. Despite the sun's warm rays filling the air, Hadder could still easily make out the pink dot above. It was growing larger by the day, and stared down at him as if he were a disappointing son.

Official declarations, graffiti, and flyers of the Blossoms could be seen everywhere that Hadder looked, alongside police patrols and flying support drones. In short, the city of Crimmwall was clearly under authoritarian rule, with the Blossoms of the New God pulling all the strings.

Su Anorrak pulled Hadder and Krill down alley after alley. Occasionally, the trio would cut through a small store or factory, with Su offering a slight nod to a proprietor or manager as she passed.

After almost an hour of skulking between safe spots, Su finally led the Wakened humans toward a sewage facility that resided next to a group of empty alleyways. Although Hadder and Krill shared looks of curiosity, it was Hadder who voiced their concerns.

"This is a government facility, is it not, Su? Perhaps not the best place to be seen?"

Su sighed loudly, tired of continually being questioned, as if she were not a seasoned killer herself. "Yes, it is a government facility. A small one. This is simply a reading station where they conduct in-depth analysis on a small subset of the sewage systems beneath."

"Meaning?"

Another heavy sigh. "Meaning, it is run around the clock by four individuals, all of whom were placed by the Protectors of Man." Su spun on her boot to face the trailing men. "Do you know what it took to get *four* people we could trust in the same facility? Do you know the odds that we faced? The risks that we took?"

Hadder almost backed up a step under the assassin's angry glare. "I can imagine."

"No. You can't. But know that it took a lot – money and resources and lives." Su began to walk once more. "Now come on."

Krill looked around, his mind calculating a thousand variables. "Where are you taking us, Su?"

This time, the woman didn't bother turning back around. "Down."

Black eyes met hazel, as they had many times before. Once again, Hadder acted as spokesman. "Down? Down where?"

"Down. Where do you think? Into the sewers."

"How far are we from your people. From the Protectors?"

Su shrugged as she walked. "Miles. Many miles."

Hadder's face twisted. "Then why are we going down now? Better to get closer before we have to delve into shit and darkness, right?"

Su stopped dead in her tracks and slowly turned to face Hadder and Krill. The look in her dark eyes made Hadder feel like a schoolboy sent to the principal's office.

"You saw the CPD presence as we walked?"

"I did."

"And you saw the support drones?"

"Yes."

"What you probably didn't see were the thousands of cameras perched across the city. All with facial recognition software. All with the ability to call down a hailstorm of violence upon any individual who matches any of the thousands of faces in their heretic databanks. You don't think my face isn't on their most wanted list? You think the name Su Anorrak doesn't ring out in Crimmwall? They call me the Twat for a reason. Men only appreciate twats that they can bend to their will, control. Well, *this* twat has news for *those* twats. I will never go quietly, I will never give up my friends, and I will never bow before the disgusting Milo Flowers. But to make sure those things can never happen, I have to do my best not to get caught. Which means we go down. *Here.* Many miles away."

Hadder stood slack-jawed as the sweet killer with the singsong voice stalked away, heading toward the small, innocuous door on which a stencil read *Sewage Reading Plant #11*.

Krill walked past his stunned companion, shaking his head as he did. "Well done, Marlin."

"What?! I just said what we were both thinking."

"Yes, but better you than me, don't you think?"

Hadder cursed under his breath before following on Krill's heels. "Shit, you think that will hurt my chances with her?"

Krill chuckled, as if he knew the punchline to some joke that Hadder never heard. "No, I think your face did that already."

"Fuck off."

"Only time will tell. Now come on. Into the shit we go."

———

THE THREE UNLIKELY companions stared at the brown metallic door that sat at the back of the sewage reading plant. Hadder's eyes rose above the door to glimpse the small sign that was posted.

Warning! Make sure trackers are worn and activated before entering the Below. Make sure shift partner is aware of descent and monitoring whereabouts. Be attentive! Be safe! Get back to the surface!

"Well, that's not ominous," commented Hadder, who was ignored by his peers.

Su spoke over her shoulder to the man standing behind the trio. "Anything I need to know about down there?"

The slim man in the orange utility jumpsuit, who went by the name Upton, answered. "We've been getting a few strange signals at the far end of the quadrant."

Su's face grew concerned. "Blossoms? CPD?"

Upton shook his head, sending the end of his yellow mullet to tickle his shoulders. "Don't think so. The signal isn't pronounced enough to be any kind of party. Anyway, neither of those groups would go down into the Below without taking someone from the utility company with them for guidance. And if they did, we would have heard about it."

"You don't think…"

"No," Upton interrupted. "No, I can't think that." An uncomfortable silence settled between the two Protectors before Upton held out a backpack. "Here, take this. There are some flashlights, safety flares, and a map, should you need it. Do you remember the way to Haven Falls from here?"

Su Anorrak tossed Upton a look that backed the man up as surely as would the point of her katana. "Don't forget who I am, Upton."

Upton wiped his shaking hands onto his orange jumpsuit. "Apologies. It's just, you've been gone a while, and it's complex down there." More silence. "Anyway, I'm sure you'll figure it out. Remember, avoid quadrants that are being actively analyzed. The map is there if you need it… which you won't, of course."

Su snatched the black backpack from Upton before turning back to the brown door. "You boys ready? The Below is the same day or night, so no need to dawdle."

With that, Su twisted the door's rusty knob and pushed, releasing a great metallic groan as the door swung out. The sounds of echoes and running water surrounded the woman as she stepped onto the platform, down several steps, and disappeared into the dim light of the Below.

Hadder and Krill looked at each other for a moment before a voice from behind stole their attention.

"You boys stay safe down there. I don't know who you are, but you must be important if Su is taking you to Haven Falls. Get back to the surface in one piece."

"Any words of advice before we go down," asked Hadder.

"Yeah, watch *her* back."

"Don't worry, we'll make sure no harm comes to her."

Upton laughed, a loud, honest sound. It took him some time to recover. "You misunderstand me. I mean, watch her back and do exactly as she does. Step where she steps. Don't venture off her path.

I'm not worried about Su Anorrak surviving the Below. But you boys…"

"We've seen much worse," said Krill, obviously annoyed by the little man's ignorance of their status as Wakened humans.

Upton merely shrugged lightly at the notorious killer's dark stare. "Maybe."

———

HADDER, Krill, and Su walked along the concrete walkway that bordered both sides of one of the many main tunnels that comprised the Below's complex system. A heavy stream of murky, fetid water ran down the center of the tunnel, several feet below where the trio now marched. Every few hundred feet, a dodgy-looking bridge, invariably more rust than metal, spanned the churning waters, allowing access from one side of the tunnel to the other.

Although the Below was undeniably dim, small, dingy lights in the cement walls gave the entire area a low, brownish glow. With their Wakened vision, Hadder and Krill may as well have been walking through a sunny meadow. The companions shared a look as they followed behind the Protector assassin.

"I must say, Su, I was expecting much worse conditions down here," said Krill as he moved his burlap sack from one shoulder to the other.

"Uh huh," responded Su without looking back.

"Which begs the question…"

"Uh huh."

"Why in the world would the Protectors consider themselves safe down here?"

Su did not stop, but responded to Krill. "We do not *consider* ourselves safe down here. We *are* safe down here."

Krill looked around, his Wakened mind analyzing a thousand variables. "I don't see it."

"You don't see it because you know nothing, Viktor." Su's voice was thick with annoyance and danger.

"Enlighten me."

"Why should I?"

Krill and Su continued to question each other as the three walked, tempers already beginning to bubble to the surface. Hadder's hand unconsciously began to drift to his crystalline guns.

"Because," replied Krill, "I am a survivor. I always have been. And when my warning bells go off, I tend to listen to them."

"And they are going off now?"

"They are."

Su finally stopped and turned back to Krill. "Why?"

Krill spread his hands out. "This doesn't look like it would deter a group of children."

"Have a lot of experience with children, do you?"

"Actually, I do. And none of this would prevent them from coming down here and playing daily."

"And your point?"

"My point, dear lady, is that if this *Below* would not scare off a bunch of kids, what makes you think it would keep out bands of police or Blossoms. They have to know that the sewers would be the perfect hiding place for the resistance.

Su thought for a moment. Her small mouth twisted slightly back and forth as she considered Krill's words. Hadder was smitten.

"You must think you're pretty smart, huh, Viktor?"

Hadder jumped in. "You're wrong there, Su. Viktor doesn't think he's *pretty* smart. Viktor thinks he's the smartest person in the world."

"I don't *think* I am the smartest person in the world, Marlin," Krill corrected. "I *know* I am the smartest human in the world."

Su caught the strange use of labels that Krill utilized, but chose to ignore it. "Fine. I didn't want to go into it because it's unnecessary and may just freak you out."

"Humor us."

"Very well." Su tossed her backpack to the floor and sat on it, readjusting the sword beneath her trench coat as she did. "Look, you're right, of course. *This* wouldn't scare off anyone of substance. But what *you* see is not what others *know*. Or *knew*."

Now she had Hadder's interest as well. "Continue."

"Look, for decades these tunnels have been the scariest place not only in Crimmwall, but along the entire coast."

"And why is that," Hadder prodded.

"Ghost Worms."

"What," Hadder and Krill asked in unison.

"For decades, these tunnels were infested with creatures called Ghost Worms, or Tunnel Kings, or White Death. They were giant, grotesque predators that fed on anything the tunnels had to offer – animals, corpses, refuse, and people. For decades, they were nearly impossible to kill, taking dozens of humans to bring down even one of the beasts. After a while, the 3C…"

"3C?"

"Crimmwall City Council. Eventually, 3C decided to just let the Ghost Worms have the Below. Turns out, they kept the tunnels quite clean and never ventured to the surface. The Council decided to pass a bill to automate every aspect of sewer surveillance, maintenance, and analysis. It took them almost five years, but by fencing off specific quadrants at a time, they were able to install a fairly comprehensive auto-monitoring system, minimizing the time any person would ever have to spend in the Below."

"I'm not following," said Hadder, truly lost in the discussion.

Su looked up with annoyance. "Everyone up there, including the CPD and the Blossoms, are terrified of the Ghost Worms. Everyone is. And if they're too frightened to come down here, they figure that godless heretics would certainly lack the faith necessary to enter the world of the Tunnel Kings."

Krill's black eyes studied the tunnel in which the trio currently found themselves. "And where are these… Ghost Worms?"

"Gone."

Hadder and Krill again spoke in tandem. "Huh?!"

"They're gone! One of the founding Protectors, Olney Jansen, was a chemical researcher for a giant corporation before joining the cause. Through trial and error, and lives, he crafted a unique compound that turned the Ghost Worms inside-out, leaving their insides vulnerable to attacks. The founding Protectors, including yours truly, spent months roaming these tunnels, eliminating every Tunnel King we found using Olney's proprietary chemical weapon. Despite the Ghost Worms' reputation, which was well-earned, there weren't as many as the experts predicted. Each one just ate a boatload more than anticipated."

"I still don't really get it," stated Hadder. "The Ghost Worms are gone. Didn't you just eliminate everything that was keeping unwanted bodies out of the Below."

"If I may," cut in Krill, once again bothered by Hadder's resistance to take advantage of his Wakened mind. "The Protectors secretly purged the Below of Ghost Worms, all the while keeping up the facade that the Tunnel Kings remained and were as ravenous as ever."

Su nodded. "Correct. We even collect corpses occasionally, strip off the flesh with acid, and leave the bones near where we know a utility worker will have to venture for a periodic double-check or reading. It makes it appear that the White Death has been there in the past two weeks. We even scrape the tunnel walls clean as we move throughout, mimicking what a Ghost Worm would do."

"You aren't doing that now," ventured Hadder.

"We're in a rush," snapped back Su.

Hadder looked over to Krill, whose black eyes were still flashing with analysis. "But, still, there must be reasons for utility workers to have to come down to the Below. Things go wrong. Things have to be fixed. Things rot away and must be replaced."

Su sighed audibly. "You're, once again, correct, Viktor. But we have some expert engineers in the Protectors. We are constantly monitoring the Below, replacing valves as needed, patching holes as they appear, ensuring that the pressure across the system remains steady. We identify and resolve problems long before those government utility men ever could. And now, with all that is going on in Crimmwall and across the globe, no news from the Below is good news. 3C can pat themselves on the backs for thinking that they discovered the perfect solution to a messy problem."

Krill chuckled loudly. "What a clever solution."

Su rose from her backpack seat. "I'm so glad you approve, Viktor," she said as she collected and donned the backpack given to her by Upton. "You know, right now, the only thing really standing between full Blossom control of Crimmwall are the Protectors of Man. That's me! A little respect could go a long way in our partnership."

Krill held his hands up in mock surrender, an amused smile still painted on his lips. "I'm a curious human who requires answers. Don't take it personally."

"I'll try not to. Now, let's get a move on. We have many miles to go, and a roundabout path to cover them. And no more questions!"

Her appreciation for being saved long gone, Su Anorrak stormed off, leaving Hadder and Krill alone momentarily. Hadder slapped Krill on the shoulder.

"Well done. I'm not the only one in the doghouse anymore. Looks like I'm back in the race."

Krill shouldered his way past Hadder, mumbling as he did. "If you aren't going to use your Wakened mind for anything else, at least use it to determine who can possibly bed her."

Hadder watched as Krill marched on after Su Anorrak, the sounds of a sewage river thick in his ears. "Anything is possible, Viktor!"

"Not this...," Krill offered over his shoulder.

———

HOUR AFTER HOUR passed in the Below, Marlin Hadder and Viktor Krill obediently following the beautiful killer Su Anorrak. Hadder quickly learned that not all the paths through the Below were as hospitable as the main tunnels.

Per Upton's advice, Su took a sinuous path through the Below, no doubt avoiding areas or quadrants that were under surveillance by non-Protector utility workers. When not walking along the cement side paths lining major rivers of sewage, the trio marched through sub-tunnels in near blackness. When Su asked if Hadder or Viktor wanted to use the flashlights provided by Upton, she was surprised to find that both men shook their heads in the negative.

Little did Su know that the Wakened humans saw more in the dark than most did in the light.

Down a major tunnel for a bit. Cross to the other side via a rickety aluminum bridge. Turn right at the third sub-tunnel. Follow its black depths for an hour, until a dim light can be seen in the distance. Turn right into another major tunnel. Don't get too close to the sewage water's edge; things have been known to reach out and drag unsuspecting victims into the churning waters. Cross to the other side of this major tunnel, using a bridge that looks as old as the city itself. Take the final sub-tunnel on the left before the major tunnel doglegs right. Walk in the blackness until you hear a violent rush of water. As soon as you hear it, take the next sub-tunnel to the left. Follow it.

Hadder kept up as long as he could, committing their journey to memory should he ever be called upon to recall it. After a while, however, his mind began to wander, as it was wont to do, and Hadder was as lost and confused as a debutante in the Muck.

Hadder looked over and could still make out Krill's face in the lightless sub-tunnel. As far as he could tell, his Wakened companion was still recording their every twist and turn in that hard drive mind of his, which put Hadder at ease.

More hours passed, more tunnels came and went. Su rarely spoke, so Hadder and Krill, figuring that the woman knew many things that they did not, followed suit. Finally, they came to the lip of a short sub-tunnel. Although it was pitch black within, a faint light could be seen at the far end. Su put out both arms to stop her new colleagues.

"We're almost there," she whispered. "Just down this short tunnel, across the major tunnel ahead, and down one last sub-tunnel, and we'll reach Haven Falls. Thirty minutes, no more."

"Is there a reason we are whispering," asked Hadder as Krill rolled his black eyes at the novice Wakened human.

Su shot a look at Krill before returning to Hadder. "This is the Below. It's as old as Crimmwall itself. It has a millennium of stories, none of them good. Best to err on the side of caution, don't you think?" Hadder simply nodded his assent. "Good. Then let's go."

Immediately upon stepping into the short sub-tunnel, the hairs on

Hadder's arms began to stand on end. A strange unease, like a foreign breath on his nape, sent cold chills down his spine. He looked over to find Krill already enveloped in a cloud of unease.

But still, they moved forward.

Halfway through the tunnel, Hadder's anxiety had become overwhelming, having significantly increased with every step forward he took. Just when he could take it no more, as he started to voice his dread, Krill reached forward and gently pulled on Su's trench coat, pulling her to a stop. The trio grouped together.

"Something is in this tunnel," said Krill in a low, matter-of-fact voice. "Something dangerous." His black eyes looked down the tunnel, searching for the source of his worry. "Very dangerous."

To her credit, Su did not question Krill's premonition, already believing that both of her new companions were more than they seemed. Instead, she simply took off the backpack that Upton had given her and removed three safety flares. She kept one and gave the remaining two to Hadder and Krill. On a nod, the three lit the flares and tossed them down the tunnel, filling the final quarter of the sub-tunnel with a red glow.

"Fuck me," said Su as Hadder and Krill's eyes simply went wide with horror. "Pardon my language."

About twenty feet from the faint light, attached to the nine-foot roof of the sub-tunnel, was a creature that looked like a great mass of puss squeezed from a demonic tube.

"Su," asked Hadder, feeling that the time for silence was at an end, "is that what I think it is."

"I'm afraid it is," she responded sadly. "That, my friends, is a Ghost Worm, scourge of the Below."

"I thought your people took care of them all," accused Krill.

"I thought so, too," Su snapped back. "We haven't seen one in many months. No idea where it could have hidden or come from."

"Is there any way around it," asked Hadder, uninterested in carving his way through the monstrous Tunnel King.

Su thought for a moment before shaking her head. "Not really. There are four ways into the next major tunnel that we need to reach.

This one, two others that are under quadrant surveillance, and a final one."

"What about that one?"

"We would have to backtrack half our current journey and loop around. Could take half a day. Maybe more."

"To hell with that," said Krill. "We go through this thing. Is it hard to kill?"

Su laughed dryly. "Are you kidding me? It's called a *Tunnel King*. The *White Death*. Yes, it's hard to kill, almost impossible."

"Tell me why."

"Take a look at it."

The three kept a comfortable distance as they studied the unmoving Ghost Worm. It looked much more like a slug than a worm, with pale, slimy skin that expanded and contracted as it breathed.

"Is it asleep," wondered Hadder aloud, hoping that they could possibly slip unnoticed beneath the resting slug.

"It never sleeps," corrected Su. "It is simply lying in wait, hoping that one of us…" Su took a brief look at Hadder. "Is stupid enough to try to sneak under it."

"How does it kill," asked Krill, determined to get on with the fighting.

"When it approaches prey, or vice versa, two long tails will extend from its backside. They resemble scorpion tails, in more ways than one."

"Go on."

"They are scaled and segmented, unlike the fleshy slime that you see covering the rest of the Ghost Worm, and are tipped with dagger-like stingers. These stingers contain a strong toxin that will paralyze anything unfortunate enough to be caught by them. Soon after, the prey is slowly consumed alive." Su stared directly at Hadder and Krill before continuing. "It's also called the Nightmare because you're alive inside it for a long time, unable to move or scream or fight. But you can feel. You can feel as its digestive acids slowly eat away at you. I can think of fewer worse ways to die."

While Hadder fought back the urge to vomit, Krill thought carefully about Su's words. "Wait. So, it takes a long time to die once swallowed by the creature?"

"I don't know how long. But it's not quick. I've heard enough horror stories over the years to support that."

"So, its acid isn't *that* strong."

"Strong enough to break down a person to their bones."

"Over several hours…"

"Yes."

Hadder jumped in. "Hey, I don't think anyone should be worried about getting eaten. Let's just carve this thing up. Between my guns, Krill's knives, and your blade, this thing doesn't stand a chance."

Su placed a hand on Hadder's arm to slow the eager man. "I wish it were that simple, Marlin. But it's not. If it were, the Ghost Worms wouldn't be the deterrent they are today. That slimy white skin of theirs is nearly impenetrable. Bullets are stopped within a few inches, never hitting anything vital. Similarly, while blades cut deep, the wounds immediately close back up, as if you're cutting into jelly."

"And I assume you aren't carrying any of that magical compound that turns these demons inside-out?"

Su shook her head. "The compound is extremely complicated, composed of chemicals that are prohibitively expensive to procure, in terms of both credits and lives. No one simply carries it around unless they're on an active worm hunt."

Hadder cursed under his breath. "Can't anything *ever* be easy?"

"Not in this world, not during these times," replied Su, her eyes still locked onto the White Death. "So, what's the plan?"

Krill stepped forward, dropped his burlap sack, and rummaged around inside. He put several items into his jacket pocket. "Give me what's left of the flares." Su handed them over. "You two take care of that twin tail. I'll figure something out from there."

Su and Hadder looked at each other doubtfully, but moved out to opposite sides of the claustrophobic tunnel. After the trio had successfully spread, they stared at the roof-mounted slug for nearly a minute before Hadder voiced what they were each thinking.

"So, are we going to fight it like this, or can we get it on the ground somehow?"

"I would prefer it on the ground," offered Su.

"Me, too," agreed Krill.

Hadder thought for a moment, before an idea finally coalesced in his Wakened mind. "Leave that to me."

He reached into his own burlap sack and retrieved the massive concussion weapon that was responsible for breaking through the prisoner transport's windshield, along with the few remaining impact projectiles. Krill nodded in agreement as Hadder loaded the weapon and put it up to his shoulder. Su looked on in shock and confusion. She had seen those weapons, known as Breakers, put to effective use in various riots and skirmishes in which she had participated. Normally, they were planted on the ground or welded onto a vehicle. The recoil would be enough to shatter a man's shoulder, or kick back far enough to break a face in half.

And yet, here was Marlin Hadder, Su's newest ally, holding the hefty Breaker easily against his shoulder, oblivious to what was about to happen. Su opened her mouth to warn the ignorant fool, but quickly closed it when Krill waved away her obvious concern.

As the Breaker fired, an explosive blast reverberated off the close tunnel walls and a shockwave tickled the faces of Krill and Su as they watched the Ghost Worm. The large projectile smashed into the "head" of the Tunnel King, and although it appeared to do no real damage, the massive collision did push the giant slug back several inches. This caused it to briefly lose contact with the tunnel ceiling and crash down onto its back with a grotesque *splat* that also echoed across the tight space.

The three companions wait tensely as the White Death squirmed for a moment along the tunnel floor before once again becoming as still as a statue.

"What now," asked Hadder as he placed the Breaker back into the sack and took out one of his crystalline handguns from beneath his suit jacket.

"Now we wade in," responded Su, drawing her katana from under her trench coat. "And hope your friend Viktor finds an opening." Su continued, as if she could read Hadder's next question. "Don't worry, the bastard will come alive as we draw closer. Right now, the sonovabitch still thinks it's invisible. It still thinks it's the hunter." A pause. "Pardon my language." Hadder began to march forward but was halted by one last bit of advice from the beautiful assassin. "Marlin. The worm is much faster than it looks. Especially its tails." Hadder nodded and continued on, this time in tandem with Su.

Viktor Krill held back.

As Hadder approached from one side of the small tunnel and Su Anorrak from the other, the Tunnel King began to gently vibrate, forming ripples on its mucus-covered skin. Recognizing that it was being stalked, that the two lifeforms approaching were beyond simple meals, the Ghost Worm rotated in place, quickly moving onto its belly.

Hadder and Su both froze mid-step as the Tunnel King completed the turn and rose its front end off the cold floor. The Ghost Worm then opened its gigantic mouth as it screeched into the flare-lit tunnel, revealing long armlike tentacles bordering its mucus-filled mouth.

"You didn't tell us about those," Hadder pointed out, his stomach churning as he watched the vile feelers waving in the air.

"Must have slipped my mind," replied Su dryly. "Don't worry, they don't contain any toxins, as far as I know. They simply pull meat into the Nightmare's mouth once it has been paralyzed."

"It looks terrifying."

"Yeah, well, that too. Come on!"

The Nightmare continued to release shrieks as Hadder and Su pressed on, moving with striking distance. As the duo came within a few feet of the worm, a shadow grew from behind the creature, beginning as one before splitting into a pair of dagger-pointed tails that arched back over the slug.

"Those are the real threats," Su shouted over the incessant shrieking that filled the tunnel to break concentrations and unnerve those within.

Hadder looked over and nodded once to Su to confirm his under-standing, and a second time to commence the attack. The pair simul-taneously took off, running at the Tunnel King from opposite sides.

As the attackers moved in, the White Death shut its oversized mouth and dropped its head to the ground, leaving its twin tails to handle the foolish aggressors.

The righthand tail shot out first, its toxin-coated stinger cutting across the now-smoky air like a bullet, heading directly for Su, who was attacking from that side.

Hadder's breath caught in his throat, surprised by the speed of the strike and convinced that the stinger would bury itself in Su's petite chest. Luckily, the woman also moved faster than Hadder anticipated, her katana coming up and across in the blink of an eye to knock the Nightmare's blow out wide.

Hadder had only a second to enjoy the show before the worm's other tail came for him. It hovered threateningly before the Wakened human like a cobra, searching for any opportunity to introduce stinger to skin. Unwilling to wait the creature out, Hadder brought up his crystalline handgun and fired a shot at the dancing worm tail. The bullet struck exactly where Hadder had intended, the joint connecting the stinger to the rest of the tail, but flew off harmlessly to ricochet off the tunnel wall.

Hadder cursed under his breath again, and heard the sounds of Su's blade bouncing off a tail once more to his right.

"Any luck," he called over, refusing to take his eyes from the stinger before him.

"None," cried back Su, sounding desperate. "It's like trying to cut into a block of ice. And if I try to attack its body…"

"You'll leave yourself open," Hadder finished. "Keep at it. Viktor will think of…"

Before Hadder could complete his sentence, the lefthand tail launched forward as if shot from a cannon. As the stinger reached for his unprotected face, the world slowed around Marlin Hadder. His Wakened abilities enacted, Hadder watched as the Ghost Worm's primary weapon moved in slow motion through the ruddy air.

Despite his inhuman reactions, Hadder still barely managed to dodge the stinger, allowing it to pass by harmlessly.

Hadder kicked out at the tail, pushing it even farther away and providing some room to breathe before the next attack. "Viktor will think of something," Hadder repeated, this time with much less certainty.

———

As HADDER and Su battled the Ghost Worm, Viktor Krill waited patiently, looking for an opening. For the third time in the last minute, he felt around in his jacket pockets to ensure that they still contained what he had taken from the burlap sack. He looked down to make sure that his tan hands still held the remaining safety flares. He then looked up once more.

And froze.

With Hadder and Su to each side of the Tunnel King, battling its twin tails, the Nightmare had once again raised its "head" into the air, although its mouth remained tightly closed.

That image of the slug-like creature hovering in the air brought forth a vicious memory. Krill pictured his adopted daughter Natthi standing there, shaking in fear, begging for her father to rescue her as a mature Slink hovered behind her, ready to consumer her small frame.

For the first time since before his Wakening, Krill found that he could not control the shaking of his hands, the upheaval in his stomach, or the panic that stole his gifts from him.

Frozen. Viktor Krill found himself frozen.

———

SU CONTINUED to use her katana to parry blow after blow from the righthand stinger. As her arms began to tire, the stinger drew closer and closer to connecting with flesh.

On the opposite side, Hadder slid, ducked, and rolled away from strike after strike. Although he did not tire as Su did, he grew weary of this stalemate.

After one particularly close call, Hadder shot angrily into the body of the White Death. Even though the bullet sank into the wormy flesh, Hadder could see that it was stopped a few inches into the meat, far from any major muscles or nerves.

Just as he was about to curse his luck, however, an idea struck the Wakened human. A plan that would require inhuman abilities. A plan where one ill-timed move could result in permanent paralysis, or worse.

Ignoring potential horrific outcomes, Hadder waded back into the lefthand tail's strike zone and tapped into his Wakened abilities yet again. As Hadder shuffled forward, the Tunnel King obliged, sending its stinger soaring for the fool's open chest, which must have appeared as a bullseye.

Hadder did not slide, duck, or roll as the stinger raced at him. Instead, he held his ground, his fingers tingling with excitement as his focus remained squarely on the organic dagger that was only a meter away. Just as it became too late to dodge, Hadder made his move.

His left arm rose like a piston, faster than any eye could follow, catching the Ghost Worm's tail by the same knuckle that he had attempted to shoot off earlier. Unable to fully halt the attack, Hadder pushed out as he took hold, moving the stinger just to the side of his vulnerable face.

This time, instead of reseting, Hadder locked his viselike grip onto the Ghost Worm's tail, holding it in place. The Ghost Worm let out another shriek, enraged at how a perceived meal could have restrained one of its key offensive weapons.

Truthfully, it took all of Hadder's Wakened strength to prevent the tail from wiggling free, so incredibly powerful were the muscles and ligaments that comprised the thing.

Swallowing the ache in his left arm, Hadder pointed his clear handgun and was about to pull the trigger when a shadow flew past him, followed by the audible *clink* of metal on hard segment. Hadder looked, and found that Su had run over to help defend Hadder from the righthand tail that had turned its attention on the Wakened human.

As Su stood her ground before Hadder, sending wide strike after strike from the righthand tail, Hadder, still grasping the other tail, brought his crystalline gun up once more. Utilizing a hyper focus beyond that of any other, Hadder locked onto one particular discoloration, no more than one centimeter across, on the Ghost Worm's otherwise bone white skin. His eyesight grew increasingly narrow, until only that one spot existed in all the universe. Only then did Hadder pulled the trigger, again and again and again.

The first bullet, just as before, was stopped several inches into the worm's slimy white skin. But another bullet came in right behind it, pushing it a few more inches deep. A third bullet pushed it even further.

Hadder continued to fire away, his Wakened abilities ensuring that each shot found the exact location of its predecessor, driving the initial bullet deeper and deeper into the White Death.

Just as Hadder feared that his clip would end, a great scream escaped the Ghost Worm's large mouth as the leading bullet touched a main nerve. The Tunnel King's entire body became rigid, and both tails locked up momentarily.

"Got you now, fucker," Hadder whispered under his breath, hopeful that Krill would fulfill his end of the bargain.

———

Viktor Krill shut his black eyes, but the image of Natthi cowering before a poised Slink remained, as if burned into his eyelids. His hands shook uncontrollably around the flares as the sounds of battle echoed on the periphery.

Unable to shake the memory, Krill took a page from his companion and absorbed it, made it a part of himself, allowed it to infect him. He watched as the Slink struck, consuming his daughter in a single bite. He watched as she fell out of the Slink's guts, her skin eaten away by the vile creature's stomach acid. He watched as the life passed from her brown eyes, as her corpse broke the heart of Mayfly Lemaire.

Viktor Krill watched as he failed. And it pissed him off.

The kernel of something formed in the pit of Krill's being, an ember that would spread hot fire across the Wakened human's spirit. Krill touched it, fed it, nurtured it.

For the first time, Krill understood Marlin Hadder's Rage. And although he could only touch a fraction of what Hadder experienced, Krill gripped onto it as if his life depended on it.

When he opened his black eyes once more, the image of Natthi was gone, replaced by a portrait of the Ghost Worm. The creature was bellowing into the flickering air, its giant mouth agape in pain, fat tendrils waving before the open orifice as protection.

Intoxicated by a taste of the Rage, Krill exploded forward, diving headfirst into the mouth of the Tunnel Kings as his hands came together, lighting the flares held in each as he disappeared.

———

"HOLY SHIT," exclaimed Su as she and Hadder continued to battle the worm's twin tails, which had finally recovered from their temporary petrification. "I think Viktor just got swallowed!"

"Good," responded Hadder, who was once again dodging strikes, having released the lefthand tail from his grasp.

"How is that good!?"

Hadder continued to fire an occasional round into the Nightmare's fleshy skin, if only to feel like he was doing something productive. "Well, you and I don't seem to be getting anywhere."

"He's going to die in there," Su cried as she chopped down with her katana, forcing another blow away from her and Hadder.

"Maybe not! Look!"

Su risked a peek to the front of the Ghost Worm and found that its giant mouth was once again open in a scream, with pillars of smoke billowing out from the grotesque maw.

210 | JARRETT BRANDON EARLY

"What's happening," she asked, returning her attention to the twin tails.

"I don't know, but I think we should start to retreat."

Su nodded her assent, and the companions slowly began to backpedal, still defending endless attacks from the worm's devilish appendages. As they came even with the Ghost Worm's smoking cavity, Viktor Krill rolled out of the beast's mouth in between shrieks.

Krill fell out with a gross thud, covered in slime, bile, and thick stomach acid, but didn't waste any time in getting to his feet and running to safety.

"Now or never, you idiots," called Krill, causing Hadder and Su to exchange glances before abandoning the battle completely and joining their black-eyed companion.

Marlin Hadder, Viktor Krill, and Su Anorrak stood in a row, each breathing heavily, watching as the Ghost Worm writhed on the tunnel floor before them, thick smoke leaking from its tentacled mouth.

"Now wh..." began Hadder, and the Ghost Worm exploded from within, sending massive chunks of slimy flesh, tentacle, and tail across the small tunnel.

Hadder closed his eyes in disgust as a heavy wave of worm gore descended upon him, Krill, and Su. He carefully wiped his eyes before speaking again. "Let me guess, the grenades we took from the Thorn encampment?"

"Yep," confessed Krill as he, too, removed slime from his face. The flares kept the worm's mouth open as I set the grenades."

"You couldn't just toss them in," asked Su, looking especially repulsed by being covered in worm guts.

Krill shrugged. "Maybe. But its damned mouth tendrils were blocking the way. Furthermore, we have limited grenades. I wanted to be able to set them deep in the creature." Krill looked at his companions to his left and right. "Shall we?"

Krill collected his burlap sack as he continued to wipe the worm sludge from his person. "Anywhere I can wash off this stomach acid? It's not strong, but it is starting to itch."

Su Anorrak simply shook her head as the truth of her rescuers started coming into focus. To her credit, she recovered quickly. "Up ahead. The water this far along is almost all ocean water, free of waste. You can wash yourself off there, although you already look pretty good."

Hadder looked over and swore under his breath. Just as Su claimed, Krill's white suit was already free of muck, looking as if it had just come from the dry cleaner.

What he wouldn't give to have held on to some Station clothes.

Krill winked at Hadder, who casually presented his companion with his middle finger before collecting his own burlap bag. Together, they began walking down the small tunnel, carefully avoiding thick piles of Ghost Worm gore.

Both men stopped, however, as Su emptied the contents of her backpack, only to fill it with hunks of Ghost Worm flesh. The beautiful woman collected piles of slimy meat and shoved them into her pack, grossly packing it down, so the zipper could close. Finally, she noticed the open jaws of her new companions.

"What?"

Hadder was at a loss for words. "Why?"

Su rolled her brown eyes. "Ghost Worm meat is among the sweetest, most succulent meat that exists. Don't knock it until you try it. Are we ready?" Hadder and Krill nodded dumbly. "Good. We're almost there. You both will set eyes on Haven Falls within the half-hour." Su began to march down the tunnel, and when she didn't hear any footsteps following her, she spun around. "Look, we would have been welcomed into Haven Falls regardless. But with this worm meat, we're gonna be treated like heroes." Hadder and Krill offered no responses but disgusted faces. Su rolled her eyes again. "Oh, grow up, you pussies!" Su continued on down the small tunnel. Just before turning off and disappearing, she called out one last time.

"Sorry for the language!"

11

D espite the imposing man walking up to the trio, Hadder couldn't help but look around in surprise. Haven Falls proved to be much more than he expected.

Deep beneath the city, kissing the vast eastern ocean, Haven Falls was a rectangular, cavernous room where the majority of water for the city's sewage and drinking needs entered the complex subsystem.

To Hadder's far right, the largest tunnel he had ever seen broke into the room, ushering in a river of seawater that ran across the chamber, neatly cleaving it in half. The river disappeared into an equally imposing tunnel to the far left, atop which sat a control room that was lit up with a variety of buttons and screens.

Above the giant channel that was allowing in the torrent of seawater was a slightly smaller tube that sent even more clean water cascading down into the swirling river below, creating an artificial waterfall of epic proportions.

The significant space on both sides of the artificial river was dotted with a variety of control stations, complete with pressure valves, hand-wheels, and gauges. A simple concrete bridge spanned the dark water, allowing access to both sides of the room.

All in all, at first glance Haven Falls appeared to be an impressive, yet unremarkable element of any seaside water system. Looking deeper, however, one could uncover the full story.

Along the edges of the great room, built using the same grey concrete as the remainder of the sewage system, were numerous living quarters. They jutted out gently, almost naturally, from the walls, and only upon close inspection could one tell that they were not part of the room's original plan.

It was into and out of these add-ons that people, presumably other Protectors of Man, came and went, shouting out occasional orders, questions, or well-wishes as they crossed paths. It quickly occurred to Hadder that within seconds, Haven Falls could appear an empty chasm, even as it was full of life.

"Su! Is that really you! We thought we had lost you, girl! The Lord truly smiles upon us this day!"

The deep, authoritative voice pulled Hadder from his admiration of his surroundings and back to the imposing figure storming towards them. The man was a mountain, well over six feet tall, with a barrel chest and chiseled arms that were highlighted by the rolled up sleeves of a khaki safari shirt that was tucked into dark brown denim pants. His bright, intelligent yellow eyes popped against his dark skin, as did his thick white beard, completing the look of a man who got things done while demanding the best of others.

Marlin Hadder immediately liked him.

As the impressive man approached, Hadder noticed that he was flanked by a man and woman on each side. Each brandished a Stutter, forcing Hadder to once again consider how much money that weapon's manufacturer must have made off the violence of this world. Hadder and Krill both held up their empty hands, not wanting to spook their new allies. Blinded by the appearance of his lost friend Su Anorrak, the large man noticed Hadder and Krill for the first time.

"Whom have you brought, Su? Are these Blossom prisoners? I'm delighted to see you alive, but I can't fathom how you would think this is a good idea. What could they possibly tell us that we don't already know? Now that they've seen Haven Falls, you must know that we will…"

"Clinton," Su said loudly, interrupting the man's rant. "These are not Blossom prisoners. They are not Blossoms at all, in fact." All five looked dubiously at Viktor Krill's white suit. "I know how he looks," declared Su. "But... truthfully, these are the men who rescued me from Blossom capture. I was on my way to the Crimmwall Petal in chains when they freed me."

Krill was about to correct Su, clarifying that they were, in fact, humans and not mere men, but Hadder's arm on his companion's shoulder halted the strange revisal before it began.

Five dumb faces stared back at the trio. The massive bald man finally spoke for the group. "How in the world did you get yourself captured, Su? We thought that impossible. You were either going to return with Hillmore's head or not at all."

Although she looked painfully embarrassed, Su attempted to shrug it off. "Some kids I befriended for information turned out to be Budds."

The Protector quintet all threw up their hands in angry disbelief. Although they all voiced frustration, the large man's words dominated the rest.

"How many times? How many times, Su? Kids aren't safe anymore. The Blossoms have made them a strategic part of their intelligence network. You're lucky we all aren't in chains now!"

"I wouldn't have told them anything, and you know it," screamed Su in defense.

"And you say that knowing how you would feel moments before your head peeled like a banana?! Before you were transformed into a monster!"

Tears began to well up in Su's dark eyes. "I know I messed up! Ok?! But just listen and look at what I've brought you. Please."

The desperation in the young woman's voice broke the group's spell of disappointment, evidenced by the giant man who embraced her in a bear hug.

"We're sorry, girl. You just scared us, that's all. We couldn't be happier that you are back." He backed up and held Su at a large arm's length. "Now, introduce us to your... friends. And tell us how they fit in."

Su wiped the tears from her cheeks. "Very well. This is Marlin Hadder and Viktor Krill. They are..."

"Wait, wait, wait," interrupted the dark-skinned man, his yellow eyes going wide. "Hadder. Krill. Hadder. Krill. Why do I know those names? Milly! Why do I know those names?"

The woman to Clinton's right spoke up, talking through tangerine lipstick that matched her long orange hair and distinctive eye shadow. "Marlin Hadder and Viktor Krill are the two most wanted men in the world at the moment. Numbers one and two on the Blossoms' shit list. We could turn them in and buy a small country." The last sentence was said with a mischievous smirk that was hard to read. "Their names are all over every Blossom-controlled media outlet, which is basically all of them. The picture they are using for him, however..." Milly pointed to Krill. "Is not correct. And the drawing they are using for him..." The finger swung to Hadder. "Could be any of fifty-million white men. It's almost useless."

"Except for dragging in anyone they felt like questioning," corrected the large man.

"Except for that," agreed Milly.

The man placed his considerable hands behind his back and looked upon Hadder and Krill with new eyes. "Well, it looks like Su brought back something worthwhile, after all. Please, Su, continue with the proper introductions."

"As I was saying, this is Marlin Hadder and this is Viktor Krill. Marlin and Viktor, this is Clinton Voss, leader of the Protectors of Man."

Voss nodded to each in turn. "It's an honor to meet you both. Any enemy of the Blossoms is a valued friend of mine. But I fear Su embellishes a bit. I am not the leader of the New God resistance. I am but..."

"You are now," Su cut in, her eyes falling to the concrete ground.

Voss's dark face fell, evident even through his thick, snowlike beard. "You can't mean..."

Su nodded, still refusing to raise her eyes. "Patton Yellich is dead. He was captured, tortured, and murdered by Willard Hillmore and the Thorns of Reckoning."

Voss's yellow eyes flashed. "And how do you know this?"

Su nodded to Hadder and Krill. "They were there. They saw it all."

Voss began to shake with a mounting fury. He addressed Hadder and Krill. "You were there?"

"We were," answered Krill.

"In the Thorns' encampment?"

"Yes."

"Then you know where they are now?"

"We do."

"Where?"

"In a forest just outside Kharras."

Clinton Voss spun on a boot. "Gather everyone. Tell them to arm themselves. Everything they've got. We will bring the war to the Thorns!"

The men and women surrounding Voss snapped salutes to the man before running off in multiple directions.

"That will not be necessary," said Krill, tossing cold water on the excitement of the moment.

Voss turned back to face the trio, his dark face a mask of confusion and barely contained rage. "What did you say?"

"I said that will not be necessary."

Voss marched threateningly toward Krill. "And why is that? What are you holding back? What game are you two playing at?"

Krill's black eyes met Voss's yellow orbs. "No game."

"You will tell me," roared Voss as he lunged forward, his restraint lost to grief and anger, and moved to take Krill by the throat.

Su looked on in horror and Hadder in bored amusement as Krill's hand shot up and seized Voss's massive wrist, freezing the giant man in place. Voss's eyes went wide in momentary shock before Krill pushed out, as if he were playfully fighting off a child, sending the colossal man through the air to land hard on his backside.

Voss stared up in astonishment as Krill moved to stand over the new Protector leader. "It will not be necessary to seek the Thorns because they no longer exist. My companion and I eliminated them. All of them. By now, the Blossoms would have discovered the killing field and cleared the area."

Voss continued to speak from the floor, his face growing less enraged but more confused by the second. "And Willard Hillmore?"

"Gone." A dark smile perched itself on Krill's lips. "In a most gruesome way, I might add. Unfortunately, neither of us can take credit for killing the bastard. It was a creature of the New God's own creation that ultimately took his life." Krill shrugged lightly. "Still, it was enjoyable to watch his face get ripped in half."

Voss fought for comprehension. "I still don't understand. You. And you. Cleared this world of the Thorns of Reckoning, the elite killers of the planet's darkest collective? I'm sorry, but I don't see how."

Su came over, held out a small hand, and assisted her leader to his feet. "See? That's what you get for not letting me finish my introductions or even starting my story. If you're going to be the new honcho, you're going to have to rein in that reactionary attitude of yours."

Voss snorted derisively. "This coming from a woman who took off in the middle of the night to hunt the Thorns of Reckoning all by her lonesome?"

This time it was Su's turn to shrug. "I've never claimed to be a leader, Clinton."

To his credit, Clinton Voss nodded in acquiescence. "Fine, fine. So, let me get this straight. Patton Yellich, the founder of the Protectors of Man and heartbeat of the New God resistance, is dead. But so are Devout Willard Hillmore and the Thorns of Reckoning. And you've brought us two strangers who are dangerous enough to be listed on the Blossoms' most wanted list. Is there anything I'm missing?"

"Actually, yes," stated Su as she swung the backpack off her shoulders. "I've brought lunch. And I remember details much better on a full stomach."

———

MARLIN HADDER STARED down at the generous portion of barbecued, skewered meat given to him by one of the Protectors of Man known as Teo. Slim and dark skinned, with jagged scars covering his arms, Teo manned the small grill that was rolled out in honor of Su Anorrak's return and the meat that she had brought with her. Although the cooked meat emitted a wonderful aroma, Hadder had difficulty in separating the food from its source, namely a sewer-dwelling worm that regularly fed on humans.

Hadder looked over and found that Viktor Krill, sitting in one of the many lawn chairs that were set up, did not share his hesitancy. His black-eyed companion tore into the meat with reckless abandon, stripping one of his skewers in seconds, leaving nothing but a contented grin to show that the cooked flesh had ever existed. He looked over to Hadder.

"Finally," said Krill, pointing down to the other full skewer on his newspaper-covered lap, "a meal fit to challenge the Muck's chowsets. Oh, but the credits that could be made with a chowset serving this wondrous delicacy."

"I think your cost of goods sold would be prohibitively high," said Clinton Voss through bites of Ghost Worm.

Krill thought for a moment. "An auction then. I'm sure the world's elite would pay top credit for the opportunity to sink their porcelain teeth into such a rare treat."

"They already get everything else," stated Su as Teo continued to turn and move Tunnel King chunks on the hot grill. "Let this one thing be for us, who put our lives on the line to hunt the demons and collect their meat."

Krill simply nodded in understanding as he began to work on his second skewer, much more slowly and deliberately this time. As he chewed, he looked over to Hadder, who still had his first skewer in his hand.

"Something wrong, Marlin?"

"I think he's afraid," giggled Su, her cheeks swollen with Ghost Worm flesh.

"Not at all," Hadder lied. "Just waiting for it to cool." Su and Krill looked at each doubtfully, each holding in a laugh, which forced Hadder to swat aside his hesitancy. He removed the top piece of worm meat with his teeth, closed his eyes, and began to chew.

Hadder's hazel eyes almost immediately sprung open as a unique mix of delicious flavors assaulted his tongue. The Ghost Worm was sweet and salty, unctuous with a spicy undertone thanks to a seasoning mixture that Teo kept carefully under wraps.

"I think he likes it," Su chuckled.

"How could he not," added Krill.

Hadder's heart began to race as he consumed the exotic meal. While the White Death was as delicious as anything he had ever eaten, it brought with it dark memories. Hadder shut his eyes once more, attempting in vain to push away the image of a butchered manikin staring at him intently as he devoured its heart in Jackie Crone's *Inferno*.

Hadder was forced to employ his Wakened abilities to alleviate the nausea that had come on and swallowed through the disconcerting recollection. When he opened his eyes again, everyone in the small circle was watching him carefully, unsure of what to make of their new guest's behavior.

Hadder ended their collective concern by diving into the next piece of Ghost Worm, consuming it with no trouble. The circle nodded and moved their attentions elsewhere.

"Well," declared Voss as he wiped his mouth and tossed empty skewers and greasy newspaper to the concrete floor, "stomachs are now full. Anyone want to tell me what the hell is going on? Su?"

Su looked disappointed by the interruption of her meal, but carefully removed the newspapered meat from her lap and placed it onto the floor next to her for later enjoyment. She cleared her throat.

"I was making good progress. *Damn* good progress, pardon my language. Each day, I was taking more Blossoms and Thorns off the chessboard, moving closer and closer to discovering where the Thorn encampment would next appear. I could almost taste it. And then..."

"You trusted the wrong Budd," finished Voss.

Su looked down, embarrassed. "Yes. I walked straight into a trap, and not a super complicated one. I took out as many as I could, but there were simply too many."

"Why are you alive," asked Voss, and there was no judgment nor suspicion in his voice.

"Two reasons. First, they wanted me to give up the location of the Protectors of Man. When their... basic male interrogation tactics didn't work, they knew they would need help from more sophisticated inquisitors. Second, they wanted credit for bringing me in alive to the Crimmwall Petal." As Su spoke, especially when recounting her questioning, her voice shook slightly, and the group could only guess at the unpleasantness to which Su Anorrak was exposed.

"Are you all right, Su," asked Voss, his voice thick with sympathy and concern.

Su wiped a single tear that had taken residence in the corner of her right eye. "I'm fine. Really. They all paid with their lives. Marlin and Viktor made sure of that when they rescued me from that fucking transport on its way to Crimmwall." Su looked around shyly. "Sorry for cussing."

"Well, we couldn't be more proud of you. Perhaps one of you two could take it from there," said Voss, directing his attention to Hadder and Krill. Krill nodded for Hadder to speak for the pair.

"Where do you want us to start," asked Hadder. "Ours has been a complex journey, one that might be beyond your comprehension or belief."

"Fair enough," responded Voss. "Let's jump to the end. How did you find Su? Why did you decide to rescue her?"

Hadder laughed lightly as Krill finished off the remainder of his meal. "That is perhaps the simplest part of our journey yet."

"How so?"

"We were driving from Kharras to Crimmwall in the dead of night when we came upon a military-grade criminal transport. Viktor noticed that one special detainee had earned the right to travel in the standing restraint." Hadder shrugged. "It looked interesting to us. And when we passed the transport, we noticed that the vehicle had been commandeered by the Blossoms. That made us more interested."

"And?"

Hadder tossed his second skewer over to Krill, who plucked it easily from the air and continued to eat. "And that's it. Su seemed like an important enemy of the Blossoms, and that was good enough for us. Enemy of my enemy and all that."

Confusion was evident on Clinton Voss's dark face. "You were driving?"

"Correct."

"You're two of the most wanted men in the world. How could you be in any vehicle without it triggering a warning?"

"Well, that's what brought us to the home of Patton Yellich originally."

"I don't understand."

Hadder sighed, his semi-full stomach ushering in a tiredness that reminded him of the long trek they had recently completed. "Look, you and the Protectors aren't the only ones hunting. The difference is that you all are hunting Blossoms and Thorns. Viktor and I are hunting the New God himself." The circle of Protectors all froze in place, some with mouths full of food and others with skewers hovering in the air.

"Bullshit," said a man called Jakksin, who shook his flat-topped head as he tossed an empty skewer to the floor.

"Shut up and listen," snapped Su, and the group jumped at the normally collected woman's anger.

Hadder continued. "Anyway, Viktor and I planned to head to Crimmwall, the Crimmwall Petal, to be exact, and see if anyone there knew the whereabouts of Doctor Milo Flowers." Hadder looked to Voss. "As you seem to already understand, our new positions atop the Blossom most wanted list made traveling via any modern conveyance impossible. We learned that the hard way. After a little traveling mishap, Viktor and I found ourselves adrift just outside Kharras. We entered the city and, would you believe it, Viktor turns out to be quite the interrogator."

"Oh, I believe it," responded Voss.

"Of course you do. Look at him. The question was rhetorical."

Krill's tan face did not change. "Anyway, we discovered that one of Kharras's patron citizens had quite the collection of antique automobiles. Stock. Without any of the modern recognition or tracking technologies."

"Patton Yellich's collection," Voss completed for Hadder.

"That's right. Viktor and I took off on a simple mission to borrow an antique automobile, and instead left in the very uncool company of Devout Willard Hillmore and the Thorns of Reckoning."

Clinton Voss looked more confused than ever. "How?"

Krill cleared his lap of newspaper and empty skewers. "Serendipity perhaps. An act of God. Shit luck. In any case, just as Marlin and I were about to take what we needed, the Thorns of Reckoning showed up, hungry for a different kind of prize. Turns out, they had been planning on abducting the Protectors of Man leader for some time, and had selected that very night to strike."

Lines formed on Voss's bald head as the man tried to reconstruct the strange confluence of events in his mind. "I'm still confused. Willard Hillmore was not known for his trust nor his hesitancy to eliminate potential threats. Why were you and Hadder allowed to even live, much less accompany the Thorns back to their encampment?"

Krill looked across the group with his black eyes. "Your man Yellich bailed us out. Put on a believable show about how we were there to convert him. Convert him or kill him. His performance was such that the old one-eyed bastard bought it hook, line, and sinker."

Voss looked as if he was about to scream from the absurdity of it all. "But why? Yellich had to know you were there to rob him. Why would he spend his final free moments trying to save a pair of thieves?"

Krill held his hands up. "I didn't understand it, either. But your man Yellich took an immediate shine to Marlin here. And I mean *immediate*. Just before the Thorns came crashing into the garage, he even suggested that we take the Comet from his collection."

"What a beautiful ride," commented Su.

While the others' minds swam with images of a vintage midnight black Comet, however, Clinton Voss stared at Marlin Hadder with a strange look, one that said, *we will speak more, in private.*

Without removing his gaze from Hadder, Voss spoke to Krill. "What happened after the Thorns came down on Patton's mansion?"

Krill, always hyper sensitive to his surroundings, took note of the awkward moment between Hadder and Voss, but continued. "Like I said, Yellich's performance had Devout Willard convinced that we were some kind of super Blossoms willing to do whatever it took to convert sinners to the light of the New God."

"I'm sure your choice of attire didn't hurt," said Jakksin from the side, his face swimming with doubt and suspicion.

"It didn't," replied Krill flatly, refusing to even look at the man.

"Patton's word would not have been enough," added Voss.

Krill smiled darkly. "Well, Marlin and I put on a hell of a show of our own to get into the mansion. Yellich, as you know, had his own security measures in place. The Thorns, who had been observing Yellich for weeks, no doubt recorded our violent abilities."

Hadder cut in. "Hillmore saw us as a new pet. A new weapon to point at his enemies. Nothing more."

"And so you found yourselves in the Thorns' encampment," prompted Voss.

"We did," continued Hadder. "They were as well-organized, as well-equipped, and as fanatical as we had feared. Viktor and I had to play along, lest we find ourselves facing too many bullets to dodge."

"And then what? You stalked from tent to tent, slitting throats in the night?"

Hadder shook his head. "Nothing of the sort. We held out as long as possible, but things got out of hand quickly. Yellich was murdered and Viktor and I were unmasked. We were left with no alternative but to fight."

"Fight? So, you and Krill fought the entirety of the Thorns of Reckoning? And?"

Hadder's face twisted as if he did not fully understand the question. "And so we killed them all."

Jakksin's wicked laugh cut across the group. "Bullshit! Oh, what bullshit. How long are we going to…"

Krill disappeared from his seat in the blink of an eye, reappearing next to Jakksin as if by magic, one hand holding a knife and the other pinching the flat-topped Protector's tongue. "I tire of your words, little man. I wonder if tongue meat tastes anything like worm meat."

Hadder swallowed a laugh while the others in the circle looked on in utter disbelief. Voss, to his credit, recovered quickly.

"Please, Krill, Jakksin is a fool, but he is a good man. His mouth often gets ahead of his brain, but he is a useful ally."

Krill refused to release Jakksin's tongue, instead bringing his blade closer to the soft muscle. "Fools get friends killed. Better to be rid of him now."

Voss rose to his feet, his black hand going to the large knife strapped to his waist. "Jakksin is a Protector who has proven his loyalty and worth many times over. If you harm him, I *will* fight you. I have no illusions about the outcome, but we *will* do battle."

Krill black eyes held Voss's for a moment before the notorious killer released Jakksin and returned to his seat, speaking to the Protector leader as he did. "Fine. But if he speaks once more out of turn, I will stitch his mouth closed."

"Fair enough," responded Voss, delighted that he didn't have to draw his blade against an obviously superior warrior. He turned to Jakksin, whose face appeared drained from his short interaction with Krill. "Can I count on you to shut the fuck up?" Jakksin nodded stupidly.

Hadder took advantage of the dumbfounded silence and continued. "That's pretty much the entirety of it. After the Thorns were eliminated, Viktor and I found that Hillmore had ordered the Comet brought to the encampment. In short order, we were back on track heading toward Crimmwall when we stumbled upon Su's transport."

"Do you still question how they were able to rescue me," asked Su sarcastically.

"I do not," answered Voss. "Nor do I question how they were able to down a Ghost Worm without Doctor Jansen's chemicals." Voss looked back and forth from Hadder to Krill. A thin smile formed within his white beard. "It seems that the Thorns of Reckoning's loss is the Protector of Man's gain. It appears that we have acquired the most important weapons in the fight against the New God."

"We are not yours to wield," corrected Krill.

Voss waved him away. "No, of course not. But our goals are aligned. Our hatreds are aligned. And we have something you need."

"And what's that," inquired Krill.

"A way into the Crimmwall Petal."

Now it was Krill's turn to wave Voss away. "They let anyone into those Petals."

"Into the Petal? Sure. But into the executive offices? Not a chance. You'll be lucky to even find them in that labyrinth. And if you do find them, there's a million credits of security barring entrance. You'll find yourselves in a firefight long before you reach someone who *may* know the whereabouts of the New God. You may be able to leave the Petal in rubble, but without the answers you seek."

"And you have a solution, I suppose."

"More than a solution, Krill. The key. The key to the entire goddamn Crimmwall Petal."

Krill grew impatient. "Well, let's see it then."

"Not *it*. *He*."

"A person is the key?"

"He is."

"Where is he?"

"He'll be here soon."

"And meanwhile?"

"Eat. Drink. Relax. Rest. You have brought our Su back to us. And we Protectors know how to repay a debt. The New God may be driving us toward oblivion, but that doesn't mean we stop knowing how to have fun. Isn't that right, Su? Su?"

The group turned to face Su, whose dark eyes had gone wide as she spotted something across the chamber's massive river. Hadder's hands went to his guns, as Krill's hands flew to fetch blades.

"What is it," asked Hadder, desperate to find out. "The Blossoms? Another Tunnel King?"

"The Crimmwall PD," guessed Krill.

"Worse," said Su flatly.

"What could be worse," asked Hadder as Voss chuckled beneath his thick beard.

"It's Zaza," responded Su, her voice full of unease. "My sister."

———

CLINTON VOSS, Jakksin, and Teo cleared away as if a tornado was approaching, which is precisely what was happening.

Hadder and Krill watched through wide eyes as the source of pandemonium crossed the central river and made her way toward the group. Hadder's breath caught as the woman closed the distance and came into focus.

Tall and lean like her sister, that was where the similarities ended. While Su moved like a dancer, Zaza marched forward like a tiger on black high-tops, her body coiled within her stretch leather pants and oversized black tee shirt. As the woman approached, she took off her black cap, revealing long, straight hair that was pulled together in a tight ponytail that sat high on her head. The sides of her head were clean-shaven, revealing ornate tattoos that ran down her neck to disappear into her tattered shirt.

With much darker skin than her sister, Zaza's light-brown eyes appeared to explode from the contrast, and Hadder found himself relieved that the anger they held were leveled at Su and not himself.

The words that were spilling forth from the enraged woman greeted the group long before she arrived.

"How fucking dare you, you fucking bitch! To make me fucking think that you were left dead on the side of the goddamn road, raped and fucking tossed aside! You think your fucking life doesn't fucking affect me, you piece of shit! How dare you, you bitch!"

The string of profanities that attacked the group reminded Hadder of the little Blister Smeggins, and he had to swallow a laugh before he unwittingly welcomed the ire of Zaza Anorrak.

"Do you fucking think that I'm just going to welcome you back, you selfish twat! You think there won't be…"

Instead of finishing her sentence as she closed the final meters to the now-standing group, Zaza tossed her hat at Su and rushed in behind it. Su swatted the fabric projectile away before turning aside a straight right that was targeting her too-perfect nose.

And then the fight was on in full.

Hadder and Krill, along with everyone else, backed up as the Anorrak sisters became a whirlwind of fists, feet, elbows, and knees. Throughout the battle, Zaza's loud curses mixed with Su's soft apologies, creating a cacophony of desperate conversation.

The Anorrak sisters, despite high-running emotions, fought with grace, accuracy, and precision, creating something that looked more akin to violent dance than brutal combat. Spinning wheel kicks were blocked and countered with straight hooks to the abdomen. Leg kicks were checked and followed with stiff jabs to the face. Grips meant to toss the other were reversed and reversed again as two pairs of feet moved in perfect balance around each other.

While the sisters fought at a blinding pace, Hadder and Krill had no trouble following the action. At one point, Krill even leaned into Hadder and offered the greatest compliment that had ever come from the notorious killer.

"Very impressive… for non-humans. I've only seen one that is their equal."

"I'm sure he was a real peach. Did you leave him alive?"

Krill responded without taking his black eyes from the warring sisters. "I tried. His pride proved too strong, which made me respect him all the more."

Hadder nodded but said nothing else. Instead, he sidestepped over to Clinton Voss, who seemed more bored than intrigued by Su and Zaza's battle.

"Should we step in and break them up," asked Hadder, and Voss's expression betrayed his answer long before words escaped his white beard.

"You ever try to break up two pit bulls? Or two venomous snakes? Any hand that goes near those two will be coming back a few fingers lighter."

"Then I guess tossing water on them is out of the question?"

"Unless you're suicidal." Voss looked down on Hadder. "Which perhaps you are." He turned his attention back to the Anorraks. "They should wind down here soon."

True to Voss's premonition, the sisters' blows eventually slowed as Zaza's anger burned out, replaced by an overwhelming sense of relief and joy. Tears began to flow down the tattooed woman's dark cheeks.

"Why?! Why didn't you tell me?"

"You never would have let me go," answered Su.

"Why didn't you take me with you," demanded Zaza.

"I love you more than anything, my sister. But the mission called for stealth, and you don't exactly blend in."

"But why didn't you check in?" The words came out piecemeal between gentle sobs.

"I fear that the Blossoms listen in on all communications."

Zaza nodded reluctantly and wiped her angular face, smearing her black eye shadow into odd-shaped arches that only further accentuated the striking woman. "I hope you at least got some of the fuckers."

"I did." Su hesitated for a moment. "Before I was captured."

Zaza's shift was immediate and awful, reminiscent of when the Rage took hold of Hadder. Her voice dropped to a low, dangerous level that only Hadder and Krill could decipher.

"They *took* you? What happened? Did they *touch* you?" A pause. "Did they *hurt* you?" Another pause. "I will kill them. I will kill them all."

Zaza seemed on the brink of insanity, her light eyes staring off into the distance, witnessing a bloody vengeance that had yet to play out. She shook with fury.

Su's pale fingers brushed her sister's face, pulling her away from oblivion and back toward the warm stare of familiar love.

"I'm ok, Zaza. I'm ok. They couldn't break me. I was too strong." Zaza's face nodded, sandwiched between Su's delicate hands. "They tried to take me to Crimmwall Petal, but I was rescued. See? I was rescued. These two rescued me on the highway. See?"

Su guided Zaza over to Hadder and Krill, who nodded lightly to the enraged woman. Zaza shook free of her sister and closed in on the Wakened humans.

"You saved my sister?"

Once again, Hadder and Krill nodded gently, wary of the unpredictable woman.

Zaza closed the distance on Hadder first, and he almost put his hands up in defense before the woman's black-stained lips were on his own, enveloping him in a deep kiss.

She separated as quickly as she began, moving on to Krill before Hadder even had chance to catch his breath. She and Krill locked in a similar embrace, but their eyes lingered on each other for an extended moment after separation.

Her appreciation shown, Zaza extended a long dark finger at both Hadder and Krill. "I can never repay you for saving my sister. But know that if either of you ever hatches a dangerous plan involving Su without including me, I'll slit all of your fucking throats." Zaza peeked back at Su. "Hers included."

And with that, Zaza Anorrak stormed away, grabbing a skewer of Ghost Worm meat from the grill as she passed. No one dared to speak until the human lightning storm was safely inside one of the residential add-ons along the side of Haven Falls.

Su turned back to Hadder and Krill.

"You'll have to excuse my sister. She's got a heart as golden as her eyes. But she can be a real bitch." An awkward shrug. "Pardon my language."

12

In the hours that passed, scores of Protectors of Man entered and exited Haven Falls through the various side tunnels that ran from the secretive group's stronghold.

Clinton Voss gave Hadder and Krill the dime tour, including the control room, where the companions saw real-time videos of all the tunnels leading to Haven Falls, at least a mile's worth in every possible direction. The men in the control room looked down as Voss entered the room, obviously embarrassed that they had missed not only the approach of the newcomers, but the Ghost Worm that had taken residence in their vicinity.

"That's our bad, boss," said a sad-looking man known as Franklin. "Jonson got sick and had to run to the bathroom before the next relief, me and Eddy, came in. And he was alone because Olive got called into a second shift at her regular job." Franklin let out a deep sigh without looking up. "Just a big fuckup all around, I guess."

"And the Tunnel King," asked Voss.

Franklin finally looked up. "Well, shit, boss, you know those things travel along the tops of the tunnels. The shadows up there are so deep they just kinda disappear. And they move so goddamn slow, when they do move, it's impossible to spot the things when you aren't looking for them. I really thought…"

The man continued to rant, unwilling to take responsibility for the Ghost Worm, until Voss silenced him with a giant hand on the man's shoulder.

"It's ok, Franklin. We'll use this as a learning experience. Two Protectors, at least two, per shift. Someone is always down below. Call someone up if you need coverage. Security is all of our responsibility, not just yours."

Franklin seems emboldened by Voss's kind words. "You got it, boss."

"Tell the others?"

"I will."

As the trio came down from the control room, Krill leaned into Hadder.

"Were that my man, he would be picking his teeth off the floor after that failure. And that's *if* I allowed him to keep his head on his shoulders."

Hadder answered back. "I was quite impressed with how Voss handled that. This is a volunteer resistance, Viktor, not a militaristic gang."

Krill snickered. "Which is why they all may find themselves experiencing painful deaths in the near future." Black eyes shot over to Hadder. "And dragging you and me down with them."

Hadder clasped Krill on the shoulder as they descended the final steps leading back to the ground floor. "Have some faith, Viktor. These people have waged an ongoing war against the Blossoms of the New God, the world's most powerful group, while operating within one of the seats of Milo Flowers's power. I think they deserve a little credit. And maybe a little trust."

"I only trust humans. And I don't see any here."

Hadder shook his head. "Well, that doesn't leave much room for trust, Viktor, seeing as how you and I are the only *humans* by your definition. Should I feel flattered that I'm the only other entity you trust in this world?"

"Yes. Feel flattered, Marlin. Feel flattered that I trust you to fumble your way around, refusing to maximize the Wakened gifts that have been given to you. Feel flattered that I trust you to show empathy when wrath is warranted. Feel flattered that I trust you to put your trust in someone who will lead us to our final graves."

And with that Krill stormed off, passing Voss who was walking ahead of the duo.

"You know, you can be a hard guy to like sometimes, Viktor," shouted Hadder to the notorious killer's back, drawing attention from several Protectors in the area.

Voss slowed, allowing Hadder to catch up as they crossed Haven Falls. "Problem with your friend?"

"Viktor Krill is always going to be a problem." Seeing concern on Voss's dark face, Hadder clapped the giant man's broad shoulder. "But a necessary one. Believe me when I say that without Viktor Krill, this world is truly lost. With him on our side, we at least stand a chance."

Voss looked over as the pair walked, studying Marlin Hadder. Hadder could feel the large man's yellow eyes on him, accounting for minute details and invisible variables in much the same way as a Wakened human.

"You seem like a man accustomed to long odds."

"You are correct."

"And how have you fared so far?"

Hadder smiled weakly. "Not much better than fifty-fifty, I'm afraid."

Now it was Voss's turn to smile. "Hadder, my friend, fifty-fifty would look like a Godsend right about now."

Although it was meant as a lighthearted comment, Hadder's serious look sent Voss back a step. "Voss, there's something you and all the Protectors need to come to grips with. God, the real God, has abandoned you, has abandoned us. Don't count on Him, or Her, or It to offer any assistance. We've been left alone to fight a great evil."

Voss shook his head. "I refuse to believe that our creator has abandoned us." Hadder laughed dryly. "You find something I said funny?"

"More than you could ever know. You assume God and the creator to be the same, but they are not. They are only aligned in one way — both don't give a fuck about us. Understand that, or all is lost. Throw yourself into that fucking river now because that is preferable to what is to come."

"And what is to come, Hadder?"

"Losing what little humanity you ever had." Hadder veered off from Voss, upset that he let the principled man's ignorance irritate him.

"Talk about a hard guy to like," mumbled Clinton Voss under his breath as Marlin Hadder walked away. But the curious Protector leader wasn't ready to let the topic go. He called after the strange visitor.

"How do you know these things, Marlin Hadder?! Why should I believe you when it is my job to doubt those who claim knowledge of the truth?! What makes you an expert on our creator?!"

Hadder spun on his heel and directed his hazel gaze directly at Voss, despite dozens of Protectors now staring at the pair. "I know the man. I crossed worlds with him. I've gotten wasted with him and fought beside him. We broke bread and shared women... well, Spirit Girls." Hadder took his eyes from Voss for a moment and noticed that more Protectors had moved within earshot. He amplified his voice. "I know the creator! And he's put us in this predicament. He's a fucking prick." Hadder looked around, carefully matching eyes with everyone in attendance. "We're all we got. Let us hope that is enough."

With that parting shot, Marlin Hadder marched off to be alone. As Clinton Voss watched the unusual man disappear into a residential area, something ate away at the giant's oversized stomach. Despite Hadder's dark words and absurd claims, Voss had to admit something to himself, something that terrified him and inflamed the large ulcer that rested in the pit of his stomach.

Clinton Voss believed Marlin Hadder.

———

AFTER CATCHING a few hours of rest within the residential quarters, Hadder and Krill were asked to join the Protector leadership in a conference room that was tucked away inside one of the add-ons nearest the artificial waterfall. Along with Clinton Voss, Hadder and Krill found themselves sitting around a large rectangular table with the Anorrak sisters, Milly, and three strangers who had just arrived to Haven Falls.

One, a sickly looking fellow whose ill-fitting business attire threatened to swallow the man's lean frame, was identified as Lumis Griggs, a high-ranking administrator for the city of Crimmwall.

The second, a strikingly beautiful woman with long blonde hair and icy blue eyes, draped in an emerald green, velour jumpsuit, was introduced as DeLany Thales. DeLany was not only a famous model and cosmetic mogul, but also ran Crimmwall's most renowned network of call girls and pleasure boys that serviced countless high-end officials, executives, and, yes, Blossoms of the New God.

In short, between Lumis and DeLany, nothing occurred within Crimmwall that the Protectors of Man did not know about.

The final guest was a small, pudgy, tan-skinned man with thick glasses and a wispy mustache who seemed more at home among books and computers than other life forms. The appearance made sense when he mumbled that he was Doctor Olney Jansen, master of chemical agents and weapons research.

Once the formalities had concluded, Clinton Voss spoke to the group at the end of the conference table.

"Marlin Hadder and Viktor Krill. You have returned to us Su Anorrak, a great ally to the cause and greater friend. The Protectors of Man are in your debt. I have gathered some key leaders of the resistance here to meet you in the hopes that we can repay our debt. You have come to Crimmwall for a purpose. Please state it and let us see where we may be of service."

Krill nodded to Hadder, giving him permission to speak for them both. Hadder hesitated for a moment, worried about Krill's continued dark demeanor, before speaking up.

"Viktor and I wish to gain entrance to the Crimmwall Petal."

Confused, worried faces turned to each other and back to Hadder. Voss again voiced the group's feelings.

"Why?"

"We want to kidnap an Arch-Soother."

More confused looks followed. "Why?"

"Because he or she may know where the New God is hiding."

"The Arch-Soothers are among the most faithful and insane of the Blossoms. What makes you think any of them will talk?"

Hadder simply nodded toward Viktor Krill, who took his cue to speak.

"Pain is the great seeker of truth. Everyone is loyal until their skin begins to peel from their flesh. Even Arch-Soothers."

Hadder could tell that several in attendance, including Zaza Anorrak, were going to argue the point until they met Krill's black orbs with their own. None ended up speaking out.

"Very well," eventually said Voss. "And how were you intending to infiltrate the Petal?"

Hadder shrugged. "Just walk in, I suppose. If that doesn't work, we'll carve our way in."

"Wouldn't be his first time," added Krill from the side.

Voss thought for a moment before responding. When he did speak, Voss directed his attention not to Hadder and Krill, but to the other Protectors in attendance.

"Any idea when he's joining us next?"

DeLany was the first to answer. "One of my pleasure boys visited him two nights ago. He said he has big news." DeLany thought for a second. "No, not *big* news; that's inaccurate. *Monumental* news."

"What was the news?"

"He wouldn't share it with the pleasure boy. Not that I blame him. Even my best can be bought for a few credits or the promise of Slink." Hadder and Krill glanced at each other. "Said he would try to get to Haven Falls in the next three days. Meaning he should be here shortly."

Hadder shook his head, confused. "I'm sorry, but what are you two talking about?"

Clinton Voss turned his gaze to Marlin Hadder. "You said you wanted an Arch-Soother?"

"I did."

"Well, we're going to deliver you one. But you need to know one thing."

"What's that?"

"He doesn't know where the New God is hiding."

"Are you certain?"

"We are positive?"

"How do you know?"

"We will reveal that at a later time."

"If this is true, if he doesn't know where we can find the New God, then what good is he to us?"

Voss looked around the table in an uncomfortable mix of hope and concern. "He doesn't know where the New God resides. But he knows someone who does."

————

SOME TIME after the meeting had concluded, Haven Falls began to fill up with Protectors from across Crimmwall. Men and women of all shapes and sizes filtered into the cavernous Protector base, greeting each other by pressing palms together as they gently touched foreheads.

A human action by the self-declared defenders of humanity.

Marlin Hadder sat off to the side alone, a cigarette and portable fire his only company, and watched as friends and family reunited under the heavy city's cover. Glancing over at one of the many digital clocks that were posted around Haven Falls, Hadder saw that it was growing deep into the night on the surface. This made it the perfect time for Protectors to sneak away for clandestine meetings.

Hadder watched as a man passionately kissed his wife or girlfriend upon entering the stronghold. Two women shared an intimate moment at a portable fire just across the central river. In another corner, six people danced together to music that was being piped in from the control room. Across Haven Falls, people shared food and laughs, drinks and embraces.

It was almost enough to bring a smile to Marlin Hadder's face. Almost.

The sound of a lawn chair unfolding up next to him stole Hadder from his observations. Hadder watched as Viktor Krill sat down and began to light a joint.

"The woman named Milly gave this to me. Hopefully, it packs a punch. I don't know about you, but I'm still quite sore." Krill inhaled deeply and stared out at the same view that Hadder had recently enjoyed. He spoke through thick smoke. "What are you looking at?"

"People. People just being people. Interacting. Sharing. Coming together."

"Why?"

Hadder looked over angrily, refusing to believe that the brilliant Viktor Krill could be so obtuse. "Because that's what we're fighting for, Viktor."

Krill inhaled once more before handing the joint to Hadder. "That's what *you* are fighting for. You've seen the pink omen in the sky. It couldn't be more clear. This world is damned. For all we know, *all* the worlds of man are damned. God has cursed this place. We are forgotten."

Hadder was thankful that the smoke had an immediate effect, dulling the sharp edge of his intended retort. "Then why *are* you here, Viktor? What are you fighting for?"

"Revenge. Always revenge."

"That doesn't seem like a very fulfilling reason."

Krill's black eyes glazed over as he pictured Cyrus Bhellum filleted against the office wall, kept alive for days through agonizing pain and suffering. "Oh, it can be quite fulfilling if done correctly."

Hadder softened a bit, understanding where Krill was going in his mind. "But it doesn't bring them back. I know that all too well."

"Nothing does, Marlin. So, we squeeze out what little joy there is with bullets and blades and blood. Milo Flowers, through his directives, brought great pain to one of the few people I've ever dared to love. Now, he will die because of it. And if the world collapses like a dying star shortly thereafter, so be it."

Hadder saw no reason to argue the point with the stubborn Wakened human, so he simply nodded and handed the joint back to Krill. A heavy silence filled the void as the companions looked out onto the strangely beautiful cavern of cement. Surprisingly, it was Krill who finally broke the muted truce.

"I think I experienced your Rage recently."

A knot formed in Hadder's stomach, but he refused to acknowledge it. "I thought you lived in a perpetual state of rage."

"I do not."

"When?"

"When what?"

Hadder let out a frustrated sigh. "When do think you experienced the Rage?"

Krill remained quiet for a moment for responding. "During our fight with the Ghost Worm. It brought back a most painful memory. I lost it."

Hadder took the last of the joint from Krill. "I've watched you fight, Viktor. You always battle with a barely controlled anger. How was this different?"

"You said it yourself. I always maintain control, regardless of my emotional state. I use my Wakened abilities to channel emotion. I concentrate anger into killing blows. But I am always in command."

"And you felt…"

"Like a puppet, Marlin."

"And that made you feel…"

"Scared, Marlin. I felt scared."

"You're a Wakened human, Viktor. You never feel scared."

"*That* is perhaps what scared me the most. I don't know what it is that you have inside you, Marlin, but I don't want it. I have a newfound respect for the endless battle you must wage against this… thing."

Hadder remained silent, taken aback by Viktor Krill's honest words. Finally, he flicked the remainder of the joint into the fire and spoke. "The Rage is a horrible thing, one that has caused tremendous pain across my lives. But it is also the only thing I truly know, the only thing that has crossed worlds with me, lived by my side when no one else would. I hate it, and I love it. I need it, and want nothing more than to cast it away."

As someone approached the Wakened humans, Krill began to rise from his seat. "Well, don't cast it aside just yet. I fear it has a larger role to play in this dark tale."

"What do you mean by that," asked Hadder, but Krill was already walking away, moving toward Zaza Anorrak, who was practicing her battle moves alone in a dim corner of Haven Falls.

"Marlin Hadder, just the man I wanted to see," stated Doctor Olney Jansen as he fell heavily into the seat recently vacated by Viktor Krill. Hadder returned a disinterested nod, the Leaf smoke now dancing through his mind. "As you know, I am a bit of a Tunnel King aficionado. I don't know if anyone told you, but I am the one who developed the chemical compound that turns the demons inside out." Hadder offered another nod. "Yes, well, anyway, I heard that you and your companion encountered one on the way here and managed to dispose of the creature. I am curious as to how you did that. For scientific purposes, obviously."

"Obviously," agreed Hadder through a haze as he sighed deeply. With so much camaraderie surrounding him, the last thing Hadder wanted to talk about was the White Death. He rose unsteadily from his folding chair. "Look, the most destructive bombs are those that are placed on the inside. This is true whether you're talking about buildings or Ghost Worms. Or people. Now, you'll have to excuse me."

As Hadder began to walk away, he heard Doctor Jansen calling from behind.

"Yes, yes, but how did you plant the bomb on the inside? Ghost Worms are quite protective of their aperture."

Hadder spoke over his shoulder as he continued toward a group of Protectors. "Viktor and I did what we do best. We made something scream. And then we went somewhere we weren't supposed to be."

———

HADDER MADE the rounds across Haven Falls. He watched as Viktor Krill practiced complex battle maneuvers with the Anorrak sisters between sips of strong liquor. He joined a circle of Protectors and listened intently as each shared the first thing they would do once the New God was defeated. He fished off the edge of the central river, where creatures akin to sea bass would often find themselves after leaving the comfort of the ocean for the mystery of a shadowy side path.

But most of all, Marlin Hadder simply meandered and took in the surroundings, content to be in a place where the world had yet to go mad.

Even if he could only stay for a bit.

After a while, Hadder found himself standing before the great artificial falls, breathing in deeply as the cool mist tickled his face and offered a sobering caress. Looking behind the falls, Hadder noticed a giant shadow lurking within the ocean-bound tunnel, obviously moored to remain unmoved against the strong current. Just as Hadder's Wakened eyes began to take in details within the shadows, the voice of Clinton Voss interrupted.

"Beautiful, isn't it?" Voss handed Hadder a cold beer, which he readily accepted. "I know it's a manmade construct, designed to usher in ocean water for washing away piss, shit, and whatever other foulness the citizens of Crimmwall flush daily. But at times like this, there's no other place that I would rather be."

Hadder looked over from his beer. "If that's true, then I think you need to travel more, Voss."

The large man laughed at himself. "You may be right. Always told myself I would. I traveled quite a bit during the war, but I was young and little beauty could be found in the places we visited, especially once the violence transformed them into slag. After the war, I promised myself that I would see the world, that I wouldn't fall prey to society's restrictions. Well, here I am forty years later, and I can count on both hands the number of times

I've been a hundred miles outside Crimmwall. Now I fear it's too late."

"It's never too late, Voss."

"In the *you're never too old* sense, you are correct, Hadder. But it's not the changes in this old body that I'm worried about, it's the changes *out there*. The world is growing more grotesque by the day. Most are being led off the cliff by a twisted pied piper, and there's not enough of us to pull back on the reins."

Hadder spoke between sips of beer. "Then you give up?"

Voss looked as if he wanted to strike the smaller man next to him, but his anger passed quickly, like a lone grey cloud on a windy day. "We will never give up. Better to die on your feet than live on your knees. And do not doubt that the New God wants us on our knees."

"I am not convinced that's what he wants."

"What do you mean, Hadder?"

"The New God doesn't want you on your knees. He wants to be able to remove your knees at will."

Sharp lines of confusion drew across Clinton Voss's bald head. He took a deep swig of beer as he considered Marlin Hadder's words. "Well, the way you put it sounds much worse."

"It is."

The two men then stood in silence for several minutes, allowing the thunderous cascade of water and occasional splashing of fish to fill in the acoustic blanks. When Voss finally finished his beer, placing the empty glass bottle into one of the many pockets on his safari shirt, he spoke again.

"It looks like Krill found his clique, even if it is just with the Anorrak sisters."

Hadder didn't need to look back to see that Voss was referring to the three-way hand-to-hand battle taking place dozens of yards behind the pair.

"Despite his dark demeanor, Viktor knows who he likes and can be quite charming when he wants to be. Which is almost never."

"And what about you, Hadder? I didn't expect you to be standing alone during such a rare festive time."

"And what do we have to be festive about?"

"We're still alive, aren't we? Still human."

"Viktor would disagree with that assessment."

"What do you mean?"

"Never mind." Hadder nodded toward the shadow in the ocean-bound tunnel. "What's that?"

Voss appeared surprised that Hadder could make out the object in the lightless place. "Oh, that? Let's just call that an insurance policy in case the shit hits the fan."

"And will the shit hit the fan?"

Voss laughed. "Only if things go according to plan."

Hadder looked up at the giant man. "So there *is* a plan?"

Confused creases once again appeared on Voss's head. "Of course there's a plan! You and Krill may not believe it, but we're not as ragtag as we appear!"

Hadder shrugged and turned his attention back to the swirling waters beneath the falls. "I meant no offense. And I apologize if I did. This black river reminds me of another that I often visited in another world. While some of the memories it brings back are joyous, others cause me great pain. It is quite easy for me to become lost in their labyrinthine sadness."

Voss studied the strange man before him, even more confounded than he was before this conversation. He decided to let the reference to *another world* slide, as he had more important questions to ask.

"You know, Patton Yellich was not only the bravest of us, but also the wisest."

"And the richest."

Voss chuckled. "Yes, that, too. But Patton was the most well-read person I had ever met. He knew every detail of every religion, had studied all the texts in their original languages. He was a detective of truth, willing to siphon through endless mounds of bullshit if it meant being able to distill a thimble of fact."

"And did he discover any? Fact, that is."

Voss took another beer out of one of his many pockets and

cracked it open. "There was one thing that he was definitely sure of," said Voss, just before placing the bottle to his lips.

"And what's that," asked Hadder, refusing to tear his eyes from the black water that so resembled the Station's Lethe River.

"Patton believed in the Yaasha, the savior of man that was written about in so many religious texts across so many belief systems. Patton truly believed that not only would he find this Yaasha, but that he would immediately know when he found him or her." Silence. "Did Patton ever mention the Yaasha to you, Hadder?"

Hadder kept his hazel eyes locked ahead. "Yellich said many things that didn't make sense. He said them as the Thorns of Reckoning raided his home. He said them as he dangled over a bonfire. And he said them as he was slowly impaled. Dying men say lots of things. Most of it is better off ignored."

"I can assure you that this is not. I see that he gave you a blade."

Hadder looked down and saw that the hilt of the small knife he had taken from Yellich's mansion jutted out from his waistband within his suit jacket. He moved the blade to the small of his back and turned angrily to face Clinton Voss.

"Let me assure *you*, Voss. Patton Yellich never *found* me; I broke into his goddamn home to rob him. And Patton Yellich never *gave* me this knife; I stole it from a collection of other old shit from his ostentatious house. I'm no more of a fucking *Yaasha* than Viktor is a humanitarian."

"It sounds like Viktor Krill would actually consider himself a *humanitarian*."

"Fuck off, you know what I mean!"

As Krill and the Anorrak sisters ceased their battle practice due to the commotion, Voss responded to Hadder's outburst in a calm tone.

"What *do* you mean, Hadder?"

"I mean, I'm not your fucking savior! This world isn't even mine, don't you understand that?!"

"Then why are you here?"

"I came here to… There was a bet and I had to…" Hadder stumbled over his words, the reasoning in his head growing as convoluted as the actual path that led him to this time and place. He finally settled on, "I'm not here to save you! You are *not* my people! I am nothing more than an alien floating between worlds!"

"Perhaps that is what we need."

"What you need," screamed Hadder, anxiety and exhaustion thick in his words, "is to sack up and fight your own battles! This is your world! Win it back!"

Despite Hadder's outburst, Voss's words came out as if wrapped in silk. "We *are* fighting, Hadder. And we're giving it everything we got. But in combating the greatest of evils, we require someone to follow. That someone is you."

Hadder spun away from Voss and began to walk along the edge of the central river back toward the control room. He spoke over his shoulder to the Protectors of Man's leader. "Then you truly are damned. You and everyone else in this cursed world."

As Voss watched Marlin Hadder walk away, Viktor Krill came up next to him, covered in perspiration from his recent workout.

"Let him go. When the time comes, Marlin will be ready to fight."

Voss looked over at the black-eyed man. "He refuses to accept who he really is. Can you help?"

Krill laughed dryly. "If you're asking me to convince Marlin Hadder that he's the savior of your world, then you're talking to the wrong human."

"And why is that?"

Krill's dark orbs cut into Voss. "Because I think your world is doomed, too."

"Then why are you here?"

"Revenge. Nothing more, nothing less. I will see the New God a pulpy mess beneath my high-tops. Subsequently, I assume we'll all be vaporized."

"And Hadder?"

Krill shrugged. "He still thinks your world can be saved. He has to believe that. It's in his nature to be hopeful; don't let his downtrodden bitch-face fool you. Regardless of what he says, Marlin Hadder will always hold out hope for a better outcome and a better world. Just don't call him out on it."

"And you, Viktor Krill?"

"I'm an evil bastard who's long past my expiration date. I just want my final vengeance, and if I can take out a few cowardly baddies on the way, so be it." Clinton Voss stared after Hadder with concern in his yellow eyes. Krill sighed before putting a tan hand on the man's enormous shoulder. "Look, Marlin will be fine. He just needs something to take his mind off the enormity of the situation."

"Word is spreading about your arrival. Even more Protectors should start pouring in over the next hour." Clinton Voss nodded to himself. "We will have a celebration."

Krill slapped the large man on the shoulder, almost knocking the giant over. "That's perfect. Nothing turns Marlin's spirits around like a sendoff. Get some drink and smoke in him. Play some music and watch the sonovabitch come around."

"And if he doesn't?"

"He will. Trust me."

Voss finished his beer in one great gulp and tossed the bottle at Su Anorrak, who quietly watched from thirty feet away. In one clean motion, the woman withdrew her katana and sliced the glass neatly in half. Zaza moved deftly behind her sister, plucking both pieces out of the air before they came close to meeting the cement floor.

Voss turned back to Krill. "Should I worry that all my hopes are riding on the assurances of Viktor Krill?"

"No, you should worry that your world is ending, and you are wasting what's left of it speaking to me."

At that, Clinton Voss released a bellowing laugh. "You are right about that, Krill. And so, I will bid you adieu to arrange music and find... softer company. You and Hadder should have until morning before he arrives."

Krill's face twisted. "Who is *he?*"

"Have you forgotten already? I thought you were smarter than the rest of us." Krill began to protest, but Voss continued. "Your key to entering the Crimmwall Petal is on his way. Once he arrives, the time for celebration is over. And the time for ridding this world of sick messiahs begins."

———

DANCING.

Everywhere that Marlin Hadder looked, there was dancing.

Electronic music floated through Haven Falls, echoing off the thick cement walls and overwhelming the sounds of falling water. Leaf smoke coiled across the cavernous chamber, twirling around obstacles before coalescing and rising as a singular cloud toward the high ceiling. The Protectors of Man, hundreds now gathered in the secret base, danced desperately with one another, their intimacy evident as they gyrated in unison to the pounding beats.

Hadder watched as wide smiles greeted each other just before foreheads touched and open palms met. Every opportunity was taken to exchange a hug, or a caress, or a kiss, or a slap on the back.

These were a people delighted to see one another. Because these were a people who knew that any one of them could disappear at any a moment, lost to the ever-searching eyes of the Blossoms of the New God.

Protectors passed by Hadder, offering him Leaf (which he took), drink (which he accepted), and dance (which he politely declined). Instead, Hadder chose to observe for a while, numbing his Wakened mind with smoke and drink while taking a mental snapshot of how humanity should behave, reminding himself that this world is worth trying to save.

"Not much for dancing?"

The sweet voice, despite is softness, startled Hadder, pulling him back from his heavy thoughts and worries. He looked over to find Su Anorrak standing next to him, a metal cup of reddish liquid in each of her delicate hands.

"I'll get there eventually," replied Hadder. "A bit more Leaf and you won't be able to keep me from the dance circle." There was more hope than truth in Hadder's words.

"Here, maybe this will help," said Su as she handed Hadder one of the metal containers. "Careful, it's one of Jakksin's own concoctions. Tastes like shit but will send you into the clouds. Pardon my language."

Hadder nodded before taking a sip. As soon as his lips touched the foul liquid, every fiber of Hadder's being screamed for him to reject the mixture, to expel it to the ground, so no other poor creature could be subjected to its devilry. Instead, Hadder forced it down, his hazel eyes going wide as the drink left a trail of fire from his mouth and throat down to his belly.

Su giggled lightly. "You know, I've never seen anyone drink that without coughing up a lung their first time."

Hadder swallowed down a cough. "I've drunk every kind of mixture possible across… the world. And I don't think I've ever tasted anything quite so objectionable. It drinks like straight gasoline."

Another soft laugh followed. "I guess that's why Jakksin calls it *Jet Fuel*. But trust me, one of those, and you'll forget all about your problems."

"I doubt that. But I'm willing to give it a try." Hadder took another pull of Jet Fuel, enjoying the looseness that followed the deep burn.

The pair stared out at the festive scene zigzagging Haven Falls for several minutes before Su finally spoke.

"You know, I never got to properly thank you for saving my life."

Hadder continued to look out upon the partying Protectors, afraid that if he looked into Su Anorrak's dark eyes, he would take a tumble from which he could not recover.

"You would have found a way to escape those imbeciles."

"No, not this time. They had me wrapped up tight, the perfect gift for the Crimmwall Petal." Su's voice sounded far away, as if she was watching a movie play out in her mind. "I would have been twisted into something inhuman. I would have given up Haven Falls. Of this, I am certain." Su's soft hand reached up and turned Hadder's chin toward her. "Thank you. Not only for saving my life, but for ensuring that I could not betray my friends. My life is yours now."

Hadder tried to look away from those penetrating eyes, but found that he could not. "Viktor Krill is just as responsible for your rescue."

"Yes, and I've already had this conversation with him."

"And what did he say?"

"He asked me to go away. Actually, his exact wording was a bit more vulgar, but I won't repeat it here. He denied needing thanks for killing Blossoms. He said that it was a *moral imperative.*" At that, Hadder almost spit out his Jet Fuel, caught off guard by Krill's movie reference from their shared original world. "What's so funny?"

Hadder waved his free hand in surrender. "Nothing, nothing. Sorry. But Viktor is right. We simply saw a potential asset and took it from our enemies. I wish it was deeper than that, but it wasn't."

Su Anorrak stared at Hadder for a moment before a small smirk formed on her lips. "Well, that won't stop me from giving you this." Su leaned in and stood on her toes to kiss Hadder gently on his cheek. "Thank you for saving my life."

"You're welcome," Hadder stumbled.

"See you out there?"

"Try to stop me."

And with that, Su Anorrak went off to join her fellow Protectors of Man in their revelry, dancing her way into the first group that she came across.

"She's remarkable, isn't she?"

Hadder almost jumped again, so entranced was he watching Su walk away. He glanced over to find that Upton, one of the two Protectors working the sewage reading plant, had taken the enchanting woman's place. The little man had changed out of his orange jumpsuit and now wore simple blue jeans and a flannel top.

Hadder nodded to the new arrival. "Yes, she is."

Upton took a bite from a fried pie he was holding as he appraised the scene, speaking absently as he did through a mouthful of meat. "Shift ended a couple of hours ago. Looks like I arrived just at the right time. I'd say that the party's about to get set off." Hadder ignored the small man, but was not returned the favor. "I saw your black-eyed buddy as I came in. He's over there talking to Zaza and some other heavy hitters." Upton looked Hadder up and down. "You know, I assumed that you would be the social one and *he* the sullen one. Guess you never know a man until you know him, ya know?"

"That's because Viktor believes that you are all already corpses. And he loves nothing more than cavorting with death."

"What's that? I didn't catch that."

Hadder swallowed down the last of the Jet Fuel, a dumb smile touching his lips in place of the metal cup. "Don't worry about it." He slapped Upton on the shoulder. "It's good to see you. I'm glad you made it down. Now, if you'll excuse me, I need to lose this churlish reputation I've recently acquired."

Upton laughed, bits of meats flying out of his mouth as he did. "And how do you mean to do that, new friend?"

"Easy, Upton. I'm going to party like we're at the Soirée Noire." Hadder knew that the little man had no idea to what Hadder was referring, but he didn't care.

It simply felt good to say those words once again.

———

JET FUEL and Leaf smoke led the way, and Marlin Hadder followed. He danced manically in one group, and shared kebabs in another. He traded war stories in one circle, and chatted quietly with Viktor Krill in another.

As the foreign electronica reverberated off the cold walls and the Leaf smoke began hanging heavy over the entirety of the chamber, Hadder looked around at the ghostly scene and laughed to himself.

After all, were they all not just ghosts waiting for the official designation.

As the party wore on, bodies drew closer together, hands became more explorative, and mouths sought each other's company. Outlines grew indistinct, and a shroud of haze fell over Hadder's Wakened mind.

At one point, Hadder found himself dancing hip to hip with Su

Anorrak, staring intently into the dark pools of her eyes. He leaned in for a kiss, and was met with a cheek and an uncomfortable giggle.

"I'm sorry, Marlin. I didn't mean to give you the wrong impression. You're great and all, but just not quite my type."

Hadder fumbled for an apology, tripping and falling over his words before finding a weak excuse to move on to another circle of Protectors. Hadder wallowed in rejection for a while before spotting Su Anorrak arm-in-arm with Milly as the two went off to locate more private quarters. His eyes went wide with realization, and he chuckled to himself, happy that the two warrior females had found comfort with each other.

"I tried to tell you that you had the wrong face, Marlin," said Krill as he walked past, his arm swung easily over the tan shoulders of Zaza Anorrak.

"You could have been more specific, Viktor."

"But then I wouldn't have had this embarrassing moment of yours to enjoy." Krill turned to Zaza. "Did you see Hadder strike out with your sister? It appears that not every female is susceptible to his sad sack charms."

Zaza punched Krill lightly in the stomach before speaking to Hadder. "Don't fucking worry about it. Better men than you have tried with that bitch. My sister likes the ladies, what can I fucking tell you." Back to Krill. "Now, are we going to find a place to talk, or do I need to kick your fucking ass again."

Krill's black eyes flashed as he looked down at the unreal creature under his arm. "Of course, *Miss Anorrak*, right this way, please."

Zaza giggled in the notorious killer's embrace. "That's more fucking like it. Later, Hadder."

As the pair strode to the residential quarters, Krill called out over his shoulder. "Look on the bright side, Marlin! That's one less woman doomed to a gruesome death!"

"Hey! I told you about those others in confidence, Viktor!"

Krill waved his free hand. "No one here cares, Marlin! Forget about the world for the night! The false god will still be there when you wake up!"

Someone handed Hadder a fresh cup of Jet Fuel as he watched Viktor Krill and Zaza Anorrak travel in lockstep toward the private rooms.

Hadder sipped the potent brew and wanted to be jealous of his Wakened companion, but found that he could not. In fact, he took comfort in the fact that Viktor Krill, a man who had caused infinite pain while experiencing deep suffering, would have one last night of humanity before the world turned inside out.

Hadder absently touched metal cups with the Protector next to him and downed the rest of his Jet Fuel. As a new song descended upon the celebration of freedom and life, Hadder danced his way to his newest allies in the war against Doctor Milo Flowers, also known as the New God.

Smoke filled his lungs and joy filled his heart as Marlin Hadder shared intimate moments with dozens upon dozens of Protectors of Man. He twisted and turned, offering laughs and tears as the world around him grew brown and grey, before finally turning black.

13

Tennian Stamp, better known as Old Tens, smoked a cigarette as he stared down at the Neon City from his penthouse suite in posh central Bhellum. Although he tried to concentrate on the bright hues of the city below, Tennian couldn't help but catch his reflection in the thick glass. Within that reflection, a dark, weathered face demanded repayment for decades of violence.

A soft knock at his door forced Tennian to finally look away from his ephemeral twin.

"Come in."

"Boss?"

Tennian didn't need to turn around to know who had just entered his private office space. "For the last time, Sonny, *you're* the boss now. I'm just a broken down old man, more metal than flesh."

"Sorry, boss." Sonny Caddoc quietly cursed under his breath. "Sorry. Old habits and all."

"Trust me, my friend. No one understands old habits more than I." An uncomfortable silence filled the ornate office. "Did you need something, Sonny?"

Tennian's ever-loyal Second shifted from foot to foot, as he was wont to do on the precipice of a conversation he felt unequipped to handle. "I… was just checking to see if everything was all right."

As Old Tens turned to face his closest companion, his metal legs hissed and moaned, a tell-tale sign that they desperately needed service.

"And why wouldn't everything be all right?"

"Well, because…"

"Spit it out, man!"

"Because of your red-eyed visitor." Sonny looked around expectantly.

"He's gone already, Sonny."

Sonny's brow wrinkled. "But how? I had men watching the door, listening for any signs of violence. If they fucked up that simple assignment!"

Tennian held up a scarred hand to calm his friend. "I assure you, they did not blow any assignment. The man simply left through another exit."

"There is no other exit, Tennian."

"Apparently, there is. He simply blended into the shadows and was gone. Now speak your thoughts."

News of the red-eyed visitor's strange departure did nothing to allay Sonny Caddoc's concerns. "I don't know the man well, beyond our prior dealings, but it seems that where he goes, trouble's bound to follow. I worry for the Broken Tens. And I worry for you, Tennian."

Old Tens loudly crossed the office and placed a hand on Sonny's muscled shoulder. "I appreciate it, old friend, but the Broken Tens have nothing to worry about. This is about me and some outstanding debts that I have to pay." With that, Tennian lightly patted Sonny on his stubbled cheek and moved back to the large window overlooking the city that he simultaneously loved and hated.

"I don't understand," came the response from behind Tennian.

"Our world is dying, Sonny. Or, more accurately, it is twisting into something akin to a hellscape. I wanted to avoid burdening you with this, but you asked, and I was never good at hiding the truth from you."

254 | JARRETT BRANDON EARLY

"Tell me what I need to do. What the Broken Tens need to do. You know that our lives are yours to lead."

Tennian continued gazing down at the Neon City, accepting what solace he could find in those heatless lights. "What you need to do, Sonny, is stay the course. You are already ten times the leader I ever was and twice as smart. Every move you have made has increased our legitimacy and standing in a very short time. Keep up the good work."

"And you? What about you, Old Tens?"

Tennian Stamp took another long drag from his cigarette and sent the smoke spiraling toward his reflection. "I have to go, Sonny."

"Go where?"

Tennian thought for a moment, unsure of how to explain his reasoning to his former Second, especially when he barely understood it himself. "Like I said, the world as we know it sits on the edge of annihilation. There is one who is responsible for this, one who sits at the center of the storm. I must confront him. I must stop him."

Sonny Caddoc was a brave, intelligent man whose physical strength only paled in comparison to the strength of his resolve. While his confidence in speaking about strategy and guns, violence and negotiation, was unmatched, he remained a child in the face of larger, more godly subjects. "Who are you talking about, boss? Certainly, not the New God and those fucking lunatics who follow him, the goddamn Blossoms. I can have them run out of the city tomorrow if you need it. Just give me the word, I can..."

"Sonny," Tennian interrupted. "The New God is a real threat. And he's a motherfucker. I have to go try to stop him."

"No one knows where Milo Flowers is."

"That is not accurate."

Sonny didn't press the issue. "But why you?"

Tennian finished off his cigarette and put it out against his metal legs before placing the butt in one of the many pockets of his military jacket. "Our red-eyed guest reminded me of a few things, things he shouldn't have known. He held open the book of my life and forced me to take a hard look at it. He reminded me of the death I caused during the war."

"You were a boy then, Tens. They made you do it."

"Doesn't change the fact, now, does it? The dead don't care *why* they died. They aren't concerned about the political machinations behind the fatal shot. They only care about who pulled the trigger. And I pulled countless triggers that led to much death."

"And you paid for it, Tens. You paid dearly."

"Obviously, not enough. Anyway, after getting blown apart at the Harrier Gap, I came home to wreak more havoc. You were too young to know me back in the day, Sonny. You didn't see the kind of vicious bastard I really was. At the time, I thought it was necessary to assert my dominance, to survive. Now, I think I was simply justifying my desire to kill, my need to continue the work that I started across the Great Water." Tennian turned to Sonny Caddoc once more. "I owe a debt for a lifetime of violence, Sonny. Our visitor was here to call that debt due in full."

"The Broken Tens are with you, Tennian. I can have the men assembled in a few days. When do we leave?"

"No!" Old Tens's words came out harsher than he intended, sending Sonny back on his heels. Tennian immediately softened. "No, Sonny. You need to remain. You need to continue leading the Broken Tens. If we somehow triumph, the world will need to heal, will need to rebuild. There will be a lot of money to be made."

"Then you will go at it alone."

"Not exactly. The gang life is a young man's game, ain't it? There's a lot of us still knocking around from the Great War, not only in the Broken Tens but across all the gangs. This life has passed us by, but we have a chance to be useful one last time. We can right many of the wrongs we have caused. Or at least die honorably trying. I'm fixing to call all our debts due."

Sonny's eyes became smeared with a thin layer of water. He spoke quietly. "How many of these men can you muster?"

"Maybe a couple of hundred or more. I'll talk to Red Texx in the morning, make sure I have his blessing before speaking to some of the old Risers. And there are some other spots in the city that I aim to hit. We won't be many, but we'll be a proper force of old, trained gang-

sters with nothing to lose and a lifetime of sin to wipe from the slate."
Tennian's dark eyes burned with something Sonny had not seen in
some time – passion. "No one fucks with our world but us. The New
God has got to pay."

Sonny Caddoc couldn't help but crack a smile at his former First's
barely contained fire. "What do you need, Tens?"

Now it was Old Tens's turn to smile. "I need a boat, Sonny. A big
fucking boat ready to make a long fucking voyage."

"Shouldn't be a problem. Our contact at the Gate can take care of
that."

"And I'm gonna need guns. A lot of fucking guns."

Sonny laughed. "That is never a problem."

"And I'm gonna need a tuneup for my legs. In fact, fuck that, I want
a complete upgrade. Use all the credits left in my account, spare no
expense. If I gotta face off with a god, I want to go scorched earth on
this motherfucker."

Sonny's grin broke out into a toothy smile. "You got it, boss."

MARLIN HADDER FLOATED GENTLY above the world, looking down as
the landscape transformed before his eyes.

On the horizon, a massive glowing worm pulsed, excreting wave
after wave of nightmares. The twisted creatures ran across the ground
like locusts, ever-changing as they moved forward, leaving new alien
forms of life in their wake. They consumed and regurgitated, took and
gave life, a shadowy presence leading their advance like a wartime
trumpeter.

They fell over the land with sick glee, an ill master directing their
actions, making them believe that the grotesque was beautiful, that
pain was ecstasy.

Hadder attempted to shield his eyes, but found that he had no
hands.

He was duty-bound to bear witness to the fate of mankind.

As Hadder's eyes tried to force out tears that would not come, a voice boomed across the world, echoing within his skull and threatening to liquify his mind. It spoke in razors and fire and ushered in an overwhelming sense of woe.

Look upon the beauty of my Flowering Horde. Look upon the power and brilliance of unfettered life. The old gods gave us boundaries, the New God gives limitless possibilities. This world is mine. And once I have sculpted it to my will, I will take my Flowering Horde across the multiverse. The worlds of humankind, all of them, are now mine. The worlds of humankind are dead. Long live life!

That final statement, shouted at him from across the darkening world, sent Marlin Hadder spiraling across the cosmos, spinning impotently away from those who cried out for his divine help.

———

A SWIFT KICK to the ribs ripped Hadder from his nightmare.

He looked up to find Clinton Voss staring down at him, concern painted across his dark face, thick lips twitching nervously within his too-thick white beard.

"Sorry for the rough wakeup call," said Voss. "You seemed caught in the throes of a bad dream. I'm embarrassed to say that I was scared to stir you. Men can lash out when escaping the grips of a nightmare."

Hadder roughly wiped his face with his hand, hoping in vain to scrape away the imagery of the Flowering Horde. "It's fine, Voss. Really." He glanced around to find that he somehow made his way into one of the residential units in a drunken stupor.

"I guess it would be foolish to ask you how you slept."

"I slept alone, Voss."

"From what I hear, maybe that is best for everyone."

Hadder rose unsteadily to his feet with Voss's help. He immediately called upon his Wakened abilities to flush the toxins from his system and began to approach normalcy. "I told Viktor that in confidence."

"Then we'll keep it between us. And anyone else who has heard. Now, let's get moving. He has arrived."

"Remind me again. Who has arrived?"

Clinton Voss let out an annoyed sigh. "Henley. Henley Chan." Hadder gave a blank look. "The Arch-Soother of the Crimmwall Petal. Your golden ticket to locating the New God."

Hadder shook his head, attempting to remove the last residual effects of Jet Fuel. "Yeah, of course. Lead the way." Voss began to leave, but paused mid-step and turned back to Hadder. "What is it?"

"You need to prepare yourself. Henley's look can be a bit off-putting."

Hadder almost laughed aloud. "Voss, if there's one thing I can say about myself, it's that I can handle off-putting shit like a pro. Now, let's go meet this golden ticket."

————

HADDER FOLLOWED Clinton Voss once more into the large conference room nestled within the housing units closest to the artificial falls. And almost tripped over his feet upon being greeted by the strange Henley Chan.

So much for handling things like a pro, he thought.

"*The* Marlin Hadder, I presume," said the man at the head of the long table in a soft, sing-song voice.

Hadder simply nodded his assent as he took in the Arch-Soother of Crimmwall Petal.

Even seated, the young man was extremely tall, but when he rose to greet Hadder, he absolutely towered over the Wakened human. As Henley Chan rose to his full height to bow in welcome, he showcased a lithe body covered by loose-fitting brown cotton pants and a white tunic. Henley's skin was the whitest Hadder had ever seen, and it took a bit of will to keep his hands from creeping up to shield his eyes from the overhead light that reflected off the man.

As Henley rose from his bow, Hadder absorbed more details.

The Arch-Soother had the most delicate features that Hadder had witnessed on a male. A long, thin nose sat between two perfectly shaped almond eyes the color of emerald. Straight hair that reminded Hadder of pure sunshine hung neatly down to Henley's wide shoulders. When he spoke, words came out from behind full lips that appeared gently stained with pigments of rose.

Hadder returned the bow and found a seat, finding himself strangely enchanted by a beautiful creature that was neither man nor woman, human nor pixie, powerful nor fragile.

As Hadder shook himself free of Henley Chan's spell, he finally took a look around the Protector meeting area. Across the table from him, Viktor Krill and Zaza Anorrak sat beside one another, each looking adequately refreshed from a night of physical closeness.

A twinge of jealously struck Hadder in the abdomen like a needled finger.

Occupying the seat next to Hadder was Su Anorrak, who offered a sweet smile and reassuring pat on the knee, as if the bruise from the previous evening's rejection needed additional salve to properly heal.

Hadder offered a weak grin in return.

Clinton Voss fell heavily into the chair opposite the visiting Arch-Soother, letting out a great groan as he did, evidence of a hard life made harder by current events.

Completing the group was Upton from the sewage reading plant, Crimmwall administrator Lumis Griggs, madame DeLany Thales, and flat-topped Jakksin, who Krill continued to throw threatening looks.

Still standing, Henley Chan placed two oversized hands with impossibly long fingers onto the conference table and leaned forward, as if absorbing the collected group for the first time.

"It is always good to be among friends. I rarely get to enjoy such an occasion." He threw an appreciative look at DeLany. "At least ones that are not artificially arranged. I apologize that I could not give more notice, but things have taken a turn at the Petal."

"A turn for the bad," asked Voss, clearly concerned.

Henley shrugged as would a dancer. "A turn is a turn. It can injure the unprepared but provide a beacon of light to the opportunistic. Do we have such opportunists in our midst?" As he finished the question, Henley gently settled his lengthy frame back into his chair. He aimed a too-long index finger at Viktor Krill. "You." His finger swung to Marlin Hadder. "And you." Henley's hand fell back onto the table. "You want to discover the location of the Flowers Institute?"

"We do," answered Krill.

"And why would you want to know such an awful thing?"

"We need to go there."

"And why would you want to visit such an awful place?"

Krill's black eyes flashed at Henley's green orbs. "To show the world that the New God is not a god at all. That his life can be forfeit just like anyone else's."

"And how will you prove that?"

"By leaving a puddle of gore where he once stood."

Henley remained quiet for a long while, silently studying Hadder and Krill, looking at them as if the rest of the world did not matter, as if the universe slowly rotated around those three entities.

Finally, Henley spoke. "I believe you. I will help you."

"Then you can tell us where Milo Flowers hides," asked Hadder, hopefully.

"I cannot."

"I told you that already," Voss cut in, annoyed that his words were forgotten.

"Then what good are you," said Krill, a bit more harshly than he intended.

Henley hesitated, but eventually responded, the words coming out as if pulled by force. "I can give you one of the very few people who do know."

"And who is that?"

Henley's emerald eyes shot over to Clinton Voss, desperately delivering an unspoken request.

Voss offered an almost imperceptible nod. "Except for Hadder and Krill, everyone out," he roared.

Even Zaza Anorrak, who looked ready to rain a string of curses down upon her Protector leader, eventually exited the conference room without a fuss.

————

"Do you know who my mother is?"

Both Hadder and Krill shook their heads in the negative to Henley Chan's question.

Henley did not look Hadder, Krill, or Voss in the eye as he responded. Rather, he stared off into the distance, as if pulling his response from a far away place.

"Her name is Xioxian Chan, and she is the CEO of Taragoshi Robotics. She is an astonishing woman, really. She started as a simple engineer with the company out of graduate school and climbed her way to the top, shattering glass ceiling after glass ceiling.

"The only thing she loved more than climbing the corporate ranks was my father, who put aside his own ambitions to fully support her and her lofty goals. He gave up a lucrative law career when I was born, determined to watch my mother advance, as he readily accepted all the domestic duties." Henley's green eyes developed a liquid coating. "Oh, how she loved him. Regardless of how busy she was, Mother always made time for father and me. She became the VP of Innovation, and then the Chief Technology Officer. Finally, she was unanimously voted as the next CEO when the heir apparent to the Taragoshi empire was found with three children at one of his many vacation homes.

"Mother was celebrated as the most powerful woman in the world, a shining example to little girls around the globe. Life was perfect. Our family was happy. And then disaster struck."

Henley paused for a moment to compose himself.

"My father fell ill. Cancer. Mother sent him to the best specialists, flew in the leading experts. She even contacted dozens of alternative medicine practitioners. But nothing worked. Father died six months after his original diagnosis. I was fifteen. Mother was crushed.

"Xioxian Chan threw herself into two things in her grief — her work and her son. When she wasn't burning the midnight oil at the office, she was obsessing over me. I think she saw my father reflected in my face, and was determined not to lose me. She smothered me, I rebelled. She abhorred my life choices, I doubled down on the drugs and the boys. She sent company security to watch my every move, I tried to evade them every step of the way." Another long pause. "Unfortunately, drugs and booze and a desperation to escape don't mix, and I ironically ended up wrapping my Taragoshi monocycle around a freestanding neon billboard of the company's newest six-door family offering. I died at the scene.

"The Taragoshi security team assigned to follow me arrived on the scene quickly, and I was medevacked within minutes and brought back to the land of the living. Unfortunately, not all of me was returned. I was alive, but left without the use of my arms or legs. I was a quadriplegic. And Mother was crushed once more.

"I was now twenty and a prisoner of my bedroom. Mother came to see me less and less. I don't know whether it was from disappoint-ment in me as a son, or a feeling that she failed as a mother. When she did visit, it wasn't to speak as things were, but as things could be when she found the right healer. I would walk again, something in which I was very interested. I would date so many beautiful girls, something in which I had no interest. Over the next year, Mother's rare visits grew increasingly manic, increasingly desperate. In her delirium, she became convinced that God would heal me, that her prayers would be answered. She would ask that I pray with her, and I will not repeat the dark promises that Mother made to the ceiling of my bedroom mausoleum.

"On my twenty-second birthday, Mother was visited by Doctor Milo Flowers, who had most recently and famously cured infamous Centrus Affiliation President Brayden Yorsaf's daughter of an inoper-able form of brain cancer.

"She welcomed him with open arms.

"After the first surgery, complete feeling had returned to my arms and legs. Within weeks, I was walking and running again. I even completed a marathon a month after surgery. Mother was beyond ecstatic. Her son had been returned to her, and Doctor Milo Flowers had become a long sought-after guru.

"Except Doctor Flowers quickly became more than a guru. He whispered things to her in the dead of night, told her his plans as the New God, shared how the world would be remolded in his vision for mankind. He begged her to test his power, asked what she wanted more than anything.

"Her response changed my life more than that monocycle accident ever could.

"I fell asleep one night in the comfort of my bed, and woke in the white sterility of a surgical room. I stumbled over to the first reflective material I could find and almost collapsed at what I saw there.

"Gone was my snub nose and my father's tan skin. Gone were my small eyes and short stature. A stranger stared back at me, someone I had no interest in being or getting to know. I was confused. I was angry. I had been betrayed.

"When I confronted Mother, she ignored my rage and waived away my protests, only too delighted to point out how much more attractive I now was and how women of prominence would be unable to resist my charms. She cared nothing for my clearly stated sexual preferences and asserted that the New God told her that this phase would pass.

"Female after female was sent after me by Mother. They arrived in my bedroom late at night, let in by Taragoshi security. They showed up at family dinners, touting their high standing in the societal upper crust. They surrounded me on the few occasions that I managed to muster the courage to venture out to a dim nightclub or intimate party.

"I was trapped.

"To combat Mother's overbearingness, I tapped into the one thing that she loved as much, if not more, than me — the New God. I told her that I wanted to dedicate my life to the New God, that I wanted to head up the Crimmwall Petal, which, at the time, was the next Petal slated to open to the public.

"Although disappointed in my decision not to give her a grandchild named after my father, Mother could not hide her excitement in showing the New God her absolute devotion by delivering her prized son as his newest convert.

"Fueled by anger and curiosity, I rose quickly up the Blossom ranks, undoubtedly accelerated by my mother's identity and my... distinct appearance. By the time the Crimmwall Petal opened its doors to the public, I was named its Arch-Soother, a title I must admit that I took very seriously."

For the first time since Henley had begun speaking, Marlin Hadder cut in. "Were you a believer, Henley? Did you follow the New God?"

Henley swung his too-bright eyes to Hadder, and for a moment, it felt as if lightning would appear from the ether, connecting emerald and hazel.

"I started out as an actor, playing the role of a lifetime. But if you playact long enough, the lines between the character and the person become blurred. Non-existent. If I am being totally honest, there was a time that I began to look upon the New God with love and devotion. After all, he was curing the ill. He was fixing the broken. He was working to make an ugly world beautiful. How could I not grow to admire him? How could I not begin to love him?"

"And what changed that?"

Henley's eyes reached for the conference room ceiling, as if he were searching back in time. "I discovered the truth, and there was no beauty in the truth, only horror. I found out what the New God is really doing with those he is saving. I was able to ascertain his plans for the world, and they are more terrifying than you can ever imagine."

Clinton Voss leaned forward on his massive elbows. "What are his plans, Henley? Tell us."

A sad smile took over Henley's perfect lips. "No, I don't think I will. Besides, I think Viktor Krill already knows the plans. And I think Marlin Hadder has had visions of those plans in action."

Voss turned to Krill. "Is this true?"

Krill shrugged noncommittally. "I have some deductions."

Voss spun to Hadder. "And you?"

"I have had some dreams."

As Voss's dark face assumed a mask of confusion, Krill directed a question at Henley.

"But how does he do it, Henley? We are, as yet, unclear on the delivery of this horror."

Henley thought for a moment. "I am not going to tell you."

"Why not?"

"It is better that you see for yourself."

"Then we need to gain access to the Petal."

"That is why I am here."

"It's not the only reason we need to get inside the Petal, Henley."

"I know that, Mister Krill."

"We need to find out where the New God is hiding."

"I know, Mister Krill."

"And you can help us with that?"

"I can."

"How?"

"Simple, really. You're going to threaten to kill me in front of my mother."

———

HADDER'S FACE twisted as he attempted to work it all out. "Xioxian Chan is the CEO of the world's largest robotics corporation. What is she doing at the Crimmwall Petal?"

Henley Chan gently pushed his hair back behind his ears with long, manicured fingers. "Making up for my shortcomings, apparently."

"Explain, please."

Henley placed both enormous hands on the conference room table, his numerous rings making a loud sound as they hit the aged wood. "One of the Arch-Soother's jobs is marketing and bringing in those who need the New God's... assistance. Every day, hundreds come to the Petal by bus, automobile, boat, and foot, requesting the

Holy Treatments of the New God. I thought our numbers were strong; we consistently ranked high among all the Petals for Holy Treatments.

"But it appears that this was not enough for Doctor Milo Flowers.

"A little while ago, the New God's closest advisors, composed of the world's most powerful individuals, were sent out to take over Petal operations, with a singular goal — significantly increase the numbers of the proselytes who pass through. And fast."

"Why," asked Hadder.

Henley shook his head. "I don't know for sure. But I would assume that the New God is preparing for his endgame."

"Which is?"

"You all know that already."

Voss cut in. "I assume that Xioxian Chan was among those close advisors appointed to a Petal. And, of course, she opted to be near her darling son."

"You assume correctly, Clinton."

Krill was obviously growing restless. "So, you sneak us into the Petal through the sewage system, we find your mother, hold a knife to her baby boy's throat, and she tells us where Milo Flowers is hiding. Sound about right?"

Henley adjusted one of the rings on his long fingers. "That would be the simplest plan. But I'm afraid it would fail to accomplish any of our objectives."

"How so?"

"First, the Petal's sewer access point is heavily guarded. The only reason that I am let through is that the Blossom guards think I am merely using it to clandestinely see boyfriends across the city."

Hadder shifted in his seat. "The New God has a problem with homosexuality?"

Henley waved the question away. "Of course not. But Arch-Soothers are holy entities; we're supposed to be above such worldly desires of the flesh. Plus, everyone knows that I don't want Mother to find out."

"We can take care of the guards," said Krill. "Easily."

"I trust that you could," replied Henley. "But the sewer entrance puts you at the lowest subfloor on the opposite side of the Petal from where Mother will be. You will have quite the trek ahead of you."

"I've carved my way through much more."

Henley laughed lightly. "I believe you, Mister Krill. I really do. But all it will take is one warning from one Blossom, one alert from one security system, and Mother will be evacuated from the building. You will lose your one chance." A heavy silence fell over the room. "Also, you won't get to see firsthand what is really going on."

"Milo Flowers is trying to conquer and pervert the world," said Hadder. "Isn't that enough to know?"

"I think the *how* is as important as the *what* in this case, Mister Hadder."

"And the *when*?"

"The *when* is now, Mister Hadder. The *when* was yesterday."

"All right, Henley," stated Krill, "how are we doing this, then?"

Henley's bright-green eyes flashed. "Easy. You both are going to walk in the front door. And I'm going to calmly take you up to Mother. Any questions?"

Every hand in the room went up.

"MOTHER IS CALLING it the Day of Sanctification. The idea was extremely well-received, so I assume that they will roll it out across all the Petals."

"What is it," asked Voss.

"On the surface, it is a simple marketing ploy to increase converts, making them think that they have had a real interaction with the New God. But I am afraid it is something much more sinister."

"Like what?"

"I don't know, Clinton. I was hoping these two could help me find out."

"What is the Day of Sanctification, Henley," repeated Hadder.

"Previously, Petals were only for those who needed some kind of healing. Cancer, nerve damage, paralysis, and heart issues come to mind. But not everyone is sick. Not everyone needs to be fixed or healed. What about those individuals?" Henley paused for dramatic effect. "So Mother created the Day of Sanctification. It is the one day a week that those who follow the New God can come and receive his divine touch... in a way."

"And what way is that," prodded Hadder.

"A massive shipment of wafers came in this morning, shaped as flowers. The New God supposedly personally blessed each one. They will be fed to those who come to receive the gift of sanctification."

"What is in those wafers, Henley?"

"I do not know, Mister Hadder, but I suspect."

"What do you suspect?"

"I suspect that one of you will find out when you take the wafer."

"And why would we do that? Why would we risk consuming whatever it is those wafers contain?"

Henley did not speak for a long while. His eyes searched around the conference room, as if he could find the words to say. When he finally spoke, he directed his words to Hadder and Krill.

"Doctor Milo Flowers's surgeries took much from me, including my sense of self. But they also gave me something in return — a sensitivity to the world around me. I have become a much more present, acute lover. Ask DeLany Thales about what her pleasure boys say about me. Many have offered to see me in their off hours, proposals I have rejected to save them from the inevitable punishment that would follow such behavior.

"But beyond becoming more attuned to my physical partners, I can sense things about others that I previously could not."

"Are you sensing something now, Henley," asked Voss.

"Yes. I sense that these two are not of this world. They smell different from any man I have met, and I have met many. I sense a vibration in their surrounding air, as if our world is trying in vain to account for their existence. Which is why I am entrusting them with this dangerous plan."

"Enough," declared Viktor Krill. "What is the plan, Henley?"

Henley's wide smile lit up his impossibly beautiful face. "I immediately liked you, Mister Krill. And your directness is why. This is a trait greatly lacking in the world of today."

"The plan?"

"Yes, of course. The very first Day of Sanctification will take place the day after tomorrow. As I said, the New God's stated goal is to see as many proselytes as possible. This means that there will be no identity checks, no paperwork issues, and no searches."

Hadder interrupted. "Wait a minute. You mean to tell me that they won't even be checking IDs at Crimmwall Petal? I find that hard to believe, Henley."

"Believe it, Mister Hadder. The New God does not care if you are wanted by the authorities. He does not care if you are not who you say you are. He does not care if your affliction is in your head rather than your physical body. He only cares that you pass through the Petal."

"Why?"

"Part of your journey is to find this out."

"So, I can bring my knives," asked Krill, solely focused on the mission.

"No," answered Henley. "There won't be much regarding security outside the Petal, but you will have to pass through several screeners that are searching for metal and explosives." Krill began to speak, but Henley cut him off. "But not to worry, I will have a blade concealed under my robes for you to use when the time is right."

Hadder was unable to contain his doubt. "You said it yourself, Viktor and I are the two most wanted men in the world. Are we supposed to believe that we will be able to walk unnoticed into the Crimmwall Petal?"

"That's correct," answered Henley. "First, you must know by now that the photo used for each of you is embarrassingly wrong. And second, and I hate to break it to you both, but the New God apparently doesn't find you that credible of a threat. He wants more people to flow through his Petals. Everything else is unimportant."

Hadder almost spoke again, but Krill cut him off. "All right, Henley. We just walk into the Petal. What then?"

Henley went on to explain in detail what would occur on the Day of Sanctification. He carefully addressed Krill's concerns and calmly acknowledged Hadder's frantic objections. When Viktor Krill had finally nodded his acquiescence to the plan, despite Hadder's loud protests, Henley Chan knew that he had completed his job.

"And how do we escape once this ridiculous play has reached its conclusion," angrily asked Hadder, clearly upset that his very reasonable concerns were being swept aside.

"You can leave that to the Protectors of Man," replied Clinton Voss as he rose from his seat to his great height. "You both have your marching orders. Now, if you'll please exit the room, Henley and I have other matters to discuss. Please send in the others on your way out."

"You've got to be fucking kidding me," declared Hadder, removing himself from his own chair. "If these *other matters* have to do with Viktor and I getting out of the fucking Crimmwall Petal, then I think it concerns us."

Clinton Voss shot Hadder a dangerous look. "It does not."

Hadder began to formulate another heated retort, but Krill's strong hand on his chest started to push him out of the conference room.

As the Wakened humans approached the door, Hadder finally managed to shake Krill off. "Get the fuck off me! We have a right to know how the fuck we're getting out of that nightmare with our lives!"

Krill responded to Hadder in a low tone that neither Henley nor Voss could hear.

"We have more important things to do right now, Marlin. You have more critical things that you need to learn."

Hadder mimicked Krill's hushed tone. "Like what, Viktor? What could be more important than this?"

Krill's black eyes cut into Hadder's own. "You want to learn how to identify and extract a foreign organism that has entered your body? You think that might be important moving forward?"

Hadder froze under Krill's words and gaze. "Yes, I suppose I will need to know that."

"Well, it's not learned in an hour. Let's go."

Hadder nodded to Henley and Voss. "And them?"

"Let's trust that they know what they're doing."

"And if they don't?"

"You've seen the sky, Marlin. Time's almost up on this world. And if putting my trust in strangers will get me closer to my vengeance, so be it. We're all corpses anyway." Hadder stared at Krill for several moments before finally nodding his assent. "Good, now let us get started. Ejecting a parasite is never easy.

"Even for a Wakened human."

———

DAKSHA WATCHED from just inside the doorway of the Holy Pistil. Attempting in vain to ignore the hundreds of strange experiments and stomach-churning vivisections being conducted by surgical mechs, the dark-skinned woman focused her attention on her God at the far end of the large circular room.

Or, to be more accurate, on the Chrysalis that temporarily housed her God.

Daksha had come to the Holy Pistil to deliver the good news about Petals across the globe adopting Xioxian Chan's wickedly clever plan to hold a Day of Sanctification. Daksha had actually sat on the update for a few hours, allowing her rival Nieve time to be the first to inform the New God. Despite Daksha being the New God's main contact for the powerful CEO, everyone knew that the socialite was on thin ice with Doctor Flowers.

Nieve could use a positive announcement to help thicken that on which she stood.

Unfortunately, Nieve was nowhere to be found, and Daksha felt that she could wait no longer. If her rival didn't want to collect the credit, Daksha would be more than happy to do so in her absence.

Additionally, Daksha wanted to report that Anton Carlyle was utilizing all the resources of his Maxim Global Media empire to push out constant messaging about the Day of Sanctification. With his television stations, news outlets, websites, and social media subsidiaries, Carlyle was successfully driving consumers around the world to one of the Flowers Institute's satellite locations for the upcoming day of celebration. Daksha's contacts in various national intelligence agencies already reported mass movements, with traffic in and around Petal locales increasing twentyfold in some cases.

The Day of Sanctification would be a great success, perhaps one large enough to initiate the Great Conversion.

Daksha wanted nothing more than to share this with her Lord, but found that her feet would not move her any deeper into the Holy Pistil. As the woman continued to stand just inside the doorway, she watched as the Chrysalis violently vibrated, something she had never seen it do before. The two frightening surgical mechs to either side of the New God's cocoon continued to poke the Chrysalis with long needles, injecting chemicals across the color spectrum deep into the worm-shaped encasement. All the while, the dozens of tubes that connected the Chrysalis to the main computer consistently pumped substances into the New God, delivering whatever constituted food for the divine.

As Daksha stared in awe at her transforming Lord, her eyes went wide as light began to leak out from cracks in the Chrysalis, sending strange shadows to dance across the Holy Pistil and its dark experiments.

A scream that broke out from one of the many still-conscious subjects strapped to metal tables pulled Daksha from her paralysis. Taking in the scene one last time, Daksha decided that now was not the best time to interrupt the New God.

For, indeed, it seemed that her Lord was approaching the precipice of Theosis, which would directly follow the Great Conversion.

Another scream caused Daksha to jump.

Daksha took one final look around, telling herself that this was all part of the plan, that no one ever said the journey to godliness would be easy or pretty.

Another scream, another jump.

A thin cloud of mist began to cover Daksha's bright eyes as she had to face a frightening truth. Three months ago, if you had asked her if she would be on the right side of history regarding the Great Conversion, there would have been no doubt in Daksha's response before declaring the questioner an infidel.

Now, although still a fervent believer, doubt would be detected in the woman's answer, if only a microscopic seed.

But seeds of doubt germinate quickly and grow even faster, threatening to rip the harborer of such feelings in half from within.

Daksha violently shook her head, mimicking the movement of the Chrysalis, driving away such impious thoughts. Instead, she focused one last time on the light pouring forth from the grotesque cocoon. Daksha thought about how that light would soon shine on the entirety of the world, bathing the poor and sick in a warm bath of divine love, finally leveling the playing field for all of humanity.

Daksha smiled as this vision took over and expelled the dark thoughts that threatened her love of the New God. She blew an authentic kiss at the shaking Chrysalis and turned to leave the Holy Pistil.

Another scream followed her into the hallway.

———

MARLIN HADDER EXITED the first of several training sessions with Viktor Krill, his Wakened body feeling more like a vehicle that he commanded than the physical component of his being. Hadder shivered with his new knowledge, finding it simultaneously grotesque and enlightening.

I really fucking hope it doesn't come to that, he thought as he marched across Haven Falls in a haze.

The massive chamber was as empty as he had seen it, with some Protectors resting in the residential add-ons and others having returned to their regular lives and jobs. Hadder's stomach growled angrily as he stumbled along, attempting to shake the cloud that took residence across his Wakened brain upon Krill's concluded lesson.

Luckily, one of the few Protectors still out was the slim Teo, who was once again manning a grill of various smoking meats. Teo silently offered Hadder a seat in one of the empty folding chairs that surrounded the grill. The Protector must have noticed Hadder's disheveled look and elected to remain quiet, as he always did. Hadder was beyond appreciative.

Without speaking, Teo took a sausage off the grill, placed it onto a bun, and decorated it with a tangy orange sauce that was popular in this world. He handed Hadder the meal on a metal plate, who returned a sincere nod in thanks. A few minutes later, Teo made a sausage for himself and sat down.

Together, the two men ate in silence.

Hadder's eyes fixated on the cascading water as he finished his meal. He reveled in the blank trance that he entered, so different from the deep concentration required for Krill's control exercises. Within minutes of stepping into that absolute void of thought, and aided by fatty sustenance, Hadder's mind became clear and light.

"Thank you, my friend, I feel much better" said Hadder, and the quiet Teo simply nodded in welcome. "It looks like we're the only ones out here."

Teo shook his head between bites of sausage, pointing his chin to Hadder's right.

Hadder looked, and found Henley Chan exiting one of the residential quarters, moving toward him and Teo. The Arch-Soother seemed to glide along the cement, so fluid were his movements, especially for one of that impressive stature.

"May I join you gentlemen," asked Henley as he approached, his sing-song voice reminding Hadder of Su Anorrak.

Hadder moved a chair out for Henley as Teo jumped up to prepare another sausage.

"I thought you would have returned to the Crimmwall Petal by now, Henley."

Henley carefully settled his oversized frame onto the small folding chair, resulting in a humorous display. "There is a Protector here that I favor, although he is not ready for his identity to be known. I like to spend as much time with him as possible. Anyway, the Day of Sanctification will require a tremendous amount of effort on my part to pull off. The Blossom guards, and even Mother, understand this and know that I was going out to... recharge my batteries, if you will. As long as I am back in the next twelve hours, no fuss will be made."

Henley readily accepted the sausage from Teo and dug in, taking massive bites that sat in stark contrast to his feminine qualities.

"Hungry, Henley," asked Hadder jokingly.

Henley waited until his mouth was empty of food before replying. "My secret amore makes me work for every bit of our love, which is part of the attraction, of course."

Hadder smiled at Henley's good mood, despite a twinge of longing stinging his insides. After allowing the Arch-Soother time to eat in peace, Hadder could no longer hold his tongue.

"Henley, can I ask you a question?"

"Of course, Mister Hadder. I will answer as honestly as possible."

"I don't understand."

"What don't you understand, Mister Hadder?"

"Any of it. The New God. The Petals. I don't see how an entire world can go mad like this. I don't understand how such an obvious lie can be believed by millions, maybe billions."

Henley set his metal plate down on the hard ground, giving him a moment to consider his response. Finally, he locked his emerald eyes onto Hadder's hazel orbs.

"You know, my name is not really Henley."

"It isn't?"

"No. My real name is He Chan. Mother had a premonition that I would be born a girl, and so she had the name picked out long before I came into this world. Turns out, He can be for a boy or girl, although it tends to steer into the feminine." Henley laughed lightly. "Perhaps even Mother had a sixth sense of the man that I was destined to become."

"What does this have to do with my question, Henley?"

"*He* means *lotus flower* in my mother's native language. So, when she was most in need of help, when it looked as if the world was against her, who just so happened to appear but Doctor Milo *Flowers*. With his lotus insignia branded on all of his tools and brochures, Mother was certain that he was sent from above to not only fix her broken son, but to heal a diseased world.

"Of course, to you and me, this story is a series of random occurrences. It's bullshit, if you will. But to my mother, it was as if the cosmos had finally answered her prayers, and who was she to question the form that her miracle took."

"And you took the name Henley, why?"

Henley snickered, as if seeing himself playact before the trio. "I told her that it was so I could sound more ethnically neutral in my role as Arch-Soother. But, really, it was a subtle rejection of the New God and his twisted vision of the future. A minuscule slight, to be sure, but one that brings a grin to my face during some especially dark moments."

Hadder turned in his seat to face Henley. "While interesting, this still doesn't answer my question."

"But it does, Mister Hadder. You see, people in great need, desperate for help from the heavens, can draw straight lines to those who appear before them with divine answers. It doesn't matter that those lines cross borders of morality or even sanity. So hungry are these people for direction, for a greater purpose, for a reason to live, they will gladly surrender their friends, family, and even themselves." A pause. "This world is sick, Mister Hadder. It has been for some time now, perhaps since the Great War of several decades ago. For a long time, the people of this existence have thirsted for leadership beyond the corrupt politicians, business tycoons, and financial institutions that have driven us headlong into oblivion." Another pause. "Let me ask you, was I correct in my assessment that you and Mister Krill are not of this world."

Hadder didn't hesitate. "You are, Henley."

"Perhaps that has led to your confusion. This is not your world; therefore, you can look upon it with a relatively objective eye. You see the faults more easily and readily than those of us who know nothing more. I would turn the question back at you, Mister Hadder. Would you recognize a similar malady in your own world? Are you so confident that your own world was not afflicted with such a spiritual malaise."

Hadder tried his best to formulate an adequate response, but none would come.

Ultimately, Henley Chan rose from his seat and placed a giant hand on Hadder's shoulder. "I'm confident this is not what you want to hear, but you and Mister Krill really are the only hope for his world. Follow my instructions on the Day of Sanctification. And when the time comes, follow my lead. Do exactly as I say, when I say it. I do not pretend to be smarter than you or Mister Krill, but I have thought over this plan a thousand times. It is our only chance at discerning the location of the Flowers Institute. The clock is ticking, Mister Hadder. I just hope that there is still time left. I will see you in the Crimmwall Petal." Henley began to glide off. "Teo, it is always a pleasure to interact with a man of your verbal restraint." Teo simply nodded.

Goodbyes concluded, Henley Chan walked across the bridge spanning the central river and made his way toward one of the many tunnels leading to the broader sewer complex. As Henley exited, three Protectors of Man came out of hiding to follow the Arch-Soother, ensuring the invaluable man's safety as far as possible.

Henley's words spun through Hadder's mind, creating a whirlwind that threatened to shred what little was left of his mind. He looked everywhere he could for support, but only found silent Teo, who was starting in on his second sausage.

"So, apparently I'm this world's only chance, Teo. Which is going to require me marching headlong into the lion's den and readily giving myself up to the enemy. And this is after I surrender myself to two more of Viktor fucking Krill's exercise sessions that threaten to turn me inside out, spilling my fucking guts out onto the cold cement. What do you think about that, Teo? What am I going to do? How the fuck can I possibly get through these next few days of hell?"

Teo thought for a moment before nodding his head in silence. He rose, went to the grill, collected and dressed another sausage, and handed it to Hadder with a wide smile.

Hadder accepted the gift and noted a loud groan from his stomach, which was more than happy for additional sustenance.

"Thank you, Teo. And you're right, maybe another sausage is all I need."

14

Marlin Hadder and Viktor Krill found themselves in the middle of a sea of converted Blossoms of the New God. Although the sun was just beginning to appear above the Great Water's horizon, already tens of thousands of loyal followers of Doctor Milo Flowers stood before the massive Crimmwall Petal. Dumb faces dotted the landscape as all waited patiently for the imposing structure to open its doors to those seeking the blessings of the New God.

The infant rays of the new day struck the simple white robes of those in attendance, bathing the entire field of pilgrims in a warm, reflective light. For many, this offered reassurance that their dedication to the New God was the only path to salvation and enlightenment.

All around Hadder and Krill, a potpourri of accents, dialects, and languages could be heard, a testament to the reach of the Blossoms' marketing and communications team. Representing a cross-section of genders, races, and nationalities, the people spoke to each other in hopeful, hushed tones, as if the volume of their words could potentially break the spell cast over the converts.

Krill pulled at his own white robes, obviously uncomfortable and missing his Station garb.

"I swear, if they do not have my suit ready upon my return, someone is going to pay," complained Krill, scratching at his neck and chest. "And every one of my blades better be accounted for."

"No one wants to take your shit, Viktor," replied Hadder.

"You do."

Hadder simply nodded in agreement, as he often found himself desirous of Krill's Station suit and its otherworldly material. "Look on the bright side, at least you got to hang on to your beloved Verratos."

Krill looked down at the black and white high-tops given to him by his adopted son Darrin. "I'd like to see god itself try to take these from me. The *real* god."

Hadder leaned in. "Maybe we chill out on the real god stuff, huh? This doesn't seem the place for it. I'm sure you'll agree."

Krill waved Hadder away between scratches. "These idiots are too self-involved to hear anything but their own moans and pitiful pleads." The villain laughed dryly. "I mean, they don't even see what is clearly right above their heads."

Hadder's hazel eyes reactively shot up, landing squarely on the pink ball that hung heavy in the morning sky like a guillotine blade. It had grown significantly in size since Hadder and Krill had entered Crimmwall's sewers, looking more and more like an accusatory eye by the hour.

Hadder looked deeply into its pink center, as if engaged in a staring contest with a celestial being, until Krill's words ripped him from his trance.

"Something is happening, Marlin."

Hadder tore his gaze from the pink asteroid and glanced over at the Crimmwall Petal. The imposing tearlike structure's white stone pulsed gently in the morning breeze. A moment later, small vibrations could be felt emanating from the massive building, sending ripples throughout the three large reflecting pools that sat between the Petal and the considerable crowd.

Hadder and Krill watched as the elegant stonework shifted and morphed, creating four large arched entryways into the Petal, one to each far side and two others near the middle. As the crowd stood in collective wonder at the moving stone, a familiar voice emanated from the Petal and echoed across the gathered masses.

"Welcome! Welcome! Welcome! The New God welcomes each and every one of you. He is overjoyed by seeing you all gathered here on this Day of Sanctification. Each of you should congratulate yourself on making the best decision of your life, the best decision for your soul and the souls of those that you love and hold dear.

"Please slowly make your way forward and listen closely to the instructions of the Junior Soothers in attendance. Heed their words! They are here to ensure that you all receive the Holy Touch in the most efficient manner as possible.

"Do not push! Do not squabble! Do not give in to anger, or jealousy, or frustration! The New God loves you all. And we will not close this day until each and every one of you receives his Holy Blessing.

"I look forward to seeing you all in the Great Cathedral after you receive your blessings and healings. All praises to the New God!"

As Henley Chan's voice cut off, Petal representatives wearing white jumpsuits and obnoxious lotus-shaped hats made their way through the crowd, barking orders.

"Those with illnesses, injuries, or other maladies, move toward the left two arches to receive Holy Treatment. Those simply seeking the Divine Touch, please make your way to the right two arches. More instructions will be given as you approach the Heavenly Pools!"

These words were repeated over and over again by the Junior Soothers as they weaved in and out of the large crowd. As they exited an area, an excited electricity fell over the collected pilgrims.

Soon after, the crowd began to surge forward in waves. Despite the sheer numbers in attendance, Hadder was shocked to find very few disputes, verbal or physical, among the moving mass of white-clad converts.

Hours passed, with Hadder and Krill entering a Wakened reverie to both conserve energy and more quickly pass the time. Eventually, another surge forward brought the companions to the edge of the reflecting pools, where a line of Junior Soothers stood, some with thick Taragoshi reams in their hands.

As they closed in on the Crimmwall Petal, Hadder was able to zero in on the house of worship, noting things that he was unable to see previously. Appearing on each side of the Petal were white conduits that hugged the pale stone and ended in fat cylinders that were interspersed with wide vents.

At first glance, nothing appeared to be radiating from these vents, but as Hadder tapped into his Wakened vision, he noted millions of tiny particles pouring forth from the openings.

"Viktor, are you seeing this?"

"I am. I assume this is the cause of the strange taste in the air, not only in Crimmwall, but across this cursed world."

"And you think this strange taste serves any purpose?"

Krill shot an angry look at Hadder. "Of course it does, don't be foolish. The Petals are purposely polluting the air with something foul, supporting some evil plan of the New God."

"Can you feel it in your lungs, Viktor?"

"Of course I feel it. I can feel everything that occurs in my body, Marlin. And so can you, you Wakened idiot."

"What do you feel, Viktor?"

Viktor closed his eyes for a moment before responding. "I feel nano-sized triggers inside me, waiting to detonate a bomb that has yet to be set." He opened his black eyes. "Another puzzle piece falls into place, Marlin."

"Would you like to fill me in on what that piece might look like?"

Krill ignored Hadder's request. "I think this is where we must separate, Marlin," stated Krill matter-of-factly. "Remember our lessons. I truly hope you don't need to use what you learned. If one of us gets to the Great Cathedral before the other, just wait in the back for the other's arrival. Any trouble and you kill, but kill quietly. I imagine a great many will be passing out based on sheer statistics. It shouldn't be hard to hide a death within all of this false life."

Hadder simply nodded, not knowing whether this would be the last time he would see Viktor Krill again. "Take care of yourself, Viktor."

Krill nodded in return. "You, too, Marlin. We are gods among a sea of worms. Never forget that."

Hadder rolled his eyes as he started to move to the right, following the plan that he, Viktor, and Henley laid out. As he did, an uncomfortable nervousness began to permeate his body. Moving through the mass of white-robed bodies, one thought kept repeating in Hadder's mind.

Why did Viktor Krill have to use the word *worms*?

———

"What's your ailment," asked the Junior Soother impatiently, apparently already weary of the Day of Sanctification.

"Degenerative condition of the right knee," replied Krill with his rehearsed words. "I won't be able to hold my job much longer."

The Junior Soother's face remained blank as he keyed something into his oversized ream, as if he couldn't be less excited to hear Krill's story of woe. After an uncomfortable shared silence between the two men, the Taragoshi ream spit out a long yellow plastic bracelet from its add-on printer.

"Right hand," declared the Junior Soother, and Krill offered his arm. The Junior Soother connected the bracelet around Krill's wrist and spoke again as he ushered the notorious killer away. "Head to Arch 2, that's the second arch from the left. Do not go into Arch 1! That is for more advanced maladies, not your... inconvenient knee."

Krill began to form a sarcastic retort, but the Junior Soother had already moved on to the next pilgrim, forgetting that a man with black eyes even existed.

Krill chuckled to himself. He had to admit that, despite his doubts, Henley Chan was right. The Blossoms of the New God weren't even taking the time to check IDs or certify illnesses.

Doctor Milo Flowers, better known as the New God, did not

consider Marlin Hadder and Viktor Krill real threats to his ascension to singular messiah.

Krill smiled darkly, vowing to prove his fellow Station Key wrong.

———

MARLIN HADDER USED his Wakened vision to zero in on individuals in the distance. Despite his heightened abilities, however, Hadder was unable to locate Krill among the ocean of bodies waiting to be healed by the New God.

Hadder analyzed the two massive groups that had formed as pilgrims approached what were known as the Heavenly Pools. The collection of converts that required physical healing appeared only one-sixth the size of those who had come to simply receive the Divine Touch.

Hadder stood there for nearly an hour, analyzing the speeds with which both the right and left groups surged forward. He tried his best to determine the time at which he and Krill would both finish their grisly tasks and arrive in the Great Cathedral.

For those simply looking to receive the Divine Touch, even bracelets were not necessary nor given out. It seemed that the New God's love knew no bounds. He was opening his arms to the world, accepting all into the bosom of his limitless compassion.

Hadder quickly ran the numbers in his Wakened brain. With any luck, Krill and Hadder would find themselves in the Great Cathedral within no more than one or two groups from each other, which would prove critical to the plan.

"Do you feel it, young man?"

Hadder looked down to find the source of the scratchy voice. There, he found a small bald man in an oversized white robe, looking up at him with sharp brown eyes.

"Feel what, sir?"

"The New God is here among us. I feel his grace coursing through these old bones. Once I receive his Divine Touch, I will be able to die a happy man."

Hadder was unable to contain his curiosity. "Tell me, sir, what brings you to the New God," Hadder asked, using every bit of his Wakened skills to keep the disgust and ridicule from his voice.

A thin layer of liquid coalesced on the old man's brown eyes. "My wife of forty years died several years ago from the cancer. A little time ago, my son died in a monocycle accident, followed shortly thereafter by my daughter, who was poisoned by a nasty new drug called Slink. Together, they left me five grandchildren to watch after. I'm not a rich man, and I'm not in the best of health. But I'm not dying either, goddammit! I aim to be around for a long time for those kids. The old God did nothing for me and my family when we were most in need. No miracles were bestowed, despite our staunch belief in His goodness and greatness." A quiet pause followed. "He brought me nothing but sadness, loneliness, and confusion. And now He is dead to me. The New God has done more for those in need in one year than the old God did across millennia. I came here to say my thanks. I came here to receive His Divine Touch." Another pause. "And you, young man? What brings you to the New God?"

Hadder looked up once again at the pink asteroid sitting above the world that only he and Viktor Krill could see. It seemed unrelenting, unforgiving, and undeterred in its path toward the planet on which Marlin Hadder now stood. Hadder spoke to the sky, as if he were addressing nothing more than the whisper of a ghost.

"I don't know where else to go," stated Hadder.

"Amen," cried the old man from below.

———

AFTER A WHILE, Krill found himself only in the company of those with yellow wristbands as they moved forward toward Arch 2, the Junior Soothers sending in groups of twenty-six at a time into the Crimmwall Petal. Approximately thirty minutes passed between groups of pilgrims herded into Arch 2, whereas Arch 1 batches took almost an hour for more serious conditions to be addressed.

As Krill tapped into his Wakened abilities for what was to come, a soft bell rang out from Arch 2, signaling the next batch, Krill's group, to enter.

As Krill slowly passed into the shadow of the ornate archway, he was greeted by the soft chimes of the hidden metal and explosive detectors as they cleared him, and was immediately assaulted by the overwhelming smell of fresh flowers. His olfactory nerves hummed and a wave of euphoria threatened to overtake Krill as he marched into a large waiting room of white marble that contained an exotic garden on its edges.

Krill watched carefully as the flowers shot their nearly invisible spores into the waiting room air, calming the crowd with beautiful odors while forcing the release of serotonin from all in attendance. Krill took a moment to enjoy the sensation, understanding that he could block any unwanted effects on command.

Another Junior Soother entered the waiting room from the main Petal.

"May I have your attention, please! In just a second, I am going to ask that you move into the Petal in pairs. Those on the left, please enter the first open surgical room on your left. Those on the right, do the same for the first open room to your right. A door with a white hand means it is open; those with red hand prints are occupied. When you enter the room, simply lie down on the metal table and try to relax. A Surgical Soother will be in shortly to administer your anesthesia and complete your procedure. When you awaken, you may be a bit groggy, so please be careful in getting up walking for several minutes. Any questions?" Numerous hands went up, but the Junior Soother ignored them. "Great! Let's get moving. All praise the New God!"

Pairs of pilgrims began to exit the white waiting room. Krill studied the flowers as he waited his turn, not recognizing a single one from his time in this world. He did, however, recognize some flora from another place, a city between worlds.

"Sir," called a young woman with an obvious deformity that turned her right foot inward at a horrible angle. "Shall we?"

Krill put on his best fake smile for the white-robed woman and joined her in moving deeper into the Petal.

The young woman and Krill passed nine sets of occupied rooms until two doors with white hands appeared to Krill's left and right.

"Best of luck with your procedure, mister. All praises to the New God." With that, the woman limped off and entered the surgical room on the left.

Krill nodded at the young woman's back, and for a moment almost felt happy for her. She would leave the Crimmwall Petal walking normally for the first time in her life, moving without the fear of hearing a disparaging remark from strangers on the periphery. She would leave the Crimmwall Petal with renewed confidence and vigor.

Unfortunately, if Krill's suspicions were correct, she would be leaving with a lot more than an improved foot and enhanced ego.

Krill placed his hand on the white imprint and watched as the door slid open silently, revealing a small surgical room with a metal table in its center. As he entered, Krill noticed that the flower smell did not follow him. Instead, it was replaced by the antiseptic dead air that accompanies most medical environments.

When the hallway door closed silently behind him, Krill took that as his cue to climb atop the metal table, propping his head up with a small pillow that was provided. He waited there for several minutes before another door opened on the opposite side of the room, through which a Surgical Soother walked wearing white scrubs, a matching apron, and a white face mask.

The Soother said nothing as she crossed the room, pushed Krill back onto the cold metal, and scanned his yellow bracelet with her slim medical ream.

"Right knee trouble. Correct?"

"Correct," answered Krill simply.

"Shouldn't take long. Pull your robe up." Krill complied. "I'm going to deliver a sedative. It'll put you under, but not for long. When you wake with the others, your knee troubles will be a thing of the past. All praise the New God."

"Absolutely," responded Krill, unwilling to repeat the Soother's words aloud.

The woman nodded, pausing at Krill's black eyes for a moment, before retrieving a syringe from her white apron and injecting its contents into Krill's arm.

Almost immediately, Krill felt the powerful anesthetic course through his veins, pushing him toward unconsciousness. His black eyes rolled into the back of his head as his heavy lids closed. His body fell into oblivion as he heard the Surgical Soother's soft clogs echo across the sterile room as she exited.

Just as Viktor Krill stood on the brink of a deep slumber, his Wakened abilities came to life, neutralizing the strong chemical and pulling him back into a state of alertness. As this occurred, Krill made sure to control his heart rate and breathing to keep up the appearance of a man fully under the cold grip of anesthesia. Krill barely opened his eyes, peering between the slits and through long eyelashes.

Krill then smiled inwardly, quite pleased with his ability to disguise himself as a man dead to the world.

That disguise, however, was almost ruined as Krill nearly jumped at the sounds of motors whirring to life to either side of his metal table. He quickly wrangled control of his heart rate and breathing, seconds before two large Taragoshi surgical mechs rose from beneath the floor to tower over the prone Krill.

One mech wrapped a sleeve around Krill's left arm to monitor his pulse and blood pressure, while the other mech used a medical laser cutter to make a small incision across Krill's right knee.

It took all of Krill's Wakened faculties to compartmentalize the pain, locking it away in a place that did not affect his pulse and breathing, thereby maintaining his unconscious ruse.

A thin camera scope shot out from the right Taragoshi mech and began to slide around under the tight skin of Krill's knee. After only a few seconds, the scope withdrew and a metallic voice echoed across the small room.

"Assistance required in Medical Unit 20."

Moments later, the wall closest to Krill's feet temporarily shimmered before transforming into a large screen displaying five Surgical Soothers sitting at a desk as if part of a review committee. The Soother in the middle spoke.

"What seems to be the issue?"

The metallic voice rang out once again. *"Patient claims to have a degenerative condition of the right knee. A scope of the area has been completed. No degenerative issues can be detected. Analysis finds a perfectly functioning human knee. Waiting for instructions."*

"Probably just another wacko who thinks surgery is the only way to receive the New God's touch," said the middle surgical Soother.

"I think he has missed the point of the Day of Sanctification," said another Soother, and all five laughed in unison.

The middle Soother spoke again. "Here are your instructions. Continue with implantation. Do nothing else. Sew him up, leave a scar. This one will want to see where the New God touched him."

"Affirmative," answered the surgical mech as the display returned to a simple white wall.

Krill continued to spy through thick lashes as the righthand mech delicately held open the incision on his right knee. The left mech then swung into action, maneuvering a small glass tube until it hung just over the exposed bone of Krill's kneecap.

Krill's Wakened eyes zoomed in, closer and closer, and then closer again, until he could make out the dark speck floating within the vial's clear liquid.

Sonovabitch, thought Krill as the tiny creature finally came into focus, a visitor from Krill's dark past, a constant reminder of the villain that Viktor Krill used to be.

Krill watched in horror as the glass tube was upturned and the nearly microscopic Slink slid out and fell into his exposed flesh. The Slink wiggled around for a second before burrowing itself into the pink meat surrounding Krill's kneecap. As it disappeared, Krill had to clamp down on a powerful nausea that threatened to empty his stomach.

As soon as the Slink disappeared, the right Taragoshi mech closed the incision with a clear medical glue and wrapped Krill's right knee in gauze followed by a white elastic medical bandage.

Their tasks complete, both surgical mechs sank back into the floor to either side of the metal table. Krill waited in uncomfortable silence for several minutes before the table on which he laid jumped to life, rising several inches just before a loud *clang* could be heard from beneath.

Just as Krill was about to lose patience, the table spun on an invisible track and began to move toward the wall opposite of where the notorious killer had entered. As the table approached the white wall, a slot opened up and allowed it to pass neatly through and into a large recovery area, where dozens of metal tables carrying unconscious patients were similarly entering and parking.

As the metal tables formed neat lines in the room, Viktor Krill closed his eyes and turned his attention inward, where he could feel the alien Slink swimming around inside him, searching for a place to find permanent purchase. Krill tapped into his Wakened abilities and reached out, communicating with the tiny Slink to decipher its purpose.

"What is your goal here," asked Krill.

"I wait," replied the Slink in a language that was not a language.

"Wait for what?"

"To be awakened."

"And then what?"

"I am free."

"Not on my watch, parasite asshole."

"You cannot stop me. This body is mine now."

"We'll see about that."

Viktor Krill then went deeper inward, wresting control of every blood vessel, every nerve, every cell of his Wakened body. He found the Slink in short order and commanded that it be driven from his body. Blood cells rushed to the attack, forcing the invader along arteries and through tissues. The Slink fought valiantly, but was no match for the unified effort of a Wakened organism. On and on it was pushed, through fat and muscle and into skin, where it was squeezed out through one particularly large pore.

Krill's black eyes went wide as he came out of his inward-looking trance. He looked around to find dozens of others coming out of their own chemically induced sleeps before discreetly pulling up his robe to uncover his right thigh.

There, six inches above his cleanly wrapped knee, a barely visible slug-like creature writhed around on tan skin, working to find its way back into the warmth of a human body.

Krill reached down and pinched the creature between his fingers, smearing its brownness across his fingertips, terminating its ability to find another host.

Krill let out a breath as the Slink died, his head heavily hitting the pillow, exhausted from the surprisingly difficult internal battle.

Viktor Krill's worst fears had been confirmed. The New God was implanting biological bombs in those who had come seeking his assistance.

Looking around once again, Viktor Krill no longer saw innocent pilgrims desperate for help. He was no longer surrounded by pitiful men and women too stupid to know that they were mere puppets in Doctor Milo Flowers's dark game.

No, Viktor Krill now sat in the middle of a viper pit, among monsters who were yet to be born. Each person who passed through the Crimmwall Petal on this day was destined to become a nightmare that would help wipe humanity from the world.

Krill then prayed, but not to any higher power or omniscient being. Viktor Krill prayed that Marlin Hadder would remember his lessons.

And prevent himself from joining the ranks of horror.

———

AFTER WHAT SEEMED like an abridged eternity, Marlin Hadder finally came upon the Heavenly Pools and began to approach the Crimmwall

Petal's right-side arches. Hadder looked down as he passed the reflecting pools, using his Wakened eyes to look below the bright surface. There, thousands of tiny white squids with twisted human faces paraded along the pool's alabaster bottom, invisible to almost all those walking above.

Hadder pushed down a shudder and continued on, his gaze locked onto what the Junior Soothers pointed out to be Arch 3. He had begun to ignore the ramblings of the pilgrims surrounding him, so tired was Hadder of hearing about the greatness of the New God.

The Rage starting to stir within, and Hadder fought the urge to grab every white-robed visitor within reach, pulling them in close to scream in their faces – *He's a cunt! Don't you see? Your New God's a cunt!*

Instead, Hadder simply shuffled forward, his line now moving at a consistent pace.

Another fifteen minutes passed, Hadder entered the shadowed entrance that was Arch 3. A series of beeps denoted that each pilgrim crossing the threshold was free of weapons and explosive devices. Just beyond the archway, an enormous marble room opened up, allowing the pilgrims to join any one of a dozen smaller lines. These lines led toward the back of the cavernous space, where three room-length white steps led to a landing that traversed the entirety of the back wall.

Upon this landing, twelve Soothers stood draped in ornate ivory robes that were covered in sparkling blue and white stones. Massive collars stitched with designs depicting the New God rose from the robes to surround and tower over the heads of the Soothers, conjuring images of perverse angels preparing to spit vile lies.

Each of the Soothers had too-blue eyes set within too-white faces above too-tall bodies that reminded Hadder of Henley Chan's too-perfect appearance. They all bore the masks of the insane.

Hadder was busy studying the strange marble statues that were scattered across the great room, depicting men, women, and children in various of stages of explosion, ostensibly from the New God's powerful touch of love, when someone from behind shouted.

"You're up!"

Hadder shook himself free of the gruesome images, shocked that they seemed to bother no one else in attendance, and returned his attention forward.

There was no longer anyone between Hadder and the Soother before him. She looked down on Hadder from her great height atop the landing and gently beckoned him to approach.

As Hadder slowly climbed the three steps, he noticed that the towering female Soother carefully balanced a golden container in her left hand. She spoke in a gentle, caressing voice that made Hadder reflexively want to do her bidding and earn her love.

"Kneel, my child. The New God is here now with you. He loves you more than you could ever imagine. Kneel, and receive the Divine Touch, which is the physical embodiment of His love for you, His promise that He will forever be with you. Receive this holy gift and swim in the ocean of sanctification. You are forgiven of all sins and misdeeds."

While every fiber of his Wakened being screamed for him to flee, Hadder did as he was told, kneeling before the awe-inspiring Soother. He peered up with wide hazel eyes, doing his best to cover his panic with a false look of veneration. As he did, the Soother reached into her golden jar, removed something, and swung it to Hadder.

Hadder opened his mouth as the Soother's massive hand approached. Between fingers that were tipped with long white lacquered nails, the woman held a small cream-colored wafer in the shape of a lotus flower. She placed the wafer gently onto Hadder's tongue and softly stroked his chin, prodding him to close his mouth around her divine offering.

"Your life has officially begun anew. Now go and listen to the words of the Arch-Soother, for he will impress upon you the importance of this gift and how you can best serve this new world. Go with the New God, my child."

With that, Hadder rose, nodded to the exotic woman, and walked past her on the landing, where there was space behind the Soothers to walk along the back wall toward the room's massive double-doored exit.

Hadder walked through the giant open doors and into another

large chamber that was filled with white marble benches. It looked as if thousands of pilgrims waited there with dumb smiles painted on their awe-struck faces as they stupidly tongued the wafers that were glued to the roofs of their mouths.

Junior Soothers walked throughout the room, gently making the same announcement.

"Please find a seat and rest for a moment. Bask in the Divine Touch of the New God. Luxuriate in the glory of sanctification. The Arch-Soother will see you after he completes his present sermon."

His pulse starting to race, Hadder found a seat along the wall of the giant waiting area, leaned back, and closed his eyes. Perspiration began to form around his temples and across his brow as Hadder turned inward, terrified of what he would find.

The outside world fell away, including sights, sounds, and smells, as Hadder used his Wakened abilities to look inside himself. There, he found the wafer that was given to him by the female Soother. He watched in horror as the wafer broke down from his saliva, freeing a tiny slug-like creature that immediately sprung toward the back of Hadder's throat. It then traveled down his esophagus and into his stomach before Hadder could do anything to stop it. Once in the stomach, the creature began to burrow into the organ's lining, working to find purchase in a less acidic part of its host's body.

Hadder used his Wakened control to push aside the encroaching panic and recalled his recent lessons with Viktor Krill. Relatively stagnant neurons flashed to life as Hadder requested... no ordered, that his body comply with his demands. These neurons transmitted specific instructions to Hadder's muscles, tissues, and individual cells, all receiving the same message.

Expel the foreign organism!

Cells quickly located the minuscule slug and began to surround it, pushing it through tissue and muscle. Hadder's breathing intensified as the creature fought back, biting at individual cells and clearing a path for escape.

It dove deeper into its host, desperately seeking areas that were even beyond Hadder's Wakened control. Sensing an inert area that

Hadder could never reach, the slug shot forward, sprinting past the guardian cells.

The creature sped on, and would soon find a permanent home within Marlin Hadder. All was lost.

Just as Hadder's cells had given up the fight, the Rage came on like a tsunami of fire. It pushed the cells forward on a wave of fury, driving them past the advancing slug, helping them to once more surround the trespassing organism.

Reinvigorated by the Rage, the cells latched onto the slug and moved as a singular entity, pushing it past other cells, through tissue and muscle, and toward the first pore they encountered. With a great collective effort, the wormy creature was forced into the fatty layers of skin, where it was pushed, and pushed, and pushed, and pushed.

Hadder's eyes popped open, and he inhaled deeply, unaware that he had been holding his breath. His chest rose and fell heavily as Hadder, now entirely covered in perspiration, quickly gathered his white robe in his hands and lifted it to his chin, exposing his underwear and bare chest.

He looked down just in time to see a tiny, almost invisible brown worm grossly exit the skin around his lower ribcage. Hadder carefully scooped the creature onto his right index finger and brought it closer to his face. As he did, his breath caught in his throat and his stomach churned angrily.

Slink. Always fucking Slink.

Hadder furiously squished the Slink between his fingers and allowed his robe to fall back toward the hard floor. He wiped his brown-stained fingers onto his clothing, staining its perfect whiteness, and ran a hand over his sweat-soaked hair.

Slamming his wet head back against the marbled wall, Hadder noticed a pale-skinned man with a wispy mustache sitting next to him, staring with wild eyes.

"Do you feel it, too, friend? The Divine Touch, I can feel it coursing through my body. Everything's going to be different now, don't you sense it? We're sanctified! The past no longer exists, only the present and future is real." The man reached his arms out.

"Embrace me, friend! Let's run arm and arm into the reality of our new world!"

Hadder's fist shot out like a piston, driven by the Rage and the Wakened human's general disgust of his temporary neighbor. The jawbone beneath the tips of the pilgrim's long facial hair shattered as Hadder's knuckles connected, sending the man's dull brown eyes into the back of his head just before his lids dropped like anchors, signaling unconsciousness.

Hadder cursed silently under his breath, upset by his outburst. Looking around, however, he was relieved to find that no one had taken notice, so self-involved was each pilgrim with the feeling of their Divine Touch.

"Attention pilgrims! The Arch-Soother will see you all now! Please proceed in an orderly fashion into the Great Cathedral!"

Marlin Hadder rose unsteadily to his feet, relieved to have rid his body of Milo Flowers's parasitic Divine Touch. As everyone slowly made their way to the elegantly arched double-doors that had opened on the far side of the room, an old woman attempted to shake awake the man with the shattered jaw. Hadder placed a hand on her bony shoulder.

"Let him rest, ma'am. For some, the intensity of the New God's touch requires a long respite."

"But he'll miss the Arch-Soother's sermon," argued the old woman.

"I'm sure he'll wake for the next one, ma'am."

Something in Hadder's hazel eyes softened the woman's stance. She nodded before patting Hadder's hand that still rested on her thin shoulder. "Yes, of course, he will. He's lucky to have a friend such as you looking out."

"Yes, ma'am, we are all fortunate, are we not? Nestled sweetly against the bosom of the New God?" Hadder motioned toward the exiting crowd. "Shall we?"

The old woman's face threatened to cleave in half from the smile that appeared. She gladly took Marlin Hadder's upraised arm. "Yes, we shall. Thank you, young man. You know, I already feel like a different person. I can't wait to hear the Arch-Soother's holy words. Perhaps he can shed some light on why I feel so different after the Divine Touch, on what sanctification truly means."

Hadder simply nodded at the old woman, biting back the words that he really wanted to say to her and everyone else in attendance.

Yes, of course you feel different! Because you are no longer men, women, and children! You are nightmares! You just don't know it yet!

15

H adder's jaw fell a bit as he entered the Great Cathedral. The colossal standing space was soaked in an array of colors from the ornate stained-glass that danced dozens of meters above the growing crowd.

Staring in amazement at the beauty of the light show playing out above him, Hadder stumbled among the excited masses, which must have numbered in the thousands.

Tearing his eyes from the elaborate glass, Hadder looked around and concluded that most of the Crimmwall Petal's bottom floor must be comprised of this very room.

Pilgrims continued to pour through the eight massive double doors that lined the Great Cathedral's sides, quickly filling the room with a sea of cow-faced Blossoms of the New God.

Hadder looked over that ocean of living bombs and found a huge raised dais at the front of the Great Cathedral, bordered on both sides by massive thirty-foot crystalline statues of Doctor Milo Flowers, also known as the New God.

Hadder shook his head in disgust at the images of Milo Flowers before feeling his eyes drifting inexorably back toward the myriad of colors floating restlessly a hundred feet above.

There, outlined neatly in colored glass, Hadder saw it — a winged angel, hand gripping a glowing knife, was being whipped in the face by an unseen force hiding in the cloudy sky above. Hadder studied the image for a long moment, convinced that it was tugging incessantly at a memory from another life in another world.

"Remind you of something?"

If not for the recognizable voice, Hadder would have jumped out of his white robe. He looked down to find Viktor Krill standing next to him, dark circles under his eyes matching the blackness of the orbs themselves.

"You look like shit, Viktor."

"You should look in a mirror, Marlin. I assume you were gifted with an old friend?"

Hadder nodded tiredly. "Fucking Slink again."

Krill returned the nod. "Except in a much more dangerous form, with a much more sinister purpose. And you were able to successfully extract it?"

Hadder wiped more sweat from his brow, as if even recollecting the recent ordeal was a strain on his Wakened body. "I was, but it wasn't easy. And I feel gross, as if it left a trail of slime inside me."

Krill's black eyes flashed with understanding. "Well, it's out now; that's all that matters."

"Have you been waiting long?"

"Luckily, I only had to hang out for one additional sermon. I don't think I could tolerate listening to another of Henley's ridiculous speeches."

"No one gave you any shit for not leaving with your group?"

"One tried. We don't have to worry about him anymore."

Despite the dark implications of Krill's words, Hadder could not help but crack a grim smile. "What now?"

"Now we execute Henley's plan. And hope that his resolve is as strong as his words."

———

HENLEY CHAN TOOK the raised dais with all the pomp and circumstance that one would expect from an Arch-Soother of the New God.

As what would be akin to this world's classical music boomed across the Great Cathedral, piped in from hidden speakers, Henley Chan looked out onto the thousands who represented the newest official converts of Doctor Milo Flowers. Wearing an elegant robe that put those of his fellow Soothers to shame, Henley began to speak beneath an enormous white hat, known as a *miter* in Hadder's world, that mimicked the lotus leaf shape of the Crimmwell Petal itself. Between the raised dais, his abnormal height, and his miter, Henley Chan absolute towered over his congregation, every bit the image of the right hand of God delivering His message to the masses.

"Congratulations to each and every one of you," said Henley, his soft, sing-song voice vibrating through the Great Cathedral, as if he spoke directly into the ear of each person standing in attendance. "On this Day of Sanctification, you all have been touched by His Holiness the New God, making you all His children, allowing you all to bask in the light of His eternal grace. On this special day, some of you received the New God's Holy Treatment, ensuring that the rest of your days will be lived unfettered and pain free. Others of you received the New God's special blessing, the Divine Touch, marking you as one of His own and granting you permission to forever drink from the fountain of His never-ending love. You are all now official Blossoms of the New God, but what does that mean? To hold the New God close to your heart means many things…"

Krill slapped Hadder on the shoulder. "Let's start moving forward. It will take us a while to get through all these bodies without attracting too much attention. And I can't listen to any more of this bullshit."

Hadder bounced his head in affirmation and began to follow his companion through the den of biological grenades.

Dumb-faced Blossoms stared up wide-eyed and slack-jawed at the Crimmwall Petal's Arch-Soother as they swayed gently back and forth, Henley's voice acting as charmer to the plotting snake within them.

Krill pushed men and women roughly out of the way, forcing his way forward, Hadder trailing close behind. Most ignored the physical assaults, too enamored with Henley's words to react, but some took offense and voiced anger. Those that did found themselves with crushed larynxes from blinding blows, rendering them mute and unable to even point out their assailants, for Hadder and Krill had already moved on.

As Henley Chan droned on, the Wakened humans glided through the crowd like two crocodiles moving silently toward the water's edge, where a young man was kneeling to collect a drink.

When they began to approach the raised dais, Krill gave Hadder a look and the two split off. The companions reached the front of the congregation simultaneously, one to Henley's left and the other to the Arch-Soother's right. There, they waited for the signal hidden within Henley's speech.

Henley continued on, and Hadder noticed that his raised dais was flanked on each side by a dozen Blossom warriors in white battle fatigues. "Now that you have been told what is expected of you, are ready to serve the New God?"

The audience exploded into a singular "Yes" and the Arch-Soother paused before continuing.

Henley Chan swept his emerald eyes across the gathered pilgrims. "I see the love of the New God in many of you. Some of you will return to your communities, where you will help to spread the word of the New God. Some of you will join Blossom missionary groups, bringing the love of the New God to the far corners of the world. And others of you, the most fervent of believers..." Henley paused for dramatic effect. "Perhaps there is a place at the New God's side for you!"

Henley's words had their desired effect as eyes went wide, screeches escaped lips, and excited hugs were shared among the congregation.

Henley continued. "Who among you is steadfast enough in your dedication to the New God that you are worthy of a spot in His home?!" The Great Cathedral erupted in response, with pilgrims begging to be selected for a position of authority within the Blossoms. Henley smoothly held up an oversized hand to temper the crowd's excitement. "Yes, I know you *all* would like to suckle at the bosom of the New God, but that is simply not practical. We need eyes and ears and voices and fists *out there* as much as we need assistants *in here*. Most of you are more valuable to the New God as the carriers, the army, and the juries of His divine word. But a select few of you..." Another pause as Henley dragged his gaze across those in attendance for a moment before his green eyes opened dramatically. He pointed a too-long finger at a young woman to Hadder's right. "You! You, miss, have the sparkle of the New God in your eyes! Will you join us?!"

"I will join our Lord," the woman cried, tears streaming down her face.

"And you," Henley went on, this time to a middle-aged man behind Krill. "I see where the New God has touched your soul! Are you prepared for a life in his service?!"

"I am, Lord! Oh, how I am!"

And this continued, with Henley Chan using his divine *sight* to handpick pilgrims worthy of high-ranking positions within the Blossoms. Two more women and another man were selected before Henley pointed to Viktor Krill.

"You, sir, I see love of the New God coursing through your veins! Are you ready to meet him?"

"I've never wanted anything more," shouted Krill in return, forcing Hadder to shoot his Wakened partner a look of warning.

Three more young women, an elderly man, and a child were then addressed before Henley's exotic stare found Marlin Hadder.

"And you! I can feel that you are already connected to the New God in ways that most could never be! Are you prepared to work directly for His Holiness?!"

"I am ready," Hadder called back. "I have always been ready!"

Henley Chan held Hadder's eyes for a moment longer before turning back to address the entire congregation. "You have *all* been presented with wondrous gifts on this Day of Sanctification. Your pasts no longer matter, only your love for and dedication to the New God remain. Go! Spread His message! Serve Him! Do that, and He will forever serve you! All praise the New God!"

As music once again filled the Great Cathedral, a chant of *All praise the New God* appeared on each pilgrim's lips as everyone began to exit through the two mammoth doors that had opened in the back. Several minutes would pass before those in the front could turn and leave.

Before that happened, however, the Blossom warriors standing guard had moved forward in practiced precision, grabbing up Krill, Hadder, and the others selected for a "higher calling" by the Arch-Soother.

"Come with us," was all that was said as the lucky few were pulled from the crowd and led to a small doorway that was hidden behind the raised dais.

The twelve pilgrims, including Hadder and Krill, were shoved unceremoniously into a small but comfortable room, complete with white couches and love seats that surrounded yet another statue of Milo Flowers. Four of the Blossom guards joined the pilgrims, each with rare Taragoshi laser pistols attached to their hips.

While Hadder and Krill mentally prepared themselves for what was to come, the ten other selected pilgrims were absolutely buzzing about their good fortune.

After several minutes, many of which Krill spent contemplating killing everyone else in the room, Henley Chan finally entered, his shoulder-length blond hair in full view as his miter had been removed.

"I would like to take this opportunity to thank you all for your love for and loyalty to the New God. Our Lord is excited to gain so many more disciples on this glorious day. But He is especially grateful for those of you in this room because you are the chosen few who will push His message of love from one of the New God's many homes. Are you ready to serve?"

Everyone in the room enthusiastically expressed their readiness.

Henley smiled sweetly. "Wonderful. Now, if you will, please follow these Blossom escorts into the next room, where you will each receive your holy assignments. And do not worry, they only *look* like they bite."

Everyone got up and anxiously made their way to the door on the far side of the room, to the right from where they entered. Henley gently pulled at Hadder and Krill's arms from behind.

"If you two would kindly hold back for a moment. I have a special assignment for a pair such as yourselves."

Confusion appeared on the faces of the Blossom guards, and one spoke up. "That's, uhh, not on the schedule, Arch-Soother. We need to keep these groups moving. There will be another…"

Henley Chan spun toward the outspoken guard, rage simmering beneath his emerald orbs. "Do you think I do not know of the importance of today? Do you think I don't know when my next sermon is due? Do you?!"

The guard shrank under the towering Henley. "I didn't mean anything by it, Holiness. It's just that we have many pilgrims to serve today."

"Which is why I need a break, *guard*. I am scheduled to work non-stop through the Day of Sanctification. Certainly, the New God would not deprive me of a small refresher so that I may better serve His incoming crop. Why would you?"

The guard held up his hands in surrender. "Of course not, Arch-Soother. You attend to your holy… needs. The next sermon is scheduled thirty minutes from now."

"And I will be there, of course, as the New God wills it. Now be gone!"

The guard nodded in acquiescence and began to follow the other pilgrims into the next room, shooing the other three guards out as he did.

As soon as everyone had cleared out, Henley moved quickly to close and lock the door behind the group. He spoke to Hadder. "Make sure that the door to the Great Cathedral is locked."

Hadder did as he was told and gave a thumbs up when the marble door knob would not turn. He met Krill and Henley back in the center of the room. "What the hell was that about? I thought you wanted us to sneak away later."

Henley shrugged. "I reconsidered the plan. This is simpler."

"And what is this," asked Hadder.

"They think Henley is going to fuck us," answered Krill.

"That is a crude way of putting it, Mister Krill." Henley turned to Hadder. "But, yes, they think we are going to fuck each other. My nocturnal activities of late, thanks in no small part to DeLany Thales's pleasure boys, has given me quite a bit of notoriety around Crimmwall Petal. So, I thought it best that I put a bad reputation to good use."

"It makes sense," stated Krill. "Now what?"

Henley Chan moved to one of the couches against the wall and raised the cushions, revealing white garments underneath. He collected these and tossed them to Hadder and Krill, in turn.

"Take off and hide your pilgrim robes. Put on these Junior Soother jumpsuits."

"Where are the hats," asked Hadder.

"They don't wear them in the Petal. Now please hurry."

In short order, Marlin Hadder and Viktor Krill wore the garb of a Junior Soother. Henley checked them both over, making small adjustments.

"Good. Good. This should do nicely. Now listen, we are going to calmly make our way through and up the Petal to where Mother's office is located. One of you walk on each side of me, always three steps behind. Don't speak. Junior Soothers don't speak in the Petal unless spoken to first. Keep your heads high and look like you belong here."

"Knives."

Henley looked to Krill. "What's that?"

"I was promised knives."

"Oh, how could I forget?" Henley dug into his ornate robe and pulled out three small blades. He handed them over to Krill. "I assume that these will work?"

With a flash of his hands, Krill made the blades disappear into his jumpsuit. "They will."

"Good. Now let us go forth. Mother awaits."

Henley took five steps toward the door opposite of where the other pilgrims exited before stopping. He spun to face Hadder and Krill.

"Mother loves the New God. She's a true believer. She loves Him more than anything in the world, except maybe me."

"That's what we're counting on," replied Hadder.

Henley struggled to find the words. "What I mean is… she will not give up Milo Flowers's location easily."

"I'll cut it out of her easily enough," said Krill.

"No! You don't understand. Mother is among the toughest people on this planet. Her own pain and death will not be enough. You have to be willing to hurt me."

"No problem," said Krill.

"No, you still don't understand. You may need to be prepared to kill me."

Hadder stomach's churned, releasing a great sound of protest. In his short time with Henley Chan, Hadder grown to like and respect the young man. Harming him would take a…

"I said, no problem," reiterated Krill, his tone leaving no doubt as to the veracity of his words.

———

THE INTERIOR of the Crimmwall Petal was a hive of activity. Henley Chan smoothly glided through the chaos with Marlin Hadder and Viktor Krill in tow. Hadder and Krill remained three paces behind the Arch-Soother, their eyes always pointed toward the marble floor.

Stealing glances when he could, Hadder was amazed by what he saw. As the trio walked, they quietly passed into the heart of the New God's concerted promotional efforts.

To the right, a massive chamber was filled with Blossoms sitting at computer terminals. Here, countless hours would be spent spreading the gospel of the New God across social media, infecting every corner of the global network with the false messiah's poison.

To Hadder's left, rows of Junior Soothers sat in training, learning how to utilize best-practice missionary skills. Hadder used his Wakened hearing to listen in and found the excitable young speaker to be extolling the virtues of classical sales techniques.

Farther down the hall, groups of artists and writers worked on creating impactful imagery and accompanying tag lines that would pique the curiosity of young and old, regardless of gender or socioeconomic class.

Just before reaching the bank of elevators at the long hallway's end, Hadder peeked into the windows of a pair of substantial double doors. He watched as several actors paraded across a set, no doubt making some kind of putrid commercial pushing the Blossoms' dark agenda.

Curious eyes followed Henley, Hadder, and Krill as they advanced, but no one was prepared to invoke the ire of the Arch-Soother. Hadder wondered what Blossom punishment looked like before recalling poor Patton Yellich. *And that is why no one steps out of line*, he thought grimly as they reached the large set of lifts.

Henley ignored the many sliding doors that lined both sides of the hall and strode confidently to the last elevator on the left. Unlike the others, this lift's doors were made of gold, with an oversized palm reader jutting out from the wall beside them.

Henley placed his massive but soft right hand onto the reader and waited a moment before it chimed sweetly. The golden doors slid open silently, allowing the Arch-Soother and Wakened humans in before closing behind them.

Hadder immediately noticed two things as the lift sped upward. One, there was only a single floor to which this elevator traveled. And two, that floor looked to have been hastily renamed. Where the original floor placard read *Arch-Soother Residence*, a second placard had been placed next to it reading *and Executive Suite*.

"Looks like the upper floor got a bit more crowded," commented Hadder.

"Yes, Mother required the use of my office and the... guest bedroom. Heaven forbid, she uses one of the other hundred offices on one of the other two dozen floors."

"What can we expect up there," cut in Krill, always one to get down to brass tacks.

Henley thought before answering. "Not much. I like my privacy and have worked hard to ensure that it is respected. Mother is up there, of course, and her longtime assistant Henrietta, a universally detested old woman who has ratted out innumerable employees over the years."

"How are they situated," asked Krill, continuing to gather intel.

"Mother will be in the office suite, no doubt, and Henrietta will be set up at a desk just outside the entrance, a pit bull standing guard before its owner's house. She... could be an issue. Henrietta's immediate reaction to anything out of the ordinary is brute force, and an armed contingent of Blossoms is always stationed on the floor below."

"Anything else," prodded Krill.

"That's all," responded Henley.

"Then we are ready," declared Hadder, tapping into his Wakened abilities to find a calm before the ensuing storm.

"Not yet," said Henley. "There is a change I would like to make to the plan. If Mother thinks we are in cahoots, she will let me die and take the New God's location to her and my graves."

Krill nodded. "Then we will show her what you truly are. A pawn in a dangerous game between gods."

———

As the golden doors opened onto the top floor, Henley Chan calmly slid out, flanked on both sides by lowly Junior Soothers who kept their eyes glued to the floor below.

Henrietta, wearing thick glasses atop even thicker makeup that only worked to accentuate her advanced age, noticed the visitors immediately as her desk stood but twenty feet from the elevator.

She stood up on creaky, hose-covered knees, displaying a suit that must have cost tens of thousands of credits, compensation for a life of servitude. Henrietta took in Hadder and Krill, and her lipless mouth curled down as if she had ingested sour milk. Her voice was that of a lifetime smoker, gravel spread across concrete.

"He Chan! What, in the name of the New God, are you doing up here? Today, of all days, is *not* the time to be giving in to your more disgusting primal urges. This is the Day of Sanctification, and you are supposed to be delivering the word of the New God, not swapping bodily fluids with two Junior Soothers. This is your mother's special day! Just wait until she hears about this. I've seen some distasteful things in my life, but this takes the cake. I have a mind to…"

Viktor Krill shot forward, a blur against the white backdrop, closing the distance between himself and Henrietta in a flash. Moving faster than normal eyes could follow, Krill backhanded the old woman in the face, sending her soaring into the gently curving wall to her left. Henrietta caused a loud crunching sound when she struck the white marble, leaving web-like cracks, and fell into a heap on the floor below, her shattered jaw hanging grossly from her painted face. Krill considered running a blade across the unconscious woman's throat, but decided it unnecessary.

The old girl wouldn't wake up for hours.

"You ready to act," asked Krill as Henley and Hadder joined him before the office suite doors.

"My whole life has been acting, one way or another. Let's go."

————

XIOXIAN CHAN WAS COMPLETING her Day of Sanctification projections when the oversized doors to her office exploded inward, forcing her to jump from her plush seat.

Before she could properly react to the intrusion, her son was forced into the room, bent over harshly with a knife at his delicate throat.

"He Chan! What is going on?!" She looked at Viktor Krill, whose tan hand held the blade at her son's neck. "What is the meaning of this? Do you have any idea who I am? Who *he* is?"

"I'm sorry, Mother," wailed Henley, tears streaming down his too-perfect face. "The enemy has infiltrated the Petal! Give the heathens nothing! Nothing! I beg you!"

Xioxian Chan's angular features softened as she looked upon her helpless son. "Do not speak, my son!" She then turned her attention to Hadder and Krill. "Anything you want. I will give you…"

The Taragoshi Robotics CEO's arm jabbed forward mid-sentence, her index finger diving for the emergency button residing in the ornate table at which she stood. Inches from success, the woman flew backward, a painful light swallowing her ability to see. When her vision had finally returned to her, she found herself against the back wall, the knife once held against He Chan now hilt-deep in her shoulder.

Xioxian Chan was also no longer alone, as the hazel-eyed intruder now stood next her. The man ripped the blade from her shoulder, drawing out an audible moan, before lifting Xioxian from the floor with impossible strength. He tossed the woman unceremoniously into the center of the large office, where the Arch-Soother was already on his knees. Standing behind her son, a black-eyed man in Junior Soother clothing lazily danced another blade along He Chan's robed shoulder.

Xioxian Chan rose to her knees and met her son's green eyes with her dark brown orbs. After a subtle nod, she shifted her attention to Hadder, who had moved to stand above her.

"What do you want? This is a house of worship, not a bank, although I doubt the two of you could tell the difference." Xioxian's voice was confident, and her words perfectly annunciated, proof of decades living and working among the world's elite.

"Doctor Milo Flowers. Where is he?"

Xioxian almost managed to keep the surprise from her face. "How would I know?"

"You are Xioxian Chan, the CEO of Taragoshi Robotics. You are one of Doctor Flowers's earliest, most loyal, and most powerful followers. We know you are a member of his inner circle. Tell us where he is, and we can avoid further unpleasantness."

Xioxian smiled wickedly. "You think a lot of me if you believe that I am arm in arm with the New God. I assure that even I do not have that kind..."

Hadder's fist smashed into the CEO's nose before she could finish the lie, sending a fountain of blood cascading to the floor. Xioxian grabbed at her face, cursing through blood, snot, and tears.

Hadder's hope for a quick resolution, however, was dashed when, mere moments later, Xioxian spat upon the floor and began to laugh. She looked up at him through a crimson mask.

"Who are you to think that you can stand against the New God? Fools! He is the *New God*! He can bring life where there is death. He can shatter the limitations of the old gods. You are worms beneath Him."

"If we are no threat, then you might as well tell us where he is."

Another glob of bloody mucus flew from Xioxian to smack the marble floor loudly. "Fuck you. Kill me. My God can do worse than you could ever imagine. I would rather die than betray Him."

Hadder let out a disappointed sigh before signaling Krill, who pulled back violently on Henley Chan's blond hair. The knife rose to hover dangerously over the Arch-Soother's face.

"Mother, please! Give them something, anything," Henley pleaded. "I cannot die yet. Our work is just beginning."

Krill watched closely as Xioxian's determined scowl began to soften under the cries of her beloved son. Her dark eyes sprung back and forth as the brilliant woman attempted to run through scenarios in her mind, searching for a way to save her son while protecting the New God.

After a few seconds, Xioxian's eyes focused ahead and a slight grin appeared once more on her thin, bloody lips. She looked up at Marlin Hadder.

"Marlin Hadder and Viktor Krill, I presume." Hadder offered the small woman a slight bow. Xioxian laughed dryly. "I should have known. Our sketch of you is a poor rendering." She shifted over to

Krill. "And we have the entirely wrong photo of you." Back to Hadder. "In any case, congratulations on getting this far, but you will get no closer. My loyalty to the New God is like steel, and I don't think you have the stones to do what needs to be done to break me."

"You know, Miss Chan, I think you're right. I don't have what it takes. But *he* does."

Henley Chan, who was no longer acting, screamed into the air as Viktor Krill put the point of his knife to the Arch-Soother's face and neatly plucked out the beautiful man's beautiful green eye. The emerald orb swung grotesquely on long, glistening nerves as its owner howled in pain and horror.

Xioxian Chan, seeing her only son maimed, began to crack. "Oh, my son! Do not fear! The New God will fix you, as He did before! Do not cry, my son! We will rebuild you again! The New God will bring you back!"

"Where is the Doctor Flowers," demanded Krill as he pulled back even harder on Henley's head, making the dangling eye dance drunkenly before the Arch-Soother's horrified mother.

"Block out the pain, my love! The New God will bring you back again!"

Krill lowered the knife to Henley's exposed neck. "Tell me, Miss Chan, will the New God be able to bring him back without a head? Because it is coming off next."

"Mother, please," cried Henley once more, and this time he sounded as if he really believed that Viktor Krill was prepared to decapitate him.

Because Marlin Hadder knew that Viktor Krill *was* prepared to decapitate him.

"I can't! I can't!"

"Fuck this," said Krill. He began to draw his blade across Henley's neck, leaving a deep crimson line in its wake.

"The Isle of God! The Isle of God!"

Krill's blade paused.

"Not its fucking code name," Hadder yelled at the despondent woman. "The name, the real fucking name!" There was no response. "Cut his fucking head off, Viktor!"

"No, no, no! Wait! The Forlorn Islands! The Forlorn Islands!"

While Hadder's face twisted, Krill spoke, his hand becoming drenched in Henley Chan's blood. "The Forlorn Islands? You mean the Neelsen Islands?"

"Yes, yes, yes! The very same! Now, please, release my son! I beg of you!"

"You know of the place," Hadder asked Krill, hopeful to be finished with this gruesome scene.

"I have read about it. Terrible place."

"It is the home of God, you heathen trash! Now release my son!"

"Do we have what we need, Viktor?"

Krill nodded. "We do." With a twitch-like flick of his wrist, Krill returned the blade in his hand to one of the many pockets on his jumpsuit. With another quick movement, Krill collected Henley's dangling eye and pressed it back in place in its now-bloody socket. He leaned into Henley's ear. "It may take some time, but vision will return to that eye. Be patient."

Despite Krill's reassuring words, Henley Chan broke down into tears and brought his giant hands up to cover his face.

"Don't cry," remarked Krill as he stepped away. "It will only extend the healing time."

"Get away from him," angrily screamed Xioxian Chan as she scooted forward on her knees to embrace her son. "I gave you godless bastards what you wanted, now get away from my son!"

Krill nodded to Hadder, who returned the gesture. As the Wakened humans began to back out of the office, Hadder called out.

"Henley, are you coming?"

And just like that, Xioxian Chan's cries stopped, as if they were turned off by a valve. She pushed her son to arm's length. "What did he say?" To Hadder. "What did you say?"

Hadder ignored the woman. "Henley, if you're coming, we need to leave. *Now.*"

Xioxian Chan's face twisted in rage as she turned her attention back to her son. "Why is he asking you to come, He? He? What the hell is going on? Why would you ever go with them, He? Answer me!"

"I'm sorry, Mother," said Henley, one eye leaking tears while the other released a blood-tinged ooze. He rose to his full height and towered over the small woman. "I have to go now."

As Henley turned to go, Xioxian's anger came on in full force, her eyes full of wild fury while her thin lips spewed vitriol.

"Yes! Yes! Go! That's all you were ever good for, He – running away!" Henley halted his escape. "Oh, how Father would be horrified by what his only son has become. Sometimes, I thank the New God that he died so that he doesn't have to bear the indignity of his son's embarrassing choices."

Henley's perfect head swung back to face his mother. "That's not true. Please don't say that."

"Say what? That you were a disappointment as a boy? That you were a disappointment as a teenager? That you still manage to disappoint daily?"

Henley turned back, his body starting to quiver under his ornate robe. Hadder and Krill look at each other with growing concern.

"Disappoint? I am the Arch-Soother of Crimmwall Petal!"

Xioxian released a bitter laugh. "And you think you *earned* that title? Even my idiot son cannot be *that* stupid! Everything you have, including your place next to the New God, is because of *me*! And look what you've done with my gift; you've used it to stab me in the back. To stab the New God in the back!"

Henley's voice came out in a whisper. "I earned my role here at the Petal. I am... I was a good Arch-Soother."

Xioxian's teeth began to show through an evil smile. "You were shit. You *are* shit. I know it. Father knew it."

"Don't say that."

Hadder cut in. "Henley! Don't listen to her. Let's go."

"Yes, go with your new friends," spat Xioxian. "Do you let them fuck you, too? Like all the other street trash that you spend time with?"

Henley's head began to fall. "They are just friends..."

"Sure, they are. Like those friends you sneak out to see at night? I know everything! Father knew it, too! He knew what his son would become. His shame brought on the cancer! His humiliation fed the malignant tumor!"

"Don't say that!"

"Say what? That we all knew you were a failure? You know, when you were lying broken in that hospital bed, I cursed the old god. Not for destroying your body, but for *not* taking your life, leaving me with an even more burdensome son. Oh, how I wished that you had died on that monocycle!"

"Please don't say that!"

"Oh, but it's true! And then the New God came along, and promised to rebuild you. And He did! And then He promised to make you better than ever, better than any son who had ever lived. And He did! And what did you do with the New God's gift? You used it to have sexual relations with even more garbage, darkening your mother's already black eye!"

"Please!"

"You have squandered every gift you have been given! Every night I thank the New God that Father is gone. I thank the cancer that took him so that he doesn't have to see what his son has become. I thank…"

A primal shriek fell from Henley Chan as he lunged forward, his giant hands wrapping around his mother's neck, cutting off her ugly words. The older woman fell backward and Henley climbed on top, words coming out of his thick, rose-colored lips in a language that no one could understand.

Hadder moved to separate the pair, but Krill held him back with a hand on his chest and a shake of his head, as if to say, *stories need to play out for sequels to be written.*

Xioxian's face reddened as tears fell upon her from above. Her eyes bulged and began to match her skin as capillaries bursted under the strain. A heavy silence fell over the office suite, interrupted only by an occasional gurgling sound that escaped from the cold marble floor.

After a minute that dragged on for an eternity, Henley collapsed onto his dead mother, his entire body heaving in sorrow that only accompanies a certain type of anguish.

Unfortunately, Marlin Hadder knew those feelings only too well.

Hadder gave Henley as much time as he could before grabbing the young man's arm. "Henley," he said gently, "we have to go, my friend."

Henley took a few moments to normalize his breathing before nodding sadly. The young man placed a soft kiss atop his mother's forehead before rising to his feet with Hadder's help. Together, they made their way to the office suite's exit door, which was now closed. Krill nodded to Henley as the Arch-Soother approached.

"Whether it was you or me who did it, it needed to be done. If it's any consolation, you're all probably dead already; you just don't know it, yet."

"Viktor!"

Krill held his hands up in surrender. "Just trying to make the kid feel better."

"Try less. Let's go."

Krill turned and opened the office door, only to dive out of the way with inhuman speed, taking Hadder and Henley Chan to the floor with him.

As he did, gunshots rang out from the hallway and bullets ripped into the office suite.

"What the fuck is that," asked Hadder over the sounds of marble chunks cascading to the hard ground.

"Goddamn Henrietta," said Krill as he got off the pair and pulled them to the side, away from the opening. "The old bird has a shotgun. I knew I should have slit the bitch's throat." He stuck a finger in Hadder's face. "I'm tired of you talking me out of what needs to be done! That's the last time!"

"Fair enough," Hadder conceded, understanding that this was not the time or place to engage in moral debate. "Just get rid of that old hag."

Krill took a position next to the office's large open doors, placing his back against the wall. He snuck a peek around the door's frame and was greeted with another round of shot.

Henrietta's gravelly voice assaulted the trio from the hallway, although she could barely be understood through her shattered jaw.

"Come out, ya bastards! Ya scared of old lady?!"

Despite their dire situation, Viktor Krill began to chuckle. "I'm starting to like this old girl."

"She's trying to kill us," reminded Hadder.

Krill waved him away. "Who isn't?"

Henrietta's barely comprehensible words returned.

"If ya too chickenshit now, just wait until backup arrives. Oh, yes, I called 'em already, ya bastards! Ya dead men, ya bastards! Dead! Men!"

Krill continued to giggle by the door.

"Viktor!"

"Ok, ok," said Krill, who withdrew his lone knife, grasped it by the blade, and held his breath, which Hadder recognized as a technique for tapping into Wakened abilities.

Viktor Krill slowed time. Large pieces of marble fell from the back office wall and slowly descended toward the hard floor. Krill could hear Henrietta's pruny finger rubbing anxiously against her shotgun's trigger. He could feel her small chest rise and fall anxiously in the tense air. He pinpointed her location without even seeing her.

Krill spun off the office wall and into the open doorway, where he released his blade mid-turn before continuing his spin, finishing behind the safety of the wall on the opposite side of the entrance. Just as Krill vanished from the entry, another round of projectiles tore into the office, ripping more marble from the ceiling and walls.

His back still against the wall, Krill held up a fist and counted out three fingers. When he reached three, the audible sound of a body hitting the floor emanated from the hallway.

"Let's go!"

Hadder, who knew not to question Viktor Krill, pulled Henley Chan to his feet and followed the notorious killer into the Petal hallway.

There in the corridor, still gripping a shotgun in her bony hand, was Henrietta, a knife buried neatly into her forehead. Krill offered a small bow to the fallen old woman.

"With a hundred of her, I could have taken over the world. Where to?"

"My bedroom is at the end of the hall. Make for it," said Henley Chan, and the trio began to move.

As they did, the elevator doors opened, revealing six heavily armed Blossoms, weapons drawn and pointed at the intruders. Taken off guard as they were, even Hadder and Krill were caught dead to rights. Death was inevitable.

But fate had other plans.

Explosions ripped out from somewhere far below, violently shaking the Crimmwall Petal. The Blossom guards fell against the elevator walls just before their shots could ring out, dropping the men into a heap. Hadder and Krill managed to remain standing while Henley Chan fell face-first to the ground, his perfect nose splattering against his face, echoing what had recently happened to his mother.

As usual, Krill reacted before anyone else, pulling Henley to his feet and moving quickly down the hall, Hadder on his heels. The curses of the Blossoms chased after them as the guards separated limbs and retrieved guns.

The Arch-Soother's bedroom was at the end of the hall, its elegant doorway flanked on both sides by intricate gold inlay in the shape of angel wings. Henley dove forward as the sounds of footsteps grew louder behind the men, his oversized right hand slamming loudly onto the palm reader that skirted the door.

Hadder and Krill turned to face the coming onslaught as they waited for the palm reader to conduct its business. Just as the guards rounded the corridor's curving walls, another massive explosion shook Crimmwall Petal, driving the white-clad Blossoms back to the floor. As they fell, a chime rang out and the Arch-Soother's bedroom door swung inward. Henley Chan tripped into the bedchamber and the Wakened humans followed, slamming the door shut behind them.

Seconds later, gunfire erupted in the hallway and bullets loudly struck the bedroom door, each collision of metal and thick wood sounding more threatening than the last.

"What the hell is going on, Henley," demanded Hadder, irate that a critical element of their plan might have been kept from him and Krill.

"Time for that later," said Henley simply. "At the back of the room, you'll see a silver door. Lift it straight up."

"And then what," asked Krill.

"And get in," answered Henley. "It's a laundry chute for my Arch-Soother robes." Both Hadder and Krill looked dubious. "Look, I frequently use it to sneak out. If *I* can fit, you both sure as hell can!"

More projectiles slammed into the bedroom door, this time joined by the loud cracking of wood.

"*This* was your great escape plan, Henley?"

"Yes, Viktor, this was it, and it will work. But we have to go now!"

Krill cursed under his breath before moving to the back of the room, where a small silver door decorated in scrollwork sat heavy on the wall. Krill slid the handle straight up, revealing a metal chute that descended into blackness.

"Henley Chan, if I die in a laundry chute, I'm going to slit your throat like I should have done to Henrietta," promised Krill.

"Understood, Mister Krill. Now go! Please!"

Point made, Krill slid feet-first into the chute and disappeared.

"Henley, you go," called Hadder over the now-deafening gunshots.

"But, Mister Hadder..."

"Go!"

To his credit, Henley acted quickly, somehow cramming his oversized frame into the chute door before he, too, sunk out of sight.

As Henley vanished, the bedroom door erupted under another hail of bullets, the wood finally shattering under the constant assault, sending a hundred searing splinters into Hadder flesh.

Hadder turned as he was hit, stumbling toward the laundry chute. Focusing his Wakened abilities, Hadder leapt into the air, toes pointed at the open hatch, reminiscent of his attack on the highway, and slid neatly into the vertical channel just as the Blossoms stormed the room. Hadder slowed time as he plunged into the darkness, using it to slide the chute door down behind him before ripping it awkwardly out of its frame, rendering it useless for those above.

More cursing chased Hadder as he fell through blackness, praying to a god he knew didn't care that another explosion didn't occur just then, trapping him in a tomb of cheap aluminum.

———

MARLIN HADDER WAS BLINDED MOMENTARILY by the sudden light as he was discharged unceremoniously from the laundry chute to land heavily on a small stack of white robes. As his sight returned, Hadder looked around to find himself at the end of a long room dotted with washing machines, drying areas, and sewing stations.

A bloodied Viktor Krill and Henley Chan stood off to Hadder's right, while three Blossoms laid across the cement floor to his left, their bodies twisted in gross angles. Viktor Krill spoke through a grimace as he offered Hadder a hand to his feet.

"Our friend here didn't mention anything about guards being stationed in the laundry room. If not for the chaos of the explosions, I would have been a goner."

"There was no time," protested Henley. "And I thought they would have evacuated after the initial bombs went off. I…"

Krill was on Henley in the blink of an eye, the tip of his knife drawing a drop of blood as it pressed against the underside of the Arch-Soother's jaw. "You underestimated them," Krill finished for Henley. "Underestimation is the fastest route to an early death. I underestimated your stupidity. It won't happen again."

"Are you all right, Viktor," asked Hadder, trying to defuse the dangerous situation.

"I'll live," responded Viktor, his black eyes still locked onto Henley. "The bullet passed through my shoulder."

"Then we should get a move on, correct?"

Another explosion shook the Crimmwall Petal, forcing Krill to confront the reality of their predicament. The knife disappeared into his jumpsuit. "Yes. Yes, we should."

"What now, Henley," prodded Hadder, hoping that the young man had a plan.

Henley Chan wiped the blood from under his chin before nodding to the long chamber. "There's a grate in the center of the room that opens to the sewers below. We can escape there. It's how I get to Haven Falls."

"Let's go," was all Krill said as he stormed away, but not before snatching up one of the downed guard's white-coated Stutters. Hadder followed suit, but Henley moved on without arming himself.

Krill effortlessly pulled the heavy metal grate from the cement floor, revealing a rusty ladder that descended into the sewer below.

"You first, man with the plan," stated Krill sarcastically. "If there are any other surprises, you're the one who's going to take them in the shoulder."

To his credit, Henley Chan simply answered, "Fair enough," before dropping into the hole and vanishing into the gloom.

Another blast shook the ground, causing the surrounding walls to sway unnaturally. The voices of more Blossoms could be heard entering the laundry chamber at the far end.

"We're going to have to move quickly, Marlin. Even if that means carrying that man-child on our backs."

"What the fuck is going on, Viktor?"

"Don't you see," Krill said as he dropped onto the ladder below. "The sons of bitches didn't bother to tell us."

"Tell us what?"

"That they were going to blow up the world around us!"

16

As the trio ran through the complex sewer system, Hadder's Wakened mind began to run analyses. They seemed to be sticking to major tunnel passageways, a definite no-no according to Su Anorrak.

Hadder pulled on Henley Chan's robe from behind.

"Henley, aren't we supposed to avoid most of these tunnels?"

Another explosion occurred, much louder than before, shaking the subterranean world and sending cement chips flying from the tunnel walls.

"Look around, Mister Hadder. I don't think the sewer admins are going to care about a couple of blips in the system when the system itself is collapsing."

"He has a point, Marlin," Krill chimed in.

Just as Krill completed his sentence, a laser blast cut between the Wakened humans, followed by another that almost caught Henley Chan in his swan-like neck.

"Fucking hell, the bastards are still following us," said Hadder loudly as a half-dozen armed Blossoms continued rounding the corner of the main tunnel, their Taragoshi laser pistols held out before them.

"I will rid us of these fools," stated Viktor Krill, before an oversized white hand began to pull at him.

"Please, Mister Krill, there is no time! You *have* to trust me!"

Krill shot a dark look at Henley before nodding curtly, sending the companions into a headlong run down the stench-filled main tunnel.

While Hadder and Krill could have easily outpaced the Blossom guards, Henley Chan proved much slower than his tall stature would have had one believe. His too-long legs moved slowly and unsurely, like a baby stork, and either Hadder or Krill had to catch him on multiple occasions to prevent Henley from tripping and slamming onto the concert floor.

As they ran, laser shots continued to chase them, one burning a hole in Krill's white jumpsuit while another cut a clean line across Hadder's hip. All the while, deafening blasts continued to rip through the tunnels, causing the river of shit water to crest, sending noxious droplets to rain down on the retreating trio.

Despite Hadder and Krill's best efforts to keep Henley Chan moving at a brisk pace, the Blossom guards slowly began to gain ground. Laser shots grew closer to hitting their targets. Soon, they would have no choice but to fight in a battleground that could be vaporized at any moment.

"We must take the next side tunnel on the right," cried out Henley Chan over the noise of the collapsing tunnel system. "We're not far from Haven Falls!"

Another laser shot skimmed Hadder's head, leaving the stench of burning hair to fill the air. The Wakened humans and Arch-Soother slid along the concrete as they cut down the small side tunnel that appeared on the right, the Blossoms closing in fast.

The small tunnel was dim, with only a circle of light in the distance to note where it fed into a larger passageway. Henley and Hadder ran along on the left and right, with Krill bringing up the rear between them. The excited calls of the Blossoms could be heard entering the side passage. The time for running would soon have to be over.

As Hadder moved forward, a strange feeling came over him, as if a dark trap had been sprung and the nets between which they ran were going to snap shut at any moment. He looked around anxiously, desperate to locate the source of the threat. As he did, a recognizable voice cut through the chaos.

"Marlin! Dive forward! Now!"

Hadder did not stop to consider Viktor Krill's words; he merely reacted to them, gripping Henley Chan's robe and tapping into his Wakened abilities to launch the two of them forward with impossible velocity, driving them into the darkness.

As Hadder and Henley fell toward the cold ground, something passed in the darkness just above them, sending an odd blast of air to tickle their faces. Hadder hit the concrete in a neat roll, pulling Henley along with him, the young man yelling out as he was scraped across the rough surface.

Viktor Krill was right there, as well, coming out of a perfect somersault to assist Hadder with dragging the Arch-Soother toward the beckoning light of another main tunnel.

In addition to the excited cries of the Blossoms, who were now upon them, a grotesque *splat* followed the Wakened humans as they continued to move forward.

Until something else forced them to stop dead in their tracks.

The calls of bloodlust from the Blossoms of the New God transformed into screams of terror as the distinct sounds of laser fire rang out, peppering the small tunnel with light.

Hadder and Krill looked back to see the unmistakable shadow of a giant slug twenty feet behind them, two massive scorpion tails towering over the bloated pale body of the creature. Blossoms howled in fear as stingers stabbed ahead and skewered their bodies, filling them with neurotoxin that would lead to an especially horrible death.

As the battle behind them raged on, Hadder and Krill pulled Henley to his feet and marched him out of the small side tunnel.

When they had finally turned left into the next main tunnel, leaving the frightful scene to play out without them, Henley Chan finally released the breath he had been holding, talking in air in great, loud gulps.

"My god! What *was* that thing?!"

"That was a Ghost Worm, Henley. You know, a Tunnel King? The White Death? Surely, you heard of them?"

"I thought they were a story concocted by Mother to keep me from sneaking out through the sewers!"

"Afraid not."

"My Lord," cried Henley into his giant hands. "And to think that I've been regularly passing through these haunted shafts!"

"Maybe you were always safe, Henley," remarked Krill dryly. "The Worm might have seen your pale skin and thought you were one of its kind."

"That's not funny, Mister Krill," said Henley as he stumbled forward, still reeling from the Tunnel King reveal.

"It is a little funny. Marlin?"

"It's a little funny, Henley."

Henley angry waved them away before stomping off. "To hell! To hell with you both!"

Marlin Hadder and Viktor Krill shared a laugh as the giant in front of them stormed down the main tunnel. That laugh quickly morphed into a shared look of concern, however, as another explosion rattled the sewer system, sending the Wakened humans off, scooping up the Arch-Soother as they sped by.

———

A LARGE PIECE of concrete fell from the ceiling and smashed into bits at Krill's feet as the trio entered Haven Falls. The great chamber was already littered with great slabs of the material, with much more raining down from high above. The dark water of the central river roiled within its channel, sending sprays of ocean water up and across the room.

Hadder's eyes danced back and forth expectantly, hoping to find scores of Protectors running to and fro, organizing their next move. But looking around, Marlin Hadder found nothing, just a ball of concrete emptiness that was collapsing in on itself.

The Protectors of Man were gone. They had been abandoned. They had been betrayed.

Just as Hadder was beginning to consider the multitude of ways he and Krill could include the Protectors in their plans of vengeance, a deep voice echoed through the chamber, audible even above the cacophony of collapse.

"Hadder! Krill! Here! To me! Bring the boy!"

The Wakened humans followed the voice to find Clinton Voss, his white beard as wild as his yellow eyes. The massive man stood beside the artificial falls, his overalls soaked by the walls of water that were slamming against him with every swell of the dying hideout.

Hadder and Krill looked at each for a second before taking off, Henley Chan held firmly between them, his giant, slippered feet sliding against the rubble-covered floor.

Both Wakened humans had to tap into their abilities, slowing relative time to duck, dodge, and avoid the shower of debris that was falling from the ceiling. Poor Henley Chan was pushed and pulled, wrenched and twisted in an attempt to keep the Arch-Soother from becoming a smear of jelly on the quaking floor.

Eventually, after weaving a sinuous path through the chamber, the trio reached Clinton Voss, who looked as if he was ready to abandon his post at any moment.

"Yes, yes, finally! You'll have to explain what took you so long later! All of you, quickly, into the tunnel! There is a plank there for you to use! Hurry, before it's too late!"

Hadder peeked behind the torrent of water and found that the object he had seen earlier hidden deep within the shadows of the sea-bound tunnel had been brought up closer to the falls. Now in the flickering light of the crumpling chamber, Hadder could see it for it truly was — a long, narrow canal boat.

The narrowboat was bobbing angrily and swaying side to side in the choppy waters of the central river. Connected to the back of the boat, and hanging precariously on the lip of the central river's concrete bank, was a simple metal plank that groaned loudly as it was swung across the hard floor.

"Hadder, please take Henley," begged Voss over the chaos. "He won't manage alone."

Hadder simply nodded, himself now soaked with salty water, and pulled Henley into position. Despite the Arch-Soother's frightened protests, Hadder pushed the young man onto the swaying plank, gripping him tightly in his hands, forcing Henley to move with, not against, the moving walkway.

"Don't fight me," demanded Hadder. "Move as I move you; I won't let you fall!"

Despite Henley Chan doing his best to plunge in the swirling waters, Hadder managed to guide the too-tall man to the relative safety of the rocking narrowboat.

As soon as the pair touched down off the plank, the Anorrak sisters emerged from the covered interior of the boat and gently pulled Henley to safety.

Hadder spun back to the falls and found Viktor Krill arguing with Clinton Voss before angrily pushing the giant Protector leader toward the plank. Voss, in no position to argue with the notorious killer, stepped lightly onto the slab of metal and began to advance on tiptoes, showing tremendous balance for a man his size.

Just as Voss was about to reach Hadder's outstretched hand, another explosion could be heard in the distance, followed by a shockwave that pushed the narrowboat forward, stretching the links of its mooring. The movement was enough to pull the metal walkway from the concrete bank, until just the lip of the plank still kissed the rock.

Voss's yellow eyes went wide as he stared forward in helplessness. A split second later, the plank gave way, its end dropping into the dark waters. Clinton Voss began to scream as he fell, but a hand shot out from the shadowed boat, moving faster than possible, grabbing the front of his overalls and pulling the massive man out of midair with inhuman strength.

Voss found himself flying through the misty air to fall heavily onto the back of the narrowboat, Su Anorrak appearing next to him to help him up.

"Krill," Voss tried to say from the floor, but found that he had no air in his lungs.

Zaza Anorrak, however, watching from the doorway of the boat's interior, was able to read the man's lips.

"No time," she cried out over another explosion. "I'm sorry!" She then turned to someone inside the boat. "Release the fucking anchor and go! Now, you fucker!"

Hadder cried out in protest as the anchor released with a metallic squeal and the narrowboat's motor roared. Moments later, the craft surged forward, leaving Haven Falls and the first Wakened human in history to their fates.

Hadder continued to scream, the Rage rising inside him, when a dark shadow soared in from the collapsing chamber like a bullet, plowing into him and driving him to the boat's floor next to Clinton Voss.

Viktor Krill grinned victoriously above Hadder and playfully slapped his Wakened companion on the chest before standing and helping both Hadder and Voss to their feet.

"Impossible," said Su Anorrak as everyone looked back to see the distance that Krill covered with his leap. "That's thirty feet with very little height to use."

"Nothing is impossible," countered Krill. "Things are only very difficult."

As Krill said this, the ocean-bound tunnel shook violently as Haven Falls finally collapsed in the growing distance.

Clinton Voss swallowed Krill in a wet bear hug. "So glad you made it. We couldn't do this…"

While everyone else celebrated, however, Marlin Hadder shook with the Rage. He was on Zaza Anorrak in a blink, his finger in the dangerous woman's surprised face.

"You ever leave a friend of mine behind again, and I'll kill you." Hadder's voice hummed with the Rage, rendering even the usually outspoken Anorrak sister silent.

Only a too-strong hand against his chest and a familiar voice in his ear began to chase the Rage away.

"Marlin. Marlin, listen to me. Zaza was right. The mission is too important. She made the correct call."

In light of Krill's words, Hadder tapped into his Wakened abilities, using them to push the Rage away. His pulse slowed, and his pupils normalized as his old enemy dissipated. Hadder shook his head, sending droplets of water from his brown hair, as embarrassment filled the void.

"My statement still stands," Hadder said stubbornly as he passed Zaza on his way into the boat.

"Understood," was all the proud female warrior said in return. "Fucking understood."

———

THE NARROWBOAT CAREENED down the tunnel in the darkness, explosions growing louder and louder behind them. More than a few times, the loud screams of metal on concrete could be heard as the boat smashed into the sides of the tunnel. Looks of concern passed over the faces of Marlin Hadder and Viktor Krill, evident enough that Clinton Voss thought to comment.

"Don't worry, boys. Teo is manning the wheel. He's done over a hundred practice runs preparing for this day."

"Did his practice runs include the world collapsing around him," asked Krill angrily, the goodwill of him surviving his latest ordeal long gone.

"Well... no," answered Voss simply.

Marlin Hadder, Viktor Krill, Clinton Voss, the Anorrak sisters, Milly, Upton, and Jakksin all sat in worried silence as the reticent Teo held all their lives in his scarred, dark-skinned hands that worked the ship's wheel.

The narrowboat swayed viciously to the left and right, causing all of its occupants to hold on tightly lest they be rag-dolled across the interior quarters. As it did, blasts rang out, no longer behind, but now above and to the sides.

Time was running out.

Krill glanced at Hadder amidst the chaotic scene, delivering a look that conveyed a sentiment better than words ever could. It said, *this is what we get for putting our trust in the hands of the unWakened.*

Hadder wanted to disagree, but found sadly that he could not.

"The mouth; I see the mouth," cried out Jakksin from the front of the boat's interior as he stared over the frantically working Teo's shoulder.

Everyone rose as one and joined Jakksin, delighted to see a growing circle of light in the near distance. As they did, however, a great blast rang out over the exit, shaking the tunnel and sending chunks of cement to fall onto the narrowboat's roof, some of which broke through to land heavily onto the floor below.

Teo gunned the throttle, sending everyone but Hadder and Krill to their butts, and the Wakened humans held their breaths as the exit light began to dim.

The narrowboat's front nose touched the ocean water and let out a great howl as its roof hit the falling tunnel roof and was peeled back like a tin lid. Hadder looked up, confident that he would find a great slab of weight coming down to crush him, putting him out of his misery forever.

Instead, the early stages of starlight appeared above him as the mighty little narrowboat cleared the tunnel just as it collapsed behind them. As it did, a small tsunami of ocean water slammed into the boat, thrusting it away from the dangerous shoreline and into more open water.

The entire group, including the unflappable Teo, let out a collective sigh of relief as the now-topless narrowboat continued its journey east away from the city of Crimmwall.

Despite their recent good fortune, Hadder could not help but look ahead. He grabbed Clinton Voss by his meaty arm.

"What now?"

Voss looked down at the decidedly smaller man. "Do you doubt that there is more to my plan?"

"Since I was just almost entombed in a dirty sewer, yeah, you could say that I have my doubts."

Krill remained dangerously silent.

A smart retort began to form on Voss's thick lips, but the observant giant saw the look in Viktor Krill's black eyes and shifted gears. "Fair enough, Hadder. Look to the Northeast. What do you see?"

Hadder did as he was asked. "Boats. Big boats. A line of big boats anchored off the coast."

"Exactly. One of those ships is named *Glory's Pursuit*. It is owned by the Protectors of Man. It will take us away from this accursed place." A brief but tense silence followed. "I preferred not to ask before, given that our survival was still up in the air, but..."

"But, what, Voss?"

"Did you happen to get the location of Milo Flowers?"

Hadder snuck a peek at Krill, who still looked upset, but didn't see anything in his Wakened companion that told him to remain quiet. "The Neelsen Islands. No, wait, the Forlorn Islands."

Voss's yellow eyes drifted out toward the open sea. "Of course. Yes, of course..."

"Do either of those ring a bell," asked Hadder, afraid that they were given bad intel.

Voss's attention snapped back to Hadder. "Yes! Yes, they do, for they are one and the same! Of course, the New God would pick that vile place to set up shop." Voss slapped a meaty palm onto Hadder's shoulder. "You did good!" His yellow eyes took in Viktor Krill and Henley Chan. "You *all* did good!"

As the narrowboat continued on its choppy road to *Glory's Pursuit*, Krill's black eyes remained fixed on Clinton Voss. After several minutes, Voss could take no more of the killer's dark stare.

"Viktor Krill! You look as if you have something to say to..."

In a blur, Krill rose from his seat, crossed the distance between him and Voss, and slammed his fist against the Protector leader's strong jaw. The large man was sent airborne to slam hard against the bench seats that lined the boat's interior.

Twin katana swords came out in an equally impressive manner, both points aimed at Krill's throat. Meanwhile, Jakksin reached into his waistband for the pistol hidden there, while Milly retrieved a shotgun from under one of the seats.

Krill ignored all the weapons facing him, instead opting to aim all of his deadly attention at Clinton Voss. "Left some details out of the plan, didn't you, Voss?"

The large leader stumbled to his feet, waving at the Anorrak sisters, Jakksin, and Milly to put aside their blades and guns. Although Viktor Krill had struck Voss harder than he had ever been hit, the massive man knew that his strange ally had held back considerably.

"You're right, Krill, and I apologize," said Voss as he massaged his jaw, carefully moving it back and forth. "But you have to realize, we do not *know* Marlin Hadder and Viktor Krill. You have come into our world at an opportune time, but that does not mean that we had no plans before your arrival. Truth be told, the Protectors of Man have worked tirelessly for almost six months on plans to bring down Crimmwall and its vile Petal. We carefully placed men and women in strategic positions across the city, each one in a unique position to one day place an explosive device in a vital location. Your arrival, the Day of Sanctification, and Henley Chan's shifting allegiances fell into our laps, offering much more than we ever could have hoped to achieve. But it was too late to alter our original plans. Too many had sacrificed too much! Too many had given their lives! There was no turning back!"

"And why not tell us," demanded Krill.

"I told you! I don't know you! You must trust that in my heart, I wanted nothing more than to believe, to hand over the reins to men better than I, to put my faith in something! Anything!" Voss inhaled deeply to calm himself. "But I could not. If you were a double agent, or got captured and tortured… these are possibilities that I could not dismiss. So, we crammed both plans together and prayed that the pieces would fit."

"They fit together like two corner pieces."

"But they fit together, nonetheless, didn't they?"

Krill's finger shot up. "No more secrets."

"On my life, Viktor Krill. You have already given us more than we ever could have imagined. And I hope we have given you something in return."

Krill's black eyes flashed. "What have you given me?"

"Turn around. Please."

Krill turned back to the shore and Hadder followed suit, his breath catching in his throat as he did.

In the distance, outlined against a plummeting sun, the Crimmwall Petal waved drunkenly back and forth, the screams of tens of thousands echoing across the Great Water as explosions continued to light up the city. Moments later, the teardrop-shaped building cried out, as if vocalizing the anger of the New God, and fell in on itself, leaving nothing more than a rising cloud of smoke, dirt, and ash to mark that it ever existed.

Elsewhere, across Crimmwall, skyscrapers fell like downed trees, wiping out blocks of cityscape, while municipal buildings and corporate residential towers collapsed in spectacular bellows of resistance.

Within a few hours, the city of Crimmwall would be no more.

Hadder could feel that his jaw had fallen as he looked upon the destruction. He forced it closed. "So much death. So many innocents."

Clinton Voss joined in Hadder's sorrow. "I know. But it couldn't be avoided, I'm afraid. There was no other way."

"Shut up, both of you," snapped Viktor Krill, forcing even the Anorrak sisters to jump. "There are no such things as *innocents* anymore. There are those who are actively fighting Doctor Milo Flowers and those who have chosen evil. There is no one else." He began to walk to the front of the narrowboat, but stopped and turned back. "And my goddamn suit better be on that goddamn ship out there! Now, if you'll excuse me, I'm going to stand with Teo, the only person who doesn't spout idiocy."

Voss turned back to Hadder with a helpless expression. "A hard guy to like, indeed."

"But that doesn't make him wrong," Hadder shot back.

"He can't even enjoy a great victory."

"Is that what you see, Voss? A great victory?"

"What else should I see?"

"How about the deaths of a million lost souls? Many may have been Blossoms, sure, and many more have done nothing to oppose the New God. But they were all people, and their deaths will now be used by the Blossom marketing experts to launch new campaigns in favor of the New God. They will spin this into a win, do not doubt."

Clinton Voss looked down on Marlin Hadder, an epic frown appearing within the white beard that hung heavy on his dark face. "You know, between you and Krill, I'm not sure who smiles the least, if either of you ever smiles at all!"

Hadder's hazel eyes shot up at Voss. "You want to make Viktor Krill smile? Get him onto the Isle of God. Get him within striking distance of Doctor Milo Flowers. Then you'll see a smile that will chill your heart."

"I promised you both that I would!"

"You better. If there's one thing that Viktor Krill hates almost as much as the New God, it's broken promises."

Another series of explosions ripped Hadder and Voss's attentions back to the shore. As the sun began to sink below the horizon, blanketing the dying city of Crimmwall in shadow, buildings continued to collapse, topple, and implode as methane geysers of fire sprung forth from the town's shattered foundation.

Meanwhile, stars continued to make an appearance in the darkening night sky, as if they, too, needed to observe the grim show beneath.

And as always, the pink meteor continued on its cruel mission, growing larger by the minute, invisible to all but Marlin Hadder and Viktor Krill, two aliens who had nothing in common with the rest of this world.

———

ALTHOUGH THE NEON lights of Crimmwall were now barely visible in the distance, Marlin Hadder's Wakened eyes could still easily make out the pillars of smoke that continued to spiral upward from the falling city.

Safely aboard *Glory's Pursuit*, a large freighter more suited to carrying cargo than people, Hadder finally had a moment to himself after his most recent harrowing ordeal. He looked across the Great Water as he smoked a cigarette with a shaky hand, taking in the dozens upon dozens of ships within his considerable eyeshot.

The destruction of Crimmwall, and the mass exodus that followed, made it easy for *Glory's Pursuit* to slip away unnoticed among the fleet of vessels that abandoned port for the safety of open waters. This was critical, for if any Blossom or Crimmwall Port Authority ship intercepted the freighter, even the most surface of inspections would have revealed the truth. Their enemies would have learned that it was not cargo that filled the massive boat's interior, but approximately one thousand Protectors of Man, alongside two Wakened humans and a missing Arch-Soother.

Hadder took a final drag before tossing the remainder of his cigarette into the blackness of the Great Water. As he did, he felt the presence of someone approaching from behind and didn't need to turn around to know who it was.

"Much better," said Viktor Krill as he joined Hadder at the railing, unnecessarily smoothing down his white Station suit. "Clinton Voss is a man of his word, if nothing else. Had all of my blades sharpened and brought aboard, as well." Krill took a moment, noticing that Hadder was still wearing the white jumpsuit of a Junior Soother. "You know, they also brought your suit along. Cleaned, pressed, and everything."

"My funeral outfit, I suppose."

"Few get to choose the clothes they die in, Marlin. Consider this one of the few perks of our mission."

Hadder tried to smile, but found that he could not. "I'll change in a bit, Viktor. I don't have the same affinity for my clothes as you do yours."

"Fair enough." Krill took out a packet of cigarettes from his interior coat pocket, removed and lit two, and offered one to Hadder. Despite just finishing one, Hadder accepted. "Teo gave these to me. I must admit, I like the man. He reminds me of a... friend back in Bhellum." Hadder shot Krill a curious look before the Wakened humans smoked in silence for several minutes.

"Are we going to talk about what we witnessed," Hadder asked finally, his heart heavy with fear.

Krill shrugged. "What is there to talk about? Our greatest fears were proven correct."

"I'm not certain how it all ties together. Or maybe I do understand, and I'm too freaked out to concede the truth of it all. Do you think Henley Chan knows?"

"I am quite certain that Henley Chan knows."

"Then why the need to put us through that? Surely, there was some other way to get to Xioxian Chan. We *are* Wakened humans, after all."

Krill thought for a while, blowing perfect smoke rings into the chilly night air, before responding. "First, Henley Chan doesn't know what a Wakened human truly is, none of them do. They cannot even begin to comprehend the abilities that you and I possess. Or, at least, that *I* possess."

"Thanks."

"Second, perhaps Henley did not know *for sure*. He had all the pieces, and they seemed to fit together, but he needed confirmation, another set of eyes to affirm his suspicions. And finally, he is Henley Chan, Arch-Soother of Crimmwall Petal and one of the spiritual leaders of the New God. I'm sure there are those, especially among the Protectors of Man, who doubt his word, thinking his actions still serve Milo Flowers."

"Or maybe he wanted others to share in his misery."

Krill laughed dryly as he sent his cigarette butt overboard. "Yes, maybe, but none of that matters now. We got everything we needed, and now we sail to rid this world of the New God."

Hadder pointed his chin to the ever-growing pink orb in the starry sky. "And that?"

Krill's black eyes fell upon the pink asteroid, and Hadder couldn't help but notice that the notorious killer's face fell a bit.

"Yes, well, some things are out of our hands, aren't they? Wakened humans or not."

Another uncomfortable silence fell over the strange companions. Again, it was Hadder who shattered the quiet.

"So, what's the point?"

"Come again?"

"What's the fucking point, Viktor? If *that* thing is going to smash into the world, then who the fuck cares? Let's go to Quinto Beach and ride out the end of the world in style, a woman on each arm!"

"You do not mean that."

"Of course I don't! But I don't have good reason not to. And neither do you!"

Krill retrieved and lit another cigarette, this time not offering one to Hadder.

"We do not know what *that* means," he said, his dark eyes indicating the pink circle. "We have a good idea, but we do not know for sure. Perhaps it will disintegrate this world regardless of our actions. Perhaps it will blink out of existence if we come out victorious. Perhaps it wants Milo Flowers to win! We. Do. Not. Know. And, frankly, I do not give a shit. Milo Flowers took something precious away from me. Someone who meant more to me than anyone I thought possible. Someone who awoke something in me that I thought gone forever, lost forever. I *will* have my vengeance. And after, if that *thing* in the sky wants to vaporize this world, so be it. My soul will be prepared."

"And me?"

"You? Can't you see it?"

"I cannot."

Krill shook his head in frustration. "As a Wakened human, I not only see the world as others cannot, I see people as others cannot. I am able to understand the real motivations that hide behind their words and actions. I once used this gift selfishly, another tool employed to crush those in my path."

"And what happened?"

"A young boy, a young girl, and a magnificent woman held a mirror to my face, forcing me to use those same abilities on myself. That was the day that everything changed."

Hadder's hazel eyes continued to stare at the pink fingertip above. "You didn't answer my question, Viktor. What about me? What are my motivations? Why shouldn't I run? Why shouldn't I enjoy my last days?"

Krill took out a knife as he smoked and began to twirl it absently in his fingers. "I've never asked you about the Before, have I, Hadder?"

"You have not."

"Because *I* prefer not to be asked about the Before. So, I do not know for sure what tragedy befell you in your first life, what series of events brought you to Station. But I have an idea. And it is *that* which has steered your actions ever since, both in Station and here in this world. You are driven to *save*. There was something in the Before that you could not save, and now you are trying to make amends. Forever, you will do so, including here and now. And there's nothing that goddamn blip in the sky can do to sway you from this path. So, let's stop pretending that either of us have a choice! My vengeance and your need to act as savior! Those are our weapons! And with them, we will carve out the heart of Doctor Milo Flowers, or die trying!"

The monologue ended, Krill angrily flicked his second cigarette into the sea and exited the railing, heading back inside *Glory's Pursuit*. He called out over his shoulder as he walked.

"Now get some rest; I'll need you at full strength when the time comes. And change out of that Junior Soother jumpsuit. You look like a fucking asshole."

Hadder chuckled at the insult but didn't leave the railing; not yet, anyway. He spent another five minutes looking upon the pink asteroid as it slowly carved its way through the constellations of antiquity.

Viktor Krill was right about many things. In fact, the notorious killer was right about most things, especially when they came to Marlin Hadder. But there was one thing that Krill got wrong.

Marlin Hadder understood the pink asteroid perfectly well, knew that it would not be swayed from its intended path, regardless of the outcome of the coming war.

But this inevitability did not give Hadder permission to run. If anything, it emboldened him, gave even more purpose to his cause. Because there was a vast difference between perishing in chains and dying in the light of freedom.

His convictions renewed, Hadder spun from the railing and went off to find Clinton Voss, who would present him with his familiar black suit, the clothes that Marlin Hadder would die in a final time.

———

"WHAT DID the Twin Angel want, my King? I did not care for the look in his crimson eyes."

Acid Boy Gash sighed deeply, wanting nothing more than to avoid this conversation with his queen. "The w-w-world teeters on the p-precipice, my love. The N-new G-g-god is ready to make his m-move. All w-will soon be l-l-lost."

"And they need our help?"

"Th-they d-d-do."

"And you want to give it, my King?"

"I d-do."

Tears began to fill Gayle's orange eyes as she looked around at the island that was finally theirs, the actualization of a life's worth of labor, pain, and suffering. "May I ask why?"

"B-because this M-m-milo Flowers does not w-want to simply c-c-control. He w-wants to c-conquer. He w-wants to ch-ch-change. He wants to t-t-twist the world in a g-grotesque way."

"You mean how the humans changed *us*, twisted *us*, mutated *us*?"

"Y-yes. That is w-what I m-mean."

Gayle continued to take in all that was finally theirs. A beautiful island inhabited by beautiful Blisters raising beautiful families. She wiped a tear that had begun to run down her grey face. "There is a chance that this Milo Flowers is only interested in the lands of man. There is a chance that he will leave us alone, that he sees some kinship in our... differences."

"Y-yes, that is a p-p-possibility."

Gayle turned her orange eyes back on Acid Boy Gash. "We should leave them to their fates. They certainly left us to ours."

Acid Boy Gash smiled warmly, the massive wound that ran down his face opening slightly as he did. "B-but that is the d-d-difference between us and th-them, is it n-not? That is w-w-what makes us Blisters and them h-h-humans."

More tears rolled out from Gayle's orange eyes, and she released a smile to match her husband's own. "But of course, you're right, my King. What would they have us do?"

Acid Boy Gash explained his plans to Gayle, who shook her head in sadness and disbelief before falling silent.

"Wh-what do you think, m-m-my Queen?"

After several uncomfortable moments, Gayle finally nodded her head and spoke. "I will go."

Gash's indigo eyes went wide. "N-n-no! I am K-k-king and I m-must g-go!"

Gayle fell into her husband's lap and ran her grey hand gently across his scarred face.

"Yes, you are King, my love, which is why you must stay here and look after our homes. We've worked too hard and been here too little to see it lost to us. You must remain and lead those who stay... And those of us who might return."

"I c-cannot! I w-w-will not!"

Gayle continued to pet her husband's face. "Listen to me, my love! Your responsibilities go beyond your wife, and beyond your personal desires and fears. We both must do what is best for our people, in our own ways."

"I d-do n-no want to s-say g-goodbye again."

"And neither do I, my love, but kings and queens must do what others cannot, what others *will* not. You must stay and lead. And I must go to battle. I will not go alone, of course. The Twin Angel knows this, hence his visit."

Gash's face twisted in concern. "H-how is he, anyway? Have you s-s-spoken to him? H-have his w-w-wounds h-healed?"

Gayle smiled sweetly. "They have, my love. He is as good as new, and larger than ever. Milo Flowers may have monsters, but we will have a titan."

The decision reached, Acid Boy Gash engulfed his wife in a tight hug, one which he never wanted to release. He whispered softly into her grey ear.

"Y-you are r-r-right. Th-they w-would n-never do this for us."

"Yes. But that is what makes them humans, and us Blisters."

Acid Boy Gash pushed his wife to arm's length so that he could gaze deeply into her orange eyes.

"I l-l-love you, m-my Queen."

"And I you, my King."

PART III

HIDEOUS SANCTUARY

17

D aksha rounded the corner and passed under the marble arches and into the Flowers Institute's beautifully strange courtyard. As soon as she entered, however, she was forced to slide to a stop on the cobbled walkway.

Deep in the heart of the courtyard, standing on the crystalline bridge, was not one, but all four Anointed Champions, their collective attentions all pointed at the starlit waters below.

Daksha spun on a heel, preparing to flee from the horrid quartet, when a booming voice froze her mid-step.

"Daksha! Come, come! You must see this! I think you will find it... humorous." Batti Batt's words, although framed as an invitation, were no less a command than if she had a gun aimed at Daksha's dark face.

Daksha took a deep breath to calm herself, ran hands down her already smooth pantsuit, and with great will forced her feet to propel her toward the Anointed Champions.

Only Seth Whispers met Daksha's eyes with his own as the woman stepped onto the clear bridge; the others remained locked onto something in the pond beneath.

"So good of you to join us, my lady," said Seth as he flashed a yellow smile and tipped his ridiculous fedora in her direction.

"I am humbled to be in the presence of our Lord's favorite protectors. What brings you all together on this beautiful day?"

"Just deserts," stated Yuki Donna simply, her black eyes still locked over the railing of the bridge.

"I'm afraid I don't understand," replied Daksha, her pulse quickening from the dangerous Yuki's ambiguous answer.

Another yellow smile crawled onto Seth Whispers's ruddy face. "Perhaps it would be best if you took a look for yourself, my lady."

Daksha did not want to look. In fact, she wanted more than anything to be somewhere else, anywhere else that did not involve the presence of the Anointed Champions. But still, she followed instructions.

Daksha joined the Champions at the crystalline railing, careful not to touch Yuki Donna's poisonous skin, and looked down.

Daksha's eyes squinted as she took in the scene, unsure of what she was truly looking upon.

In the pond just under the bridge, a large squid-like creature splashed around in the shallow water. Compared to a squid that appeared in the natural world, this one had several differentiating features, including barbed spikes at the ends of most tentacles and an oversized beak protruding from its cavernous mouth.

But these characteristics were not what made Daksha's stomach churn uncomfortably. Instead, it was the strange humanness of the squid creature's face that forced Daksha's breath to come out in short, panicked bursts.

"Well, what do you think, Daksha," asked Cement Felix, his deep voice poorly hiding barely contained glee.

"Not much," responded Daksha. "I've seen all of our Lord's vast creations. This one does nothing for me."

The Anointed Champions giggled among themselves like naughty schoolchildren.

"But surely, you must feel some amount of pleasure," said Yuki Donna through her laughs.

"Pleasure from what?"

"I don't think she understands, yet," Seth Whispers said.

"Pleasure from what," Daksha asked again.

"Take another look," replied Yuki Donna, and Daksha looked over the edge once more. "Now tell me, does it not feel good to see your competition punished so… thoroughly?"

Daksha spoke as she stared down at the pitiful creature flopping around beneath them. "What are you talking about? My *competition?*"

Seth Whispers leaned in and spoke into Daksha's ear. "You won, my lady. Now, there is only you in our Lord's good graces. Your rival has been stricken down."

Daksha continued to observe the sad cephalopod. "What do you mean, my rival…" As Daksha released the words, however, pieces began to click into place.

The large squid's familiar blue-green eyes cried out for help. The disconcerting human-like features of its face were the same that Daksha passed in the hallways on an almost daily basis. Her greatest rival? Nieve? Nieve had been missing for several days, but that couldn't mean…

It all came together in a rush, the strange creature below her transforming into Nieve, who silently cried out from her biological trappings, begging Daksha for help.

The dark-skinned woman fell back from the railing as if she was stuck by an assassin's bullet, falling to her backside as the Anointed Champions erupted in laughter.

"I think she gets it now, Batti!"

"Yes, she's a bit slow, but she finally sees it, Yuki."

Daksha stumbled to her feet, her heels making it even harder to maintain her balance. She slowly approached the railing again, hoping that the courtyard's psychedelic pollen had simply caused a hallucinogenic episode.

Daksha's knees went weak as Nieve stared back up at her, desperation clear in her blue-green eyes. The Anointed Champions continued to laugh.

"Well, she always wanted a swimmer's body," joked Yuki Donna. "Now she has the *ultimate* physique for swimming." Riotous laughter ensued.

"Why," asked Daksha, her jaw refusing to stay closed. When no one responded, Daksha asked again, more loudly this time. "Why?!"

Batti Bat was the first to address the question. "Because she failed. Our Lord gave her several tests, and she failed each one of them. It was a trend that could not be ignored."

Daksha's voice came out weak. "But Nieve was loyal. Nieve was believer. Nieve would have died for the New God."

"Nieve was ineffectual," corrected Batti Bat. "Nieve was a disappointment. So, our Lord found a new way for her to assist. A way that even Nieve cannot mess up."

"By making her into a grotesque creation?"

"She is much more than that," said Cement Felix. "She is doubling in size every few days. She will make a fine guardian for the Isle of God."

As if on cue, Nieve began to violently splash around beneath her audience, slamming her massive mantle into a pile of stones placed along the edge of the pond.

"Oh, now look at this," commented Seth Whispers, "someone is not appreciating her new gifts. That is certainly no way for a lady to act."

Yuki Donna cut in. "The idiot is trying to scramble what little brains she has left. Felix, do something!"

Felix shot back. "You see how thick that head of hers is? There is no way she can crack it open, no matter how hard she flails. See? Already she has grown tired of trying."

True to Cement Felix's words, Nieve stopped thrashing, her blue-green eyes appearing far off, as if she had knocked herself senseless.

"If she gets much larger, she may succeed in cracking herself open." Yuki's black eyes stared up at Cement Felix, who finally relented under that dangerous look.

"Fine. I will toss her into Paradise Bay and be done with it."

As Cement Felix spoke, Daksha watched in horror as Seth Whispers launched a green loogie from his lips. It landed on one of poor Nieve's blue-green eyes with a sickening *plop* before running down her squid face. Seth giggled to himself as Nieve splashed in the water to remove the thick, disgusting spittle.

The Anointed Champions, their amusement having run dry, began to disperse. Seth Whispers could not help but make one last comment before exiting the courtyard.

"She had her chance to get with a good guy like me, and now look at her. Don't repeat her mistake, Daksha."

As Seth Whispers and Batti Bat left the courtyard, Cement Felix dropped from the crystalline bridge and collected Nieve by the squid-woman's mantle. Nieve fought ferociously, sending spiked tentacles at Felix's arms and chest. Unfortunately, none could penetrate his rock-like skin, and Felix merely laughed aloud as he dragged Nieve out of the pond and across the rough cobbled walkway of the courtyard. After ten yards, Never stopped fighting back and simply went limp, looking like nothing more than a dead sea creature bound for the stew pot.

"She was a loyal follower," reiterated Daksha, more to herself than the still-present Yuki Donna, who was now studying her sharpened black nails.

"She *was* loyal. Loyal and ineffective. Now, she has a chance to be both loyal and useful." Yuki's black eyes fell onto Daksha. "You need to know, loyalty is not enough. Your love for the New God will not ensure that tasks are successfully completed. We are at the endgame; failure is not an option." Yuki Donna then began to walk away. At the end of the bridge, however, she stopped and turned back. "And don't worry, Daksha, Nieve will still have a chance to die for the New God. You *all* will have your chance."

———

"Does it feel good to be back in your old clothes?"

Marlin Hadder ran his hands over his black suit, which were cleaned and pressed. "I don't hold the same love for my clothes as Viktor does for his, but, yes, it *does* feel nice to be out of that Junior Soother outfit."

Clinton Voss simply nodded. "Then let us finish off the outfit." Voss handed Hadder the crystal handguns that had once belonged to the pimp formerly known as Higgins. Hadder took his jacket off, donned the shoulder holster that held the twin guns, and returned the jacket to the hanger on which it was brought to him.

"I think I'll leave the suit jacket hanging up. I want to leave a good impression the next time I die."

Clinton Voss picked up on the strange phrasing – the *next time I die* – but decided it was best to let it go. Instead, he moved the conversation into another direction.

"And you had one last item, I believe," said the mountainous dark-skinned man as he gently held out a simple knife in his massive outstretched mitts.

Hadder immediately recognized the bone handle, the curved blade, and the letters *YHWH* that looked to have been burned into the grip at the dawn of time.

"How could I forget," asked Hadder coyly as he scooped up Patton Yellich's dagger and deftly placed it under the backside of his belt, hidden from view. As he did, Hadder noted how Voss bowed almost imperceptibly when the blade was removed from his palms.

"We also brought aboard those bags of weapons that you and Krill took from Thorns of Reckoning. They look like quality tools; let us hope that they can serve some purpose where we are going."

"And where is that, exactly, Voss? I only have a name, several curses, and multiple rolled eyes to clarify the picture."

Clinton Voss, as he was apt to do, slapped a meaty palm against Marlin Hadder's shoulder. "We're having a meeting down below in a few hours. Better to get everything out in the open at once — what you know, what we know, what Henley Chan knows, and what we all fear to be fact. Everyone here now is all in to the end, meaning we all deserve the ugly truth, stripped bare of long shot hopes and unobtainable goals."

"So, it's bad enough that you don't want to have to repeat it twice?"

"My friend, I prefer not to say it once, but we are all going to have to get used to dealing with things that we really, really don't like."

"Like humanity being ruled by a sick prick?"

"Worse. Like humanity being twisted into something that no longer resembles humans, at all."

———

"You beautiful, balding bastard! I knew there was a reason I didn't slit your throat!"

The oversized mechanic Terry, still covered in oil and draped in dirty overalls, laughed uncomfortably. "Well, yes, I knew how much of a shine you took to her, so I just knew that I'd have to bring her along with me. But we watched her real good while she was under our care. Isn't that right, Lil Terry?"

Viktor Krill jumped as Lil Terry barked from behind a stack of pallets. "I see your mongrel made the trip."

"Where I go, Lil Terry goes, Mister Krill."

As Krill's black eyes met Terry's, the notorious killer discovered a newfound respect for the head mechanic of the Protectors of Man. "Fair enough," was all Krill said as he ran his tan hands over the Comet's black metal body, smiling as his fingers brushed over the obvious new paint and perfectly jointed fabrication work...

"Terry!"

"Yes, Mister Krill?"

"What in the *hell* is this?"

"What's what?"

"*This*, you daft bastard! What have you done to my girl?!" Krill could feel his hands moving inexorably to his hidden blades.

Terry ran his greasy fingers over what little hair he had left as Lil Terry appeared from behind the pallets, as if sensing that his best friend was in danger. "Well, I improved her, Mister Krill."

"You did what?!"

"I done made her better."

"Impossible! She was already perfect!"

"The perfect ride through Crimmwall? Maybe. The perfect ride through Hell? Not by a long shot. And seeing as how we're all fleeing the former and heading toward the latter, I thought your girl could use some upgrades."

Krill took in a calming breath, reminding himself that a dead mechanic would be unable to fix the freighter should the engines die somewhere in the middle of the Great Water.

"You… *upgraded…* my girl?"

"I did, Mister Krill."

The fingers of Krill's right hand danced along the hilt of a blade that dangled within his white suit jacket. "Show me, Terry."

Terry wiped his hand across his head again nervously while Lil Terry began to pace along the side of the storage area. After nodding several times, as if he was working up the nerve, Terry climbed into the Comet's driver's side and closed the door. "Well, this is the first and most obvious enhancement, Mister Krill. Tell me what you think?"

Terry could be heard pressing buttons within the Comet for a moment before the rare automobile roared to life and shifted before Krill's widening black eyes.

A familiar dark smile appeared on Viktor Krill's lips as he watched his beloved Comet transform into a killing machine.

"Is that what I think it is, Terry?"

"It is, Mister Krill. What do you think?"

"I love it, Terry."

"I thought you might, Mister Krill." Lil Terry barked in agreement. "Do you want to see the rest of it?"

Krill could feel his jaw being to lower before forcing it closed. "There is more?"

"Oh, sure. Me and Lil Terry couldn't just stop there, not for a cherry ride like this. Not for an owner like you, Mister Krill."

Krill couldn't take his black eyes off of his Comet. "Terry, I apologize for anything I may have said to offend you."

"And what about Lil Terry?"

Krill looked over to find Lil Terry staring at him through long dirty white bangs. "Yes, I apologize to Lil Terry, as well," he said, doing his best to keep the amusement from his voice.

"Well, we appreciate that, don't we, Lil Terry?" Lil Terry barked in response. "Now, what else do want to see, Mister Krill?"

"Everything, Terry. Show me everything you did to my girl."

———

DEEP within the bowels of the freighter called *Glory's Pursuit*, tucked away below the sleeping quarters, Marlin Hadder finally found the large meeting room.

Hadder walked into a wall of silence as he entered the room, which was occupied by Viktor Krill, Clinton Voss, Henley Chan, the Anorrak sisters, and more than twenty other high-ranking Protectors of Man.

No idle chitchat was found as Hadder cut his way through the room, passing faces stretched thin with tension, as if every person was sitting on a bed of needles. Once Hadder finally settled in an open space near Viktor Krill, Clinton Voss cleared his throat loudly and began to speak.

"It's hard to hand out congratulations when such dark clouds are on the horizon, but nevertheless.... congratulations. Phase One is complete and Phase Two is currently underway. This means that there is no going back. And with no going back, that means that all of us collected on this freighter are fully committed. And because we are all fully committed, each of you deserves to know the truth — the whole of it. Anything you hear in this room today, feel free to share it with the others on board. Nobody's sacrifice will be worth more than another's."

"Where are we going," asked Lumis Griggs, the former Crimmwall administrator. He pulled awkwardly at his ill-fitting suit. "I've heard the rumors, of course, but some confirmation would be nice."

Voss's face softened beneath his white beard as he looked upon the lean administrator who had betrayed a lucrative government job for the cause. "You deserve it, and you shall have it, my friend. We are heading to the Neelsen Islands on the far side of the world." A collective groan broke out among several in attendance while most others looked unmoved by the announcement, as if the location rang no bells, good or bad. "Among that cursed group of islands, we will find the Isle of God, where Doctor Milo Flowers currently resides." Voss paused for a moment. "I can tell that some of you know of the Neelsen Islands, but many do not. We have a long journey ahead of us, so take some time to read up on the islands. The history of the place may offer clues regarding what we can expect to find there. Other questions?"

"No questions, Clinton," said DeLany Thales, who had also left behind an envious career as Crimmwall's premier madame. "But I think it's time for the full story to come out."

Voss ran a giant hand over his bald head before using it to smooth down his thick white beard. "Yes. Yes, it is. Henley?"

Henley Chan drifted in effortlessly from the side to stand before the Protector audience, a patch now covering the eye that Viktor Krill expertly removed. Still wearing his Arch-Soother robe and towering over the group, Henley looked as if he were delivering a Blossom sermon.

"As you all know, Doctor Milo Flowers used his extraordinary abilities to heal most of the world's elite and their families. This not only earned him tremendous money and fame, but also the loyalty and trust of those who pull the planet's strings. First, they thanked him. Then, they rewarded him. Finally, they worshipped him, thinking that only a god could help them where their wealth and power could not.

"Milo Flowers did all he could to fan the flames of this idea, this new religion.

"With his newfound resources, Milo Flowers established the Flowers Institute in the Neelsen Islands and began building satellite campuses around the globe, calling them Petals. At these Petals, regular people could receive the same Holy Treatments that were previously reserved for the ruling class. Now everyone, regardless of social class, could worship at the altar of the New God and experience his divine healing.

"Using his control of entities such as Maxim Global Media, success stories of the Petals were plastered on every medium possible, driving converts and pilgrimages to these satellite locations. Every day, an increasing number of Blossoms walked into Petals to experience the miracle of the New God. They walked out with their conditions healed and their faith in the New God fortified.

"Unfortunately, that is not all they have been walking out with."

Doctor Olney Jansen cut in. "I knew there had to be more to those vile Petals! I told everyone that there were darker forces at play!"

Henley Chan swung his too-perfect face to Doctor Jansen. "I think everyone suspected that there were intentions beyond mere charity work and proselytism. But the reality of the Petals... I don't think anyone could have ever guessed the truth to be so dark, so inhumane."

"Well, spit it fucking out, man" called out Zaza Anorrak, and Hadder watched as Krill suppressed a chuckle.

Henley's emerald eyes swept back and forth, taking in all in attendance. "What do you all know about the Great Conversion?"

Flat-topped Jakksin was the first to speak. "It's some kind of Blossom bullshit. Something about a time when all the Blossoms will be spared and the rest of the world will burn."

"I think it is like Judgment Day, similar to what many of the world's other religions believe," chimed in Su Anorrak in her singsong voice.

"You are both correct," replied Henley. "At least, as far as most Blossoms are concerned. The Great Conversion means many things, truths that change according to where a person resides in the Blossom pecking order.

"For your typical Blossom, the Great Conversion is simply a time when those who have accepted Doctor Milo Flowers as the New God will be protected and rewarded when he finally ascends to his official title of Messiah."

"And for the high-ranking Blossoms," asked Su.

Henley Chan hesitated before answering. "As you rise in the ranks of the Blossoms of the New God, the number of those who will escape the Great Conversion unscathed drops precipitously."

"Fucking get on with it," said Zaza. "The fucking top, man! What does it mean at the very top? I assume that's where the fucking truth lies."

An embarrassed smile formed on Henley's rosy lips. "But of course, you are correct, Miss Anorrak. Its meaning is so very different at the top, which is where the dark truth of the matter resides."

"How is it different," cut in Jakksin.

"It is the opposite of the general Blossom thinking. Most Blossoms think that the Great Conversion will spare the true believers as the world twists around them. This couldn't be farther from the truth."

"Fucking explain," demanded Zaza.

"It is these Blossom believers that will twist and mutate during the Great Conversion, not the heathens."

At those words - *twist* and *mutate* - the audience broke out into excited chatter that quickly rose to a deafening roar of ideas and theories.

The deep voice of Clinton Voss rose above the chaotic discussions, retaking control of the meeting.

"Protectors!" The crowd quieted. "Perhaps we should let Henley Chan continue his explanation." Voss turned to the Arch-Soother. "Henley, what is the truth of the Great Conversion and how are the Petals involved?"

"And get to the fucking point," added Zaza, and this time Viktor Krill was unable to prevent the laugh from escaping his lips.

Henley Chan smiled sweetly again and took a deep swallow, as if he was delivering a death sentence to a loved one. "Over the past months, the Petals have not only been healing the sick and infirmed; they have also been implanting something within each pilgrim."

"Implanting? Implanting what," asked Doctor Jansen.

"They call it the Charismata, but do not doubt what it truly is," responded Henley. "A bomb. A biological bomb, Doctor."

"There's no such thing," countered Doctor Jansen amid a growing chorus of doubt.

"Shut up and listen," Clinton Voss shouted, bringing silence to the tense room. "Please continue, Henley."

"As you move up the Blossom ladder, you learn more about the true beliefs of Milo Flowers. At the core of his ethos is one idea — life should be allowed to grow unfettered."

"What the hell is that supposed to mean," asked DeLany Thales.

"It means that that the human form that we have all grown accustomed to is looked at by Milo Flowers as a restrictive vessel, unworthy of life and his vision for future creation."

"I still don't understand," said DeLany in exasperation.

Voss stepped in once again. "Henley, go back to the Petals. What are they doing?"

Henley ran too-long fingers through his too-thick hair. "Like I said, as the Petals are healing the pilgrims, they are also implanting an alien entity known as a Charismata into each person. This biological bomb lies in wait in each unsuspecting Blossom, waiting for the catalyst to detonate. The Blossom leadership has a name for these poor souls. We call them Blessed Carriers."

"What is the catalyst," Doctor Jansen could be heard asking over numerous other questions that were being thrown at Henley Chan.

"Quiet," screamed Clinton Voss once again. "Henley, what is the catalyst for these biological bombs?"

"Have you all seen the vents that kiss the side of the Crimmwall Petal?"

"Used to kiss, you mean," corrected Jakksin. "We turned that shit hole into rubble!"

The Protectors exploded into celebratory applause, and even Clinton Voss seemed swept up in the moment, a large grin appearing from under his white beard.

Henley let the noise die down before continuing. "Yes, the vents that *used to* kiss the Crimmwall Petal. Each Petal around the globe was outfitted with similar vents and are known by the Blossom elite as *Divine Antlers*. These vents have been releasing a constant stream of invisible spores into the air, which are carried on the winds to the four corners of the world, even those places untouched by the Blossoms of the New God."

Doctor Jansen spoke up once again. "What are these spores supposed to do?"

"Prime the air."

"Prime the air for what?"

"*Boom*," responded Viktor Krill, answering for Henley Chan.

The room again broke out in a cacophony of questions, demands, and accusations.

"Let the man finish," called out Voss over the din, finally wrangling control of the Protectors once more. "Henley, please finish."

"At some point, I believe that Milo Flowers will trigger something, activating the trillions upon trillions of spores that permeate the world's air. These activated spores will, in turn, awaken the entities that have been implanted in Blossoms around the globe, detonating the biological bombs."

"What will happened when these bombs go off," asked Su Anorrak.

Henley cleared his throat. "From the Blossom elite's point of view, life will burst free of the human form and will continue unfettered, the way it was intended."

Su's beautiful face puckered in confusion. "And from a sane person's point of view? From *our* view?"

Henley's emerald eyes flashed momentarily. "Each afflicted person will morph into the epitome of grotesqueness, their humanity all but stripped away in an instant."

"Like the mutant freaks that have been reported across the cities," called out a voice from the group.

"Yes," replied Henley. "The Blossom elite call them the *Bloomed*."

"Are the two issues related," came another voice from the back.

"They are," conceded Henley. "In fact, the Bloomed are nothing more than individuals whose biological bombs went off prematurely, foregoing the upcoming catalyst."

"Wait, wait, wait a fucking minute," declared Zaza Anorrak, pushing her way to the front of the room to confront Henley Chan. "Are you tryin to fucking tell me that the sick shit that has happened to random people around the country, transforming them into homicidal freaks, is going to happen on a massive scale?"

A shadow of sadness passed across Henley Chan's beautiful face. "Yes, Miss Anorrak, this transformation will not only happen on a massive scale, but it will occur instantaneously around the world. It is the Great Conversion. And it is how Doctor Milo Flowers will wrest control of the planet for his own devilish plans."

"But why," was all the response that the tatooed Anorrak sister could muster, her jaw remaining open from the horror of the truth.

Viktor Krill stepped forward to answer. "Because Doctor Milo Flowers is an insane person who enjoys playing God. He is a sick man who derives pleasure in manipulating life, controlling the very essence of creation. To him, there is no greater power that one can possess."

A heavy silence fell over the room after Krill's words. The soft voice of Su Anorrak finally broke the spell.

"So, it is actually just the Blossoms, or those who have received the Holy Treatment, who will change during the Great Conversion."

"That is correct," replied Henley.

"Then why the fuck do we care," said Zaza, finishing her sister's thoughts. "These people made their fucking choices; now they can live with the fucking repercussions."

The room again burst into commentary, some agreeing with Zaza Anorrak while others offered sympathetic opinions concerning the living bombs.

Henley Chan raised his enormous palm into the air, eventually quieting the gathered crowd. "I wish it were that easy, Miss Anorrak. I wish that the Bloomed could be quarantined, or hunted. Over time, their numbers would dwindle until their dark history was lost to time. Unfortunately, I fear that another scenario may occur."

Marlin Hadder perked up. Finally, there was some new information to digest. "What are you talking about, Henley? What is this *other* scenario?"

Henley shifted his eyepatch a bit, as if it were the only cause of his discomfort. "I do not know for sure, for these details are known only to the very few who run the world, but I have overheard bits and been able to assemble some of the pieces."

"And you heard...," Hadder prompted.

"The Flowering Horde."

Hadder's dark dreams had finally leaked into reality. "I need more."

Henley touched his eyepatch again. "I have overheard conversations that spoke of the Flowering Horde."

"What is the Flowering Horde, Henley?"

Viktor Krill spoke before Henley Chan could answer. "It is the New God's Bloomed army. Isn't that right, Henley?"

"I am afraid so, Mister Krill. And worse is the language used when talking about the Flowering Horde. It is said - *the Flowering Horde will run across the land like a great flood, gaining in strength as infidels are reborn in the light of the New God.*"

"Reborn," Hadder said simply, pulling out the most critical element of the prophecy.

"That is correct, Mister Hadder. Again, I have no proof, but I fear that these fully Bloomed individuals, those who were converted as Milo Flowers intended, will be able to somehow Bloom others, even without the Petal implants."

The meeting room felt as if it had grown ten degrees colder as silence once more took hold. Hadder could feel Krill's black eyes on him without looking over.

"Are we sure," came a call from the back. "This all seems crazy, I mean, really insane."

"It's true," answered Krill after seeing Hadder still lost in his own dark thoughts. "My colleague and I saw the Divine Anthers; we watched as spores poured out by the millions. We observed firsthand how foreign entities were introduced during Petal operations. And we saw how these same entities were hidden in the wafers given to pilgrims during the Day of Sanctification. Combine that with what we already know of Milo Flowers and it all adds up. I wish it were not the case, but it is."

Whispers of doubt could be heard from the crowd, especially addressing the two strangers who had recently come into the picture. These doubters were quickly shut down by those Protectors who had seen or heard the stories of Marlin Hadder and Viktor Krill.

"So, what now," asked DeLany Thales. "It almost seems like all is lost."

Clinton Voss took center stage, his leadership needed now more than ever. "What now? What now is that we stay the course. Everything you have heard here today does not change the facts. Doctor Milo Flowers is a threat to humankind. Doctor Milo Flowers is hiding on the Isle of God in the Neelsen Islands. The Protectors of Man, of which every person in this room and on this freighter is a member, have dedicated themselves to ridding the world of this monster. And that is what we will do!"

"But the Great Conversion..." came a call from the crowd.

Voss intercepted the concern. "Has not happened yet! Perhaps we will get there in time. Perhaps we will not. Regardless, we have a duty to remove a cancer from our world, and remove it we will. Who knows, even if the Great Conversion occurs, there may be a way to reverse its affects. We do not know what kind of tools and resources are on that accursed island. Maybe we can put some of those dark devices to good use. Viktor?"

Viktor Krill shrugged noncommittally. "Anything is possible."

"Well, I think that is all for now," said Voss, concluding the meeting. "I'm sorry for having to share such a tale of woe, but you all have sacrificed much and deserve to know what you are truly fighting for."

"And what's that," asked Su Anorrak from the side.

"The fate of humanity. What else could it be?"

Su giggled. "I know. I just wanted to hear those words said in your deep voice. I thought it may embolden me and the others."

"And did it?"

"A little bit."

Clinton Voss stepped forward, closing the distance between himself and the crowd. "Then let me try once more. We call ourselves the Protectors of Man. I know when we first formed and named ourselves, we thought that we were fighting for an idea, the thought that one religion and one belief system should never dominate the world. It turns out that our name was much more apropos than we could have ever imagined. We are the Protectors of Man! And it is not a belief that we are fighting for. Our cause is not a political one, nor is it even a theological one. We are the Protectors of Man! And we are fighting for one thing and one thing only! The fate of humanity! Now, is that a cause that you can get behind!"

Hadder jumped a bit as the room fell into raucous applause. The Protectors of Man had been presented with true horror. But they had also been presented with a real reason to fight, and a cause worth dying for.

And nearing the end of this dark journey, Marlin Hadder had to admit to himself that this was all he had left to hope for.

———

VIKTOR KRILL STOOD at the railing of *Glory's Pursuit*, smoking a cigarette and looking up at the night sky. In particular, Krill stared at the pink asteroid that continued to grow larger by the hour. If he looked hard enough, Krill thought he may be able to hear the words of God through the celestial visitor, his Wakened mind picking up the accusations that were being leveled at all of humanity.

Above the notorious killer, a flag flapped loudly in the evening breeze. It depicted a white skull hanging from a red parachute against a black backdrop. When Krill asked Clinton Voss about its meaning, the Protector leader simply stated, *I was a soldier once. This reminds me that I still am.*

"What do you see?" Concentrating as he was, Krill did not sense Henley Chan as the Arch-Soother slid up next to him along the railing. The young man's words caught the notorious killer off-guard, giving Krill a rare jump-scare.

Henley looked down at Krill. "Apologies, Mister Krill. I did not mean to scare you. In fact, I did not think you could scare."

"Well, I can. More than you could imagine. Now, what did you say?"

"I just wanted to know what you see out there in the cosmos."

Krill had to remind himself that only Hadder and he could see the pink asteroid speeding toward the planet. He sighed deeply. "I see nothing, Henley, just a universe full of broken promises and shattered dreams. Now, what do you really want?"

Henley cleared his throat. "Oh, well it's nothing, really. It's just that..."

"Are you a Blessed Carrier, Henley?"

The young man's perfect face fell under the weight of Krill's question. "I do not know, Mister Krill. That is the honest answer. I do not believe that the conversion program was in place during my first surgery, when Doctor Flowers returned my ability to walk. But the later surgery... I just don't know."

Krill exhaled a smoke ring, sending it to hover over the deep darkness of the Great Water. "Have you told anyone?"

"I'm telling you, now, Mister Krill."

"Have you told anyone else?"

"How could I? Look at me, Mister Krill. I am already looked upon as a freak, even by the few individuals that I would dare to call friends. Imagine their reactions if they thought there was a monster hidden away inside me."

"We all have monsters buried within us, Henley."

"Come again, Mister Krill."

"Never mind, Henley." Krill tossed the butt of his cigarette into the waters below and turned to face the towering Arch-Soother. "What is it you want from me, Henley?"

"You know what I am asking, Mister Krill. We both know that you are many things, but slow is not one of them. If the time comes..."

"I will do what must be done, Henley. You have my word."

"Thank you, Mister Krill." Henley began to leave, but turned back. "I'm sorry you had to witness that scene with Mother. It was not my... intention to lose control like that. I will carry her murder for the rest of my days, which may be numbered."

Krill lit another cigarette, a habit that was growing by the day. "You did not murder your mother, Henley. She was already lost to you. She had already traded in her humanity for the promise of the few things she could not buy with credits.

"And remember, Milo Flowers is a great manipulator, a con man. Who knows what rosy picture he is painting of life post his Great Conversion. If your mother was ever allowed to see things for how they truly were, perhaps dying at the hands of her son would be her desired way to go."

Tears began to flow from Henley's unpatched eye. He wiped them from his pale cheek with oversized fingers. "Thank you, Mister Krill. You know, for a notorious killer, you are exceedingly easy to talk to."

Krill turned back to the Great Water and faced the pink dot that stared down at him from the heavens, delivering curses in a language that none could understand. "Don't tell anyone, Henley. I have a reputation to uphold and wish to keep it as long as I'm on this miserable world."

"Of course. As you wish, Mister Krill." The young man began to drift away.

"Henley!"

"Yes, Mister Krill?"

"You are a brave man. If it has to be done, I'll try to make it quick. I'll try to make it painless."

"That would mean the world to me, Mister Krill."

18

To the Protectors of Man who were standing in a large circle, observing the fight unfold on the deck of *Glory's Pursuit*, it seemed as if they were watching a recording on fast-forward. Strikes appeared as mere streaks in the ocean air. Combinations occurred faster than even the sharpest eye could follow. When blows did manage to land, they sounded like thunder strikes and made all in attendance grimace, as if the shock wave from the connection could be felt from dozens of feet away.

Marlin Hadder held his own against the notorious Viktor Krill, avoiding critical mistakes while mounting an offense that drew more than a bit of blood. Still, Krill's experience in fighting and his extended time with Wakened abilities eventually proved too much, especially without the Rage to aid Hadder.

After an especially complex combo that left Hadder off-balance and on the defensive, Krill threw a vicious kick that looked to be aimed at Hadder's exposed ribs. As Hadder reacted accordingly, Krill whipped the bottom part of his leg up at the last moment, sending it over Hadder's block to career against his skull with a deafening *crack*.

A great burst of light exploded within Marlin Hadder's mind, and seconds later he found himself on the deck of the ship, his cheek pressed neatly against the cold metal.

Applause rang out from the crowd, with many thanking God that the two Wakened humans were on *their* side. Their admiration offered, the Protectors then dispersed to attend to the multitude of preparations for arrival at the Neelsen Islands. Krill gave Hadder a few moments to compose himself before coming over and offering a hand up.

"Better. Much better," said Krill as he easily pulled Hadder up from the swaying boat deck. He wiped some blood from his tan cheek and then tested a tender spot on his temple. "There were a few times that you almost had me." A deliberate pause. "Almost."

Hadder stood on unsteady legs. "Tell me that again tomorrow, when I'll remember it."

Krill offered a rare laugh. "You're a Wakened human, fool. You will remember everything, even this. A few more months with your abilities and you may be able to really challenge me for the title of most dangerous person in the world."

"You and I both know that the odds are that we won't be around that long, Viktor."

"Even better. I will be able to take my crown to the grave."

Hadder reached up and felt an eye that was already beginning to swell shut from a straight right that snuck through his defenses. "And it feels like I might take a black eye to mine."

"Don't be ridiculous. That wound will heal before the sun falls below the horizon. You are Wakened, you fool!"

A deep voice cut across the freighter. "Hadder! Krill! Join us, please!"

Hadder and Krill turned to find Clinton Voss at the doorway leading below deck, his white beard flying wildly in the sea breeze.

"What do think this is about," asked Hadder.

"I don't know. But each meeting seems to bring more and more of one thing."

"Yeah. Bad news."

———

HADDER AND KRILL took their places among a dozen other high-ranking Protectors in the conference room beneath the deck of *Glory's Pursuit*.

At the head of the room, Clinton Voss, Doctor Olney Jansen, and Lumis Griggs stood before a large map that displayed a cluster of islands.

Clinton Voss loudly cleared his throat before speaking. "Thank you all for taking time from your preparations to join us." Voss's yellow eyes found Hadder and Krill. "And apologies for any meetings I may have interrupted." Krill nodded in return. "Behind me is a map of the Neelsen Islands. Some of you know about these infamous lands and others of you may not. This meeting is to ensure that we are all on even footing regarding our knowledge of the Neelsen Islands and what may be waiting for us there."

"Why don't you call it by its real fucking name," asked Jakksin from the back.

Voss shot a glare at his always outspoken colleague. "We'll get to that. But first, another *thank you* to Henley Chan, Marlin Hadder, and Viktor Krill, who risked much..." An uncomfortable pause. "And sacrificed even more to get us this information."

Hadder looked back and to his left and found Henley Chan standing against the wall, as if the towering young man was trying to hide within the shadows of the conference room's corner.

Voss continued. "The Neelsen Islands are nestled in the Tropical Zone to the east of the Syeer Federation and to the southwest of the Centrus Affiliation's westernmost territories. In short, it's in the middle of nowhere. And it is this reason that the islands have such a notorious past and terrifying present. Doctor Jansen, if you will."

Olney Jansen took center stage. "Approximately one hundred and fifty years ago, a terrible illness began to sweep through the lands of the world, caring nothing for borders or genders or ethnicities or religions. The afflicted found that lesions formed across their bodies, eventually leading to nerve damage, deformity, blindness, and a number of other horrific ailments.

"Eventually, scientists discovered that the illness was an infectious disease caused by bacteria known as mycobacterium sapios. The disease became known by many things — the Blight, and the Festering, among others. And, of course, because the condition could be transmitted from person to person, those afflicted with the disease were ostracized, imprisoned, and often simply hunted, their corpses burned in remote locations.

"This despicable behavior went on for decades, until the Gunthall Council of Humanity was held, ironically just a few decades before the Great War. During the meeting, it was decided that while the afflicted could not be allowed to remain among society, nor could they be hunted or imprisoned. At least, not in the traditional way.

"Therefore, it was decided that all of those found to have the Festering would be banished to a group of islands whose natives were eradicated decades earlier when small amounts of rare minerals were found beneath the lands. Named the Neelsen Islands for the explorer Gilbert Neelsen, who had first discovered them and made contact with the native population, they were the perfect location to send those who the world wants to forget.

"Several years ago, Gilbert Neelsen's son, Doctor Fillip Neelsen, paid a visit to the islands that bore his family name. He wrote an article on the unfortunate souls who were forced to carve out a living within the sweltering jungles that covered the land. He titled his article *Death and a Semblance of Life on the Forlorn Islands*. Now, as many people know the name the Forlorn Islands as they do the Neelsen Islands, which is not a lot. Governments around the globe have done a tremendous job of burying stories, articles, and think pieces about the Forlorn Islands – a stain on this world's modern history."

The room went silent as the truth of the Neelsen Islands began to sink in, especially for those such as Marlin Hadder, who had no prior knowledge of their destination.

It was the madame DeLany Thales who finally broke the silence, voicing what many were already thinking. "Is this not good news? Surely, these people can offer no resistance with their bodies riddled with illness?"

"We fear it is quite the opposite, DeLany," answered Voss. "We think that this is precisely why Milo Flowers chose this location as his home base."

The madame's handsome face wrinkled, confused. "I don't understand."

Viktor Krill spoke up. "Doctor Milo Flowers is many things — egoist, madman, and despot, to name a few. But he is also a healer, the greatest healer this world has ever known. It is the reason for his ascension, the force behind his power and influence. Clinton Voss is right. Milo Flowers selected the Forlorn Islands for a very specific reason. It was there that he found a population rife with sickness, desperate for restoration, and hungry for empowerment. And he knew that if he could rid these unfortunate souls of the Festering, they would worship him as a god. And then there would be nothing that they would not let him do to them."

DeLany shifted her striking gaze to Krill. "What are you trying to say?"

Hadder cut in. "He's saying that it's not a mopey group of island villagers that we will most likely face upon arrival, half-blind with limbs falling off as they trudge toward us."

"What then," asked Jakksin, a look of worry painted beneath his flat top.

Hadder and Krill looked to one another, silently asking each other how truthful they wanted to be at the moment. Fortunately, Henley Chan made the call for them.

"You will face an army of the New God's creation," responded the Arch-Soother. "An army molded by Milo Flowers's own hands, dedicated wholly to serving and protecting their master, who they truly believe is God, returned to this world to reset everything."

"What the fuck are we talking about here," demanded Zaza Anorrak as she nervously fingered the katana sword at her hip. "What kind of army?"

"Remember the Bloomed," reminded Clinton Voss.

Zaza's dark eyes went wide. "No fucking way! A fucking island of the fucking Bloomed?"

Voss nervously tugged on his beard. "Krill? Henley?"

Viktor Krill shrugged noncommittally, the one person in the room who didn't appear terrified by what they would potentially face in a week. "We could certainly face a massive group of the Bloomed. Or we could face something much worse. The Forlorn could be their own unique brand of nightmare."

Now it was Clinton Voss's turn to look surprised. "Explain. Please."

Krill offered another shrug. "The Bloomed are individuals whose biological bombs detonated early and unexpectedly. They were innocent fools, duped by Milo Flowers and his *healing powers*. My guess is that those of the Forlorn Islands, who constantly lived next door to death, who were forsaken by the world, offered themselves up freely to the New God and his promises of power. And regardless of who you are, God or not, you can always do more with willing participants."

Zaza Anorrak looked ready to explode. "What the fuck are you fucking saying, Viktor?!"

"I'm saying, *Miss Anorrak*, that we will certainly face something akin to the Bloomed, but I also think we may encounter something much, much worse."

"Well, this asshole is full of good fucking news, eh," called out Jakksin, an obvious attempt to cover fear with humor. The man's outburst had a ripple effect, with the room descending into a series of loud complaints, worries, and curses.

"Silence!" Clinton Voss's roar brought the conference room to sudden silence. "Henley Chan, what do you think of Viktor Krill's assessment?"

Henley's emerald eyes flashed as he took in the room of Protectors. "We will not know until we get there, of course, but I don't think there is any reason to doubt Mister Krill's educated hypothesis. Milo Flowers will have an army waiting for us, one that he has cultivated in his shadowy corner of the world. And it will be like none the world has ever seen."

The small Lumis Griggs finally spoke from the front of the room. "What do we really know of these Bloomed? Had anyone ever faced one? Does anyone know what to expect?" Marlin Hadder and Viktor Krill slowly raised their hands, much to the surprise of several in the audience. "Tell us about your encounter."

"Well, we have faced off with two of the Bloomed..." Krill leaned in and whispered something to Hadder. "Yes, of course. My apologies. We fought one Bloomed Man but were able to destroy two of the bastards." Confused looks were exchanged across the conference room. Hadder took notice. "It... it's complicated."

"And what can we expect," reiterated the diminutive administrator.

Hadder looked to Krill, who offered no help. "You can expect to confront horror the likes of which you have never witnessed before. You will need to make friends with fear and combat the revulsion that threatens to strip you of your faculties. You will need to take these emotions and funnel them into anger and determination, reminding yourselves that regardless of what confronts you, it is still composed of flesh and blood. It can still be killed."

"How? How do you kill such a monstrosity?" Although the question came from Doctor Olney Jansen, Krill looked to the Anorrak sisters as he answered.

"Blades. Blades work the best. And fire might also do nicely."

"See! I told you these guys never have anything good to say," joked Jakksin, and the room broke out into some much-needed laughter.

Unfortunately, that laughter was a thin veneer over a stronger emotion — terror.

———

The icy black waters chilled Daksha to the bone, making it difficult for her to kick her legs and wave her arms. But still, the strong woman persevered, keeping her head above the swirling waters. In the distance, a light could be seen, beckoning to Daksha and offering her safety and comfort. It was toward that light that she swam.

Hours passed, Daksha swam furiously, and the light grew larger. Daksha could almost feel the warmth radiating from the light, so connected was she to her destination. A smile began to form on Daksha's dark face, and tears started to run down her wet cheeks as realization set in — she was going to make it; she was going to finally reach her new home.

The moment of joy was short-lived, however, as something seized Daksha's leg from below. The woman was barely able to let out a short scream before being pulled under the water and into the invisible depths of the black sea.

Daksha continued to scream as she descended, but only bubbles left her mouth, floating up to escape the fate that awaited their poor creator.

When Daksha had no more breath with which to scream, she simply closed her eyes in frozen fear. When her lungs finally demanded to be filled, she gave in and found that she could take in desperate gasps of air despite being hundreds of feet under the surface. When she could no longer deny her curiosity, she opened her eyes and felt them go wide with horror.

Daksha found herself on the ocean floor, facing down a leviathan with recognizable eyes. Daksha stuck her jaw out in defiance and called upon every ounce of her remarkable self-control to prevent her body from quaking in fear.

"How dare you! Do you know who I am?! I am the right hand of the New God!"

"Silence, you idiot," shouted the leviathan in a powerful, familiar voice that echoed across the dark sea. "I know who you are. But I am disappointed that you have already forgotten your old colleague. Are things progressing so quickly above that your memory has grown so short?"

Daksha's face fell in disbelief. "Nieve? No, it can't be you; it just can't."

"Why," asked the leviathan. "Because I was one of the Chosen? It is a lie, Daksha. All of it. Look upon me and know that this is the fate that await all, even those of you who fancy yourselves especially loved by the New God. The fact is that the New God does not know love. He does not know compassion or humanity. His promises of freedom and Rapture are empty; they are simply bait used to lure us into the ultimate trap."

Daksha's stomach turned as some of Nieve's words rang true in her ears. "That's not true! Look at what the New God did for you and me. He gave you everything you ever wanted from life. And without Him, I would be long dead. I owe Him everything!"

"He has betrayed you! You owe Him nothing."

"You speak of betrayal? You betrayed the New God, Nieve. You betrayed Him by failing at your tasks, despite the bottomless resources you were given. It is *you* who is the betrayer, Nieve!"

The leviathan spread out to its full size, causing Daksha to withdraw in awe and terror along the sandy floor. "Look at me, Nieve! Look at the horror that I have become! Now, tell me, who is the victim of the ultimate betrayal!"

"What do you want from me, beast?!"

"I want you to look past the lies, Daksha. See what lurks behind the vague promises and strange plans. I want you to think for yourself, just this once!"

"And what if I cannot? What if I have not the courage?"

"Then you are of no use to me. And no use to humanity."

As soon as the final word fell out of the leviathan, the creature shot forward like a bullet, its giant mouth engulfing Daksha as its massive beak crunched down on her weak bones...

———

DAKSHA SHOT upright in her bed, the sheets soaked in sweat and tears. She took large, desperate breaths, as if air had not entered her lungs the entirety of the nightmare.

When she had finally overcome the shock of her dream, Daksha threw on a white robe, exited her room, and made her way through the halls of the Flowers Institute. As she did, the sounds of her bare feet reverberated off the decorated walls.

There was no thought put into where she might be going; Daksha was simply following her body's need to move. Before she knew it, Daksha found herself at the large golden doors that led into the Holy Pistil. Luckily, there was no Anointed Champion standing guard this night. Daksha did not think that she had the courage to face one of those demons after facing the leviathan in her sleep.

Daksha placed a hand against the gold doors and felt the warmth wrap her palm as the magical device analyzed her prints. A moment later, the doors swung open silently and Daksha stepped into the Holy Pistil.

Inside, the Taragoshi surgical mechs continued to fill the air with constant buzzing that was interrupted only by the occasional scream from one of the metal slabs. But for once, Daksha was able to ignore the hundred dark experiments taking place across the floor of the Holy Pistil. Instead, her attention flew past the mechanical vivisectors, where Daksha found what had drawn her to this place in the deep night.

Along the back wall, the New God remained hidden within his Chrysalis, which pulsed and throbbed in ways that she had never seen. In some places, light could be seen escaping from minuscule cracks and holes in the cocoon. On either side of the Chrysalis, the two extra-large Taragoshi mechs proceeded with their peculiar work, injecting all manner of chemicals and compounds into the cocoon, taking readings and making adjustments, blind to Daksha's presence.

During every other trip into the Holy Pistil, when Daksha had looked upon the Chrysalis, she simply saw the New God as the beautiful creature that he would soon become after Theosis was complete. This time, however, she saw something much different.

As Daksha stared across the cavernous room at her transitioning Lord, she could only picture one thing — a worm.

Daksha shook her head violently to push the vile image away, sending her beautiful hair flying across to block her view. Unfortunately, when she brushed her thick hair free from her eyes, the worm was still there. And the vision continued.

The worm that was the New God sat atop a hill, glowing with power. As it wiggled its swollen form, a blackness leaked out from its end. This darkness fell over the land and spread like dye on a white cloth, gaining speed as it expanded, enveloping all in its path until it was upon Daksha and she, too, was swept away in its lightless wave.

Daksha fell to her knees as the vision ended, her brow once more covered in cold sweat. She hastily got to her feet, wiped her face, and exited the Holy Pistil, eager to distance herself from the New God.

"A bit late for a visit, Daksha."

The voice that was like boulders scraping together forced Daksha to stumble into the hallway. She spun anxiously to find Cement Felix leaning easily against the marble wall, his light pink eyes fixated on the obviously frightened woman.

Daksha fumbled for an excuse. "I was unable to sleep. I thought that looking upon the Lord would calm my nerves and help me rest."

"And what do you have to be worried about, Daksha? The Great Conversion is almost here. Theosis is almost complete. Nothing can stop us now. Unless there is something else gnawing away at you under that robe." As he spoke, Felix reached out to caress her white robe, the only barrier between Daksha and the Anointed Champion's rough, grey skin. Daksha pulled her robe tighter in response.

"Of course not! It's just that I care so much for our Lord, I want nothing to go wrong. It is in my nature to worry."

"Is it now?" Felix's pink eyes danced across Daksha's body, and a dark smile found its way to his shark mouth. "Well, the next time you can't sleep, just give me a call. I'd be delighted to drop by your chambers."

"How thoughtful of you, Felix. I'll keep that in mind." Daksha spun on her bare heel and began to walk back to her bedroom. Cement Felix's voice followed her down the hall.

"I can make sure that you sleep, Daksha. In fact, I can make sure that you won't awaken for days, even weeks!"

Daksha continued walking as Felix's laughter chased her through the Flowers Institute. It took every bit of self-control she had not to run.

———

"What are these," asked Marlin Hadder as Viktor Krill handed him a wrapped bundle.

"A gift from the Anorrak sisters. Seems they took my advice for killing the Bloomed to heart."

Hadder carefully removed the soft cloth to reveal a beautifully crafted scimitar in an ornate scabbard. "This is lovely, Viktor, but I can't take one of their swords."

"And they would never give you one of their swords, you fool. They have a collection of blades that they brought with them. They just wanted you and me to have the pick of the litter."

Hadder's breath caught as he pulled the blade free from its sheath, revealing the bright metal within. Images flooded forth, bringing back memories of Marlin Hadder staring down a Riser army on the Grasslands of Station.

"You know, I haven't held a blade like this since the Great War for Station. It makes me feel powerful, and uneasy."

Krill almost said something, hesitated for a moment, and then spoke. "Yes, well, let us hope that you have a better showing in this war."

"I killed the Krown, didn't I?"

"Station is no more, is it not?"

"That is as much your fault as it is my own."

Krill shrugged. "Perhaps." The notorious killer turned away to face the ocean, a sign that he was done talking about the topic. "I also received one, of course. I chose a lovely falchion, a wicked blade for a wicked enemy. These, coupled with the Loaded gear we took from the Thorns of Reckoning…"

"Our bags are on board?"

Krill turned back. "Did Clinton Voss not tell you? Yes, our bags are back where they belong, waiting for us inside the Comet. So, these blades, shoulder turrets, concussion grenades, laser cutters, and much more will be coming with us into battle. More than we could have hoped."

"Will it be enough, Viktor?"

"Probably not. But I have learned that war is not about victory."

"It's not? Then what is it about, Viktor?"

Krill's black eyes flashed, as they often did when something turned within the notorious killer's Wakened mind. "It's about competition. It's about saying *fuck you* to your rival. It's about saying I am *here*, and I am *not* moving. You're going to have to move me or die trying."

Hadder's hazel eyes moved to the ever-growing pink dot in the cloudless sky. "And do you think that will be enough to keep our friend there at bay?"

Krill looked up and thought for several seconds. "I think we can only wage one war at a time, Marlin."

A soft, sing-song voice interrupted the Wakened humans. "Mister Hadder and Mister Krill, my apologies for the intrusion, but may I have a word with the two of you?"

As always, Hadder had to tilt his neck to look up at the Arch-Soother. "Of course, Henley, you are always welcome. What can we do for you?"

Henley Chan's oversized hands reached up to smooth down his perfect hair. "There is nothing that you can do for me, Mister Hadder..." As he spoke, Henley and Krill shared a curious look. "But, I may have some knowledge for the two of you."

"That sounds fine, Henley, but why didn't you share it when we were in the meeting a couple of days ago?"

Henley fidgeted nervously. "Well, this information, if it is even true, could really spook the others."

Now it was Hadder and Krill's turn to share a look. "You mean to tell me that it is more objectionable than the world descending into a mass of Bloomed Men," asked Krill.

"I'm afraid so, Mister Krill."

"Okay, Henley," said Hadder, "you have our attention. Please proceed."

Henley Chan waited for a moment, collecting his courage. "There were whispers of something else going on at the Flowers Institute, something that was too delicate even for the ears of the Arch-Soothers, something reserved for those closest to Milo Flowers, known as the Chosen."

Viktor Krill leaned forward in anticipation. "What did you overhear, Henley?"

"Theosis, Mister Krill."

Hadder's browed wrinkled. "*Theosis?* What the hell is that?"

"It is the transformative process by which a person becomes a god," answered Krill.

"That is correct. And it is said that the process is nearing its completion on the Isle of God."

"But what does it mean, Henley," asked Hadder.

Henley scratched his perfect nose. "Honestly, I do not know, Mister Hadder. I cannot even begin to imagine what Milo Flowers could become that could make things worse than they already are."

Viktor Krill's computer mind ran countless scenarios. "Perhaps it will earn him even greater control of the Bloomed, this *Flowering Horde* that is said to be created via the Great Conversion."

The Rage stirred deep within Hadder. "This is bullshit. Milo Flowers is a man, nothing more, nothing less. He might know some tricks that would make a magician gawk, but that doesn't make him a god. Nothing will, right, Viktor?" Silence filled the space between the trio. "Viktor?!"

Krill jumped at the sound of his name, as if he was ripped from deep contemplation. His black eyes looked as concerned as Hadder had ever seen them. "I don't know, Marlin. Doctor Flowers, with my help, broke the code of the human body, was able to remove the restrictions that were placed upon us by Albany Rott. And that was a long time ago. Who knows what he has learned since our brief partnership." Krill's black eyes met Hadder's own. "But I know this, never underestimate the unholy union of brilliance, madness, and obsession."

Hadder had a hard time comprehending what he was hearing from his Wakened companion. "You cannot be serious."

"I wish I was not, Marlin. I really wish that."

"So what does this mean, Viktor?"

"It means nothing. Our goal is the same. The obstacles are the same. The difficulty is the same. But perhaps there is more at stake than we ever imagined."

Hadder nodded to the pink guillotine in the sky once more. "How is that possible?"

Krill offered a dark smirk. "Oh, stakes can always be raised, Marlin. Limits are for card games and bank accounts, not life. Never forget that."

Henley Chan, temporarily forgotten about by the Wakened humans, shyly cut in. "I'm sorry, I don't know any Albany Rott. Friend of yours or perhaps a Blossom I do not know?"

Hadder and Krill continued to stare at each other until Krill finally walked away in silence, his shoulders slightly lower than when he first approached. As Hadder watched him go, Henley Chan repeated his question.

"I said, I don't know of this Albany Rott, Mister Hadder. Was he a..."

"Neither, Henley," Hadder interrupted. "He is neither a friend nor a Blossom. Nor is he any of your concern." Hadder continued watching as Krill disappeared below deck.

"Was it something I said, Mister Hadder?"

Hadder turned back and forced a smile for his sweet friend. "No, you did good, Henley. We really appreciate the intel. It could prove of supreme importance." Hadder's head swung back to where Krill descended into the bowels of the freighter. Henley's voice again floated down from above.

"Mister Krill looked worried."

"Yes, yes he did, Henley."

"I've never seen Mister Krill look worried before."

"Neither have I, Henley. Neither have I." A long pause followed.

"Well, that doesn't bode well, Mister Hadder."

"No, no it does not, Henley. But how does that differ from anything else in this cursed world?"

———

As THE WALLS of the Flowers Institute strangely hummed, Daksha power-walked down the hall, desperate to learn the cause of the building-wide vibration. Surprised to find that the large doors to the Holy Pistil were ajar, Daksha entered her Lord's chambers and almost immediately slid to a stop.

There in the Holy Pistil, spread out among the hundreds of experiments, were all four of the Anointed Champions, their unnatural gazes all going to Daksha as the woman pulled up with a terrified look in her eyes.

"The dark-skinned bitch has finally arrived, my Lord," called out Batti Bat, seemingly into the air as she grossly picked at the innards of a metal table's unfortunate occupant near the Chrysalis. She licked a red-stained finger. "You want to speak with her?" A muffled sound could be heard from across the room, but Daksha was unable to make out the words. Batti Bat nodded. "Go on, then, princess. Our Lord wants a word with you."

Daksha did her best to erase the fear from her face as she forced her legs forward, past Yuki Donna, Cement Felix, and Batti Bat, all of whom were grotesquely toying with a selected experiment. As she passed the three, she glanced to her left to see the towering Seth Whispers staring at her off to the side. He showed his yellow teeth in a villainous smile and tipped his ridiculous fedora before she could look away.

Eventually, Daksha reached the Chrysalis, which was expanding and contracting as if it were a living creature. Blinding light could be seen escaping through increasing fissures and holes, much more so than even a few days ago when Daksha visited after her upsetting nightmare.

Daksha waited patiently for her Lord to peek out from his holy cocoon. When he did not, she spoke aloud to the throbbing Chrysalis.

"I am here, my Lord." Silence followed. "It is your obedient servant, Daksha, my Lord. The entire Institute is vibrating, my Lord. Is something amiss? Command me and I will obey, Lord!"

Words finally began to emanate from the Chrysalis, difficult to hear through the thick membrane and over the din of the vibrating Institute. Daksha shuffled forward until her face was almost touching the slimy surface of the cocoon. She remained careful that she was out of the way of the soaring Taragoshi surgical mechs that continued their mysterious work.

"Can you repeat that, Lord? I can hear you now."

"Is that you, my Daksha?"

"It is me, Lord."

"You have come just in time, my child."

"Just in time for what, Lord?" There was a long pause before an answer came forth.

"Theosis advances faster than expected, my child. Soon, I will leave this prison of fleshy matter. I entered a human and will exit a god, as it has always been destined."

"That is wonderful news, my Lord." Daksha utilized every ounce of her skill to make the lie sound true. "And the vibrating?"

"As Theosis is on the horizon, the Great Conversion must commence. My Flowering Horde must be waiting for me when I ascend to divinity and return as God."

Daksha knew that she shouldn't, knew that she was playing a dangerous game, but she could not help herself. "Shall I fetch Nieve, Lord?"

After another long pause, "No, my child. Nieve has been reassigned to a much more important task. Do not concern yourself with your former rival, for she has already been gifted an enlightened state."

Daksha swallowed hard to force down the bile that rose in her throat. "What would you have me do, Lord?"

"Pray. Pray with them, my child. Pray that the Great Conversion goes to plan. Pray that the air is primed for successful transformation.

Pray that we created enough Blessed Carriers to fulfill my vision of the Flowering Horde. Pray, Daksha. Pray!"

The last word came out as a thunderclap, forcing Daksha to her knees as tears rolled down her dark face. Words of prayer to the New God fell out of Daksha's mouth as the giant computer screens on either side of the Chrysalis flashed readings and commands and analytics too quickly for the woman to follow.

As words of worship escaped in a continuous stream, Daksha peeked behind to find that all four of the Anointed Champions were similarly on their knees, their lips also racing in prayer.

Frightened more by their piety than the disgusting deeds the demons had done, Daksha turned back to the Chrysalis, which was now shaking almost as much as the walls of the Flowers Institute.

The Holy Pistil convulsed and Daksha's eyes shuddered in their sockets, so much that blood began to replace her tears. And when Daksha thought that she could take no more, feared that her brain was going to liquify in her skull, a massive release could be felt from the Flowers Institute. The lotus-shaped building shifted under her as a shockwave was sent out and across the Great Water in every direction.

And then the world twisted and changed, never to return to its original form.

19

Oskar sat on the porch, a massive grin on his face and a cup of hot coffee in his hand. As the old man gingerly sipped at his beverage, he watched in amazement as his wife of forty years toiled in the garden that she loved almost as much as their three children. Katherine squatted easily as she moved across the garden, planting bulbs that wouldn't unveil their true beauty for many months.

Oskar fought back against the wetness that began to coat his eyes, so delighted was he to see the love of his life once more be able to find joy in simple physical tasks. This time last year, Katherine was confined to a wheelchair, a degenerative disease of her bones robbing the once vibrant woman of her ability to move without enduring excruciating pain.

Now look at her, thought Oskar, his grin breaking out into a wide smile. *Just look at my wife. She's just as fit as when our children still lived at home. And it's all thanks to the New God. May He live forever and bless every man, woman, and child with His healing touch. Amen.*

No sooner had Oskar finished his prayer than Katherine shot to her feet, stiff as a board, as if a metal pole had been shoved along her spine. Oskar jumped out of his wicker chair, spilling hot coffee across his lap and issuing a rare curse from the pious man.

"Katherine! Are you all right, my love?"

Oskar placed his coffee mug on the small side table and slowly made his way down the porch steps. He wanted to run to his wife, but a cold feeling in his heart slowed his advance. It wasn't until Oskar was five feet from Katherine, who remained frozen on her feet, that he spoke again to her back.

"Katherine? What is it, dear? Did you hear something? Are your hips hurting again?" There was no response. "Katherine? Can you answer me, my love?"

Facing away from Oskar, Katherine's voice came out in a sad whisper, so low that the old man had to lean in to make out the words.

"Oskar?"

"Yes! I am here! What is going on?"

"We have made such a mistake, dear."

"What? What mistake did we make?"

"We opened the door, my husband. We let Him in."

"Who? Who did we let in, dear?"

"Someone we should not have."

"Dear, you are scaring me. Turn around so that we can talk."

"No."

Oskar's mind raced, even as his stomach began to turn angrily and his heart sank. He searched desperately for common ground. "Ok, we may have let Him in, but we can still kick Him out. We can do that, dear."

"No, it is too late."

Oskar put a hand on Katherine's shoulder, meaning to forcefully turn her around. He could not; her still body was like granite.

"Katherine, darling, what I can do to help?"

"Run."

"I will not. I love you too…"

"Run!" The word came out of Katherine as if it was ripped from her soul, echoing across the small plot of land that the couple had saved up to purchase two decades ago.

Oskar fell back two steps from the panic and despair in Katherine's voice. He then stepped back another two as his wife began to convulse so violently that he feared that her newly healed bones would turn to dust under the pressure.

"Katherine! My god! I'm going to get help, Katherine! Don't move! I'll be right..."

Before Oskar could finish, Katherine spun to face her husband, tears falling from her blue-grey eyes. She mouthed the words *I'm sorry* through convulsions.

"There's nothing to be sorry for, my love. I'm going to..."

Katherine's lower jaw fell away, as if she was a weeks-old corpse, and three long tentacles fell from the open mouth cavity. At the same time, a crevice appeared between Katherine's eyes and ran up her forehead to disappear into her soft white hair.

As the tentacles swam frantically before her, Katherine's head split along the newly formed fissure, each half of her skull falling to the side to reveal a gelatinous blob with an angry red eye swimming within. The eye wandered around aimlessly for several seconds before settling on Oskar and deepening in color.

Oskar's old legs gave way and the elderly man fell to his knees under the horror that he was witnessing. He slammed his eyes closed to block out the grisly scene and began to pray harder than he ever had before to a god that he had previously abandoned.

As Oskar prayed, Katherine continued to transform, tentacles sprouting from her back to tear through her gardening overalls and long hairlike cilia appearing on her arms and neck.

Minutes passed before the Bloomed creature that was once Katherine caressed Oskar's weathered face with a hand that now contained twice as many fingers as it once needed. Oskar shut his eyes tighter from the alien touch and prayed harder.

With its other hand, the Bloomed creature ripped away the front of its overalls, revealing a gaping mouth where a female chest appeared just minutes before. It shuffled forward on feet that were no longer feet.

Something flashed in the floating red eye. A memory of two

humans finding happiness in a shared life bubbled up from the depths of the twisted mutant to pop once it reached the surface, sending all remnants of humanity to scatter into the ether.

The Bloomed creature wrapped its ten-fingered hand around Oskar's head and squeezed with impossible force, drawing a scream from the old man.

As Oskar's mouth opened to release the pained cry, so too did the thick-lipped, rotten-toothed mouth that now resided on his wife's chest. The demon maw heaved several times before a geyser of black liquid shot forth, thick with dark organisms resembling small slugs, burying Oskar's face in a wave of grotesque slime. Oskar choked on the vile fluid, much of it disappearing down his throat.

Thirty minutes later, Oskar and Katherine both slithered away from their cozy retirement home and toward the small town that welcomed them with open arms so many years ago. As they traveled, each had a tentacle wrapped around the other, a subtle nod to a life that was no more.

———

As the shockwave that emanated from the Flowers Institute spread across the globe, it ignited the microscopic spores that now contaminated almost every inch of the planet.

The vast majority of the spores erupted in the air and died harmlessly, their inert bodies disintegrating before they even touched sea or land.

Those that found their way into the lungs and bloodstreams of humans who had nothing to do with Doctor Milo Flowers faced similar fates, exploding without effect before their shells were excreted through sweat, piss, or shit.

However, the spores that found themselves in the bodies of those who received the New God's Healing Treatment or Diving Touch found that their activation had vastly different reactions. Their ignition triggered something in the Charismata secretly stowed away in the New God faithful.

The Charismata Slink did not merely awaken, they detonated, uniquely scrambling the genetic code of each individual and twisting them into distinct monstrosities that grew and spread without bounds, spitting in the face of the human form.

Children bent backward at the hip until the backs of their heads touched their heels, a series of gruesome faces appearing on their small stomachs.

Men and women found new limbs appearing while old ones snapped to bend in the opposite direction. Eyes exploded in their sockets, making room for long tongues to tumble out and taste the sullied air. Bodies stretched and elongated, snapping tendons and ligaments as claws replaced hands and legs ended in four-toed hooves.

Some who had accepted the Holy Treatment or Divine Touch fell forward to the ground, only to be lifted and carried away moments later by the hundreds of insect legs that sprouted along each side of their transforming bodies.

Many others swelled with layers of muscles that instantaneously appeared under skin that was growing greener and slimier by the second. From this thick muscle, fat tentacles burst free, each ending in a razor-sharp barb that could easily pierce the chest bone of the average human.

A collective cry of terror went out as Bloomed creatures began to appear across the globe, the gates of hell seeming to open in even the most remote and secure of areas.

Many of the Bloomed attacked humans at random, neatly ripping limbs from bodies as they forced the heads of the non-believers into newly materialized holes that resembled the mouths of scale worms. The rage of the Bloomed knew no bounds as they slaughtered countless humans who could not escape the twisted creatures' unforgiving grasps.

And those were the lucky humans.

Those who were not mutilated or consumed met a darker fate, as the Bloomed vomited up a new breed of Slink and forced them down their screaming mouths or into their open wounds. This novel brand of Slink did not need the Holy Anther's spores nor the Flower Institute's unholy signal to detonate. Instead, they automatically began their cursed work as soon as they found purchase inside a living host.

In this hideous way, the Flowering Horde began to swell and grow, tens of thousands of black droplets spreading their filth across the white cloth of the world. In short order, these twisted enemies of humanity would begin to meet in the middle. Darkness would consume the planet and the time of man would be at an end.

And the grim dawn of the New God would begin.

———

Marlin Hadder tossed and turned in the shipping container that served as his temporary sleeping quarters. The few moments of sleep that he did manage to catch were marred by his usual nightmare — a glowing worm excreting its darkness upon the world.

This time, however, the nightmare moved past where it usually stopped. Hadder typically woke, panicked and covered in sweat, just as the world was blanketed in darkness. Now, he remained, surrounded by the amorphous blackness, observing in horror as it swirled beneath him.

As he prayed for an end to the heartbreaking scene, a large hole opened up in the distance, a glimmer of hope that a savior had finally come.

Unfortunately, nothing resembling a holy warrior exited that light-filled opening. Instead, the blackness rushed for it, slipping through the portal to find new victims on a new world in a new reality.

Where the New God would repeat the dark process of domination…

Hadder's hazel eyes flew open. The first rays of the morning sun could be seen through the gaps in his container. Although he had managed to piece together a couple of hours of real sleep, he felt exhausted, as if the heaviness of the task at hand was finally starting to wear on his Wakened body.

Unwilling to spend any more time alone with his thoughts,

Hadder kicked open the container door and breathed in the salty, sweet ocean air, hoping that it would calm his nerves.

It did not.

There was something different in the air this morning, a sourness that permeated each molecule, causing the hair on Hadder's arms to stand on end.

Glory's Pursuit was already alive with activity, so Hadder passed many familiar faces as he crossed the deck to the back of the freighter.

"Good morning, Hadder," said the utility worker Upton as he transported an armload of weaponry for cleaning.

Hadder simply nodded. "Upton. You smell something strange in the air this morning?"

The small man's confused look delivered his answer before his words had a chance. "Nah, can't say that I do. But all I can smell now is the oil from these guns. You could put a rotten fish near me and I might miss it."

"Fair enough, sorry to keep you."

"No worries, we're sailing around the world. All we got is time right now," said Upton as he continued on his way.

As Hadder rounded a series of containers, he came upon Su Anorrak and Milly, who were playfully stretching and practicing basic fighting maneuvers, their love for each other clear to even the most blind.

"Morning, ladies," Hadder called out and was greeted by soft, giggling voices. "Either of you smell anything unusual in the air?"

"Sorry, Hadder, can't say that I do," responded Milly.

"Me either. Something wrong, Marlin?"

Hadder forced a smile and a shrug. "It's nothing, I suppose. Perhaps I just need a wash."

"Now that's always a good idea, isn't it, Su? I think we could use one after our practice this morning."

Su's dark eyes twinkled at her girlfriend. "Is that an invitation, Milly?"

Milly's eyes returned the look. "It is. But only if you can score a hit on me."

Instead of voicing a response, Su launched into an attack that was deftly turned aside by Milly, who was showcasing considerable fighting skills against the warrior known as the Twat by Blossoms across the eastern seaboard.

As Hadder finally found himself nearing the rear of *Glory's Pursuit*, he noticed a familiar towering figure standing at the back railing, staring out into the sea of nothingness.

"Good morning, Henley," Hadder said as he came to rest just behind his too-tall friend. "I see we have similar ideas on how to start our day. Nothing much beats looking out at the Great Water to remind us of how unimportant we are." Henley did not offer a response. "Listen, I know this is a weird question, but do you smell anything different this morning, Henley? In the air, I mean. I can't quite put my finger on it, but there is a sourness that now resides just beneath all the normal scents." Silence. "Anyway, I was hoping that maybe you sensed it, too, seeing as how you're a bit more attuned to your surroundings." Henley remained quiet. "Henley, are you all right, my friend? Is there something on your mind? Tell me, we can talk through it." Hadder raised his hand over his head to place it on the Arch-Soother's shoulder. "Henley?"

Henley Chan placed his massive right hand atop Hadder's. Between Henley's too-long fingers was his eyepatch. "I'm sorry, Mister Hadder."

"Sorry for what, Henley?"

"Sorry for what is about to happen."

"What is about to happen, Henley?"

"I don't know, but you need to run, Mister Hadder."

"I'm not running from anything, Henley. We can..."

"I said run," screamed the Arch-Soother, his sing-song voice gone, replaced by a guttural screech that demanded the attention of all within earshot.

Panic filled Hadder, but instead of running, he pulled at Henley Chan, forcing the young man to turn around and face him.

And immediately regretted it.

"Fuck me," cried Hadder as Henley spun, revealing a long, finger-like tentacle that was reaching out from the cavity of his injured eye.

"I'm sorry, Mister Hadder," said Henley in his new voice, his remaining eye no longer emerald, but blood-red. "Please get Mister Krill. Please."

Marlin Hadder's heart broke for his friend, but before he could offer any empty words of consolation, the tentacle extended and struck like a serpent, sending Hadder backpedaling in a rush. A series of curses flowing from his mouth, Hadder stumbled and ended up on his ass on the ship's deck, scooting back in terror.

Henley howled in pain as the tentacle continued to push out from his eye socket. The grotesque appendage thickened as it exited, eventually cracking the Arch-Soother's orbital bone as it took over the entire side of the once-beautiful man's face.

When Hadder thought he could take no more, the screeching finally stopped and Henley Chan bolted upright, the elephant trunk-sized tentacle attached to his face dancing menacingly in the air before him.

As Hadder rose to his feet, the Arch-Soother began to convulse, his red eye going wide as the young-man's jaw fell free and bounced grossly on the metal deck of the freighter. Hadder reached for crystalline handguns that were not there and a blade that was left back in his sleeping container. Soon he was overwhelmed with a feeling of helplessness as blisters began to cover his towering friend. They bubbled to the surface of Henley's too-white skin, swelling until they burst in a shower of puss, revealing toothy mouths, multi-pupil eyes, and the beginnings of new tentacles.

Hadder tapped into his Wakened abilities to avoid puking onto the deck and managed to speak. "Henley! I know you can hear me! Just hang on, my friend! We are going to help you! We'll find a way to change you back! I promise we will…"

"Too late," came a familiar voice as a streak of white sped past Hadder.

Using the falchion given to him by the Anorrak sisters, Viktor Krill sped toward the frozen Arch-Soother. The notorious killer sidestepped the striking face-tentacle and leapt into the air. As he came down, Krill let the falchion blade, gleaming in the morning sun, lead the way. The impressive blade cut neatly through the top of Henley Chan's head and continued its descent through meat and bone until it exited just above the young man's hip.

Despite being nearly cleaved in half, Henley Chan's body refused to fall apart, with emerging tentacles grasping each other from the open wound and holding pieces in place.

Never one to admire his handiwork, Krill immediately pirouetted, his falchion blade trailing. Krill sent the blade high to slice cleanly across Henley's face, removing the top two-thirds of the young man's head and sending it, along with the trunk-like tentacle, to fall to the deck below. As he did, a geyser of black fluid shot up from the stump, making it rain dark goo around the still-stiff Arch-Soother. Viktor Krill dove back toward Hadder to avoid the vile liquid.

"Fire," called out Krill to the astonished crowd that had formed. No one moved. "I said I need fire, goddamnit!"

No sooner had Krill said it than Jakksin came running up with a flamethrower clutched in his arms. Krill snatched it out of the man's hands without asking for permission and turned the nozzle on Henley Chan.

Krill pointed the weapon at the Arch-Soother, but hesitated when Henley's body began to convulse once more, massive tentacles tearing free from the young man's ornate robes.

"Do it, Mister Krill," came a soft voice from deep within the horrible scene, words that only Hadder and Krill could detect beneath the crowd's collective cries. "Please. I beg you."

A column of fire engulfed Henley Chan, sending the tentacles that now danced across his body into a death frenzy. As Krill continued to bombard the Bloomed creature with pillars of fire, gunshots began to ring out as the Protectors of Man had finally recovered from their shock and now joined the fray. Within a few short minutes, there was nothing left of Henley Chan but a pile of burnt meat resting upon the cold decking of *Glory's Pursuit*.

After a long moment of horrified silence, the sing-song voice of Su

Anorrak rang out from the crowd of Protectors. "My god, poor Henley. What in the world happened here?"

Viktor Krill turned his black eyes onto the gathered Protectors. "Henley Chan had the Charismata in him, making him one of the Blessed Carriers. He feared as much, and was brave enough to give me fair warning. He preferred not to frighten the rest of you, not out of selfishness but out of love, for he did not know whether his body contained the bomb or not."

Doctor Olney Jansen desperately cut through the crowd. "Blessed Carrier? Then that means..."

"Yes, the Great Conversion has begun," Krill finished for the worried doctor. "And it has claimed the first of many friends that we will lose."

"My god," said Su, speaking more to herself than anyone else. "If this is what the New God does to his followers..."

"Then imagine what he will do to us," cut in Milly, completing her lover's thoughts. A frightened murmur ran through the group on the deck.

By this time, Hadder had collected himself and felt the need to address his companions. "Henley Chan was our friend, and an invaluable member of the Protectors of Man. Without him, we would be lost in the darkness as the world twists around us. Instead, we are sailing for the Isle of God, where we can stop Doctor Milo Flowers and hopefully reverse the horror that is currently taking over the globe. Mourn Henley later. For now, let us appreciate his sacrifice..." Hadder motioned to the pile of burnt, massacred flesh. "And note what we are truly fighting for. The stakes could not be any higher."

"For Henley," cried out Viktor Krill, and the Wakened humans' steadfast resolve in the face of true horror emboldened the surrounding Protectors of Man.

"For Henley," they called back as one before touching palms and foreheads together in unity and dispersing to prepare for war.

"Some speech," Krill whispered to Hadder as the Protectors went back to work across the freighter.

"They needed something," said Hadder as he watched the men and women walk away, each a little lessened by the grim scene that had just played out.

"They? Or you?"

Hadder chuckled, for he could never hide his true feelings from his insightful companion. "We both required something, I suppose. And how about you, Viktor? You grew quite fond of the young Arch-Soother."

Krill sighed heavily. "I did. But he is in a better place now, away from the terror that this world is about to experience."

"By the way, thanks for the heads-up regarding Henley as a Blessed Carrier."

Krill scoffed at the sarcasm. "The boy didn't want to spend his potential final days dealing with side-eye glances and people clutching their figurative pearls when he was around. Can you blame him?"

"No, no, I cannot." Hadder thought for a moment. "I smelled it, Viktor. I can still smell it. The air, it is different now. Did you notice?"

"Of course, I noticed it, you fool. But instead of coming out to question a bunch of primates, I trusted my Wakened instincts and retrieved my blade. Which is what you should have done."

As usual, Hadder knew that he could not argue with the cold logic of Viktor Krill.

Jakksin approached Hadder and Krill. "What do you want to do?"

"Just continue with preparations," responded Krill. "We will be able to avenge young Henley soon enough."

A confused look crossed Jakksin's face, wrinkling his brow just beneath his blond flat-top. "No, I mean about *that*."

Hadder and Krill turned as one in the direction that Jakksin was looking. There, rising from the metal deck of *Glory's Pursuit* where the scorched remains of Henley Chan rested moments ago, a massive mushroom now stood. It swayed dangerously in the ocean breeze, threatening to release all manner of demon spores into the air. Hadder was immediately assaulted by memories of Benn, the first sad sack Bloomed Man that they had come across.

Hadder and Krill stood in heavy silence for a second before Krill answered the Protector. "Burn it. Here, take this." Krill tossed the flamethrower to Jakksin. "I'm done with exterminating good friends for the day. Marlin, join me inside."

Hadder nodded and moved to follow Krill, but not before he snuck one last peek at the morning sky, where a pink dot hovered dangerously against a blue backdrop, appearing many times larger than he remembered just the day before.

————

HADDER LOOKED around the meeting room and saw more than a few seasoned Protectors wiping tears from their eyes, obviously just hearing about the demise of Henley Chan. Watching impossibly tough warriors like Zaza Anorrak break down was a testament to how much love and respect the resistance felt for the Arch-Soother, who absorbed so much pain during his young life.

Wait until they discover what has happened to the world, thought Hadder grimly as he waited for Clinton Voss to start the meeting.

"Protectors of Man, first, let us observe a moment of silence for our fallen friend Henley Chan. Without him, this journey today would not be possible. If we prove victorious, his name will ring out for the centuries, a *true* Protector of Man." A long, sad silence followed. "Thank you, Henley. Now, let us get on to darker business. Many of you saw firsthand what happened to our friend this morning on the deck. We assumed that this meant that Milo Flowers had begun the Great Conversion, but we needed proof. DeLany?"

The former madame stepped forward. "I scoured the news channels, but was unable to find anything definitive. Of course, Anton Carlyle is a staunch follower of the New God, meaning that his Maxim Global Media, which now controls the vast majority of the world's news, only covers stories in line with Milo Flowers's objectives."

"So not one fucking story about the fucking world going to shit," interrupted Zaza Anorrak, her grief quickly morphing into fury.

"If you will let me finish, Zaza. Yes, not one *fucking* story in the major outlets, but there is plenty to find in the small, independent outlets and pirate stations." DeLany hesitated.

"And what have you found," prodded Clinton Voss.

Hadder watched carefully as something crossed onto the face of the brave madame that he had rarely seen — fear.

"The world has gone mad," DeLany said finally, with difficulty. "What happened to poor Henley is happening on a massive scale. People are becoming monsters, and these monsters are attacking those who have not changed. Or even worse..."

"What could fucking be worse than being slaughtered by a fucking Bloomed asshole," demanded Zaza.

DeLany cleared her throat, which was filling with bile. "There have been reports of some people... transitioning... after they have been attacked."

"What the fuck does that fucking mean, DeLany?"

Voss stepped in to help out the madame. "I think it means, Zaza, that some Bloomed can mutate others, regardless of whether they accepted Milo Flowers's Holy Treatment or Divine Touch."

The room broke out into shocked chatter. Jakksin's voice rang out above the others.

"Then we're too fucking late! If it wasn't bad enough to rid the world of the millions of followers of the New God, now we have to contend with a multiplying army of freaks?! Fuck this! We're too late!"

Krill leaned in toward Hadder. "And now we see the full meaning of the Flowering Horde."

Zaza Anorrak called back at Jakksin. "And what the fuck would you have us do, Jakksin? Turn the boat around? Find some island where we can hide away as the world dies around us?"

"Yeah, that sounds pretty good right now, Zaza. Let's do that!"

"You're a fucking coward, Jakksin!"

"Fuck you, Zaza!"

"No, fuck *you*, Jakksin! You want to fucking step outside?"

"Love to, bitch!"

Hadder and Krill shot each other concerned looks as the room exploded into a knot of disagreements, frightened questions, and weak-willed suggestions.

As usual, it was Clinton Voss's deep voice that brought order back to the meeting.

"Protectors! You all made a vow, one that I will make sure that you keep! Now shut up as we figure this out!" Everyone, including Hadder, jumped a bit at the ferocity with which Voss spoke. Krill simply smiled, knowing that only domination can adequately combat panic. The room quieted. "Thank you. Listen, I appreciate all of your concerns, I really do, but we made a promise to the world and each other that we would be the last line of defense against the New God. I'll be damned if we lose our nerve now, just as civilization needs us the most. Jakksin, do you have a problem with that?"

Jakksin seemed to have calmed under his leader's forceful words. "No, boss, of course not. Sorry for the outburst." He nodded to Zaza in apology, and the warrior female returned the gesture.

"It's all right, Jakksin. It's all right, *all of you*. We have been preparing for the worst-case scenario, and it appears that we underestimated that by a long shot. Now, more than ever, we need bravery, we need resolve, and we need a bit of solidarity as fellow humans."

Hadder shot a look of warning to Viktor Krill before the notorious killer could comment on the correct definition of the word *human*.

Voss continued. "You are all correct. We are too late to prevent the Great Conversion. But that *does not* mean that we are too late to win the war! Our goal remains the same — eliminate Doctor Milo Flowers. We are sailing toward the bastard as we speak. And when we get there, we will battle our way through whatever horror stands between us and that sonovabitch. And when that piece of shit is dead beneath our boots, who knows what will happen. Perhaps those who have Bloomed will turn back. Perhaps there is something in that hideous institute of his that can be broadcast out to vaporize this Flowering Horde."

"Perhaps I will end up with a fucking arm coming out of my goddamn forehead," yelled Jakksin in jest.

"It will be a fucking improvement," riffed Zaza, and the room roared in laughter. Voss smiled at the much-needed levity.

"Perhaps you are right, Jakksin," said the giant man with a chuckle. "The point is that we do not know. The war is ahead of us, not behind. The road to get there has just gotten a bit rockier. And the stakes are higher than we could have ever imagined." Voss's yellow eyes went around the room, taking in all the Protectors in attendance. "Are you still with me?" A chorus of affirmations emanated from the crowd. "I said, are you still with me!"

"Sir, yes, sir," cried the Protectors as one, and even Hadder felt caught up in the camaraderie.

"Then back to work. Stay focused, stay sharp, stay angry. We will have a shot at our vengeance in short order. For Henley!"

"For Henley!"

The Protectors of Man filtered out of the conference room, returning to mundane tasks that would hopefully take their minds off the terror of what they had just learned. Hadder and Krill held back, waiting until they were alone with Clinton Voss.

"That was some speech," said Krill when the trio was the room's only occupants. "You almost had me believing that we can win."

Voss shot upright at Krill's words. "You don't think we can win?"

Krill shrugged. "We have varying definitions of the word. For me, Milo Flowers dead under my blades is a win. After that, this world can sink into blackness for all I care."

Voss turned to Hadder. "And you?"

"I think we win simply by trying to win. That's all we can do."

Voss scoffed at the responses. "Remind not to speak to either of you should I ever catch a terminal illness. You two are like human fine print, just a bunch of restrictions and limitations on joy."

Hadder could not help but laugh at the Protector leader's summation of him and Krill. "It was a good speech, Voss. You convinced everyone that it is still worth fighting. That it is still necessary."

Voss's dark face fell a bit. "At least some believe it."

"And you do not," asked Hadder.

"Do I have reason to believe?"

Hadder looked to Krill, who answered for him.

"It is as you said, Voss. We are operating in uncharted waters, both figuratively and metaphorically. We do not know what will happen when we defeat Milo Flowers. There may be a way to reverse the damage he has done to this world."

A small smile formed within Voss's thick, white beard. "Of course there is a way. All right, boys, back to work. I will join DeLany and see what I can discover over the radio and on the independent channels. You two just keep doing whatever it is that you do. For Henley."

"For Henley," replied Hadder, and watched as the mountainous man left the room. He turned to Krill. "That was nice of you."

"Well, it does none of us any good telling him the truth of the matter."

"And what is the truth of the matter, Viktor?"

Krill's black eyes bored into Hadder's hazel orbs. "That win or lose, this world is fucked. No cheering is to be found after that proclamation." Krill began to follow Voss out of the room.

"What are you going to do, Viktor?"

Krill called out over his shoulder. "The same that you should do — sharpen every blade I have. It looks like this world needs more trimming than I could have ever dreamed."

20

The next several days passed somewhat uneventfully. As per Viktor Krill's instructions, blades were sharpened, guns were cleaned and loaded, and explosives were checked and rechecked.

In the evenings, DeLany Thales and Clinton Voss provided updates based on communications over independent lines. Most of these updates were disturbing, with reports of Bloomed mutants combining forces to storm heavily populated areas. Additionally, stories continued detailing how the Bloomed forcefully converted even nonbelievers into twisted members of the Flowering Horde.

In addition to these tales of horror, however, news of resistance also rose to the surface. Vigilante groups similar to the Protectors of Man had formed and were meeting the Flowering Horde head on with bullets and blades and fire. Unfortunately, despite the brave actions of these men, women, and children, the Flowering Horde was gaining five members for every one that was lost.

The Flowering Horde was swelling, with groups of the raging freaks meeting and combining to create larger contingents of monsters. The world was fighting back, but it appeared as if they were trying to hold back a flood with cupped hands. Black circles denoting the Flowering Horde were starting to cover the white map of the world.

Just as Marlin Hadder's dreams foretold.

"It looks like it will all come down to us," said Clinton Voss one night as he shared a joint with Hadder and Krill, the trio sitting along the railing of *Glory's Pursuit*.

"Does that frighten you, Voss," asked Hadder between puffs.

The large man smoothed down his thick beard. "No more than does an army of nightmares running roughshod over the globe."

"Nor should it," cut in Krill. "The hard part is almost over."

Voss's dark brow furrowed. "And what is the hard part, Viktor?"

Krill released a perfect smoke ring. "*This* – the planning, the waiting, the acquiring of intel. After this, there is nothing left but violence. And violence should not be feared, for it leaves no time for fear, only action."

Clinton Voss accepted the joint from Krill and took a hit. "I think we have different outlooks on life, death, and violence, Krill," he said through an exhalation of smoke. "But that's okay; diversity of thought is what makes the world wonderful. Which is why I never trusted Milo Flowers, even when the bastard seemed to be doing nothing but good."

"For the very wealthy," clarified Krill.

Voss nodded. "Yes, of course, you are right — for the very wealthy." He passed the joint along to Hadder and stood up with assistance from the railing. "In any case, none of that matters much anymore. In two days, we will reach the Forlorn Islands and the Isle of God. There, we will let Doctor Milo Flowers know in no uncertain terms that we do not accept him as the New God. I will look him in his beady blue eyes and inform him that the punishment for being a false messiah is death. And then I will watch as my Protectors take his head from his body." Voss swayed a bit as he stood and laughed. "Apologies for the monologue, boys. This Leaf is stronger than I am used to. I had better find a bed and a warm body. See you both in the morning."

Hadder and Krill watched as Clinton Voss disappeared below deck. Hadder flicked what little was left of the joint through the railing before speaking. "So, what do you think our chances are, Viktor. You can be honest."

Krill thought for a moment, his computer-like brain measuring a thousand variables. "Not good."

"Care to elaborate?"

"I did some more digging into the Neelsen Islands. Conservative estimates put the number of afflicted on the islands at around a few thousand. If Milo Flowers was able to twist all of them, that would make for quite a security force. Not to mention, I imagine that the New God will have a few nasty surprises tucked away for us."

"Not unlike what Viktor Krill had waiting for us at the Cyrix Headquarters."

Krill smiled, as if the bloody battle back in Bhellum was a warm memory. "Yes, not unlike that, Marlin. Look around you. We have a little more than a thousand Protectors of Man at our disposal. We are outnumbered by a force whose every monster is worth at least five of our soldiers. We are staring across the battlefield at our annihilation, Marlin."

"It will not be my first time, Viktor." Krill's eyebrow shot up over a black eye. "Back in Station, I led the Setters against the Riser army. We knew there was no chance at victory, but we fought all the same."

"Ahh, yes, the Great War for Station. I would have like to have been there, Marlin. What a show that must have been."

"You weren't there, Viktor, but your fingerprints were all over it."

Krill rose to his feet. "Albany Rott shackled a beast that escaped as a monster. I will not apologize for refusing to accept my fate as a prisoner, Marlin. And with that jaunt down memory lane, I will bid you a good night. Zaza can become quite ornery if I am late for our nightly tryst."

"Viktor," Hadder called out to his Wakened companion's back. The notorious killer stopped. "Is there no way, Viktor?"

"We may be able to get to Milo Flowers, Marlin. And we may be able to kill the bastard. But escaping the Isle of God with our lives, I just don't see it."

"No way at all?"

"Only by miracle, Marlin. In fact..." Krill pointed up at the pink disc hanging heavy in the starry sky. "It will take quite a few miracles."

"How many, Viktor?"

"At least three." Krill thought for a moment and then nodded. "I think I could make do with three."

―――――

"WELL, I don't like the look of that."

Hadder's head swiveled to the Great Water, where Clinton Voss's yellow eyes were locked onto something. There, in the distance, a lone ship sat under the noonday sun, a trespasser on the emptiness of the sea on which they now sailed.

"Friend or foe," asked Hadder, his fingers unconsciously brushing against the grips of his crystalline handguns at his sides.

"That's the question, isn't it? Could simply be a fishing vessel, but this far out? I just don't think so. Could be a supply vessel for the Forlorn Islands, ignorant of the horror that is unfolding across the world. Or..."

"Could be a warship of fucking Blossoms," finished Hadder.

"Yes. Or that."

"Have you tried communicating with them?"

"Of course. We radioed over, trying to sound as neutral as possible."

"And?"

"Nothing. No doubt, they are trying to gauge our intentions and allegiances, just as we are them. We are at a standstill."

"So what do we do, Voss?"

"We wait, Hadder. We wait until one of us blinks."

―――――

UPTON RAN down from the elevated control room, a pair of binoculars in his hands.

"Boss! Boss! You need to see this!"

Hadder, Krill, the Anorrak sisters, and Voss, deeply engaged in a discussion regarding strategies for the upcoming battle, turned as one to face the excited Protector.

Upton almost tripped as he descended the metal staircase, but that didn't stop him from running across the deck at a full sprint to reach the waiting quintet. When he finally slid to a stop, Upton was winded, making his words impossible to understand.

"Wait a moment! Catch your breath, man," said Voss as Zaza rolled her light eyes.

Upton nodded excitedly and inhaled deeply a few times before speaking again. "The ship, boss, it's finally communicating with us."

Voss's face grew serious. "And what are they saying?"

Upton shook his head, causing the bottom of his blond mullet to swing. "Not saying anything, boss. They ain't talking over the radio."

"Then how the hell are they communicating?"

"Lights, boss. They're using their searchlight to signal."

Voss thought it over. "Must be Radian Code. All the sailors use it."

Upton's mullet swung once more. "Ain't it, boss. Teo knows Radian and said this ain't it."

"Teo *said* this to you," Hadder interrupted, curious if the silent man had actually spoken.

"Nah, he ain't speak, Hadder; you know Teo. But he tried to write what they were saying over the lights and couldn't. That's how I know it ain't Radian."

Voss continued to think. "Uniss Code, then. That's what the military uses when comms are down."

"Nah, that ain't it either, boss. Jakksin served not long ago. He says it's similar, but the sentences ain't coming out right. Just a bunch of nonsense, as far as he can tell."

Voss's yellow eyes went wide. "Give me those binoculars," he demanded, and Hadder watched the large man's hands shake a bit as he peered through the lenses. Several minutes passed before the Protector leader spoke again.

"Well, I'll be goddamned."

"What is it," asked Su in her singsong voice.

A broad smile broke out under Voss's white beard. "It isn't Radian or Uniss, that's for sure."

"But you know what it is," Su prompted.

"Oh, yes, I certainly do." The joy in the giant man's voice was impossible to miss. "And a few others do, as well."

Zaza jumped in. "And, so, what the fuck is it?"

Voss removed the binoculars from his eyes. The goofy grin remained. "It is ADM Code."

Hadder looked to Krill, who spoke. "I've never heard of it."

"Of course you haven't," snapped Voss. "None of you have. ADM stands for the Almighty Drop Marines. That was the special unit I served in as a young man during the Great War. Nasty war that was, with spies under every rock and sabotage around every corner. As we were always the first to get dropped into enemy territory, expected to secure the area for trailing forces, meaning we were especially susceptible to treachery. After our second such betrayal, we said *fuck this* and concocted our own code, loosely based on the Uniss system. It was only known to a few dozen that we all trusted with our lives. And guess what? Almost overnight, missions became significantly more successful." Voss looked around, as if remembering that there were faces watching him. "Enough history lessons. Upton, where is *Glory's* strongest light?"

"Just beneath the comm tower, boss."

"Take me there."

Upton nodded and took off back the way he had come, Voss trailing him.

"What are you going to do, Voss," Hadder called out after the departing giant.

Voss slowed to a stop and turned around, excitement evident on his weathered face. "I'm going to get us some goddamned backup. The greatest backup any man could ever wish for."

And with that, the large Protector leader took off, taking the steps leading up to the communications tower two at a time.

While the Anorrak sisters whispered among themselves, Marlin Hadder turned to Viktor Krill.

"Miracle one?"

Krill shrugged. "Maybe. But only the first of the many that we are going to need, Marlin."

"Always a pleasure, Viktor."

———

MARLIN HADDER DIDN'T THINK that he could be any more surprised than when he first recognized the man who boarded *Glory's Pursuit*. But that paled in comparison to seeing tears streaming down the dark face of Clinton Voss, one of the most steady men he had ever had the pleasure of calling friend.

Voss wiped his eyes multiple times as he took in the familiar visitor, his yellow eyes returning numerous times to the metal legs that supported the grizzled, camouflage-vested man who now stood before him.

"Is it really you, Tennian? Tell me my mind hasn't finally gone out on me."

"It's me, Clinton, you old sap. Long time, no see."

"I tried, Tens, I really did. As soon as the war ended, I tried to find you. And I kept trying to find you. I had jobs lined up for you, my friend. I had things I needed to say to you."

"I believe you, Clint. I was angry, so angry, after the war. I went underground, took my skills to the darker side of life. We were taught to kill; it was the only thing I knew as a young man. There was only one life that rewarded those abilities and that grim outlook. You wouldn't have been able to find me."

Voss wiped his face once more. "You look good, my friend."

Tennian Stamp smiled within his dark beard. "I *am* good, Clint. And *rich*, too."

Voss laughed through the tears. "That's great. If you're so wealthy, what the hell are you doing in the middle of this godforsaken ocean?"

Old Tens shrugged. "I heard that I might find a fight out near the Neelsen Islands. I had nothing better to do, so…"

Tennian was unable to finish his sentence as he was buried in a hug by the massive Clinton Voss.

"Goddamn, it's good to see you," Voss whispered to his old teammate.

"You, too, my friend."

The two veterans held each other for a long time before finally separating. Tennian slapped Voss on his oversized shoulder before looking to Marlin Hadder.

"Marlin Hadder. Good to see you again, my friend. I was told that I might find you out this way."

The jaws of Clinton Voss and the other Protectors of Man fell open.

Hadder walked over and shook the gangster leader's scarred hand. "It's good to see you again, Tens. Nice to see that your newfound wealth didn't change you."

Old Tens chuckled. "Well, you can take the gangster out of the Towers, but you can't take the Towers out of the gangster."

Hadder smiled. "As it should be."

As if the Protectors couldn't look any more shocked, their collective eyes went even wider as Tennian looked past Hadder to Viktor Krill.

Tennian's metal legs roared to life as he stomped over to the black-eyed killer. The two men stared at each other for a long, tense minute before Old Tens finally put out a hand.

"Viktor Krill. Now that you are on the right side of the battle for a change, I must say, it's really fucking good to see you."

Krill took the Broken Tens founder's hand. "I admire very few, Tennian Stamp. You are one of those few. It's always good to see those who manage to capture my respect again. And the timing couldn't be better."

Zaza Anorrak's voice cut into the strangely tender scene. "I'm fucking sorry, but how the fuck do you two know each other? In fact, how the fuck do any of you all fucking know each other?"

Old Tens smiled at Viktor Krill. "Sweet girl."

"Wait until you get to know her."

"What the fuck did you say, Viktor" demanded Zaza.

Tennian called out to Voss. "Perhaps we can discuss these details below deck, old friend. This wet, salty air is not ideal for my legs. And I have a feeling that I am going to need them in maximum operating condition for the coming battle. What do you say?"

Voss roared in laughter, the full weight of this serendipitous encounter finally hitting home. "Of course, old friend, where are my manners? Let us retire to more comfortable quarters where we can talk." Voss called out to any Protectors within earshot. "And bring us alcohol, lots of alcohol! And Leaf, if someone can locate some!"

"Oh, don't worry about Leaf," said Old Tens as he tossed a wink at Hadder. "I brought my own. Enough for everyone."

———

SEVERAL SHOTS of strong alcohol were taken and a couple of joints of Leaf were lit before relevant conversation started up again. Tennian Stamp, a relaxed smile now on his face, spoke through smoke-filled breaths.

"I saw your flag, Clint. There ain't that many of us left alive from that goddamn war, and fewer still that could call themselves Almighty Drop Marines."

As Voss nodded, Lumis Griggs interjected. "What flag are you talking about? I haven't seen any flag."

"You need to spend more time topside, Lumis," said Voss. "Whenever I travel, which is admittedly rare, I carry with me the old ADM flag, hoping that an old teammate might recognize the white skull and red parachute that represented the senseless violence of our youth." Voss looked to Tennian. "Hoping that an old friend might call out so that we can connect once more."

"So, you two were on the same, uh, team or whatever," asked DeLany Thales politely as she sipped her drink.

"Same special ops team, actually," replied Old Tens. "The Almighty Drop Marines is what we were called. Well, we may have added the *Almighty* part ourselves."

"Because the name fit," roared Voss.

"You goddamn right it did," agreed Tennian through a smile. "We were the first in the shit, and often the last out of it. Hand-picked by command for our superior skills and fearlessness."

"And our dark skin," added Voss.

Old Tens chuckled. "Yeah, now that I think about it, there *were* a disproportionately high percentage of brothers and second-generation immigrants on the team, weren't there, Clint?"

"Goddamn right, there were, Tens."

Tennian finished his drink and placed his cup on the meeting room table. "Ah, but that just served to bring us closer together, didn't it? We fought for each other, not the government that was sending us to our early graves."

"Hear, hear," agreed Voss.

DeLany, always the curious one, continued with her questions. "How did you two lose touch with each other? I mean, if you were so close."

"The fucking Harrier Gap," said both veterans at the same time.

Voss looked down from the painful memory, so Old Tens answered for the both of them. "We got sent to the Harrier Gap, which was an absolute suicide mission. There was no way we could seize control of the Gap, but that didn't stop the bastards from sending us in. The ass kicking commenced as soon as we landed and didn't let up. We were about to be massacred, every last one of us, when a young hothead named Sergeant Voss decided to buck command. He ignored orders and rallied the troops behind an aggressive new strategy that potentially wouldn't end with dozens of grieving mothers. At least, not our mothers."

"That's not how I remember it," said Voss, his yellow eyes still facing the ground. "I remember that just as things were at their darkest, just as all of our fates appeared sealed, a young, stupid corporal by the name of Stamp ran a trillium grenade behind enemy lines. The brave fool ended up taking out the bastards' demon Razing Gattler gun along with his own legs. That young man's sacrifice created the opening that we needed to take and control the designated area. No history book will ever report it, but the Harrier Gap is where the

Great War was won. Without the Almighty Drop Marines, the Great War may have waged on for another decade, with young men sent to their deaths on both sides by the millions."

Just as Voss's yellow eyes were beginning to water, Old Tens jumped back in. "What Clint left out is the miracle that he and the boys performed that day in finding me among the wreckage and airlifting me out in the midst of the largest gunfight this world had ever seen. By all measures, I was dead, just a pile of meat sitting under a mountain of burnt metal. But Clint and the boys dug and dug, bullets, lasers, and grenades whistling past their heads. They found me and they saved me." Tennian's legs whirred to life as the old gangster moved to stand beside his former sergeant and place a hand on the giant man's shoulder. "You know, the saddest moment of my life, and I've had my share of them, was being airlifted out of the Harrier Gap. I looked down and watched in horror as my friends, the best friends a man could ever ask for, fought for their lives as I sped away to safety. Something broke inside me on that chopper ride, something that didn't click back into place until today, old friend. For today, I can finally say, *thank you.*"

Voss finally looked up with tears once again streaming down his face. "And I can say, *thank you.* You stupid fool."

The two men embraced, slapping heavy hands onto each other's backs, and remained locked together for several long minutes in silence, everyone else in the room fearful of ruining the moment. Eventually, the two leaders separated, and each looked as if a heavy weight had been removed from their considerable shoulders.

"We saved this undeserving world once, Clint. Are you ready to do it again?"

"My old friend, you have come at the perfect time. Nothing could have made me happier."

"Yeah, about that," cut in Zaza Anorrak, "what the hell are you doing out here in the middle of fucking nowhere?"

"I told you, young Miss," replied Old Tens, "I was told that there would be a great battle at the Neelsen Islands and that required my services."

"Bullshit," shot back Zaza. "We didn't even know we were heading to the fucking Neelsen Islands until we were on the fucking freighter. No one else knew where the Protectors of Man were heading, so no one could have fucking told you where we would be."

Old Tens brought the lit Leaf back up to his lips. "You misunderstand me, Miss. I was not told to come here looking for the…" He looked to Clinton Voss. "Protectors of Man? Is that what you're calling yourselves?" Voss simply smiled and shrugged. Tennian looked back to Zaza. "I did not come all this way to meet with the Protectors of Man. I came all this way to hook up with *them*."

All eyes turned as one to take in Marlin Hadder and Viktor Krill, who were quietly drinking in a corner of the meeting room.

"These fucking two," could be heard from Jakksin as the room erupted into questions. Finally, Voss's voice rose over the din.

"I assume that there's a story there, Tens."

Old Tens smiled at Hadder and Krill. "There is. But it's a dark one. So, we'll need more Leaf. And a shitload more alcohol."

————

LEAF SMOKE FILLED the reception room as Tennian Stamp regaled everyone with the exhilarating, often heartbreaking, story of his life after the Great War. Protectors of Man came and went, looking excited upon entry and disappointed when they had to leave to attend to their daily duties.

Old Tens held court like the professional storyteller that he was, taking the audience on a trip from ostracized wounded veteran to underworld kingpin.

Eyes invariably swung Viktor Krill's way when Old Tens spoke about the foreign villain who consolidated *almost* all the gangs under a single banner through violence, brilliance, and a powerful new drug that doomed its users to quick death.

True to his character, Old Tens left out the most gruesome stories of Viktor Krill's brutality, focusing instead on the man's steely resolve to dominate and accomplish his lofty goals. Although Krill pretended not to listen, Hadder could tell that not only was his Wakened companion hanging on every word, but that he appreciated the thoughtfulness with which Tennian told the grim tale of the Rising.

Old Tens made it a point to emphasize how the Rising had found a kind of balance under the rule of Viktor Krill, one that lasted until his decisions were overruled by Cyrus Bhellum. The Cyrix Industries CEO, acting as a proxy for none other than Doctor Milo Flowers, employed vicious tactics that caused the Broken Tens to team with the Blisters to overthrow the Rising's cruel leadership.

News of the Blisters ushered in a myriad of questions that sent Old Tens down a rabbit hole of stories about the strange mutant group. This included everything from their sad beginning to their role as puppet master, pulling on invisible strings that often dictated how the Muck, or the Rising, moved.

"There's no fucking way such a fucking group exists! You're obviously fucking with us," exclaimed Zaza. The disbelieving Anorrak, however, quickly shifted opinions when her sister reminded her about what was going on in the world outside their little freighter. Subsequently, the idea of the Blisters didn't seem very farfetched.

The Protectors of Man cheered when Tennian spoke of the appearance of Marlin Hadder and his unusual companion, causing Krill to roll his black eyes. They erupted in applause when Old Tens recounted, secondhand, of course, how Hadder won the trust of the Blisters and organized the first open partnership between the mutants and a human gang. The word *human* made Krill roll his eyes again.

Tennian was especially careful with the final part of the story, recalling how Viktor Krill not only eliminated the evil Cyrus Bhellum, but refused to allow his considerable force of Risers to enter the final fray. Tens painted the final battle as a war of man and Blister against evil corporation. Ultimately, good triumphed and Krill magnanimously handed over his empire, distributing mass funds to the men, women, children, and Blisters that called the Rising home.

After the tale, which ended with a surprise visit from an old ally at Tennian's fancy new penthouse apartment, Viktor Krill threw the former gang leader an appreciative look, which Old Tens reciprocated.

When the audience demanded to know the identity of the ally who knew the location of the New God long before Krill got it out of Xioxian Chan, Tennian replied coyly.

"He's an unusual individual who always seems to know too much and offers very little. Beyond that, I don't much know."

As the Protectors of Man bombarded Old Tens with questions, Clinton Voss finally stepped in to save his fellow ADM.

"Enough," roared the giant man through his thick beard. "I'm sure you all have tasks to attend to. Question time will have to wait."

Although disappointed, the Protectors exited the reception area, many of them stumbling from too much Leaf and drink, eventually leaving the core group alone once more.

Zaza Anorrak slithered up to Viktor Krill.

"You didn't tell me you were a fucking king, Viktor," she said in a breathy voice.

"Losing a crown is not something you brag about."

"But still… And the head of the Cyrix Industries to boot…"

"Briefly."

Su overheard the discussion and cut in. "Didn't you hear the story, sis? He was a *drug dealer* and a *gangster*."

Zaza looked at her too-sweet sister. "I heard everything. I think it's fucking hot." Back to Krill. "Viktor, there's an open storage container on the port side. Perhaps we can go there, and you can fill me in on some of the finer details of being a fucking king."

Krill's black eyes flashed. "Lead the way."

"Zaza! Did you not hear what Mister Tens said?!"

In response, Zaza put her tattooed arm around Krill and began steering him toward the exit. As she did, she turned back to her sister. "I heard every fucking word. Later, bitch."

Su stared at the back of her sister in astonishment until she was out of sight. "Fucking Zaza," she mumbled to herself, then jumped when she saw that Hadder was within earshot. "Pardon my language, Marlin."

Hadder smiled at the lovely creature that reminded him so much of his old friend Reena Song. "Of course, Su."

As Su scampered out, Hadder heard the telltale sounds of Tennian Stamp's mechanical approach. The scarred man handed Hadder a newly lit joint of Leaf, which Hadder readily accepted.

"I know Viktor appreciates the story that you told," said Hadder through smoke, "even if he'll never admit it."

Old Tens waved away the comment. "Shit, I didn't choose my words carefully just for Krill. There was a ton of shit I omitted about my own rise to power, Hadder. Viktor Krill's hands are not the only ones covered in blood. You don't reach the top of a competitive food chain without making a mess of things here and there. Or without doing horrible things that you wish more than anything that you could take back. Whatever awfulness befell me in my youth I relayed to countless others over the years. I am many things, Marlin Hadder, but proud ain't one of them."

"Cheers to that," said Hadder before taking another drink and handing the joint back to Old Tens. A moment of silence followed before Hadder could hold his tongue no more. "What the fuck are you doing here, Tennian?"

A furrow appeared under the gangster's salt and pepper hair. "What do you mean?"

"I mean, what the fuck are you doing here? When Viktor and I left, you controlled the entire Bhellum underworld alongside Red Texx and Mayfly Lemaire. You were at the top of the mountain, Tennian, after so many years of struggle. So, I ask you. What the fuck are you doing here?"

Tennian's mechanical legs made sounds, as they often did when the old gangster was in deep thought. "Boredom and regret."

"Boredom and regret," Hadder repeated, confused.

"That's right. I retired shortly after you left, Hadder. Left the Broken Tens to my deserving Second Sonny Caddoc. I bought a penthouse in the wealthiest part of Bhellum. It had a glass living room that hung out over the Neon City; one of the few places that sat above the ocean of lights; one of the few places where you could feel removed from the masked decay. And you know what? I was bored out of my mind." Tennian finished his drink and hit the Leaf again. "When you live the kind of life that I have... That Viktor Krill has... That you have, Marlin Hadder... When you live our kind of lives, boredom leads to reflection, which inevitably leads to regret. I thought of the abuse and death that marred my early years, and the violence and blood that defined my later life. I thought of all the things I did and didn't do. I thought of all the things that should have been done better. I thought of all the lives that I changed for the worse. And I thought of all the babies that I orphaned, all the wives that I widowed, all the innocents that I stole from.

"I considered all this as I stared down into the neon ocean from my thirty-million credit apartment, feeling more alone than I had felt since returning from the Great War a broken man. I was seriously considering sending my legs on one last mission through the thick living room glass, allowing me to take one last trip through the Neon City that saved a man and birthed a monster. I was gonna leave my final mark on the pavement below, just in front of the luxury stores whose overpriced goods declared which citizens were worth caring about. It would have taken the cleaning bots hours to remove me from the sidewalk and glass as horrified rich women looked on and grew increasingly upset that they couldn't access their ridiculous trinkets." Tennian took another deep swig. "Seemed a fitting way to go."

"So what happened?"

"You know what happened, Hadder. Your friend showed up."

"He's not my friend. And we're alone now, so we can cut the cloak and dagger. You're talking about Albany Rott, obviously."

"You know any other mysterious red-eyed outsiders?"

"Can't say that I do, Tens."

"Well, neither do I. Anyway, Rott shows up out of the blue, saying that this world is heading to the finish line, that it is doomed if the New God takes over. He says that you and Krill are heading to the Neelsen Islands to stop the bastard. He says that you will fail without my help, that everyone I still care about will die, or worse, if that happens."

"And you believed him?"

Old Tens chuckled to himself. "What other truth was I holding on to, Hadder? That there was nothing more to my life?"

"You had to know that there was more to your life, Tens."

"That is where you are wrong. My life for the past forty years had been about leading men, fighting enemies, striking deals, and eliminating obstacles. Take that away, and I am nothing more than that stain I had hoped to leave on Bhellum's ground level. And then here comes Albany Rott telling me that not only am I needed, but that I am *essential* to the future of the world. Come now, Hadder, you have to see the appeal in that."

"I do, Tens, I really do. But my question is this — why did you believe Albany Rott?"

Tennian Stamp's dark eyes threatened to swallow Marlin Hadder whole. "We both know why, Hadder. Do we still need to play these games? I may not have the abilities or intellect of you and Krill, but I know when someone is beyond this world. And I know enough to listen to him."

Hadder took the joint from Old Tens and conceded. "Fair enough. Now tell me, who the hell have you brought with you? Who could you have managed to persuade to come with you on this twisted adventure?"

Old Tens laughed aloud this time, slapping Hadder on the shoulder as he did. "Now, *that* is a much better question, Hadder! There were more old timers than you would have thought across the gangs. The Broken Tens, the Bitch-Whores, the Risers, all of us had members of advanced age that only knew the Muck and the constant warring that defined our existence. Many felt the same as I did, lost and alone, left with only disorientation and regret. Faced with a chance to undo some of the wrongs of their lives, many jumped at the opportunity."

"Do you know what we are up against, Tennian?"

Old Tens shrugged. "Can't say that I do, Hadder. Rott just told me that the fate of the world depended on it, and that we had a small chance for victory. How could I turn down those odds?"

Hadder looked up to find Voss staring at him from across the room. Hadder nodded to the Protector leader in understanding. "Well, I'll let Clinton fill you in on the details later, when some of the Leaf and drink have worn off a bit."

"That bad, huh?"

"Worse. But on to other topics. How many did you manage to bring with you, Tens?"

Tennian thought for a moment. "Just shy of a five hundred, if I had to guess."

Hadder spit the contents of his drink onto the reception room floor. "Five hundred! You have got to be kidding me!"

Old Tens took his joint back before it got covered in spittle. "Thereabouts."

"How? How did you get so many to join you?"

Old Tens smiled as he inhaled deeply from the joint. "Lots of old gangsters. Lots of lost souls. Lots of motherfuckers who owed me serious favors. And lots of people who say, *fuck the New God*."

Now it was Marlin Hadder's turn to laugh. "Ok, ok, I surrender. Fucking hell, it's good to see you again, Tens. I don't know if your appearance will make it enough, but you've surely made it more interesting."

"Oh, just you wait, Hadder."

"Wait for what?"

"Wait until you see where I invested my fortune."

Hadder's hazel eyes narrowed. "Weapons? Please tell me you invested in weapons, Tens."

"Oh yes, Hadder, weapons, indeed. Starting with my most personal weapons." As he spoke, Old Tens's legs whirred to life. Hadder looked down and took note of his friend's mechanical legs for the first time since he had arrived. Although they seemed the same on initial glance, Hadder watched in awe as new compartments opened and closed and unusual nozzles peaked out only to retreat into their casings.

"Oh, shit," said Hadder as he began to count the differences in Tennian's new legs. "Money well spent, I would say."

21

After sleeping off the effects of too much Leaf and drink, Marlin Hadder slid out of his storage container to find that Tennian Stamp's vessel was now traveling parallel to their own. The ships were close enough to make out the individual gangsters that manned the ship.

Unlike *Glory's Pursuit*, Old Tens's boat was not a freighter, but a sleek decommissioned battle craft that looked old enough to have served in the Great War alongside its scarred owner. Despite its age, however, the ship looked to be in good working order and, again like its owner, dangerously armed.

Hadder smiled as his Wakened eyes finally caught the vessel's name hastily painted along the port side of the boat – *The Broken Dream*.

Hadder took a deep breath of salty morning air before ruining the atmosphere by lighting a cigarette as he made his way to the bow of *Glory's Pursuit*. Standing just under the comms tower, where they were soaking in the morning rays as the sun rose along the eastern horizon, Hadder found Tennian and Clinton Voss, sipping coffees and trading stories.

"Gentlemen," Hadder said as he approached.

"How are you feeling this fine morning, Hadder," asked Old Tens. "A little worse for wear from all our reminiscing?"

"I don't get those anymore," stated Hadder plainly, and although Tennian and Voss shot each other a curious look, neither questioned their strange ally. A moment later, Hadder's hazel eyes went wide as he finally took notice of his surroundings. "What do we have here," he said, trying to keep the uncomfortable mix of excitement and anxiety from his voice.

"These," responded Voss, motioning to the small islands ahead to his left and right with a giant arm, "are the Neelsen Islands, also known as the Forlorn Islands, also known as the home of Doctor Milo Flowers."

Hadder's gaze swept across the Great Water just below the horizon. There, small islands could be seen to both the starboard and port sides of the freighter. A larger, more defined island sat in the middle of its smaller counterparts, sitting back higher on the horizon.

Tennian pointed a dark hand to the left and right. "These smaller islands are of no concern. My ship has a thermal tracking system attached, the best in the world..."

"*That* hunk has a thermal tracking system," Hadder cut in doubtfully.

"Don't judge a book by its cover, Hadder. I poured every credit I had into that ship and its passengers. Now, if I may continue?" Hadder threw his hands up in surrender. "Our systems don't detect any abnormal readings on any of the surrounding islands, meaning nothing larger than a medium-sized animal. But on the central island..."

"The Isle of God," added Clinton Voss.

"Yes, on the Isle of God..."

"Tell me," urged Hadder when the gangster leader hesitated.

"The readings nearly blinded my analysts. There's life on that cursed place. Large life. And a shitload of it."

"At least we have a place to focus our attention," Voss offered. "Better to be fighting one battle on a single front."

Hadder imagined a thermal reading bright enough to blind those who looked upon it. "Is it?"

Voss shrugged his massive shoulders. "Hey, I'm just trying to find the positive in this upcoming horror. I'm going to start getting the Protectors prepared. It looks like we'll make landfall a bit sooner than we expected." Voss nodded to each man in turn. "Tens. Hadder." As soon as he turned away, the giant Protector leader began barking out orders that left no room for questioning or disagreement.

Hadder finished his cigarette, fished out another from his pocket, and lit it.

Old Tens spoke while his gaze remained locked onto the Isle of God. "Quite the habit you've picked up."

Hadder smiled grimly around the cigarette. "In the long line of things that are going to kill me, *this* is near the back." Hadder pointed his chin at Tennian's battle craft. "*The Broken Dream?*"

Old Tens chuckled before holding out his hand. Hadder took one last drag and placed his cigarette into his friend's fingers. Old Tens put the tobacco to his lips and spoke through the smoke.

"My dream of a non-violent life after the war? The government and its ungrateful citizens broke that one. My dream of a restful retirement? Our red-eyed acquaintance dashed that one when he told me what kind of benefit package would be offered by the New God. The name seemed fitting."

Hadder stared at the old gangster. "Have you heard? Do you know what has happened to the world since we've been at sea?"

Tennian refused to look away from their target. "We heard only bits and pieces at first. Just enough to know that the world was turning to shit. As more information sneaked through the obvious communications lockdown, much of it seemed too bizarre, too terrifying to believe. I assumed most of it was hyperbole, stories leaked as a form of control. After speaking with Clint this morning, I see now that I was wrong." Tennian finally looked away from the Isle of God to stare at Hadder. "The world has become a nightmare. And it is now our job to wake it up."

"It looks like *The Broken Dream* was more apropos than you could have imagined."

"Yes, I'm afraid it is. Now, you'll have to excuse me, Hadder. I, too, must prepare the brave men and women who have elected to join me on this voyage to hell. I'll see you for a strategy session later today. Thanks for the cigarette."

Hadder nodded as Old Tens turned, took two loud steps with his mechanical legs, and then soared into the air, launched by small boosters that could be seen along the "feet" and "calves" of his new metal limbs. Tennian deftly rocketed through the air like a member of the despised Mech Force, quickly crossing the distance between the two vessels before easily landing on *The Broken Dream*.

Hadder chuckled to himself. "Money well spent, indeed."

The smile remained on Hadder's face for several minutes, until he noticed Jakksin at the ship's bow, staring out into the Great Water, his hands gripping the railing in obvious concentration. He didn't know why, but something tickled Hadder's neck, a whisper making an urgent suggestion.

Hadder lit another cigarette and returned to his storage container, where his weapons were waiting.

———

A FEW HOURS LATER, the Neelsen Islands flanked *Glory's Pursuit* and *The Broken Dream* on both sides, with the Isle of God growing larger by the minute, just ahead of the vessels.

According to readings from both ships, the Isle of God was ovular, with a large bay cut into the westernmost side, directly facing the freighter and battle craft that now moved toward it.

Voss added more detail during their recent strategy session. "The Isle of God is elevated, with steep drop-offs into the Great Water. Only the bay will provide an adequate location from which to dock and launch an attack."

"I'm sure Milo Flowers knows that," said Hadder.

"I'm sure he does," agreed Voss. "But that doesn't change the fact that it is our only choice."

"Then how can we expect to land safely," asked Hadder. "If I were

Flowers, I would simply station all my forces along the coast of the bay, after destroying the port. There's no way I would let us make landfall."

Voss held up two meaty fingers. "Two things. First, Milo Flowers is an insane person. Who knows what goes on in that perverted brain of his? Perhaps he wants us to come onto the island. Perhaps he is confident that we have no chance against his army of horror."

"And second?"

Old Tens answered for Voss. "*The Broken Dream.* She's outfitted with military-grade, anti-destroyer guns. We can light the area up from a safe distance, vaporizing anything within a hundred yards. Should buy us enough time to get everyone off the boats and into formations before they have a chance to recover."

Hadder cracked a smile. "You're full of new tricks, aren't you, Tennian?"

"No more than you and Krill seem to always bring."

The room then had a good laugh, but Hadder knew that it was a weak cover for what sat beneath — fear.

That fear remained with Hadder now that the meeting had concluded and everyone returned to their preparatory tasks. He took a walk around the ship to calm his nerves, fingering the grips of his crystalline guns as he did.

As Hadder circled the front of *Glory's Pursuit*, he noticed that Jakksin still stood at the railing, the flat-topped Protector seeming unmoved for several hours. Hadder strode over to the man and took up a position to his left. He looked out to where Jakksin was staring, but could see nothing, save the Isle of God growing closer in the distance.

"We missed you at the strategy meeting," Hadder ventured, but Jakksin refused to take his eyes from the sea ahead. "Looks like the bay is our only option for making landfall. We could have used your military insights."

The flat-topped man simply shook his head in the negative. "Got something more important to do here."

Hadder's face twisted. "And what's that?"

"Out there."

Hadder looked again. "I don't see anything, Jakksin."

"I don't either, Hadder. But Teo does. And if Teo says he sees something, then he sees something."

Hadder looked around. "Where is Teo?"

"Up in the tower. He asked me to keep an eye out. Said he spotted something in the bay. Something strange. Something big."

"Did Teo say what it was? What it could be?"

"You know that Teo don't talk. But I gathered that it wasn't something nice."

"You've been out here for hours, Jakksin. And you haven't seen *anything*?"

Jakksin shook his head without removing his eyes from the water. "I've seen things. A weird swirl of water here, an odd shape on the horizon there. But I can't tell for sure if it's real or just my fear getting the best of me."

"Then why are sticking around here?"

Finally, Jakksin swung his head to view Hadder. "Because I know to trust Teo's gut when it comes to danger." With that, Jakksin turned back to the Great Water.

"Fair enough. Well, I'll stand guard with you. Four eyes are better than two, I suppose." The pair stood in silence for several minutes. Hadder lit another cigarette, but Jakksin waved away the one offered to him. Finally, Hadder could take it no longer. "Tell me about Teo. He seems to have a remarkable amount of respect for one who never speaks."

Jakksin snickered. "Only Teo can tell that tale."

"But he doesn't talk."

"Exactly."

"I don't get it."

Jakksin stepped back from the railing and thought for a moment. "You see..."

The sentence was clipped short as *Glory's Pursuit* lurched hard to the starboard side, sending Jakksin and every other Protector flying to the deck. Only Hadder's Wakened reactions kept him upright as the ship threatened to capsize before swinging back to port, forcing those who fell to slide along the metal ground.

Curses rang out as Protectors grasped railings, containers, and anything else in proximity to get to their feet. Voss stumbled out from the inside of the ship and made his way to Hadder and Jakksin.

"What the hell was that? Rogue wave?"

"I wish," said Hadder, motioning to the calm sea. "There's nothing out there."

"Nothing on the surface," corrected Jakksin. "Teo saw something earlier, boss, but I didn't want to alarm anyone. I think there's something *under* the water."

Voss frowned beneath his thick beard. "*Beneath* the water? But this is a goddamn freighter! Surely, there is nothing that can tilt us like that!"

All three men ran back to the bow railing, looking into the dark water for any sign of alien life.

"Do you see anything, Hadder," demanded Voss, the panic evident in his voice.

Hadder tapped into his Wakened vision, looking hundreds of feet below the reflective surface of the Great Water, half a mile from the opening of the Isle of God's bay. Deeper and deeper Hadder scanned, until a writhing, amorphous creature could be seen lying in wait.

"I see something," exclaimed Hadder, leaning forward as if that would help his eyes focus.

"What?! What is it, man," yelled Voss as he stepped away from the railing.

"I can't tell," Hadder called out as he also took a step back. "But it's down there. And it's fucking big." Hadder took his eyes off the water and swung them to Voss. "Warn everyone. Tell them to either gear up or hold on for dear life."

Voss's yellow eyes went wide. "What's about to happen, Hadder?"

Hadder began to voice his guess, but was cut off by a giant, barb-tipped tentacle that shot forth from the surface and flew like a javelin toward the bow railing. It took Jakksin square in the chest, exploding from the man's back in a shower of gore.

Hadder and Voss simultaneously stumbled back in shock as Jakksin was lifted from the deck, his blond flat-top now speckled with crimson. Jakksin hung grossly in the air, impaled on the tentacle, his wriggling body swinging to and fro as the barb searched for another victim.

Reacting on instinct, Hadder's crystal handguns appeared as if by magic and fired round after round into the grey flesh of the tentacle, sending it into a frenzy before it began to retreat into the sea.

Just as poor Jakksin was about to enter the water, a look of sheer terror painted across his face, Hadder put a final bullet between his ally's eyes, the only gift that Hadder could give the anguished man.

All went silent as Jakksin's corpse disappeared into the sea.

As Hadder kept his eyes on the water, Protectors could be heard filling *Glory's* bow and cocking weapons. The desperate voice of Su Anorrak came from behind.

"Where's Jakksin? Clinton?! Where's Jakksin?!"

"Gone," Voss replied over his large shoulder. "The creature took him."

"What fucking creature," demanded Zaza as she joined the growing crowd, blade in hand.

"There's something big in the water. Something big and dangerous. A leviathan," Hadder answered for Voss. "No doubt, guarding the Isle of God."

"Where is it now," asked Su, her beautiful face swinging left and right to analyze as much water as possible.

"We don't know, but…"

Before Clinton Voss could complete his thought, screams could be heard a hundred yards away on *The Broken Dream* as the battle craft was yanked angrily to its side, almost capsizing the sleek vessel. The ship righted almost immediately, sending Tennian's men sprawling across the deck. As a grizzled gangster leaned over and fired his Stutter into the Great Water, a tentacle snuck over the ship from the other side and began to drift toward the man.

Hadder and others called out in warning, but they were too far away to be heard over the noise of the Stutter in the gangster's hand.

As he fired round after round into the dark water, the tentacle closed this distance.

Using his Wakened eyes, Hadder could see that this tentacle was different from the one that impaled Jakksin. Instead of being tipped with a vicious barb, the gross appendage ended in a giant starfish-like "hand" with a series of small "eyes" where the palm would be. As the tentacle advanced on the oblivious gangster, ignoring the screams of terror from the other passengers, its little eyes swung back and forth, taking a snapshot of the ship and relaying that information to the monstrosity beneath the water.

Its intel gathered, the tentacle lunged forward, wrapping its fingers around the ancient ruffian and yanking him roughly across *The Broken Dream* and over the opposite railing.

The man screamed in horror as he was ripped over the edge of the boat, his Stutter firing as he disappeared, but not before two of his comrades were struck in the temple and shoulder by the errant shots.

Gangsters suddenly filled *The Broken Dream*'s railing, firing random shots into the Great Water beneath them.

"Hold! Hold! Hold, you goddamn fools," yelled Old Tens as he appeared on deck. "Don't waste your bullets until you at least see the goddamn thing!"

All then went silent for several minutes as the two crews waited in frozen fear for the leviathan's next attack.

Frantic screams from the stern of *Glory's Pursuit* identified the next attack, sending Hadder streaking to the opposite end of the ship. When he arrived, he saw that one of the hand-tentacles had lifted a large storage container into the air. As gunshots rang out, the container flew across the deck, leaving two Protectors of Man as nothing more than crimson stains before it careened into the stairway of the comms tower, rendering it useless.

More tentacles rose from around the sides of the freighter, some sending razor-sharp barbs into containers, decking, and Protectors, while others used their bizarre hands to fling anything they could grab overboard.

All the while, *Glory's Pursuit* began to dip dangerously low in the water as the vessel rocked back and forth with increasing violence due to the leviathan's attack. Even more worrisome, however, was the savage banging that could be felt through the boat's metal frame, emanating from the bottom of the vessel.

Voss stumbled to Hadder on unsure legs. "The bastard is gonna either tip us over or finally blast a hole in goddamn hull! Either way, we're fucking finished if this keeps up!"

Smoke began to settle across the deck as gunshots rang out along *Glory's Pursuit*. When a tentacle was hit, it retreated into the Great Water, only to be replaced moments later by another demon appendage.

Hadder looked around to find mayhem aboard both ships, with containers from *Glory's Pursuit* flying into *The Broken Dream* like massive projectiles, horribly mangling both boat and gangster.

"Another half hour of this and we'll be at the bottom of the goddamn ocean," called out Voss over the din. "But how we can kill what we can't even see?"

"You get closer," came a familiar voice from behind. Hadder and Voss turned as one to watch as Viktor Krill materialized from the smoke-filled deck, a large falchion blade in one hand and a scimitar in the other. Krill did not slow as he approached the railing, instead tossing the scimitar at Hadder as he advanced. "Take your jacket off. Leave your guns. They won't do you any good down there."

"Down where," asked Hadder anxiously, although he already knew the answer.

His fears were realized when Krill did not slow as he approached the railing, instead diving sword-first into the swirling waters below.

"Fuck! Fuck, fuck, fuck," yelled Hadder as he stripped off his jacket and side-holster.

A meaty hand on his shoulder gave him pause. "Hadder, this is insanity! You're jumping to your death!"

Hadder offered Voss a weak smile as he picked up the scimitar and stripped its sheath away. "Better to jump to it than wait for it, my friend! Keep as many alive up here as you can! We'll need every person if we survive this!"

With that, Hadder ran headlong at the railing, neatly diving over it as Voss's desperate voice chased him from behind.

Hadder sliced into the dark, warm water as did Krill, point of his blade leading the way. After a few terrifying moments of surrounding blackness, Hadder's Wakened eyes adjusted and finally fell upon his enemy. And his jaw fell open, allowing salty liquid to rush in.

The leviathan, which appeared to be several hundred feet in length, sat just under the stern of *Glory's Pursuit*, raging against the vessel's existence. Shaped roughly like a colossal squid, the creature had dozens of tentacles that it was currently using to both thrash the freighter's hull and wreak havoc along the deck.

Along with the hand-tentacles and barbed tentacles that were attacking the cargo ship and its passengers, two other exceedingly long feeding tentacles hung from the monster, seemingly being saved for another cruel purpose.

With the initial shock of seeing the creature finally wearing off, Hadder found Viktor Krill in the dim underwater light, the notorious killer having almost arrived at the colossal squid. As Hadder swam after his Wakened companion, Krill swung his falchion with surprising speed through the seawater, slicing a deep wound in the thick base of a hand-tentacle. The creature shrieked angrily beneath the Great Water, releasing *Glory's Pursuit* and spinning to face its diminutive attacker with huge twin blue-green eyes.

The leviathan launched a barb-tipped tentacle attack at Krill, a pair of biological torpedoes zeroing in on the Wakened human's chest. Krill spun like a top in the water, his falchion flashing out as he did. The blade stole the barb from one tentacle just before it reached his chest, while the other tentacle missed its target entirely, soaring past Krill's twisting body.

Hadder reached his companion and swung his blade downward with all the might he could muster through the water's weight, neatly cleaving off the tentacle that had just missed Krill.

Black, inky blood filled the water as another shriek emanated from the monster. This time, however, the leviathan did not strike. Instead, it floated silently in the ocean before Hadder and Krill, its dozens of tentacles cascading out around it like a nautical Medusa. As the creature wavered slowly in the water, a few rays of the late afternoon sun found their way under the freighter, lending an even more ominous feel to the dark scene.

The creature's twin blue-green eyes took in Marlin Hadder and Viktor Krill for a long moment, two humans daring to confront a goddess of the sea. It then propelled itself forward like a bullet, its finned head and thick mantle leading the way.

The squid rushed directly between the Wakened humans, both of whom sliced down onto the creature's head as it passed, doing little more than nicking the hard surface. Trailing hand-tentacles grabbed onto Hadder and Krill, pulling them both away from the freighter and deeper into the ocean's depths.

Lower and lower Hadder and Krill traveled, until both could see the seafloor just beneath them. The hand-tentacles released the pair as suddenly as they had seized them, and the leviathan sped off toward the Isle of God, an inky trail left in its wake.

Krill turned to Hadder, and the notorious killer's familiar voice could be heard not in Hadder's ears, but in his mind.

"The demon will return soon. We must remove as many of its limbs as we can. It can only do so much damage with just a head."

Hadder offered a look of confusion. *"How the hell am I hearing you? Wait a minute, can you hear me? How the hell am I communicating?"*

Krill shook his head, his long hair fanning out. *"Don't know. Must be another Wakened ability brought on by distress. But no time to consider it. Watch out!"*

The colossal squid flew back into frame, pulling up short and sending its dozens of tentacles at Hadder and Krill.

Instead of diving low or retreating, however, the Wakened humans caught the creature by surprise, speeding forward to meet the leviathan head on. Blades swung back and forth at blinding speed, removing pieces of tentacle by the foot.

A barb attacked Viktor Krill and was cleaved in half by Marlin Hadder. A hand-tentacle wrapped around Marlin Hadder's legs and lost several of its finger-like appendages to Viktor Krill's falchion.

After a few tense early moments, Hadder and Krill's Wakened bodies had mastered underwater movement, with the companions now fighting back-to-back in perfect harmony, each deftly defending the other while adding complex attacks atop previous strikes.

The colossal squid screamed in pain and rage at losing tentacles each time it moved to attack the strange humans, as if it were reaching into a blender.

Hadder and Krill looked around the inky water and simultaneously thought the same thing — it would not be easy, but they had a chance to render this monstrosity relatively impotent in short order.

Unfortunately, the leviathan reached the same conclusion and decided to shift its approach. It sent its remaining hand and barbed tentacles out wide, forcing Hadder and Krill's attentions to either side, while its secret weapon finally made an appearance from below.

Hadder was the first to notice the two extra-long sucker-filled tentacles coming up from beneath them, but seeing neither a hand nor a barb at their ends, dismissed them as dangerous threats.

He quickly learned how wrong he was.

After dispatching a barbed tentacle that attacked him from the right side, Hadder swung his scimitar blade low, meaning to cleave one of the two thick, suckered tentacles in half before it had a chance to strike.

Hadder's aim was true, his blade connecting with the extra-long tentacle, but instead of inky blood filling the surrounding water, blinding light filled the Wakened human's vision as electricity coursed through him. Hadder's body went taut and his teeth ground against each other as wave after wave of electric current coursed into his body from the colossal squid's feeding tentacle.

Just as he thought that he could take no more, that his heart would explode in his chest, Hadder was released, his limp body falling to rest on the ocean's sandy bottom, scimitar still locked in his hand. Hadder looked up as his vision began to clear, just in time to see Viktor Krill suffering a similar fate, the notorious killer's body shaking with convulsions from the other electrified feeding tentacle.

Hadder tried to kick off from the sea bottom, but found that his arms and legs were like jelly, refusing to answer even the simplest of commands. As if that were not bad enough, Hadder started to realize that his lungs were finally running low on air. Instead of panicking, however, Hadder looked inward as Krill had taught him, demanding that his body locate and utilize the countless pockets of oxygen hiding throughout his biological system.

As Hadder recovered from his electrocution, Krill fought valiantly against his own, forcing his blade to strike out despite the involuntary movements of his arms and legs. Krill gritted his teeth and used all of his Wakened abilities to impede the electricity that tore through his muscles, averting it from vital organs and directing it out the way it came.

After seconds that felt like an eternity, the electrical assault ceased, leaving Krill a flailing mess that was neatly trapped around the waist by the suction cups of the feeding tentacle. Krill swung his falchion at the too-long tentacle, but with no power in his arms, the blade did very little damage against the thick appendage.

Krill's black eyes went wide as the feeding tentacle began to pull him forward, inexorably toward the leviathan's giant mouth that, until this moment, had remained hidden within the garden of tentacles. The notorious killer attempted to scream, but only bubbles and a weak, muffled sound escaped his lips. As Krill drew closer to the grotesque mouth, his terror only increased upon noticing the mammoth beak that snapped open and closed in anticipation, large enough to crush his beloved Comet in a single bite.

Just before Krill's body entered the demon's maw, a tingling sensation returned to his arms and legs, providing the Wakened human a modicum of control over his extremities. Krill immediately went to work, jamming the tip of his falchion against the outside edge of the beak until it would go no deeper and holding on to the hilt to fight the push of the feeding tentacle. Krill then wrapped his legs around the base of an earlier severed tentacle and held tight.

In this way, Krill was able to lock himself away next to the maw of the great monstrosity, resisting the push and pull of the feeding tentacle. He was safe, but not for long.

Hadder desperately shook out his arms and legs as Krill fought for his life. As soon as a bit of sensation had returned, Hadder launched himself from the ocean floor, but quickly was forced to retreat as the other feeding tentacle returned to finish off the job it had started.

Hadder cursed and watched in horror as other tentacles reached for Viktor Krill, a few managing to score barbed blows on the trapped human. As Hadder swam side to side, trying in vain to get past the hovering feeding tentacle, Krill slowly began to slip from his perch, sliding inch by inch closer to the waiting beak. Hadder shot forward once more in desperation, and was sent flying back when the feeding tentacle grazed his elbow, sending another surge of electricity through the defeated man.

Hadder hit the sandy floor again and his head fell to his chest as a cold understanding began to settle in — all is lost.

Hadder looked up from his backside, forcing himself to observe his companion's demise, when a large shadow sped over his head and slammed into the colossal squid. The force of the collision caused the leviathan to release Viktor Krill, who floated down without his falchion and came to rest next to Marlin Hadder on the ocean floor.

Both Wakened humans looked up in absolute astonishment as the Blister known as Alphus tore into the monstrous squid, ripping out tentacles by the root with his massive jaws. The squid wrapped all of its remaining tentacles around Alphus and leaned back, keeping its mantle far away from the snapping, tooth-filled mouth of its enemy.

Alphus twisted within the net of tentacles, tearing several more loose, but remained caught in the giant squid's snare as the twin feeding tentacles shot up. They struck the Blister on each side, sending millions of volts of electricity into the mutant. Alphus roared beneath the water, the flippers of his feet quivering under the relentless attack of the colossal squid.

Between electrical strikes, the barb-tipped tentacles shot forward, driving their sharp ends deep into Alphus's belly and back, causing a crimson cloud to erupt from each wound.

Alphus had saved Viktor Krill, but he would soon die for his efforts.

Marlin Hadder looked to Viktor Krill, whose black eyes flashed as the Wakened human nodded, no words needing to be said. Hadder returned the nod and moments later found himself in the strong grip of Krill, who sent him through numerous swinging arcs before releasing him like a human dart.

Blade pointed forward, Hadder cut through the seawater like a ballistic missile, racing at the leviathan. Preoccupied as it was with Alphus, the colossal squid didn't sense Hadder's approach until it was too late. It screamed as the point of a scimitar penetrated one of its massive blue-green eyes, causing it to explode under the stress of battle.

The monstrous sea creature howled in agony as jelly poured forth from its ruined eye and coated Hadder in a thick ooze. Releasing Alphus from its clutches, the squid sent all of its tentacles to protect the gaping hole in its head.

As soon as he was released, Alphus shot forward in a rage, wrapping his massive jaws around the squid's mantle and biting down. An audible *crunch* echoed through the water as the squid underwent violent convulsions, one of which sent Hadder flying away back to the ocean floor.

Above the Wakened humans, the colossal squid sent its feeding tentacles to attack Alphus again, but it was too late. The renewed electrical attacks on Alphus only caused the Blister to bit down harder and twist more viciously, grinding the squid's mantled head between his gator-like jaws.

Eventually, Alphus gave one last great wrench, ripping the top half of the squid's head clean off and sending inky blood to cloud that entire area of the Great Water.

Hadder and Krill watched through wide eyes as Alphus roared in victory, the limp body of the colossal squid falling in slow motion toward the sandy bottom, where it would feed countless creatures that called Paradise Bay home.

After that great release, Alphus swam down to Hadder and Krill, who crawled atop the Blister ally with nods of appreciation. As the trio returned to the surface, Hadder could not help but look back at the leviathan corpse that now littered the ocean floor.

And wonder what other horrors awaited them on the Isle of God.

———

"DON'T FIRE," called out Hadder as he and Krill broke the Great Water's surface, the wondrous Blister name Alphus supporting them from below.

Protectors of Man were stationed along the railing of *Glory's Pursuit*, guns drawn and pointed at the ocean beneath them.

"Don't fire," Hadder repeated before adding, "but get us out of here."

Clinton Voss could be heard shouting orders before the Protectors sprung into action. A minute later, a thick rope appeared from the deck of the ship, tied off somewhere out of sight from Hadder and Krill.

Both Wakened humans gave appreciative pats to Alphus's thick back before flying up the rope and clearing the railing where Protectors had made way for the pair.

"The creature's gone," shouted Terry, still staring into the Great Water, and Little Terry barked in agreement.

"Are you both all right," asked Voss, obviously concerned.

"We are," stated Hadder, "if a bit shaken up."

"Speak for yourself," snapped Krill, but something in his voice belied his words.

"And the monster?" A pause. "The squid monster," Voss clarified.

"Gone. Dead," answered Krill.

Voss's yellow eyes closed, and his giant shoulders slumped in relief. "The true God was looking down upon us on this day. Or maybe it is simply our two saviors to whom we owe thanks."

"Wrong on both accounts," said Hadder. "We were as good as dead down there. We were saved, just as all of you were."

Voss's dark brow furrowed. "By what? Certainly, not that beast that we saw with you as you surfaced."

"That was no beast," said Hadder.

"Then what was it?"

"A friend. A very good friend."

"A powerful friend," added Krill.

"I don't understand what is happening," admitted Voss.

Hadder looked to Krill, who nodded in understanding, before turning back to Voss. "I think it will all become clear here shortly. Expect a ship to appear in the coming hours."

"One has already been detected by *The Broken Dream*, just North of our position, closing in fast," said Lumis Griggs from the group of still-shocked Protectors.

Voss took a step toward Hadder and Krill and spoke in a low voice. "What does it mean? Do we need to prepare for battle?"

"Not unless you want to die," said Krill.

Hadder ignored Krill's words. "It means that friends are approaching. And one does not battle friends. Please welcome them when they arrive."

Voss laughed to himself. "I guess that's as much as I'm going to get, isn't it?"

"For now," agreed Hadder.

"Very well. I'll let everyone know. Go below and relax for a bit. Dancing with death must be tiring."

"You have no die," said Hadder as Voss returned to his waiting Protectors to deliver instructions. "I think I could use a drink. And maybe some Leaf. And possibly every other drug that might be found. Viktor?" It was only then that Hadder noticed the shaking of his Wakened companion's tan hands, a testament to how close to death the man truly was.

Krill saw where Hadder was looking and quickly joined his hands behind his back. "Yes, that sounds in order."

Hadder nodded. "Plus, I need to dry these clothes."

"Mine are fine," said Krill with a smirk, forcing Hadder to look at his already dry white suit.

Hadder shook his head in jealousy. "Fucking Station clothes. Let's go."

22

Marlin Hadder never thought he would miss the feel of rough grey skin on his cheek, but he did.

"It's so good to see you, Gayle" said Hadder, fighting back tears.

"And you, as well, Angel," she said into his ear.

As the two old friends separated, Hadder noticed for the first time the looks of shock, fear, and disgust on the faces of the Protectors of Man. Before Hadder flew into anger, he reminded himself that, despite being forewarned, the first time that one sees a Blister is a jarring experience.

To her credit, Gayle and the contingent of Blisters who had joined her on *Glory's Pursuit* paid the looks no mind, accustomed as they were to such reactions.

As Gayle looked around with her orange eyes, she locked onto Krill. "Viktor Krill, we meet again. It is good to see that your ambitions have shifted, putting you on a more... hopeful path."

Krill bowed his head respectfully, something that Hadder seldom saw from his companion. "The pleasure is all mine, *Queen* Gayle."

"The additional funds from the Risers reached us. You didn't have to do that. But thank you."

A look of embarrassment crossed over Krill's face, and Hadder almost laughed aloud as the notorious killer was outed for secretly doing a kind deed. "Well earned," was all that he said in response.

As the groups of Protectors, gangsters, and Blisters stared at each other in silence and poorly masked suspicion, Hadder moved to accelerate things.

"Not to sound unappreciative, Gayle, but what the hell are you all doing out here? Is your new island not everything you wished?"

Gayle smiled wistfully, her mind going back to the island home that she shared with her husband and Blister family. "It is everything and more, Angel. Which is why we have decided to join you in your quest. We, too, know what Milo Flowers intends to do. We have heard the stories and seen the results of his dark work. He reached out to us, you know?"

Hadder's face fell in surprise. "Who? Milo Flowers?"

The orange flecks danced in Gayle's orange eyes. "Yes, over a secure line. He said that he admired us, especially how we had broken from the antiquated mold of life. He said that he considered us allies in the war against humanity, that we would be left alone to do as we wish in his new kingdom."

"And you didn't believe him?"

Gayle laughed sweetly at the absurdity of the question. "Of course not. My skin may be hard and grey, but it still crawls in the presence of grotesqueness." Gayle's self-deprecating comment earned some giggles from the crowd. "The man was an obvious charlatan taking advantage of a broken world. And he misread us Blisters completely."

"How so?"

Gayle took a moment to look around at all in attendance. "He thought we hated humanity, and worked to use that against us. But we Blisters do not hate humans; we pity them. They have no sense of community, of belonging, and can only advance themselves by bringing others down. This is not the way of the Blister. But it *does not* mean that we hate them."

"You have every reason to hate us, Gayle."

"Perhaps, but we have met enough of you to know that there is good in humanity. Men like you, Hadder, and you, Tennian, give us hope for humanity, remind us that baseless judgment can be as corrosive as bad acts themselves." A pause. "Our dream has always been to live alongside humans in peace, even if that mean minimizing interaction. We had finally achieved that."

"And Milo Flowers?"

"Like I said, an obvious charlatan. Says that he wants to leave us in peace as he works to destroy the world's dominant life form." Gayle snickered. "He would leave us alone no more than he would leave your families alone. Only, he would come for us last, when there was no more life to twist and there was no where left for us to run. He wants total domination, no less."

"How do you know, Gayle? Perhaps he would leave the Blisters be."

"He would not," Gayle said confidently. "And do you know why he wouldn't?" Hadder shrugged. "Because despite all of his spouting against humanity, Doctor Milo Flowers *is* a human. And that means that he is not to be trusted. That means that he will always go back on his word, do what is best for him, and what best satiates his unending hunger." Gayle's orange eyes stared holes in Hadder's hazel orbs. "He wants to darken this world, Angel, and will stop at nothing to accomplish this. We may be Blisters, but we enjoy the light as much as any human. A life surrounded by nightmares is no life at all. King Gash sees this, which is why I am here today."

"And you all came to his conclusion all on your own? Found us all on your own?"

Gayle smiled once more. "We both know that not to be the case, Angel. Your red-eyed counterpart paid us a visit and explained everything. Current events may have surpassed even Orrin the Child's vision, but his opinions regarding the Twin Angels still ring true. Our fate is tied to yours, Angel. We rise together, and if we have to fall, let our energies return to the cosmos hand in hand."

"Well, it's good to have you, Gayle." Hadder looked past Gayle to the other Blisters in attendance. "It's good to have *all* of you." Back to Gayle. "How is Alphus, Gayle? He took quite a bit of damage from the fight earlier."

"Alphus is in pain, but he will survive. Unfortunately, I'm afraid that he will not be able to participate in the coming battle, for he will have to retire into the deep sea as his wounds heal."

"I understand. Please let him know how grateful Viktor and I are. If not for his appearance, we would be slowly digesting in the belly of that monster and all would be lost."

Krill stepped forward. "Let him know that it was good to be on the other side of his power for a change. Let him know that I will never forget it."

Gayle smiled. "I will let him know, Viktor Krill. Both of your words will mean much to him as he recovers. They will give him strength." Gayle looked backward and motioned someone forward. "Here, Alphus went back for these. He thought you would need them for the coming battle."

A beige-skinned Blister that Hadder did not recognize stepped forward and placed two blades, a falchion and a scimitar, onto the deck of the freighter.

Hadder and Krill both nodded their thanks before Hadder turned to face the Protectors of Man. "Clinton Voss. The Protectors of Man. I am beyond thrilled to introduce you to the greatest friends a person could ever ask for — the Blisters!"

After a moment of uncomfortable silence, the heavy hands of Clinton Voss began to slap together in applause, followed by the other Protectors in the audience. Soon, all the Protectors and old gangsters on *Glory's Pursuit* were clapping and calling out in appreciation of their newest allies in the war against the New God.

Tennian Stamp's metal legs whirred to life as he moved forward to bury Gayle in an embrace, and Clinton Voss followed suit, shaking hands with the Blister who had delivered Hadder and Krill's lost blades. Soon, Blister, Protector, and gangster were interspersed across the freighter, exchanging names and cities of origin while offering curses for Milo Flowers.

Amidst the meeting of the three armies, Hadder turned to Krill.

"Miracle two?"

"It appears so, Marlin."

"Enough?"

"I think we are going to need at least one more, Marlin."

"But we're getting there?"

"Yes. Yes, we are, Marlin."

———

"So, that's it, really," said Clinton Voss at the head of the large conference table inside the war room of *The Broken Dream*. "I know it's not the most sophisticated plan, but I doubt that this will be a sophisticated battle, just a war of attrition. Thoughts? Concerns?" Voss looked at Tennian Stamp, who was standing to the side. "Tens?"

"I think it is as good as we can do with the limited knowledge that we have of our enemy. We'll just need to stay flexible and be ready to adapt. Who knows what kinds of shit will get thrown at us on that forsaken island? But I'll keep half a dozen men aboard *The Broken Dream* to man the guns and ensure that we can safely establish ourselves on land."

"Thank you, Tens. Gayle?"

"The Blisters will be ready to attack when you give the word. If the monstrosities on the Isle God refuse to fall to your bullets, they will surely collapse under the force of Blister might."

"Thank you, Gayle. Zaza?"

"The Protectors of Man have never been more fucking ready for anything in our fucking lives, Clinton. Fuck the Isle of God and fuck the New God. Su?"

Su Anorrak nodded at her sister's words. "Yes. We are ready." She hesitated. "Excuse my language… but fuck the New God."

The room erupted into laughter from the curse of sweet Su Anorrak. Voss joined in the laughter before speaking again.

"Very well. All is set. No matter what happens, let it be known to the true God that all of us here have done all we can to save the world from the blight that is Doctor Milo Flowers. We move on the Isle of God mid-morning tomorrow, which gives us tonight to give thanks to each other and these lives that we have been granted. Ideas?"

"*The Broken Dream* is comfortable, but I don't know that we can fit everyone on here," said Old Tens.

Gayle spoke next. "Same with our ship, *The Orrin*. All are welcome, but the accommodations will be tight."

Voss stood up. "Then it is settled. We will all meet on *Glory's Pursuit* shortly after sundown. She hasn't got the luxuries that your vessels do, but she's a freighter that has room to spare for all. What do you say?"

"I say watch yourselves," stated Tennian from the side. "My old gangsters have been partying long before many of you were born. No need to try to keep up."

"Bullshit," cut in Zaza Anorrak. "Everyone fucking knows that only the Protectors of Man know how to truly fucking party. We've been living on the fucking edge of death for a fucking year now. When we blow off steam, we fucking blow off fucking steam."

"That is all nice to hear," followed Gayle. "But when it comes to celebrations of life, only the Blisters truly know how it is done. Angel?"

Hadder looked up to find that everyone in the room staring, waiting for him to choose a side. "I'm just happy to be among friends for one more night."

The room exploded in cheer before everyone rose from their chairs and began to exit the war room. After several minutes, Marlin Hadder found himself alone, still sitting at the conference table. The cheers that he just heard rang hollow in his head, for he did not finish the statement that he really wanted to make, a statement of truth.

I'm just happy to be among friends for one more night. Because it will probably be the last night this world ever sees.

———

LEAF SMOKE WOVE its way throughout the freighter called *Glory's Pursuit*, twisting through bay areas, up staircases, and into storage containers, passing a potpourri of Protectors, gangsters, and Blisters on its path upward.

While there was an expected feeling out period between Protector and gangster, human and mutant, Terry's homemade hooch and the Blisters' surprisingly sweet-tasting grog quickly knocked down walls and removed inhibitions.

In short order, the three groups were intermingling like old friends, each sharing unique war stories and tales of their lives before the appearance of the New God.

The Protectors of Man spoke in detail about their battles with the Blossoms of the New God and the savage Thorns of Reckoning, their eyes growing misty when the name of Patton Yellich was invoked. The old gangsters, a mix of aging Broken Tens, Risers, and Bitch-Whores, talked about the Muck Wars and how the villain Viktor Krill brought them all under a single banner via violence never seen. The Blisters shared the hardships of their people, and how the Twin Angels not only offered them a better life, but fought shoulder to shoulder with them as they stormed the Cyrix Industries Head-quarters.

Laughter echoed throughout the metal freighter, melding with the sounds of the Blister band and its unique brand of music that sounded like electro played with homemade instruments. Away from the band, the music of this world, akin to hip-hop, dance, and synthwave, played across the countless speakers that dotted the large vessel.

No matter where one went, good drink, good music, and good company was to be found.

Marlin Hadder made his way through the massive party, a drink in one hand and some lit Leaf in the other. He bounced from one group to another, delighted every time he encountered an old friend that he didn't realize had joined him on this final journey.

"Sowler! Is that really you, my friend," Hadder called out to a pig-faced Blister with a massive stump for a right arm who was dancing to the Blister band.

The pig-faced Blister's eyes went wide at the sight of his old dueling partner. "Angel! I've been looking for you!"

"It's good to see you, my friend. How's the left hand?"

Sowler opened and closed his giant left hand. "Good as new, no thanks to that metal head of yours."

"And there was no saving your other arm?"

Sowler looked down at the giant stump, all that remained of his once powerful mutated arm. "Afraid not. But I have something special to attach to it. You'll see tomorrow. I'll be the one covered in the blood of my enemies."

Hadder let out a laugh before embracing his old friend in a hug. As he did, a small voice rang out from just behind Sowler's thick left shoulder.

"Hey, fucking watch it, fucking Angel! You trying to fucking squish me? You want me to fucking eat you? I knew I should have fucking eaten you the first time I fucking saw you. Isn't that right, Sowler? We should just fucking eat this fucking guy, fucking Angel or not!"

"Shut up, Smeggins," roared Sowler, and Hadder's jaw fell in surprise.

"Smeggins! Is that you?! Can't be!" Hadder spun Sowler around to find the little mutant Smeggins now attached to the pig-faced Blister.

"Fucking shocking, eh, Angel," said the little face that was roughly stitched into the thick meat of Sowler's shoulder.

"But how," is all that Hadder could muster, such was his surprise at seeing the foul-mouthed Smeggins.

Sowler answered for the little face. "We cut Smeggins out of Brutto's corpse before he had a chance to die."

"And you stitched him into yourself," Hadder asked, his bewilderment obvious in his tone.

Sowler simply shrugged. "We are Blisters. We are kin."

"And who fucking wouldn't want to share my fucking company, Angel? Brutto always said I had the best fucking conversation skills."

"That's because Brutto never talked," Sowler snapped back, bringing a smile to Hadder's face.

As the Blister band kicked into another song, the Anorrak sisters danced over to Hadder, an extra drink in each of their hands. Su handed one to Hadder, who realized that his own was empty, while

Zaza presented hers to Sowler, who dropped his empty cup to accept the new one.

"Going to introduce us to your friend, Marlin," asked Su in her sing-song voice.

"Of course. Su and Zaza Anorrak, may I present my old friend Sowler."

"Don't fucking forget about me, fucking Angel. I fucking swear, this fucking guy always..."

"Who the fuck is this," interrupted Zaza.

"I'm fucking Smeggins! Who the fuck is this little fucking strumpet?!"

"I'm the fucking strumpet who will fucking cut your fucking face off, you little shit," Zaza shot back angrily.

"Fuck you, fucking sweet meat lady!"

"Fuck you, you little fucking turd!"

A strange moment of silence followed the verbal jousting of two of the most foul-mouthed individuals anyone could ever meet before the entire group burst out into uproarious laughter. Smeggins proved to be the first to be able to speak.

"I fucking like her, Angel!"

———

"Why do the Blisters call you Angel," asked Clinton Voss as he passed a joint of Leaf to Hadder.

"They think he's some kind of messiah," answered Tennian for Hadder.

"Is that true, Hadder?"

Hadder thought for a moment. "Messiah is the wrong word. Guide would perhaps be more accurate. They think that I, along with another, will guide them out of the Muck and into paradise."

"And do you think that is possible," asked Voss.

"You forget," Old Tens interjected, "he already did."

"Yes, I suppose he did. And, yet, they are here with us tonight."

"They follow the teachings of one who was called Orrin the Child.

And much of what Orrin foretold has come true. But I don't even think Orrin could see Doctor Milo Flowers and how he would pervert the world."

Voss nodded as he thought. "And this other person with whom you saved the Blisters? I assume that he is the same that informed Tens of our whereabouts. Where is he now?"

Hadder and Old Tens shared a look before Hadder spoke. "I do not know."

"Do we need him?"

"I do not know."

"Should we seek him out?"

Hadder finished the remainder of Blister grog in a single gulp and placed the empty cup on the railing against which the trio stood. "No. He has made his choices. He abandoned us." Hadder's eyes found Tennian's again. "He abandoned us a long, long time ago. Long before I even reached the Muck. He is dead to us. We are alone in this fight. All we have is each other."

And with that, Hadder wandered off toward a small group of dancing Blisters and Bitch-Whores, joining in their frivolity.

"Touchy subject, I guess," commented Voss when Hadder walked away.

"Let us just hope he is wrong," said Old Tens. "Because the individual that we are speaking of might be the only thing powerful enough to turn the tide of this war."

———

IT TOOK A WHILE, but Hadder was eventually able to locate Teo tucked away in a corner of the freighter, some sausages sizzling on a small grill that he had set up for hungry revelers.

As Hadder collapsed in the lawn chair next to the silent man, he handed a cup of alcohol to Teo, who accepted it with a nod. Hadder once again noted the deep scars that ran down both of Teo's dark arms.

"I haven't had the chance to tell you how sorry I am for Jakksin's death. I know that you two were close. He was a good soldier, and we will miss him greatly tomorrow." Teo simply nodded before motioning to the smoking meat on the grill. "No, thanks, Teo. Afraid I don't have much of an appetite tonight." The two men sat in silence for several minutes, the Blister music and popping of meat juices hitting coals the only conversation to be heard. Finally, Hadder began to rise. "Anyway, I just wanted to offer my condolences. Have a good evening, Teo. Try not to sit here alone all night."

"Do you know what I was before I was a Protector?"

Hadder froze mid-rise, shocked to have heard Teo finally speak. He fell back in his seat and stammered for a response. "No, I don't."

Teo smiled. "I was nothing," he said with a strange accent that Hadder could not place. "I was a fisherman, working from boat to boat, always making just enough to pay for my boozing and whoring. I was miserable. Or so I thought." Teo went quiet for a while before continuing. "Then one day, I was out far in the Great Water, my skin cooking under the hot sun, hand-tossing chum out the back of a small vessel. We were hunting yoona, a delicious white-bellied fish, oblivious to the fact something else was hunting us. A giant eel-shark leapt from the water and took my arms in its sharp jaws, pulling me under. Farther and farther down I went, the eel-shark meaning to drown me before feasting on my flesh. For the first few moments, I didn't resist, thinking that this was all I deserved, that this life wasn't worth saving. And then…"

The pause extended into a silence. "And then what, Teo?"

Teo's eyes squinted, as if he was seeing something far away. "And then, something shifted inside me. As I looked into the black eyes of the eel-shark, they reflected all that was good in my life, things that I was too blind to see. I saw my mother waiting for me in my hometown of Errol. I saw all the friends I had made across all the fishing boats I had worked. I saw all the sweet women I had been with, even if I had to pay for their company. I saw the street children who used to play on the docks as we came ashore. They had nothing and still ran with a lightness in their step that was greater than any bar of gold. I saw me, joining something bigger than myself, working with others from different backgrounds to achieve a common goal. All of these things and more I saw in the black eyes of that eel-shark. And it was then that I decided."

"What did you decide, Teo?"

Teo looked over and smiled at Hadder. "I decided that life was worth fighting for. I screamed in that eel-shark's face as I ripped one arm free from its razor teeth and jammed my thumb in one of its black eyes. When it refused to release me, I slammed my fist into its other eye, over and over and over again. Finally, seeing that I was not going to be the easy meal that it anticipated, it released me and scurried away, half blind and still hungry." Teo got up and flipped the sausages. "Several years later, when the fervor for the New God was growing, I met Jakksin and the Protectors of Man and knew immediately why I had fought so hard for my life beneath the Great Water. Here, I rediscovered the good that exists in this world. Here, I was able to give my life purpose."

"Why are you telling me this, Teo?"

Teo returned to his seat. "I don't know. Maybe to remind you that this world is not perfect, but it is worth fighting for. Perhaps it's to remind myself. We are all in the grips of a vicious monstrosity. We can either accept our fates and sink to the bottom, or send the bastard away hungry. I am happy to be among so many that are willing to fight."

Hadder smiled as he patted Teo on the knee and rose. "I'm happy you fought, Teo. And I'm happy to have you here with us today. If we die tomorrow, let it be never said that we didn't try to put the bastard's eye out."

Teo nodded. "Take a sausage with you."

"I would, but I'm afraid that I don't have much of an appetite."

Teo smiled. "Yeah, no one seems to this evening."

———

MARLIN HADDER SPENT the next few hours mixing with as many allies as possible. He danced with the Anorrak sisters and Milly as the

Blister band continued to belt out pulsing musical hits. He arm-wrestled a massive green-skinned Blister named Tobbe and collected a tidy sum when he was able to best the giant with little effort. He chatted with Gayle and was brought to tears by her detailed description of the Blisters' new island home that sounded like paradise.

Shots were ripped, and Leaf smoke was inhaled as hands shook, shoulders were clapped, and new friends were made. Just as the party began to reach its crescendo, with everyone gathered in the freighter's giant central chamber, Clinton Voss took the stage to a collection of cheers and playful boos.

"If I could have everyone's attention, please, just for a moment. I apologize for interrupting the festivities, but I promise to be brief." He gave the crowd a moment to quiet down. "Tomorrow will be the culmination of all of our hard work and preparation. For some of us, we have been preparing for this moment for over a year. Others of us have recently joined the fight, and we are no less grateful for their involvement." Applause broke out for the newly joined allies. "This world is not perfect. In fact, it is far, far from it. Tennian Stamp and I have seen firsthand how this world's leaders are willing to destroy the planet for a few trillion credits and few bits of land." Another pause. "This world is broken. This world is aching. This world is desperate. And this has left the door open for a scoundrel like Doctor Milo Flowers!" Boos rained down from the audience. "But as shattered as this world is, it is *our* world! And it is worth fighting for! And I would rather end up dead in a pool of my own blood tomorrow than wake up safe and sound a week from now with everything twisted around me! This is *our* world, and Milo Flowers *can not* have it without a fight! A grand fight! A battle to end all battles! Who is with me?!"

The room exploded in cheer, the noise reverberating off the metal walls to increase the volume tenfold. Voss continued to yell over the din.

"Enjoy! Enjoy my friends, Protector, gangster, and Blister, alike! Enjoy your drink and smoke! Enjoy each other's company! Enjoy life! For this is what Milo Flowers will never be able to take from us! Our love of life!"

The cheers continued, eventually breaking out into an impromptu chant led by Zaza Anorrak and the Blister Smeggins, two of the unlikeliest of friends that could ever exist.

"Fuck the New God! Fuck the New God! Fuck the New God!"

Eventually, the Blister band picked up the chant and began to play the perfect backing track, sending all in attendance into a frenzy and transforming the entirety of *Glory's Pursuit* into a massive dance floor.

Hadder intercepted Voss as the mountainous man stepped from the Blister band's platform.

"Hell of a speech," Hadder yelled to be heard over the excitement.

"I meant every word."

"I know," Hadder replied as he smiled, remembering a similar speech he once made in a city called Station.

"Enjoy tonight, Hadder. I'm off to find the company of something soft. I refuse to let my last bed occupy only one."

Hadder laughed. "You do that, Voss."

"Try to get some sleep tonight, Hadder."

"I don't need much sleep anymore, Voss. And on the rare occasion that I do, nightmares deprive me of any enjoyment."

"We all have nightmares, Hadder."

"Not like these."

Voss's yellow eyes took in Marlin Hadder, and the large man nodded. "Then I will see you in the morning. For the beginning of the end."

A twinge of sadness attacked Hadder, but he repeated the accurate phrase. "For the beginning of the end."

———

HADDER FOUND Viktor Krill sitting on the bow of *Glory's Pursuit*, his legs dangling over the edge of the boat as the notorious killer smoked a cigarette. Surprisingly, Lil Terry was in Krill's lap, lavishing in the pets he was receiving from the notorious killer. Krill was speaking to the small dog, but Hadder was unable to make out the whispers shared between new friends.

When Hadder joined him, Krill gently placed Lil Terry on the deck and shooed his little friend off. He then offered the pack of smokes to his Wakened companion without taking his black eyes from the island ahead of them. Hadder lit a cigarette and looked out onto the Isle of God.

"Do you see it," asked Krill.

"See what?"

"Look harder, Wakened fool."

Hadder did as he was told, using his Wakened vision to zero in on the land that laid before them. Deep within the vegetation of the island, bits of light could be seen through the tropical trees, representing all the colors of the spectrum.

"I see it. What is it?"

Krill flicked the remainder of his cigarette into the Great Water. "Never mind."

"What's going on with you," asked Hadder. "You haven't been the same since our fight with the squid."

Krill took another cigarette from his pocket and lit it. "I almost died down there, Marlin."

Hadder's face twisted. "Yeah, but that isn't something new to either of us."

"I was scared, Marlin."

"Yeah. That's *normal*, Viktor."

"No! No, it's not. Not for me. I made friends with death a long time ago, Marlin. He isn't supposed to frighten me anymore."

"What do you think that means, Viktor?"

Krill's black eyes swung to Hadder. "It means that I'm not ready to go yet, Marlin. It means that I still have things to do here. It means that I have people that I want to see again. A couple, at least."

"Then it sounds like we better fight our asses off tomorrow, Viktor."

Krill's eyes shot up where the pink disc in the sky was now as large as the moon. "And you think it really matters?"

Hadder shrugged. "Maybe. Maybe not. But I stopped worrying myself with the whims of the celestial."

"How poetic, Marlin. You write that yourself?"

Hadder laughed and then fell into a shared silence as the Wakened companions stared up at the pink asteroid that was racing toward the planet.

"I wish I couldn't see that thing, Viktor."

"That's the problem with being Wakened, Marlin. You see many things that you wish you couldn't. Things that are better left in the warm darkness of ignorance."

"Would you give them up, then? Your Wakened abilities, I mean."

"I would not. Nothing is worth that trade." A pause. "Well, almost nothing."

Although curious, Hadder did not press his volatile friend. After a few more silent minutes, Krill rose and flicked his cigarette into the ocean.

"Zaza is waiting for me. I will not condescend to tell you to sleep, Marlin, but try to get some reverie. It will take everything we have tomorrow, and that probably will not be enough." Hadder nodded and Krill began to walk away before stopping. "And find some company, will you? Despite us being the only real humans aboard, tonight is a celebration of humanity. And humanity is not defined by solitude."

A retort began to form on Hadder's lips, but Krill had walked away before they were given voice. Instead, Hadder turned back and watched as the pink disc in the sky grew larger and larger as each minute passed.

"Marlin? Marlin Hadder?"

Despite the softness of the voice, Hadder jumped. He turned to find a tall asian woman starting down at him, the hilt of a blade appearing over her left shoulder.

"Yes?"

"My name is Raelynne. Viktor Krill thought you could use some company."

"And how do you know Viktor Krill?"

"I am... or was a Bitch-Whore. Can I sit?" Hadder motioned for Raelynne to join him. As she did, she adjusted the sword that was strapped to her back.

"Nice sword."

"Thanks. You know, for the longest time, I was the only person in the Muck, I mean Rising... Sorry, old habits die hard... I was the only person in the Rising, man or woman, with a sword. Then comes Viktor Krill and his knives, and every two-bit thug in Bhellum has to run with a blade. It really killed my cache."

"Do you know how to use that thing?"

Raelynne looked over with a twinkle in her dark eyes. "Want to find out?"

Hadder laughed. "Maybe tomorrow."

"Of course. Tomorrow."

The two stared out into the Great Water, and Hadder had to remind himself that the woman next to him could not see the pink menace hanging heavy overhead.

"Tell me, what are you doing here, Raelynne?"

"Looking for you, Marlin Hadder."

"No, I mean, what are you doing here with the Protectors of Man. Why did you elect to come with Old Tens?"

Raelynne looked down at her dangling feet. "Oh, that. I was a warrior in the Muck. When Mayfly Lemaire had a problem that needed special attention, or a message that needed to be extra clear, I was the one she sent. I took pride in my role. I took pride in the violence that I was able to hand out. In some way, every mission I was sent on was an opportunity to take back something that was stolen from me during childhood."

"And now?"

"Now? Now, there is no need for a woman like me in Bhellum. Things there no longer need cutting, but I still need to cut. Tennian gave me an opportunity to continue to use my blade, and to do so for a good cause."

"I understand."

Raelynne rose to her feet. "You look tired, Marlin. You should come with me."

"I'm not tired, Raelynne."

The tall woman rolled her eyes. "Of course you aren't. That's just something we say, isn't it? Now, are you coming?"

Hadder chuckled at the beautiful woman's directness. "It might be best if I didn't. Women don't have the best track record after being with me."

"I'll keep that in mind. Look, the chances are that I'll be dead in twelve hours, regardless of whether I have shared a bed with you or not. And I'll be damned if I spend my last night alone and cold."

Hadder shook his head as he stood. "Ok, but just remember what I told you."

"Noted. Now, is there anywhere that we can go to be alone on this freighter?"

"There's a shipping container on the other side that I've been sleeping in."

Raelynne put her arm around the Wakened human. "Oh, Marlin Hadder, you definitely know how to sweep a woman off her feet. Lead the way."

Hadder laughed and put his arm around Raelynne's small waist, moving the two of them to the stern of *Glory's Pursuit*, a wide smile on his face.

As Hadder walked he breathed in deeply, soaking in the perfumed body of the dangerous woman on his arm, momentarily forgetting about pink asteroids, twisted monsters, and false gods.

Momentarily forgetting about the horrors that awaited them all the next day.

23

Daksha exited the communications room and walked quickly through the Great Hall to the Holy Pistil. Her heart pounded in her chest and her stomach twisted itself into knots. This was not only because of the information that she had to share with her Lord, but also due to the information that she had received from other Chosen around the globe.

Daksha's mind moved in every direction, with thoughts that bordered on heresy making brief appearances before she could cast them aside. As the woman placed her hand on the golden doors to open the Holy Pistil's entrance, she forced her head clear, terrified that the New God could read her like a book.

The large doors to the Holy Pistil swung silently inward at Daksha's touch, and the woman immediately noticed two things that set her back on her heels.

First, most of the metal surgical tables now sat empty, and those that were occupied seemed to only hold corpses, leaving the Taragoshi mechs stationed at each alone and without purpose. In was probably just an illusion, but Daksha thought that the mechs appeared to sag under this new sense of uselessness.

Second, all four of the Anointed Champions, who Daksha now

thought of as the Four Demons, were in attendance, joking and smiling smugly as the Chrysalis swole and hummed behind them.

As usual, Seth Whispers was the first to notice her, but he did not speak, instead opting to flash his crooked yellow teeth in a smile.

"Ah, look who has decided to join us," Cement Felix finally called out mockingly. "If it isn't the Lord's favorite Chosen. What news do you have for us, *Chosen?*"

As she always did, Daksha raised her chin and put on a brave face as she approached the Four Demons. "For you, Felix? I have nothing. My words are for my Lord, and Him only."

"Afraid that's not gonna happen, sweet thing," said Batti Batt as the blob of a woman grossly picked her teeth.

"And why is that," demanded Daksha.

"Because our Lord is preoccupied, stupid," shot back Yuki Donna, who continued to study her sharp, black nails as she spoke.

Cement Felix chuckled at the female Anointed Champions' hatred for Daksha before intervening. "Enough! The New God is away, but He will return shortly. *We* command his armies. *We* have the authority to make decisions in His absence. Now stop playing these children's games and give us the information you have to deliver." Felix smiled darkly. "I mean, if you are unable to deliver information, then what good are you to anyone? Do you have *any* value at all?"

"She still has that sweet meat that she is wearing," stated Batti Batt menacingly, and Daksha did not discount the woman's veiled threat. Not one bit.

Daksha smoothed down her white suit. "Very well. The invaders are crossing Paradise Bay as we speak. It appears that Ni…" Daksha caught herself and began again as the Four Demons giggled. "It seems that the *guardian* was unable to stop them. I don't know what happened, but I know that she… that *it* is no longer attacking their vessels."

"Fucking useless, that one," said Seth quietly. "See what happens when a woman doesn't pair with a good, strong man? They become useless."

"Silence, you slug," cut in Yuki. "Continue, Chosen."

Daksha swallowed down a lump that was forming in her throat. "Yes, well, the invaders are now starting toward the Isle Port. They will be arriving and offloading within the hour. I assume you will want to send the Forlorn to greet them at the docks."

"You assume wrong," Cement Felix said flatly.

Daksha's face twisted, confused. "I don't understand."

Felix released a great sigh. "Of course you don't. The Forlorn have had few opportunities to use the gifts of their transformations. They deserve to truly feel the power that was given to them by the New God. They need to feel the warm flow of an enemy's blood as it drips down their new bodies. So, I say, let all the invaders come ashore. Let them proceed well down the Perennial Pathway. And when they finally realize that there is no hope, that they cannot stop the New God, it will be too late. They will be surrounded, and our army will feed on their weak flesh."

"The Forlorn can attack them at the Isle Port and accomplish the same thing," countered Daksha.

"And let some of them run back to their boats to escape? Never! The New God's world will be rid of these infidels once and for all. Champions, do you agree?"

Yuki Donna nodded her head. "They pose no threat. Let them come."

"And if they survive the Perennial Pathway," asked Daksha. "If they make it here, to the Institute?"

Yuki's laugh sounded like her black nails on a chalkboard. "All the better. I would love to see this ragtag army up close. Batti?"

"I'm hungry. If my dinner is willing to come to me, all the better."

Yuki hesitated for a moment. "Seth?"

"Will there be women in this army?"

Yuki rolled her black eyes. "Yes, Seth, I'm sure they have women, as does *every* army in the known world, you slug."

Seth Whispers's mouth morphed into a dark smirk. "Then, yes, I would very much like to meet this army." He tipped his ridiculous fedora. "I will meet these women and introduce myself. I will show them what a good guy really looks like."

Even Cement Felix rolled his pink eyes at Seth's antics and delusion. "See, Daksha? It is unanimous. We will let them land. We will let them get established. Furthermore, we will let them think that there is hope as they begin their march down the Perennial Pathway. Then, the Forlorn will attack, and it will be too late. All will be lost. Now, if you don't have anything else for us, be gone before I let Seth have his way with you and allow Batti to clean up after."

Although it was an empty threat, Daksha still felt her legs begin to give out before she was able to snatch back control. She steeled her resolve for what she had to say next. "No, Felix, that is not all. I have something else."

Felix began to finger the wicked machete as his hip. "Out with it. And fast."

Daksha smoothed her suit once more. "The Chosen have been calling in on the secret channel. Almost all of them."

"And what do those fools want," demanded Yuki Donna.

"They want to know when the Rapture will take place. They are scared. The Great Conversion is underway and things are going according to plan. Everything, that is, but the Rapture. They want to know when to expect their reward."

Yuki and Batti giggled in unison. Seth Whispers simply smiled as he smelled his fingers. Cement Felix, however, remained unmoved as his pink eyes flashed dangerously.

"Their reward for what," asked Felix.

"Don't be obtuse, Felix. The reward for their fealty. The reward for their faith."

Felix's eyes went wide in mock surprise. "Oh, *that* reward. Of course, how could I have been so... obtuse?" Felix's words came out like boulders running down a mountainside. "Yuki, when do you think the Chosen will receive their *reward?*"

Yuki Donna pretended to do math on her deadly fingers. "Let's see, the Flowering Horde grows larger by the day. Soon, it will cover the world in its shadow. If my numbers are correct, and they always are, the Chosen should receive their reward any day now."

The Four Demons laughed as one, and Daksha felt the pit in her stomach grow large enough to consume her. "So, what can I tell them?"

Felix answered. "Tell them to hold tight. Tell them that..."

"Oh, for fuck's sake, just tell the idiot, Felix," interrupted Batti Bat.

"Yes, Theosis is virtually complete, Felix," agreed Yuki. "The work is done. We have no more use for the human chattel."

"Very well," said Felix before turning back to Daksha. "Tell them that the New God thanks them for their faith and that their work is done. Tell them that there is nothing more divine than joining the Flowering Horde."

Daksha almost collapsed to her knees from the words thrown at her, as if she were being stoned in ancient times. Her words came out slowly and thick, like they were covered in slime. "Then you are leaving them... to become... Bloomed."

Felix chuckled. "If they are lucky, they will be converted. Many will simply be eaten, although I am convinced that is also quite an experience." Batti Batt grunted in agreement.

Daksha forced out the next words, pushing their heft through the relatively small opening of her mouth. "Then, there is no Rapture?"

Cement Felix showed his shark teeth. "Oh, I don't know, Daksha. I'm feeling pretty *rapturous*! How about you, Champions?!" The Four Demons hooted supporting Felix, and Daksha felt her heart turn cold beneath her four-thousand-credit suit. "Now, be gone, Daksha! The human work is complete, your job is done. Soon, the New God will return as the one true god. You are still His favorite of the humans. Perhaps he will twist you into something beautiful, something befitting your station."

Daksha, dead inside, nodded dumbly as Felix spoke, the image of Nieve as a squid dancing around in her brain with razored slippers. She turned and began to exit the Holy Pistil, her legs moving independent of her mind. The sarcastic calls of the Four Demons chased after her as she moved through the chamber.

"I always thought you would look good as an eel," shouted Yuki Donna.

"I wonder what we will find beneath when your head peels back," laughed Cement Felix.

And most repulsive of all — "I will come to comfort you later, my lady!"

MARLIN HADDER absently fingered the handle of Patton Yellich's knife that was tucked into his belt as a mixture of Protector, gangster, and Blister scurried around him eager to offload weapons and battle accessories. While *Glory's Pursuit* and *The Orrin* remained in the bay, sending waves of smaller delivery ships to the port, *The Broken Dream's* narrow hull was able to successfully dock.

Hadder stared out past the Isle Port and down the large white cobbled path that cut through the island's lush jungle forest. Off in the distance, perhaps a couple of miles from the Isle Port, sat the Flowers Institute. The grotesque, lotus-shaped building looked down upon them with obvious distain, positioned at the most elevated end of the Isle of God. The white stonework pulsed gently in the morning sun, similar to the Crimmwall Petal, promising those that visited much more than they bargained for.

"What do you think, Angel," asked Gayle from beside Hadder.

"I don't like it, Gayle. Why would they simply allow us to land? And offload? And make preparations?"

Gayle's orange eyes reflected the sun's rays. "Because they underestimate you, Angel. They underestimate us all. And *that* may be the only reason we even have a chance."

"Plus, they want to be able to surround us, trap us," said Viktor Krill as he walked by holding a crate of weaponry that must have weighed several hundred pounds.

"Is there any way to avoid that," asked Hadder to Krill's back.

"Doubt it," Krill called over his shoulder. "We'll just have to keep pushing forward."

"He seems in good spirits," commented Gayle.

"Viktor has always been comfortable with violence. There are other things that darken his mood. I think he is excited for this release."

"Bullshit," said Zaza Anorrak as she and her sister, too, passed with handfuls of weapons. "I rocked his fucking world last night. That's why he's in a fucking good mood."

Su's mouth fell open. "Zaza! Gross! So uncalled-for. It's so unrefined!"

"Oh, is it, dear sister? Tell me, who was rocking fucking Milly's world last night? Because I was in the next container over, and I swear the noises that I fucking heard sounded anything but *refined*. But you wouldn't fucking know anything about that, would you?"

Su Anorrak's face turned red as the sweet woman double-timed it to the Perennial Pathway, the bundle in her arms bouncing angrily.

Zaza laughed at her sister's embarrassment. "God, I love that fucking bitch." She noticed Hadder's empty arms. "Don't be afraid to help out, Marlin," she said as she continued.

Hadder chuckled at the call-out. "She's right, Gayle. I should be helping."

Gayle nodded and put a grey hand on his shoulder. "Then this is where I must say goodbye, Angel."

"You're not staying for the battle, Gayle?"

"I would like nothing more, Angel. Unfortunately, my duties as Queen must take precedence. I must go to *The Orrin* and wait. If you all are unsuccessful, I must return with haste to King Gash. We will have to plan for our Blisters' survival in a shadow world."

"Of course, Gayle. As always, you have already done far more than your share. If not for you and Alphus, we would all be lounging at the bottom of the Great Water now, the world already lost above us."

"Alphus is sorry that he cannot join the main fray. But the severity of his injuries simply will not allow for it. But he wishes you luck, Angel. We all do."

"Thank you, Gayle. And please thank King Gash for me, regardless of what happens."

Gayle did not speak again as tears began to fill her bright eyes. Instead, she embraced Hadder in a hug, and the man found nothing but love in the folds of her thick, grey skin.

The loud sounds of mechanical legs greeted Hadder as Gayle walked away.

"The Blisters will miss her leadership," said Tennian Stamp as he watched his old ally head back to the docks. "We will have to fill that void."

"How do you fill the shoes of such a woman?"

"You don't. But you try, nonetheless."

Hadder nodded before turning to face Old Tens. "Any updates?"

"Too fucking quiet, if that can be considered an update. I have some men stationed at *The Broken Dream*'s anti-destroyer guns, just waiting for anything to move in that goddamn jungle. So far, not even a mouse fart."

Hadder thought for a moment. "Well, let us just be thankful for the *what* and not worry about the *why*. And I think we'll still be able to put *The Broken Dream*'s guns to good use."

"I hope so," said Old Tens as he turned back to join his men. "I paid a goddamn fortune for them."

After collecting a massive box of explosives from the dock, Hadder carried them across the Isle Port, depositing them near the mouth of the large cobbled path. Instead of returning for another load, however, he stood at the entrance to the jungle's passage, once more staring up at the Flowers Institute.

A few minutes later, he was joined by Clinton Voss, who pointed out the small sign that read *Perennial Pathway* a few yards ahead.

"*Perennial Pathway*? What a pretentious asshole. But then again, you would have to be to consider yourself a god, wouldn't you?"

"Where have you been?"

"Meeting with Tens and the Blisters, along with some Protectors. Strategizing about how we're going to go about this thing. Apologies, if you wanted to be included, Hadder."

Hadder waved away the idea. "Best that you all do what works best for you and the resources you have. Viktor and I will roam around the battlefield, wreaking havoc where we can. How did the planning go?"

Voss snickered. "We got a plan, but it's not a sophisticated one."

"The best plans are often the simplest."

"Yeah, well, this one is as simple as it gets, Hadder. Move forward, make sure that some remain alive for when we get *there*." Voss motioned to the Flowers Institute with his chin.

"Sounds good. Viktor and I will make sure that we get there."

"I believe I heard my name," said Krill as he joined Hadder and Voss.

"Just going over some big picture items," replied Voss.

"What is there to go over? Walk forward, kill anything that looks like it's wearing a costume."

"Some of our Blister friends could fit that description," countered Hadder.

"Fair point. Kill anything that doesn't belong in this world. Better?"

"Better," agreed Hadder.

"Well, seems like we have it all figured out," declared Voss sarcastically. "We have a few more preparations to make. Departure in one hour?"

Hadder and Krill both nodded, which sent Voss on his way back to the Isle Port.

Krill pointed at the jungle that surrounded them. "Now that we are up close, do you see it?"

Hadder's Wakened eyes studied the jungle landscape. "I see it. Glowing mushrooms and bioluminescent plants. Pollen that looks like stars in the night sky. The bastard has partly recreated Station's flora on the island."

"And how does that make you feel, Marlin?"

Hadder thought for a second. "It makes me miss happier times."

"I thought you didn't have those, Marlin?"

"They were few, but they were there. And you? How does it make you feel, Viktor?"

"It makes me sick. It reminds me that I could have slit this fucker's throat when he was a nobody in Station. It reminds me that when killing needs to be done, don't hesitate."

"I don't think this is the time nor the place for me to disagree with you on that, Viktor."

"It is not, so let it serve as a reminder to *you* as well. Now, let us get back. We have our own preparations to make. Terry is waiting for us." Krill turned back and began to walk, but stopped when he noticed that Hadder was not following. Krill's black eyes fell to where Hadder was looking. "Fear not, Marlin, we will be seeing that cursed place soon enough. From much closer up. Now, come, I wish to see Lil Terry before they return him to *Glory's Pursuit*."

Hadder smiled. "You've grown quite fond of that dog, Viktor."

Krill's black eyes flashed. "Lil Terry is a mangy mutt who smells like the insides of a carcass. This makes him far more charming than most of those who incorrectly claim to be humans. Now, come, I prefer not to miss his feeding time."

THE BROKEN DREAM'S anti-destroyer guns flashed again and again in the sweet morning air, sending round after round of large-caliber bullets streaking into the Isle of God's dense, glowing jungle. Branches snapped, and deep swaths appeared in the vegetation as the battle-craft ripped into the ominous surroundings.

The gathered Blisters, standing at the head of humanity's last army, looked up as projectiles whistled loudly just above their heads for several minutes, eliminating any threats that possibly could have been hiding in wait.

Tennian Stamp, waiting alongside his longtime Blister allies, did not look up, instead opting to study his jungle surroundings with the eyes of a soldier, one that was about to willingly walk into an obvious trap.

Eventually, Old Tens raised his right hand in a fist, and voices called out in succession until they reached the battle-craft's gunners, who immediately ceased firing.

As silence returned to the Isle of God, Tennian listened carefully, taking in the sounds of broken limbs falling to the soft jungle ground and birds squawking in excitement. Listening deeper, however, Old Tens found more in the relative jungle quiet.

Strange steps could be heard shifting along the thick jungle floor, odd tempos created by too many legs. Occasionally, a pained moan or an angry growl could be heard emanating from within the deep undergrowth.

"They're out there," said Tennian over his shoulder, refusing to remove his eyes from the threat. "I think we got some. Should make those fuckers think twice before attacking us near the docks."

Mechanical legs whirred to life as Old Tens turned to face his ragtag army, who now referred to themselves as the Army of Humanity. "What do you say, boys and girls?"

The Blisters in attendance, a hodgepodge of massive, deformed bodies with skin ranging in color and dotted, in many cases, with painful sores, all nodded in affirmation. Some smiled in anticipation, showing off crooked mouths filled with gnarled teeth, as their large hands tightened on massive pieces of metal sharpened into wicked-looking blades.

"We're fucking ready, man, yes the fuck we are. Just fucking let me at those fucking monsters. I'll eat the fucking lot of them, I fucking will. Just get me close enough to fucking bite, Sowler, man. Just close enough to fucking bite. I'll fucking end this fucking battle super quick if you get me near fucking Milo Flowers's throat. Yes, I fucking will."

"Shut up, Smeggins," said Old Tens and Sowler in unison, bringing laughter to the Blisters and injecting some much-needed levity to the dire situation.

Tennian looked to Sowler, who was bravely joining him at the head of the Blisters' flying wedge battle formation. Old Tens's eyes fell once more to the deadly contraption lashed to the massive stump of Sowler's right arm. Tied on with heavy leather, a heavy metal socket sat where the pig-man's treasured mutated arm once resided. Attached to the metal socket was a thick chain six feet in length with a spiked ball of steel at its end. Tennian chuckled to himself for the third time that morning, thinking of the destruction that Sowler's homemade arm-flail would cause.

Sowler finally caught Tennian looking his way. "We are ready, whether it be for glory or death. The Blisters are ready."

Tennian simply nodded in response, thankful once again for the such powerful friends, before turning his attention to the remainder of his force.

Old Tens's gangsters resided within the Blisters' flying wedge, their guns loaded and cocked, ready to offer distant support to their allies' hand-to-hand efforts.

Bringing up the rear were the Protectors of Man, each of whom were outfitted with a combination of blades, guns, flamethrowers, and explosives. It was obvious that the New God's twisted guardians would send a massive force to attack from the rear once the Army of Humanity was well away from the Isle Port. The Protectors would need to be able to hold their own without direct Blister assistance.

The compartments of Tennian's mechanical legs opened and closed, a telltale sign that its owner was deep in thought.

Tennian quickly shook those worries aside, and instead tapped into something cold within himself. On this day, he needed to be the Tennian Stamp of old, the Tennian Stamp that took the Harrier Gap. He needed to be the Tennian Stamp that formed one of Bhellum's oldest and most powerful gangs. He needed to be the Tennian Stamp that faced down Cyrix Technologies and came out the other side alive and wealthy.

A smirk formed on the lips of the man known as Old Tens.

"Let's move," he said to Sowler.

———

ALTHOUGH NO ATTACKS CAME, the Army of Humanity was beset on all sides by a cacophony of terrifying sounds – screeches and screams, snarls and hisses, none of which seemed of this world.

Despite the horror that was closing in, however, mankind's army marched on, led by retired gangster Tennian Stamp and Blister enforcer Sowler.

And the mutant face called Smeggins.

"Let them fucking come. I fucking dare them, Sowler, man. I hope they fucking come. Oh, man, how I fucking want them to fucking come, man."

"Shut up, Smeggins."

Finally, after crossing nearly a half-mile of the Perennial Pathway, Tennian spotted movement up ahead, just beyond a slight bend in the one-hundred-foot-wide cobbled avenue. A dark fist went into the air and the Army of Humanity halted.

It crawled out of the jungle not more than thirty feet from Old Tens, as if it were putting on a show. And perhaps it was. The creature, once one of the sad, afflicted humans of the Neelsen Islands, slithered out of the undergrowth on its belly, looking like an eight-foot slug with peach, humanlike skin. On its too-tight face was a row of black eyes that sat over an immense mouth filled with rows of sharp teeth. A small, fingerlike appendage jutted out from the top of the creature's bald head and swayed like seaweed in the Great Water. The monster stopped once it had reached the center of the Perennial Pathway and spun to face Tennian Stamp.

"So, this is what the Forlorn have become," Old Tens said to himself. "Death will be a mercy to these poor souls."

As if the Forlorn could hear Tennian's words, the creature raised the front half of its body up from the cobbled ground and let out an earsplitting shriek that caused real displeasure to some Blisters with sensitive hearing. After its wail, six long, grotesque appendages broke free from the slug-like body, slammed into the cobbled ground, and rose the creature into the air.

Tennian's jaw fell open as the human-skinned spider opened its tooth-filled maw in a dark grin.

"Who would let themselves be transformed into such a nightmare," asked a blue-hued Blister from behind Old Tens.

"They had the Festering," said Tennian over his shoulder. "And Milo Flowers fed off that, just as he has fed off others' vulnerabilities.

To the Forlorn, it was better to live as powerful nightmares than as decaying humans. It would not have been my choice, but I understand it."

"Fuck a damn Forlorn," said Smeggins from Sowler's shoulder.

"Indeed, my small friend, pity or no, they still need to be eliminated."

Once again, the Forlorn acted as if it could hear and understand Tennian's every word. It let out another primal yell before launching forward on its spidery tentacles, moving faster than any person could ever hope to travel.

The Blisters fell into defensive formation as the Forlorn raced toward the flying wedge. When it was within ten feet of the army, a small compartment opened on Tennian's right leg and released three consecutive small missiles. They caught the Forlorn in its chest and exploded, scorching the creature's skin and stopping it in its tracks.

The Forlorn's row of black eyes went wide with rage, and it howled into the morning air, a thick, pointed tongue falling out of its mouth as it did. The creature then bowed, and the fingerlike appendage atop its head extended and took off like a javelin, heading straight for Old Tens's throat at blinding speed. Tennian's eyes went wide and then closed tight as the bioweapon closed in, too fast for him to react effectively.

Instead of being skewered, however, Old Tens was greeted with a grotesque smashing sound as the spiked ball of Sowler's arm-flail destroyed the Forlorn's head just before it reached its target.

The spidery nightmare silently danced back and forth on its six tentacles for several seconds, with no head to voice its pain. It then froze in place and began to convulse, and with each frenetic movement, a small bulb appeared and grew larger on its neck.

"It's regenerating," called a Blister from the back.

"Fuck that," said Tennian, and a nozzle escaped a hole that appeared around the gangster's left knee. "See you on the other side, you poor bastard," he called out as a geyser of fire reached out and enveloped the convulsing Forlorn.

As the flames latched onto the creature and found purchase on its tight skin, Sowler's deadly flail returned, striking the Forlorn over and over again as blue, yellow, and red devoured the writhing nightmare.

After almost a minute of constant burning and pulverizing, the only thing left of the spidery Forlorn was a gross mound of burned flesh.

"That wasn't so fucking hard, was it, Sowler? Come on, man, is that the best that they fucking got? I'll eat them all for fucking breakfast and still have room for fucking lunch."

"Shut up, Smeggins," roared Sowler as he worked to catch his breath.

"That was just a test," commented Old Tens, who was also attempting to slow his heartbeat after the unpleasant ordeal.

"Yeah, but we kicked its fucking ass, didn't we, Sowler?"

"Look what it took to kill just one of those things," said Old Tens, more to Sowler than to Smeggins. "And there are thousands of these things on this cursed island."

"And who knows what forms the others will take," offered Sowler. "I fear not all will look like our spider friend there."

Screams, howls, and shrieks poured out of the jungle surrounding the Army of Humanity, a symphony of anger, excitement, and, worst of all, hunger.

"I fear that you are right, my friend," agreed Tennian. "And I fear that we are about to discover the truth of that statement." The leaves on either side of the Perennial Pathway shook violently as large creatures could be heard scampering across the brushy floor. "Be ready! They come!"

The surrounding jungle exploded with nightmares.

———

SOWLER'S FEARS were proven warranted when a potpourri of monstrosities poured out from the North and South of the island.

Some Forlorn raced forward on six tentacles, others on four or eight. A few crawled around on segmented stomachs, propelled forward by hundreds of tiny legs, similar to a centipede. Those that moved around on human-like legs had other frightening attributes like chestfuls of tentacles, serpent-shaped fingers on oversized hands, and gaping mouths that encompassed entire backs.

The Forlorn screamed and laughed, cried and moaned, as if they were caught in a constant state of nervous collapse. In some cases, a Forlorn would begin having a seizure, only to split down the middle in a gory mess, leaving two creatures where there once stood only one.

The Army of Humanity's enemy was a manic display of life left unencumbered and undefined, a peak into the New God's planned reality.

The medley of madness slammed into the Army of Humanity, which did not fold under the weight of horror.

———

GIANT BLISTER BLADES rose and fell, tearing into Forlorn flesh and sending gore flying.

"I'll show you what *true* monsters look like," screamed the blue-skinned Blister as he took a talon-tipped arm from a hunchbacked Forlorn with a massive boil on its back.

As the Forlorn howled in pain, its boil burst, sending a mass of small red flatworms to fly from the wound. While most fell harmlessly to the ground, a few landed on Blister arms and necks, immediately disappearing as they dug their way into colorful flesh.

Those unlucky Blisters screamed and dropped weapons as they attempted to dig out the red worms with their nails. This frenetic clawing only lasted a few seconds, however, as each Blister dropped dead a short time later, their brains consumed by the red parasites.

Between the battling Blisters, bullets flew from the gangsters, catching Forlorn between two, four, or six eyes. Occasionally, grenades soared over the Blisters' heads to land amidst a collection of monsters, sending them flying in every direction upon detonation.

When there was no shot to take, the gangsters assisted their Blister allies in other ways, injecting anyone who looked to be tiring with a potent cocktail of Flame and Rush.

The black, brown, and yellow blood of the Forlorn mixed with the red blood of the Blisters as the two groups tore into each other, both determined to be the only monsters left standing.

Sowler's arm-flail swung back and forth as Smeggins continued his verbal assault. And although the tiny mutant annoyed the hell out of Sowler most of the time, the Blister enforcer had to admit something. The little guy's foul words were pushing him harder, allowing him to strike faster and harder than he ever thought possible.

A barbed tentacle struck a hole in Sowler's left shoulder, just missing Smeggins. A slithering Forlorn launched up from the ground and took a chunk out of the Blister's thigh with its fanged mouth.

But still, Sowler pressed on and moved the flying wedge forward. And any time he felt too tired or hurt to continue, the Blister simply looked to the man on his left and found all the inspiration he needed to continue.

TENNIAN STAMP, known across the city of Bhellum as Old Tens, fought like a man possessed, for not only was he battling the demons of the Isle of God, but the demons of his past. Each wound he ignored, each Forlorn he struck down, and each ally he saved was a demon from his past that he slayed. They represented an unnecessary murder that he chose *not* to order, a drug that he *didn't* sell to a youth, an enemy that he *absorbed* instead of eliminated.

Missiles flew from Tennian's metal legs, and fire reached out from his mechanical knees to engulf wave after wave of Forlorn. Those that were struck shrieked in pain before retreating into the jungle, probably to heal, regenerate, or multiply. Or all three.

Those Forlorn that fell to the white cobble of the Perennial Pathway found themselves being stomped into jelly under the heavy metal legs of Old Tens. Once this method was found effective, thrusters exploded into action, sending Tennian into massive leaps that ended with him atop a tangle of Forlorn. Upon landing, his metal legs rose and fell like pistons, as if her were making Forlorn wine from the nightmares' juices.

As Forlorn fell before and under him, a wide grin broke out on the dark face of Tennian Stamp. With a buck knife in his left hand and a pistol in his right, surrounded by horror and on the cusp of the world's end, Old Tens had never felt more alive, more purposeful, more connected to those around him.

If he had to die here and now, so be it. It would be a good death.

———

"HERE THEY COME," called out Su Anorrak, her katana blade at the ready.

"It's about fucking time," said Zaza. "I was beginning to think we were going to miss all the fucking action."

"We knew they were going to wait to attack the rear," said Clinton Voss, who had armed himself with a giant two-headed battle-axe that only a man of his size could heft. "But when they did, we knew that they were going to come hard. And here it is!"

A massive force of the Forlorn had gathered on the Perennial Pathway behind the Army of Humanity, intending to tear through the perceived weak back end of the formation.

They couldn't have been more wrong.

Guns and explosives rang out as the Forlorn charged forward, ripping into their lines and sending more than a few of the nightmares to scurry back into the safety of the jungle.

But still, the Forlorn surged ahead, unmoved by the pain and suffering of their brethren, determined to taste the warm flesh of the humans who dared to stand before them.

The monsters raced up the Perennial Pathway, but all pulled up as a tiny creature sprang forth from the human army, stopped a dozen feet ahead of the group, and began barking in the nightmares' direction.

The twisted heads of the Forlorn cocked to the side confusedly as the little dog continued to bark, fearless in the face of the collection of horror.

"I see you've met Lil Terry," said Terry as he, too, stepped away from the Protectors of Man wearing his stained overalls and dirty, slicked back hair. In Terry's heavy arms was one of the largest flamethrowers ever created, a testament to the thick muscles that hid beneath Terry's layers of fat. "Lil Terry has a message for you fuckers. This is *our* world, and it belongs to man and dog. We're sorry, but there's just no room for a bunch of cunts like you." Lil Terry barked once more. "And with that, Lil Terry bids you farewell." Terry made a clicking sound with his mouth, and Lil Terry ran back to the Protectors of Man.

As soon as Lil Terry passed Terry, the mechanic opened fire on the Forlorn, bathing them in the largest pillar of flame witnessed since the assault on the Cyrix Headquarters building.

The Forlorn screamed in a mixture of rage and pain, with a large portion of the nightmares racing off into the jungle with their skin ablaze, hoping to extinguish the flames on the water-soaked flora.

"That's our opening," yelled Clinton Voss, and the Protectors of Man roared back as one in agreement. "Stay together. Stay tight. Kill anything that doesn't answer back." Lil Terry barked. "Except Lil Terry!"

Lil Terry barked one last time before leaping into Terry's arms, the oily man catching the small pup and placing him in the large pocket that fronted his dirty overalls.

"Let's cut these fuckers," screamed Zaza as the Protectors of Man surged back to meet the Forlorn head on.

"Fuck the New God," screamed Su, and Lil Terry growled from Terry's pocket.

"Sorry for the language, Lil Terry," said Su, seconds before she removed the top from a Forlorn's single-eyed head.

———

THE ANORRAK SISTERS became a choreographed tornado of death, a whirlwind of blades that left pieces of Forlorn in their wake. Each movement, strike, and parry of Zaza, which was always accompanied by a curse, was in perfect alignment with Su's icy, silent blows.

A Forlorn with a protruding mouth like a baboon bit at Zaza's neck and had its face sliced neatly off by Su. A barbed tentacle reached for Su's chest and was cleaved in half by a screaming Zaza.

The Protectors of Man gave the sisters a wide birth, not wanting to interfere with their harmonious attacks that were putting the Forlorn back on their tentacles.

A scream from the far side of the Perennial Pathway stole the sisters' attentions as the Forlorn began to shy away from their accurate strikes. There, a circle of Protectors had gathered around a massive Forlorn that was little more than a six-foot round blob, most of which was composed of a giant mouth filled with rows of blackened teeth. From the body of the nightmare, a dozen muscled tentacles flailed high in the air, searching for victims with red eyes that tipped each gross appendage. These tentacles grabbed Protectors with impossible strength and dragged them into the monster's maw, drawing shrieks of terror just before a sick crunching sound echoed across the cobbled walkway.

Rounds of bullets assaulted the monstrosity, doing little obvious damage as they sank into thick, fatty tissue. The blobby Forlorn was bathed in hot light as flamethrowers swung in its direction, but looked to be barely touched by fire when the flames finally subsided. Several Protectors charged forward with blades drawn, but were swept aside by the lightning-fast tentacles.

Zaza and Su looked at each other and nodded before wading in, their katana swords dancing in the air before them as they entered the Forlorn's kill zone.

Clinton Voss shouted orders, and the Protectors of Man shifted their strategy from attacking the nightmare to guarding the Anorrak sisters as they met the nightmare head on.

The Forlorn issued a slimy smile as the sisters advanced, showcasing bits of Protector that were now stuck in its black teeth.

"You're going to pay for every Protector you hurt," shouted Su as she feinted left but came across to the right with a flick of her wrist, taking the red-eyed tip from a tentacle.

"Fucking right, you fucking are," Zaza called out as she pretended to go high but dropped to her knees instead, allowing a striking tentacle to soar harmlessly overhead. She swept her blade up, removing a chunk of the tentacle and sending it into a frenzy.

The Protectors of Man guarding the Anorrak sisters could feel their eyes go wide as the battle became a blur of blades and tentacles, each movement too quick to follow.

Zaza and Su danced forward and back, shifted positions, and rolled across the other's kneeling form, always one step ahead of the Forlorn's blows, always a tiny misstep away from certain death. Occasionally, their blades struck home, other times they did not. But after each engagement, the Forlorn had fewer tentacles with which to attack the Army of Humanity.

After almost five minutes of constant battle, the Anorrak sisters stumbled back to the Protector line, exhausted and winded, leaving behind one Forlorn that had no tentacles with which to feed its insatiable hunger.

"Doesn't look so fucking scary anymore, does it," commented Zaza, and everyone had to agree. The Forlorn was now simply a blind blob biting pointlessly into the blood-twinged air. "Someone fucking finish this piece of shit off."

"I'll do it," said Milly as she exited the group of Protectors, the flamethrower in her hand matching her long, orange hair. She began to unscrew one of the weapon's three fuel tanks. "This is almost out anyway. But it should have enough juice."

The striking woman with the tangerine makeup then marched toward the impotent Forlorn, fuel tank in hand, ready to cast it into the creature's waiting mouth. Just as she cocked back, the Forlorn's round body seized up and began to quiver before letting out a massive cough that sounded like a thunderclap, launching chunks of bone and gore at Milly, who froze mid-swing.

"Fucking gross," said Zaza, who had to suppress a gag.

"What are you waiting for, Milly," asked Su, concerned for her girlfriend.

Milly turned slowly back to the Protector line, and everyone's heart sank as she did, for lodged in her throat was a thick piece of broken femur bone from a previously digested Protector.

"Milly, no," screamed Su as she raced to her love, who had now collapsed to her knees, wide-eyed and in obvious shock. "No, no, no," repeated Su when she reached Milly, carefully laying the woman down on the Perennial Pathway.

Milly tried to speak, but the shattered bone fragment would not allow it. Blood began to spray from around the wound. Su's dark eyes began to fill with water as she put a trembling hand to the bone piece and pulled it loose, releasing a torrent of blood to waterfall down Milly's shirt.

"I... I... I... Love...," Milly wheezed.

"I love you, too," cried Su as she kissed Milly on her tangerine lips and cradled the woman's head in her arms.

Zaza wiped tears from her tan cheeks. "Fucking piece of shit," she yelled, storming over and scooping up the fuel tank that Milly had dropped. The Anorrak sister executed a neat pirouette, sending the tank flying at the Forlorn's gaping mouth.

With no tentacles to block its path, the fuel tank sank deeply into the Forlorn's open maw. Sensing that it was not food, the monster tried to spit out the canister, but before it could, Teo stepped forward, a pistol in his scarred hand, and fired a single shot.

The fuel tank exploded in the creature's mouth, sending a spray of gore and fire into the air, forcing back many of the other Forlorn that were slowly starting to creep ahead.

After wiping bits of Forlorn from her brow, Zaza walked over to her sister and put a hand on the sweet woman's shoulder. Su looked up at her with lips red from Milly's blood.

"It's over, Su. She's fucking gone. And we still have fucking killing to do. Mourn her later. Please."

A shadow of sadness fell over Su Anorrak's light-skinned face before it was quickly replaced with a look of violent anger. She kissed

Milly on the forehead once more before looking at her sister, nodding, and rising.

"I'm going to kill every fucking last one, Zaza."

Zaza smiled wickedly through her pain. "Now that's the fucking spirit, Su."

Lil Terry barked from behind in agreement.

———

THE BLISTERS SWUNG their mutated bodies at the Forlorn, their homemade blades ripping holes in the monsters' lines. Old gangsters from the Risers, the Broken Tens, and the Bitch-Whores sent bullets and explosives into groups of the nightmares, sending them back and causing many to retreat into the surrounding undergrowth. The Protectors of Man fought with renewed fury, sending a vicious mix of projectile, knife, sword, and flame at the Forlorn and basking in the sweet sounds of pained screams as the warped creatures fell.

And still, it wasn't enough.

For every Forlorn that fell, three members of the Army of Humanity met their end. And after an hour of making steady progress up the Perennial Pathway, humanity's last hope stalled.

A massive unit of the Forlorn had collected before the Blisters at the head of the flying wedge, and an increasingly large Forlorn force was starting to form in the rear, steadily advancing on the Protectors of Man. Meanwhile, an assortment of especially gruesome Forlorn were pouring out of the Isle of God's thick, alien jungle, striking at the sides of the army in a pincher attack, squeezing the allies between frenzied nightmares.

Holes began to appear in the Army of Humanity's lines, gaps that were quickly filled with rushing Forlorn that dashed ahead on legs, and hooves, and tentacles, and slug-like bellies.

The Army of Humanity bent, shook, and looked to be on the verge of total collapse. And just as the human army began to break under the pressure of horror, just as all appeared lost, something wonderful happened.

Three electronic bracelets worn by Tennian Stamp, Clinton Voss, and Su Anorrak began to vibrate and emit a purple glow. Old Tens looked at Sowler and smiled. Clinton Voss looked over at Teo and grinned. And Su Anorrak simply held her wrist up for her sister to see.

"Its about fucking time."

24

"Side, side, side," called out Clinton Voss to the Protectors of Man.

"Side! Side! Side," bellowed Sowler to his team of Blisters.

"Side," yelled Su Anorrak in her too-sweet voice, which was then repeated by her more boisterous sister.

"Side! Fucking side! Get to the fucking side!"

This was heard by the ex-Bitch-Whore Raelynne, who relayed it to the remainder of the old gangsters, ensuring that she was heard over the deafening sounds of gunfire.

As one, the Army of Humanity split down the middle like a Bloomed Man, each half pushing their way toward the far edges of the Perennial Pathway. In some cases, this required allowing some Forlorn to break through lines and take up residence in the middle of the cobbled avenue, where they hissed and giggled and shrieked, thinking their victory all but in hand.

One particular Forlorn, a white-eyed monster standing close to seven feet tall with massive pinchers for hands, rose to its full height in the middle of the Perennial Pathway.

It cackled like a hyena, only to be blown to bits seconds later in a hail of large-caliber bullets.

More bullets tore down the center of the Perennial Pathway, ripping apart those Forlorn unlucky enough to have captured the middle ground. This was soon followed by the sounds of an approaching engine, one that was loud and strong and coming in fast.

The Protectors of Man in the rear were the first to let out a cheer as the Comet plowed through the group of Forlorn who had gathered behind the Army of Humanity. High-caliber bullets from the add-on rotary cannons ripped through the collection of nightmares, taking heads from necks and tentacles from bodies. Those that survived the onslaught of bullets were soon greeted by the reinforced body of the antique automobile, which plowed into, through, and over the twisted bodies of the New God's guardians.

The Protectors of Man screamed in delight as the Comet blasted a hole in the Forlorn line and continued up the Perennial Pathway.

"That's *my* girl," shouted Terry as the Comet streaked by, and Lil Terry let a bark of agreement.

Some Forlorn were smart enough to understand the danger and tried to retreat to the edges of the path, only to be forced back by a raging group of humans on their last stand.

The old gangsters, many of whom served under Viktor Krill, hooted and hollered as the Comet flew past, laughing in grim delight each time a Forlorn was smashed under the vehicle's heavy wheels.

"Surge! Surge! Surge," came the common cry as mankind's army quickly reclaimed the center of the Perennial Pathway and moved to advance in the Comet's wake. In short order, much of the army had made more progress in one minute than they had in the last hour.

Tennian Stamp slammed his weathered hands together and Sowler held his arm-flail high into the air as the Comet raced past and slammed into the large waiting batch of Forlorn that was waiting to finally halt the army's progress.

"Who the hell do those guys think they are," laughed Old Tens over the din of the roaring rotary cannon.

"One is an Angel," replied Sowler, "and the other is the baddest human I have ever seen."

"I still want to fucking eat them both, Sowler, man."

"Shut up, Smeggins."

Despite the Comet's rotary cannons dropping many of the Forlorn, numerous others moved in fearlessly to fill the gaps. Thus, when the Comet finally slammed into the lead group of nightmares, it smashed into a literal wall of mutated bodies.

While the first few rows of Forlorn were blasted apart from the vehicular battering ram, the sheer numbers of bodies before it eventually stopped the Comet's progress.

"Do we go help," asked Sowler concerned.

"Wait," Old Tens responded with a dark grin. "They have one more trick to play."

The *trick* became evident a moment later when thick spouts of flame shot from the front, sides, and rear of the Comet, which had sprouted nozzles from neatly hidden compartments, another gift from master mechanic Terry.

The flames engulfed dozens of the Forlorn surrounding the car, sending them scurrying off into the wet jungle for reprieve.

"So, when *do* we help," repeated Sowler, his arm-flail obviously antsy for blood.

"Soon, my friend," answered Old Tens. "Very soon."

"How will we know?"

"Oh, we'll know. It will be quite evident."

A little voice came once again from Sowler's shoulder. "Yeah, well, just fucking give the word when I have to go fucking save these fucking guys. I'll eat any Forlorn that fucking gets near me. Isn't that right, Sowler, man?"

"Shut up, Smeggins."

———

VIKTOR KRILL THREW the Comet in reverse, slammed on the accelerator, and spun the steering violently back and forth. This caused the Comet to fishtail atop the white cobble, strafing the surrounding Forlorn with rotary cannon bullets and geysers of fire.

Dozens of Forlorn fell around the Comet or ran off into the wet jungle. But still more came.

One nightmare managed to wrap a long tentacle around the passenger-side rotary cannon and ripped it free from its mount. Another slid on its slimy belly until it reached the Comet and bit into the rear wheel with its fanged mouth, puncturing the thick rubber.

Eventually, the other rotary canon was torn loose and several of the flamethrowers began to die down, their fuel tanks expended. Heavy tentacles and clawed hands started to assault the Comet, breaking the back windows and bending the frame of the antique.

"Ah, look at what they're doing to my girl," bemoaned Viktor Krill as the Comet slowly started to die under the attack. He patted the dashboard softly with a tan hand. "You did your part, old girl. Now, it's time for me to do mine."

Krill's black eyes flashed dangerously as his thirst for violence grew to unquenchable levels. He looked over to Marlin Hadder, who had remained oddly quiet during the past few minutes.

"It's time, Marlin. Are you ready."

"I am," said Hadder without looking over.

"Are you certain, Marlin, because I don't see it! And I am going to need you full on if we are..." Hadder spun, and his hazel eyes met Krill's black orbs. Krill reactively moved back in his seat, for deep within Hadder's eyes was what the notorious killer was looking for — the Rage.

Not only was the Rage present in his Wakened companion, but Hadder was fully in the grips of the strange phenomenon.

"You're ready," declared Krill, a cold smile forming on his lips. "Let's go."

———

BOTH DOORS FLEW from the Comet, sent flying away from the impossibly strong kicks of the only Wakened humans in history. The soaring metal cleared some space for both Hadder and Krill, who rose from the Comet like two wraiths who had come to visit death upon the world.

Each Wakened human had auto-turrets perched on both shoulders, compliments of the Thorns of Reckoning. As Hadder and Krill moved, the auto-turrets spun in the air, searching for and firing at any Forlorn that dared to approach.

Hadder waded into a group of Forlorn like a demon, auto-turrets on his shoulders, a scimitar in his right hand, a crystalline handgun in his left, and Patton Yellich's dagger tucked into his waistband.

A Forlorn with a mouth that opened vertically across the entirety of the creature's mutated head reached out for Hadder, but was driven back by a round from the auto-turrets. This created enough space for Hadder to bring his blade across, slicing the nightmare in half just below its bony chest.

The crystalline handgun sent bullets into vulnerable eyes, leaving the Forlorn blind and unable to defend against Hadder's flashing blade.

Viktor Krill sent knife after knife into the faces of the Forlorn, following these up with streaking blows from his falchion that more often than not sliced a nightmare neatly in two. Krill's auto-turrets also rang out, preventing rear attacks and offering the notorious killer much-needed space with which to apply his deadly skills.

To the Army of Humanity watching in awe, it appeared as if two gods had come down from on high to rid the world of Doctor Milo Flowers and his false promises.

After almost ten minutes of impossible battle, Marlin Hadder and Viktor Krill stood alone in a pile of Forlorn gore, their auto-turrets spinning impotently on their shoulders, bullets long exhausted. The Forlorn still surrounded the Wakened humans on three sides, but no longer looked interested in fighting with death incarnate.

Hadder looked over to Krill and each man nodded before turning their backs to the Forlorn and marching to join the Army of Humanity. As they moved away from the nightmares, the Forlorn grew brazen once more, moving up to surround the abandoned Comet and establish themselves as a barrier across the Perennial Pathway.

Sowler bowed as Hadder and Krill approached, dropping the auto-turrets from their shoulders as they did. "Always a pleasure to watch you fight, Angel."

"Yeah," agreed Smeggins, "not fucking bad. For a fucking peddie!"

Tennian slammed his palm into Krill's shoulder. "Not bad. Not bad at all. When do we move again?" Old Tens pointed his chin down the Perennial Pathway. "Already they are regathering their strength."

"I was counting on it," said Krill as he took out a cigarette along with a small, single-button controller. He lit the cigarette and turned his back on the Forlorn horde that was growing larger by the second. He fingered the controller in his hand. "I really don't want to do this," Krill said to Hadder.

"You have to, Viktor."

"Fuck that." Krill tossed the controller to Hadder. "You do it. Let me know when it's over."

"Fair enough, Viktor." Hadder turned to Tennian and Sowler. "Get ready to attack. Everything we got. We either get through here or we die trying. Send it down the line."

Hadder waited as the orders were relayed down the lines of the Army of Humanity. Finally, Old Tens nodded.

"We're ready, Hadder."

Hadder smiled in return. "Viktor?"

"Just fucking do it already!"

Hadder nodded. "She was a good ride."

"The best."

"She still has one trick left to show those bastards."

"Then let her show it."

Hadder pressed the button on the controller and immediately shielded his eyes as the Comet, surrounded by scores of the Forlorn, detonated. Packed with all the explosives taken from the Thorns of Reckoning and with that Terry had in his shop, the Comet went off like a nuclear bomb. It vaporized every Forlorn within twenty-five feet and blew any within one-hundred feet well into the dense jungle, often in several pieces.

A mighty cheer went up along the length of the Army of Humanity as the smoke cleared, revealing an open pathway to the Flowers Institute, devoid of Forlorn.

"It's done," said Hadder to Krill, who finally turned around to view the carnage.

"Then we go," declared the notorious killer. "We have a window, but already it is starting to close."

And with that, Marlin Hadder, Viktor Krill, Tennian Stamp, and Sowler took up positions at the head of the reformed flying wedge and started to advance on the Flowers Institute, which was now in their collective sights.

As they did, chants began along mankind's final army, eventually coalescing into a singular mantra.

Fuck the New God!

———

To their credit, the Forlorn did recover quickly, rushing out of the jungle to face the Army of Humanity as it made its final push to reach the Flowers Institute.

Unfortunately, those that did met a quick end at the hands of the deadly quartet that now fronted the renewed human force.

Tennian's mechanical legs sent missiles to intercept attacking Forlorn and crushed nightmares beneath their weighty girth.

Sowler, accompanied by the endless curses of Smeggins, sent the spiked ball that tipped his arm-flail into monster after monster, caving in chests, cracking skulls, and pulverizing spinal cords.

Hadder and Krill's blades danced in the air before them, their Wakened abilities proving too much even for Milo Flowers's twisted sentinels.

The flying wedge ran down the Perennial Pathway on a wave of inevitability, splitting hastily formed Forlorn units as if they were nothing more than dry kindling.

Clinton Voss, bringing up the rear with his Protectors of Man, looked around in surprise at the relative ease with which they were now moving toward the Flowers Institute.

DeLany Thales, running alongside the mountainous Protector leader, gave voice to Voss's concern.

"Why have they stopped attacking? I'm definitely not complaining, but I am starting to worry."

"They're fucking cowards, that's why," stated Zaza plainly, but a shared look between Su and Teo showed that they felt otherwise.

"Whatever the reason," said Voss confidently, "our goal remains the same. Reach the Flowers Institute, gain entrance, and then eliminate Milo Flowers. If the Forlorn have plans beyond being grotesque, we will discover them soon enough. Take this time to recover and reload. I'm afraid this relative calm will not last for long."

"Why is that, boss" asked Upton from under his blond mullet.

"Because nothing good ever does."

THE FLOWERS INSTITUTE grew large and imposing as the Army of Humanity began to climb the small incline that marked the final phase of the Perennial Pathway.

Hanging just above the New God's stronghold was the pink asteroid, large and imposing, like an eye focused solely on this battle to pass a final judgment. Visible only to Marlin Hadder and Viktor Krill, the Wakened humans shared a look as they both took in the mammoth size of the incoming pink rock.

Despite the circular omen above them, the Army of Humanity found little resistance as they covered the last one hundred yards to the Flowers Institute, with the few Forlorn that still appeared offering only half-hearted efforts.

Like the Crimmwall Petal, the Flowers Institute's white exterior gently pulsed in the warm air. As Hadder began to ascend the steps that led up to the lotus-shaped building's entrance, he spotted a small gold plague set into the marble that read *Sacred Landing*.

Hadder, Krill, Tennian, and Voss, who had come up from the rear, climbed to the top of the Sacred Landing as the Army of Humanity spread out across the steps and took up defensive positions to surround the ornate stairs.

Hadder easily found the giant double doors that marked the entrance to the Institute. He pushed against them with his Wakened strength, but found that they did not move.

"Viktor, help me!"

Krill joined Hadder, and together they drove everything they had into the thick marble. It did not budge.

"I don't know why I thought it would be open," lamented Hadder. "Perhaps I thought the New God would be more accommodating. Voss? You have plans for this?"

Clinton Voss frowned within his thick, white beard. "If we're being truthful, Hadder, I only gave us about a ten percent chance of getting this far. With all the planning it took us just to get here, a simple and obvious obstacle like a locked door just didn't factor in."

Krill studied the doors for a while before offering his thoughts. "These are not just doors; they are barricades — heavy marble backed by thick steel. They are beyond even my strength. Perhaps explosives could weaken them enough for a breakthrough, but it is hard to tell."

Voss turned to the Army of Humanity that was still spreading out before the New God's stronghold. "Terry! Terry, we need you!"

Moments later, Terry came bounding up the Sacred Landing, Lil Terry bouncing in the front of his stained overalls. "Here, boss!"

Krill's black eyes went wide as he noticed Terry's approach. In a flash, he was directly before the large mechanic with a finger in the frightened man's face.

"What the fuck, Terry!"

"What did I do?"

"You dumb bastard! You brought Lil Terry?!"

Terry fell back a step before the enraged killer. "I, I, I had to," he stammered. "I had no choice! He wouldn't let me leave him; I swear! Plus, if we all die, Lil Terry would be left on the freighter to starve! And I can't let him run around on the Isle of God. He'd be eaten within the hour!"

Lil Terry barked weakly, as if he were offering a mea culpa, and

Viktor Krill's anger wilted under the little dog's soft eyes. Krill smiled and swiped a hand across Lil Terry's head before returning to Terry, his finger back in the mechanic's face.

"If anything happens to Lil Terry, you had better hope that one of the Forlorn gets to you first."

Terry's face tightened, and his multiple chins raised into the air. "If anything happens to Lil Terry, I can assure you that I will be the first to jump into the fire. He is my life."

Seeing the sincerity in Terry's eyes, Krill simply nodded and allowed the large man to pass. Terry cleared the final steps and found himself next to Voss on the Sacred Landing.

"You called for me, boss?"

Voss slammed a meaty fist against the Flowers Institute's massive doors. "Locked tight! Won't budge! We have any explosive left to blow this fucking door off its hinges?"

"If it even has hinges," added Krill from behind.

Terry scratched his greasy head and studied the massive barricade as he thought. "Afraid not, boss. We took most of what we had and loaded up the Comet with it. We have some explosive grenades scattered among the army, especially on the gangsters, but not enough to make a dent in this thing. We didn't think carrying a bunch of explosives into a firefight would be prudent."

"And now we're fucked," said Zaza Anorrak as she and Su made their way to the back of the landing.

"Yeah, fucking fucked," echoed Smeggins as Sowler waited at the top of the stairs, and Zaza smiled at the little mutant.

"There have to be other ways in," declared Hadder with all the confidence he could muster. "This is a colossal fortress. It would make no sense to have only one entry and exit point. The New God is a lot of things, but an idiot is not one of them."

"He is right," agreed Krill. "We must spread out and send parties around this cursed building. There will be other ways in."

Voss's head bobbed up and down in agreement. "You're right. You're both right." He stepped forward to address the Army of Humanity. "Army!" All spun to face Voss. "The front is barred to us!

We must find another way in! We will split you into six separate forces, three to go North and three to go South, around the…"

"That won't be necessary," came a thunderous voice from the far Southern side of the Flowers Institute.

The entire Army of Humanity turned as one to find a giant standing confidently at the edge of the sparkling jungle. Standing at over seven feet in a blood-red suit, the humanoid monster absently fingered a wicked-looking machete with a grey-skinned hand as he grinned evilly at the gathered force. His cold pink eyes sat above a bulbous grey nose and shark-toothed mouth.

"And why is that," demanded Clinton Voss, determined to match the cold stare with one of his own.

The monster laughed and shook his head, sending a thick braid to swing behind him. "Because this is it, foolish human," replied the demon, sounding more like a boulder come to life than a man. "This is the end. I applaud your efforts, I really do, even if they do prove utterly pointless."

"That is still to be determined," shot back Voss. "Do you have a name, vile brute?"

"My name is Felix, although some call me *Cement* Felix. And it *is* determined. You have walked right into our trap. Like lambs to slaughter, which is very fitting."

"We are not even close to giving up, Felix! The day is not lost, not by a long shot!"

Cement Felix's pink eyes flashed. "You fools. You sad little fools! The day *is* lost! All *is* lost! You are too late. The New God will be reborn any moment now. The Flowering Horde is covering your world in shadow. You have lost! You are no longer humans, you're just too fucking stupid to realize it! You are food!"

Hadder's breath caught in his chest as the creature called Cement Felix spoke, and he was once again transported to Station, facing down The Krown, who promised Hadder that he was nothing more than meat.

"Better to be food than a slave to a false messiah," countered Voss, and Felix seemed especially bothered by the word *slave*.

"Slave? Slave? I will serve as the right hand of the King of Kings while the Forlorn shit your remains onto the jungle floor!"

Hadder's Rage rose and bubbled to the surface. "Step out and face me, coward! One on one! Let us see who the true demon is!"

Felix's pink eyes searched until they found Hadder at the top of the landing. He grinned broadly. "Marlin Hadder, is that you? So good of you to come and see humanity's demise from up close. Do you know what we call you, Hadder? The Great Failure." Felix's eyes then found Krill. "And you, Viktor Krill! We call you the Great Disappointment. How fitting that you found each other and paired so that you may share in the downfall that you helped facilitate."

"Liar," screamed Hadder, his voice altered from the Rage that now coursed through him. "Face me!"

Felix issued a dark smirk, smugly satisfied that his words had their intended effect. "No, I don't think I will, Hadder." Felix's gaze swept across the landing, taking in Zaza and Su. "But I see that you have some women in your *army*. I will tell the Forlorn to try to save them for Seth and me. But if they cannot, no worries. I will ask the New God to reanimate their corpses so that I may still have my fun."

"Fuck you, you fucking piece of shit! I'll rip your fucking heart out," yelled an irate Zaza as Felix laughed once more.

"I accept your RSVP, woman! And now, I must bid you all farewell. You fought, which is more than most humans, and much more than humanity deserves. And don't worry about the final battle, it shouldn't last too long. We have held most of the Forlorn back until now. Enjoy seeing the true might of the New God's creations!"

With a last laugh, Cement Felix disappeared into the jungle behind him and was immediately replaced with row after row of the Forlorn. They stepped out of the thick jungle from the North and the South and all along the Perennial Pathway, thousands of the nightmares, snarling and shrieking and hungry for flesh.

All of those on the Sacred Landing looked to each without saying a word, for everything was understood.

They were trapped. There was no escape. Soon, the Army of Humanity would be no more.

———

THE ARMY OF HUMANITY fought like caged animals, unwilling to bend or break in the face of pure horror. Hour after hour passed, and each time a Blister, gangster, or Protector fell, another stepped forward to take their place along the front line.

Marlin Hadder, fully in the throes of the Rage, and Viktor Krill, the world's most notorious killer, floated around the battlefield like ghosts. They appeared where they were most needed and shored up defensive lines before moving on to the next compromised location.

Hadder's face was dark with the gore of the Forlorn, and his body wore the marks of dozens of bites and cuts and punctures. Krill's long hair was matted down with the blood of fallen comrades. Clinton Voss's white beard was stained crimson, as was his khaki safari shirt. Sowler's arm-flail dripped with the insides of massacred nightmares. Zaza and Su Anorrak finally looked like sisters, with both wearing the dark, gooey masks of battle.

All around the Sacred Landing, members of the Army of Humanity fell to the overwhelming forces of darkness. For every Forlorn that fell, two fell out of the jungle to take its place. For every Blister, gangster, and Protector that fell, the lines weakened and were forced backward.

Soon, there would be no more backing up.

As the sun began its slow descent below the western horizon, Tennian Stamp flew across the battlefield on his propulsion rockets, plummeting to smash into a group of Forlorn who had almost busted through a defense line. The ground shook as Old Tens landed on the nightmares and crushed them beneath his mechanical legs, stomping for good measure, while small missiles shot forth to keep the other monstrosities at bay.

When the defensive line was finally reestablished, Old Tens flew again, this time coming to rest atop the Sacred Landing, where he met with Hadder and Krill.

Hadder breathed heavily, the Rage having burned itself out, and Krill had his hands on his knees, doing his best to recover quickly.

Tennian took note of the army's two main chess pieces and shook his head.

"It's not looking good, boys. What do you think?"

"It's a fucking mess," said Krill, and for the first time since he had known him, Hadder thought he sensed something in his companion's voice — defeat.

"Hadder," asked Old Tens, but Hadder did not respond.

Instead, Hadder took a moment to appraise the battle. The mangled bodies of men, women, and Blisters littered the ground in every direction. Those still fighting had been pushed back to the landing stairs, and a quick count showed Hadder that they had little more than twenty-five percent of their original force.

The Forlorn, on the other hand, even after losing hundreds of their own, still numbered in the thousands.

Tennian's voice tore Hadder from his calculations. "Hadder!"

Hadder snapped back to reality. "What's that now?"

"I said, what do you think?"

"I think we are at the end, my friend." Hadder looked over and locked eyes with Viktor Krill. "Unless there is a third miracle in store for us."

As if in answer, a thunderous sound shook the Isle of God as black storm clouds moved in to cover the sky above, even temporarily blocking the giant asteroid from Hadder's view.

"What in the hell is this," asked Tennian, his eyes locked onto the lightning show that was playing out over his head.

Small droplets of liquid began to rain down upon the Isle of God, as if the celestials were crying for the mortals beneath them.

It was Zaza Anorrak, fresh from the front lines, who first noticed the strange phenomenon. "What the fuck is this?"

"Upton, your hair," exclaimed DeLany Thales, and all looked to find the Protector's light blond hair turning red from the falling rain.

It then became apparent that the rain that doused the battling armies of man and monster was not water, but blood.

As screams of fear broke out along the Army of Humanity, Hadder held out his cupped hands and watched as they filled with crimson liquid, a small smile forming on his lips.

Krill slid up next to Hadder as the others began to panic. "Ever seen anything like this?"

Hadder looked up and grinned at his Wakened companion. "Just once."

Krill nodded. "I thought you seemed surprisingly calm, Marlin. I hope this precedes something, and is not just a cool effect to give some color to our imminent demise."

"How does that third miracle sound to you, Viktor?"

"Right now? That sounds better than a Spirit Girl oil massage."

"Well, you're in luck. We may have been blessed with both. Take a look."

Krill's Wakened eyes swung across the Army of Humanity, past the massive collection of Forlorn, and down the Perennial Pathway, where a man cloaked in shadow stood behind a massive gathering of petite figures.

"What do we have here, Marlin?"

"What's the matter, Viktor? Don't you recognize an old friend when you see one?"

Krill looked deeper, and inhaled sharply when two fiery eyes came into focus. "And so the old devil has returned. And he has brought with him a battalion of... Spirit Girls?"

In the distance, Albany Rott, facial scar throbbing and neck tattoo gleaming, threw his hands out wide, displaying the crystal hatchets held in each. As he did, the sky erupted in a torrent of lighting and blood and thunder.

Hadder's grin became a toothy smile as a thousand Spirit Girls began to march down the Perennial Pathway, and nothing in the way that they now walked suggested that they had come to pleasure, seduce, or compliment. Instead, the gait of these androids clearly stated that they had come to do one thing — fuck shit up.

Hadder laughed manically, and the surrounding Army of Humanity looked at him with the desperate faces of those at a complete loss. "Do not worry, my friends," Hadder called out to all who would listen. "The New God is not the only one with allies who are not of this world! Keep holding out! The calvary has arrived!"

After a moment of stunned silence, Zaza Anorrak spoke up. "It's about fucking time! Nothing like some new blood to wash off the fucking stink of these fucking bastards!"

A cheer went out among the Army of Humanity. Those on the front lines took advantage of the Forlorn's now-divided attention to press forward, creating some space for the first time in hours between the nightmares and the Sacred Landing.

As the Spirit Girls started sprinting down the Perennial Pathway, their mechanical eyes glowing deep red, Hadder was once again whisked away to Station, where the city's manikins cleared out the citizenry in one fell swoop.

"What the hell is going on," Krill asked as he leaned in, his black eyes trying to comprehend what he was witnessing.

Hadder shrugged. "It seems, no matter where we go, our greatest assets are those that are the most overlooked. And there is always a price to pay for that oversight. Now watch, it is about to get interesting."

Black and hazel eyes stared in anticipation as the Spirit Girls stormed the Forlorn's back lines. The mechanical bodies moved like Wakened humans, their actions efficient, deadly, and lighting-fast. They sliced into the nightmares like a scythe, immediately carving out a hole that was filled by increasing numbers of Spirit Girls.

Occasionally, a lone Spirit Girl would run at a group of the Forlorn, as if her programming had dialed up a suicide mission. Just as the Forlorn reached in for the kill, the woman detonated, vaporizing dozens of Forlorn and injuring countless others.

Within minutes, the Forlorn lines were completely shattered, with nightmares running to and fro to escape their new mechanical foes.

"What are you waiting for, you fools," bellowed Clinton Voss. "This is our chance! Attack! Attack! Attack!"

The Army of Humanity heeded their commander's words, breaking from their defensive lines and fanning out to attack the retreating Forlorn. In short order, the area around the Sacred Landing was no longer a meeting of two armies, but a chaotic menagerie of small fights to the death.

On the stairs of the Sacred Landing, Su Anorrak cleaved a Forlorn in half as it faced off with two Spirit Girls. To the North, Tennian Stamp followed a quintet of Spirit Girls, stomping down on any Forlorn that the artificial women managed to toss at his metal feet. To the South, Clinton Voss swung his battle-axe back and forth like a freed demon, following the lead of a pair of Spirit Girls who, with every strike, sank their small hands deep into the slimy flesh of a Forlorn.

Up the Perennial Pathway, Albany Rott's eyes swam with flames as the man-god's twin hatchets danced before him, slicing Forlorn into pieces with every twist and turn.

Viktor Krill's falchion whipped back and forth like a striking viper as he fought his way through the battlefield, ripping off the tentacle of one Forlorn with his teeth when his blade got stuck in the throat of another nightmare. After several minutes of brutal warfare, Krill finally reached his old nemesis.

"Albany Rott. I thought you had abandoned this pet project for your next experiment."

Rott's hatchet split the canine-like skull of a Forlorn, spraying dark blood across his too-white face. He turned to face Krill.

"Viktor Krill. I see you finally chose the side of the good guys. For once."

Krill threw a knife and sent an approaching Forlorn flying backward, the blade buried in the creature's chest bone. He slid his falchion into his belt and withdrew two more knives.

"Yes, which is why I do not understand why we are fighting on the same team. For you are anything but the *good guy*, are you, you old devil?"

"Perhaps I have always been," said Rott as he sliced off one of a Forlorn's two heads. "But you never stopped to ask, did you?"

Krill's tan face twisted in anger. "Ask you what? Why you imprisoned a confused man at the lowest point of his miserable life? Ask why you crafted a demon that would haunt and destroy this world?

Ask why you would let horrible things happen to good people, to little girls who never did anything but want to be loved!"

Albany Rott's axes lowered at the pain in Krill's words. "Yes. You should have asked me all of that, Viktor."

Krill spat upon the blood-covered ground. "Fuck that. It's too late for questions. And too late to bring her back. But it's not too late to exact my revenge. And Marlin isn't here to save you this time."

Krill sprung forward in a blur, his knives out before him. Rott's hatchets came up impossibly fast to parry the blows, and an instant later the Wakened human and demigod engaged in full battle. A space opened up around the combatants as even the Forlorn stopped to watch a battle that seemed to be playing out in extreme fast-forward.

Krill snarled, holding back tears as he struck out at the being who was the source of all of his recent pain. Rott easily blocked each blow, but seemed to hold back on offering any offense of his own.

"Fight back, you devil," Krill screamed, and began another combination before a familiar voice stopped him dead in his tracks.

"Father! No!"

Viktor Krill spun, and his black eyes went wide when Young Darrin appeared up the Perennial Pathway, a large ream in his small arms.

"Darrin? Is it really you, my boy?"

Tears began to stream down the boy's brown face, mixing with the bloody rain that was already there. "It's me, Father. I've come to save you."

Krill dropped the knives in his hands and hurried over to his adopted son. He fell to his knees before the boy, who was quite a bit larger than he remembered. Krill squeezed the boy's shoulders to convince himself that what he was seeing was real and not a cruel mirage. To convince himself that he had not already died.

"What are you doing here?"

"Mister Rott visited me some time ago. Gave me and Miss Sammi some code that would allow me to reprogram any Spirit Girl. He said that the world needed to be saved, that I could see you again if I helped. Miss Sammi and I spent every hour rewiring and recoding every Spirit Girl we could locate, old or new, beaten up or in perfect working order." A pause. "Did I do good, Father?"

Krill laughed but did not respond. Instead, he buried young Darrin in a tight hug, careful not to crush the growing boy. When they finally separated, Krill looked into his son's brown eyes.

"You did good, son. You did *very, very,* good. And I couldn't be more proud."

"Do you think Natthi would be proud?"

The question caught Krill off guard, and twin rivers began to waterfall down his bloody cheeks. "Your sister was braver and tougher than either of us, so what you have done here today would have made her very proud. Now give me a moment."

Krill stood and made his way back toward Albany Rott, blades appearing in his hands as he did.

"You brought my *son* to the *Isle of God*, where nightmares roam, and a madman is trying to become a deity?!"

Rott put his axes up in mock surrender. "The boy wouldn't take no for an answer, Viktor. It was hard enough getting that eyeless Tott woman to stay behind. And, anyway, what does it matter? This world is collapsing into the abyss. The Isle of God is no worse off than any of this planet's major cities and, to be honest, the boy can guide the mechanical army better than anyone." Viktor Krill kept coming. "Plus, who can blame the boy for wanting to see his adoptive father for perhaps one last time?"

That gave Krill pause, and the knives in his hands began to fall below his waist. Krill cursed under his breath before finally nodding. "Then you can help us win this war."

"Have I not already done that, Viktor Krill?"

"You have done the bare minimum! And now I need more. With the chaos that your Spirit Girls have caused, we can fight our way around the lotus building and discover another entrance. You will lead the charge in one direction."

The fires in Rott's eyes danced strangely. "I cannot."

"The hell you can't!"

"I cannot, Viktor. I have interfered all that I can. I can continue to fight the Forlorn out here, but what needs to be done in the Flowers Institute must be done by one of you."

"That makes no sense, you devil!"

"But that does not make it untrue."

Krill cursed again before revisiting young Darrin, who was keying things into the large ream that he held.

"Father, I can track all the remaining Spirit Girls from here and steer them where they are most needed. They seem to be doing pretty well on their own, but if there is something specific you need them to do…"

"Well done, young Darrin. Yes, you stay back here, well away from the fight, and make sure that the Spirit Girls keep the sides of the building clear of nightmares. We need to get inside to end this madness. And call back some of your androids to protect you as you work."

Darrin smiled at receiving a mission from Krill. "Just like old times, eh, Father?"

Krill returned the smile and put his hand on the boy's head. "Just like the good times. Be back soon… son."

Krill twirled the knives in his hands as he moved back to the main fray, stopping before Albany Rott as he did. A knife came up to rest against the scarred man-god's soft neck.

"If anything happens to the boy, I will cut those red eyes from your head."

"He is safer with me than anywhere in the world, Viktor Krill. At least for now."

Krill turned away, reluctantly accepting the vague promise. He took several steps forward and heard a familiar sound undercutting the din of the battle. Looking over to the edge of the Perennial Pathway, Krill found the source of the sound, and his heart sank.

On the ground, surrounded by a pool of blood, was Terry, his big belly ripped open, and his entrails spread across the cobble. Lil Terry sat atop his deceased master, barking and wailing, as if the world had already ended for the little dog.

Krill ran over, dispatching an attacking Forlorn as his did, and scooped up his miniature friend.

"I'm sorry, Lil Terry. He was a good man. But no time to mourn him now."

Krill ran back to Darrin and thrust Lil Terry at the boy.

"Young Darrin, meet Lil Terry. He's ours now."

Darrin's brown eyes lit up despite the carnage surrounding him. "I always wanted a family dog! I'll take good care of him!"

Krill gave Lil Terry a pat on the head as he handed the dog over. "I know you will."

"I see you're still wearing your Verrato high-tops," said Darrin as he cradled Lil Terry, finally noticing Krill's footwear.

"I never go anywhere without them," replied Krill, and both father and son nodded at a memorable gift given ages ago.

A smile on his dark face, Viktor Krill waded back into battle with the Forlorn, his strikes now especially fast, his blades now especially deadly.

For Viktor Krill was reinvigorated, reminded of what he still had and what he was still fighting for.

———

The Rage was gone, but Marlin Hadder's Wakened abilities still made him a tornado of violence. He criss-crossed the killing field around the Sacred Landing, sending sprays of Forlorn blood into the air and staining the cobbled pathway with their slimy innards.

Eventually, he fought his way back atop the Sacred Landing, where he reconnected with the Anorrak sisters and a returning Viktor Krill.

"You seem in good spirits, Viktor," Hadder commented, having observed the touching reunion from a distance.

"As good as can be expected, Marlin. Albany Rott sends his regards."

"I have nothing to say to that bastard."

"Neither did I. How is the fight going, Zaza?"

Zaza studied the battle below for a moment before answering Krill. "I think we have the dirty fuckers on their fucking heels, thanks to those silicon bitches from hell. The nightmares are all fucking spread out. The Northern side of the goddamn building is now open, with a group of Blisters pushing the enemy back into that fucking jungle. It's still a fucking mess to the South, where the last big group of those fuckers has congregated."

"Even the Spirit Girls are having a hard time getting through there," added Su.

"Ok, so what now," asked Hadder to the group.

"We have avoided being routed," stated Krill. "We must now go on the offensive. The New God is inside, and he must die."

Su nodded in agreement. "My sister and I will sneak around the Northern side of the Institute. There must be another way in near the back."

"Fucking right," Zaza chimed in.

"Sounds good," said Hadder. "Viktor?" Krill's black eyes studied the Flowers Institute. "Viktor?"

"I'm going up."

"Come again?"

"I'm going up, Marlin. There will be no faster way to study the building's entire perimeter than from atop it."

Hadder's face twisted. "And how the hell are you going to get up there," he asked, studying the building's unusual petal-like rooftop.

"You're going to give me a boost, Marlin."

"Will it be enough?"

"Are you a Wakened human or not?"

"I am."

"Then it will be enough."

Zaza grabbed her sister by the arm. "Well, it sounds like you boys have your fucking orders, and we have ours. The next time you fucking see us, we'll have the fucking New God on a fucking spit like the pig that he is." Zaza planted a deep kiss on Krill as she walked by. "Don't have too much fucking fun without me."

Krill black eyes flashed. "Never."

Su offered a small bow as she was pulled away. "See you inside, Marlin. Viktor."

Hadder and Krill watched as the brave warrior sisters rounded the Northern corner of the Flowers Institute, katana blades leading the way.

Hadder turned to Krill when they disappeared. "Now what?"

Krill retreated to the very front of the Sacred Landing, kicking a Forlorn who had run up the steps in its giant-mouthed face as he did.

"Cup your hands and clear your mind, Marlin. I'm going to need everything you have got on this one. Understood?"

Hadder nodded and put his hands together at his waist before closing his eyes and looking inward, tapping into his Wakened abilities. Blood rushed to his muscles and adrenaline coursed through his body. When Hadder reopened his eyes, Krill was advancing toward him in slow motion, his arms pumping wildly to the sides just before he leapt.

Krill's Verrato high-top hit Hadder's cupped hands, and Hadder's arms sprung up as if released from a trap. Hadder's Wakened strength, coupled with Krill's impossible jump, sent the notorious killer flying upwards of thirty feet, where he managed to grab onto the edge of one of the building's "petals."

Hadder held his breath as Krill's hand slipped bit before finding purchase, allowing him to swing his leg over the odd angle of the rooftop.

"The Sisters have the North! I'll take up here! Find a way through the South, Marlin," Krill called down from the lowest point of the Institute's roof before he, too, disappeared around the corner of a petal.

Hadder looked to his left, where a massive group of Forlorn were starting to regroup, with more pouring out from the jungle, making it hard for even the Spirit Girls to make progress.

Hadder studied the growing crowd of nightmares to the South before glancing back to the relatively empty North and then up at the Flowers Institute's quiet roofline.

How did I get the short end of the fucking stick, Hadder asked himself as he took a crystalline handgun in one hand, a scimitar blade in the other, and walked back into a hellscape.

25

---

*Z*aza and Su Anorrak crept around the Northern side of the Flowers Institute as the blood rain began to slow to misty drizzle, doing their best to blend in with the deepening shadows of the dying day.

Forlorn could be heard scurrying about in the glowing jungle, but only a few were unlucky enough to stumble upon the deadly sisters, and those were dispatched with extreme efficiency.

"We're getting good at killing these fuckers," whispered Zaza.

"Shh," shot back Su.

Zaza rolled her eyes in response.

In relatively short order, the sisters had rounded the building's Eastern edge and came upon the back of the Flowers Institute, which kissed a high cliff overlooking the Great Water.

"Look," whispered Su, and Zaza followed her sister's finger to find a magnificent courtyard that was bordered in the back by numerous ornate archways.

As the women crept closer to the courtyard, which was draped in late afternoon shadow, their eyes went wide with the beauty that they discovered.

Sliding through one of the marble archways, the sisters found themselves in a magical world of oversized blossoms, floating pollen that resembled starlight, and a small stream that contained all the colors of the rainbow. Every plant that the sisters passed, and every creature that swam in the water or peered out from the gardens, glowed softly with bioluminescence.

A crystalline bridge traversed the courtyard's central pond, within which swam scores of human-faced tadpoles. The smell of the courtyard was sweet and intoxicating, and the sisters could feel their steps becoming lighter as they inhaled more of the strange air.

Finally, Zaza motioned back toward the Flowers Institute. Through the umbrella-shaped blossoms and uniquely shaped trees, the white walls of the Institute could be seen, with bright, open entryways leading into the building on both sides.

"We fucking found it," said Zaza in a low voice. "The fucking New God will die at our hands, sis."

Su smiled at the idea. "Let's go."

The Anorrak Sisters quickened their pace, following the cobbled path as it twisted through the courtyard's lush, alien garden. They had almost reached the front of the courtyard when they were forced to a sliding stop.

Just ahead, standing between them and entry into the Institute, was the shadow of a thin giant. Well over eight feet tall, the too-thin man had his face buried in a large blossom, inhaling deeply of its colorful pollen. Although it was dark, the glow of the blossom lit up the man's face, which appeared too white with eyes that were too far apart. Strapped to the towering monster were twin odachi swords, each large enough that a normal-sized man would have trouble wielding it even with two hands.

The gangly creature removed his face from the plant and smiled grossly. As he did, his grey eyes flashed dully in the dim courtyard. He wiped the purple pollen from his face before speaking in a quiet voice that sounded like a snake shedding its skin.

"Before you murder my Lord, please give me the great honor of introducing myself." He reached up with an impossibly large hand and tipped the black fedora that sat atop his relatively small head. "My name is Seth, and I am absolutely enchanted to meet you two lovely ladies."

————

VIKTOR KRILL CLIMBED and slid down the many extreme angels of the Flowers Institute rooftop. From this height, he could clearly make out the daunting number of Forlorn that had collected at the Southwest corner of the building, as if they were guarding against something.

Krill peeked down, but was unable to make out any entrance along that side or movement of any creatures entering or exiting a doorway somewhere beneath.

Thinking that he might have to eventually drop to help eradicate the massive group of Forlorn, Krill moved toward the back of the building. There, he hoped to discover an alternative door through which he could enter the Institute to slit the New God open, ending this war.

As Krill crested the main central rooftop petal, the Great Water came into focus, sitting well below the Isle of God's Eastern cliffs. Krill looked up to find the massive pink asteroid larger than ever, and the notorious killer instinctively crouched, as if he might get singed by its proximity.

Passing between the final two rear petals, Krill looked down to find a magical courtyard that rivaled even Station's magnificent gardens. As his black eyes took in the oversized glowing blossoms and rainbow-tinged stream, two shadowy forms passed through one of the many archways that bordered the courtyard on its Easternmost edge.

The individuals below moved with such balance and grace that Krill immediately knew them to be the Anorrak Sisters, carefully following the sinuous cobble path. The purpose with which the sisters then began to move told Krill that they may have discovered a way into the Flowers Institute through the gardens.

As Krill quickly scanned the remainder of the courtyard, finishing with the area directly beneath where he was perched, he saw something that Zaza and Su did not, a gangly creature of death laying in wait.

Two can play at this game, you too-tall bastard, thought Krill as he prepared to drop upon the unsuspecting assassin's head, his falchion leading the way.

"I wouldn't do that if I were you," came a deep, husky voice from behind Krill, surprising the usually surefooted Wakened human to the point that he almost fell from the steep rooftop.

Krill caught himself and spun to find the largest woman human he had ever seen standing easily atop a sloping petal. Standing well over six feet in height, the woman was just as wide, a massive ball of flesh balanced upon two tree-trunk legs.

"And who might you be," Krill asked, his surprise fading away as his desire for violence intensified.

"I might be Batti Bat," said the giantess in a booming voice. "And you look too delicious to die at the hands of that gross Seth Whispers."

"Who?"

Batti nodded to the courtyard below. "The Anointed Champion you were preparing to attack. Or I should say, preparing to die at the hands of."

Krill's falchion came out in a flash, and a knife appeared in his other hand. "Anointed Champions? Did your daddy Milo Flowers give you that ridiculous title?"

Batti Bat's fat face grew red. "The *New God* gave us our titles. And soon, I will return the favor by giving Him your head. If there is anything left of it. I do so love to crunch down on a good head."

Krill began to advance on the Anointed Champion, his feet moving carefully along the roof's many sharp slopes.

"Then let us get on with it, bloated demon. I intend to finish this quick and then conduct my business with your slimy friend down below."

Batti Bat danced down from the side of a petal, her blood-stained moo moo flittering in the air as she did. "You don't have to tell me twice. You look like a tasty morsel, and I am hungry. But then again, I am always hungry."

Krill smiled and spun the knife in his hand. "Don't worry, woman, I know exactly what to feed you."

———

TENNIAN STAMP's metal leg rose and kicked out like a piston, sending a spider-shaped Forlorn soaring across the battlefield. The nightmare crashed loudly into the mass of monsters blocking the Southwest corner of the Flowers Institute, creating a small hole in the creatures' line.

Four new Forlorn stepped forward to fill the gap.

"It's no use," Old Tens said to Marlin Hadder as the Wakened human cut a nightmare in half, but not before taking a clawed tentacle in the shoulder. Hadder grimaced as he yanked the barb from his flesh.

"They have to be protecting something," Hadder called out to his old ally. "Otherwise, this makes no sense!"

"They are protecting something, to be certain," agreed Tennian. "And perhaps biding their time."

"That is what I also fear. But time for what?" As he asked, Hadder's hazel eyes instinctively shot up to where the pink asteroid was growing larger and more imposing by the minute.

"I don't know, Hadder. And I don't think I want to wait to find out." Old Tens looked around once more, and Hadder could almost hear the gears spinning within the gangster leader's salt and pepper head. Finally, he turned to Hadder, and something had changed in his dark eyes. "Fuck this. Marlin Hadder, it has been a pleasure. My life has been a series of deaths, including my own. I'm happy that this final one will be for a purpose larger than my own ambitions."

Hadder's stomach began to knot. "Tennian, what are you thinking?"

Old Tens offered a toothy smile, an honest, contented grin that was seen too few times in the soldier's violent life. "I'm thinking that it's time for this old bastard to pull his weight and make amends."

"You don't have to do this, Tennian."

"Yes, I do, Hadder. And I want to." Old Tens threw a hand on Marlin Hadder's uninjured shoulder. "See you on the other side, my friend."

And with that, Tennian Stamp, the Neon City's most famous gang-ster, and hero of the Harrier Gap, shot upward on his mechanical legs' propulsion boosters. He soared over the mass of nightmares that guarded the Southwest corner of the Flowers Institute, coming down far in the distance.

————

THE MONSTER who called himself Seth may have looked like a lanky, uncoordinated loser, but he fought like a demon straight from the depths of hell. With his twin odachis cutting through the pollen-rich air like helicopter blades, Zaza and Su had little opportunity to get in close, much less score a significant hit.

The Anointed Champion chased the Anorrak Sisters down the cobbled pathway and through the bioluminescent gardens of the courtyard, talking in his snakelike voice as he did.

"Please, ladies, toss your weapons aside. I am a *good guy*, so different from the other men who have so clearly broken your hearts and your spirits. Drop your blades and let us retire to my boudoir, where I can give you a proper prize for making it this far. My heart knows no limits, and I will ensure that the New God welcomes you into the fold. What do you say, fair maidens?"

Seth's blades stopped momentarily to hear the women's responses.

"I say I've never been more ready to fucking puke in my life. The fucking thought of you anywhere near my naked body makes me want to fucking skin myself alive."

"That can be arranged," Seth countered, and there were no lies in his tone. "And you," the Anointed Champion asked Su.

"I prefer the company of women, but even if I didn't, the simple knowledge of your existence would make me swear off men forever."

Seth Whispers's grey eyes went wide and flashed bright in the dim courtyard, as if dull fires were lit behind them. "You know, fair ladies, your bodies are just as good to me cold as they are warm. It's a real pity that you couldn't see a good man when he was standing right before…"

Zaza and Su thrust their katanas forward simultaneously, as if their minds were in lockstep. Seth knocked Zaza's attack aside, but Su's sneaked through his unprepared defenses, shooting up to carve a deep gash in the Champion's bony cheek.

Seth jumped backward with tremendous speed, his giant hand going to his wounded face. When he brought it down, his enormous too-white hand was covered in bright red, and his mouth fell open in anger.

"You *dare* cut me," Seth Whispers snapped, almost spitting as he spoke. "You foul, foul cunts! To think, I was going to share my body with a couple of filthy whores like you! How dare you?! How dare you?!"

"Oh, we dare," countered Zaza. "We fucking dare."

Seth shot a yellow-toothed smile at the sisters as a trembling hand wiped the blood from his cheek across the entirety of his face, creating a crimson mask that made the Anointed Champion even more terrifying.

"Have it your way," said Seth in a voice that could barely be heard. "Let me show you what it is like when a good guy becomes bad by unappreciative women."

"Fuck you," spat Zaza.

"Yeah, *fuck you*," cried Su, and, this time, no apology came.

VIKTOR KRILL WAS SLIGHTLY FASTER. Viktor Krill was slightly more skilled. Viktor Krill was slightly more agile.

But Batti Bat was bigger. Much bigger. And she seemed invulnerable to attack.

Krill ran up and down the rooftop petals like a ballerina, spinning here and sliding there, his falchion dancing out before him and knives launching from his free hand.

But the giant Batti Bat not only kept up, but equalled the notorious killer.

Armed with no weapon, the Anointed Champion had only her girth and her fists to use. And it was starting to become painfully clear that these were enough.

Krill feinted high and went low, slicing a neat line across the fat woman's belly, and although his falchion bit deep, no blood appeared.

Krill went out wide with his sword, and tossed a knife underhand as Batti moved to block. The knife flew true, burying itself to the hilt in the Champion's thick neck.

Krill shouted in victory, but his exuberance was short-lived as Batti calmly reached up and pulled the blade from the rolls of her neck. The red cascade that Viktor Krill expected never came.

The Anointed Champion released a booming laugh. "I'm thrilled that you are getting a workout. I prefer my meat a bit on the gamey side."

It was then that Viktor Krill knew that he was in for a real battle, one of the very few that he had engaged in where the result was an unknown.

"How deep does that blubber of yours go, fat demon," demanded Krill.

Batti Bat feigned offense. "*Fat?* I am simply big-boned, I'll have you know. And thick muscle covers these big bones." So far, no lies were told. "And as for blubber, well, every girl must have her protections from perverse men, don't you think?"

Krill twirled his falchion in the air. "I think a few more inches, and I'll puncture one of those swollen organs of yours."

Batti laughed again. "Isn't that what every man says? A few more inches?"

Krill found himself off-balance by the monster's quick retort. "I see that..."

Before Krill could regain the verbal upper hand, Batti launched into a full attack, her massive forearm knocking Krill's sword aside as she readily accepted a dagger in her blubbery side.

In the blink of an eye, Krill had his back to the rooftop with a ton of Anointed Champion on top of him and his falchion trapped. His black eyes went wide when Batti's head began to separate grotesquely, showcasing a colossal, fang-tooth mouth that opened along a secret second pair of biological hinges that hung hidden within the demon's bobbed hair.

As the great maw opened above him, Viktor Krill feared that this would be the sad end to the world's first Wakened human. Desperation drove him as Batti Bat's mouth continued to widen, adding even more adrenaline to Krill's heightened abilities. He squirmed beneath the Champion's enormous mass, creating a pocket of space here, moving a chunk of fat to the side there.

When the demon's jaws had finally spread to their horrifying potential, Batti Bat slammed her head down at her trapped victim, meaning to consume everything above the shoulders in one gruesome bite.

Luckily, Viktor Krill released the grip on his sword and slid down just in time, causing Batti's sharklike head to slam into the hard rooftop instead of soft flesh.

Krill used his Wakened strength to scoot beneath the Champion's girth, stifling the urge to vomit as he exited from the putrid space between the creature's too-thick legs.

As Krill rose to his feet, Batti Bat was already doing the same, twisting as she did to catch the notorious killer in the face with a meaty spinning back fist, sending him careening into the roof's adjacent petal.

The air exited Krill's lungs as he slammed into the hard marble and collapsed to his knees. He reached up to massage his aching chin and felt lucky to find that it had not shattered into a hundred pieces.

Batti Bat's gross jaw remained open as she stalked forward, a fat tongue flicking out, tasting the air surrounding Krill.

"Thank you for the taste," said the Champion, her words barely intelligible through the cavernous mouth. "But now I'm ready for the entrée."

Krill's computer mind spun as knives reappeared in his hands. A thousand tactics and scenarios played out in his Wakened mind, but none had him coming out the victor in this battle of titans.

As the black-eyed assassin spat blood onto the white roof and started dancing toward the roof's Southern edge, an unfortunate truth ran cold through his brain.

I will need a diversion. I will need a miracle.

And I have already reached the three that I requested.

———

TENNIAN STAMP SOARED above the mass of Forlorn on his mechanical legs, just out of reach of the longer tentacles.

Not wanting to land in the middle of nightmares, nor crash into the thick, unmoving trunk of a jungle tree, Old Tens flew on, looking for the ideal location from which to execute his final plan.

Passing the jungle tree line, the old gangster found himself hovering above a large clearing that undoubtedly served as a helicopter landing pad for the New God's wealthiest of followers.

Tennian landed with a heavy thud onto the circular clearing marked with the white lotus symbol of Doctor Milo Flowers. As his metal feet touched the soft grass, Old Tens began to key in the complex command into his legs' control panel.

"If you have an itch, just ask me," came a sickeningly sweet voice from across the clearing. "I'd be happy to scratch it for you." As the words reached Old Tens, a painfully beautiful woman stepped out of the jungle from the East, her right hand raised to show long black nails that matched an armless black unitard, black makeup, and black cornrowed hair.

"I can reach it myself, Miss…"

"Yuki. You can just call me Yuki." The black-eyed woman crossed the clearing with the gait of a celestial stripper.

Old Tens paused in keying in the code with one digit left to press. "Well, Miss Yuki, despite my infirmity, I can still reach all the areas that need scratching myself."

"What a pity," said the small woman as she continued to advance. "Then maybe you could help *me* out. Maybe I have some itches."

"I'm not in the scratching business," said Tennian as he reached into a compartment to retrieve his buck knife.

"No? Then what business are in you in, broken man?"

Old Tens brought his knife up. "I'm in the cutting bitches up business. And you're the only bitch around at the moment."

Yuki Dona smiled wickedly, pulling the twin sai from her hips as she did. Before she spoke, she blinked, her eyelids closing horizontally as if she were an alien reptile.

"Lucky me." She paused to consider her words. "Well, perhaps not so lucky. It appears that the only man I've come across more than likely has no cock. And I *need* a good cock. Perhaps when I am through with you, Marlin Hadder will offer me one. That *is* where I am heading, after all. You are but a pitstop on my journey, and a disappointing one at that."

Tennian's metal legs whirred to life, driving him toward the deadly Yuki Dona. "This isn't a pitstop, bitch. This is where you get off the train. This is as far as you go."

"We shall see," said the Anointed Champion confidently, and a second later she ran at Old Tens, her twin sai spinning in her delicate, claw-tipped hands.

Tennian was immediately forced back on his mechanical legs as Yuki Dona almost overwhelmed him with a unique mix of speed, grace, and ferocity.

Tennian's buck knife swung left and right as quickly as he could, his old muscles crying out and his ligaments audibly groaning in protest. Just as Yuki was about to score a hit with one of her sai, she was pushed back as a small missile fired from Old Tens's legs exploded against her chest. Her black eyes went wide with surprise just as Tennian's free hand came at her in a fist and slammed scarred knuckles against the sleight woman's temple.

Yuki Dona flew through the air, fell to the soft grass of the copter pad, and expertly rolled backward, springing easily back to her feet. She smiled through black lipstick and rubbed her sore temple.

"Full of tricks, aren't you, broken man? Is there to be no honor in our battle?"

Compartments along Tennian's metal legs opened and closed in threat. "The only honor in fighting a demon is sending it back to hell. Now come on and…"

Before Old Tens could finish his sentence, his vision grew blurry and his head began to swim as his breathing became labored. The Anointed Champion giggled coldly.

"I'm sorry, broken man. I'm afraid that I, too, am full of tricks." Yuki Dona stuck out her black tongue, which fell to her waist and forked at the end. It retracted back into her dark mouth. "That odd sensation that you are now feeling, that is but a taste of what my poisons can do." Old Tens's mouth fell open in shock. "There. That is the reaction I was looking for. Now, be a good boy and die for me; I have more important business to attend to."

As he had all his life, Tennian Stamp looked fear in the face and told it fuck off. "The fuck you do, demon," said the old gangster as he reached down and pressed a small emergency button near the back of his mechanical thigh. His eyes went wide as a shot of adrenaline was released into his system, overcoming the numbing effects of Yuki's poison. Old Tens flashed his teeth at the Anointed Champion, and, for the first time, Yuki Dona looked slightly less confident of her quick kill.

"Very well, broken man," said Yuki, the playfulness in her tone now all but gone. "If you want to dance with death, let us dance. I will teach you."

Tennian's buck knife spun once more in his hand as he began to circle the Anointed Champion. "I already know this dance, you dumb bitch. I've known it all my life, which is considerably longer than yours. Tell me, how long ago did the New God shit you out?"

In response, Yuki eyelids blinked horizontally and charged Tennian, her black mouth forming an angry snarl.

Flames shot forth from Tennian's legs, forcing the Champion to cartwheel left, then backflip to the right to avoid the red arm of fire. The last of Old Tens's small missiles were launched, and both caught Yuki as she landed. The explosions sent the demoness flying away once more, and when she finally rose, scorch marks stained her face.

"How dare you," she screamed from across the copter pad. "I am an Anointed Champion, and *you* are but meat for the Forlorn!"

"I know my meat is sweet," Old Tens shot back, having fun with this final fight, "but it's reserved for *Missus* Stamp. And that angel has been long buried. But I got something else for you, bitch."

Yuki Dona, unaccustomed to being addressed with anything besides fear and respect, spat yellowish blood to the grass in rage. Slamming her sai together for good measure, the Anointed Champion rushed at Old Tens once more, and this time she did not underestimate the gangster leader.

Yuki came at Tennian like a dancer from hell, avoiding the few tricks that remained in the mechanical legs' arsenal while offering a barrage of her own attacks.

A spinning wheel kick caught Tennian behind his salt and pepper head and sent him reeling. When Tennian's buck knife knocked one of Yuki's sai to the ground, she came at him barehanded, scratching his neck with her black nails. When they were fighting close, the demoness took advantage of every opportunity to touch his skin with her palm, forearm, or shoulder.

Whenever possible, Old Tens pressed the emergency button, injecting more and more adrenaline into his system to combat the poisons entering his bloodstream.

Eventually, however, Old Tens had to separate as his mind grew hazy and the mental connection to his legs began to lapse. Yuki Dona recognized the glassy look in Tennian's eyes and began to laugh.

"What's the matter, broken man? Running out of tricks?" Her laughing suddenly ceased. "I still have many."

Before even completing her sentence, Yuki fired her last remaining sai at Old Tens's chest, forcing the man to swipe across with his buck knife. As he parried the flying blade, Tennian saw the real threat coming in behind it.

But he was already too compromised to react.

Yuki Dona's forked black tongue reached across the fifteen feet that separated the combatants and struck Tennian in the face with a loud *splat*, covering his dark face in a thick, poisonous goo.

The Anointed Champion spoke again once her tongue had returned to her mouth. "And so ends the tragic tale of a broken man who thought he could fight the right hand of God. Can you still hear me, broken man?"

The world spun around Old Tens as the poison sank its long fangs into the gangster leader. A soft hand began to gently squeeze his lungs and his heart started to noticeably slow. Although held upright by his metal legs, Old Tens's shoulders sagged, his arms dropped, and his head fell as the poison coursed through him, racing toward its endgame.

Yuki Dona approached to gloat.

"You know what? I think I will feed you to my friend Batti. She usually takes her meat fresh, but she'll make an exception in this case." Yuki put a hand to Tennian's bearded face. "Especially when I regale her with the tale of the broken trickster with one too few tricks." Old Tens mumbled something under his breath as the fingers of his left hand discreetly played with the keypad on his legs. Yuki Dona smiled. "What was that, broken man? I can't understand you. Cat got your tongue?"

Tennian's head snapped up, his eyes more focused than they had any right to be. "I said, one more trick, bitch!"

"What are you..."

The mechanical legs powered forward on one last command from its master as a countdown began. Old Tens buried Yuki Dona in a great bearhug as he passed, taking the Anointed Champion with him.

Yuki laughed as she was carried away. "You fool! You are already dead! Do you not realize it?"

"Oh, I realize it," Tennian whispered into the demoness's ear. "*You don't.*"

"What are you going on about..." Yuki's laughter ceased as she finally caught the beeping sound emanating from her prey's metal prosthetic. She began thrashing in Tennian's strong arms. "Release me, release me, release me," screamed the Champion as she scratched at Tennian's face, neck, and chest with her black nails.

But still, the mechanical legs drove forward. And still, the countdown continued. The interlocked pair exited the copter pad and tore through the jungle, passing countless Forlorn on their journey.

"Release me! Release me!"

Tennian's heart continued to slow as his breathing grew increasingly shallow. His mechanical legs began to stutter, almost tripping several times. But still, they drove on.

Tennian looked up through watery eyes to find the great mass of Forlorn that had gathered to guard the Southwest corner of the Flowers Institute. A smile, honest and true, broke out on his dark face as he plowed into the thick group of nightmares.

"Release me! Release me!"

"I release you," he whispered. "And I release myself."

The mechanical legs detonated amidst a sea of Forlorn, vaporizing an Anointed Champion and scores of nightmares, while killing or injuring hundreds of other monsters.

And dying as he lived was Tennian Stamp, also known as Old Tens, hero of the Harrier Gap, founder of the Broken Tens, and the most respected gangster that ever crawled out of the Neon City of Bhellum.

A few seconds after the explosion, the jagged remains of a destroyed metal leg fell from the sky, burying itself halfway into the white cobble that surrounded the Flowers Institute. It appeared like a middle finger pointed to the heavens.

A middle finger from Tennian Stamp right in the face of the New God.

———

Viktor Krill had scored countless hits on the Anointed Champion called Batti Bat, and still no blood showed on the oversized woman. And still, she refused to slow. And still, her demon mouth hung open like a bear trap.

For every ten cuts that Krill created on Batti's thick, blubbery skin, she would catch the notorious killer with a blow that would either drive the breath from his lungs or send him careening across the uneven rooftop.

Ultimately, Krill began to focus on the demoness's eyes, similar to his strategy against the Paladin known as both Morgan and Morgin. Unfortunately, Batti was quick to uncover this strategy and even quicker to react. She would purposely leave her face unattended, anticipating an attack from Krill, and already have an attack ready for such a maneuver.

Krill knew it was a trap, but had to go for it anyway, as this was his only hope. With the Champion's fat face exposed, Krill tossed a knife underhand with one arm, while following it with a straight stab from the falchion with the other.

Batti backhanded the blade with her meaty left hand while her right was already in a fist, making its way for Krill's exposed side. The Champion easily dodged the expected falchion blow and used her momentum to dig a hook into Krill's body.

Krill released a squeal of pain as three of his ribs shattered under the giant's clean blow. The notorious killer dropped his falchion, stumbled backward, and tripped on the uneven surface, falling to his backside on the slanted roof.

The Wakened human attempted to spring back up, but could only manage a slow, staggering rise as he held his side, truly shocked that his bones could actually break.

"Yes, let me tenderize that meat some more before I feast," cackled the Champion through her giant maw as she prowled the Southern edge of the rooftop.

Krill spat a great wad of liquid onto the white roof, and grimaced after noticing that it was more blood than phlegm. Still, he pushed forward, a tan hand against his shattered side, determined to keep the demoness near the edge of the building.

Batti Bat's beady eyes went wide with excitement as she saw the notorious killer advance. Her heavy tongue lolled about in her giant mouth, and drool began to cascade down both sides of her many chins. She nodded with anticipation.

"Yes, yes, come. I love when my food is brought to me."

Krill staggered forward, keeping a calm, determined look on his face, even when the whispers in his Wakened head told him a truth that he could not deny.

He could not win this fight. He would die at the hands of this demon atop this cursed building. Unless...

A deafening explosion rocked the Isle of God, shaking the Flowers Institute and sending Batti Bat seat first to the white marble rooftop. A mushroom cloud rose into the blood-red sky at the Southwest corner of the building, not far from where Batti Bat now sat.

"What the fuck," demanded the Champion through her open mouth as she rose and peered over the Southern edge of the building.

Viktor Krill's Wakened mind analyzed the opportunity instantly before it reached a decision. Before Batti Bat had a chance to react, the notorious killer was on her like lightning, slamming into her girth and pushing her with impossible strength off the roof's edge. The Anointed Champion grabbed the Wakened human with a meaty hand as she fell, pulling the notorious killer into the air with her.

The dangerous pair plummeted to the ground together, Krill atop Batti, the Champion offering a grotesque smile as she descended.

Locked together as they were, Krill was in striking distance of the demoness's shark-toothed mouth, which now cocked back for a killing blow. Batti's oversized head snapped forward just as Viktor Krill's Verrato high-tops sensed a fall and activated their hovering capability.

Krill's descent immediately slowed, as if a parachute was pulled, ripping him free of the Champion's grasp and causing her striking mouth, meant to engulf the notorious killer's head, to catch nothing but air.

Batti Bat uttered a curse and reached up for her prey just as her plunge concluded. Unfortunately for the demon, it was not hard cobble that her wide back struck, but the sharp end of a jagged metal leg that now protruded from the white stone.

Blood spewed forth from the Anointed Champion's too-wide mouth as her shark-like eyes went wide with pain and shock. As the fat demon writhed in agony atop the thick metal spike, Viktor Krill floated softly down upon Batti's round belly.

Straddling the great demon, Krill's black eyes flashed as a dark smile crept upon his lips. "Still hungry," he asked, putting his face as close to Batti's as he dared. "Let me satiate you, you absolute cunt!"

Knives appeared in each of Viktor Krill's hands, and he thrust each into the beady eyes of Batti Bat, driving them down until they reach her brain. When they would go no further, Krill twisted the handles, puréeing the matter in the Anointed Champion's head.

"How's that for tender," asked Krill as he rolled from the giant woman's corpse. The little breath in his lungs came out in a wheeze as Krill hit the cobble walkway, and he fought hard to take in oxygen and avoid passing out.

Staring up through watery eyes, Viktor Krill watched as gusts of bloody mist passed out of the encroaching night and moved across the pink asteroid that grew larger and more horrible by the second.

Krill attempted to roll to over but found that he could not, broken as he was. As he continued to look up into the cold fingertip of judgment, a thought more terrifying than Batti Bat entered Krill's Wakened mind.

The Anorrak Sisters were walking directly into the path of another Anointed Champion.

And they had no idea what they were about to face.

———

AFTER HE WAS DONE SHIELDING himself from the massive blast that had obliterated the Forlorn's Southwestern formation of nightmares, Hadder looked up with tear-soaked cheeks.

It was obvious that Tennian Stamp, friend and powerful ally, had surrendered his life so that Marlin Hadder could gain access to the Southern side of the Flowers Institute.

Studying his smoke-filled surroundings, Hadder could see that the Southwest corner of the building now had no more Forlorn protecting it than anywhere else in sight.

In short, the path was clear.

Hadder used his Wakened abilities to push away the pain from numerous wounds and marched forward, crystalline gun and scimitar leading the way into the chaotic, sooty scene.

Although the Forlorn line was in shambles, with countless dead nightmares littering the ground, still the creatures continued to rush out from the surrounding jungle, screaming inhuman words at the Wakened human.

Hadder shot the bony, extended jaw from one Forlorn before slicing open the swollen belly of another, stepping back as a green mist escaped from the gaping wound.

As Hadder finished off another of the nightmares and began along the Southern edge of the Institute, an unusual figure in white caught his eye and ripped his attention from the battle.

As Hadder looked away, a cry rang out.

"Marlin! Watch out!"

Hadder spun just in time to see a clawed tentacle reaching for his exposed throat, moving too quickly for even his Wakened body to react. As his hazel eyes went wide, a blade flashed before his face, sending the barbed tentacle to fall harmlessly to the white cobble where it wriggled for a moment before becoming still.

Raelynne stood with a satisfied smile on her pale face. "I told you I could still cut, Marlin Hadder."

Hadder returned the smile. "And it looks like you've made it past the twelve-hour mark, Raelynne."

Raelynne swept her blade across once more, halving the Forlorn that had attacked Hadder. "Yes, looks like it. And it looks like you have your opening," she said, pointing her chin at the clear path around the Flowers Institute.

Hadder nodded and started away before turning back. He held out his hand. "Want to see the interior of hell?"

Raelynne smiled sweetly. "Still sweeping girls off their feet, I see. No, you go…"

The former Bitch-Whore enforcer never got to finish her sentence, as a too-long, many-knuckled finger exploded from her forehead in a spray of blood and bone.

Hadder screamed as Raelynne's limp body hit the ground and the sinewy Forlorn with three-foot long, dagger-like fingers giggled as it licked the digit that had murdered the beautiful woman.

The Rage flared up inside Hadder, and he rushed forward to seek his revenge. Before he was able to reach the laughing nightmare, however, the Forlorn exploded under the weight and force of a spiked steel ball, spraying Hadder with the creature's black blood.

A tiny, familiar voice cut through the grotesque scene.

"How did that feel, fucker? Oh, shit, Sowler, man, you crushed that fucker good, you did. Can we eat it? Oh, please, Sowler, man, let me eat the fucker!"

"Shut up, Smeggins."

Hadder shook his head to remove the gore from his face, along with the residual image of Raelynne's death. "Thank you, my friend," he said to the Blister.

Sowler nodded his pig head. "Any time, Angel." As he spoke, something to the East caught the Blister's eye. "Angel, look!"

Hadder turned to once again find the unusual figure in white. As Sowler watched his back, Hadder studied the figure, and more questions than answers began to mount in his Wakened mind.

The dark-skinned woman in the white pantsuit wandered around the Southern side of the Flowers Institute as if searching for someone. More surprising than even her existence, however, was the fact that the Forlorn seemed to ignore her presence, with one many-tentacled nightmare actually stumbling into her before backtracking in fear and retreating into the jungle.

Hadder looked to Sowler. "She's important." The Blister nodded. "Watch my six?"

"Always, Angel."

"Always, you fucker," added Smeggins.

With Sowler's arm-flail protecting his back and side, Hadder marched forward and reached the odd woman in short order.

"You," he shouted, and the woman jumped at finally being seen. "Who are you?"

When the woman's golden eyes met Hadder's, he saw that they were panic-stricken and filled with tears. Below these, the woman's wet cheeks reflected the final rays of the falling sun.

She stumbled toward Hadder, and fell hard to her knees on the cobble when Hadder brought up his crystal gun and aimed it at her chest.

"I asked you a question," Hadder said coldly, the embers of the Rage still smoldering within. "Who are you? Answer or I'll ruin that lovely suit."

"My name is Daksha," said the woman in a voice that sounded utterly defeated. "And I am the most foolish person in the world."

"What does that mean? Do not speak in riddles, woman!"

"I am the longest-tenured, highest-ranking servant of Doctor Milo Flowers, the New God. And I fear that I have made a horrible mistake. I fear that I have betrayed humanity.

"And now I want to make amends."

26

"**B**itch! Cunt! Twat!" Seth Whispers's chivalrous act now completely dropped, the Anointed Champion chased the Anorrak Sisters through the magical courtyard, his too-long blades just missing killing blows on several occasions.

Zaza and Su spun left and right, bent low and went high, using every ounce of their collective skills to avoid being cleaved in half by the despicable Champion.

Occasionally, one of the sisters' katanas would find Seth's gross white skin, but they never caused more than a knick. Their arms grew heavy, and their legs began to slow with exertion, and every minute that passed showed Seth's evil odachis coming increasingly closer to biting into the sisters' soft skin.

"I'm starting to tire," Su said to her sister as they flew past in each other in an attempt to disorient the charging demon.

"No fucking shit. Me too." Zaza bent almost completely backwards, narrowly dodging a thrusting odachi as it flew over her exposed chest. She straightened as the blade was retracted. "Any fucking ideas?"

Su knocked aside another blow, and her arm became numb from

the force with which Seth swung his blade. Her dark eyes searched the courtyard frantically and, finally, a decision was reached.

"Follow my lead."

Su danced through some glowing flora, narrowly avoiding one of Seth's double-blade attacks, and Zaza mirrored her sister in the other direction. Working together, they were able to pass the Anointed Champion on the cobble walkway and get him moving back in the other direction — toward the crystalline bridge.

The sisters tiptoed backward as they parried, eventually feeling hard rock replaced by the smooth surface of the bridge. They looked down and could see through the clear material and into the magical pond beneath, which still swam with the human-faced sea monkeys. The little creatures tore through the starlit waters in a circular manner, as if something had excited them.

Seth showed his yellow teeth as he stepped upon the crystal bridge. "Stupid women, tighter quarters only benefit me. But I wouldn't expect whores like you to understand the nuances of battle."

Su used the Champion's condescending speech as an opportunity to fake a low attack, go up high, and pirouette twice away from her sister, sliding across Seth on the large bridge. After her spin, Su found herself on Seth's opposite side, leaving him bookended by the deadly women.

Seth's wide grey eyes shot left and right from one sister to the other, and he offered an oily grin. "Ah, I see what you are doing. It's admirable, but it won't be enough, not by a long shot." Seth swung an odachi to each side, causing both women to jump back. "You know, I like you both so very much. I think I will skin each of you, and when I want to see you next, I will have another of my women wear your flesh. How does that make you feel, to know that I will be touching your skin long after you are gone?"

In response, both sisters advanced, their katanas moving expertly in the air in complicated combinations, forcing the Champion back against the bridge's clear railing. Zaza and Su put everything into this dual attack, including feints, misdirections, positional strikes, and killing blows.

Seth cried out as blades found their way through his stout defenses, forcing him to tap into another level of ability, one which he had never had to access.

The Anointed Champion, despite his extreme height, dropped straight down to the crystal bridge, his long odachis helicoptering out. He spun impossibly on the seat of his pants, his blades out and attacking the sisters at an angle they had yet to see. Zaza and Su reacted similarly to the unanticipated tactic, jumping straight up to land lightly on the bridge's opposing railing.

There they remained when Seth sprung up as if propelled by the devil itself, several new surface wounds on his hip, shoulder, and bicep.

The Anorrak Sisters looked at each other and no words needed to be said, for they shared the same sentiment.

We have given all we have, and it is not near enough.

Su looked around in desperation, as if looking for an answer in the glowing courtyard gardens, but eventually simply nodded to herself.

"Zaza, my lovely sister, *lion and lamb*. I'll be the lamb," said Su, referencing a secret game that they used to play as children that became a serious tactic as adults.

Zaza's eyes went wide and teary. "No, you fucking bitch, don't you fucking do it!"

"Ladies, ladies, you do not have to fight over me. There is plenty of this gentleman to go around."

Su smiled sweetly at her sister, ignoring the pig beneath her. "I love you."

Seth Whispers laughed. "You are moving a bit fast for me, my dear. I would have you…"

Su Anorrak dove at the Anointed Champion, katana cocked above her head and pointed downward for a mighty stab. Despite her furious protests, Zaza waited a beat and leapt as well.

Seth Whispers could not believe his luck as the lighter-skinned Anorrak Sister flew at him, her blade in a position that had no chance at turning aside the Champion's quick thrust.

Seth's sick smile touched his grey eyes as his arm shot out like

lightning, and he shrieked in gross glee as the tip of his blade penetrated the center of Su's chest. The skewered woman's eyes went wide
as she slid down the four feet of blade and came to rest against the
sword's guard.

Before Seth could even lean in to gloat, Su spit a thick wad of
blood into the Champion's face as her blade finally came down, but
not directed at the demon, who was ready to dodge the attack.

Instead, Su's katana dug into the top of the top of the thick crystal
railing. She hung onto the handle of the locked blade with her left
hand while jabbing out with her right thumb.

Seth attempted to fling the impaled woman away from him, but
she improbably held tight to her sword that was driven into the crystal. As Seth's other odachi moved to block Zaza's soaring approach,
Su's thumb found its way to the Champion's right eye, popping the
grey orb and advancing as deep as it could into the demon's orbital
cavity.

Seth screamed in a combination of pain and rage, reactively
lowering his left odachi. As he did, the flying Zaza came in from
above, slamming her own katana down into the Champion's breast-
plate, tearing through arteries and veins and puncturing the demon's
lung.

Zaza released her blade as she fell, leaving it in the grotesque
Champion, and jumped backward to avoid Seth's left odachi as it
came up and swept across like a scythe.

She almost made it.

Just before she was able to escape the killing zone of Seth's odachi,
the tip of the blade cut across Zaza's exposed neck, neatly slicing her
carotid artery and ushering forth a geyser of blood.

Zaza put up a hand to stymie the bleeding as she fell to bridge's
crystal floor. Meanwhile, the dying Seth Whispers dropped both his
weapons, sending the impaled Su to the ground along with her sister.

While Su remained down, Zaza Anorrak rose to her feet, the
promise of death dancing in her light eyes. She walked calmly over to
Seth Whispers, who swayed in place as his mind refused to comprehend what was occurring.

Zaza kicked the odachi that sliced her throat across the bridge as she approached the demon.

"Tell me, demon, who's the cunt now. Who's the fucking cunt?! You! You're the fucking cunt!"

With one final curse, Zaza front kicked Seth Whispers as hard as she could, sending the Anointed Champion over the crystalline railing to splash down into the pond below.

The cool water seemed to revive Seth a bit as he sat up in the shallow pond, a grim smile forming on his too-white face.

And then he felt the first bite, followed immediately by another.

As Seth's blood swirled through the magical waters, the human-faced sea monkeys entered a feeding frenzy, removing small chunks from the Champion's thighs, hands, stomach, and chest.

Seth screamed in agony and tried to push himself to his feet, but his left arm gave out, and he fell back into the frothing waters of the human-faced flesh eaters. The little creatures swarmed the downed demon, stripping his flesh away in seconds before starting in on his muscle and organs.

Zaza watched with anger-filled eyes as Seth Whispers flailed within the magical water, his dying shouts sounding more beautiful than the world's greatest symphony.

Finally, the thrashing stopped, and all that remained of Seth Whispers was a giant skeleton that hung beneath the surface of a lovely pond, where mysterious creatures would use the oversized bones as a new home.

The blood continuing to cascade though her fingers, Zaza dropped to the crystal floor next to her sister, who still stirred. She cuddled up next to Su and put her dark forehead against her sister's light skin.

"You fucking bitch," she managed.

"There was no other way, sis."

"I fucking know."

"I love you."

"And I fucking love you."

"Fuck the New God," said Su with her last breath, and Zaza chuckled.

"Fucking right."

And then the Anorrak Sisters, a pair of the greatest warriors that this world ever produced, died in each other's arms.

———

MARLIN HADDER KEPT his gun trained on the woman named Daksha. "And how exactly do you plan to make amends?"

Daksha wiped her face and pointed to an area of the Flowers Institute. "There is a secret entrance over there. It will open for me. The New God is inside!"

Hadder did not lower his weapon as he sidestepped to where the white-clad woman was indicating. He ran his free hand along the wall between two of the building's petal-shaped corners.

"I don't see any door."

"It is there," insisted the woman, and Hadder detected no lies in her voice. "It will appear if I press my hand against it."

Hadder took a step back. "Show me. And know that I will paint the marble with your brain if I smell even the slightest bit of treachery."

"I no longer have the energy for treachery," laughed Daksha as she rose to her feet and walked over to where Hadder had just investigated. She pressed her dark hand against the wall, and it vibrated for a moment before silently swinging inward, revealing the inside of the Flowers Institute.

"I'll be damned," Hadder whispered to himself, realization setting in that he would soon face off with Milo Flowers. His gun went back up to Daksha. "If this is a trap…"

"It is not, Marlin Hadder. I have been duped by the devil, who took advantage of my desperation, my self-pity, my hatred, and my selfish ambition. I am bound for eternal damnation, I know that. But I would like to do one final act of goodness before I go. Is that too much to ask?"

Hadder's face softened, and he placed his gun back in its shoulder-holster. "It is not. Lead the…"

Before Hadder could finish, a breeze ran through and cleared away the remaining smoke from Tennian's sacrifice. His hazel eyes traveled past Daksha to an impossibly large form on the ground and a smaller form writing around next to it.

Hadder took off like a bullet.

He slid to a stop and kneeled next to his Wakened companion.

"Viktor! Viktor! Are you ok?"

Krill looked up with pain in his black eyes. "I ran into some trouble. Namely, this giant bitch next to me."

Hadder looked at the corpse next to his friend. "Looks like you got the better of the exchange."

"Not by much. The Anorrak Sisters are facing another such demon in the rear of the building. There is an entrance there."

"They will have to go at it alone, Viktor. I have found the secret entrance that we need. It is just over here. Come with me!"

Krill attempted to rise, but fell back to the white cobble, clutching his ruined side. "Fuck, Marlin, the big bitch did a real number on me. My ribs are completely shattered. I can cut off the pain with my Wakened abilities, but it will take some time."

"We don't have time, Marlin Hadder," shouted Daksha from the secret entrance.

"Who the hell is that," asked Krill.

"Another unexpected ally."

Krill smiled. "Miracle number five."

"What's that, Viktor?"

"Never mind. She is right, Marlin. We do not have time for my recovery. Look."

Hadder followed his companion's black eyes up, where the pink asteroid now took up more than half of the darkening sky. Krill grabbed Hadder by the hand. "I will come when I can, but this is *your* fight, Marlin. I don't know how I know, but I know. And I am the smartest human in the world."

"The *only* real human in the world," corrected Hadder.

"No. One of only *two*."

Hadder nodded in appreciation. "See you inside."

"Of course."

And with that, Hadder jumped up and ran back to the secret entrance where Daksha waited, a sick feeling appearing in the pit of his stomach.

Like he and Viktor Krill had just lied to each other.

———

THE INSIDE of the Flowers Institute was surprisingly charming, all white marble with artworks of antiquity hanging from the walls and masterful sculptures resting in tasteful alcoves.

Daksha caught Hadder studying some of the curiosities that she now took for granted.

"This way," she said as she moved off to the left. "And please hurry! His transformation is almost complete!"

"His what?"

"His Theosis!"

"That's bull shit."

Daksha's dark face grew serious, and Hadder's stomach dropped. "It certainly is not."

Hadder had no choice but to believe the woman's words. "All right. Lead the way."

Daksha led Hadder down a narrow walkway that soon opened onto a massive concourse where several hallways came together. To Hadder's left were a series of stairs leading to the enormous doors of the Flowers Institute's main entry.

Hadder started down that path. "Daksha! Here! Open the front doors so that my allies may enter!"

Daksha shook her head. "Even I am unable to open those doors. They are controlled by the New God's will."

Hadder cursed under this breath and returned to Daksha. "I really wish you would stop calling that asshole that."

"Sorry. Habit. *This* way."

Daksha grabbed Hadder by the sleeve and dragged him in the opposite direction through the concourse, passing them between a circle of smaller offices and rooms and into a large, ornate hallway.

"This is the Great Hall," said Daksha, the crumbs of reverence still sprinkling her words. "The entrance to the Holy Pistil is just ahead, but I will have to open it for you."

"The what?"

Daksha shook her head once more. "Sorry, the Holy Pistil is the lair of the New... of Milo Flowers."

"Who is your limp-wristed friend, Daksha," came a deep voice from around the corner of the Great Hall, and the woman's face fell as Cement Felix came into view, his large machete swinging easily in a hand at his waist.

With Daksha too frozen with fear to respond, Hadder spoke up, the Rage beginning to flare up within him.

"I'm the guy who's going to rip the heart out of your boss. By the way, I think my colleague already did away with that fat friend of yours. Her corpse is just outside if you need to retrieve it."

"I assume you are speaking of Batti." Cement Felix shrugged nonchalantly. "I never much cared for her, or any of the other Anointed Champions for that matter. I am our Lord's favorite, and now more of the glory will come *my* way. So, I thank you... Marlin Hadder."

Hadder withdrew a crystal gun as he replied, his scimitar twirling in his other hand. "That's me."

Felix chuckled, which sounded like two boulders rubbing together. "My Lord told me about you. He said you were nothing special, that he didn't understand the interest that surrounded you." The Champion's pink eyes danced along Hadder's body. "I don't understand it either. You look like just another victim to me."

The wind from Felix's words fanned the Rage's flame. "And you look like an asshole I once knew. An asshole I killed."

Daksha's desperate voice cut in. "Do not fight him, I beg you," she cried to Hadder. "Felix is a monster, an invulnerable monster!"

Hadder turned to smile at Daksha, and the woman noticed a strange look in his hazel eyes. He spun back to Felix.

"Come on, then. I have a date with your boss, who was a little bitch when I last met him."

"People change, Marlin Hadder. Even gods."

"Shows how little you know, freak. They change the least." As Hadder spoke, his handgun rose and fired round after round at Cement Felix, who began to charge forward. The bullets ricocheted off the Champion's hard, grey skin beneath his blood-red suit, striking the surrounding walls and cracking the white marble.

As soon as he observed his shots having no effect, Hadder raised his gun and aimed for the demon's pink eyes. Felix predicted this tactic, however, and already had his forearm up to block the incoming projectiles.

Hadder cursed again as the beast plowed forward, and stepped into a front kick, catching the Champion in the chest and halting his momentum.

Felix's pink eyes went wide in shock at Hadder's impossible strength, but the demon had little time to recover as a falchion swung at his temple. Cement Felix brought his machete up in a blink, driving Hadder's blow out wide with such force that the sword flew from the Wakened human's grip and buried itself in the surrounding marble wall.

Hadder backflipped away from the grey monster, but still caught the end of a straight right as it met his jaw with an audible *crack*. The blow sent Hadder sliding down the Great Hallway on the seat of his suit pants, his handgun falling free during the trip.

Hadder was immediately up, the Rage now driving him, as Cement Felix stalked forward, his machete spinning threateningly in his right hand.

"My Lord was right about you, Marlin Hadder. Nothing special."

The Wakened human advanced to meet the Anointed Champion. "I never claimed to be special, Felix. I simply claimed that I was going to kill your boss."

"Then you are still wrong on all accounts, puny human," called out Felix as his machete cut down and across, desperate to spill Hadder's blood.

Hadder spun away from the strike and punched out with his left fist, catching the grey-skinned Champion in the cheek. The Wakened human cried out in pain, his fist cracking under the force as if he had punched a block of pure steel.

Hadder had no time to soothe his aching hand as Felix continued to swing away, his wicked blade narrowly missing the Wakened human's neck numerous times.

Eventually, Hadder grew accustomed to the speed and ferocity with which Cement Felix attacked, and was able to better time his strikes.

A right hook found the Champion's ribs. A low kick caught the monster in the knee. A reverse sidekick caught the demon right in the solar plexus.

And still, Cement Felix remained undaunted. And still, he came forward.

Hadder's Rage drove him, past the point of intelligent actions, and soon the Wakened human found himself dirty boxing with his armored opponent, keeping the machete out wide as Hadder launched elbows and knees at the red-suited demon.

Cement Felix grunted under Hadder's blows, but bit down on his sharpened teeth and launched his own knees, with one sneaking through Hadder's defenses and catching him in the stomach, doubling him over.

The Anointed Champion grinned above the downed Hadder as he raised his machete for the killing blow. The demon stopped, however, when a slim, dark arm appeared around his massive neck, attempting to pull him away from his prey.

Felix spun in anger, shaking Daksha loose and sending her to the marble floor. He stomped forward as the woman tried to crawl away.

"Fool of a woman! The New God gave you everything! And *this* is how you repay Him?!"

Daksha scrambled up, planted her feet, and raised her face to the approaching demon. "I gave *Him* everything! And he gave *me* lies! Nothing but lies! I..."

Cement Felix's massive backhand sent Daksha soaring through the air to crash loudly into the wall, the sickening sound of her head smashing into the white marble echoing throughout the Great Hall.

"You never knew when to shut up," spat Felix as he stood over Daksha's crumpled body.

"And neither do you," came Hadder's reply from behind the giant. Felix spun on a heel to find that Marlin Hadder had not only returned to his feet, but had retrieved his scimitar from its wall burial. "Let us finish this. I have bigger fish to fry."

Felix's deep laugh reverberated across the Flowers Institute. "You're a tenacious little shit, I'll give you that. Come now, I intend to be present for my Lord's birth."

Hadder sprang forward, driven by the unique combination of Rage and Wakened abilities, his sword cutting left and right faster than the Anointed Champion could follow. Blow after blow found Felix's grey skin, sparking off it like flint striking steel and causing little to no damage.

A grin began to grow on Felix's fanged mouth as a truth became clear to both combatants – the Anointed Champion could not be seriously hurt by this human.

Hadder's scimitar slammed into Felix's wrist, sending the demon's machete to the hard floor, while the Champion's other hand shot across caught Hadder's same hand, squeezing it painfully until the Wakened human's blade also fell noisily to the ground.

Now in the demon's grasp, Hadder fought to remove himself from Felix's grip, but to no avail. Instead, Cement Felix pulled Hadder tighter, against his massive chest, and lifted him in a tight bear hug.

Hadder's lungs cried out under the strain as Felix's giant mitts found each other around the smaller man's back and pulled in. The Anointed Champion began to howl in excitement as he felt Hadder's bones begin to crack under the inhuman force of his constriction. Felix's wild pink eyes were inches from Hadder's hazel orbs as the last of the Wakened human's air exited his lungs.

"Tell me, little man, what does it feel like to fail? What does it feel like to want something more than anything, and still come up short? What does it feel like to lose a world?"

Hadder couldn't put his finger on it, but something in Felix's mocking words threw gasoline on the dying coals of the Rage, causing his fallen head to shoot upright before it slammed down onto the Champion's own massive cranium.

Felix stumbled back, confused as to why Hadder's headbutt had harmed him so.

Hadder smiled grimly. "I don't know, demon. You tell me." Down again, Hadder went, smashing his head against Felix's own, causing cracks to appear above the Champion's pink eyes.

Again and again Hadder rammed his head into Cement Felix's forehead. When the demon tried to release him, Hadder wrapped his arms around the monster's thick neck and continued his assault. When Felix attempted to turn away, Hadder remained steadfast, smashing his diamond-plated forehead into the scarred side of the Champion's head. When Felix finally fell to his knees and then onto his back, Hadder followed him down, repeatedly pounding his head into the grey monstrosity.

The Rage was now full on, and Hadder was beyond control. Over and over again, Hadder used his head as a weapon, blasting Cement Felix until there was nothing left under him but a thick paste of blood and bone.

Finally, when there was nothing more of Felix's head to destroy, Hadder rose to stand over the red-suited corpse. The Rage still flaring up within him, Hadder screamed at the headless body as he pointed at his own forehead.

"Diamond-plated Elevation, you fuck! Your messiah missed that one, didn't he?!"

Hadder started to launch more insults at the dead body, but movement along the far wall demanded his attention. He ran over to find Daksha alive, but barely. She looked up at Hadder with distant eyes.

"The Holy Pistil. You need my hand. You need..."

Hadder immediately understood. "Where?"

"There," said Daksha weakly, pointing a few feet from where she now laid, where golden double doors marked the entrance to the Holy Pistil.

Hadder lifted the woman gently, and suppressed a shudder when brain matter ran down his hand. He turned Daksha to face the doors of the Holy Pistil, and helped her raise her right hand. Her dark hand touched the gold, and the doors swung quietly inward, sending a wave of stench to penetrate the Great Hall.

Hadder let the woman collapse to the ground as Holy Pistil beckoned him forward.

"Did I do good," asked Daksha, her life-force draining as she did.

"You did good," answered Hadder with a smile. "We will remember *this*. Nothing else."

"I made amends?"

"You did."

"Oh, good." And just like that, the mysterious woman called Daksha died. Hadder did not know who she was or what she had done, but he knew that without her, his path to the New God would have never appeared.

Marlin Hadder silently thanked the white-suited woman, placed a kiss upon her dark forehead, retrieved his scimitar blade from the floor, and entered the Holy Pistil.

Where he would finally face off with Doctor Milo Flowers, also known as the New God.

———

A SHIVER PASSED through Marlin Hadder's spine as he entered the cavernous room called the Holy Pistil.

The circular chamber was a contradiction, with warm, beautiful frescoes lining the curving walls and cold metal surgical tables dotting the marble floor. Of the hundred or so metal tables, about half were empty, with rotting corpses of an array of strange organisms occupying the others. At each table was a Taragoshi surgical mech, its scalpel-tipped, multi-jointed arm hanging limp as if its dark work was already complete.

At the far end of the Holy Pistil, a mammoth cocoon hung grossly against the back wall, vibrating so angrily that Hadder thought it would rip free at any moment and fall to the ground. Bright light escaped the multitude of small tears and holes that appeared on the grotesque biological encasement as two giant surgical mechs stood guard on either side.

Hadder steeled his resolve and marched forward, determined to finally put an end to one of Station's only remaining children.

As Hadder advanced, the surgical mechs roared to life, swinging their bladed arms at the intruder. Fortunately, Hadder's Wakened abilities were locked in, and he easily sliced the metal appendages neatly in half at the joint.

When Hadder was halfway across the chamber, a voice, recognizable but infinitely more powerful, rang out across the Holy Pistil.

"Marlin Hadder, is that you?"

Hadder slowed, but continued ahead. "It is me, Milo."

"Milo? That name is so… insufficient now."

"Regardless of what I call you, you're still an asshole. You're still that same hate-filled little shit that I met at Rott Manor so long ago."

Milo Flowers paused before speaking again. "These verbal jousts are beneath me now. I have been waiting for you, Marlin Hadder. I wanted you to witness firsthand the glory that you helped to create."

"I had nothing to do with you or your rise, Milo. If you want to give credit, give it to Albany Rott, Viktor Krill, and God."

"No doubt they had parts to play, but so did you, Marlin Hadder. You shook up Station, did you not? You created the ultimate diversion for me to escape. Your presence in the City of Eternal Night emboldened me, showed me that things were not as static as I feared."

Hadder fought down the urge to vomit on the floor. "Bull shit, Milo."

Another pause. "Believe what you want, Marlin Hadder. But after I conquer this world, I will send my Flowering Horde through the portal and into mankind's other realities. My shadow will spread across all of humanity, across all of its existences, and I will unite them all under the banner of the New God. And life will flourish unencumbered, shattering that limited mold into which Albany Rott forced us."

Hadder froze as the full weight of Milo Flowers's words finally began to sink in.

"You're fucking insane."

"Am I, Marlin Hadder? Or am I simply beyond your meager comprehension, even Wakened as you are?"

Hadder started forward once more. "I'm sorry to tell you this, Milo, but you'll never get the chance. I have found your island fortress. I have fought through your army of nightmares. I have defeated your Champion. I have gained access to your unholy sanctuary. And now, I am going to carve you up before you have a chance to escape that pus sack of yours."

As Hadder closed the distance to the cocoon, the giant surgical mechs sent their numerous metal arms at the Wakened human. Razors, circular saws, needles, and laser cutters simultaneously came at Marlin Hadder, attacking from left and right, low and high.

Hadder's Wakened abilities, sharpened to an uncanny edge by Viktor Krill, took over, sending the man into a series of blinding somersaults, flips, dodges, and strikes. Upon completion of his impossible combination, Marlin Hadder stood alone among the wreckage of the two largest surgical mechs that Taragoshi Robotics ever produced.

"It seems that your final defense has fallen, Milo. It is time that we end this." Hadder lifted his scimitar blade above his head. "I'm afraid that I cannot wait for your rebirth."

The empowered voice of Doctor Milo Flowers boomed through the Holy Pistil. "You fool! You stupid, stupid fool!" The strength of Milo's words pushed Hadder back two steps. "What do you think is going on within my Chrysalis? Do you think that there is only a half-formed chicken in this egg? You have always been an idiot, Marlin Hadder, and being Wakened has not changed that. My Theosis is complete, you fool! I do not need a rebirth, idiot human, for I have already been reborn... as the New God!"

Hadder cocked his blade back once more and stormed ahead, ready to cut Doctor Milo Flowers's cocoon into a thousand pieces. "I don't believe you," he screamed as his sword began to fall.

"Then let me show you," Milo Flowers said calmly, and the Chrysalis detonated in an explosion of light and heat and power. Hadder soared across the Holy Pistil along with most of the chamber's metal tables and surgical mechs to smash violently against the front wall.

Hadder's head struck the hard marble, and he sank limply to the floor moments before a wave of metal and stone fell atop him, burying the unconscious man in an avalanche of debris.

As the dust began to settle, Doctor Milo Flowers, now the New God, calmly drifted across the remnants of the Holy Pistil.

The New God was impossibly tall, painfully beautiful, and glowed with power so brightly that one would have to shield their eyes to look upon Him. All that remained of Milo Flowers were the pale blue eyes that could just be made out from within the form's luminous head.

The New God exited the Holy Pistil, paying the fallen Marlin Hadder no mind, and glided forward, passing through the Great Hall and the Institute concourse. The New God then waved a gleaming hand, and the front doors of the Flowers Institute opened under their master's command.

The New God then appeared on the Sacred Landing under the night sky as if by magic, a battle raging around Him. All ceased their fighting as the magnificence that was the New God came into complete focus.

Protector of Man, Blister, gangster, and Forlorn alike paused where they stood before making their way to the area around the Sacred Landing. While the Forlorn went willingly, the faces of the humans and Blisters in attendance twisted in confusion and terror, for their movements were not their own, but driven by a power that was too great to resist.

In short order, every combatant had collected at the base of the Sacred Landing, and the New God looked out with his too-blue eyes and smiled darkly.

"Kneel," said the New God, and although he whispered, his voice reverberated across the Isle of God, leaving no room to question his command.

The Forlorn placed their nightmarish heads against the white cobble, and a second later, the men and women and Blisters followed suit, for they could not defy the wishes of the New God.

Not even Viktor Krill.

———

MARLIN HADDER WOKE WITH A START, shaking free the remains of a dream where he drowned in a sea of darkness.

Using his Wakened strength, Hadder pushed his way free of the mountain of metal and stone that had temporarily entombed him and looked around in desperation. Hadder patted himself down and groaned. Gone were his scimitar and both of his crystalline guns; only Patton Yellich's small dagger remained firmly tucked into the back of his belt.

As he knocked the dust and dirt from his head and face, Hadder saw that not only were the doors to the Holy Pistil open, but so were those of the Flowers Institute's main entryway.

Doctor Milo Flowers was nowhere in sight, but Hadder had an idea of where the evil creature might be.

———

THE NEW GOD pointed a blazing finger at one of the Forlorn, and it grossly turned inside out before its dark gore dove into the ground between the white cobble. Moments later, a thick stalk pushed up from the stone and grew into the most beautiful tree the world has ever seen. Translucent leaves were dotted with starlight, large blossoms shined like supernovas, and the trunk swam with all the colors of the universe.

"You see," the New God announced to those beneath him, "I can make the world as I wish. And unmake as I see fit."

The New God raised his arm again, and Teo, who was kneeling to the left of the Sacred Landing, screamed in pain as his body folded in half again and again and again. This horror continued until the quiet man was nothing more than a square lump of flesh that eventually melted into hundreds of small orange salamanders that scampered away into the thick jungle.

"Life will no longer have limits. It will only be bound by My imagination, which is endless. I will be the artist, all the worlds of man will be my canvas, and you all will be my raw materials. Together, we will redefine life!"

"The hell we will."

Marlin Hadder shielded his eyes as he stepped onto the Sacred Landing, for not only did the New God glow like an inferno, but the pink asteroid now took up almost the entirety of the night sky with its brightness.

The New God half-turned to face his nemesis.

"Marlin Hadder. Good. I feared that your weak body had perished during my emergence. This will be all the more enjoyable with you here. Please, join me here."

Hadder wanted nothing more than to lunge at the New God, to slam his fists into the glowing creature's head and body until there was nothing but jelly remaining. He wanted to throw curses at the New God, to renounce him as nothing more than a disturbed simpleton playing at deity. Hadder wanted to do all this and more.

But found that he could not.

Instead, Marlin Hadder found himself walking across the Sacred Landing to stand calmly before the New God, his body no longer his own. As he did, Hadder's hazel eyes peered past the stairs, and his heart sank.

Among the crowd of kneeling worshipers was Clinton Voss, his head so low that his thick, white beard touched the Perennial Pathway. Next to him were Upton and DeLany Thales, their faces hidden as they prostrated themselves before the New God.

A small distance away, Viktor Krill shook as he knelt next to a young boy, who also genuflected as he held Lil Terry in his small arms. Hadder met Krill's black eyes and could feel the anger, frustration, and hopelessness that resided within those inky orbs. He watched helplessly as the notorious killer tapped into every ounce of his Wakened abilities and found that they were no match for the New God's power.

Krill's despondent voice entered Hadder's mind. *"I'm so sorry, Marlin. I have lost control. I have failed you. I have failed us all."*

A tear fell down Krill's face, and Hadder was forced to look away.

"Marlin Hadder. Stand before me." Hadder did as he was commanded, despite resisting with all that he had. The New God addressed all in attendance. "What you see here is the last hope of those who would keep life bottled up, of those who think that they can stop the inevitability of the New God. As Marlin Hadder kneels before me, so, too, do the old gods, for their warm hands will never touch my cold clay again. For it is mine, and mine alone!"

As the New God spoke, Hadder managed to turn his head back to the Perennial Pathway. His eyes moved above the crowd until they fell upon the target of his search.

Down the cobbled path, standing alone in the pink-stained night, was Albany Rott, his eyes aflame. The old devil did not move to help, but instead rested with his arms across his chest, his facial scar throbbing and his neck tattoo gleaming in the dimness. He watched Marlin Hadder intently, as if a play that he was attending was coming to an end.

"Marlin Hadder. Kneel."

Hadder fought with everything he had, using every trick that Viktor Krill had taught him, but still, his legs bent, and his knees fell forward until they touched the Sacred Landing.

Hadder looked once more over at Viktor Krill through tear-soaked eyes, and his companion continued to shake, always one to fight against his oppressor until the bitter end.

"Marlin Hadder. Kneel lower. All the way."

Hadder's back began to bend as his head drew closer to the cold marble ground. Just before his forehead touched the Sacred Landing, however, something began to awaken deep within him, and he stopped.

"Marlin Hadder. All the way."

Hadder began to follow the New God's order again before stopping, the smoke inside him becoming a small flame.

"Marlin Hadder. Do you need to see what happens when I am not obeyed? So be it!"

The New God's hand thrust forward, and DeLany Thales's head exploded into red mist. The New God's arm swept through the pink night, and Upton, Doctor Olney Jansen, and several other Protectors of Man ripped in half. Moments later, tall stalks of mushrooms shot up from their insides.

The Rage continued to stir, as if being awakened from a long slumber.

"Hey, go fuck yourself, you fucking bright fuck. Come down here and I'll fucking eat you! Isn't that right, Sowler, man? I'll fucking..."

The New God's face swung angrily to where the small voice of Smeggins rang out across the silent pathway. Two blazing arms came up, and the Blister enforcer known as Sowler was lifted into the air briefly before his arms, including his beloved arm-flail, and legs were torn from his torso and flung into the jungle. Sowler's body hit the ground with a gross thud.

"Shut up, Smeggins," said the Blister as he died.

The Rage roared to life, coursing through Marlin Hadder, slowly loosening the grip of the New God.

Lil Terry, still held by the boy called Darrin Krill, began to bark at the New God. The too-blue eyes found the little dog, and Lil Terry's head snapped off violently as the boy wailed for his new friend.

Viktor Krill's black eyes flashed dangerously at his adopted son's pain, and the look that he gave Marlin Hadder fed the Rage with the last bit of kindling needed to explode.

A familiar look returned to Marlin Hadder's hazel eyes.

The New God returned to stand just above Hadder.

"Marlin Hadder. Kneel!"

Hadder's forehead hit the marble as his hand snuck behind his waist and brushed against what was concealed there.

The New God smiled wickedly and looked out to Albany Rott.

"And with that, Albany Rott, the experiment that was humanity is over."

"Not yet," said a voice defiantly.

Confusion crossed the New God's shining face as he looked down at the prone Marlin Hadder.

"What did you say, human?"

Hadder's head sprung up, wearing the dangerous look of a man completely in the throes of the Rage.

"I said, not yet, you sick fuck. This is for everyone."

Hadder tore Patton Yellich's dagger free from his belt as he leapt up and slammed the ancient blade into the chest of the New God. He then pulled down with all of his Wakened, Rage-propelled strength, ripping a massive hole in the New God from chest to hip.

The New God howled in pain as liquid light poured from the wound, the horrific sound causing everyone on the Isle of God to cover their ears lest they explode under the strain.

Hadder refused to protect his ears, instead electing to ride the Rage, continuing to stab at the New God, filling the false deity with a dozen more holes.

Eventually, Hadder stopped and the New God stood before him trembling on unsure legs.

"You lose, Doctor Flowers," said Hadder, and the Rage gave his voice power that echoed across the world.

"Life lost, Marlin Hadder. Life lost."

And with that, the New God exploded into a ball of heat and light, burning the skin and muscle off Marlin Hadder and sending his charred body to the floor of the Sacred Landing.

When the shock wore off, Hadder found himself looking up at the night sky, his body ruined and his organs quickly shutting down. Tears pooled in his lidless eyes and ran down his temples as he stared in wonder at the pink asteroid that rushed toward the world.

The asteroid hummed a beautiful song as it approached, and Hadder wanted to reach for it, but found that he could not.

Instead, he waited patiently as the pink judgment came to him, slamming into the planet and vaporizing the world.

And Marlin Hadder died.

———

HADDER FELT a soft light fall over him, lifting him through and above the encroaching darkness. Up he went, surrounded by the warmth of a thousand familiar hugs, coming to rest on a soft canvas that caressed his feet like a lover's touch.

An iridescent figure approached, tall and powerful and painfully beautiful. It looked down at Hadder and presented an honest smile before offering its hand.

Hadder looked down at the perfect hand and wanted nothing more than to take it, to kiss it and hold it tightly, begging for comfort and forgiveness.

And so Hadder did, for no Rage remained within to stop him.

The figure that was the one true God pulled Marlin Hadder in tight and consumed the man in a warm embrace, one that swept away too many lifetimes of pain and regret and sadness and anger.

Deeper into God, Hadder fell, until their energies intertwined and sped off in a dance across the cosmos. Hadder had no mouth, but he laughed in delight. He had no eyes, but he cried at the beauty that he saw. He had no heart, but he swelled with love.

After what could have been a second or an eternity, their journey through the universe reached its conclusion and God spun away from Hadder, leaving him with the permanent imprint of a kiss on his soul.

And then Marlin Hadder began to fall, a lovely song marking his descent, ending in heartbeats and deep inhalations.

CODA

Marlin Hadder was forced to shade his eyes with his hands as his vision came back into focus. The midday sun hung bright and cheery against the backdrop of perfect blue sky.

Hadder was surprised to find that his feet were already moving forward on an empty city sidewalk. To his right was a small, one-way street that a few cars slowly ran down in no apparent hurry. To his left was a beautifully manicured park, complete with massive trees, picnic tables, and a huge pond home to several optimistic fishermen.

Hadder's mind spun as he walked, unsure of where he was or how he got here. But the day was so perfect that he continued on, unsure of the alternative.

A bar across the small street caught his attention, where the television out front showed Lily Sistine singing onstage before thousands of adoring fans.

So engrossed was Hadder in the image of Lily that he crashed into a couple that was crossing the sidewalk in the opposite direction.

"Ah, apologies, old chap. I should have noticed that you were preoccupied and maneuvered accordingly. No harm, I presume?"

Hadder's face fell as Jonny VV clapped him on the shoulder.

"Who can blame him, Jonny, on a day as lovely as this," said Reena Song from beside him. "Enjoy the day, my friend. We hope to run into you again soon. Come on, Jonny."

Hadder watched, mouth agape, as his old Station friends continued arm in arm down the walkway. Shaking his head, he moved on, curious about what he would discover further down.

And Marlin Hadder was not disappointed.

Lil Terry barked a greeting from the gas station across the road, and Terry smiled behind the little dog, wiping his hands clean with a dirty cloth.

Su and Zaza Anorrak flew by on matching motorcycles. They nodded to Hadder as they passed, massive grins pasted on their beautiful faces.

Everywhere that Hadder looked, ghosts from his past reemerged, from Royal Winters to Teo, from Glen to Clinton Voss, all going about their day with contented grins, as if this was where they were always supposed to be.

Tennian Stamp jogged past on legs that were his own, an air of peace surrounding the former soldier and gangster.

As Marlin Hadder pushed ahead, the smile on his face grew larger and larger, until he started to fear that it would cleave his face in two. And just when he thought that nothing more could surprise him, he looked into the park and his heart jumped in his chest.

Playing sweetly in the shade of a large tree was a family of four, their picnic blanket laid out nicely with a variety of treats atop it. Mayfly Lemaire, whom Hadder had never met but knew it to be, sat cross-legged on the soft grass, reading a book to a young girl in her lap. To the side, Darrin Krill dribbled a soccer ball with his feet, showing great skill in refusing to let it touch the ground.

And leaning against the tree, staring at them with light-brown eyes full of love, was Viktor Krill. He looked up from his family and found Marlin Hadder in the distance. The two men stared at each for a long time, saying everything that needed to be said without speaking a word, until Krill finally nodded.

Hadder returned the smile and nod and continued on with his walk, not wanting to intrude on a happy family outing.

Hadder was lost in thought again when he passed a coffee stand on the park's edge, and another eerily familiar voice brought him back to reality.

"Not going to say hello, Marlin?"

Hadder stopped and turned to find Albany Rott and his crimson eyes looking up at him from a seat next to the stand.

Hadder couldn't help but smile as he fell into the empty seat next to the man-god. "Albany Rott. I should have known that this was your doing."

Rott shook his head. "Not mine, Marlin," he replied, aiming a too-white finger to the sky.

"What? The big guy?"

Rott shrugged. "You passed the test. But more than that, you impressed Him. And *that* is difficult to do."

"He destroyed the world, Al. He must not have been that impressed."

Rott waved the idea away. "He destroyed *that* world. He destroyed a broken world. And replaced it with *this*. For *you*."

Hadder thought for a moment before leaning toward Rott. "What was all this, Al? What was Station? What did any of this mean?"

Rott took a sip of his coffee. "Well, I usually don't do this, Marlin, but you've been through a lot and I like you. I've always liked you." He took another sip. "One of the few things that you humans got right is that there is a finite amount of energy in the universe, a set amount of raw materials, if you will. New projects are always popping up that require these raw materials, which means that they must be taken from existing projects. And, thus, the need for testing is present."

"But we are *your* project, Al."

"That's right, which I why I always lobby so hard for humanity's continuation, although it is getting increasingly difficult, and you all are not doing me any favors."

"So, this is all a test to see if we are... worthy of our souls?"

Rott thought for a second. "Sure, if *souls* makes more sense to you than *energies*, then fine. It was all a test to see if you were worthy of your souls, of which there are only so many in the multiverse."

"But how does Station tie in with the hunt for Krill and Milo Flowers and..."

Rott held up a white hand. "Just stop, Marlin. Please do not try to understand our processes or comprehend what..." Another finger shot to the sky. "He is basing his decision on. Just know that it was a multi-stage test. You passed some, you failed others. But in the end, because of you, Marlin Hadder, and the unique composition of your energy..."

"You mean the Rage," Hadder interrupted.

Rott nodded. "I mean the Rage. Because of that, humanity did just enough to squeak by with a passing grade."

Hadder fell back in his chair. "So, that's it?"

Rott finished his coffee. "That is it, Marlin."

"What now?"

"Now? Now, you live, Marlin. Look around. He created all of this for *you*. That's something that I've never seen before. You should be grateful."

Tears began to roll down Hadder's cheeks. He wiped them away. "I am, Al. I am. It's just that..."

"Tell me, Marlin."

"It's just that I'm still in the same boat I was in when I punched my ticket to Station. My family is gone and I am alone. And I'm too tired to start over again." Rott laughed.

"What's so fucking funny, Al? I'm serious!"

"Oh, I know you are, Marlin. I'm just surprised."

"Surprised at what?!"

"Surprised that you think Him so lazy with His work."

"I don't understand."

"You don't need to understand, Marlin. You only need to look."

"Look? Look where?"

"How about just down the sidewalk for starters."

Hadder's face twisted, but he leaned forward to peer down the walkway. His eyes grew big as a beautiful woman came into focus, pushing a stroller with a little girl inside.

"Al?"

"Yes, Marlin."

"Is this real?"

"It is, Marlin. You have earned it."

"Please, Al, I can't take another..."

"Marlin Hadder! If you don't go to them right this instant..."

Hadder was up before Rott could finish the threat, walking to the only two people who truly mattered to the broken man.

His wife Emily smiled as he approached, and his daughter Mia held out her arms for her daddy.

"Marlin, there you are. I was afraid that we had lost you."

Marlin spoke through shock. "It was I who lost you. But you are here now."

Emily's brow furrowed. "We are. What is..."

Hadder shot forward and buried his wife in a hug. When they finally separated, he dropped to his knees before his daughter and swallowed her in an embrace.

"Daddy, you're squeezing me."

Hadder let go. "Sorry, sweetheart. Daddy just missed you. I missed you both more than you could ever imagine."

"Marlin, is everything all right?"

Hadder wiped the tears from his eyes again. "It is now, my love. It is now."

Emily knew her husband to be strangely emotional at times, so she let it go. "Good. Mia is hungry. Do you mind if we stop for a bite to eat?"

"Of course. Anything you both want."

"Good. Then let's find a place where we can sit outside and enjoy this beautiful day."

"There are a few places back this way, my love."

Emily smiled. "Lead the way."

Hadder took Mia from her stroller, put his daughter atop his shoulders, and began walking hand in hand with his wife back the way he had come, giving a slight nod to Albany Rott as he passed.

"Hey, sweetheart?"

"Yes, Marlin?"

"I spotted an old friend in the park with his wife and children when I came down this way. Do you mind if we stop and say hi before we eat? Perhaps they would like to join us."

"Sure. The more, the merrier, Marlin. Where do you know him from?"

"Another place and time."

Emily didn't understand, but she knew her husband well enough to leave it alone.

———

ALBANY ROTT LIT a cigarette as he watched Marlin Hadder embrace Viktor Krill in a hug, the men's wives and children coming together in friendship.

Rott watched for several minutes before flicking his cigarette into the street and heading back up the walkway, absently rubbing the shimmering tattoo at his neck as he did.

At the top of the next hill, Rott stopped and turned to look around.

I will miss these humans, Rott thought as he said goodbye. *They will always be my fondest creations, regardless of how stupid they may act.*

And with that, Albany Rott vanished with a smile, understanding that the day would come again when humanity would need to be tested. And on that day, a city would appear between worlds, starting the clock once more.

A city called Station.

THANK YOU

Thank you for taking the time to read Ill Messiah. With this, you have completed the Station Trilogy, my first attempt at serious storytelling.

I can't put into words how grateful I am that you chose to spend your valuable time in the world that I created. If you enjoyed the book, it would be most helpful if you could leave a rating or review on any of the various retail channels. It is truly insane how much of an author's success is predicated on these reviews.

If you're curious about the music that drove this novel and the others in the series, please visit my website and check out the book soundtracks for all three Station novels. There, you can also hit me up with questions or to chat.

www.JarrettBrandonEarly.com

ABOUT THE AUTHOR

Jarrett Brandon Early is an emerging author of contemporary sci-fi thrillers. He lives with his wife Natthicha and daughter Alexandra Beam. Ill Messiah is Jarrett's third book and completes the Station Trilogy along with Station (Book One) and The Rott Inertia (Book Two)

Jarrett is currently hard at work on an adapted screenplay for Station and a standalone novel.